THE

WOMEN OF LONDON

DISCLOSING

The Trials and Temptations

OF A

WOMAN'S LIFE IN LONDON

WITH OCCASIONAL GLIMPSES OF A FAST CAREER

With Twenty-four Original Illustrations

LONDON

GEORGE VICKERS, ANGEL COURT, STRAND

1863.

CONTENTS.

LIST OF ILLUSTRATIONS.

THE
WOMEN OF LONDON
𝔄 Romance.

JABEZ CLARKE CORRECTS HIS DAUGHTER.

CHAPTER I.

AN UNPROTECTED FEMALE—THE WAY OF THE WORLD—
MADAME CERISE—THE FATAL CARD—SMITHERS—THE
TABLES TURNED—A FRIEND IN NEED—THROWN ON
THE WORLD.

"HELP! help! oh, help!"

These exclamations proceeded from a young woman who was running quickly up a back street which ran parallel with the magnificent thoroughfare of Regent-street. She was apparently about sixteen years of age. Her features were of that Saxon type so well known in this country.

Her hair was fair—almost golden; her mouth was small; her lips red and rosy; her nose had a narrow escape of being "retroussé;" her complexion was light and delicate —in short, she was a blonde.

The cause of her alarm was not so easily discovered.

It was broad daylight, scarcely past two o'clock in the afternoon.

It was ridiculous to suppose that she was afraid of thieves.

Equally so to imagine that she was terrified by a mad bull, for the Metropolitan Cattle Market was some miles off.

What, then, could have caused so much terror and alarm in one so young and beautiful?

That was the question.

And although one apparently intricate and difficult of solution, the interpretation was not so far off as might have been expected.

Not far behind her walked a well-dressed, handsome-looking young man.

If you can judge a man's age from his whiskers and the hair he wears upon his face, he was about six or seven and twenty.

But this is never a sure standard to go by.

Whatever his age might have been, one thing was certain—he was as good-looking a young fellow as you would meet in a day's march.

His complexion was dark, as well as his hair and eyes. And he had a look of "*insouciance*," which sat well upon him. His clothes were well made, and he knew how to wear them.

In a word, he might have been taken for a nobleman; but he could never have been mistaken for a lawyer's clerk.

This young man, with a few rapid strides, overtook the trembling and shrinking girl.

Then the mystery which at first hung over the whole proceeding was rapidly dispelled.

As he neared her, he exclaimed, in a low yet manly voice—

"Don't be alarmed, little one. I shall not hurt you. I am not an ogre, to eat up little girls!"

And he gazed tenderly upon her.

At the first sound of his voice she made another effort to escape her pursuer, but, finding that he had seized her hand, and that the attempt was useless, she looked up, and replied, in a tone which she evidently meant to be not only indignant but defiant—

"Why do you talk to me? I do not know you."

"Possibly, my child," he answered, coldly, almost sarcastically; "possibly, what you are pleased to state may be correct, but I am sanguine enough to hope that we may eventually become better acquainted."

"Oh! let me go!" she cried. "Why do you detain me thus?"

"Am I such a monster, then?" he demanded, smiling.

"Oh! I know not what you are," she replied. "Pray Heaven you mean me no harm."

The stranger appeared to muse a moment. Then he said—

"You are young—inexperienced. You may like me better when we next meet. Come, tell me, where do you live?"

"Where I live can be of no consequence to you," she answered, boldly.

A cloud passed over her interrogator's brow at this response, and for a moment he again appeared plunged in thought.

His reverie, however, was interrupted by a beseeching appeal from the girl whom his grasp detained.

"Oh! do let me go!" she exclaimed; "do let me go! Were I seen with you it would be my ruin!"

For a woman to be seen talking with a man in a street contiguous to the Haymarket is nothing very wonderful, as most people are doubtless aware; and consequently, although these two had been standing together for some minutes during the scene we have been describing, the passers-by manifested no astonishment whatever, but quietly pursued their several ways without bestowing more than a casual glance as they hurried past.

"Well! well!" said the stranger, at last; "take this card, and if ever you want a friend call on Bernard Leslie."

At the same time he released her hand, and she sped up the street as if her life depended upon her fleetness.

"Now, there is a contumacious piece of innocence," he muttered to himself. "How I detest innocence! Well there is one consolation—it is a fault easily cured. Adam and Eve were innocent once. The tree of knowledge still flourishes, and I suppose we all pluck its fruit, and eat it some time or other. Women are the fools, and men the deceivers ever. Well! 'Tis the way of the world."

During these reflections of Mr. Bernard Leslie, as he called himself, the young girl whom he had so rudely waylaid had entered a house having a frontage on Regent-street. Over the back door, through which she had entered, were written the words—

"MADAME CERISE."

The girl crossed a yard and passed through a passage which led her to an open door, which revealed a room containing from twenty to thirty young women.

They were milliners, and worked for the celebrated and fashionable Madame Cerise, the well-known "*modiste.*'

Most of them were too busy to look up as the girl entered.

There was one, however, whose duty it was to see that the "young ladies," as the work-women were in the cant language of the business called, were punctual in their attendance, and also that a due amount of work was diurnally—and nocturnally, too, for the matter of that—extracted from them.

This woman's appearance is summed up in the popular and expressive words, "a hag."

Who else would have been a slave-driver and a task-mistress?

Her name was Smithers, and she was a distant relation of Madame Cerise—so report had it.

Smithers approached the girl, who, through the circumstances we have detailed, had made so tardy an entry.

"Well, Miss Clarke!" she exclaimed, in an acrimonious tone of voice; "you are late to-day. You ought to know as well as the other 'young ladies,' that we cannot afford to allow skulking here. You are all paid liberally."

Here an exclamation of dissent was audible in every part of the workroom.

Smithers, at hearing this, appeared to be vastly incensed.

"Let that be repeated!" she cried; "and everyone in the room shall be fined a day's wages."

The poor creatures, who were sacrificing their health, their very life, for their daily bread, dared not but respect the warning so solemnly given.

"What have you to say?" demanded Smithers, turning sharply to Miss Clarke.

"If you please," she replied, "I could not come quicker. I will make up for it."

"Of course you will!" exclaimed Smithers; "no doubt about that, my dear. You are not paid half-a-crown a-day for nothing—oh! dear no, don't flatter yourself!"

The girl was turning away to go to her seat, when Smithers cried—

"Stop a bit! I have not done with you yet, Miss Agnes Clarke!"

Agnes stood still, looking timidly at the floor of the room, which was destitute of carpeting, and rather dusty than otherwise, owing to the number of people continually walking over it and the excessive heat of the weather, for it was the middle of summer.

"You forget, Miss Clarke, you have not told us yet what made your ladyship so late this afternoon," began Smithers.

Agnes made no answer.

"Our young ladies," continued Smithers, "are allowed half-an-hour for dinner, and you have taken an hour."

"I couldn't help it," repeated Agnes.

"That's all very fine—you told us that before, I think. I suppose the truth is, you have got a sweetheart—a lover, eh?"

As Smithers said this, all the girls in the room looked up, and fixed their eyes upon Agnes.

But she boldly returned their gaze, and, with honest indignation, although her unsophisticated heart fluttered a little, replied—

"No, I have not; and whoever says so tells a bad, wicked story."

"Oh, indeed!" said Smithers. "Then what is the meaning of this?"

And with a sudden movement, Smithers dexterously snatched the card, which Agnes still held in her hand.

This was the fatal card given her by Bernard Leslie!

She had retained it, almost without knowing that she held it in her hand, and little dreaming the unmerited obloquy it would expose her to.

Smithers read the name and the address—Albany, Piccadilly—aloud, and then, pointing the finger of scorn at Agnes, she said—

"Young ladies, this must be instantly communicated to Madame Cerise, my respected relative, and she shall determine whether so hardened a hussey is to be allowed to pollute, by her presence, the rest of her former associates?"

"Stay, I implore!" cried Agnes. "It is true I had the card in my hand——"

"We know that too well," said Smithers, with a sardonic grin.

"Oh! indeed I am innocent!"

And she fell on her knees before her accuser, who never having in her own proper person known the delights of love, could by no possibility make any allowance for another accused of so grave an offence in the eyes of a British matron or a British old maid.

Smithers pushed her rudely away, striking her clenched hands with a small cane she always retained, to enforce order amongst the "young ladies" under her care.

"We don't want any acting, Miss Clarke," she said, coldly.

"Oh! I am innocent," sobbed the unhappy girl; "a gentleman ran after me and pushed this card into my hands, and when he let me go I ran away as fast as I could."

"A very likely story," replied Smithers, with an incredulous air; "a very likely story, indeed; only, unfortunately for you, Miss Clarke, I don't believe it."

At this a low laugh ran all round the room.

The "young ladies" were not a bit more charitable than their amiable task-mistress.

"It is true. Oh! it is, really," sobbed Agnes still more vehemently.

"I appeal to your companions," said Smithers, "whether such a story as you have told us is true, or anything like true. What do you think, ladies?"

A chorus of noes followed this adjuration.

There was, however, one exception. A rather dashing-looking girl, good-looking, but pale from over-work, and want of fresh air and exercise, with hair and eyes dark as the night, exclaimed—

"I believe her!"

"You do! Who are you?" asked Smithers, contemptuously.

"I suppose you know as well as anybody else," replied the girl; "my name's Saunders—Charlotte Saunders—and Saunders is better than Smithers any day."

The girl who spoke so boldly seemed to have come to a sudden determination, and to have made up her mind to risk everything to protect and stand up for her friend.

"Indeed!" replied Smithers. "We'll attend to you presently, Miss Saunders."

"I think you will attend to me now or not at all," said Saunders. "I brought Agnes Clarke to this hole, I am sorry to say, and I have known her for years to be a good and virtuous girl, and I wont have her abused and bullied by you."

"I wish I could say half as much for you," replied Smithers, in a great passion; "but this is evidently a plot, a conspiracy; you shall both suffer for it though. I will have you dismissed, both of you, without your wages, and then see what you will come to."

Charlotte Saunders threw down the work she was engaged upon, at these words, and walked up to Smithers before that disreputable old lady could guess what was going to happen to her, and violently snatching the little cane we have before mentioned out of her hand, she seized her by the right arm, and for the space of a minute administered so severe a castigation that the sufferer's breath was completely taken away, and she sank exhausted with rage, pain, and fear, upon a chair.

During the chastisement, Charlotte Saunders refrained from making any remark, but when she had punished the task-mistress to her satisfaction, she cried, "You old hag, you are nothing better than a murderess: you know you drove three girls, within the last year, to commit suicide; and one died here in her bed the other day; and if I hadn't lived at home you'd have killed me too, most likely; but I have had enough of it for some time past, and I had made up my mind to cut it, only it didn't seem to suit me till to-day."

Agnes during this scene had remained perfectly passive.

"Agnes," said Charlotte, addressing her.

The girl looked up inquiringly.

"Come, child," said her friend. "Put on your bonnet again; you know, I suppose, you can't stay here after this."

"Yes," replied Agnes, "only I am so sorry, dear Charlotte, you should have spoilt your chance by taking my part."

"Oh! don't talk nonsense; dress yourself, and come with me, if you don't want to be kicked out."

Smithers made a movement as if she wanted to get up.

"Not if I know it," exclaimed Saunders. "When I have done with you—not before, Miss Smithers."

And she struck her a sharp blow over the knuckles to enforce obedience.

When Agnes was fully equipped, Charlotte attired herself, and nodding farewell to her associates of the workroom, led the way out of the place.

No attempt was made to follow them, and in a short time, they emerged arm-in-arm into the street.

"Oh, what an unlucky day!" cried Agnes. "I am again thrown on the world."

"Never mind," replied her friend, "there are more ways than one of gaining a living, and I for one am tired of dress-making, I can tell you."

"I dare not go home," said Agnes.

"Why not?"

"Oh, father, you know, will be so angry; and mother is not much kinder."

"I tell you what, Agnes, I have my doubts," said Charlotte, "whether those people are your parents."

A strange flutter agitated Agnes' heart at these words. She too had had an intuition to the same effect.

"What do you mean?" she asked, anxiously.

CHAPTER II.

NORAH NOLAN—DOING A DRAIN—NO BETTER THAN SHE SHOULD BE—VIRTUOUS INDIGNATION—JABEZ CLARKE—"THE COKE AND TATUR LINE"—A FEVER DEN—A FOUL BLOW—TAKING A WIFE DOWN A PEG.

BEFORE Charlotte Saunders had time to reply to her friend's question, her attention was arrested by a showily-dressed young woman, who, walking on the same side of the way, had almost run up against them.

It was evident that Charlotte Saunders and the new comer were acquainted, for a rapid greeting passed between them.

Turning to Agnes, Charlotte said in a low voice, "Norah Nolan, a friend of mine, and a good sort, too."

Norah Nolan might have been pretty some years ago, but dissipation and excess had left their mark upon her, and although when dressed and made up, she was still tolerably decent, she was but the shadow of her former self.

Nevertheless, she cut a very respectable appearance in a black bonnet, with strings and trimming to match, a black shawl, and a moiré antique dress of the same colour.

"Why have you not been to see me?" asked Norah.

"Business," replied Charlotte. "I am not so free and independent as you are."

Norah could hardly repress a sigh at these words.

"How, then," she asked, "are you about now?"

In a few words Charlotte told her friend what had happened at Madame Cerise's, at which she laughed heartily.

"You see," she said, pointing to her attire, "I had gone into mourning for you already, for few women, as I know, last more than a year or two at that slave-driving business."

"What, have you been a milliner?" asked Charlotte.

"What haven't I been!" she replied. "But come and have a drain somewhere. Where will you go?"

"Anywhere," was the reply.

Accordingly the trio went into a public-house where Norah seemed to be well known.

"What will you have?" she asked Agnes.

"I never drink spirits," said Agnes, timidly.

"Oh, nonsense! have a drop of brandy. It wont hurt you. Here! three drains of pale, please."

"Three drains of pale, Miss? Yes, Miss," replied the barman.

After this, Norah insisted upon Charlotte and her friend's coming up to her rooms, which were in a neighbouring street, and hardly knowing what to do, the young women accepted her invitation.

Norah opened an unpretending-looking door with a latch-key, and ushered her friends into a dimly-lighted corridor, leading to a staircase which eventually conducted them into some handsomely-furnished rooms on the first floor.

"Here's my crib," exclaimed Norah; "what do you think of it?"

Agnes thought she had never been in so beautiful a suite of rooms in her life—her untutored and inexperienced mind could compare it to nothing but Madame Cerise's show-rooms.

Going to a cupboard, Norah produced a bottle of gin, saying—

"You know women can never do anything without a drop of gin."

The pictures on the walls were certainly not works of high art, but those tawdry Parisian prints, which are what is called a little free without being positively indecent.

When Agnes had looked at them, and opened one or two gaily-bound books lying on the table, an idea suddenly came into her head that, in popular language, her new acquaintance was no better than she should be.

This was a discovery that any one but one so young and innocent as Agnes Clarke would have made half an hour ago.

Yes; Norah Nolan was a gay woman. She was one of those ephemeral butterflies who regard those moments wasted that are not devoted to pleasure.

Agnes did not wish to make a mistake about her new acquaintance, so she went up to Charlotte, and said, in a whisper—

"I say, Charlotte, is your friend gay?"

"What's that to you?" replied Charlotte. "Perhaps you'll mind your own business."

"Well, if you are going to stay here I shall go," said Agnes, firmly.

"Go!" cried Charlotte; "go where?"

"Oh! anywhere away from here;" and rising, she made towards the door.

"What's the matter?" asked Norah.

Charlotte told her in half a dozen words.

"Oh! Bless her little heart, let her go," laughed Norah, good-humouredly.

"Well, I shall remain here," said Charlotte. "And look here, Miss Fastidious, mind you don't come to the same thing sooner than you expect."

"Remember, I shall be glad to see you, if you want a home or a friend," exclaimed Norah.

Unheedful of these exclamations, Agnes quickly made her way out of the room, and was soon standing in the street.

Where was she to go to?

If she went home her father would be sure to scold her, and most likely beat her.

Her mother was powerless to protect her.

They would be expecting some money, too, for it was nearly the end of the week, and they relied a good deal upon the small sum that Agnes brought home weekly.

Jabez Clarke was a tradesman in a small way, we may say in a very small way indeed. In fact, he was in the 'coke and tatur' line. And although he had, for the last ten years, been hoping to rise to coals every successive week, yet his lofty ambition had unhappily never been gratified.

Mrs. Clarke was a poor, sickly woman, who always seemed at the point of dying, but yet had the appearance of not being able to make her mind up on the matter.

The unfortunate daughter of this worthy couple was in a dilemma.

She had lost her employment, and she had quarreled, with her friends, and now she was afraid to go back to her paternal abode.

Yet she could not remain in the streets. She was becoming hungry. She felt faint and weary. So, summoning up her courage, she turned her steps in the direction of Clare-market.

Here, in this poverty-stricken neighbourhood, was the domicile of Jabez Clarke, Coke and Potato Merchant.

It consisted of the ground floor only, the rest of the house being let to other tenants. The front room was, of course, the shop, while the back one was the sitting-room, kitchen, and bedroom of Jabez Clarke, his wife, and daughter.

So much for the boasted civilization of the nineteenth century.

Sometimes they have small-pox, scarlet fever, and typhus in the neighbourhood. And people shake their heads and wonder at the high rate of mortality in the poorer districts.

Let them come to us; we could enlighten them, and show them what to do with Mr. Peabody's money.

As Agnes entered the shop, Jabez was sitting on a heap of coke, smoking a short clay pipe; "arf a pint o' porter," as that gentlemen himself would have called it, stood on a table by his side, which also supported the remains of an ounce of the best Virginia.

He looked up as the girl made her appearance, and said, in a tone in which surprise and displeasure were mingled—

"What! You 'ome urreddy."

"Yes, father. I've lost my place," replied Agnes, thinking it best to plunge into her troubles at once.

"You 'ave, 'ave yer? Come 'ere!" he exclaimed.

As the girl approached, he seized her by the arm, and drawing her towards him, gave her a heavy blow on the side of the head with his open hand, which had the effect of partially stunning her.

She staggerd a moment, and then, with a low cry, fell on the floor.

Mrs. Clarke was during this scene engaged in the kitchen, cooking a bit of neck of mutton for the repast of the husband, and humming to herself—

" "Tis the song of the poor, the sigh of the weary,
    Hard times, hard times, come again no more;
Many days have you lingered around my cabin door,
    Oh! hard times! come again no more."

but when the noise of her daughter's fall aroused her, she exclaimed—

"Here's Jabez up to some of his games now."

"Missus!" cried Jabez, through the half-opened door.

But Mrs. Clarke did not require calling, she was in the room in a second.

"Oh! deary me, deary me, what be here?"

"Pick her up, you fool," said her husband, with an oath, "or I'll serve you the same."

The poor woman did as she was told, and raised Agnes up.

The girl opened her eyes, for she was more stupified than hurt, and rising to her feet, followed her mother to the back room.

"What's the matter, child?" she asked.

"Matter," suddenly exclaimed Jabez, who had followed them in from the shop; "why, there's lots the matter."

"Let her speak, will you, Jabez, now?" asked his wife.

"She shall speak fast enough, or I'll know the reason why," he replied.

"I've lost my place, mother, that's all. I'm very sorry; I couldn't help it."

"And who do you suppose is a-goin' to keep you in idleness," demanded her father, gruffly.

"I don't know," sobbed Agnes.

"No, I suppose you don't. No more don't I."

"How was it, child?" asked her mother.

"Why, mother," explained Agnes, "I was going back, when a gentleman ran after me, and wanted me to talk to him, and I wouldn't; and he gave me a card, and when I went in I forgot the card; but Miss Smithers saw it, and said I had been doing wrong, and I am sure I hadn't. And so I had to go."

"Where's the card?" demanded her father, roughly.

"Miss Smithers kept it," was the reply.

"Well; you'd better find it, and go to the gentleman who seemed to take such a fancy to you. I aint going to keep you, that's flat," said Mr. Jabez Clarke, brutally.

"Don't talk like that, Jabez," expostulated Mrs. Clarke; "it aint right."

"She's no child of mine," cried Jabez, incautiously, "and I don't care what becomes of her."

"She's listening, Jabez," said his wife. "You'll spoil all."

"Spoil, indeed! I don't see what there is to spoil," he returned.

"You're a fool, Jabez," replied his wife, with unusual boldness, for her.

"Am I?" he cried. "You don't call me fool again!" and he violently pushed the woman to the floor, and her head came in contact with an old iron fender.

Jabez turned on his heel, and walking out of the room, went to the bar of his favourite public-house, and there remained to drink and smoke with other congenial, though ruffianly spirits, to whom he could boast how he had taken his old woman down a peg.

"Oh! mother, mother!" cried poor Agnes, falling on her knees beside her mother's inanimate body.

"What shall I do? what shall I do?" she sobbed.

But the necessity for action forcing itself upon her mind, she got up from her recumbent position. Then going to the sink, she drew a little water in a basin. This she sprinkled with her fingers over her mother's pallid, though blood-stained countenance.

But no signs of animation showed themselves.

Agnes then thought of using a little vinegar, as she had seen that used as a restorative at Madame Cerise's when any girl happened to faint.

Getting on a chair, she took down the vinegar-bottle from a shelf on which it was kept, and bathed her mother's brow, also putting a few drops just underneath her nostrils.

This treatment had the desired effect. Her mother in a

short time recovered her senses, and with her daughter's assistance, laid herself down on the wretched paillasse which served them for a bed.

Agnes ventured to express a hope that her mother was better.

But she replied—"No, child; no. He has done for me this time. However, there is something you must hear before I go."

Agnes' sobs choked her utterance, and she listened to her mother in silence.

CHAPTER III.

THE DEATH-BED—DISCLOSURES—THE CREDULITY OF WOMEN—THE FRUIT OF CRIME—THE OLD STORY—DEATH—ADRIFT.

"OH! mother, mother, dear mother!" cried Agnes, "don't say so."

"Why, my child, should I disguise the truth?" asked Mrs. Clarke.

"But it is so horrible, so dreadful!" said the poor girl.

"Ah! it is a bad world, Agnes, and there are many dreadful things enacted in it," replied the wounded woman.

"It was cruel, it was unmanly, to strike you, mother," said Agnes; "as for me, why I am young, you know, and I can get over such things."

"If you knew all, dear girl," answered her mother, "you would indeed pity me."

"If I knew all?"

"Yes, all, child. I said all, for at present you know next to nothing."

"Are—are you not——" she stopped, for the question almost choked her.

"I know what you would say," her mother replied. "I am——"

Here a sudden faintness came over her, and Agnes was obliged to have recourse to the friendly bottle of vinegar which was of so much service on a former occasion.

When signs of vitality again appeared, Agnes tremulously exclaimed,

"Yes, dear mother, I am listening."

The injured woman recalled her scattered senses, and continued,

"I am your mother."

"Thank God for that!" cried Agnes, overpowered with emotion.

"But——" murmured Mrs. Clarke, in a gentle tone.

"But what, mother?" said Agnes. "Oh! tell me all. I can bear anything but the loss of you."

"Well, the time has come. You shall hear all."

"Yes, all; let me hear all," repeated Agnes.

"Jabez Clarke," said the sinking woman, "is my lawful husband; but he is not your father."

"Oh, Heaven!" said Agnes, clasping her hands, "am I, then, the child of shame?"

"Hush! hush!" cried her mother, "add not fresh pangs to my present misery."

"No, no," answered the unhappy Agnes, "I would not for the world grieve you, dearest mother, for you are my mother, but this is sudden—so sudden."

"Would that I had never sinned!" said the dying woman.

Agnes buried her face in her hands, and seemed rapt in grief or meditation.

Her mother gasped for breath; it was evident that she had not long to live.

Always weak, and subject to anxieties of many kinds, her overtasked mental and corporeal system had for some time been ready to succumb to the first great shock which fell upon them; this had at last come in the shape of the cowardly and brutal attack which had been made upon her by Mr. Jabez Clarke, coke and potato merchant, in Clare-market.

Suddenly Agnes looked up, and said, with evident traces of agitation about her,

"Mother, may I ask you a question?"

Mrs. Clarke looked up at the sound of her daughter's voice, and said,

"Yes, child; speak."

"Who, then, is the author of my being?"

A tremor passed over the features of her mother, as she replied,

"It is hard indeed to publish my shame to my own daughter, but——"

Here a fit of coughing interrupted her utterance, and her frail frame seemed on the point of dissolution.

"Oh, speak, mother, speak!" exclaimed Agnes, in an indescribable agony of expectation.

"Oh! avoid my fate, my daughter," said her mother.

"His name; let me know my father's name, mother, I conjure you!"

"You shall," she answered, faintly. "His name was—is—for I know not that he is dead——"

"Yes, yes," said the expectant girl.

"But to me he is dead," resumed her mother, "yet to you he may be alive. His name, I say, was Leslie."

"Leslie!" cried Agnes, the reminiscences of the afternoon flooding her already over-crowded memory.

"Yes, Leslie—Bernard Leslie."

"Oh! let me hear all."

"You shall, but briefly; my life is ebbing fast."

"Oh, say not so!"

"Why disguise the truth? Yes, my time has come, but there is yet enough life left in this feeble frame to tell the story of my guilt. May my confession be some slight reparation in the sight of Heaven for my offence."

Here the wretched woman paused a moment, while her daughter listened intently for the resumption of her all-absorbing communication.

"I was young," she continued, "and men told me I was beautiful. I was admired by many. How should a poor farmer's daughter escape from the meshes that were cast around her? Let it suffice that I fell: how, you shall hear. The son of the owner of most of the land in our neighbourhood was a young, good-natured boy of between twelve and thirteen; his mother had been dead about a couple of years. Well, he would come to the wakes and festivals held in the village, and when they made me Queen of the May, he danced with me on the village green, and afterwards asked me into the domain of the hall, to fish and take part in other sports which his father's place was famous for."

Mrs. Clarke here broke off abruptly in her narrative, and said,

"Some water, child; some water! I feel a fire consuming me."

Agnes complied with her mother's command as speedily as possible, and she resumed,

"One day your father saw us together, and he spoke to me, told me he was glad to see so beautiful a flower flourishing on his poor estate, and paid me similar compliments—but why dwell on the history of my disgrace—he took me to London, and I became his mistress. You were the only child of our union."

"Oh! my poor mother," sobbed Agnes, leaning her head upon her mother's outstretched hand, "how I pity you!"

"At last, my child, he left me. The usual fate of women who

'Love not wisely, but too well.'

But before he did so, to save his own reputation and character, he married me to one of his dependants."

"And that was Jabez Clarke?" suggested Agnes.

"You have guessed rightly," said her mother, "the man I married was Jabez Clarke, and bitterly have I rued the day he called me wife."

"You have not told me all, mother?" said Agnes inquiringly.

"No, child, no, but you shall hear. For a time Mr. Leslie made us an allowance, but suddenly this stipend was discontinued, and the agents said they had no authority to continue it. Their principal, they told me, had gone abroad, and left them no instructions."

"Horrible!" groaned Agnes. "Can such base ingratitude exist?"

"Oh, yes; men are ever deceitful," responded her mother; "but to my tale. Being deprived of the little pension for which Jabez Clarke married me, he grew peevish and morose, and never lost an opportunity of hurting and ill-treating me; and you see, my child, to what his ill-treatment, and Bernard Leslie's desertion, have brought me."

"You have been cruelly treated," said her daughter.

In vain she waited for an answer. Her mother, overcome by the ill-treatment of her husband, and her painful recollections combined, had succumbed to their united influences, and swooned away.

She was destined never to awaken.

A crimson tinge dyed her lips.

The ill-fated woman had broken a blood-vessel in the intensity of her emotion, but even had this event not taken place, she would have expired of sheer inanition, so exhausted was her system from want of proper food, and the worry brought on by the perpetual ill-treatment of her dastardly husband.

On receiving no reply, Agnes looked in her mother's face wonderingly.

She was filled with an undefined dread—could she be dead—was it possible that she had lost her only friend in this world?

Alas! It was only too true. Mrs. Clarke had breathed her last in this world.

Unaccustomed to such scenes as she was, Agnes could not disguise from herself the fact that her mother had departed this life.

Overcome by her feelings, the girl fell upon her knees by the bedside, and breathed a prayer for the repose of her mother's soul.

If ever a wrong was forgiven, the wrong done her by her mother, was forgiven by Agnes.

"It is not for me," she said, "to cast the first stone."

For some time she remained rapt in meditation and prayer.

When she had partially recovered herself, the great question which had more than once perplexed her that day—"what was to be done?"—again presented itself.

Alone and friendless, she might almost say homeless, what was she to do—what *could* she do?

'Twas a question more easily asked than answered.

If she remained at home she would have to accuse her father at the inquest, which would undoubtedly be held.

To accuse him of the murder of her mother, or at any rate to depose to the fact of his having struck her most brutally, which, combined with his habitual ill-treatment, undoubtedly hastened the poor woman's death.

Such would be her ungrateful task, yet were she to go away, where would she go to, and what was there before her? The very ground seemed to be, by a series of accidents, cut away from under her feet.

Agnes could not help thinking, in the midst of her grief, that it was a singular coincidence that her mother's seducer—her father—should bear the name of the stranger who had that day accosted her near Madame Cerise's, who had given the unlucky card which seemed the forerunner of so many evils.

For misfortunes, as many people can attest, never come singly.

It was her duty, however, to follow her mother's remains to the grave.

But could she brave her reputed father's anger? Would it not be better for her to leave him to his fate, and to go away altogether?

She thought it would; let us not then blame her. Youth is always a series of contradictions. Sometimes right, sometimes wrong.

Impressing a fond, long, loving, lingering kiss upon the placid brow of her inanimate parent, without touching anything in the house to which she might, or might not, have had a good title, she sallied forth from the dwelling, and wandered she knew not whither.

CHAPTER IV.

DESPAIR—A FRIEND IN NEED—AN ABDUCTION—THE HOUSE NEAR GRAY'S INN LANE—MRS. WIDDICOMB—SUSPICIONS—A MAN WITH A MYSTERY.

AGNES CLARKE, destitute and forlorn, left her father's house—that house in which her mother's corpse was lying.

Yet her steps did not falter.

After walking for some time without any well-defined purpose, for the poor child's brain was in a whirl, she sat down upon a doorstep.

She was still in the squalid neighbourhood of St. Giles's, not far from those seven branching thoroughfares, which, converging upon a common centre, give it the name of the "Dials."

The two squares, Soho and Golden, are the only oases in this desert of filth and wretchedness.

Agnes began to cry.

This was no uncommon spectacle, and attracted little attention.

We should be in error though, were we to say that the fit of weeping passed wholly unnoticed.

A young man, apparently about two-and-twenty, paused in his onward way, at beholding the spectacle of the young girl's grief.

He gazed compassionately upon her, and exclaimed, "Can I assist you in any way?"

Agnes shook her head.

"Come, tell me," he said, "what the matter is. Those eyes are far too beautiful to be spoilt by weeping."

Agnes was roused at these words. She wanted help and assistance of a practical sort.

"Compliments are poor food for misery to feed on, sir," she cried. "It is not manly of you to insult a helpless, unprotected girl."

And at the thought of her isolated position her tears flowed afresh.

"Calm yourself," said the stranger. "I will not harm, I will help you, if I can,"

"I am indeed in want of help," sobbed Agnes.

"Then trust in the honour of Marmaduke Wilson, and all will be well," said the stranger, in a voice that thrilled through Agnes, it seemed so full of genuine compassion.

She repeated his words, "All will be well," mechanically. Her head was becoming a little confused.

It must be remembered it was now evening, and she had been some hours without food.

The exciting scenes she had gone through, too, had had an effect upon her nervous system.

"I will give you shelter," said he, who called himself Marmaduke Wilson; "say, will you accept my offer?"

Agnes made no reply; her head drooped gently on one side, and had he not supported her she would have fallen on the pavement.

"What shall I do?" hastily muttered the stranger to himself. "She is evidently poor and friendless, perhaps homeless."

The conclusion his cogitation led him to was speedily made manifest by his hailing a four-wheeled cab, that luckily happened to be passing at this critical juncture.

With the cabman's assistance, Agnes was lifted into the vehicle, and on receiving an address from Marmaduke Wilson, which was spoken in a low voice, the man drove off rapidly in the direction of Holborn.

After a while the cab stopped at a house in a quiet and respectable-looking street which led out of the Gray's-inn-road.

By this time Agnes had opened her eyes, but was still too faint and ill to realise her position or to offer any resistance.

The cabman on receiving a liberal fare touched his hat and drove off, leaving Agnes leaning on the arm of Marmaduke Wilson.

The latter personage produced a key from his pocket, with which he opened the door of a house, ushering in his fair prisoner, for so she might almost be called, then with a celerity which showed him to be well acquainted with the premises, he lighted the gas in a little parlour on the ground floor.

Gently conducting Agnes to a comfortable-looking armchair, he exclaimed—

"There, little one, sit down; you are at home now."

Agnes stared round her in a bewildered manner.

"I think," said Marmaduke Wilson to himself, "that a glass of wine would not be amiss here."

So saying, he went to a cupboard and produced a black bottle.

He evidently despised that refinement of civilization—a decanter.

Pouring out a glass, he offered it to Agnes, and pressed her to drink it.

She took the proffered cordial and drank it off.

It had the effect of restoring her worn-out energies.

"Where am I?" she asked a little nervously.

"This is your home, now. I found you fainting on a door-step in St. Giles's, and I brought you hither. The apartment you see is only homely; I am not rich, although I have enough to live upon, but what I have is very much at your service, until we can communicate with your friends."

"Oh! thanks! thanks!" cried Agnes, "how good you are! But——"

"But what?" he said, smiling; "let me hear anything you have to say."

"But, can I trust you?" she asked, timidly. "How do I know who or what you are?"

A slight cloud passed over his good-looking countenance as he answered,

"I am a man of honour, and as such bound to protect a woman in distress. You are safe in my hands, so be not uneasy. These are your apartments. That room communicating with this is your bed-room."

"And you?" she asked; "I am turning you out of your apartments."

"Oh, never mind me!" he said, laughing; "I can take care of myself. I dare say my landlady will be compassionate enough to give me a shake-down upstairs; and, with your permission, I will send her to you. You are, doubtless, in want of some refreshment. I will order some supper."

Before Agnes could utter her thanks he had left the room.

In a short time a good-natured, motherly-looking old woman made her appearance.

Agnes felt from the first that they would be friends, and the few cheering words with which she greeted Agnes confirmed this impression.

"Mr. Marmaduke, my dear, has sent me to ye," she began; "he says that you are an old friend of his mother's down in the country, and have come up to London to see some of the sights, but that you are powerful tired, and have lost your box at the railway station."

Agnes at once saw the tact and delicacy which had induced her preserver to invent this little history.

"Dear me!" continued the garrulous old woman; "them railway stations is awful—awful, my dear; I always loses myself. And then there's Bradshaw: why, it's so writ that none but a scholard from Oxford or Cambridge can make head or tail of it, let alone a poor body like me; but laws! if I ain't a talking away without ever thinking of you; and you so tired, poor dear!"

So saying, Mrs. Widdicomb, for such was her name, led the way into what was up to this time Mr. Marmaduke Wilson's bed-room.

"There are some of Mr. Marmaduke's things about, my dear," said the old woman; "but they're goin' upstairs directly, and I can lend you something to go on with; for Mr. Marmaduke says I'm to be a mother to you while you stop in town, so you musn't mind what I say, for I have taken a fancy to you already."

Agnes smiled her thanks.

"Now," Mrs. Widdicomb ran on, "now, my dear, take off your bonnet and your shawl; we will go out shopping to-morrow, and buy lots of things. To lose your luggage like that, poor dear! Come, never mind, never mind."

After a time the various arrangements consequent upon the new arrival were made; and after partaking of some supper—the wing of a chicken, and a glass of bottled ale—Agnes retired to rest, as Mr. Marmaduke Wilson had sent word to say, that as she must be very tired he should not trouble her again that evening, but he would have the pleasure of breakfasting with her at nine o'clock, if she would kindly permit him to do so.

When Agnes woke in the morning, all the strange occurrences of the past day, which had been so eventful in the history of her life, rushed like lightning across her memory, and her only feeling was one of unmitigated thankfulness to Providence for its care and protection.

At breakfast the next morning she frankly told Mr. Wilson everything—who she was, and how she came into the position in which he found her.

She saw from the expression of his countenance that he believed her. So she added—

"And you can now exercise your own discretion, Mr. Wilson, in extending your shelter and protection to Agnes Clarke."

"My dear Miss Clarke," he replied, "your remark implies a want of knowledge of my character, which I trust a very short time may remedy."

Agnes expressed a hope that she might soon be able to procure some work, so that she might not be altogether a burden upon him.

"Rest perfectly easy about that," he answered, with an intelligent smile. "I may, perhaps, ask for a reward for my poor services some day; but of that, more anon."

He then told her that he was a commercial traveller, and out a good deal; but he would supply her with books, money, &c., and recommended Mrs. Widdicomb as an honest, if not entertaining companion.

Time passed on, and Agnes settled down in her new home. She assisted Mrs. Widdicomb to get the dinner ready for her preserver on his return home, and contrived to make the time pass pleasantly enough.

Her new friend, too, interested her strangely. Did she detect a tenderness in his manner towards her rather more than that prompted by friendship?

Or was it her fancy—her vivid imagination?

Who shall say?

Again. Did she not sometimes detect an air of melancholy—even of utter sadness at times, about the noble features of Marmaduke Wilson?

Yes; she could not conceal from herself that there was a mystery about this man.

CHAPTER V.

LOVE—A DECLARATION—THE SCENE UNDER THE CEDAR-TREE—THE WARNING—A SUDDEN STORM—TAKING A LEAP IN THE DARK—AGNES IS MARRIED—THE WOLF IN SHEEP'S CLOTHING—TROUBLOUS TIMES—THE IDOL DASHED TO PIECES—THE DISCOVERY—A HIGHWAY ROBBER—REVELATIONS—THE POLICE ARE AT THE DOOR.

IT was summer still; the month of August was waning, but it was summer. Glorious, gorgeous summer! The rays of the setting sun were dancing over the waters of the silvery Thames, and steeping in a deluge of golden light the fair and lovely gardens of Hampton-Court Palace.

Under the shelter of a stately spreading cedar-tree, a fit rival for those of Lebanon, sat two people.

What need of disguise? They were Agnes and her protector. A blush mantled her beautiful face, and then the crimson tide rushed back again, leaving her pale as monumental alabaster.

Was he murmuring words of love in her untutored ear? Alas! yes.

"Agnes, dear Agnes," he was saying, "I have long loved you; from the first moment these eyes fell upon your peerless form, I have loved you. You must have seen it."

Agnes, with her eyes, sought the ground.

"Yes; my love has been constant as it was sudden," he continued.

Agnes felt that a crisis in her fate was approaching. And as she sat with her lover and protector under the spreading branches of that solemn cedar-tree, an undefined presentiment of coming evil stole over her.

Why or wherefore she knew not.

Yet it was so. However, she was the child of fate, and she felt that she must pursue her destiny, whatever the consequences might be.

At last the declaration she had looked for came.

"Agnes!" he exclaimed, in a voice that trembled a little with emotion or with anxiety; "will you be my wife?"

She had often asked herself how she should reply to him when he asked her this momentous question.

For she had felt assured, for some days past, that such was his intention.

But now, when the occasion was actually at hand, and she had to decide, she hesitated.

She could not conceal from herself that Marmaduke Wilson's handsome face and pleasing gentlemanly manners had made a deep and lasting impression upon her.

But there was that intuitive feeling of coming, if not of present evil. A still, small voice it was, which she found it impossible to smother.

She knew that when trouble came, though it was at first like a little cloud no bigger than a man's hand, on the verge of the horizon, it generally, as it passed over, assumed formidable dimensions.

For misfortunes never come singly.

Yet if she loved him, why not marry him? She was friendless and destitute, and his proposal was definite, he offered her a home. His intentions were honourable. Why, for the sake of some girlish scruples, some superstitious nonsense, should she make him and herself miserable?

And, in spite of the prompting of her better nature, she determined to accept him.

"You hesitate, Agnes," he said, in a hoarse voice. "Oh! let me hear my fate! This suspense is worse than death itself!"

She opened her lips, but so agitated was she that the words refused to come.

During the short conversation we have detailed, a sudden change had come over the heavens.

Dark clouds drifted rapidly past.

A cold wind hissed and soughed through the branches of the trees.

The waters of the river bubbled and boiled and foamed restlessly along, as if they, too, were about to take part in the coming conflict of nature.

This change, however, was unnoticed by the lovers, so absorbed were they in themselves.

"Speak, speak, my darling Agnes!" exclaimed Marmaduke. "If you do break my heart, I will try to forgive you. Then, for the love of heaven, speak!"

Agnes put her little hand in his, and replied, "Marmaduke, I love you; I will be your wife."

No sooner had these words passed her lips than a vivid flash of lightning cleaved the air.

And hardly had a second elapsed ere a terrific clap of thunder burst, as it were, over their very heads.

Did the earth seem to tremble at the shock, or was it mere fancy?

Imprinting a burning kiss upon her brow, Marmaduke caught Agnes in his arms, and strained her to his breast.

Her bosom rose and fell, and their hearts beat in unison.

Oh! the rapture of that moment!

Both in after years recalled the happy scene, and it was ever a pleasant reminiscence when worn down by battling with a cruel and heartless world.

But the storm aroused the feminine fear of Agnes.

Large drops of rain were falling on the thirsty sward.

Marmaduke speedily removed his precious charge from the dangerous vicinage of the tree.

He then as quickly sought the shelter of the Palace.

And under the cloisters that had once re-echoed to the foot of Wolsey and the loud laugh of the sensual and voluptuous Eighth Henry, these two young people pledged their troth.

The storm continued for the space of a quarter-of-an-hour to rage with great fury.

The terrible thunder-claps shook the venerable pile.

And a bolt, some people said, had been seen to descend into the river, hissing and boiling like a thing of evil.

Was the tempest but another warning to the astonished girl?

She dared not think—she shut her ears to everything but her present happiness.

Was she not to be Marmaduke Wilson's bride? and was not that enough to send her wild with joy?

For, in spite of her strange warnings, she knew she loved him—fondly, dearly, as well as truly, as ever man was loved.

And he—he, too, was wildly happy.

Well, they have the joy cup at their lips—let them drink, drink, drink deeply. They know not how soon the bitter gall lying at the bottom may be reached.

When the storm passed away, they sought the station and returned to London.

The next day—so anxious and eager was Marmaduke—they were united.

Agnes Clarke became the blushing bride of the man she loved.

Things went smoothly and pleasantly with Agnes for a few brief blissful weeks.

After that it was evident that she had been born under the auspices of a stormy constellation.

Those vain suspicions which had already agitated her mind were destined before long to assume some reality and consistence.

One night her husband came home rather later. He was palpably annoyed by something.

All his art was not sufficient to conceal this fact from his wife.

She, with all the tenderness she could compress into her manner, inquired the cause of his uneasiness.

He replied that it was nothing. He was not very well, and with this excuse he jumbled up the heat of the weather.

"Dear Maramduke," she said, "do let me into your confidence—you know how I love you."

He made no answer.

"Oh! there is some secret," she cried, "which you conceal from me! Why am I never to be part of your own inner self?"

Marmaduke Wilson was visibly agitated, but yet he made no sign.

"Marmaduke," said the young wife, "I insist upon knowing—I have a right to ask, to demand your confidence."

"You had better not, my own darling," he replied, sadly.

And he seized one of her hands, and kissed it passionately.

"Oh! Marmaduke," replied Agnes, "you will break my heart if you hide anything from me. I am prepared to share your perils as well as your joys."

At these words he looked up incredulously, as it were.

"I can never forget," she continued, "that you saved me from destitution, starvation, from something, perhaps, which I have always regarded as worse than death itself. I gave you my hand and my heart; and I do not think you could tell me anything which would alienate my affections from you. Indeed, I am sure that such an occurrence is utterly impossible from the love I bear you."

Marmaduke Wilson rose from his chair, and taking her head between his hands, gazed fondly upon her upturned countenance.

"My poor child," he said, slowly, almost solemnly; "do not ask me any questions."

"But I will, Marmaduke," she replied; "*I must.* I cannot live in this dreadful state of anxiety."

"Well! she must know all some day," he said, as if speaking to himself; "so why not now—at once."

Agnes caught these last words, and exclaimed, "Yes, now—at once. Oh, Marmaduke! if you love me, tell me all."

"How can I publish my own shame to her?" he said; "but yet it must be done. Oh! would to God I had never seen her."

Agnes threw herself at his feet, and said, "Oh, do not say that! anything but that. You cannot—do not hate me!"

And she burst into an agony of tears. Marmaduke Wilson soothed his lovely wife as best he could, and taking her in his arms, placed her on the sofa.

When her paroxysm of weeping was past, she sobbed rather than said—

"Oh! recal those dreadful words, or rather kill me at once. I could not live—if deprived of your love."

Then he whispered words of kindness, of love, and of encouragement in her ears, until she said—

"Forgive me, Marmaduke; but little women are so foolish sometimes, and I *do* love you, my own."

He kissed her tenderly, and a tear-drop stood in his eye.

Well, it is a weakness we like to see in men—it shows they are not utterly hardened, and depraved by contact with a bad, money-making world.

"Now, love, you will tell me, will you not?" she asked, with a winning smile.

He heaved a deep sigh, and replied, "Dear Agnes, you will hate, despise me; I know you will, you cannot help doing so when you know my secret."

"God forbid," cried Agnes, solemnly, "that I should despise my husband, for I do not think I could ever hate him. Oh, speak, Marmaduke, speak! You raise strange terrors in my heart. Let me, in Heaven's name, hear the worst!"

"Suppose, Agnes," he said, as if he were feeling his way—"suppose I am one of the pariahs—the outcasts of civilization—suppose that society was against me, and that my personal liberty is never safe?"

"Oh, my God!" cried Agnes, "you cannot mean that you are——"

Here she stopped, waiting for him to complete the sentence.

"Yes, Agnes; it is but too true, I am——"

"What? what? Oh, this will kill me! What are you? tell me, oh, tell me!"

"I am—yes, you shall know it—I am a *thief.*"

"Oh, Heaven!" exclaimed Agnes, "this is indeed hard to bear."

"I knew you would hate me," he said; "but now you have heard part you shall hear all."

"Yes, yes," she murmured, faintly.

"The officers of justice are even now on my track, and a reward is offered for my apprehension."

Agnes clared her hands in mute amazement.

MARMADUKE WILSON AND AGNES FIND SAFETY IN FLIGHT.

"A price is set upon my head," he continued.

It was strange that this young woman, whose whole soul was centred upon the man who stood before her, should not have fainted, or have lost consciousness, at the recital of a story fraught with such horrors to herself. But no. She bore up heroically.

There are some natures which in times of very great danger become sublimated by the misfortunes and calamities which menace them.

Hers was one of these. She did not faint. She even repressed her tears.

Sitting up on the sofa upon which he had deposited her, she exclaimed, with a strange fortitude, "Let me hear every thing now! You know what I mean."

"Agnes," he said, while that sad look we have before remarked, came over his face, and gave it an almost Byronic beauty, "you have sacrificed much for me, and when you hear my history, perhaps some touch of pity may penetrate your heart for a man who has been more sinned against than sinning."

"I am listening," she answered, quietly, without moving a muscle of her countenance.

"I am the son of a gentleman, Agnes, who had considerable property. This has long since passed from his possession, but it lasted long enough to educate me. You will smile, perhaps, when I tell you that I have been at Oxford; yet such is the case. I kept four terms at that classic seat of learning, and then my father, who was a merchant, failed. My mother I never knew, she died when I was born."

Here he paused a moment, as if overcome with unpleasant recollections.

"And your father?" asked Agnes.

"My father," he replied, "committed what people call a crime. When he found his affairs becoming involved, instead of giving up his property to his creditors, and either becoming a bankrupt or making some arrangement, he collected all the property he could, and turned it into money; he also raised money on accommodation bills which had but a short time to run, but before they became due, he had sailed with a mass of property for America, I believe; but from that day to this I have neither heard nor seen him."

"Is it possible!" cried Agnes.

"He left me a thousand pounds," continued Marmaduke Wilson, "and he wrote me a letter saying that the best thing I could do was to be called to the Bar; but I had not the elements of hard work in me, Agnes, and my father's disgrace recoiled upon myself; my friends cut me at College, and I left in disgust. I gained a fellowship though before I left. It was only thirty pounds a year for three years, but low as I have sunk, I have hitherto avoided detection, and the College authorities pay me the annual stipend I gained, not by the sweat of my brow, but by my brain."

He laughed a low laugh of triumph as he said this.

"I was born a gentleman," again he went on; "my father was a younger brother, but he came of a good stock. Men call me *now* Marmaduke Wilson, but I am a Leslie."

"Leslie!" cried Agnes; "again that name. Do I hear aright?"

"How!" he said; "does that name excite memories in your mind?"

"It does," she replied. "Some day you shall hear, but at present it does not press. Let me hear your tale."

"You shall," he answered. "My thousand pounds, as you may imagine, did not last long. I gambled, I raked, I—pardon me—I amused myself with women——"

"Oh!" cried Agnes, "you have, then, loved before you met me?"

"Never!" exclaimed Marmaduke, "before Heaven, I swear it!"

"Well, well," she said, in a hollow, heart-broken voice, "it is my fate; I must bear it. Go on!"

"There was one who was my mistress, she called herself Norah Nolan."

"What do you say?" said Agnes, with some impetuosity.

He repeated the name, and asked, "Do you know *her?* Oh, Agnes! can it be possible that I have been deceived in *you?*"

"Yes," answered Agnes, confidently, "I know her."

"Oh! this is too much," he exclaimed, as if to himself. "I counted upon her love. I thought her young, and pure, and unsophisticated. Can I have been deceived?"

"No, Marmaduke, you have not been deceived. I am all you ever in your fondest moments thought me; but still I am in a manner acquainted with Norah Nolan."

"May I ask you to tell me?" he said.

"Oh, yes, you shall hear." And she told him the history of her acquaintance with Charlotte Saunders, and their accidental meeting with Norah Nolan.

"Pardon my suspicions," he said tenderly, with a penitential air, "but to lose faith in you would utterly demoralize me."

"Be as brief as you can in continuing your narrative," responded Agnes; "these things pain me."

"Norah Nolan was my mistress," he continued; "she involved me in debts and difficulties, and one by one my former associates cut me. At last I found myself without a halfpenny, and Miss Nolan quietly wished me good-morning. This did not break my heart, for I had only made her acquaintance because it was the custom of all the men I knew at college to do the same thing; and as she was the first I came in contact with, I protected her, as the phrase is."

"Is that all?" asked Agnes.

"No; not all. I then became a frequenter of billiard saloons, for I could play a good game of billiards, but I did not make enough money at that to satisfy my purposes, so I in a manner took to the highway."

"The highway!" ejaculated Agnes.

"Not exactly to Hounslow Heath," he answered, with a smile; "but what I mean to say is, I made other people who had plenty of money contribute to my wants. I have been to public balls, and concerts, and choice gatherings of the cream of society, and I have put some of the visitors at those festive scenes to the expense of obtaining new diamonds and new watches, and all that sort of thing. There, Agnes, now you know. Have I not told you enough?"

He left off with an exclamation of annoyance which was almost immediately followed by a reckless laugh.

"Yes," said Agnes, "I have heard all you are, Marmaduke is your name Marmaduke?" she asked, calmly.

"Yes," he replied; "my christian name is Marmaduke, and to all but you I am Marmaduke Wilson."

"Well, be it so. You are, as you truly told me, a thief."

"Yes; that is no news to me," he said, bitterly.

"Marmaduke," she said, gravely, "I have made up my mind."

"Yes; I expected it," he replied, with a wild, careless laugh; "and you will leave me, I suppose?"

"No," she answered, "I shall not; you are my husband, and with all your faults I love you."

"Are you in earnest?" he cried, not crediting the evidence of his senses.

"Perfectly," was the reply. "Let this kiss prove it."

So saying, she held out her arms, and was instantly clasped in a close embrace.

"I will never leave you, Marmaduke; come what may, I am still your own Agnes."

"God bless you for those words, my sweet angel!" he replied.

At this moment came a loud knocking at the door.

"Good heavens! what can that be?" exclaimed Agnes.

"I know not," he replied, "but I must expect the worst." Rising on tip-toe, he gently raised the blind and peeped through the window.

One glance sufficed to convince him of his danger. Returning to his wife, his agitation assured her that there was something wrong.

"Oh! tell me, Marmaduke," she said, "is there danger? If there is I will share it with you."

"Yes; and the danger is imminent," he replied.

"What can it be?" asked Agnes; "is it——"

"You are right," he said, "*the police are at the door!*"

CHAPTER VI.

THE MYRMIDONS OF THE LAW—HOW TO ESCAPE—THE BACK-DOOR—SURROUNDED ON ALL SIDES—THE ROOF—A FRIENDLY TRAP-DOOR—ON THE TILES—THE ATTIC WINDOW—SAVED.

THE terrible reality burst like a thunderclap upon Agnes and her husband.

The police were at the door.

That was the dreadful fact. And their mission was to arrest *her* Marmaduke—the man to whom she had just vowed a devoted allegiance.

How was the danger to be avoided?

Marmaduke Wilson soon solved the question, by saying—

"My love, I must escape somehow or other. If I am taken by these myrmidons of the law, my fate, I am afraid, is certain."

"Alas! yes," said Agnes.

"And to be separated from you," he replied, "is intolerable. No, it shall not be."

Again the knocking was heard at the door, and this time more loudly and imperiously.

The delay arose from the fact of Mrs. Widdicomb being safely ensconced in bed.

This good lady, hearing the noise, was hastily donning her apparel; but she felt it inconsistent with her dignity to appear in her nocturnal attire.

"Oh! Marmaduke, dear Marmaduke, what will you do? I am worse than a child, I can suggest no plan whatever," said Agnes, tremulously.

"Fear nothing," replied Marmaduke; "I have a plan. God bless you, darling! Kiss me."

Agnes did as he bid her, and in an instant they were locked in a fervent embrace.

"Here is money!" he exclaimed, putting some into her hands; "take it, and meet me to-morrow, at one o'clock, at the National Gallery."

"Oh! no, I cannot—will not leave you," she said.

"Yes, you must; indeed you must."

"No, no; a thousand times no. Where you go, there I will go."

"Oh, Agnes!" he said, "do not destroy me. We shall meet again to-morrow."

"Well, be it so. If I can secure your safety by any sacrifice, it shall be done."

Imprinting one kiss upon her lips, and uttering the word to-morrow, he left the room, and entering the passage, made towards a window which opened upon a small yard in the rear of the house.

Opening this, and gazing outwards, he perceived several policemen, who had somehow or other gained admittance to the rear of the house.

At this juncture the knocking was more furious than ever.

Marmaduke Wilson's first idea had been to escape by the yard at the back, but finding that occupied by his enemies, he was obliged, on the spur of the moment, to organize a new idea.

This he was not long in doing.

Running quickly along the passage, he reached the front door, and with the greatest carefulness drew the key out of the lock.

This he put in his pocket. Then, imitating the voice of an old woman, he said, "Who is there?"

"Police," was the reply; "and you had better make haste."

"Very well," said Marmaduke. "Don't be in a hurry, and you shall be let in."

"Now," exclaimed the leader of the police, "now, we want Marmaduke Wilson, and if you don't let us in we shall break the door down."

"Oh, dear! oh, dear!" said Marmaduke, still counterfeiting his landlady's voice, "how dreadful! but you must wait, gentlemen, indeed you must. I have been and left the key in my bedroom."

"Well, look sharp, that's all," replied the policeman, "or we shall not be long in effecting an entry."

With the agility of an antelope Marmaduke leapt upstairs, meeting Mrs. Widdicomb at the top of the first flight.

One vigorous push sufficed to send the old lady on her back. Then, seizing her by her shoulders, he pushed her into her room, and taking the key, locked her in.

It was the work of an instant after that to rush to the top of the house, to seize the steps, and to open the trap-door leading to the roof.

The roof was unoccupied.

Then, with equal celerity, Marmaduke descended the stairs, and going to the door, said—

"Oh, dear, gentlemen! do be patient, you do worrit a poor lone widow so. I have lost the key, and if you flurry me I shall never find it."

"Make haste, my good woman," said the head of the police force, "or we shall force an entry."

"Oh, wait a minute, dear, good sir!" said Marmaduke, in the quaking voice of an old woman.

"Well, we will wait two minutes longer—no more," replied the officer, "so look slippery."

"Yes, yes, sir; I will, I will," said Marmaduke.

Then gliding along the passage, he entered the sitting-room.

Agnes was stretched upon the sofa, her hair disheveled, and her eyes red with weeping.

"Come, Agnes!" he said, "we will not be separated except by the grave."

Joyfully she sprang up and followed him, without asking a single question.

He led the way up-stairs to the roof, and as they passed Mrs. Widdicomb's chamber, they heard her bellowing like a mad bull—

"Thieves! fire! thieves! fire!" until her voice was as hoarse as a raven.

It did not take Marmaduke long to re-open the trap-door and to lift Agnes through it.

When they were once safe upon the tiles, their first anxiety was to fasten the trap-door as well as they could.

Having accomplished this by employing some loose bricks and tiles they found lying about, they had to consider what was next to be done.

Their only course was to hasten along the edge of the roof as quickly as they could.

For there was little or no doubt that the officers would eventually effect an entry.

This being the case, their only chance was clearly to escape as quickly as they could.

With this purpose in view, and hand in hand, they passed over the roof of several houses.

At last they espied a window, leading, they supposed, into an attic. This window was open.

It seemed to be their only chance. It was now between eleven and twelve o'clock, and if they were to make their escape it must be done quickly.

There was certainly a moon to guide their footsteps, but its light also enabled them to see that if they pursued their onward course much farther they would come to the end of the row of houses, as a cross street intervened, and then what was to become of them? The thought was dreadful. Agnes, by sharing her husband's flight, had to a certain extent involved herself as an accomplice, and although it would be difficult to prove her guilt in his malpractices, still she would lay herself open to grave suspicion.

At all events she would be exposed to much annoyance, and most probably many insults at the hands of the police.

This thought struck her husband, and urged him to fresh exertions.

He could have suffered himself, but he was determined that the fair creature whom he had married should have as little cause as possible to regret that marriage.

So, whispering a few words of encouragement in her ear, he boldly entered the open window.

Without making the slightest remonstrance, she passively followed him:

The moonbeams penetrated a part of the room, and showed the intruders that a female—probably a servant—occupied the apartment. She was fast asleep, and had evidently left the window open to relieve herself from the severe heat.

Marmaduke's plan was soon made, and in a low tone he communicated it to Agnes.

She made no opposition: she seemed disposed to follow him blindly wherever he led her—such is the force of love.

Their movements were so gentle and so quiet, that their entry did not arouse the slumbering maid-servant.

After they had entered, Marmaduke carefully closed the window and bolted it.

Then he, with as much gentleness as he could command, undid the door of the attic into which he had penetrated, and with Agnes descended the stairs.

Although they accomplished the descent with the utmost caution, they could not avoid making a certain creaking noise.

For stairs at night always creak and groan if any one trusts himself upon them.

This noise aroused some one who slept on the second floor of the house.

It was most likely the landlady or owner of the house. Anyhow, Marmaduke and Agnes heard a door creak upon its hinges, and in a moment a form emerged clothed in the garments of a vestal virgin.

"Who is there?" demanded the form, which might have been mistaken for a ghost, only the voice was too unmistakeably human.

Marmaduke pressed forward and replied—

"My dear madam, myself and my wife are strangers in London, and we have only just arrived from the Great Northern Railway. Not wishing to incur the expense of putting up at an hotel, as we have heard so much of the rapacity of hotel-keepers, we have made up our minds to look after lodgings. So we told our cabman to drive slowly along various streets until we saw a house we liked. We saw yours, and, as you see, we have made an application."

"But I did not hear you knock!" exclaimed the lady of the house.

"No, I dare say not," replied Marmaduke, carelessly.

"Then how did you get in?" she demanded.

"My dear madam," said Marmaduke, "servants, you know, will be servants."

"Well, sir——"

"And the fact was we found the street-door open, so at first we took it for an hotel, and as it looked so eminently respectable——"

"Yes, sir, I trust it is respectable, as you are good enough to say," replied the landlady; "but it is not an hotel, and how the door came to be left open I cannot conceive. It must have been that Dinah, who sleeps in the attic. Dinah, sir, is my servant."

"Very likely it was Dinah's carelessness," answered Marmaduke. "But, my dear madam, the question is whether you can accommodate us for the night?"

"Certainly I can, sir," replied the landlady; "but my terms are rather high."

"Name them," replied Marmaduke.

After some slight conversation these preliminaries were arranged, and Marmaduke and his wife took possession of some decent apartments where they could for the moment take refuge.

Marmaduke explained that they had left their luggage at

the cloak-room of the railway station, and that they would call for it to-morrow.

He also gave the old lady a couple of sovereigns as the first week's rent, since she had intimated a wish to be paid in advance.

After all these things they retired to rest in a room into which the old lady ushered them, and she herself slept none the less soundly, for they assured her that they had fastened the front door securely after they had entered the house.

———

CHAPTER VII.

THE GREY DAWN OF THE MORNING—INSPECTOR WYMAN —THE POLICE ARE ON THE WATCH—A SUBTERFUGE— A DISGUISE—THE WIDOW—THE SHOEBLACK—TOWER HILL—ARE THEY PURSUED—THE STRUGGLE—FREE-BLUEGATE-FIELDS.

ALTHOUGH Marmaduke Wilson and his lovely and confiding bride had succeeded in obtaining a temporary refuge, neither of them dreamt of retiring to rest.

The danger which beset them was imminent — so imminent that at any moment the police who are not wont to be beguiled by subterfuges might be upon them.

Is it to be wondered at then that Agnes's heart was full of alarm and terror? She had just sworn everlasting allegiance to a man whom up to the present time she had looked upon as faultless. Now she knew him to be what her inmost soul shrank from. Yet she did not cast him out. She clung to him. He was her husband. She had loved him. She loved him now, and whatever his faults might be, she determined that she would neither cast the first nor the last stone.

Who shall determine the subtleties of a woman's nature?

It was well for them that they were on their guard, for the police, as relentless as bloodhounds, were still on their track, and pursuing them with unremitting ardour.

The chief of the force which had come in the night time, armed with a warrant for the arrest of Marmaduke Wilson, was Inspector Wyman. Ever a man of great determination, he united with this quality that of extreme cunning. Altogether, Inspector Wyman was a foe worthy of a courageous antagonist.

It was not long before Wyman effected an entry into the house in the small street leading out of the Gray's-inn-road. But it would be superfluous to say that he found that his trouble had been taken in vain, as the birds were flown. The manner of their escape has been already detailed to our readers.

Inspector Wyman, however, was not a man to be baffled in this way. He argued, and very justly, that they could not have escaped either from the front or back of the house, because he himself had been keeping guard in front, and a trustworthy detachment were by his orders doing the same in the rear.

There remained, then, but the roof, and this Wyman carefully examined. But his examination was without any practical result. One thing, however, he felt assured of, and that was, that Marmaduke Wilson could not have emerged from the block of houses in one of which he had hitherto lodged.

About Agnes they knew nothing. She was as yet utterly unknown to the police, and in this fact, as will be seen, lay Marmaduke Wilson's great hope of safety.

Inspector Wyman contented himself with setting a guard in every position from which Marmaduke could possibly make his escape. That done, he betook himself to his home, where his wife and family were awaiting him. Not that the charms of home would have been an inducement powerful enough to withdraw Inspector Wyman from the scene of his duty, only he esteemed the precaution he had taken amply sufficient, and he thought that he might safely return to the bosom of his family without detriment to the public service.

Marmaduke Wilson came to the conclusion that the entire street would be strictly watched, but he was also of opinion that the police would not venture to disturb the inhabitants by searching every house. And after some consideration, it seemed to him that Agnes and himself might snatch a few hours' repose, and fortify themselves for the coming events of the morrow.

The morning, grey and misty, was not long in making its appearance. Marmaduke knew well how to exercise the important power of waking when you will. Accordingly, at cock-crow, he was on the alert.

And he racked his brain to devise a means of escaping from the danger which threatened him. The only plan which occurred to him was one fraught with great risk and peril, but from its very audacity likely to be successful. This, after some deliberation, he determined to adopt.

Breakfast was duly brought them by their new landlady, and discussed in silence by themselves. When Marmaduke considered that the time for action had arrived he exclaimed—

"Dear Agnes, if you will be guided by me, and seek your own safety, I can, without difficulty, dictate the means."

"Never, Marmaduke," said Agnes; "where you go there I will go."

"But, my child," he replied, "consider the risk you run; would it not be better for us to separate, and meet again subsequently?"

"If you tell me to leave you," she said, "why, I suppose I must; but I would rather—much rather, share your risk—and who knows but that a woman's ready wit may, some time or other, stand you in good stead?"

"It may, Agnes; it may," he answered; "but I am indeed loth to expose you to the endless annoyances which must, I know, follow, since the police have commenced to persecute me."

"Marmaduke," said Agnes, after listening to him attentively, "we must not separate. I feel it. It will be better for us both that we hang together. You remember the bundle of sticks; when they were tied together no one could tear them asunder, but, once separated, they fell an easy prey to all who chose to pluck at them."

"What you say is true, my own darling, and I thank you for your courage and devotion. We will not part," responded Marmaduke; "at least not voluntarily," he added.

"What then is your plan?" she asked, anxiously.

"My plan is simply this——" And he talked earnestly to her for a few minutes, but in a very low voice.

"I think that will do," she replied.

"You think so," he exclaimed. "Very well, let us then act upon it."

Agnes descended the stairs, and sought an interview with their landlady, who seemed glad to make the acquaintance of the new lodger, who, as she afterwards declared, was such "a nice, soft-spoken body."

"And what can I do for you, my dear?" demanded the old woman, whose name was Hughes; "I am sure I am right glad to see you."

"Well, Mrs.——" began Agnes, but not knowing her name, she hesitated.

"Hughes, my dear, Hughes," suggested the landlady. "And it's an honest name, if it isn't an aristocratic one."

"Well, Mrs. Hughes, you can go shopping for me, if you will. I have promised to send my aunt in the country some mourning. She has just lost her husband, so that she wants it as quickly as possible. Look, here is some money; will you go?"

"What should you want, think you?" asked Mrs. Hughes.

"Let me see," responded Agnes. "A black crape bonnet, of course, and a black dress trimmed with crape, and a black shawl, and other little things, Mrs. Hughes, which the men at the shop will suggest to you."

An idea seemed to strike Mrs. Hughes, for she looked grave for a moment, and then suddenly exclaimed—

"You wont be offended, my dear, but when poor dear Hughes died"—here a not over clean pocket-handkerchief was brought into requisition—"I, you know, went into mourning."

Agnes did not know, but she accepted the declaration as matter of fact, although she did not perceive the drift of her companion.

"Yes, Mrs. Hughes," she said. "Pray go on!"

"And that mourning, my dear, is still in this very room, in that identical chest of drawers," replied Mrs. Hughes.

"And what then?" asked Agnes.

"Well, my dear, if so be as you are not too proud, there it is, and you shall have it cheap, too, although it isn't much worn, considering I was in weeds twelve months."

The truth then burst upon Agnes. Mrs. Hughes had kept her mourning by her since the death of her husband, but now, seeing a chance of parting with it on advantageous terms, she agreed to sell it to Agnes, who, most probably, was the first bidder.

Finding, by an inspection of the melancholy-looking attire, that it would answer her purpose, Agnes agreed to buy it of the considerate Mrs. Hughes, and cheerfully paid the price demanded by that rapacious old lady, which was about ten or fifteen per cent. in excess of the cost price.

Agnes had the mourning apparel brought up-stairs into her bedroom, and told Mrs. Hughes that she would pack it up, and get her servant to take it to the Parcels Delivery Company.

Then she sought her husband, and told him upon what terms she had effected a purchase.

Was it not strange that this simple announcement seemed to fill the breast of Marmaduke Wilson with delight and joy?

Of what possible use could these old clothes be to him, or indeed to his wife either, for that matter?

We shall shortly see of what use they were. Marmaduke Wilson was not the man to act without an object.

He disappeared into his bedroom, and in a short time emerged, fully equipped in the despised widow's weeds.

As he entered the room he looked in the glass, and turning to his wife, who had assisted him in his *toilette*, said—

"Shall I do, Agnes?"

She responded in the affirmative.

"You think that, disguised like this," he continued, "I may defy detection?"

"I am sure I hope so, dear Marmaduke," was the reply. "And indeed I think so; but the issue is in the hands of Heaven."

"It is so," he said, "but we must still rely upon ourselves. Well, let us make the venture. Do you, Agnes, send the old woman out for change of a five pound note. Tell her you will not trust the servant, and if we follow her closely we can emerge from the house without being exposed to her scrutiny."

Agnes complied with these directions, and then, having hastily put on her bonnet and shawl, they descended the stairs together.

Just as Mrs. Hughes' portly figure disappeared round the corner of the street, Agnes and her husband left the house which they had so unceremoniously entered the night before.

They were not calculated by their appearance to excite any particular attention; a widow and her daughter are not uncommon spectacles at any time.

There was one thing in their favour, too. As they had proceeded up the street in their flight of the previous night, they would be spared the necessity of passing Mrs. Widdicomb's house.

This was fortunate, because had that good lady been looking out of the window, as was her diurnal custom, she would infallibly have recognised Agnes.

Marmaduke Wilson looked carefully up and down the street, but he saw nothing to excite his apprehension. This apparent quietude did not exactly please him. Things were too quiescent to denote perfect security.

The street was perfectly deserted. No one appeared to be moving either one way or the other. It is true that it was a very quiet, out-of-the-way street, but still it was suspicious that there should be no one standing about, either as a spy or a sentry.

This very circumstance ought to have put Marmaduke Wilson upon his guard. And so it did, to a certain extent; but not sufficiently, as will be seen in the sequel.

At the corner of the street stood a shoe-black. He was not one of the ordinary sort, for he had not a red coat on, nor was he of what we may call the orthodox size or age. He appeared to be a poor, ragged fellow, about nineteen or twenty; but he was evidently awake to the exigencies of trade, for, as Marmaduke and his wife passed, he exclaimed, addressing Marmaduke—

"Boots cleaned, sir! Clean your boots, sir! Polish your boots."

Marmaduke, for a moment forgetting his disguise, replied, "No, thank you; not this morning."

Directly the shoe-man heard this reply, he scrutinized the pair closely, and the result of his scrutiny was that he abandoned his stock-in-trade—blacking, box, brushes, &c.—and followed Marmaduke and Agnes sedulously, although at a respectful distance.

"I did not like that man, Marmaduke," exclaimed Agnes, "who spoke to you at the corner of the street."

"Which one, darling?" he asked.

"Why, the man who asked you if he should black your boots. There was something which struck me particularly."

"And that was——" said Marmaduke, smiling.

"That was he addressed you as sir, and you, my pet, were foolish enough to answer him."

"You are a very clever little woman, Agnes," answered Marmaduke, "but I think you have discovered a mare's nest this time. However, we shall know, and come what may, I hope and think I am a match for one man."

"I am sure you are, Marmaduke," replied Agnes. "But be careful what you do, and, above all things, be on your guard."

Marmaduke hailed the first cab they saw, and as they got into it, he said to his wife—

"Agnes, you must trust implicitly to me. I am not going to take you into the neighbourhood of Belgravia, but I am going where I think I shall be safest for a time."

Agnes's only reply was to press his hand tenderly.

"Go to the Whitechapel-road," exclaimed Marmaduke, addressing the cabman; "I will pull you up when I wish to stop."

After entering the cab Marmaduke took the precaution to look out of the window to see if he was followed. A few moments set his mind at rest upon that point. The man who had accosted him at the corner of the street, asking to be allowed to black his boots, had, notwithstanding his seedy attire, hailed a cab, and, as Marmaduke was looking on, he was pointing towards his cab, and evidently giving the man instructions either to follow in pursuit, or else to keep the other one in sight.

Marmaduke fell back in the cab, and began to reflect. It was clear that his silly answer to the shoe-cleaning man had aroused that individual's suspicion, and that, in spite of his attire, he was suspected.

He could think of nothing except to allow his pursuer to follow him to some of the small, deserted streets about the Tower of London, and there meet him, and, boldly confronting him, ask him why he was following him, and if his reply was not satisfactory, to knock him on the head or burke him.

Desperate diseases require desperate remedies. Marmaduke's cab slowly pursued its way through Holborn and the City till it reached the Bank, when Marmaduke let down one of the front windows, and told the driver that he wished to go to the Mint on Tower-hill.

He was not long in arriving. When he had done so, he got out, and handed Agnes out. Another mistake, which a prying pair of eyes not far off noticed with a gleam of satisfaction.

Marmaduke paid the cabman liberally, and plunged into a narrow street leading to St. Katherine's Docks.

Huge mountainous masses of houses arose on every side; they were, however, only inhabited in the daytime. They were storehouses for grain and various other articles of merchandize.

Those warehouses cast a gloomy shadow over the footway upon which not many people travelled at the busiest of times.

When Marmaduke and his wife had progressed about one-half of the street he turned round in order to reconnoitre.

Yes! there was the boot-cleaner but a few yards behind him. He must, then, be a police-spy; there could be no doubt about it.

What was to be done?

Marmaduke was a man who never lost much time in thought.

Without saying anything to Agnes beyond "Be quiet, all will be well," he turned round, and began to retrace his steps as quickly as he could.

The police-spy also endeavoured to retreat, but Marmaduke was upon him before he could go many feet.

"My friend!" exclaimed Marmaduke, "it appears to me that you take a great interest in my movements."

"So much so," replied the man, "that I arrest you in the Queen's name."

"Not so fast, my boy," said Marmaduke; "not so fast. I shall have a word to say to that."

"I am Wyman, the Detective Superintendent of the C Division," cried the boot-cleaner; "and it is useless to resist."

"Then take that, Wyman!" said Marmaduke, striking the detective a blow in the face, and immediately afterwards, before he could recover from the blow, seizing him by the throat, and strangling him till he grew black in the face.

When he thought he had gone far enough in order to accomplish his purpose without committing actual manslaughter, Marmaduke let go his hold, and Wyman the detective fell heavily on the ground.

During this scene no sound had been uttered by either party, and strange to say, no one had passed by on either side of the way.

Certainly Marmaduke had calculated the chances before he embarked in his perilous contest.

But now there appeared several people coming each way. In a few minutes quite a small crowd surrounded Marmaduke, the officer, and Agnes.

"What is the matter?" asked one.

"The poor man is in a fit," replied Marmaduke. "Look to him, some of you, and unfasten his neck-tie, while I go and get a cab to take him to the hospital."

The bystanders thought what a benevolent old lady it was, and proceeded to carry out her instructions to the letter.

Marmaduke, accompanied by Agnes, made the best of their way out on to Tower-hill again; and seeing an empty cab standing still, they hailed it.

The man, however, said he was engaged, but on Marmaduke's offering him half-a-sovereign, he accepted the fare, and rapidly drove them in the direction of Whitechapel. When they had passed Leman-street a few hundred yards, they alighted, and paid their fare.

Agnes remarked that the cabman seemed to look after them as if he was watching them; but she said nothing to her husband, who led her at a smart pace through numerous small streets, until they stopped in a neighbourhood which we will describe more fully in the next chapter.

Suffice it to say that Mr. and Mrs. Marmaduke Wilson were in the precincts of Bluegate-fields.

CHAPTER VIII.

THE SUBTERRANEAN DWELLING—AN APPARITION—WHAT IS IT?—THE DWARF "STUBBLES"—A TEMPORARY REFUGE—"STUBBLES" SMELLS A RAT—WYMAN AGAIN —THE FUGITIVES IN A FIX—MARMADUKE OVERHEARS AN IMPORTANT CONVERSATION—WILL THEY ESCAPE?— WYMAN ON THE WATCH.

MARMADUKE WILSON did not pursue his peregrinations much farther. After passing up a long street lined on either side with low-looking, squalid, tumble-down houses, with four small streets on either side running out of the main thoroughfare laterally, he turned round to see if he was followed.

But after throwing a searching glance in every direction he appeared to be satisfied.

There were a few children playing about in the road. These unfortunates seemed steeped in the utmost wretchedness and poverty, if not crime. Their fathers were most likely out thieving, or undergoing a term of imprisonment for some former offence.

When a man returns from transportation or imprisonment he returns to his wife and family, if he be possessed of these incumbrances, and supposing his dwelling is situated in Tiger Bay or Bluegate-fields, the inhabitants turn out, and his return is celebrated with much rejoicing. And the orgie of rum and gin is kept up until early in the morning, when men, women, and children seek their disgusting, vermin-ridden beds, and snatch a few hours of broken repose in a reeking and pestilential atmosphere.

Such is Bluegate-fields, and such its inhabitants.

Marmaduke, we say, saw nothing to arouse his suspicions, so he turned down a small street, which was one of the miserable-looking arteries we have before alluded to. It even seemed more ruinous than the rest. The very doors which gave ingress to the houses were so rotten and out of repair that they refused to move on their hinges. The glass in the windows was broken here and there, and pieces of dirty rag were stuffed in to exclude the wintry blast, which at times seemed to penetrate the very marrow of the bones of the inmates.

Marmaduke stopped at one of these houses, which appeared to be untenanted, so very desolate did it look. The door hung by one solitary hinge. The windows were so obscured with dirt and rags that to penetrate the interior visually from outside would have been impossible.

Entering the passage Marmaduke put his fingers to his mouth and blew a shrill whistle.

After the lapse of a few seconds this was responded to. It was evidently a signal.

Presently, what in the dim light of the mouldy passage appeared to be a horrible monster made its appearance.

Yet it had the semblance of humanity.

Its hair was long and shaggy, its eyes gleamed fiercely, its finger-nails were long and gnome-like, and its head was fixed deeply in its shoulders, as if nature had omitted to give it a neck in a moment of forgetfulness: add to all this its insignificant stature, scarcely exceeding four feet; it was an apparition calculated at first sight to inspire terror in the breast of the bravest.

"Stubbles!" ejaculated Marmaduke.

"Is that you, captain?" asked this hideous dwarf in a shrill voice.

"Use your eyes, and you'll see," responded Marmaduke. "Is there anyone here?"

"No one, Captain," answered Stubbles, who indulged in what was the very ghost of a laugh, but which evidently denoted the height of enjoyment or amusement at something or other.

"What now, you abortion?" exclaimed Marmaduke.

"You does the widder well," replied Stubbles, with another and more prolonged cachinnation.

"Lead on!" exclaimed Marmaduke, impatiently; "we are tired, and would rest."

On receiving this summons, Stubbles entered what was once the kitchen, but which was now deserted by all but the mice, and rats, and black-beetles, some of the latter crushed beneath your every other foot-fall, so numerous were they.

Having traversed this, the dwarf led the way down some steps into a subterranean apartment, the existence of which few would have suspected. It was nothing more than a cellar, but the damp and slimy walls had been securely hidden by double layers of thick carpeting, and the floor was likewise protected. It was a spacious apartment, but its dimensions were rather contracted by a partition which had been put up for the purpose of forming a sleeping chamber. Some luxurious pieces of furniture gave it an air of comfort. There were two arm-chairs and a sofa, and the room was lighted by two candles placed on a table at the further end.

This hiding-place was, as Marmaduke explained to Agnes, only known to a few—half-a-dozen at the utmost—who resorted to it in times of danger. Of course this half-dozen were all of one fraternity, but Marmaduke had become acquainted with them, and had by them been initiated into the mysteries of the underground apartment in the old house in Bluegate-fields.

Stubbles, the dwarf, was the ostensible tenant, and he paid a slight rent every quarter to a grasping and avaricious landlord. The dwarf acted as the servant of the men who frequented the cellar, and Marmaduke was well known to him.

"Do you think, Agnes," asked Marmaduke, "that you can stay here with me until the storm blows over?"

"If anything is good enough for you," she replied, "you know it is for me."

"Very well; but your patience and goodnature will be a good deal tried, I warn you. But now to change these garments."

Retiring behind the curtain which formed the partition, he in a few minutes returned dressed as a bricklayer.

"You see," he said, smiling, "that we keep all sorts of dresses here, so that we are prepared for any emergency."

Stubbles, without waiting for instructions, produced a flask of wine, some cold ham, and the remains of what was once a fine goose.

"Fly-by-night and the Surrey Wolf were here last night, Captain," he said, by way of explanation.

Stubbles then sat down on a stool in the corner of the room nearest the door, as if on the watch.

"Marmaduke," said Agnes, "will you make me a promise?"

He readily consented to do so.

"Then," she said, "leave off this dreadful life, and go abroad with me to Australia or New Zealand."

This request took him somewhat by surprise.

"I would do so," he replied, "but I have not the means. It is easier to propose such a thing than to accomplish it."

"But this life I am sure will kill me."

"It is unkind of you to reproach me," he said.

"I am not reproaching you, Marmaduke; I am advising you for your good. Begin a new life in Australia, and forget the dreadful past; why not?"

She said this earnestly, but he shook his head.

"Some day perhaps, Agnes," he replied, "but not now. It is impossible."

Agnes's eyes filled with tears; a feeling of profound compassion found a home in her breast for this handsome, misguided young man, who was, she felt convinced, rushing upon a terrible fate.

If he fell into the hands of the police, penal servitude would be his doom, and she would be once more alone in the wide world.

Oh, that she had accepted the omens which agitated her in the gardens of Hampton Court Palace!

But no; she would not say so. She would not now look back. She would cling to her husband, and endeavour to reform him. She knew she had great influence over him, and she did not despair of effecting his reformation in the long run.

Every man's hand might be against him, yet should not hers.

Suddenly Stubbles rose to his feet, and holding up his finger, cried "Hush!"

Instantly the silence of the dead reigned in that cellar in Bluegate-fields.

Gliding stealthily, like a snake in search of its prey, Stubbles crept up the ladder which conducted to the kitchen.

Having brought his head on a level with the floor, he placed his ear to the ground and listened.

He remained a minute, perhaps more, in this singular position. It was a time of awful suspense to the couple remaining below.

Then he descended as carefully as he had gone up, and advancing towards Marmaduke he uttered the single word, "Slops!"

"The police! good Heavens! Am I again environed?" cried Marmaduke.

"Indeed I fear so," said Agnes. "Heaven help us in this our hour of need!"

Marmaduke boldly, though with the utmost caution, ascended the ladder as Stubbles had done a few minutes previously.

It was unmistakeable that two people were conversing either at the doorway, or in the passage of the old house.

Marmaduke could hear their voices, though not very distinctly. He could, however, glean enough from their conversation to discover that he was the object of it.

"You say that you saw them enter this house?" exclaimed one.

"Sartain sure, master," was the reply.

"And what were they like?"

"One was a widdy, uncommon tall she was, too, and the other a young 'oman as might ha' been her daughter, though ekally she might not ha' been."

"And you have not seen them emerge?" asked the one who was interrogating him.

"'Merge, master," asked the respondent; "what may that be?"

"Come out, you fool! I mean come out."

"Fule yersel, for the matter of that; why don't yer tauk English? then a body could onderstand; but that aint 'ere nor there."

"Will you answer my question?" demanded the other, angrily.

"Sartainly, but aint you lost something, mister?"

"Lost something? not that I am aware of," was the reply; "have you found anything?"

"Oh, it don't matter!" said the other, "only I thought, mebbe, you'd lost your temper."

"Thunder!" exclaimed his companion. "I'll make you speak. Now, answer me, have you seen this widow and her daughter——"

"I didn't say it was her daughter."

"You didn't, eh! Then perhaps you'll listen to me."

"Sartainly, but that aint neither 'ere nor there."

"Will you hold your tongue?"

"Sartainly; will you?" was the provoking reply.

"Now, once more——"

"Yes, once more. I's ready, I is."

"Did you see this widow and her daughter——"

"Tell you I never said so."

"Confusion!" shouted his companion; "you must be mad, drunk, or an idiot."

"Ijjit! Ijjit yersel. Who are you a calling fules and ijjits?"

Marmaduke could not help smiling at this colloquy, although he had, indeed, great cause for alarm.

While listening he had made a discovery—a discovery fraught with tremendous danger to him.

The man who was making all these inquiries was *Wyman*. Yes, Wyman, the detective—Marmaduke's inveterate and sleepless foe, was again on the track.

He had evidently recovered from the assault made upon him by Marmaduke on Tower-hill, and now he would add personal pique to his official duty.

Truly Marmaduke had cause for fear, but he had not much time to think over his desperate position; the conversation was resumed, and it was important that he should overhear it in its minutest detail, as he would shape his future movements by those of the detective.

"Come," said Wyman, after a moment's consideration, in a conciliatory tone, "come, you've had half-a-crown——"

"'Arf-a-crown—bull, I *should* say—yes, I 'ave, and you've had more'n 'arf-a-bull's worth of information."

"Granted, my friend," replied Wyman; "and here is another for you."

"That's business," said the man.

"Well, let us resume. You say you saw the woman and her supposed daughter——"

"That's right, that is."

Wyman resumed without noticing the interruption—"supposed daughter enter the house, and you have not seen them come out?"

"Right you are, sir."

"Very well, then," said Wyman, "if you will take a note for me to Scotland-yard, I will give you another half-crown."

"'Arf-bull, I says."

"Will you go? yes or no."

"I'm your man, capting, although that's neither 'ere nor there; what I mean is, I'll go."

Wyman took a note-book from his pocket, and hastily scribbled a few lines. He then folded the paper in a three-cornered form, and giving it to the man, said—

"You'll make the best of your way, my man?"

"Sartainly."

"Then off you go, and I shall wait here for the answer."

The man started off at a good round pace, and Wyman, after watching him out of sight, entered the passage of the old house, leant against the wall, and indulged in what appeared to be a reverie.

Marmaduke was a silent witness of all this.

One thing was clear, Inspector Wyman was convinced that his prey was safely housed; but not liking to indulge in a hand-to-hand conflict with Marmaduke without some assistance, he had despatched a message to Scotland-yard for help.

Why he had not sent to the station at Spitalfields, or at Leman-street, Whitechapel, was not clear. Perhaps it was an unintentional blunder. Even the cleverest men are not always infallible.

Certainly it was a blunder, and in Marmaduke's favour, because it gave him more time.

It may appear singular that Inspector Wyman should have been able to trace the fugitives so quickly and with such certainty.

But it was not mysterious or singular when all was known. The cab-driver who had driven Marmaduke to Whitechapel had really been waiting for the inspector, but, tempted by Marmaduke's half-sovereign, he had taken the fare, afterwards returning to see if his first fare was still on Tower-hill.

A little cold water, and a drop of brandy, supplied by some of the spectators, had revived Inspector Wyman; and when he was able to walk he asked to be assisted towards Tower-hill, where he had left his cab.

It fortunately drove up again just as the little crowd emerged on the Hill.

The Inspector got in, and drove first of all to a public-house, where he alighted, and went into the parlour, beckoning the cabman to follow him. It was from this worthy that he derived information which determined him to go to Bluegate-fields. Here he again made inquiries, and with what result our readers already know.

Wyman still remained upon the watch.

CHAPTER IX.

A BOLD RESOLVE—THE DWARF ARMS HIMSELF—WYMAN IS SURPRISED—MARMADUKE'S REVENGE—THE UN-PLEASANT PREDICAMENT IN WHICH AN INSPECTOR OF POLICE PASSED A MORNING IN BLUEGATE-FIELDS—THE ESCAPE—THE "FENCE"—MIRIAM MOSS.

IT will have been perceived by this time that Marmaduke Wilson was not only a man of resources, but also a man of rapid invention. And in the present crisis it was fortunate indeed that he was possessed of those sterling and valuable qualities.

He took in his position at a glance. He was concealed in what had hitherto been considered a secure hiding-place, but it was now no longer so. Marmaduke Wilson's deadliest enemy was awaiting him in the passage of the old and lonely house in Bluegate-fields.

Escape seemed out of the question. Buried, as it were, in the cellar, he could only escape by walking over Wyman's body.

Another danger menaced him. He knew, from the conversation he had overheard, that in a short time a force of constables would be upon the ground, so the moments were precious. If anything was to be done it was clear that it must be done quickly.

Marmaduke conceived a bold idea, and with the help of the dwarf Stubbles, he proceeded to put it instantly in execution.

As may be readily imagined, Agnes was terribly alarmed. This sort of life was new to her, and she could not conceal her trepidation.

Marmaduke whispered some words of consolation in her ear, which served in some measure to reassure her, for her confidence in her husband was unlimited and unbounded.

She knew his bold and fearless nature, but she also knew that he was far too clever to do anything rashly or without sufficient deliberation to insure thorough and complete success.

So she pressed his hand tenderly, and with a throbbing heart awaited the sequel.

Marmaduke was totally unarmed. Not so the dwarf, he carried in his left hand a deadly-looking weapon resembling a poniard or stiletto, only longer. This was evidently to be reserved for emergencies, but if the occasion required it, it was evident from the determined air of the dwarf that he would not scruple to employ it.

Marmaduke trusted more to his muscular strength and agility, for if it could be avoided he had a great objection to shedding blood, and he was never known to have done so or to have countenanced by his presence any scene where such atrocity as the murder and assassination of innocent victims was perpetrated.

Closely followed by Stubbles, Marmaduke once more ascended the ladder, and having reached the level of the kitchen, he looked cautiously around him; then he gradually drew his body free from the aperture which revealed the descent into the cellar.

Stubbles was not long in following; and as these two rose up in the semi-darkness which pervaded that part of the old kitchen, they might have been taken for two ghosts, so strange were their movements, and so weird-like their appearance.

Gliding very quietly over the floor with all the subtlety of a Red Indian on the war-trail, Marmaduke took up a position from which a view of the passage leading to the street might be obtained.

Having accomplished this to his entire satisfaction, without making so much noise as might have aroused a fly, he commenced to reconnoitre.

It was as he suspected: Wyman was in his old position, only he did not seem to be particularly vigilant, his eyes were fixed upon the opposite wall. It might be that he had not altogether recovered from the severe attack made upon him that morning by Marmaduke. And if the truth were known, he had a legitimate cause for feeling a little dizzy or faint, as Marmaduke's hug was like that of a grizzly bear.

However it might be, Inspector Wyman did not, to use a popular phrase, seem to be "all there."

It was evident by this time that Marmaduke's plan was to take his enemy by surprise, for he commenced moving along the passage with the same quietude that he had observed all along. Stubbles following closely at his heels.

The adventurous couple had arrived within a few yards of the unwary inspector, when that individual chanced to glance in the direction from which they were advancing.

With that intuitive keenness of perception which is habitual with thief-takers and detectives, Inspector Wyman comprehended everything in an instant.

He had been discovered by his enemies, and they were even now upon him. That they had come with an hostile intent he could not doubt, or why such excessive caution?

He turned then to fly. It was his only chance. Once in the street he could arouse the neighbourhood, which, bad as it was, would scarcely suffer any deed of violence to be done in broad daylight in an open thoroughfare before their very eyes.

But with a bound like an antelope and a spring like that of a tiger, Marmaduke Wilson was upon him ere he had time to reach the threshold.

"For your life, silence!" exclaimed Marmaduke.

But Inspector Wyman was not the man to be taken without a struggle, and he boldly grappled with his assailant, meanwhile shouting at the top of his voice; but Inspector Wyman, clever as he undoubtedly was, was evidently not clever enough on the present occasion. Besides, he was not acquainted with the dwarf Stubbles.

This latter rendered Marmaduke good and effectual assistance—he seized the inspector by the throat, and flourished the dagger we have already mentioned before his eyes. Wyman in addition to being a bold man was a prudent one; and when he saw himself outflanked by a strange, uncouth-looking monster with a dangerous weapon in his hand, he considered it best to surrender at discretion.

Besides, his strength was not so great as it had been in the morning, and he felt that altogether the conquest was unequal.

Another reflection which consoled him not a little was, that in a short time his men would arrive from Scotland-yard, and then how gloriously he would turn the tables!

Of one thing he was certain; his captor's did not intend to offer him any violence, or they would have done it at the first attack.

Marmaduke hastily improvised some bonds with which he secured the hands and feet of his captive, and stuffing some pieces of old rag into his mouth he gagged him to his satisfaction; for although a few cries in that part of the town were not taken much notice of, as being of too frequent occurrence, still, if they were repeated for any length of time curiosity must have been excited.

Having captured and secured Wyman, Marmaduke's next thought was what to do with him. As it happened there was a water-butt in the little bit of a yard at the back, and Marmaduke determined to make use of it.

Leaving the inspector in charge of Stubbles, he walked into the yard and had a look at it. It was certainly not very savoury; in fact, a rather disagreeable smell arose from the pestilential water which the butt contained. The water which had probably been there unchanged for years, except when diluted by a fresh shower, was full of animal life, and formidable-looking tadpoles might have been seen disporting themselves upon the surface.

Returning to Stubbles, Marmaduke, with the dwarf's assistance, carried the inspector into the yard, and, with a little difficulty, placed the unhappy detective feet downwards in the water-butt; which was of such a size that it only permitted the head of the prisoner to appear above the iron rim which surmounted the tub.

With his chin resting on this, and the gag in his mouth, Inspector Wyman presented a pitiable, but, at the same time, a ludicrous appearance.

"He wont hurt there for half an hour," said Marmaduke. "His men are sure to find him, and, at any rate, he is out of mischief."

"That's true, captain," replied the dwarf, with one of his elfin grins.

There was no time now for delay, and Marmaduke knew it, and he turned to go downstairs and prepare Agnes for immediate flight; but before he went he could not resist the temptation of saying to Wyman—

MARMADUKE WILSON IS CAPTURED BY INSPECTOR WYMAN.

"You have got a cooler this time, Mr. Wyman, and I think it would be only prudent in you to give up the chase."

The inspector shook his head violently to express his dissent from this opinion.

"Very well," returned Marmaduke; "at all events, this time the laugh is on my side, and I don't think you will catch me without getting up very early in the morning. Good bye, Mr. Wyman. I hope you wont forget the morning you spent with me at my residence in Bluegate-fields."

So saying, Marmaduke sought his wife, who was anxiously awaiting his return. Their preparations were soon made, and in a few minutes, they, accompanied by Stubbles, left the house.

A question arose as to where they should go. Marmaduke only knew one place of refuge; and that was the house of a celebrated receiver of stolen goods, with whom Marmaduke had often done business.

The hospitality of the "fence" was well known, but then he made his visitors pay handsomely for their accommodation.

There was, however, one little objection. When Marmaduke once had occasion to seek the shelter of the "fence's" house, a little adventure befel him.

Mike Moss, as he was called, had a daughter.

Marmaduke was then both young and free. It followed that he made love to Miss Miriam Moss, who thought him the most accomplished cavalier she had ever had the good fortune to encounter.

Such being the case, a mutual passion was the result, which, as usual, was much deeper on the part of the young Jewess than on that of the man.

Not that Marmaduke was a gay Lothario or a Don Juan.

But shut up in the old Jew's house it was a nice amusement for him to flirt with and make love to a pretty young girl.

They swore eternal constancy those two young people.

Miriam Moss set her whole heart upon Marmaduke. He was her idol. But the time came when Marmaduke was called away, and after he went he forgot all about Miss Miriam Moss.

Not so Miriam. *She* was constant ever, and impatiently awaited the return of her lover.

But how could all this prejudice a visit to the old "fence" now that danger threatened.

Miriam might be jealous of Agnes.

It was this fear that made Marmaduke hesitate. He knew that if Miriam had not supplied herself with another lover she would consider herself badly treated.

The sight of his young and beautiful bride might inflame her anger. And the fury of a vindictive woman, when her passions are aroused, is not a thing to be laughed at.

Still, it was important that they should have an immediate shelter, and that of the securest description.

And Marmaduke with some reluctance decided upon going to the house of Mike Moss.

He dispatched Stubbles to a thieves' haunt in Westminster, where he would most likely meet with Fly-by-night and the Surrey Wolf, so as to put them on their guard: for it was clear the police would hold possession of the old house in Bluegate-fields for the purpose of making captures.

Then getting into a cab, Marmaduke drove with his wife to an outfitter's in the Minories, where he obtained some decent attire, and then proceeded to the Foundling Hospital, where he alighted. He did this so as to prevent pursuit or identification of any particular house by the cabman.

Then threading the streets about the hospital, he at last entered one which seemed eminently respectable, but so old-looking and so deserted that you would have thought it inhabited by a colony of ghosts. Everything had a mouldy look as of long continued-neglect and decay.

At one of the houses in this street he stopped and rang the bell. They were instantly admitted by Mike Moss himself, who greeted Marmaduke very kindly, but stared inquiringly at Agnes.

"My wife," said Marmaduke.

The old man bowed.

But just as the words were uttered, a shrill scream was heard, and Miss Miriam Moss, who had just descended the stairs, fell heavily upon the floor of the entrance-hall.

Marmaduke guessed the cause of her agitation, but he seized her by the waist and took her into the dining-room. exclaiming—

"The heat, sir, probably has affected Miss Miriam's health."

Agnes seemed rather astonished at this scene, and did not seem to exactly like *her* husband carrying a strange woman in his arms.

"Ma tear," said the old fence, addressing his daughter, "you ish not vell."

Miriam soon opened her eyes and complained of a headache, adding, she would retire to her room, but as she left the apartment she cast a glance so full of hatred at Marmaduke, that even he trembled.

That look boded Marmaduke Wilson no good.

The "fence" drew Marmaduke into the recess of a window and said—

"Have you got anything to shell?"

Marmaduke explained that he wanted protection for a few days till a certain unpleasant affair blew over, and Mike Moss readily agreed to afford it him.

So Marmaduke and his wife were duly installed as inmates of the quiet, mouldy-looking house in the vicinity of the Foundling Hospital.

But in the mean time, neither Miss Miriam Moss nor Inspector Wyman were idle.

The latter personage had, as Marmaduke predicted, been discovered by his men on their arrival.

When taken out of the water-butt the inspector looked like a drowned rat, and shivered as if he had the tertian ague.

He swore a very big oath that he would have a terrible revenge on Marmaduke Wilson.

How he kept his promise will soon be detailed.

CHAPTER X.

MIRIAM DETERMINES TO BE REVENGED—AGNES BEGINS TO DOUBT—IS SHE A VICTIM?—WYMAN FINDS THE TRAIL—MARMADUKE WILSON'S PERIL—TREACHERY IN THE CAMP—AN EXCITING MOMENT.

WHEN the beautiful young Jewess, Miriam Moss, retired to her bed-chamber her mind was tormented with doubts and fears. At first she could scarcely bring herself to believe in Marmaduke Wilson's treachery, even when there was the clearest evidence of it before her eyes.

So prone are people to hope against hope and cling to shadows.

Although Miriam could love well and fondly, she could also hate, as Marmaduke Wilson was to discover to his cost. The girl whose affections had been blighted by his senseless folly and heartlessness was not one to tamely submit to an insult. Miriam Moss determined that she would be revenged.

But when the first feeling of anger had passed away a spark of compassion glowed in her breast.

"Perhaps," she thought, "the woman I saw is not his wife after all. She may be his sister, or a friend. Let me then ascertain this beyond a doubt before I act, so that I may do him no injustice."

With this intention, Miriam descended the stairs in order to interrogate Agnes as to her relationship with Marmaduke Wilson.

Miriam found Agnes alone in the sitting-room into which she had been ushered on her first arrival at the "fence's."

She was reclining upon a sofa, but rose as Miriam entered. She was a little pale and appeared fatigued. Evidently the excitement and worry of the morning had been too much for her. At any other time Miriam would have done all in her power to make her feel comfortable and at home, but now there was a consuming fire at her heart which burnt up or smothered all her better feelings.

Although there were traces of languor and harassment on Agnes's face she still looked very beautiful; and Miriam could not conceal from herself that her rival was a young and lovely creature. This fact, however, only increased her rage, and made her hate the unsuspecting girl more than ever.

"Your husband," began Miriam, laying a stress on the last word, "your husband is not at home, I presume?"

"No," replied Agnes; "he has stepped out to attend to some business, but he will not be long before he returns."

"She admits that he is her husband," thought Miriam; and she added to herself, "Well, let me see how my poison will work. It has been doubly distilled, and ought to accomplish its end well."

"Ah! Marmaduke is a sad fellow," said Miriam, with an insinuating smile.

"What mean you?" asked Agnes in alarm.

"Oh! nothing much," was the reply. "Marmaduke, as I dare say you know, is a very old friend of mine."

"Indeed! I was not aware of the fact," answered Agnes, agitated, she hardly knew why.

"Perhaps you will tell me that you did not know we were engaged once, Marmaduke and I?" said Miriam, carelessly.

"You and Marmaduke engaged? What is this? Oh! let me hear more?" exclaimed Agnes, now painfully aroused.

"I have nothing more to tell," replied Miriam, a little coldly.

"Nothing more! Oh! yes; there is some mystery hidden in your words," said Agnes.

"I would spare your feelings, poor child!" replied Miriam, whose basilisk glance certainly rather belied her words, for there did not seem too much compassion in it.

"But you have said either too little or too much," said Agnes. "You have made me uneasy. Oh! I pray you, tell me all you know!"

"I could tell you," replied Miriam, "how Marmaduke Wilson was an acknowledged suitor for my hand."

"Yes," gasped Agnes.

"He vowed eternal constancy. Sooner might the stars fall from their places," he said, "than his love for me could wane; but I made timely discoveries and rejected him."

"Oh!" cried Agnes, as if a great weight had been taken off her heart; "I see what you mean now, he was not good enough for you. You knew him to be what, unfortunately for him, the world calls dishonest. I, too, know all that; but that is totally different from what I thought you meant."

And Agnes positively laughed—a small laugh of joy—as if she had escaped some dreadful danger; and then she began to scold herself for being so naughty and foolish as to distrust the man of her choice.

"That was not my meaning, Mrs. Wilson," said Miriam, bitterly.

"Not your meaning," repeated Agnes; "what, then, in Heaven's name do you mean?"

"I, too, could have forgiven the faults you pardoned, but there were others of a nature a woman never overlooks or pardons."

Agnes sat still, speechless with amazement, wondering what singular disclosures her companion was about to make. But after firing this last shot Miriam remained silent, occasionally glancing at her to see what effect her words had produced. They had, it was easy to see, raised a tempest of suspicions of various kinds in the mind of Agnes. This was what she wished, and she protracted her silence in order that Agnes might demand some more of the "doubly-distilled poison" she had prepared for her.

She had not long to wait, for in a short time Agnes looked up and said, "Will you go on with what you were saying; you would not keep me in suspense, I know, if you were aware of the interest I take in the subject we are discussing?"

"You will not accuse me of being unfeeling?" inquired Miriam.

"Certainly not, whatever may be the effect of what you are about to tell me, I shall have brought it on myself."

"In that case I am prepared to tell you what caused me considerable pain at the time I heard it. Marmaduke Wilson is not what he assumes to be; he is a heartless libertine, and I should have been one of his victims had I not found him out in time. He amuses himself with a woman for a time, and when he is tired of her, he deserts her, and throws her friendless and heart-broken on the world."

"It is a base fabrication!" cried Agnes, indignantly.

"Just what I said myself, my dear, when I was told of it; but I found out the truth of it," replied Miriam, quietly.

"Oh! no, no! I cannot believe it. He is so good and true," said Agnes, the tears starting to her eyes.

"Well, you may please yourself about believing it," answered Miriam, rudely; "but you will discover before long that what I say is only too true; and then you will be able to distinguish your friends from your enemies."

Agnes remained with her head bent down and her eyes fixed upon the carpet, as if plunged in the deepest melancholy.

"There is one thing I must discover before I leave her," murmured Miriam. "It is essential to the success of my plans. Your husband is in some little trouble, I suppose?" she demanded, in a careless tone.

"Yes, indeed, he is in great danger," replied Agnes, innocently, not suspecting the subtle nature of the crafty Jewess, Miriam Moss.

"In great danger?" said Miriam. "Indeed, you surprise me. I deemed him much too clever to allow himself to be so hard pressed."

"You see," said Agnes, in a low voice, "Wyman, the detective, is hunting him from place to place."

"Wyman, the detective," repeated Miriam, mentally making a note of the name.

"Yes," replied Agnes; "from Scotland-yard, you know."

"Ah! Then he is in danger, for Wyman is a sleepless foe; and your husband does well to seek the shelter of my father's house."

"You have made me very miserable," exclaimed Agnes.

"Nonsense!" replied Miriam; "if Marmaduke loves you he may treat you better than the rest. At all events, never meet troubles half-way. There are as good fish in the sea as ever came out of it."

Poor Agnes! These were very sore tidings for her. To have her faith in Marmaduke undermined was sufficient to break her heart almost, so fondly did she love him, and so implicitly did she trust in him.

After this conversation Miriam Moss quitted Agnes, on the pretence of attending to some pressing domestic business.

"So," she thought, as she quitted the room, "so Marmaduke is in trouble. Inspector Wyman is on his track. This is great news to me. I once loved him, but now, when I look upon the little chit whom he has made his wife, I lose my patience. I have a right to be revenged upon him for his perfidy."

Miriam had convinced herself by the questions that she had put to Agnes that Marmaduke Wilson had made her his wife.

This thought was intolerable to her, for she had, up to the present time, indulged a hope that he might be hers.

Being of a passionate and headstrong nature, Miriam resolved to be revenged upon the man who had so ruthlessly trifled with her feelings.

By talking to Agnes as she had done she had aroused the demon of suspicion, which is almost as fatal to domestic happiness as the green monster, jealousy.

This was part of her system of vengeance, and when she gazed upon the pale shrinking girl before her, she rejoiced to see how her scheme had succeeded.

But her great work was as yet unaccomplished. Marmaduke Wilson was still at large. She would, however, swoop down upon him as a falcon on a dove, and dash all his hopes, his plans and aspirations, to the four winds of heaven.

Miriam Moss was a creature of impulse—most women are, and she was no exception to the rule. If she conceived an idea she must carry it out immediately. In fact, with her to conceive was to execute.

Accordingly she dressed herself, and leaving her father's house, went rapidly towards the west.

At length, after much walking, the young Jewess reached Scotland-yard.

It was now plain that her purpose was to betray Marmaduke to the police.

Entering the station, she found herself in a large room. A man in uniform was sitting at a desk in a corner; busily engaged in writing, on benches placed in various parts of the apartment, were seated policemen who had either come off duty, or who had come to make some report at headquarters. One of these latter rose as Miriam entered, and politely asked her what she wanted.

"Be good enough," she replied, "to tell Inspector Wyman that a lady wishes to see him."

The man bowed, and went on his mission. When he returned, he requested Miriam to follow him.

After conducting her through several small and rather dismal-looking passages, her guide stopped before a door covered with green baize. Pushing this open, he beckoned to Miriam to enter, and doing so, she found herself alone with the astute, but at present baffled detective.

The walls of the apartment were garnished with bills offering rewards for notorious offenders, and amongst these she saw one headed "Marmaduke Wilson—100l. reward." Then followed a description of his person. "So," she thought, "the hounds of the law are still baying at his heels. Perhaps my information will stimulate them to a little increased exertion."

"To what, madam, am I indebted for the honour of this visit?" inquired Inspector Wyman, with a low bow.

The inspector was always polite to ladies.

"Are we alone?" asked Miriam.

"Certainly. Speak freely, and without fear; though," added the inspector, with characteristic caution, "if you come to accuse yourself of any offence, I must warn you that what you say will be used against you in evidence afterwards."

Miriam smiled, and replied, "Indeed you quite mistake the object of my visit. I come to give information about others, not about myself. I am too much afraid of the law and its satellites to put my poor little self in its power."

"I shall be happy—I may say, very happy, to hear anything you have to say. Pray proceed."

"Marmaduke Wilson," began Miriam, when she was interrupted by the detective, who exclaimed—

"Did I hear aright? Who did you say?"

"Are you, then, unacquainted with the gentleman?" asked Miriam, laughingly.

"On the contrary," said Wyman, "I have such a regard for him that I should like to have him near me at this moment, and if you can assist me nothing would give me greater pleasure than to renew my acquaintance with Mr. Wilson."

"Very well. So far we are in accord."

"There is a reward offered," said Wyman. "You know, I suppose, that it is customary for the informer and the captor to share it."

"Money is no object to me," replied Miriam, a little haughtily; "I don't want any pecuniary reward, Mr. Wyman; do with that as you think best. If I am once assured that Marmaduke Wilson is in the hands of justice I shall rest contented."

"Some case of revenge, I suppose," thought the inspector. "Well, it is nothing to us what her motive is; but it is a fine thing for me. Why, if the women did not peach on their pals, where should we be? I don't believe we should catch a quarter as many as we do now."

"Will you answer me a question?" asked Miriam.

"With pleasure," replied Wyman.

"What I want to know is what punishment will be allotted to this man Wilson when apprehended?"

"Most probably six years' penal servitude, perhaps more, according to circumstances."

Although she had made herself acquainted with the terrible doom she was bringing on the man she once loved, she never wavered a moment in her purpose.

"You are always here, I suppose," she asked; and being answered in the affirmative, she continued, "Very well, then, if I send you information at any time, you will be prepared to act upon it?"

"You may rely upon that," he said, with a chuckle. "This fellow has given me so much trouble, that I will spare no pains to secure him. I have not forgotten a morning I spent with him at Bluegate-fields. No, no; in a case of this sort you don't catch Wyman, the detective, napping. I will lay all my plans so well that even Jonathan Wild himself couldn't have done them better."

"You shall hear from me, then, Mr. Wyman," said Miriam, "very shortly, and I will send you such information as must inevitably lead to his capture."

So saying she wished him good morning, and left the police-station to return to her father's house.

It may be asked why she did not at once say where Marmaduke was concealed, and have returned with a party of constables to effect the arrest then and there.

But the objections to this course are obvious. For instance, to bring the myrmidons of the law to her father's house would have been to betray him as well, and besides, she would have annoyed and irritated her father beyond measure if she had given his enemies the least clue to his whereabouts, or his pursuits.

She had determined then to listen carefully and find out if Marmaduke went to see any of his companions, and if so, having discovered when and where, to forward the information to Inspector Wyman.

Miriam Moss had not long to wait before an opportunity of carrying out her vindictive purpose presented itself. She was seated at the window engaged on some embroidery work, when her father and Marmaduke Wilson entered. Miriam's form was partly concealed by the window curtains, and it is probable she was not noticed, but her father placed implicit confidence in his daughter, and would not have hesitated to speak before her at any time.

The conversation overheard by Miriam was somewhat trivial in its import, but of great consequence to her.

Marmaduke informed the old "fence" that he had seen his friends Fly-by-night and the Surrey Wolf, who had some plunder to dispose of, and as they were in concealment as well as himself, they did not like to show themselves in open day.

But Marmaduke, being of a bold and adventurous disposition, had undertaken to visit them at night, at the Three Tuns, in Westminster, where they were staying, and to bring the watches and jewellery they wished to dispose of back with him.

The Jew was much pleased with this arrangement, and told Marmaduke to tell his friends that although diamonds were quite a drug in the market, nevertheless he would give a handsome price for all they could send him.

Miriam Moss carefully treasured up in her memory the address of the Three Tuns, Westminster.

Sitting down at a desk, she wrote on a sheet of paper, "To Inspector Wyman. Marmaduke Wilson will be at the Three Tuns, Westminster, to-night, with the Surrey Wolf and some others. Fail not to be there."

This notification was written hastily, and as hastily dried on some blotting-paper. Then, folding it up and addressing it to Inspector Wyman, Miriam put on her bonnet and shawl, and wended her way to the police-station, in order to betray her father's guest.

Now she would be revenged upon the man who had, by his cruelty, broken her heart and crushed her finer feelings into dust.

But an accident happened upon which she had not reckoned.

Marmaduke Wilson made an important discovery.

CHAPTER XI.

THE USE OF BLOTTING-PAPER IN THE NINETEENTH CENTURY—MIRIAM'S TREACHERY—IS IT THE JEW?—MIKE MOSS EXCULPATES HIMSELF — MIRIAM CONFRONTED WITH MARMADUKE—THE JEW'S PASSION—MARMADUKE WILL KEEP HIS APPOINTMENT—SHE MUST DIE THE DEATH.

No sooner had Miriam Moss quitted the room than Marmaduke Wilson, by one of those strange chances which influence a man's whole life, re-entered it.

Certainly there was, at the first sight, nothing extraordinary in his doing so, but the event became of great moment by what followed.

It would seem that he was desirous of writing a letter, for he went to the desk that Miriam had just left, and commenced turning over the blotting-paper as if in search of some writing-paper.

Suddenly he stopped with a convulsive start. And his eyes appeared to dilate with astonishment.

What strange sight was it that met his view?

Miriam Moss had dried her letter there, and her note to Wyman was as legible on that blotting-book as if it had been on paper.

Yes, there it was in black and white. His place of meeting—his name. In fact, it was so self-evident that there was no room for doubt.

Yet could he believe his eyes? Was it possible that the gentle and confiding Miriam could so far play the traitress as to place him in the hands of justice?

Alas! there was the evidence; it was not circumstantial, it was plain, and to the point.

"This is a lucky chance," exclaimed Marmaduke. "Fortune seems to favour me. What could have been this girl's motive? Can it be slighted love? No; she could never have thought me serious, and yet her faint—her agitation. Yes, Miriam Moss loves me, and rather than see me the husband of Agnes she betrays me to the police, or——"

Here he clenched his fist, as a new idea struck him.

"Is this," he continued, "a plant of the Jew's to sell me? There is a reward offered for my apprehension. Of that I am well aware. Can he have sold me? By Heaven, if I thought so I would give his rascally old carcase to the worms! Let me seek an interview with the Israelite. I will question him shrewdly, and if he prevaricates, the worse for him."

True to his purpose Marmaduke Wilson hastily sought the Jew's private apartments, where many of his nefarious transactions were negotiated. Many an usurious bargain had he here completed, for Mike Moss was a bill-discounter as well as a "fence."

Making a signal without which the Jew never opened the door of these rooms, Marmaduke was admitted.

"Vat is it, my young friend?" inquired Mike Moss. "I am busy, my hands are full of bishness."

Marmaduke gazed around him for a moment to see what pressing business was engrossing the Jew's attention. Happening to look under the table he discovered a fine lobster on a tray.

The Jew's eyes followed Marmaduke's searching look, and when he saw that he was found out, he exclaimed—

"Ah! yes. I see you have found out my dinner. It is 'tryphor food,' but I shall eat 'cosher' to-morrow."

In fact, Marmaduke was slightly surprised at discovering shell-fish in the old Jew's apartments, for the Jews look upon a lobster as "tryphor" or unclean, and Jews of all sorts are usually as strict as Mohammedans about their food.

But without taking any further notice of that, Marmaduke

exclaimed, "I have known you for some time, Mike Moss, and you have always behaved well to your customers and friends."

"Yes," said the Jew.

"And if I thought that you were capable of selling a pal, I would wring your old neck where you sit."

"Take a shair; be seated," said the fence in evident trepidation and alarm, "and tell me vat all this is apout."

Marmaduke Wilson took a chair, and drawing it near to where Mike Moss was sitting, leant a little forward, and said in an impressive voice—

"I trusted you, Jew; but my confidence has been requited with treachery."

Had a serpent stung him, Mike Moss could not have been more astounded. "By Abraham!" he cried, "I know nothing of it, Mr. Wilshon. Nothing vatever, s'help me Heaven."

The man's manner was so evidently genuine and sincere, that Marmaduke was constrained to believe him.

"I had thought that you might have been hankering after the reward," he said; "and the circumstances of the case were certainly suspicious, as you will admit when you have heard them."

"Tell me, tell me, Mr. Wilshon," cried the old fence, letting his spectacles fall upon his papers in his agitation.

"I went into your dining-room when I left you just now," said Marmaduke.

"Yes, yes, Mr. Wilshon."

"My purpose was to calculate what was a fair price for you to give for some little trinkets I was to bring you to-night from Fly-by-night, as we had arranged."

"That ish true."

"In order to do that I went to a writing-desk to obtain a piece of paper, but while turning over the leaves of a blotting-book, what was my utter surprise to see——"

"Jehosaphat! vat did you see?" demanded the Jew.

"I will tell you what I saw, Mike Moss," replied Marmaduke Wilson, sternly. "I saw your daughter's hand-writing."

The Jew gasped for breath.

"And that handwriting convinced me that she had betrayed me, either by your orders, or by her own inclination."

The Jew expressed a wish to be further enlightened.

"The note she had evidently just written, and it contained the name of the place, where, as you know, I am to meet my friend, Fly-by-night, this evening. The writer strongly impressed upon her correspondent the paramount necessity of taking a large force with him in order that my capture might be secured."

"Ha!" exclaimed Mike Moss.

"And if you doubt that the writer of that letter was your own daughter, Mike Moss, you can easily undeceive yourself by looking at the handwriting."

"This is pad work, very pad work," said the fence, when Marmaduke had finished his narration.

"I can think of nothing to account for it," continued Marmaduke, "except——"

"Ah! she wanted the monish—the reward. Miriam is a sharp girl, but a pad one to shell her friends," interrupted the Jew, with a laugh.

"No, old man," replied Marmaduke; "your daughter did not want the money. Her object, as I was about to tell you when you interrupted me, was revenge."

"For vat should she vant revenge?" asked Mike Moss, opening his eyes.

"She loved me," replied Marmaduke, quietly.

The effect of these words upon the Jew was indescribable. He instantly became violently agitated; his countenance was convulsed with passion, and his whole frame trembled with rage.

"Vat!" he cried, "my daughter love a Christian—a dog. Bah! I spit at you. No, it ish too pad; too dreadful. But," he added, getting a little calmer, "if Miriam has cast the eye of affection upon a Gentile, she must die the death."

What these words portended was a mystery.

Marmaduke took no notice of the old man's rhapsody, having for some time known his antipathy to all who were not of his own faith.

Just then a timid knock was heard at the door.

"Ha! 'tis Miriam!" cried Marmaduke.

"Hush! be shtill," said the Jew, holding up his finger warningly.

In his natural voice he then bade her enter.

Miriam entered boldly, but on seeing Marmaduke, shrank back a little involuntarily, but in a moment she recovered her former confidence, and advanced towards the middle of the room, and seated herself on a chair which Marmaduke presented her with.

She had sought her father, she said, to ask him some questions of domestic interest, but Mike Moss replied—

"My shild, listen to me first."

Miriam, although a little uneasy, expressed her willingness to do so.

"Where have you been now?" demanded her father.

"For a walk, and to do some shopping."

"But you write letters, ma tear. Do you not?"

"I? No; very seldom," was the reply.

"Vat did you write this afternoon?" asked the Jew, with a searching glance.

"Nothing, father," answered Miriam.

"Prevarication is useless here, Miss Moss," interrupted Marmaduke; "your secret has been discovered, and by me."

Miriam was much astonished at this announcement, and she felt greatly mortified at the ill success of her scheme.

"I regret that any secret of mine should have been discovered, sir," she answered boldly, "for it argues badly for my skill and care and prudence. I am at a loss, however, to guess what particular secret you allude to."

Marmaduke Wilson drew himself up to his full height, and with a withering look replied—

"Miriam Moss, you are a traitress!"

She started visibly at the denunciation.

"Yes," he continued, "you are a traitress of the blackest dye—you have betrayed your father's guest—you would have had me fall into the hands of the police this evening, and I charge you with having even now been in communication with them."

"Your proofs, sir—your proofs!" exclaimed Miriam. "You insult me by these suspicions."

Marmaduke bowed, and quickly left the room, returning in a few seconds with the tell-tale blotting-pad.

"Here," he cried, "are my proofs!" And holding the paper up to the light, her treachery was manifest to all. The evidence was so straightforward, and so damning, that Miriam saw there was no escape from it.

"You cannot deny you wrote that letter," said Marmaduke.

Miriam hung her head as the full conviction of her treachery was placed before her.

"Your motive, Miriam Moss?" asked the man she had so deeply, cruelly wronged.

"Can you ask me?" she replied, her eyes flashing, and her face pale and red by turns—"you, who have trifled with my affections, and who changed my love to hatred—you, who have blighted my whole life, and made me entertain bad and wicked passions? Will not the trodden worm turn upon its oppressor, think you?"

At these words the old fence rose, and going towards his daughter took one of her hands in his, and said, in a gentle, coaxing tone—

"My shild—my Miriam."

"Father, I am listening," she replied.

"Tell me I am mishtaken. Shay you did not love that man. It ish all lies, ish it not, my Miriam?"

The expression of the old man's face was pitiable as he thus pleaded with the child of his age.

The reply came slowly, but distinctly.

"Father, it is true. I loved this man; but now I hate—yes, hate him even unto death."

At these words the Jew's face became once more convulsed with rage, and casting his daughter's hand violently away from him, he said, in a voice hoarse with anger and concentrated passion—

"She has defiled her father's sepulchre. She must die the death——"

Again those words! Surely some awful significance must dwell beneath them.

She must die the death! Of a verity the clouds are gathering over the doomed head of Miriam Moss.

"Stay! deal not harshly with her," interposed Marmaduke.

"I want not *your* pity," said Miriam, scornfully. "Were I in want of bread *your* charity would choke me."

"Peace, girl!" cried her father. Then, turning to Marmaduke, he said, "Her punishment rests with me. Rest assured the full measure shall be meted out to her."

"You are saved this time, Marmaduke Wilson," exclaimed Miriam; "but you shall yet feel the effect of my hate. My vengeance shall never sleep! I swear it! By my father's grave, I swear it!"

Marmaduke smiled disdainfully.

"Ah!" she said, "you are congratulating yourself on your escape. The police will seek in vain to-night, but a time will come."

"You are wrong, Miriam Moss," answered Marmaduke. "I shall keep my appointment this evening at Westminster."

"What? Do I hear aright?" she cried.

"Yes; my friends must be put upon their guard. And I fear not the police. My time is not yet come."

"You know not that," she replied, rather astonished at his audacity.

It was a bold resolve of Marmaduke Wilson's, but he rejoiced in dare-devil adventures, and trusted to his ready wit and his good luck to get him out of any sudden danger.

"Yes," he said, "Inspector Wyman shall have another chance; but to be forewarned is to be forearmed."

All this time the Jew was occupied with his own thoughts. The discovery that his daughter once loved a Christian seemed to have completely upset him.

"Jew!" exclaimed Marmaduke, "to your charge for the present I confide my wife; and remember, I shall claim her from your hands. Should aught happen to her while under your roof—should a hair of her innocent head be injured—I will exact a terrible revenge."

With these words he left the room, and sought the companionship of Agnes.

Miriam and her father remained absorbed for some minutes after Marmaduke's departure. At length the Jew looked up. The traces of a severe mental conflict appeared upon his features; and as he gazed upon his daughter his face was stony cold, and compassionateless.

"Yes," he said aloud, "she must die the death!"

Miriam became alarmed at the iteration of this ominous phrase, and rising, walked towards the door, intending to leave the room, but the old man with a bound reached the door before her, and, locking it, put the key in his pocket, and confronting her, said in a severe voice—

"Thou must expiate thy sin."

CHAPTER XII.

MARMADUKE AT THE THREE TUNS—KEEPING HIS HAND IN—MAKING FRIENDS—THE DWARF SEES AN OMEN—WHAT MARMADUKE SAW WHEN HE SOUGHT THE SURREY WOLF—THE DWARF DEFENDS THE PASSAGE—MARMADUKE WILSON IS CAPTURED BY THE POLICE—WYMAN'S TRIUMPH.

MARMADUKE WILSON kept his promise to his friends. When the clock at Westminster struck the hour of twelve, he entered the old hostelry which had been selected for their meeting.

The publichouse was situated in a very low part of Westminster, near Tothill-fields. As Marmaduke passed through the bar, he perceived a number of low-looking ruffians, with a sprinkling of women, swearing and drinking, and although they were mostly thieves and pickpockets they looked at him wonderingly, not recognizing him as one of their own profession.

There was one man in particular who attracted Marmaduke's attention; he was dressed in shabby-genteel attire, but he rejoiced especially in a gaudy-looking waistcoat which, in addition to its own particular glories was adorned with a thick massive-looking chain, highly suggestive of "Brummagem" manufacture.

At beholding this, Marmaduke determined to try his skill at the expense of the man with the massive-looking chain.

As he passed him he stumbled carelessly against him, and in an instant with great dexterity possessed himself of the other's chain. So quickly and expeditiously was this done, that the man was totally unconscious of his loss.

Marmaduke begged the man's pardon for his clumsiness in falling against him and added, "You don't want to buy a gold chain, master, do you?"

The man replied in the negative, saying he had already got one.

At this, Marmaduke produced the chain he had just robbed him of, and said—

"This is the chain. Perhaps when you see how handsome it is you may change your mind!"

At the sight of his own chain in another's possession, the man muttered a few words highly impregnated with the odour of blasphemy.

Looking down at his waistcoat, he saw that his own chain was gone, and he had no doubt whatever then that the one Marmaduke held in his hand had just been taken surreptitiously from him. Instead of being annoyed he smiled—it is true rather grimly—but still he smiled and said—

"You wasn't born yesterday, I can see." And turning to the crowd about them, he added, "I say, pals all, this bloak 'ere copt my ticker-chain; but I guess he didn't twig it was a duffer."

They seemed immensely delighted at the idea, and some shouted jocularly, "Where's the police! it's hodd the bobbies is never at hand when they's wanted."

At this there was a roar of laughter.

"Here, my friend," said Marmaduke; "here is your chain; and I wish for your sake it would spout for a fiver. I am, as you have sagaciously guessed, an old hand, and perhaps you will consider it no disgrace to have been robbed by Marmaduke Wilson."

When they heard who it was that had amused himself by performing on one of the "family," their delight was unbounded, for some of Marmaduke's exploits had been pretty well bruited abroad.

"Glasses round," said Marmaduke, addressing the barman, and throwing down a couple of sovereigns to defray the expense.

"Hurrah!" cried the crowd.

When the liquor was served out to them, Marmaduke exclaimed, "My friends, I don't suppose you would like to see a brother pal lagged?"

"No, no," shouted everybody.

"Well," he continued, "if I don't look about me to-night, I shall be in the unpleasant position I have indicated."

"Not if we know it," said the crowd.

"Not as long as I can lift a finger," cried Leary Ned, the man whom Marmaduke had deprived of his chain.

"Thanks, thanks!" replied Marmaduke. "I thought I could rely upon you all, and I will tell you how you can assist me."

A breathless silence reigned, while every ear was strained to catch Marmaduke's words.

Every eye was fixed upon him.

"Inspector Wyman has been informed that I am to meet two friends of mine here, and Wyman, with several officers, will most likely be here in search of me in half-an-hour."

"We'll fight for you."

"We'll pitch the police out of window."

"They'll go faster than they came, I warrant."

These and similar exclamations greeted Marmaduke's ears at the conclusion of his address.

"Now I will tell you what to do," continued Marmaduke. "One or two of you must keep watch outside for the peelers, and at their approach, some one must come up-stairs and give me warning. Then extinguish the lights and fight as well as you can, and in the scuffle I shall make my escape. You may wonder why I came here after having such explicit information. I answer you that I came because I love daring for its own sake, and I think it is a bad plan to show the police that you are afraid of them."

"So it is. Hurrah! we'll do it," responded his auditors.

The Three Tuns was a night-house, and frequented almost entirely by thieves and pickpockets and ruffians of all descriptions; there are not many such houses, but those that exist are pretty well patronized.

Consequently there might have been from thirty to forty men and women in the Three Tuns.

These would have caused a great deal of annoyance to the police, and have given them so much trouble, that Marmaduke had not calculated badly when he reckoned that he should, with their assistance, succeed in again escaping from the clutches of his inveterate foe, Wyman.

As Marmaduke turned to ascend the stairs, in order to

join his friends, who, for certain reasons best known to themselves and the police, thought it better to remain hidden in some apartments upstairs, the door of the public-house swung open, and the dwarf Stubbles, looking rather troubled and careworn, entered.

He walked directly up to Marmaduke, whom he instantly recognised, and said, in a hurried tone, "I saw three moths fly into a candle this evening, captain, and I knew by that sign that there was danger in the wind."

"Danger, my Stubbles," answered Marmaduke, with a laugh. "Well, for once you are right—there is danger."

"I knew it," answered the dwarf, "and I have been up to warn you."

"Be not alarmed," said Marmaduke; "I am a match for Wyman any day in the year."

"Be not too positive."

"Bah! Stubbles, you are afraid."

"Afraid!" cried the dwarf, angrily. "Am I afraid? You shall see, captain, when the time comes, if I am afraid or not."

"Well, well, follow me; I am going to the Surrey Wolf."

Marmaduke, closely followed by Stubbles, ascended the rickety stairs which led to the upper regions.

Stubbles was armed with a bludgeon, heavily loaded with lead.

Marmaduke had a brace of pistols in each pocket of his coat.

Having arrived at the top of the stairs, they walked unsuspiciously along the corridor.

When he came to the door of the room occupied by Fly-by-night and the Surrey Wolf, Marmaduke paused and listened.

He heard no sound.

The silence of the great Sahara seemed to reign in that room.

The noise of the half drunken revellers assembled below ascended the stairs and floated along the corridor.

But not a sound emanated from the apartment he was about to enter.

This silence appeared ominous to Marmaduke.

How could it do otherwise?

"Stay! What was that?"

Was it a subdued groan?

Marmaduke thought so—but no. It might have been the offspring of his imagination—it might have been the creaking of the rafters, or the floor, or the soughing of the wind outside amongst the gables.

Whatever it was, it had the effect of making Marmaduke Wilson hesitate before he turned the handle of the door before him.

But it was a time for action, and after a moment's consideration he resolved to enter.

There was a gas-lamp in the passage, which gave faint light, but quite sufficient to show Marmaduke that Stubbles was behind him.

Placing his hand boldly upon the door-knob, Marmaduke threw the door open.

Scarcely had he done so, when, by the light of a solitary candle burning on a table, aided somewhat by the gas in the passage, Marmaduke saw that he was environed with danger.

On the floor near the window lay the bodies of Fly-by-night and the Surrey Wolf securely bound and gagged.

It was from one of these that the sound resembling a groan had emanated. Standing in a row near the wall were seven policemen all with their truncheons drawn. As the door opened one stepped from the rank, and advancing to Marmaduke, exclaimed, in a voice replete with joy and triumph—

"Marmaduke Wilson, you are my prisoner!"

This man was Wyman.

His hand was upon Marmaduke's arm before he could recover his astonishment.

"It is useless to resist," said Wyman. "The house is surrounded, and all hope of escape is cut off."

As he uttered these words Stubbles, who had not hitherto been perceived by Wyman, raised his bludgeon.

By a chance, fortunate for the detective, the dwarf missed his aim, and his blow, instead of falling on the head, slipped a little on one side, and grazing his right temple, descended upon his shoulder. With a howl of pain, Inspector Wyman relinquished his hold of Marmaduke, who, taking advantage of the opportunity, sprang forward into the corridor.

As the men under Wyman's command saw this catastrophe they bounded forward after the fugitive.

The dwarf remained valiantly in the door-way and disputed their passage.

Fearful execution was done by his formidable weapon, and in a shorter space of time than it takes to write it, three policemen were lying on their backs dangerously wounded.

"Fly! fly!" cried Stubbles, between his strokes.

But although Marmaduke had the inclination he found it impossible.

Impossible, because as he reached the end of the passage he perceived the staircase crowded with policemen, who had been concealed in another part of the house, and who hearing the noise of the affray had gone to take part in it.

From the noise, and groans, and shouts, it was apparent that a fearful struggle was going on downstairs.

Certainly, some souls would be sent to their last resting-place that night, for the Three Tuns was the scene of a terrible conflict.

When Marmaduke found himself confronted by the police he was bewildered—he knew not what to do. Stubbles alone, by his determined bravery, prevented Wyman and his gang from rushing forward; and every now and then the harsh voice of the detective rang out through the passage.

"Take him! take him! Dead or alive, a hundred guineas for him!"

Pulling a pistol from his pocket Marmaduke thought of selling his life dearly.

But he considered on reflection that the odds against him were too great to make any way against.

If he fired all four of his pistols, and took as many lives, how would it assist him?

It would only aggravate his offence; therefore it would be better for him to surrender at discretion, and to trust to his ingenuity to devise some means of escape subsequently.

There was one thing he could do, though, one thing he was bound to do, if he could possibly effect it in any way, and that was to secure the safety of his two friends, Fly-by-night and the Surrey Wolf, and also of the valiant and faithful dwarf, Stubbles.

The policemen at the top of the stairs had, up to the present time, hung back, deterred at the sight of Marmaduke's pistols.

Turning his eyes in the direction of Stubbles, Marmaduke saw him at last succumb to the force of numbers.

The dwarf fell heavily to the ground beneath a vindictive blow from one of his adversaries' truncheons.

With a shout of triumph Wyman and two men, for only two had escaped the furious onslaught of the dwarf, darted forward, but they were confronted with Marmaduke's pistol.

With his back against the wall he stood, a pistol in each hand, awaiting his enemies.

Inspector Wyman was somewhat impressed with Marmaduke's determined manner, and stopped suddenly in his onward career.

Those pistols, and especially the one pointed at himself, were enough to make the bravest man shrink back, for they carried death with their discharge.

Seeing that the police on either side of him had made a temporary halt, Marmaduke exclaimed—

"Inspector Wyman, I will deliver myself into your hands on one condition."

"And that is—?" said Wyman.

"That condition is the safety and liberation of my three friends, Fly-by-night, the Surrey Wolf, and the dwarf."

Wyman was sufficiently pleased with the capture (which was indeed inevitable even if he had fought for an hour) of Marmaduke, and he thought he could readily make the required promise, but he did not, however, instantly comply.

"What if I refuse?" he said.

"If you refuse, you die by my hand," answered Marmaduke, sternly.

And any one who had seen Marmaduke at that moment would have known from the determined light in his eye that he was fully prepared to carry out his threat.

"Well, it shall be as you request," replied Wyman; "your friends shall have their liberty."

"I have your word for that?" demanded Marmaduke.

"You have," replied the inspector.

Marmaduke knew that he could rely upon this promise,

and he accordingly threw down his weapons, and quietly allowed himself to be bound and handcuffed.

"Now it is my turn," hissed Wyman in his prisoner's ears.

"Mine may come again," responded Marmaduke, in the same tone.

The police had been equally successful downstairs, having cleared the house of the rioters.

And Wyman conducted his captive, without molestation, to Vincent-square, where he was safely immured in the strongest cell of the police-station.

CHAPTER XIII.

MIKE MOSS MAKES A TERRIBLE RESOLVE—THE JEW'S VICTIM—THE WINDING STAIRCASE—THE OLD CHAMBER—A SKELETON—DOOMED TO DIE—THE SUBTLE VAPOUR—DESPAIR—SAVED AT LAST.

WHEN Marmaduke Wilson quitted the room, Michael or Mike Moss was alone with his daughter.

After having placed the key in his pocket, as we have related, he assumed a threatening manner.

Alarmed at her father's strange, unwonted behaviour, Miriam approached him softly, and exclaimed in those gentle tones which belonged to her—

"Father, what mean you by these strange proceedings? you frighten me."

The old Jew looked sternly at his daughter without replying for the space of half a minute, at the expiration of that time he said slowly and emphatically—

"Miriam, thou hast offended, insomuch as thou hast committed an unpardonable sin."

"I! father?" cried Miriam; "oh! how have I offended so greatly?"

"In loving a Christian lies thy sin," answered Mike Moss, still keeping his basilisk eyes upon her.

"Oh! trouble is indeed the lot of our doomed nation," sobbed Miriam.

"Not so, schild; ours is a glorious race, but disobedience brings its own punishment."

"Say what you have to say, father, and let me go," said Mariam, recovering herself, and looking up at the Jew as if conscious of innocence.

"I have little to shay," replied her father; "but that little interests you mosh."

"Say on; I am listening."

"Your mother, Rachel, hated the Christians, and vowed that as long as she lived you should never be the bride of a follower of the Nazarene, and swore that if you sho mosh as cast your eye favourably on a Christian, you should die the death."

"Again those dreadful words! Oh! father, you alarm me, let me go. I will go; I cannot stay with you; would you murder me?"

"Your mother's fate is yours," he replied.

"My mother's fate! oh! what of her?"

"Before the chief rabbi in our synagogue, she vowed to love me."

"Yes; oh, yes."

"And well she kept her word—"

"I could have sworn it, oh! my sainted mother."

"Until one day, when a Gentile, unclean dog as he was, came to my house," continued Mike Moss, "to borrow monish. I let him have it. But as Heaven and Abraham willed it, he saw your mother; what followed, child, would not, before you met Marmaduke Wilson, have been fit for your ears. But now you have eaten of the tree of knowledge of good and evil."

"Oh! no, no," sobbed Miriam.

"And thou hast chosen the evil from amongst the good."

This time Miriam made no answer, but sobbed without speaking.

"Thy mother," continued the Jew, "dishonoured her nuptial couch."

"Oh! this cannot be. It is not true," cried Miriam; "you malign the dead."

"Schild Miriam," said the old man, angrily but firmly, "thou hast heard the truth."

"And—and, what became of her," asked Miriam, timidly,

trembling in every limb, and pale with anxiety and excitement.

"She died the death," replied the Jew, solemnly.

"The death! oh! what new horror are you reciting?"

"I speak the simple truth—by Abraham, the simple truth!"

"And I?"

"You?—your hours are numbered."

At these words Miriam was sensibly agitated.

"Oh! what means this?" she cried.

"The very minutes that you have to live are reckoned," said her father, in a low, determined voice.

"Oh, father! have you no pity?" pleaded Miriam.

"In that room," said Mike Moss, "thy mother Rachael breathed her last. There shalt thou also expiate thy sin. I have sworn it."

As he spoke he pointed upwards; and as Miriam followed the movements of his hand she guessed that he alluded to a chamber above, but in the rear of the one she was at present in.

"How did she die?" asked Miriam.

"No violence was done her. But ask no questions, schild, thy turn has come."

"No, no! I will not be thus killed in cold blood. Help! help!" shrieked Miriam.

"You cry in vain," said her father. "These walls ish padded, and the windows have double frames. No soul, even here, can hear your cries."

"Oh! Heaven help me," moaned Miriam.

"Call not on Heaven; for thy sin's sake, it has deserted thee, and has delivered thee, like Sisera, into my hands."

Gazing at her for a moment, Mike Moss, without changing a muscle of his stony countenance, exclaimed, "Follow me!"

Miriam arose almost mechanically, and followed her father, who crossed the room, and opened a small door in the wall with a key of peculiar workmanship.

Entering this he led the way up a narrow flight of stairs, closely followed by his daughter, who went passively like a lamb to the slaughter.

After ascending for some time the Jew stopped, and touching a knob in the wainscoting, which was easily discernible by the light of the small taper he carried in his hand, he threw open a panel in the wainscoting, which afforded an aperture sufficiently large to admit of the passage of a human body.

"Enter," he cried, addressing Miriam, and making way for her to pass him; but the young girl shrank from the perilous enterprise.

At this juncture a gust of wind extinguished the somewhat feeble light held in his hand.

With a curse and an exclamation of disappointment Mike Moss descended the stairs to fetch a more trustworthy light than the one he had formerly held.

But ere he did so, he said to Miriam, "Daughter, await my return. Nothing will harm thee."

Miriam awaited his return in the close oppressive atmosphere of those old-fashioned stairs, and huge spiders played at hide and seek in her jet black tresses, yet she heeded them not as she stood with her head against the cobwebbed wall awaiting her unnatural father's return.

In a short time, which, however, appeared an age to her, he made his appearance.

"Didst thou hear anything?" he asked, rather anxiously.

"Nothing," was the reply.

"Then follow me, and fear nothing."

Miriam followed her father, who soon disappeared through the aperture formed by the sliding panel.

An extraordinary sight met her eyes as she entered that room.

From its appearance it seemed to have been deserted for years.

The furniture was covered with thick layers of dust, and the carpet threw up clouds of the same impalpable substance as soon as a footfall descended upon it.

The door appeared to be securely fastened, and so begrimed with dust and dirt was the window, that to all intents and purposes of a practical nature, the room was destitute of any ventilating or light-admitting apparatus.

Miriam gazed around her in blank amazement.

The light her father carried in his hand was sufficient to reveal the decayed and mildewed nature of the apartment.

MIRIAM MOSS MAKES A TERRIBLE DISCOVERY.

It was evident that those articles of furniture had not been visited for years.

Miriam, actuated by a curiosity the motive for which she could not exactly define, advanced towards an aged sofa she perceived in the centre of the room.

Upon this she sat down, but almost as quickly sprang up again.

What was the cause of her alarm?—what made her rise so suddenly from her position?

She had sat upon a skeleton!

The bones jingled and ground together beneath her pressure.

A horrible idea possessed her.

It was probably her mother's remains! her father had hinted at such a consummation.

Oh, Heaven! such a thing was too horrible. She could not stay in such a frightful place.

At all hazards she must make her escape. She would appeal to her father's better feelings.

She turned to address him, and had prepared a plaintive appeal which no man possessing anything like a heart could have withstood.

But what was her astonishment to perceive that her father had left the room.

She could not, at first, believe her eyes.

The evidence was, however, conclusive. The lamp still remained upon the table where Mike Moss had placed it.

But all traces of the Jew had disappeared.

What a horrible situation for a young girl, her nerves already strung to the highest pitch, to be placed in.

Alone in a sepulchral-looking chamber! Not a soul within call! At the mercy of a fiendish, cruel, if not mad old man.

And worse than all, alone with a skeleton, and that skeleton, for all she knew to the contrary, the skeleton of her erring, but oppressed mother.

Truly this young girl's position was horrible beyond conception.

But she could escape!

She had come up a flight of stairs into the fatal room, and if so, why could she not descend by them?

Certainly this was a fair deduction from a reasonable premiss.

Miriam Moss advanced towards that portion of the wall through which she had recently entered the room which she could only now regard as her mother's grave.

But what was her chagrin, surprise, and amazement to discover that all traces of the hidden panel had totally disappeared.

In vain she searched the wall from end to end. No signs of the panel rewarded her patient investigation.

"This is absurd," cried the poor girl; "I must have been mistaken somehow or other. Let me try again."

But still her efforts were utterly fruitless and without result.

Mike Moss had taken care, as he made his silent and crafty retreat, to leave no trace of the sliding panel; so cleverly and sagaciously was it made, that once closed, without you know the secret, it defied detection.

Miriam, in a paroxysm of fear, rage, and terror, attacked the paper on the walls with her finger nails.

Large strips of paper rewarded her exertions in this direction, and that was all.

In time she desisted from those childish efforts, and subsided into a quiet, miserable, hopeless state of mind.

"Oh! he cannot have left me here to die of starvation," she thought; "he is my father, and some spark of pity must linger in his heart for his offspring. Perhaps he is trying to frighten me.

"He will, most likely, come this evening and liberate me, making great fun of my fright.

"Oh! yes; I have no doubt he is amusing himself at my expense, and being a little angry at what I have done, he wishes to alarm me a little into the bargain."

Ah! What is that on the dusty old table-cover, near the lamp?

Papers, by the look of them.

There can be no great harm in my investigating their contents, I should think.

So saying Miriam Moss approached the table, and seized a bundle of papers tied with red tape.

To slip the tape off did not take her much time.

The papers were indorsed outside, "Papers belonging to the Leslie Family."

Opening the packet, which seemed to have been placed there for her inspection, Miriam perused several letters, which placed her mother's guilt beyond the suspicion of a doubt.

Bernard Leslie appeared, according to the signature, to have been the man who had destroyed the old fence's happiness. In addition to the letters were some notes of hand, bills of exchange, and post-obit bonds of Bernard Leslie, and one or two sheets descriptive of the history of the family.

But in these details Miriam took no interest.

It was enough for her to know that her mother was guilty of the crime imputed to her by her father.

Her brain felt in a whirl.

She was utterly bewildered, and knew not what to do.

Throwing herself into an arm-chair, which threw up a perfect cloud of dust as she sat down upon it, she began to ruminate upon her forlorn and desperate position.

Her father had evidently deserted her, and she began to realize the meaning of those fearful words, "Thou hast committed an unpardonable sin, and thou shalt die the death."

Her father meant, it was clear, to abandon her to starvation.

As this thought took possession of her, Miriam Moss almost gave herself up to despair.

But as she sat on that faded, moth-eaten, dust-begrimed arm-chair, another and a sweeter reflection came upon her.

She had done nothing positively wrong, and why should she not hope for the interposition of Providence in her behalf?

She prayed to the God of Abraham, Isaac, and Jacob, and she did not think that she should be deserted in the hour of her greatest peril and her utmost need.

As she was reasoning in this way she became conscious of a strange scent in the apartment.

A subtle odour filled the chamber.

It seemed as if all the perfumes from Araby the blest had been concentrated into one cloud, and that cloud was now within the chamber occupied against her will by Miriam.

Denser and denser grew the cloud.

Stronger and more subtle seemed the essence.

But suddenly a great dread took possession of Miriam.

Was not the perfume she was inhaling with such apparent pleasure having an extraordinary effect upon her?

Had not an intoxicating feeling taken hold of her and invaded her senses?

Oh! what a fiendish refinement of almost superhuman cruelty was this!

As the idea gained strength in her mind that she was to die in the inebriating embraces of that dense and all-pervading vapour, a feeling of panic seized on Miriam.

Even as the inhabitants of the forests of the Far West run panic-stricken before the fuliginous cloud of smoke, which tells them that the woods behind them are in flames, so did Miriam rush wildly from place to place, in a vain attempt to escape from her terrible thraldom.

Oh! for one breath of fresh air, if only one; never had she before known the blessing of the pure air of heaven.

Oh! if one little zephyr would float in upon her, and snatch her from her frightful doom.

Or the atmosphere of the sewers of fetid and underground London—anything in the world would be preferable to these insinuating fumes.

As these thoughts occurred to her, Miriam ran wildly about the room, without any fixed purpose or plan, shrieking wildly and fearfully.

She beat upon the walls with her poor hands till they were lacerated, torn, and blood-stained.

But all to no purpose; that secret sliding panel defied every attempt at detection.

But then there was the door—she would try that. Alas! for it was securely fastened—how did not appear; but it resisted all her attempts to open it.

An idea struck her. That door must communicate with some other apartments; she would put her lips to the key-hole, and send shriek upon shriek, to alarm the inmates, if inmates there were any.

But to her intense annoyance, she discovered that the keyhole was plugged and stopped up with putty or some such substance.

Taking a penknife from her pocket, she hastily scraped away the impeding matter from the orifice.

In the midst of this operation her knife broke in half, but she worked on bravely with the remains.

Worked too with a frantic eagerness, for she felt that if she once sat down and gave way to the subtle essence about her, she would never wake again.

This was indeed an incentive to labour.

At last the keyhole was free from obstruction, and bending down, Miriam sent her fierce lamentations travelling through it.

Would they be heard, and if so, would she be rescued from the devilish ingenuity which was encompassing her death?

These were the anticipations which agitated the breast of the unhappy Miriam.

Again and again did those weird, unearthly shrieks, as of a woman in her death-agony, peal with horrible distinctness through the narrow aperture.

But no response followed.

A strange light danced in Miriam's eyes. She heard strange noises, and her brain felt sublimated, as it were.

A feeling like that which animates drowning people when their senses leave them stole gradually over the girl, who was rapidly becoming unconscious.

One more effort for life and liberty! It was the last struggle of her strong and vigorous nature against the soul-oppressing effects of the mysterious vapour, which was slowly but surely leading her to her doom.

Yet another shriek! more weird, more wild, more unearthly than the preceding ones, rang through the orifice, and with a strange laugh the unfortunate maiden fell heavily on the floor.

Ere her senses entirely left her, did she indeed hear a sound, as of friends, coming to her rescue, or was it some fiend mocking her last moments?

Pale and ghastly was she as she lay in that dreadful room her sole companion a hideous skeleton, and that in all likelihood her mother's.

Suddenly a sound, as of some one endeavouring to open

the door of the room, was heard, but these glad tidings did not reach the ears of the captive, who was too far gone to notice them.

Heavy blows resounded upon the aged panels, and one more vigorous than the rest sent the old rusty lock flying into the apartment.

This, however, was no great achievement, owing to the antiquity of everything connected with the apartment.

It required no party of sappers and miners to effect the forcing open of that door, which had, owing to the want of proper weapons, resisted all the exertions of Miriam.

The heroine of the achievement was no other than Agnes, Marmaduke Wilson's wife, and the weapon she used was a stout poker, snatched up in a hurry at hearing those terrible shrieks, each of which had, to Agnes' astonished ears, sounded like a death-wail.

Agnes gazed about her for a moment, and then discovered Miriam Moss. To bear her to the light and air was the work of a moment.

As this was accomplished, a howl of rage emanated from some mysterious corner, and the subtle vapour began to disappear as strangely as it had arisen.

One fact, however, remained. Miriam Moss, through Agnes, was snatched from the very jaws of death!

CHAPTER XIV.

NOURISHING A VIPER—MIRIAM LEAVES HER FATHER'S HOUSE, AND PERSUADES AGNES TO ACCOMPANY HER—SEEKING A NIGHT'S LODGING—AGNES LOSES HER TEMPER—THE CHASE—POLICE! POLICE!—MR. TODD'S SILVER SPOONS—ASSAULTING WITH INTENT, ETC.—LOCKED UP IN A POLICE STATION.

MIRIAM MOSS, with a deathlike pallor spread over her countenance, lay upon a sofa in Agnes' apartment.

Was she indeed dead, or was it but the semblance of death? Her inanimate form gave great room for the former supposition.

Agnes gazed anxiously upon the countenance of the young Jewess, to detect any signs of returning consciousness, but for some time her expectations were disappointed.

She had bathed her temples with water, and thrown open the window to allow a little air to penetrate to the sufferer, and meander gently through the tangled masses of her long dishevelled hair.

Better would it have been for Agnes had Miriam Moss died then and there.

Yes, better had she died upon that sofa, whither she had been carried after her rescue from the fatal embrace of that suffocating and mysterious vapour.

But the events of the future were not revealed to Agnes.

She had no friendly Cassandra to warn her of approaching evil.

Had the contrary been the case, she would have avoided the society of one who was in heart her deadliest enemy, even as Wyman was her husband's inveterate foe.

Agnes was in truth, innocently enough, nourishing a viper in her bosom.

A venomous reptile which would inevitably, as soon as it was strong enough, fold its spiral coils, and darting upon her, sting her to the heart.

But, alas! prescience is not an attribute of frail humanity.

Slowly Miriam Moss opened her eyes, but almost instantly again closed them.

"Oh, speak, Miriam!" cried Agnes. "Tell me that you live once more."

At the sound of a friendly voice, Miriam roused herself, and with an effort sat up.

"Oh, thank Heaven, you are better! I feared the worst." Miriam uttered a long-drawn sigh. "What has happened?" continued Agnes. "Something dreadful, I know, must have befallen you."

"Indeed, yes," replied Miriam, for the first time opening her lips since her swoon. "My father—oh, it is horrible. I cannot, even now, persuade myself that it is not a hideous shapeless dream!" Miriam after uttering these words shut her eyes, as if to keep out some frightful vision.

"It is all too true, I am afraid," replied Agnes; "but one thing is certain, whatever fate was in store for you, dear Miriam, it has providentially been averted, for you are now free and scathless."

"That is true."

"There, you see, is the old door I battered open when I heard your dreadful shrieks, which sounded shrilly through the house. Guided by them I found this door, and perceived that some one must be in trouble and in great peril; so I effected an entry as well and quickly as I could."

"To you I owe my life," said Miriam.

"Talk not of that. It was a fortunate chance, and I rejoice to have been able to come in time."

"Let me see that room once more," exclaimed Miriam, "to be sure that I am not the sport of some hallucination, and I shall be satisfied."

"Do not excite yourself, Miriam. You are not yet strong enough. I would wait awhile until you are somewhat recovered."

Waving her hand imperiously, Miriam rose to her feet, and walked into the room, followed closely by Agnes. Having entered it, she gazed around her, and her glance first sought the skeleton that lay upon the sofa.

"There lie my mother's remains," she cried, with a hysterical sob. "Her fate was indeed a sad one, as my experience can testify. There have her bones bleached unsepulchred and untended."

"Horrible!" ejaculated Agnes.

"Yes, it is horrible, but still more so when the murderer is one's own husband."

"Her husband! What mean you?"

"My father's fiendish malice and ingenuity slew my mother, and would have slain me, had you not, by the help of Providence, saved me from destruction," replied Miriam, looking at Agnes.

"Is such cruelty possible?" asked Agnes, in astonishment. "Such things make one's blood freeze and curdle in one's veins."

"Ah! truth is often stranger than the wildest fiction," replied Miriam.

"Of what crime was your mother guilty?" inquired Agnes.

"In that she loved another than my father."

"How know you that?"

"I am too sure."

"You should have good proof. It is not well to malign the dead; you may do your mother great injustice," said Agnes.

"Was not her fate sufficient evidence of her guilt?" replied Miriam, almost fiercely; "if more confirmation were needed, it could be found in that packet of papers lying on the table."

Casting her eyes in that direction, Agnes discovered the bundle in question.

But she started as if a serpent had imprinted his fangs upon her flesh. "Papers belonging to the Leslie family," she exclaimed. "By what strange concatenation of circumstances am I doomed ever to meet with that name?"

"Yes, there are the proofs of my mother's weakness, and my mother's shame," said Miriam. "But come, let us leave this horrid atmosphere, I feel half-suffocated still," and with an exclamation of disgust she left the room.

Actuated by an irresistible impulse, Agnes seized the packet of papers, and hastily concealed them in the folds of her dress. Having accomplished this she followed her companion.

"This house is no place for me now," exclaimed Miriam. "I shall quit my father's roof, and seek shelter beneath that of strangers. My life is not safe."

"I feel sincerely for you, Miriam," replied Agnes, kindly.

It was strange that no sooner had Miriam Moss fully recovered her senses, than she renewed her determination to destroy the happiness and peace of mind of Agnes.

It was now late in the evening, and she calculated that from the fact of Agnes being alone, Marmaduke Wilson had gone out to keep his appointment with the Surrey Wolf and Fly-by-night, for he had, with unparalleled audacity, declared his intention of doing so.

Of the result of such an interview she felt pretty confident.

In a few hours, she argued, Marmaduke Wilson will be in the hands of the police. Once secured, Wyman is not the man I take him for if he allows the bird to escape.

Accused as he will be of numerous offences, conviction is inevitable.

At present this silly fool who calls herself his wife must know nothing of it, or my plans will be foiled. I must lead her to suppose that her affectionate Marmaduke has deserted her, as I predicted the other day he would. She will be loth to believe it, and indignant with me for supposing such a thing; but as day after day glides by, the suspicion will become a certainty, and then she may pine away and die as soon as she likes.

It was diabolical thus to plot against the very life of a girl who had a few short hours before saved her life; but when a woman determines to be revenged, she seldom hesitates at the means wherewith to accomplish her end.

Miriam now considered herself wronged and injured by Agnes, insomuch as she had enthralled and married Marmaduke Wilson.

And as she had been slighted and trifled with by the latter, she resolved to punish both of them.

Marmaduke Wilson's forebodings after leaving Bluegatefields were terribly realized; better would it have been for him and his young unsuspecting wife to have slept under the Adelphi arches than to have entered the old fence's house in that retired street near the Foundling Hospital.

For misery and misfortune had dogged their footsteps ever since, and was still following fiercely on the trail.

"Will you fly with me, Agnes?" asked Miriam, pleadingly.

"I cannot leave my husband."

"Your husband will follow us, for we can leave word for him."

"But he may return to-night, and he would wonder at my absence."

"Well, you must please yourself," returned Miriam, with a look of deep disappointment. "I had reckoned upon your friendship in my hour of trouble."

"And so you may," cried Agnes. "Anything that I can do for you, dear Miriam, rely upon it, I will; but I cannot desert my husband."

"If he were mine," said Miriam, spitefully, "I would not allow him to go out at night; how know you where he goes, or how his time is spent?"

This speech threw fuel on Agnes' already roused suspicions. "Surely," she thought, "if other people remark these things, there must be something for me to complain of. Miriam, I think, evidently knows something about Marmaduke, or she would not have said what she did say the other morning. Oh! I am very unhappy!"

"Deserted by my father, with the corpse of my mother lying in that room, and with no one to care for me," exclaimed Miriam, "I am indeed friendless!"

Touched at these words, which were uttered in a heartbroken manner, Agnes seized her friend's hand, and replied,

"I am your friend, if you will only think so. Say, what can I do for you?"

"Ah! you do not mean what you say? I want some one to lean upon—some one to comfort me, until my nerves recover the terrible shock they have sustained."

"I will do all that to the best of my ability."

"You will?" cried Miriam, joyfully. "Then let us leave here at once."

"Leave here?" responded Agnes; "and wherefore?"

"I cannot stay! I fear some fresh attempt on the part of my father to destroy me. Baulked in the execution of his original scheme, he will endeavour to compass my death in some new way. Even now I tremble for my life."

"You would have me leave Marmaduke to go with you?" said Agnes. "You place a heavy tax upon our newborn friendship."

"Were he my husband," muttered Miriam, as if talking to herself, but yet loud enough to let Agnes hear every word she said,—"were he my husband, I would go away for a day to punish him for his irregular ways. If a man takes to staying out late at night, the best way for a wife to cure him of the habit is to stay away too, and when he finds that two can play at the game, he generally reforms."

"What do you say?" asked Agnes.

"Oh! nothing. I thought I had a friend, but I find I was mistaken."

Taking up her bonnet and shawl, Miriam attired herself, and put away all her trinkets she could get at, as some were locked up in her father's safe, and with a little money in her purse she prepared to depart.

"Good-bye!" she said, a little coldly, to Agnes, adding, in a feeling tone, "May Heaven be kinder to you when your evil day comes than you have been to me! Misfortune's clouds may even now be gathering about your head."

"Stay, Miriam!" cried Agnes, as Miriam was moving towards the doorway.

Miriam stopped, and looked inquiringly at her.

"I will go with you. You shall not accuse me of coldheartedness."

"Heaven will bless you!" answered Miriam, pretending to be much moved.

Agnes was soon equipped, and, following Miriam, descended the stairs with some caution, lest the old fence should overhear them, and endeavour to dispute their right to leave the house.

They reached the landing on the ground floor in safety without having met anyone. The solitary servant kept by Mike Moss had hours ago retired to rest.

Gently opening the huge nail-studded oaken door, these two adventurous girls sallied into the street.

"I breathe once more!" exclaimed Miriam, "now that I have left the detestable house of my unnatural parent."

It now became a question what they were to do with themselves.

Alone and unprotected in our modern Babylon, without knowing where to go, is anything but a nice position for two good-looking young females to be placed in.

They walked for some little distance without stopping or conversing. At length, when Miriam considered that they had placed a sufficient distance between themselves and their pursuers, if pursuers there were, she halted to hold a council of war.

It was not, as we know, the first time that Agnes had been bewildered in the streets of London.

Therefore she was not much alarmed; and Miriam was too overjoyed to be at large once more, to feel any particular anxiety as to her present position.

Yet it was necessary to do something. The girls could not sleep in the open air. Miriam proposed that, as it was too late for two women to procure lodgings anywhere that night, the best thing they could do would be to get a bed at some coffee-house, and with that intention they walked towards Tottenham-court-road.

The shops were all shut up, but there were still several people about, as is always the case in large and frequented thoroughfares. The public-houses seemed to be well filled to judge from the noise that issued from the half-open doors.

A quiet, genteel-looking coffee-shop arrested their attention.

"Here!" cried Miriam. "This, I think, will do for us. Let us go in, and ask what their charge is for a night's lodging."

They passed underneath the lamp, upon which an inscription was placed informing the public that Mr. Todd was prepared to let good beds.

A neatly oil-clothed passage led them to a coffee-room. Here a man of the rough and ready order was serving some customers. This was Mr. Todd, who rejoiced in being his own waiter.

When he perceived the two girls, he looked inquiringly at them, and waited for them to speak.

"What do you charge for beds?" asked Miriam.

"Half-a-crown," was the surly reply.

"Have you two vacant?"

"Maybe I have. Who are they for?"

"For my friend and myself," answered Miriam.

"Then I don't let 'em, and that's flat," replied Mr. Todd, who, from his manner, certainly appeared to have taken something stronger than coffee during the evening.

"You don't let them—why not? Just now you said they were vacant."

"I don't choose to let my rooms to a parcel of women who come running about after lodgings at this time of night. That's not me, I can tell you!" said Mr. Todd, with some asperity.

"We can pay you what you ask. See here, I have got money," replied Miriam, her face flushing scarlet at his insolent speech, as she drew her purse out of her pocket.

"I don't want your money. My house is respectable, and, please God, I'll keep it so," said Mr. Todd, whose meaning was now no longer doubtful.

"If I were a man," cried Miriam, her face all aglow, "you would not dare to insult us thus. Never mind, there are, I have no doubt, several places where a civil landlord will be glad to take our money, which is as good as yours any day in the week."

"Your money! yes; lightly got, lightly gone!" cried Mr. Todd. "Out of my house, or I'll help you in going, you shameless things!"

It will be perceived that Mr. Todd was, as country people say, like a hedgehog after an immersion in water—"when he's wet he's open;" and if he had, as there was a reasonable presumption, been indulging in a copious libation, it had certainly had the effect of opening him very considerably.

But his insults were rather more than either Agnes or Miriam could bear. Miriam's fingers moved about uneasily, as if she contemplated making an assault on the somewhat bloated physiognomy of Mr. Todd; while Agnes, who hitherto had taken no part whatever in the conversation, exclaimed—

"Before I go I'll give you something to remember me by!" and she looked about her for some weapon wherewith to carry out her threat. Her eye almost immediately fell upon a rather massive tumbler: with the rapidity of thought, before anyone could prevent her, she seized it, and, with unerring aim, hurled it at the insolent coffee-house keeper.

With such precision was it thrown that it struck Mr. Todd upon the forehead, between the temples, with considerable violence.

The man staggered a few paces backwards, but maintained his footing, and, in a second or two after the occurrence, rushed forward, followed by his customers, to secure Miriam and Agnes, and hand them over to the tender mercies of the police.

But, unfortunately for his purpose, those young ladies had disappeared.

Taking advantage of the confusion, they had levanted, and were fast vanishing in the darkness.

Determined not to be baffled, however, Mr. Todd shouted "police" as hard as his stentorian lungs allowed him.

Streaming with blood, he rushed into the street continuing his cries, which were taken up and echoed by several others.

"Police! police!" rang through the neighbourhood of Tottenham-court-road.

Wonderful to relate, two policemen, attired in the sombre uniform of the force, appeared upon the scene of action, and joined Mr. Todd and his friends in search of the fugitives.

"Here they are, round the corner!" cried a voice, causing the crowd to turn round a corner in the direction of Torrington-square.

"Stop thief! stop thief! police! police!" resounded on all sides.

Hunted like so many deer, Miriam and Agnes ran on until fatigue and want of breath compelled them to stop.

"Oh! this is dreadful, Miriam," cried Agnes; "those dreadful men are close upon us!"

"Let us hide under the shelter of these railings!" said Miriam, crouching down.

Her advice was acted upon; but the security gained by this step was only momentary.

Almost directly the crowd of fierce pursuers bore down upon the shrinking girls.

Bulls'-eyes flashed their lightning gleams in all directions.

Suddenly a shrill cry of triumph burst upon the air, denoting that the fugitives were discovered.

A rude grasp was placed upon the arms of the two girls, who, in custody of two policemen, were marched through the streets, followed by a crowd of a miscellaneous nature.

Mr. Todd presented rather a ludicrous appearance, although there was still a large amount of ferocity apparent upon his florid countenance. In his eagerness to follow the two girls, he had snatched up a night-cap instead of a hat, and the immaculate purity of his skin and linen was stained with blood.

"I'll pay you!" he cried to Agnes. "I'll give you six months, or my name aint Nathan Todd."

"Will you?" replied Agnes. "I don't doubt your inclination, but I doubt your ability."

"Now come on, young woman!" said the policeman in whose custody she was; "I've no time to spare for you to stop chattering here."

"I'll give it you in the morning!" said Mr. Todd; "but now I must go back and look after the shop."

So saying, he was about to return to his coffee-shop, when one of the policemen said—

"Hullo! guv'nor, where are you off to?"

"Off to! why going home to attend to business. It's all right, isn't it?"

"It's all wrong, I think," responded the policeman.

"What do you mean, eh?"

"Mean! I mean what I says. You've give these young girls here into custody, and you'll have to come to the station and charge them before the inspector, that's all!"

"But I can't; who's to look after the business, I should like to know?"

"You should have thought of that afore."

"Well," said Mr. Todd, "sooner than let these designing, artful, violent women escape the punishment they deserve, I would lose everything I've got, except my silver spoons."

"Oh! blow the silver spoons," said the policeman. "Are you coming, or are you not? that's a plain question; so give it a plain answer, if you please."

"I'm with you," replied Mr. Todd. "There's my son Tom about somewhere, and I suppose it will be all square."

In due time the procession arrived at the station, and Mr. Todd proceeded to charge Agnes with assaulting him; and he declared vehemently that Miriam was her accomplice, and aided and abetted her.

But the inspector shook his head, and said to Miriam, "If you can give a satisfactory account of yourself, I shall feel it my duty to liberate you; but we will proceed with the first case. Now, young woman, what is your name?"

"Agnes Wilson," was the reply.

"Where do you live?"

"Nowhere, at present," answered Agnes.

"You refuse your address?"

Agnes made no further reply.

"Very well; that is enough." And at a sign from the inspector, Agnes was taken away and locked up in a cell.

"Your name?" demanded the inspector on duty to Miriam.

"Miriam Moss," she answered.

"Your address?"

"I have none."

"Um!" muttered the inspector; "what are you?"

"Nothing. I have never had to get my own living yet; my friends have supported me until to-day, when I left home with my friend, owing to a family quarrel."

"Indeed!" said the inspector, drily, "and who are your friends?"

"I refuse to answer," replied Miriam. "It is nothing to you."

"Where do they live?"

"I refuse to answer," again replied Miriam.

"Um!" muttered the inspector a second time. "I don't think I should be doing my duty if I discharged you. The whole of the circumstances are so very suspicious. You both of you refuse to give an account of yourselves, and as far as you are concerned, if you gave me a good account I would liberate you directly, as I told you before, but on mature consideration I think you must be confined with your friend."

Miriam said nothing, and was just about to be taken away to join Agnes, when a red-headed lout of a boy rushed into the place.

Mr. Nathan Todd was at the time rubbing his hands and asking the police to come and have a "drain" somewhere. He was inwardly highly delighted that both Miriam and Agnes were to be locked up.

Suddenly his rapture was disagreeably dissipated by a voice exclaiming—

"Oh! father, they've been and gone and done it."

"Done it! Done what?" replied Mr. Todd turning pale, as he recognised his son Tom, to whose care and vigilance he had confided his shop and silver spoons.

"Two on 'em," said Tom.

"Two what? And what have they done? Speak, boy, or I'll break your neck," vociferated Mr. Nathan Todd.

"I come out with you, father, to see the thieves took, them as you've just locked up——"

"I'll skin you for it," interrupted Mr. Todd, savagely.

"And when I got back," continued Tom, blubbering, "I found two fellows a-coming out of the shop. They pushed me on one side and hooked it, but all the plate's gone."

"Gone!" said Mr. Todd; "are the spoons gone? Don't say the spoons are gone, anything but that. The spoons aint gone Tom, are they now?" he added, as a lingering hope possessed him.

"Yes, they be," said Tom, doggedly.

"Oh! my spoons, my silver spoons. It's your fault, you scoundrel. I'll give it you," shouted Mr. Todd, springing on his son, but that young gentleman cleverly evaded the parental grasp, and getting into the street "made the running," closely followed, however, by his infuriated father.

"How about your silver spoons?" cried Miriam, as he left the room.

Mr. Todd turned round for an instant, glanced savagely at her, shook his fist menacingly, and disappeared.

"Well, Agnes!" exclaimed Miriam, as she joined her friend in their novel apartment, "at all events we have got a night's lodging for nothing, and that's something."

CHAPTER XV.

AGNES AND MIRIAM ARE BROUGHT BEFORE A MAGISTRATE—MR. SOLOMON ISAACS—AGNES IS COMMITTED—NATHAN TODD'S DELIGHT THEREAT—THE CHARGE AGAINST MIRIAM IS DISMISSED—MIRIAM RETURNS HOME—A HORRIBLE SIGHT—THE GASH IN THE THROAT—THE JEW'S DEATH—AGAIN AN OUTCAST.

THE night was not passed very pleasantly either by Agnes or Miriam Moss; a police cell is at best a sorry hostelry.

They had, however, one consolation, the cell was all their own—no drunken men or women were thrust in upon them.

No thief, or wife-beating ruffian, disputed possession with the two friendless girls.

Their apartment was artificially warmed by some hot-water apparatus, so that even in the middle of winter it would not be uncomfortable, except for the associations.

There was no bed, however, that was a little too much to expect. A narrow sort of ledge, or locker, ran round the cell, upon which the prisoners were at liberty to recline if they had the mind.

If not, they might sit up with their backs to the wall, and make the best of it.

Agnes sobbed and cried a little at first, but after she had been incarcerated for an hour or so, she became more composed.

Miriam sat with her hands folded upon her knees, looking stately and dignified, as if she had made up her mind not to be overcome by any accumulation of misfortunes.

But the truth was, she was brooding over her revenge. She had sworn most solemnly to be revenged upon Marmaduke Wilson for his perfidy and treachery. If revenge upon him could be compassed by human means, she would undoubtedly achieve it.

At length the girls fell asleep, and when they awoke the morning had long dawned.

Yes, the morning had dawned, but it dawned upon misery, despair, and doubt.

Doubt on the part of Miriam, misery and despair on the part of Agnes.

The girls were hungry and thirsty. A friendly policeman, who came in the morning to inquire if they wanted anything, consented, upon being paid by Miriam, to get them some coffee and some bread-and-butter.

This infused new life into them, for although it was not super-excellent, it stayed the gnawing pangs of hunger which had before possessed them.

At ten o'clock the sergeant on duty appeared at the door of their cell, and opening it with a key he carried with him, told them to follow him. This they did; and passing along a passage they at length emerged into the street.

As may be imagined, their appearance was not so prepossessing as it would have been had they had an opportunity of making their toilette.

But the Commissioners of Police for the metropolis do not undertake to supply the refractory population of London with combs and looking-glasses.

Nor are soap and water attainable.

But by assisting one another as well as they could, they contrived to look passably respectable.

Crossing the road they were conducted through a small crowd into the Police-court, which was opposite the station-house.

Both Agnes and Miriam blushed deeply at the scrutiny the public bestowed upon them.

Both girls were beautiful in their way.

Agnes, as we have said, was a lovely blonde, Miriam was dark as the night; and as their attire was a little ruffled, by their having been in such unpleasant quarters all night, the spectators freely canvassed their social status.

Of course they were set down as wandering beauties, who, like bats, disport themselves in the hours of darkness.

These remarks, which were distinctly audible, were very disagreeable to both Agnes and Miriam. The former shrank back involuntarily, but the strong grasp of the policeman was soon upon her arm, and in a stern voice he told her to go forward.

They were not alone in misfortune. The other cells contained prisoners, who, as well as themselves, were marched across the street.

One was a woman of the town, who had assaulted a barman at a public-house, by throwing a jug of hot water over him, which so scalded him that his eyebrows and moustache fell off like the hair from a scalded pig.

Another was a man who had indulged in the pastime of "picking up," or looking out for drunken men, and then picking their pockets.

A third was an inmate of St. Martin's Workhouse, who had had permission given her to go and see her friends, but who had abused the kindness of the authorities by a very flagrant breach of discipline.

She had brought a flask of gin in with her, and had got very respectably drunk.

For this offence she was given in charge, and was now about to take her trial.

Agnes and Miriam were first placed in the dock, and their hearts trembled at their novel and most unpleasant position.

Visions of a prison passed before their eyes, and they trembled with apprehension.

Miriam felt more secure than Agnes, because she had not actually committed the assault.

But they were both in a dilemma.

The policeman who took them in charge entered the court with them.

Then the charge-sheet was read, and he got into the witness-box to give his evidence.

When he had finished, Mr. Todd, the coffee-house keeper, took his place, and said everything he could think of to prejudice the two girls.

In fact Mr. Todd rather overdid his case; if he had not been quite so demonstrative he might have done better.

"Is anything known about these females?" asked the magistrate.

The policeman replied that they were unknown at that court, and that the gaoler was unacquainted with their features, but he had no doubt, if his worship would grant a remand, he could discover something about them.

The magistrate replied that he did not recognise any point in the case which would justify a remand.

At this juncture some one in the court below the dock where the girls stood touched Miriam Moss's hand.

That young lady, dreading some new indignity, started back, but as she did so her fingers closed upon a piece of paper.

Thinking it might be a communication from some friend, she lost no time in perusing it.

The piece of paper contained these words: "If you wish to be defended and rescued from your unpleasant and dangerous position, give a sovereign to Mr. Solomon Isaacs, and the thing is done."

Miriam reflected a moment, and thought that this might be a device of some clever rogue to obtain a sovereign from her for nothing.

But when she considered their desolate position, she hesitated no longer, but took out the requisite sum from her purse, and handed it down to the individual who had presented her with the piece of paper.

He immediately spoke to another man who was standing near him, and it was evident from what followed that one of them was a solicitor, and the other his clerk, who had been doing what is commonly called in the profession "a little touting."

Directly Mr. Solomon Isaacs saw the fee, he rose and said, "I appear, sir, for the prisoners at the bar; and I quite agree with your worship, that there is no possible reason why they should be remanded.

"If your worship will permit me, I can point out several weighty and cogent reasons why the case should be summarily dismissed."

"I shall be glad to hear you," replied the magistrate.

"Your worship is kind—very kind," said Mr. Solomon Isaacs. "I will not take up much of the time of the court, but it is clear a case of this importance cannot be disposed of without a clear and impartial hearing.

"Fair play is the prerogative of an Englishman, and I sincerely trust of an Englishwoman also.

"My unfortunate clients left their homes last night owing to some family squabble, as has been already given in evidence.

"Looking for a night's lodging, they were unlucky enough to meet with Mr. Nathan Todd, coffee-house keeper in the Tottenham-court-road.

"Your worship will be good enough to bear in mind that my fair clients were not only able, but willing, to pay for the accommodation.

"But Mr. Nathan Todd, whose conduct I will not animadvert upon in case I might overstep the bounds of propriety, by his insults and general conduct, brought upon himself a chastisement which, with all submission to the court, I cannot but think he most fully deserved."

"But how about the assault?" inquired the magistrate.

"I have it on my notes that an assault was committed by one Agnes Wilson upon one Nathan Todd—to wit, by throwing a tumbler composed of glass at the aforesaid Nathan Todd, and doing him grievous bodily harm."

"Your worship," said Mr. Solomon Isaacs, "an assault was undoubtedly committed, but it was one of a very trivial character, and nobody but a coward and a dastard would think of prosecuting these two poor helpless and friendless girls, whose only fault has been in possessing sufficient spirit to resent an insult when it was offered them in the most gross and open manner.

"I may speak with some warmth, sir, but the occasion requires it; and I call upon your worship to mark your sense of the injustice of the case by dismissing the charge against Miriam Moss, and by fining Agnes Wilson a few shillings for the ridiculously trivial assault she committed upon Nathan Todd, the Tottenham-court-road coffee-house keeper."

"I have listened to your arguments attentively, Mr. Isaacs," said the magistrate, gravely; "and although you have long practised in this court, both to your satisfaction and my own, yet I cannot remember your having placed a case before me in so bad a light on any previous occasion.

"Here is an assault committed upon a respectable tradesman by a female of dubious character, who refuses her address.

"And I feel it my imperative duty to convict without a fine in the case of Agnes Wilson.

"The sentence will be fourteen days' hard labour."

Mr. Nathan Todd rubbed his hands. To see the anguish of the fair girl standing in the dock was some slight reparation to such a brutal, unfeeling mind as his for the loss of his silver spoons.

"But, your worship, there is clearly no case against the other prisoner, Miriam Moss," said Mr. Solomon Isaacs.

"I am of the same opinion," said the magistrate, "and think she must be discharged. However, let her beware how she comes here again. Do you hear, young woman? Do not let me see you here again, or the consequences may be as serious, or more so, than they have proved to your companion."

"Never mind, Agnes," exclaimed Miriam to her friend, who was weeping bitterly; "I will come and meet you at the expiration of the time, and I will, in the meantime, get a nice little place ready for you to come into. Cheer up, it is only a fortnight."

"Oh! it is not the time," sobbed Agnes, "it is the disgrace."

And she cried as if her heart would break, as she was led away to await the coming of the prison van.

Miriam, finding she could do no more for Agnes, left the police-court, after thanking Mr. Solomon Isaacs, the Jew attorney, for his eloquent advocacy, and wended her way in search of some apartments.

It was rather singular that Miriam seemed to be elated at the result of the magisterial investigation.

The long and the short of it was, that Miriam was glad to have Agnes removed out of the way for a while, because it was clear no communication could possibly take place between her and Marmaduke Wilson while they were confined in different prisons.

And Marmaduke might be tried and convicted during his wife's imprisonment.

Miriam knew from the papers that the Old Bailey Sessions were progressing at that time, and she hoped that the man who had trifled with her tenderest and dearest feelings would be transported before he could have news of his wife.

If she could only break both their hearts at one blow, what a triumph it would be!

This was the diabolical plot of Miriam Moss!

Marmaduke Wilson could only suppose that his wife had deserted him in his hour of need.

Agnes would, through the wiles and insinuations of Miriam, suppose that Marmaduke had left her for some new victim.

Truly the plot was worthy of Machiavelli!

It was a great relief to Miriam to think that both husband and wife were safely disposed of.

She knew that at four o'clock the van would come round, and that the gentle Agnes would be rudely pushed into one of its prisoners' compartments, and carried off to prison, where she would be detained until a fortnight had elapsed.

That, at present, was enough for her.

The question that most engrossed her mind on leaving the court, after her acquittal, was what she was to do with herself.

It was a question easy to propound but difficult to answer.

She had a faint idea of returning to her father's house. "He will not kill me in cold blood," she thought. "I may as well risk the chance. Perhaps he has relented by this time.

"My absence and after events may have changed the current of his thoughts."

Eventually Miriam Moss determined to return to the old house in the neighbourhood of the Foundling Hospital.

It was a strange resolution; but women are so odd and whimsical, that it is impossible to criticize their actions as you would a man's.

After a sharp walk she reached the door of her father's house a little before one o'clock in the day.

She both knocked and rang, but no one came to the door.

Again and again she made application for admittance, but with no perceptible effect.

"Oh! the fact is he wont let me in," thought Miriam; "he can see me through the window-blinds, and he intends to keep the door locked."

"Oh! how very fortunate," she suddenly exclaimed, "I have found a latchkey in my pocket. I had no idea it was there; but if the door is not fastened on the inside, I have no doubt it will open it."

She was right in her conjecture.

The key fitted the lock to perfection, and opened it without the least difficulty.

Entering the house, and carefully closing the door behind her, Miriam went across the hall towards the room usually occupied by her father. Listening carefully outside for some time, and perceiving no noise or movement, she turned the handle, and throwing open the door, entered the apartment.

The room was empty.

Her father was nowhere to be seen.

Miriam Moss walked towards the centre of the room and suddenly came to a dead stop.

She trembled from head to foot, her eyes were glazed, and her cheeks blanched.

What on earth could have agitated her to such an extraordinary extent?

Was it the events of the morning which had unnerved her, and caused her to be penetrated with grief at the absence of her unnatural father?

No. There was some dreadful mystery beneath her strange behaviour.

And when this is explained, no wonder her cheeks blanched and her eyes were distended with horror.

A sight met her gaze, as she crossed that room, which might have sent that young girl raving to a lunatic asylum for the rest of her days.

For at her feet lay the lifeless body of her father.

Yes, Mike Moss's lifeless corpse lay like so much carrion before her.

He was weltering in his blood.

A deep gash ran from ear to ear across his throat.

He had not only severed the carotid artery, but he had frantically hacked the windpipe in two.

With a cry of alarm and disgust, the girl stepped back, for she had placed her foot in a pool of clotted blood.

It was horrible to think that her foot had dabbled unwittingly in her father's vital fluid.

There he lay, stiff and cold and lifeless.

No doubt agonized by soul-deadening recollections, and mortified by the ill-success of his plans, he had killed himself.

Or had he, as flashed across his daughter's mind, had he been murdered.

Miriam imagined that she might be accused of complicity in the fatal deed.

Accordingly, taking one last look at the hideously mutilated corpse of her father, she left the room, and afterwards the house, half mad and distracted, and wandered she knew not whither. Overcome and horrified by her father's dreadful fate, she felt for the time stupified, and cared not what became of her. Death, she thought, would be preferable to life.

But she had yet to discover that the more you seek for death the less likely you are to find it.

CHAPTER XVI.

MIRIAM'S DESPAIR—SHE TRIES TO DROWN HERSELF—THE HUMANE-SOCIETY'S DRAGS—THE CASUAL SICK WARD—AGNES MAKES AN ACQUAINTANCE—A RIGHT SCREW—THE PRISON VAN—TOTHILL FIELDS—IN PRISON.

MIRIAM MOSS rushed wildly, frantically out of her father's house.

She went she knew nor cared whither. The sight of the old man with those frightful gashes in his throat maddened her.

Badly as he had behaved to her, and she had reason to suppose to her mother also, yet most dreadfully had he expiated his sin.

The shocking sight had, as it were, been photographed upon the retina of her eye, for, open or shut, she could not exclude the scene that she had just quitted.

The old fence lying in a pool of blood—his gaping wounds—the agonized expression of his countenance—were ever before her.

She could not rest—she could not stop.

Like the Wandering Jew, who is condemned to perpetual motion, she felt some invisible power urging her on.

At length she found herself in Hyde Park, and soon the black, murky waters of the Serpentine revealed themselves to her gaze.

She stood a moment on the bank, as if hesitating, but the next she threw herself, with a wild shriek, into the deadly embraces of the treacherous wavelets.

Her body disappeared under the water, and it was some time before it reappeared.

It being broad daylight, a crowd of people were soon on the spot, and messages despatched to the receiving-house of the Royal Humane Society.

A park-keeper arrived with drags, and with the assistance of the bystanders drew Miriam's body towards the land.

But she was inanimate—no breath issuing from her pale and bloodless lips. Her eyes were dull and glassy.

Her long hair, released from the bondage of a bonnet, hung wet and dishevelled over her fair shoulders.

Was she a corpse? Had the vital spark left her frame?

Indeed, there was reason to suppose so.

Soon the body was laid upon a stretcher, and conveyed, amidst a throng of eager, wondering people, to the receiving-house. Its hospitable and charitable doors opened to admit the melancholy cortège, but the public were, of necessity, excluded. Restoratives were at once applied, and the body was immersed in a warm bath.

For a long, long time no symptoms of vitality were apparent, although she slowly opened her eyes; but her reason seemed to have left her.

She spoke incoherently, and sometimes jabbered nonsense, like an idiot.

Her mind was wandering—her senses had deserted her.

It was not part of the system of the Humane Society to keep patients for days, and weeks, and months.

They did not keep a hospital, but only temporary houses of refuge, so Miriam was conducted by one of the officials, as soon as she could walk, to St. George's Hospital.

Here they refused to admit her, as not being one of their cases.

No address could be found on Miriam, and the official, for a moment, knew not what to do.

Ultimately he made up his mind to take her to the workhouse.

The nearest one he knew of was in Mount-street, Grosvenor-square.

Finding that Miriam had some money in her pocket, the official divided it equally between himself and his fair charge, concluding that by so doing he was behaving very handsomely to her.

With an air of importance he hailed a cab, as he descended the steps of the hospital.

But the first man he stopped refused to take him, thinking that it might be some fever case, or some small-pox convalescent.

At last, by dint of perseverance, he found a man who was willing to take them.

Arriving at the workhouse, he made application, and stated his case.

After some demur, the relieving officer consented to receive Miriam in the sick ward of the casual ward.

And, after sending for a pint of beer, the Humane Society's officer went back to his duties by the banks of the Serpentine in Hyde Park, jingling the money in his pocket as he went.

Miriam Moss, on being admitted into the workhouse, was found by the surgeon to be delirious, and in a high state of fever.

She was put to bed, and carefully attended to.

There we must leave her, and return to Agnes.

She was taken weeping and sobbing out of the court; but she evidently had the sympathy of the public who had penetrated the precincts of the court in order to hear the night charges.

"Never you mind, my dear," said one, as she passed by. "You'll do that lot on your head."

"Silence in court!" said the usher.

"Kyus!" cried a low-looking ruffian, with a red kerchief round his throat in lieu of a shirt collar.

Most of the auditory being thieves or their associates, knew that "kyus" was the slang term for "Be quiet," and silence again reigned in the police-court.

Agnes had a few shillings in her pocket, and she gave the policeman who had charge of the cells half-a-crown at his own suggestion to get her something to eat.

The poor thing was too much distressed to think of anything but her own misery.

It was fortunate for her that she had some money, for had she been destitute of that very necessary article in this sublunary sphere, she would have had to go without anything until the prison van deposited her at the House of Correction in Tothill-fields.

She thanked the policeman for his sympathy, and ate the bread-and-butter and the cold sausage he brought her—not because she had any appetite, but because she felt faint and ill, and knew that she wanted something.

A cup of cold tea sufficed to quench her thirst.

Agnes had some hours to wait before she was removed, and, sitting down upon the hard seat of her prison, she gave herself up to her grief.

"What," she thought, "will my husband suppose? But no doubt Miriam will instantly communicate with him, and let him know the position I am in. Oh! if what Miriam suggested should be true—if he should have deserted me for some one else—but it cannot be. I will never believe it! Oh, no! Marmaduke has always been too true and good to me. I will not credit so gross a calumny!"

Her meditations were disturbed by a drunken woman being pushed into her cell.

She seemed more hilariously drunk than anything else, for she instantly commenced singing in a loud voice—

"One night I got a drop of liquor,
And went and copt an old bloak's ticker.
Oh, dear! oh, dear!

"I hadn't got a blessed mag;
And so I went to sell the swag.
Oh, dear! oh, dear!

"But then I found the dirty slops
Had been and gone to all the shops.
Oh, dear! oh, dear!"

"I say, in there!" exclaimed a policeman, pushing back the grating in the door, and looking in; "I can't have that you know, Betsy; it wont do!"

CHAMBERS IN THE ALBANY.

"All right, my dear," replied the woman. "How's your mother?"

Shutting the grating, the policeman departed, and directly his retreating footsteps had died away in the distance, Betsy continued her song—

> "And so my kidment was no go;
>   The ticker wouldn't pop about Soho.
>   Oh, no! oh, no!
>
> "At last they lagged me on the booze,
>   And to go, why I couldn't refuse.
>   Oh, no! oh, no!
>
> "The beak he gave me six months 'ere;
>   And didn't I feel uncommon queer?
>   Oh, dear! oh, dear!"

"I say," she suddenly exclaimed, as she finished her song, "what have we got here?"

She looked at Agnes from top to toe, but could not make her out.

Walking up to the end of the cell where Agnes was sitting she said, in a jeering tone, "Little Miss Twoshoes been out for a spree?"

Agnes made no answer.

"Well, you're civil, anyhow. Can't you answer a lady when she speaks to you?"

"Oh! I am too miserable to talk to anybody," replied Agnes.

"That's the way, is it?" said Betsy. "You're a green hand, I suppose. What are you in for?"

"I am to be imprisoned for a fortnight for throwing a glass at a man's head because he insulted me," answered Agnes, crying.

"The moral to that is, my little Bo-peep, that you should not shy glasses at blokes," said Betsy.

"I couldn't help it," replied Agnes, innocently; "you would have done the same thing, I daresay, if he had said to you what he did to me."

"And what was that, eh?" asked Betsy.

"Why, he called me a fast woman, and I am sure I am not."

"Oh!" replied Betsy, with a prolonged whistle, "if this ain't fine!"

Agnes stopped her tears. The fact of her having some one to talk to, seemed to have freshened her up a bit.

"Have you got any of the ready?" asked Betsy.

"The what?" said Agnes.

"Blunt, tin, needful, cash, couters, quids, skivs, bobs, kicks, flimsies, fivers, tissue?" replied Betsy, with some volubility; "will *that* suit you?"

"If you mean money," replied Agnes, upon whom a light began to dawn, "I think I have."

"Bleed, then, my little booty," said Betsy.

Agnes looked up for an explanation. Her new friend's language sounded rather oddly in her ears.

"Part, my little toolip," continued Betsy, holding out her hand.

Agnes understood this, and gave her five shillings.

"Strike me blind, a bull!" exclaimed Betsy; "that's prime! Now we will have some white satin."

"What is that?" asked Agnes.

"Blue ruin, cream of the valley, Old Tom, gin, you little fool!" replied Betsy.

"But how will you get it?" inquired Agnes, "you cannot get out."

"Out? No, not if they know it. But I have got a right screw here. You wait a bit, and you'll see."

Going to the grating in the door, she whistled shrilly through it. Presently a policeman was heard approaching.

"Get us a pint of Old Tom, will you, Mat?" she asked, as he drew back the grating.

Taking the money she gave him without making any answer, he said in a rough voice, "Now, young woman, you be quiet, will you? I shall come and have another look at you presently, and you'd better mind your p's and q's."

"That's for a blind," explained Betsy to Agnes; "he is as right as ninepence, and no mistake. He will soon come back with the lush."

Betsy was right in her conjecture; in a short time the man returned with the gin, and handed it in through the grating, saying in a low voice, "Here you are, Mrs. Lushington."

He then, as before, began to talk roughly, and soon after retired.

"Why didn't you give him some?" asked Agnes.

"Give him some! You must be a flat," said Betsy; "there isn't much to spare out of a pint, and as I gave him your five bob, he has made something nice out of it, seeing as how a pint of the best Old Tom only costs two bob."

"Oh! I see," said Agnes.

Betsy drank a quantity of the fiery liquid, and then handed the bottle to Agnes, who, in order to keep her spirits up, followed her volatile friend's example.

Soon after the van came up to the court, and the prisoners were led up one by one and placed in separate compartments.

Agnes blushed deeply at the disgrace of her position as she crossed the pavement through a gaping crowd.

Soon the van drove on, and deposited its freight at the door of the Westminster House of Correction, in Tothill-fields.

Agnes stepped out of the van and followed her companions in misfortune, passed a nail-studded iron-bound door, and stood, for the first time in her life, in a prison.

CHAPTER XVII.

LIFE IN PRISON—THE MATRON—IN THE "DARK"—PICKING OAKUM—THE SILENT SYSTEM—FREE ONCE MORE—AGNES IN DESPAIR—NO HOME—THE PRECIOUS PACKET—WHO ARE THE LESLIES?—AGNES FEELS THAT SHE IS ON THE EVE OF MAKING STRANGE AND STARTLING DISCOVERIES.

AFTER entering the prison, Agnes had to submit to numerous indignities, although having her hair cut off was one that, owing to the short term of her imprisonment, and the comparatively trivial nature of her offence, she escaped.

Yet almost immediately on her arrival she was conducted by the matron, or female gaoler, to a bath-room, and compelled to plunge into cold water.

When this involuntary ablution had been performed, she found a suit of prison clothes awaiting her, her own having been made into a bundle and stowed away until her term of punishment should have expired.

Those clothes were neither new nor over clean, they having been used on innumerable previous occasions by other prisoners.

There was what one might almost call a prison effluvium about them, and it was with a feeling of very great disgust that Agnes put them on.

But how was she to help herself? The iron hand of the law had laid its irresistible grasp upon her, and she could not help but submit.

Unhappy Agnes! Already had she begun to taste the bitterness of adversity, and that, too, in its most unpalatable form.

Lucky, indeed, was it for her that she recked not the still greater calamities Fate had in store for her.

Had she entertained the slightest inkling of the fate the future had in store for her, she would inevitably have pined away and died.

A kind Providence, however, conceals the events of the future from the children of men.

It was late when Agnes arrived at the House of Correction and work for that day was over.

She had her supper given her in the cell to which she was conducted.

It consisted of some brown bread in the shape of a roll, and some weak gruel.

The cell itself was of narrow dimensions—possibly twelve feet by six. The bed was something like what is, on board ship, called a hammock.

The canvas part of it was fastened to some hooks in one side of the wall, and when it was unrolled it stretched to the opposite side, and was then attached to two other iron staples. The rest of the bedding was rolled up in the canvas, which served as bed and mattress. This Agnes had to unfasten for herself, and she was obliged to arrange it and fasten it up in the morning at five o'clock, when the matron summoned her to get up.

When she was up and dressed, a piece of thick, tarred rope was given her.

In surprise she demanded its use. The reply was that she would not be long before she found out.

"That," said the Matron, "is what we call hoakum, and you've got to pick it."

"But how shall I pick it? What do you mean? It will make my fingers all over tar."

"Shouldn't be surprised if it does," replied the matron.

"I don't deserve it," cried Agnes, passionately, "and I wont do it."

"Oh! hoity toity, what next?" exclaimed the matron.

"Well, although you have got me here in this horrid place, you cannot make me do what I don't like."

"Can't I? We will see about that. If that there piece of hoakum ain't picked clean and nice, full weight too, you'll catch it hot and strong," answered the matron, roughly.

"What will you do to me, if I refuse to pick it, at least you might tell me that?" asked Agnes.

"You have so much work to do every day, and you will be kept here till it's done; and if you remain imperent and disobedient, why we have a way of taming you," said the matron.

"What mean you?" asked Agnes.

"We put you in the 'dark' when you disobey rules."

"The dark! what is that?"

"You try your little game on, and you wont be long before you find out."

"But at least you might let me know the worst I have to expect," pleaded Agnes, her determination not to work a little shaken at the words of the matron.

"The 'dark,' my dear, is a sort of cellar, or dark place, where you are shut up all alone, and without any food to speak of, for a certain time, which depends upon your offence."

"Oh, how dreadful! I should go mad," exclaimed Agnes.

"Nobody wants you to do that, so you had better do your work quietly," replied the matron.

"But if I must do it will you tell me how it is to be done, and how I am to begin?" said Agnes.

"Certainly, and if you had said that at first you would have saved all this time and conversation. It is this. Now look here. You take the rope and untwist the strands of which it is composed, and having done that, you untwist the cords themselves, and that will give you some fine stringy matter, and that you shred as well as you can, and it then becomes fluffy and feathery-like. Why, bless you! that piece of rope there will make a heap of stuff that will come up to your knees a'most."

" Really!" said Agnes, rather interested in this description, although she was not a little dismayed at the prospect before her.

" And after you have done it," continued the matron, " you will have to bring it downstairs and see it weighed; if there is anything short, you will have to make it up, I can tell you, before you go away from here. And now, good morning. I will bring you your breakfast at the proper time."

The hard rope tore Agnes' tender skin, and made her fingers bleed, and the tar stuck to her hands and made her uncomfortable and irritable, and altogether she felt very miserable and unhappy.

But she knew that the punishment had to be undergone, and she suppressed her sighs and tears, and got on with her work as well as she could, although a tear would now and then fall upon her poor, lacerated fingers, and make her wounds smart afresh.

On those occasions her efforts to force back her welling tears were fruitless, and the hapless girl sobbed audibly.

Her breakfast in due time made its appearance. It consisted simply of brown bread and gruel, and this was the food she entirely subsisted upon during her fortnight's incarceration.

Until a prisoner has been three weeks in the House of Correction he is fed on the same homely diet; at the expiration of that time he is allowed a small quantity of meat, which is gradually increased until the maximum allowance is reached.

And this melancholy privilege of a little meat three times a week, said the enemies of the late Sir Joshua Jebb, is infamous and disgraceful.

In the morning Agnes was summoned by the matron into the yard of the prison for exercise, and took her place amongst a number of women of all ages and of every description.

Silence was strictly enjoined, and any breach of this injunction would have entailed severe punishment on the defaulter.

The prisoners walked with a saddened air, one after the other, round and round the interminable, everlasting gaol-yard, until the given time expired, when they were reconducted to their cells, to continue their work.

In the evening, when she was summoned to have her day's labour weighed, Agnes had finished, and her contribution to the general stock was found to be full weight.

In this manner were her days passed, until the time came when the prison opened its gates, and she was liberated.

Although she had done nothing very serious, yet she could not help feeling that she was what pious people call a gaol-bird, and this reflection had a very injurious effect upon her.

It made her feel bad and wicked, and her eye shrank from encountering the gaze of the people she met in the street.

Of course her first object was to see if her husband had been uneasy about her. She thought she would at once return to the house of the old Jew fence, and fly to the arms of Marmaduke Wilson.

Alas! That such a pretty dream was destined never to be realized.

"Miriam Moss will, of course, have communicated with Marmaduke in some way," thought Agnes. "If she has not seen him herself, she has doubtlessly written him a letter or sent him a message."

Agnes had still a little silver left, and calling a cab, she entered it, and ordered the man to drive to the quiet, lone street near the Foundling Hospital. Having arrived there, she told the cabman to knock at the door. He did so, but no response was made.

Again and again did he repeat his summons, but with the same result.

Agnes was at a loss to understand such strange conduct. At last the cabman came to the door of the vehicle, and told her that it was his impression that the house was empty.

"Perhaps," he suggested, "the people you want to see, miss, have gone away for a holiday, and locked the place up, or perhaps they may have left altogether. Anyhow, there is no one there now, unless they be asleep, and if they do be asleep," he added, with a grin, "why, all I can say is that they sleep confounded hard."

Agnes, much against her will, was fain to come to the same conclusion, and what to do she did not know. Alone, friendless, almost penniless, forlorn indeed was her sad condition.

She was at a loss, also, to account for Miriam Moss's non-appearance at the House of Correction that morning.

"She has forgotten her promise," thought Agnes; "or she has deserted me. Oh! I am truly wretched! I have no friends! And my husband, shocked at the disgrace I have incurred, has also deserted me! or, as Miriam suggested, he is no longer true to his marriage vow, and, glad of any excuse, has sought a new victim. Oh! what shall I do?—my heart is full to bursting!"

"Now, miss, if you please!" exclaimed the cabman. "My fare's half-a-crown, and two shillings an hour for waiting."

At the sound of his voice Agnes awoke to a consciousness of her present position.

The cabman even thought there was something suspicious about her. Had she not better discharge him, and walk about the streets and think?

Certainly this was the best course she could pursue; and taking three shillings from her pocket, she gave it the cab-driver, and alighted from the cab.

Walking slowly, she turned her footsteps in the direction of the Regent's-park, where, after about an hour's walking, she found herself.

Sitting down upon a bench under some trees in a secluded spot, she gave herself up to reflection.

She knew not what to do. She was literally adrift upon the ocean of life.

She could only suppose that her husband had deserted her; or if he had not deserted her, he was behaving in a very strange manner to her; and at all events, she could not by any means at present discover his whereabouts.

She could not return to Clare-market; for she could not, for half an instant, suppose that Jabez Clarke, coke and potato merchant, was still there.

If he had not been arrested by the police for the man-slaughter of his wife, he had no doubt run away to some more secure place when he saw the fatal effects of his violence.

What, then, should she do? Miriam Moss was nowhere to be found, and Mike Moss had, as she supposed, gone away to some other locality.

As she thought of the old fence's house, an idea came into her head.

It will be remembered that when she so providentially rescued Miriam from suffocation in the old room, the door of which she battered down, she had made a discovery.

A bundle of papers lay upon the table.

These documents were labelled, " Papers relating to the Leslie family."

These, as we have already related, she had determined upon taking with her, and, in furtherance of this resolution, she had placed them in her bosom.

They were there still. They had not been disturbed at the prison, but had been given to her with her clothes when she left.

Up to the present time, so great had been her mental perturbation, that she had totally forgotten all about them. But now she thought she could not do better than investigate the contents of the mysterious packet.

Taking it from the bosom of her dress—what fairer resting-place could it have had?—she untied the piece of red tape which bound the papers together.

Her heart fluttered a little as she did so, for she could not help feeling that she might be on the eve of making some grand discovery. What if she might by this means obtain some clue to her parentage, and be enabled, through the agency of these musty, moth-eaten writings, to unravel the tangled skein of evidence and facts her mother presented her with as a dying bequest?—a mortuary legacy.

It was something more than strange that she should be confronted at every other turn in her career with the name of Leslie.

She had evidence enough to show that her father's name was Leslie.

She knew, from her husband's confession and assurance, that, although men called him Marmaduke Wilson, yet his real name was Leslie.

And she was also certain that the destroyer of the old fence's happiness and domestic felicity was also called Leslie.

This was passing strange; and, as she thought of it, it raised strange doubts and conjectures, strange hopes and fears, in her mind.

And it was with her heart upon her lips, and with her hands trembling with expectation, that she undid the tape which bound the mysterious but precious parcel.

CHAPTER XVIII.

AGNES LOSES A HUSBAND, BUT DISCOVERS A BROTHER—SHE SEEKS BERNARD LESLIE—ON THE WAY SHE HEARS NEWS OF JABEZ CLARKE—AGNES IS SUPPOSED TO BE THE MURDERESS OF HER MOTHER—HER INDIGNATION—THE ALBANY—A JACK IN OFFICE—DISAPPOINTED AGAIN—NO CLUE—MORE ADRIFT THAN EVER.

THE first documents Agnes examined were among some letters written by one Bernard Leslie.

At first they were filled with expressions of ardent affection. These gradually toned down, until it was clear a feeling of indifference had succeeded to the hot love that possessed the writer at the commencement of his amour.

The letters were all addressed to the unhappy mother of Miriam Moss, who came to so untimely an end by the fiendish machinations of the old fence.

Certainly Mike Moss had good cause to punish his wife, but no offence could extenuate conduct so madly brutal as his.

Agnes glanced over all the letters, from the first to the last, and a passage in one of them interested her very much.

"If you will quit your husband," said the writer, "and come and dwell with me in foreign lands, I will love and cherish you. Your image is shrined deeply in my heart, and I always bless the necessities which, by inducing me to visit your house, in order to investigate the contents of your husband's money-bags, introduced me to so charming a member of her sex as yourself. I am a widower, without any incumbrances. I have but one son, who bears my name; he is provided for, and with the proceeds of my only partially encumbered estates, we can fly England, and live a life of happiness. Yes, my Miriam, of happiness and bliss in luxurious Italy, or the still more dreamy East. Be mine, and a life of devotion on my part shall reward your sacrifice."

After reading this letter, she turned to a somewhat obscure paper, written apparently by the Jew. It ran thus:—

"I have discovered him to be a licentious ruffian, a libertine, and a debauchee. Heaven doubtlessly has its own peculiar punishment in store for him, but if I ever should have the chance——"

Here the manuscript broke off abruptly, but seemed to have been continued again at a later period.

"Yes; all I hear of Bernard Leslie is correct. My wife was not his first victim—one had to make way for my Miriam. This unhappy creature was first heartbroken by his perfidy and cruelty, and then with a living pledge of her affection for a worthless villain, was, in order to save her shame and the character of her seducer, married to a drunken wretch, who happened to be a groom of Bernard Leslie."

"Can this be my mother?" exclaimed Agnes. "I cannot doubt it; yes, it must indeed be so. How strange that thus my parentage should be revealed! My mother, on her deathbed, told me that my father's name was Leslie, and the researches of the old fence throw additional proof upon the assertion. He had a son too, my father says in one of his letters; can he be that Bernard Leslie who worked me so much evil in a thoughtless manner? If so, I find a brother and a father by this strange coincidence. Oh! mine is indeed an eventful existence. I find undreamt-of relatives, and as I find them, I am deserted by my husband, whom I love more than all the world besides."

The thought of her husband raised fresh emotions in the breast of Agnes.

"Where is he?" she said, "and how can I once more communicate with him?"

But, alas! she could obtain no answer to her earnest query.

Agnes, like most women, was quick at resolving, and after the impulse had sprung into existence, execution was not long delayed.

Her common sense told her that, whether Marmaduke

Wilson had deserted her or not, it was nevertheless morally and physically impossible for her to find him, except Heaven interposed a miracle in her behalf.

But this prosaic age, unhappily for such an occurrence, is not prolific in miracles or supernatural marvels.

This being so, for the present Agnes placed a meeting between herself and Marmaduke Wilson without the pale of possibilities. That is, she ceased to think about it.

Very well; this being the case, it was necessary that she should do something.

But what?

The conviction was overwhelming, but, as we have said, Agnes was equal to the emergency. Her resolution was briefly this. She would seek her brother. Yes, her brother; for although she was a natural daughter, yet they both had the same paternal blood in their veins. Though born out of wedlock, Agnes was, to all intents and purposes, as closely related to Bernard Leslie as we have stated.

That is, always provided the statements in the budget of papers, which she had culled so strangely yet so carefully, should turn out to be correct.

If they were not so, all her suppositions were of no more use than so much bright and silvery moonshine.

If they were not so, then all the glittering, tempting fruit she had placed in so fascinating a light before her straining eyes would vanish like the apples that grow on the shore of the Dead Sea, and turn to ashes directly they are touched.

But even granting them to be correct in every particular, still numerous obstacles arose.

Might not a proud man, and one no doubt devoted to pleasure, repudiate such an unexpected and low-born connexion?

It was far from improbable.

Or might not Bernard Leslie, the rich, the young, the courted, with an exclamation of disgust spurn his illegitimate sister from his doorstep?

Agnes did not try to shut her eyes to these facts, yet she determined to brave every danger in order to try to improve her social position.

Her efforts might fail, but there was always the consoling chance that they might not.

And on this frail peg Agnes hung all her great expectations.

No sooner had she finally made up her mind, however, than a new difficulty had nearly arisen.

Where did her newly-found brother live?

Was it not like looking for a needle in a bundle of hay to seek for a stranger in labyrinthine London without the least clue to his address?

But Agnes had a clue to the residence of Bernard Leslie.

It will be remembered that when the Task-mistress Smithers snatched the fatal card from Agnes' hand she read aloud the name, Bernard Leslie, and the address, Albany, Piccadilly.

This circumstance flashed like lightning across Agnes' brain.

It was clear, then, that in order to find Bernard Leslie Agnes must proceed towards the fashionable neighbourhood of Piccadilly.

Fastening up her papers, and placing them once more in their snowy resting-place, she left the Regent's Park, and began her walk.

When she got to the bottom of Tottenham-court-road she thought of Clare-market, and of her unnatural soi-disant parent. She felt a desire to penetrate the murky streets and inquire as to his fate. The idea gained strength, until it acquired such formidable dimensions that she could not resist it.

A little hurried walking brought her to the vicinity.

She passed by the shop—it was still open—and the present proprietor was in the same line of business, as coke and potatoes were the staple ingredients of his trade.

Could she believe her eyes?

Was that her mother's murderer—was that Jabez Clarke, attending to the wants of a customer?

It certainly was.

Here then was some frightful mystery. By what strange combination of circumstances had Jabez contrived to escape the penalty of his crime?

It was a mystery that Agnes felt she must fathom.

Hastily retracing her steps, lest she might be seen by that monster in human shape, who would most likely involve her in some fresh trouble, she eluded the gaze of Jabez Clarke, and twined round, and stopped not until she reached a small shop, where she never remembered having dealt.

They could not then remember her features, and so think it odd that she should be asking questions.

Entering the shop, she made some slight purchase, and said, "Is Jabez Clarke, coke and potato-man, still living in these parts?"

"Yes, child, he be," replied the motherly-old woman behind the counter.

"Did he not lose his wife some time back?" continued Agnes.

"He did so."

"Do you remember the particulars?" asked Agnes; "and, if so, do you mind telling me briefly? I used to know Mrs. Clarke, and I take an interest, you see, in anything that relates to her."

"Quite so—only nat'ral, my dear. Well, you see, the thing made a bit of a stir in these parts. This Jabez Clarke and his wife had a daughter—a civil, well-spoken, young body, I've heard tell, although I never see her; at least, not to my knowledge. And this daughter—Hagnes, I think they called her—worked up in Regent-street as a dressmaker. But one day she got the sack, because something was found out between her and a gentleman."

"It's not true!" exclaimed Agnes, passionately.

"Did you speak?" inquired the old woman, her informant.

"No; that is, I said simply that she was a bad girl."

"And so she was; anybody who knows how many beans make five could tell that. But as I was a saying, she got the sack, and had to go. And when she came back her and her mother 'ad words about her a losing her sitivation. And it's supposed that she must have struck her mother and killed her; for when Jabez come back from the public, where he'd been to get arf a-pint, why he found his ole woman dead, stark and stiff. Then he rushed out mad-like, a crying, 'Who's been on to my missus?' and the neighbours they all come in. But that artful hussey of a gal warn't nowhere to be seen or found. Then he says, says Jabez, 'I left my darter Hagnes with the ole woman; where is she?' Nobody knew. Then the people began to suspect her, and Jabez, he says, rather cut-up like, 'It ain't a pleasant thing for a cove to accuse his own darter, but I can't help thinking as she's done this 'ere.' And everybody was of the same opinion; and the police was called in, and a reward offered, but she got clean hoff. And Jabez, he's doing well now; the neighbours all deal with him, cos of his misfortins. And now, my dear, you knows all about it, and you'll find Jabez down there in his shop belike, if so be as you're going to drop in friendly-like and have a chat."

Agnes thanked the worthy woman, and with her heart swollen to bursting almost with rage and indignation, left the shop.

It was intolerable to her to think for a moment that she had been accused of the cowardly and dastardly murder of her unfortunate mother.

Should she at once go and expose Jabez Clarke?

Alas! what chance had she of being believed? the evidence in her favour was almost nothing.

Prejudice had taken possession of the public mind, and, when that is the case, to convince an English mob is as difficult as proving black to be white.

Yet it was galling to see the ruffian Clarke thriving upon his baseness. He seemed more prosperous than ever.

For a moment Agnes forgot that retribution is swift, and sooner or later overtakes those who do wrong.

She was not so silly as to hide from herself, however, that she was powerless to annoy Jabez Clarke.

Supposing she came forward to denounce him! The first consequence of such an act would be her own instant arrest by the police.

Circumstantial evidence would be against her. She was some time alone with her mother; then she suddenly left the house, and had never been seen in the neighbourhood since.

Yes! horrible as the imputation was, she could not help sitting down as the supposed murderess of her mother!

Yet her conscience held her guiltless, and that was some slight satisfaction.

Truly it was a clever device of Jabez Clarke to turn public suspicion from himself upon the innocent and guileless Agnes.

Sighing deeply, Agnes continued her journey, and got away from the dangerous vicinage of Clare-market with as much speed as possible.

As she neared the stately precincts of the Albany her heart trembled a little.

How should she approach this newly-found brother? Should she be open and straightforward and candid with him?

Should she tell him that she was the wife of a thief, who had in all likelihood deserted her?

Should she confess that a charge of murder was even now hanging over her head, and a reward offered for her capture?

It was true that she was no more actually deserving of shame for these fortuitous occurrences than the man in the moon.

That, however, was not the question. How would Bernard Leslie take such revelations?

Agnes felt that she must be circumspect. It would not do to be too open and confiding. So she resolved that she would tell the truth, but not the whole truth. She would conceal certain things, and gloss over others, and make herself appear as respectable as she could.

Agnes displayed considerable knowledge of the world in coming to this determination. But, as the sequel showed her, honesty in everything is the best policy; and if you disguise facts, and the entire truth is subsequently discovered, the consequences of your concealment are, to say the least, excessively unpleasant.

Going to the porter at the entrance to the Albany, Agnes demanded, in a timid voice, if Mr. Bernard Leslie was in town.

"Left here," replied the man. "Don't know nothing about him."

"Left!" cried Agnes. "Is it possible? Where has he gone to?"

"Tell you I don't know nothing about him, young woman," answered the porter, roughly. And taking up his newspaper, he continued reading, as if utterly oblivious of her presence.

Here was a disappointment for the unlucky girl! She was, indeed, the sport of Fortune and the football of Fate.

With all her hopes dashed, what should she do? It was clear this Jack-in-office either had nothing to tell her, or that his native insolence was so great he would not take the trouble.

Agnes was again adrift, and this time more hopelessly than ever; and, with a despairing look, she turned away from the Albany, and walked mechanically along the street —she scarcely cared whither.

CHAPTER XIX.

AGNES MEETS HER BROTHER—SHE TELLS HER TALE— BERNARD LESLIE WAVERS—HE RECOGNISES AGNES AS HIS SISTER, AND INTRODUCES HER TO HIS AUNT— MISS LAVINIA—AGNES' HORROR WHEN SHE DISCOVERS THAT SHE IS ABOUT TO BECOME A MOTHER.

AGNES had hardly gone more than fifty yards when a voice, whose tones seemed familiar to her, struck upon her ear.

Turning round, she found herself confronted with Bernard Leslie!

Her brother!

The very man she had wished so much to meet. He had apparently just left the Albany, and was walking along with his arm entwined in that of a friend, to whom he was talking in an easy, flowing, light-hearted way.

Very likely they were conversing about some of those trifles light as air which engross the attention of young and frivolous men.

The last opera and the star of the ballet.

Some new actress, or the merits of a new burlesque.

The result of a pigeon match, or how far that famous mare, Black Bess, could trot against time.

Bernard Leslie was passing by Agnes, without in the least recognising her.

Here was at last a chance. It was the forelock of opportunity within her very grasp.

And should she allow it to elude her?

No—a thousand times no!

Her throat was husky with emotion and agitation as she exclaimed, "Good morning, Mr. Leslie!"

Bernard Leslie took off his hat, and returned her salutation, adding, "'Pon my word, you must excuse me. I have not the honour of knowing—that is, of recollecting—eh! really you have the advantage."

"Do you not remember me?—ah! I see you do not."

"No, indeed," he replied.

His friend looked on rather amused at all this.

"I have something of the utmost importance to communicate to you, Mr. Leslie, if you are not too much engaged.

"I shall be glad to hear you," he said. "But I think the public street is hardly the proper place to hold a colloquy in."

"I quite agree with you," said Agnes, "and it was quite by chance that I accosted you in the street, only the porter at the Albany told me you had left your chambers some time ago, and that he did not know where you were gone."

"Oh! Thomas told you so, did he?" exclaimed Mr. Leslie. "You know he did not mean anything offensive or impertinent; but the fact is, I never see women at my chambers, and if any females ask for me, Thomas is instructed to deny me. But will you allow me to ask of what nature your communication is?"

"I would rather not enter into particulars here," she said; "more especially as I have some papers to show you."

As she said this, Agnes took the bundle of papers she had so recently examined in the Park out of the bosom of her dress, and held them up for Mr. Leslie to look at.

He instantly recognised the handwriting, and cried, in some astonishment—"My father's writing! This is curious! How came those documents in your possession, eh?"

"That is what I am desirous of telling you, Mr. Leslie, if you will give me the opportunity."

Bernard Leslie turned to his friend, and said, "Will you excuse me this morning? This little woman has found some papers that interest me, and I want to look over them. Can you make it convenient to look in at chambers in a couple of hours?"

"Certainly," replied his friend, with a faint smile. "I will call upon you in the afternoon."

Raising his hat slightly to Agnes, Mr. Leslie's friend left them together.

It must be borne in mind that Agnes was by no means poorly dressed. The things she had on were expensive, and had been bought for her by Marmaduke Wilson. And, although her attire was plain, she was still of a ladylike appearance, and, what was of equal importance, very lovely.

She wore on this eventful morning a rich black silk dress without flounces, which was surmounted by a handsome French cashmere shawl, and a plain straw bonnet trimmed with black ribbon.

When his friend had departed, Bernard Leslie turned to Agnes, and said, "Have you any objection to come to my chambers in the Albany; we shall be free from interruption there, and be able to converse more freely?"

"I have no objection," replied Agnes. "I will go where you like."

"We can go to a confectioner's if you wish, or have a private room at some hotel."

"No. I think it would be better to go to your chambers, Mr. Leslie," answered Agnes.

"Please yourself," he said. And offering her his arm, which she accepted without hesitation, they retraced their steps, and entered the passage of the Albany.

In a few minutes Agnes found herself in Mr. Leslie's chambers. His sitting-room was, as may be supposed, handsomely furnished.

Finely executed proof-prints of pictures by the best masters hung in splendid frames upon the handsomely-papered walls.

The carpet was of the richest description of "Turkey," so much so that the foot sank into it at every step.

Gorgeous inlaid cabinets and tables adorned the room here and there.

The chairs were of the costliest manufacture.

Mr. Leslie presented Agnes with a chair, and begged her to be seated.

Then ringing a bell he told the servant who answered this summons to bring some wine.

Opening one of the cabinets, he produced decanters and glasses and retired.

Mr. Leslie poured out some wine and offered it to Agnes. Then he said, "I shall be very happy to hear what you have to say to me, Miss ——"

"My father's name is like your own, Leslie," replied Agnes.

"Leslie!" he cried; "really you quite bewilder me.

"Do you remember once meeting a girl in a street near Regent-street," said Agnes.

"Perfectly, now you recal the occurrence."

"I am that girl."

"Is it possible?"

"Then I was in ignorance of facts which have since come to my knowledge."

"To what facts do you allude," he asked.

"The reason that I have called upon you to-day is that I have been led to believe that your father is also mine."

"How! what mad assertion is this," cried Bernard Leslie, starting from his chair.

"Calm yourself," said Agnes, "and you shall hear; but first of all answer me one question—is our—is your father alive?"

"He is," was the reply, "but more than that I cannot at present tell you; but to the matter in hand—your proofs?"

"Are here," she said; "that is to say, partially; but I am prepared to substantiate what I have asserted by other circumstantial evidence."

Bernard Leslie eagerly took the packet of papers Agnes extended to him, and carefully perused them.

When he had finished he said, "This affair is strangely involved and entangled, but by perseverance I think I can put its discordant elements together.

"In the first place, one Bernard Leslie goes to an old and notorious Jew to borrow money.

"During his visits at the moneylender's house he sees his wife, and falls in love with her.

"He seduces her affections from their legitimate object, and the Jew vows revenge if ever he gets the opportunity.

"With this object in view, he makes inquiries about Bernard Leslie who has destroyed his domestic happiness.

"One of the results of these inquiries is that Bernard Leslie has only just deserted a girl whom he marries to one of his grooms in order to get rid of her?"

"Yes," said Agnes, "you are right so far."

"This latter girl," he continued, "has a child. Is it not so?"

"It is."

"And there the matter ends so far as this chain of evidence goes."

"Not so," said Agnes, "for I am that child. The unhappy offspring of Bernard Leslie's illicit love."

"Is it indeed so?" he cried.

"It is," replied Agnes. "Listen to me, and I will tell you the words of my mother on her deathbed."

"I await your words with impatience," he said.

"My mother told me that my father's name was Leslie, and she so corroborated her statement that she left no room for doubt. But it comes to this: do you refuse to recognise me as your sister?"

Bernard Leslie hesitated.

"Are you afraid to acknowledge me before the world as your relative," persisted Agnes.

Still Bernard Leslie refused to come to any decision, for he remained silent and passive.

"By all human ties and obligations I am your sister," said Agnes, "except the fatal one of wedlock."

Bernard Leslie looked at Agnes, and thought that she was very beautiful, and that although she was not apparently accomplished, yet she was not too old to learn the arts that genteel society cultivates.

He thought, too, that it would be an amusement to him to introduce his sister to the fashionable world.

There was, however, a still more cogent argument that he made use of while reasoning with himself, and that was that through the instrumentality of Agnes he might get introductions into certain families which had hitherto, owing to his excesses, rather excluded him.

And he considered that in addition to all that we have recapitulated, that even if he did not find an opportunity of marrying some heiress himself, yet he might have sufficient influence over Agnes to induce her to marry some imbecile old nobleman, who would leave her all his wealth and estates when he died, and settle a handsome sum upon her when his marriage took place.

These considerations had their weight with Bernard Leslie, for although he had a certain sum to live upon, and that a very handsome one, yet he had fallen into the hands of the Jews, and was fast dissipating his paternal acres.

Exclusive families had shut their doors upon him, and he

was partially debarred from the sort of society his position in life, his birth, and his fortune entitled him to move in.

He had been living so hard a life, that, to speak figuratively, the candle had been burning at both ends.

And, in consequence his fortune was reputed to be dwindling away.

Here was a chance to retrieve his excesses.

He could introduce Agnes, and she would probably make a good match. In other words, he would speculate with her as well as he could.

After reflecting thus, Bernard Leslie rose from his chair, and taking Agnes by the hand, exclaimed, "In future we will be brother and sister."

"Oh! this is indeed kind of you. How can I ever thank you?" cried Agnes, throwing herself on his breast, and sobbing for joy.

"I will tell you how you can thank me," he replied. "By trusting me implicitly, and obeying me as a brother has a right to be obeyed."

"I will ever do that," answered Agnes, with a faint smile. "To trust and obey you is, methinks, not so very arduous a task now I am Agnes Leslie, your acknowledged sister. The past——"

"Let that be forgotten," he exclaimed, hurriedly; "I wish not to know anything about it. The consideration of the past could only be harrowing and disagreeable both to you and to myself."

"It shall be as you wish."

"Then let it sink into oblivion, Agnes, and from this day forth begin as it were a new life."

Agnes, quite enraptured with her new position, readily promised compliance with his request, although she felt inclined to tell her brother something about Marmaduke Wilson. But as he had imposed silence upon her with regard to the past, she found herself stopped at the very commencement.

Little did she know that by the course of conduct she was pursuing, she was sowing the seeds of a consuming fire, and placing herself on the site of a slumbering volcano.

Bernard Leslie, immediately after acknowledging Agnes as his sister, went out and procured some lodgings for her in a fashionable street in May-fair. He then supplied her with money to purchase dresses and jewellery.

A few days after these things were accomplished he called upon a maiden aunt of his—a Miss Lavinia Leslie. This lady lived in Hill-street, Berkeley-square; and although she had enough to live upon, she was not rich enough to give parties and to keep up her position as a lady of fashion. Bernard Leslie thought that were he to offer his aunt a certain sum of money every month to introduce Agnes to her friends, she would readily accept his offer, as she would be glad to go about with a very lovely young lady.

For young ladies who are good-looking engross the attention of the men, and then aunts and mothers also receive some of the homage which is so lavishly scattered at all times on a pretty woman.

"Anyhow, I can but try," he thought; "most likely she will fall into my views, and, if not, I must try some one else."

Bernard Leslie explained to his aunt that he had no idea his sister was living until a few days before. But that she had been respectably brought up, although the people she had lived with were poor. And he added, "It will be better, I think, to abstain from asking her any questions as to the past. Take her for what she is, a good and lovely girl."

Miss Lavinia Leslie agreed to do so, and cordially entered into her nephew's plans.

Agnes was installed in Hill-street, and went to one or two parties; but as the season was nearly over, she had little opportunity of showing herself that year.

A few weeks passed and Agnes, by mixing with a different set of people, and by surrounding circumstances, became quite metamorphosed.

Few would have recognised in the well-dressed, well-behaved, and rather stately-looking lady, the former timid and shrinking milliner.

She learned to ride, and pursued several other studies, by her aunt's desire, with a view to becoming well educated.

Bernard Leslie came very frequently to see her, and placed a brougham at her service.

Agnes tried to forget everything connected with her past life, and although the effort was not an easy one, she had nearly accomplished it.

"Every one that I knew formerly has deserted me," she said to herself; "and why should I break my heart about them?"

And Agnes after the lapse of some weeks began to feel comparatively happy; but Heaven had a severe trial in store for her, which she never dreamt of, or, if it had struck her as a possible contingency, she had dismissed the idea from her mind as one too disagreeable to be dwelt upon.

Poor Agnes! tossed about as she had been upon the stormy fate-ocean, she had proudly dreamed that she had floated into a haven of rest and repose.

But, alas! it was not so.

A fact which would at any other time have been hailed by her with joy and gladness was making itself more patent, day by day, to her startled imagination.

Young and innocent as she was, Agnes could not disguise from her unsophisticated mind that she was about to become a mother.

CHAPTER XX.

AGNES IN A DILEMMA—MARMADUKE WILSON'S FATE—HE VOWS REVENGE ON HIS WIFE—AGNES SEEKS AN INTERVIEW WITH HER AUNT—THAT GOOD LADY'S ASTONISHMENT AT AGNES' REVELATIONS—AGNES IS EVENTUALLY FORGIVEN—WHAT NEXT?

To become a mother in her present position was a reflection fraught with the greatest danger and most serious inconvenience to Agnes.

At any other time she would have hailed the fact with rapturous delight, but now the affair was totally different.

So true it is that circumstances alter cases.

Her newly-discovered aunt would in all human probability drive her with ignominy from her doors, and regret that she had ever harboured her at all.

The fact must be discovered sooner or later, and what discredit would it not reflect upon the stately and fashionable Miss Lavinia Leslie?

There was only one chance for Agnes—only one loop-hole through which she could hope to escape the very imminent peril that at present threatened her—and that was an alternative that she shrank from.

It was simply this: When the inevitable discovery took place she could only confess that she was a married woman, and throw herself on her aunt's mercy.

What that would consist of it was premature to attempt to divine. Her heart might relent on hearing the unhappy girl's melancholy tale. But it was idle to speculate on an event at present only looming in the distance, because it would have been impossible to ascertain the issue with any amount of accuracy.

Therefore, all Agnes could do was to cling to the chance, and, making a full confession, implore her aunt's clemency.

It was the more annoying to Agnes, as she could not help thinking of the father of her child, her own dear Marmaduke, whose image and whose memory she had done her part to bury in oblivion. And she had done so because her pride dictated such a course to her. She imagined herself deserted by one who had sworn to love and cherish her through good and evil report, and who had taken her for better or for worse.

Under these circumstances, with Marmaduke Wilson's apparent desertion staring her in the face, her pride came to her rescue and peremptorily commanded her to erase from the tablets of her heart the image of the man who proved himself fickle and false to her.

In addition to all this, Agnes had become habituated to her new mode of life. She had taken a fancy to it and she had made the very natural discovery that to be a lady is much better than being a sempstress.

Item, as the lawyers say, she had found out that riding in a carriage is more comfortable than walking or riding in an omnibus.

Item, that living in a nice house in May-fair, with every luxury around her, was to be preferred to Jabez Clarke's miserable tenement in St. Giles's.

Item, that the society of ladies and gentlemen is infinitely to be preferred to that of thieves and ruffians.

Now, her unsophisticated mind, in the fulness of its

generosity and kindness, had looked over the fact of Marmaduke Wilson's moral delinquencies!

He had acknowledged that he had been driven by circumstances to break the eighth commandment, but she had magnanimously forgiven him.

Now, however, having had a better example placed before her eyes, she began to regret ever having met Marmaduke Wilson; and, under her aunt's able tuition, she began to acquire that worldly feeling that all who mix with the world sooner or later acquire.

Mankind are like the pebbles on the seashore, which, washed by the waves, in time, from the simple fact of their being continually rubbing against one another, acquire a smooth and polished appearance.

And Agnes was certainly very much changed during her residence beneath the hospitable, but worldly roof-tree of her astute aunt.

A feeling of shame, too, took possession of Agnes when she reflected that she had ever been the wife of a thief—of a professional breaker of the laws of the land.

And this was surmounted by a feeling of intense anger that Marmaduke should have, as she thought, thrown her over for some one else in the heartless manner he had done.

One thing is certain, Agnes Leslie, as we must now call her, was changing in a very palpable manner; and it is to be feared that prosperity was spoiling her, as it has done many a man and woman before her.

Since the fortunate chance, as she esteemed it, which threw her into her brother's society, she had stifled all her better feelings as well as she could.

But when her maternal instincts were aroused, she could not shut out Marmaduke Wilson from her mind.

For Marmaduke Wilson she had entertained as fond and as pure a passion as ever woman did for man.

She had thought that any separation from him would be worse than death itself.

Thus have many women reasoned; but they have ultimately discovered that they have had love enough left to enable them to bestow their hearts on half a dozen men in succession.

Yet Agnes could not help her thoughts travelling back to her husband. But when they were most tender, the idea that he might at that moment be in the arms of another, and a rival, stung her to madness.

Women, however, are such contradictions, that Agnes, notwithstanding these bitter reflections, resolved to love her child for its father's sake.

That father whose fate we may as well enlighten our readers about now as later.

Marmaduke Wilson had been tried and found guilty, and he had been sentenced to be transported beyond the seas for the term of seven years.

In vain had the unhappy man endeavoured to find out his wife's whereabouts. Letter upon letter had he written, and, by the aid of his friends, despatched to the old fence's, and every other spot he could imagine she was likely to have gone to.

But all to no purpose. And, almost heartbroken, the wretched man submitted to his hard fate.

"If I had only had her love to comfort and refresh me during my period of enforced captivity and toil, I think I could have borne it.

"But now I shall never rest till I find her. I will do my utmost to escape from captivity; and I will search the globe to the utmost limit, in order to discover so perfidious a traitress!"

Then his mood would change.

He would abuse himself, and endeavour to exculpate Agnes.

And in this contradictory state of mind we for a time take leave of the gentleman thief, Marmaduke Wilson.

Agnes, in resolving to confess the circumstance of her marriage to Miss Lavinia, felt that she had nothing very shameful to acknowledge. She had been beguiled into the union before she knew the antecedents of her husband. In fact, she was totally ignorant of his real character.

And she had some small hope that her aunt would look favourably upon her, owing to her youth and innocence.

Still, supposing that her aunt forgave her, and estimated her as highly as ever, there was a very great difficulty to be surmounted.

And that was, that the fact of her being represented as an *unmarried* woman, and the little circumstance of her having a child, would not only prejudice her acquaintance against her, but utterly exclude her from their society.

This was a thought which tormented Agnes night and day. But she little knew the resources of her aunt's intellect, or she would not have made herself ill at ease with regard to that difficulty.

The fact was, that Agnes was entirely ignorant of her aunt's character. She knew that she was a worldly woman, esteeming money very highly; but she did not know that she was a Yorkshire woman, who thought more of the main chance than anything else.

In truth, what is known as the Yorkshireman's coat of arms was, to a certain extent, applicable to Miss Lavinia Leslie.

A Yorkshireman's coat of arms is by his enemies popularly supposed to be a flea, a fly, a magpie, and a flitch of bacon.

A flea, because a flea will bite dead or alive, and so will a Yorkshireman.

A fly, because a fly will drink out of any man's cup, and so will a Yorkshireman.

A magpie, because a magpie will chatter to anybody, and so will a Yorkshireman.

A flitch of bacon, because a flitch of bacon is never worth anything until it is well hung; no more is a Yorkshireman.

This is rather severe, and whether there is any truth in it we will not pretend to say, as we might utter a wholesale libel upon a very deserving race of men.

Had Agnes been thoroughly acquainted with her aunt's mind she would not have sought her presence with such evident trepidation as she did on the present occasion.

Miss Lavinia Leslie was, on this particular occasion, reclining upon a couch. The room was delicately shaded by elaborately-contrived Venetian blinds, which allowed a soft, luxurious light to penetrate the apartment occupied by Miss Lavinia.

That lady herself was engaged in perusing the columns of the fashionable chronicle, the *Morning Post*.

She looked up as Agnes entered, and exclaimed—

"Be seated, child; you will utterly ruin your complexion if you continue to run about in the sun in the way you are at present doing."

"Oh! no, aunt; do not be afraid," replied Agnes, with a sickly smile; "I take a great deal of care of myself,—more than you give me credit for, I have reason to think."

"Well, well, so much the better. Young ladies of a marriagable age, who have their fortunes to make, cannot be too careful, because their success depends, in a great measure, upon their personal appearance."

This beginning rather disconcerted Agnes. It was not what she considered a fortunate one.

Miss Lavinia continued to read her paper, without taking any further notice of Agnes, who seated herself, and restlessly turned over the pages of the last year's *Keepsake*.

"Well! I may as well say what I have to say at once," said Agnes to herself. "It must come out, sooner or later; and what is the use of beating about the bush? I know it will be a trying interview, but I must hope for the best."

"Aunt!" she exclaimed.

"What is it, child?" asked Miss Lavinia, a little petulantly. "Do you not see I am engaged at present? You know very well that I dislike excessively being disturbed when I am reading the paper. Cannot you practice, or draw, or something?"

"Yes, I can certainly," replied Agnes; "but the fact is I want to talk to you rather particularly just now."

"Will not some other time do?" said her aunt.

"If you insist on it, I suppose it must; but I would infinitely prefer saying at once what I have to communicate."

"Is it of such a pressing nature, then, that you cannot wait an hour or so?"

"Yes; it is a matter of great importance to me; and as you must know it some day, you may as well be enlightened at once."

"How strangely the girl talks!" thought her aunt; "I wonder if some man has proposed to her. If so, that would at once account for her agitation."

"Has any one made you an offer, then?" she inquired.

"No; your conjecture is wrong," replied Agnes, the blood rising to her face, she knew not why.

"Oh! I thought probably that Lord Marchmont might have done such a thing. He is here a good deal, you know,

SNATCHED FROM THE JAWS OF DEATH.

and he pays either you or me very marked attention. Which is it, eh?" added the old lady, with a laugh.

"I am not in the humour for banter, dear aunt," said Agnes, impressively. "I have that to tell you which at present engrosses all my thoughts."

"Well, then, let me, by all means, have this terrible secret revealed without any further delay," replied Miss Lavinia, throwing down her newspaper.

"It is a strange confession for me to make, dear aunt," preluded Agnes, "but I hope you will not be too surprised."

"No, indeed. You have been admiring some diamonds at Hunt and Roskell's, I suppose, and you want me to tell your brother Bernard of it, eh?"

"It is not that, aunt. I can tell you the whole affair in half-a-dozen words."

"Do so, then, by all means."

"Dear aunt, I am much to blame for not informing you before, but I am a married woman."

"Are you mad, insane, crazy?" cried Miss Lavinia Leslie, in a tone of bitter disappointment, commingled with almost abject fear.

"Alas! it is too true. Would to God it were not so!"

"Does your brother know of this?"

"He is entirely ignorant of it."

"And your husband, where is he?" demanded Miss Lavinia. "Tell me instantly, I request; where is your husband?"

"He—he is dead," replied Agnes, having come to a sudden resolution.

"You are well advised of that?"

"I am," was the reply.

"What else?" asked her aunt, after a moment's pause.

"I am—why disguise the fact?—I am about to become a mother," replied Agnes, after a few moments' hesitation.

So completely did her aunt seem surprised and dumb-founded at this most unexpected declaration, that she made no answer, no remark, no comment.

"Dear aunt, I have been very wrong, very wrong indeed, in concealing all this from you, but I throw myself upon your clemency."

Still Miss Lavinia made no response. Probably she was making up her mind how to act in such an emergency.

"Have you no pity for me, aunt?" pleaded Agnes, in an agonized tone of voice.

Miss Lavinia was calculating in her mind whether she would succeed better in a pecuniary point of view by forgiving Agnes and looking over her faults, or whether it would be better to open her doors, and say to her, "You have defiled my threshold. Get you gone."

There were several weighty considerations, which had to be duly pondered.

In the first place, Agnes's husband, whoever he was, was dead, at least she had Agnes's assurance to that effect.

Secondly, Agnes was, under her tutelage, in a fair way to make a good marriage, which would, of course, be so far beneficial to Miss Lavinia, inasmuch as she would, by having a claim on Agnes's gratitude, be able to help herself to the wealth of her husband's coffers.

Then, on the other hand, there was the trouble, and worry, and annoyance of the peculiar and interesting condition in which Agnes was, and its consequences.

In Miss Lavinia's opinion, however, it appeared that the former reasons were the weightiest, and she resolved to take Agnes to her bosom, and hold out the hand of forgiveness.

This gracious determination was not come to without serious deliberation, as we have already stated; and during her aunt's cogitations Agnes was tormented by doubts, and fears, and horrible presentiments of evil.

These atrabilious reflections gave way to others of a more pleasant nature when Miss Lavinia exclaimed, "You have done very wrong in not placing implicit confidence in me ere this, my dear Agnes; but I hope and trust it is not too late now to rectify what, with some people, would have been a fatal mistake."

"I hope not, indeed, dear aunt," replied Agnes, trembling with delight at still having Miss Lavinia as her friend.

"Your husband being dead, you see you can marry again, and make your fortune in the way I have often suggested to you."

Agnes made a gesture of assent.

"And as for the child," continued Miss Lavinia; "well, it is of no use looking difficulties in the face until they actually arrive."

"What am I to understand by that?" asked Agnes, a little suspiciously.

"Do not ask questions, child—it is a bad habit; you shall know when the time comes. In the meanwhile, leave me to consider the position. (This was a favourite phrase of Miss Lavinia's.) At all events I have forgiven you; so be easy on that score."

Agnes bowed and left the apartment with her mind considerably relieved.

CHAPTER XXI.

MISS LAVINIA'S VISITING LIST—P. P. C. CARDS—BLOCK-HAVEN, ON THE SCOTCH COAST—LORD MARCHMONT—ON BOARD THE "FAIRY"—A STRANGE SHIP—NO. 401—THE CONVICTS ON BOARD—AGNES RECOGNISES MARMADUKE WILSON—HER HORROR—HEAVILY IRONED—AGNES VOWS REVENGE AGAINST MIRIAM MOSS.

THE result of Miss Lavinia Leslie's considering the position was in a short time notified to Agnes, who waited impatiently the result of her aunt's deliberations.

The season was nearly, if not quite, over in London, and there would be nothing extraordinary in Miss Lavinia, accompanied by her niece, retiring for a few months to the sea-side, or withdrawing into the recesses of the Welsh mountains.

And it was determined that they should at once withdraw from the festive scenes of fashionable life.

In short, that for a time the pomps and vanities of the world should be renounced.

"You see, my dear," said Miss Lavinia, "I have carefully considered the position, and I feel confident that the only safe and reasonable course we can pursue will be to leave town."

"I am of the same opinion," replied Agnes.

"There is nothing whatever to detain us here, and therefore the sooner we quit London the better."

"To-morrow, aunt, if you like; I am ready at a moment's notice."

"Well, well, I can excuse your impatience, but I do not see the necessity of such very great haste."

"But why linger?" demanded Agnes, with a gesture of impatience.

"I do not counsel any lingering, but as you must know, there are certain forms and ceremonies to be gone through before one leaves one's home."

"I did not think of that."

"And were those forms omitted, rumour would be busy and scandal active."

"Would it indeed be so?"

"Take my word for it, it would," replied her aunt; "I do not make my assertions lightly."

"Let us, then, commence these forms and ceremonies," said Agnes, "and we shall get them over quicker."

"We will do so."

"What, then, is the first thing to be done?" asked Agnes.

"Get me our visiting list, and I will tell you."

Agnes rose, and going to a writing-desk she unlocked it, and took from it a sheet of paper with many names written on it.

On seeing it in Agnes' hands, Miss Lavinia said, "Now just run your eye over it, dear, and try and remember who are still in town, and who have gone away."

"Well, first there is Lady Bigbustle," said Agnes, reading from the list.

"Ah! she's gone, and no loss to anybody, an old hypocrite! She is at Baden, and there she may stay, for what I care. Who is next?"

"Next? Let me see. Oh! Mr. Pleader and his wife, the parliamentary barrister, you know."

"Pleader, Pleader—ah! yes, I remember; very vulgar people, but very well off. Give good parties. Once met the Chief Baron there. We must call and leave a P.P.C. card upon them."

"A P.P.C. card, what is that?" asked Agnes.

"That simply means that you are going to take leave," replied her aunt. "They are the first letters of three French words. Go on to the next."

Agnes continued to read the names of the people with whom her aunt and herself were upon visiting terms, until the list was exhausted, and all those people whom they imagined were in town they called upon, as they had previously determined; and having accomplished this arduous task, and having gone through sundry other little tedious forms that the inexorable Goddess of Good Society entails upon her votaries, they were in a position to pack up their things and depart from the attractions of the modern Babylon.

Then arose the question "Where should they go to?" Of course it was easy to name a hundred places; but this one was too noisy, that one too full of people, and at the other place "you will be sure to meet every one you know," said Miss Lavinia.

"I did not think of that," replied Agnes.

"Yes, I daresay; but, my dear, in this world, where every one has a part to play, it is necessary to think occasionally."

"So I suppose," said Agnes, yawning.

"My dear child, whatever you do, do not yawn; nothing is so detestably vulgar as yawning," exclaimed Miss Lavinia, in horror at such a flagrant exhibition of bad breeding.

Agnes apologized, and her aunt continued: "You see we want to go to a quiet place, where nobody knows us, and where everything will pass off quietly."

"Quite so," replied Agnes; "that is it exactly."

"Very well; then we will at once put the Continent out of the question. For I am not at any time particularly fond of foreigners; indeed, I think the attraction of the Continent, with most English people, lies in the novelty of the scenery, and the chance of meeting a great many of one's friends at the table-d'hôte, or the kursaal, or on the promenade. But I have a proposition to make."

"Well, aunt, what is it? I will agree to anything; I should prefer quietness and peace to noise and revelry," answered Agnes.

"In that case we shall agree perfectly. My idea is this: I know a nice, a very nice, quiet place in Scotland, on the coast of Kincardine. It is called Blockhaven, and is not more than twenty miles from Aberdeen."

"Oh! that is capital—that is famous!" exclaimed Agnes. "It is the very thing; nothing could be better."

"So I think; only you must confess, my dear child, that I am making very considerable sacrifices for your sake."

"Sacrifices! how—in what way?"

"Oh, how simple you are! why affect to be so dull of apprehension?" said Miss Lavinia.

"Indeed I affect nothing," responded Agnes.

"Oh, nonsense; you know very well you do. It is impossible that a girl of your age and your sense can be ignorant of the sacrifices I am making for you."

"Perhaps, if you will condescend to enlighten me," said Agnes, "I may comprehend."

"Well, then, in the first place, I am going into exile with you, as it were, for some weeks."

"Yes, that is true. It must be a banishment for you, dear aunt."

"And I am so fond, as you know, of my fellow creatures," exclaimed Miss Lavinia, with a hypocritical sigh.

"Then why go at all?" said Agnes. "Leave me to my fate."

"Not so; I never desert my friends," replied her aunt, sententiously.

This declaration was to a certain extent true; for Miss Lavinia never did desert her friends when she found it was her interest to adhere to them.

"No," she continued; "I will be your ally, and see you safely through your present trouble. We will say no more about my sacrifices. You, I know, are a warm-hearted girl, and will be grateful in proportion to the services I do you."

"Indeed, you may safely rely upon my everlasting gratitude, dear aunt," exclaimed Agnes. "You have already been so very kind to me, that were I to live a thousand years I could never forget it."

"Ah! it is very well to say so, but we shall see; time will show," said her aunt, with a smile.

"Yes, time, the revealer of all things, will show," repeated Agnes, earnestly.

"In the meantime, it is decided that we go to Blockhaven, on the Scotch coast. It is unfortunate that it is such a distance from here, as the railway is expensive, and it is a dreadfully long journey."

"Why not go down in a steamer, or a yacht?" suggested Agnes.

"Ah! a yacht—let me see—who has a yacht? It would do capitally."

"Why, Lord Marchmont, to be sure," said Agnes. "He has a fine yacht, seven or eight hundred tons burden, I know, because he once told me, and he has repeatedly asked me to come down to the Isle of Wight and sail upon the waters of the Solent with him."

"Lord Marchmont!" repeated Miss Lavinia. "To be sure; I totally forgot him. That is a clever idea of yours. It would, I think, be judicious to accept his lordship's offer, and once on board, we will soon induce him to take us on to the coast of Scotland."

"Yes, indeed, I will answer for that," replied Agnes, laughing. "I think the poor man would do any single thing I told him."

"So much the better. But do not talk so loud: walls have ears, you know; and if one should consider Lord Marchmont an eligible *parti*, there is no reason why one should tell the listening walls so."

"No, indeed; I agree with you, aunt, that one can never be too cautious or too circumspect."

"Then always bear that in mind, child."

The next morning a letter fortunately arrived from Lord Marchmont, repeating his invitation to Agnes and her aunt. The letter was dated Southampton, and his lordship begged an immediate reply, as the weather was so charming and delightful, that the *Fairy* was positively longing to fling her canvas to the breeze.

Miss Lavinia looked upon this as a fortunate circumstance, and told Agnes to write by return of post, to say that they would have very great pleasure in accepting his lordship's very kind invitation.

Accordingly, the next morning they left town for Southampton, and putting up at the best hotel in the town, inquired for the yacht *Fairy*.

They were told that it was lying at anchor a short distance out.

Miss Lavinia then sent a letter on board, inviting Lord Marchmont to dinner that evening.

The guest accepted the invitation, and pressed them to come on board the next morning.

This they agreed to do, but Agnes said, "I wish you would take us for a long cruise—I am a capital sailor."

"Where would you like to go?" he replied. "Shall I take you to Iceland?"

"Not quite so far; but I want to go to Aberdeen. I have some friends there, and railway-travelling is so tedious."

"Yes, it is; but Aberdeen is a long way, and the coast is stormy and dangerous."

"Oh! if you are a coward, and distrustful of your vessel or your seamanship, there is an end of the question," said Agnes, laughing rather scornfully.

"I am not afraid of anything," he replied, his face reddening at the imputation; "and rather than you should say or think that, I would take you to the coast of Norway, and go down the Mäelstrom with you."

"No, thank you; I am not tired of my life."

"But, seriously speaking, do you really wish to go to Aberdeen?" he asked.

"Yes, I do. Do we not, aunt?"

Miss Lavinia supported Agnes, and Lord Marchmont replied, "That being the case, I shall be very happy to take you; and as the weather is fine and steady, we will start to-morrow, if you like."

"By all means," said Agnes. "Let us go at once."

The next day Miss Lavinia and her niece were rowed by two sturdy sailors on board the *Fairy*, where Lord Marchmont and his skipper graciously received them. They remained on deck for some time, admiring the novelty of everything.

While standing, telescope in hand, a strange incident befel Agnes.

As they left the harbour, the *Fairy* passed a dull, sombre-looking ship, hull-down in the water.

The tide was just turning, and as the crew were busily engaged in heaving the anchor, it seemed that she was about to leave her moorings and commence her voyage.

The *Fairy* passed quite near to this strange-looking ship.

But what made the vessel appear stranger than anything else was, that its decks were crowded with human beings.

They were not the crew. Were they passengers?

Perhaps so; but their dress was of a peculiar description. All the men who thronged the decks of that singular ship were clad in the same way.

Each wore a yellow jacket with a number on the back, and canvas breeches.

What could be the meaning of so singular a scene? thought Agnes, but in vain she asked herself the question.

They were now close to the ship, and those in the *Fairy* could distinguish the features of the men leaning, some sadly, some listlessly, some excitedly over the bulwarks.

All at once Agnes appeared strangely agitated; something as she gazed upon the sea of faces gazing at the yacht, seemed to raise the most violent, the most irresistible emotions in her heart.

"Oh! no, no," she cried; "it cannot, cannot be."

With trembling hands she raised the spy-glass to her eye and looked at the vessel.

Instantly she stood as if paralyzed, and the glass fell from her hands and struck the deck violently.

Lord Marchmont was standing at the other end of the ship, talking to Miss Lavinia, and did not notice Agnes's agitation.

Had he done so he would instantly have flown to her assistance.

Erect and motionless, more like a beautiful marble statue than aught of flesh and blood, Agnes stood upon the deck of the *Fairy*.

Her eyes distended and her mouth open, her hands were clenched, and her finger-nails penetrated her soft and tender flesh.

At the same time a slight commotion was visible amongst those on board the strange vessel.

It appeared as if a man, who was numbered 401, with his eyes glaring like a tiger's, with a demoniacal expression upon his pale and somewhat attenuated countenance, was endeavouring with all his might to precipitate himself bodily into the sea.

Strong hands and arms, however, held him back, and his frantic efforts were frustrated.

It was frightful to see this man's struggles. Twelve men were scarcely sufficient to hold him, and raving like a madman he was dragged down into the ship's hold, where securely manacled hand and foot, he lay blaspheming heaven and earth like an evil spirit.

When this man disappeared, Agnes, as it were, melted again into her former condition.

She was, however, frightfully pale, and her lips were blood stained, as if she had bitten them to prevent herself from crying out, or shrieking aloud. Turning to a seaman, she asked, "What ship is that?"

"Convict ship, Miss—the *Argoy*—convicts going to Australia, Miss. A rum lot them be."

As the sailor made this reply to her somewhat simple question, it looked as if Agnes would have fallen to the ground.

But recovering herself by a great effort, she walked towards her aunt and said, "I feel a little giddy, dear aunt, if you and Lord Marchmont will kindly excuse me I should like to retire to the cabin and lie down for a little while."

"Certainly," replied Lord Marchmont; "by all means, my dear Miss Leslie. But I hope we may expect the pleasure of your charming society at luncheon."

"I will try," answered Agnes, with a faint smile; so faint as to be scarcely perceptible, "but at present, I am not indeed in a condition to talk, so you must excuse me."

Having descended the stairs, Agnes entered her own private state-cabin, and throwing herself upon a sofa, gave way to a passionate fit of weeping.

Unhappy Agnes! On board that fatal ship she had made a terrible discovery. One fraught with the most dismal consequences, for it destroyed her peace of mind for ever.

The wretched girl wished herself at the bottom of the sea, upon whose placid surface the *Fairy* was swiftly sailing.

For she had *recognised her husband*.

Yes, on the deck of that convict ship, dressed in the hideous vestments of the prison, typical of the class of offenders to which he belonged, she had seen and recognised the well-known features of Marmaduke Wilson.

Condemned perhaps, she thought, to a life of horrible slavery. Stamped and branded with shame and infamy for ever.

It was a terrible discovery for her to have made.

There on the bosom of the ocean, even now within a few hundred yards of her, lay the father of her child.

It would be better for them had they been both dead.

She had seen his frantic efforts to throw himself overboard, doubtless with the intention of joining her, but ruthless men had dragged him from her agonized sight, and left her weeping tears of blood in her heart at so cruel a catastrophe.

This then explained everything. He had unfortunately fallen into the hands of the police and had been prevented from communicating with her.

Or if not that, he had written and sent to her; but beguiled away from the old Fence's house in the lone street near the Foundling Hospital, as she had been by the wiles of Miriam Moss, Marmaduke Wilson had been, as a matter of course, totally unable to trace her.

He thought her cold and heartless. She thought him false and villanous.

Oh, what a tragedy of errors.

How heavily was the iron hand of fate descending upon them.

Agnes had not even held out her hand to him. So he would doubtless still think her perfidious and deceitful. But as for her, she at least now knew that her husband had been true and good to her.

The veil was lifted, and she saw every circumstance which before had been as black and as obscure as night, as clearly as the light of day.

Bitterly did she curse the hour she had been born.

But at last a sullen resolve to live on and battle against fate, took possession of her.

"I at least am the victim of circumstances," she thought. "Things happen to me very strangely, but I am only the passive agent in the hands of some occult power."

She thought, too, of Miriam Moss, and she could entertain no doubt of her treachery. "She doubtlessly loved Marmaduke, and hated him for having married me," said Agnes, to herself. "But I doubt not a day will come when

Miriam Moss and myself may meet again, and then shall I demand a terrible reckoning. No one shall trample upon and play with my feelings with impunity."

And Agnes registered a deep and terrible vow of revenge against Miriam Moss, the treacherous Jewess.

CHAPTER XXII.

AGNES RECOVERS HER EQUANIMITY—HAIDEE—HOW THE LION CUB FIRST TASTED BLOOD—THE DEATH OF TINY—AGNES OVERBOARD—THE LAST GASP—LORD MARCHMONT TO THE RESCUE—JUST IN TIME—SNATCHED FROM THE JAWS OF DEATH—AGNES FEELS GRATEFUL TO HER PRESERVER.

YACHTING is a pastime that the English pre-eminently delight in, and a very proper amusement it is for a maritime people and the inhabitants of an island home.

But Agnes, for reasons well known to the reader, did not take that amount of interest in the nautical proceedings of Lord Marchmont that that extremely susceptible young nobleman had a right to expect.

His lordship attributed Agnes's indisposition to the effects of the sea, and surmised that she would feel better in a day or two.

He did not guess very incorrectly, for, at the expiration of the third day, Agnes appeared again upon deck, outwardly serene, whatever her mental distress might have been.

Her aunt and Lord Marchmont congratulated her upon her recovery.

Everything on board the *Fairy* was of a luxurious description.

The champagne was of the first vintage, and, it must be confessed, that it flowed freely.

Time works wonders, and, by degrees, Agnes regained her spirits to some extent, although the shocking scene on board the convict ship threatened to haunt her to her dying day.

The remembrance of that day lay like a lump of lead upon her heart and her senses.

But outwardly she was calm and smiling.

And to look at her, no one would have thought for a moment that her husband was being led into a hopeless captivity, or that his last despairing wail was in imagination ringing in her ears.

Agnes bowed her head to the inevitable, and behaved with all the fortitude inherent in her nature.

Lord Marchmont thought her a little pensive and sad, but he was far from guessing the real cause; and, with a view to amuse and interest her, he took her all over the ship, and showed her everything which he thought would be likely to assist her in recovering her spirits and wonted hilarity.

One thing particularly struck Agnes's attention, and that was a small lion cub which Lord Marchmont had picked up a short time ago at Algiers, during a cruise in the Mediterranean.

"Will it hurt me? Does it bite?" she asked.

"Oh, no! It is as quiet and tame as a rabbit—you need not be at all afraid of it."

"Oh! how nice! I should like to have it so! Have you any objection to let it come on deck?"

"Not the slightest," replied his lordship.

And, turning to a seaman, he said, "Bring Haidee on deck."

"What do you call it?" said Agnes.

Lord Marchmont repeated the name; and Agnes, as soon as the animal was brought up, approached it, saying, "Come here, Haidee—come along."

But the cub hung back, as if it was not very desirous of making her acquaintance.

It was a fine specimen of its species, although as yet very young. It was regarded by the sailors quite as a pet and plaything; and it had never yet shown any of its savage instincts, therefore no one was afraid of it, and it was often brought upon deck.

One thing they were particular about, and that was its food, which was always of a farinaceous nature.

For it is said that when a wild animal once tastes blood it becomes terribly ferocious, and utterly unmanageable.

Agnes, seeing that the cub did not approach her, wondered

at the reason, and looking round her, she espied a favourite little dog of her aunt's, called Tiny.

"I wonder," she said, addressing Lord Marchmont, "if it is afraid of the dog?"

"Well, no, I should think not; but now I think of it, it has never been confronted with a dog before, and it may possibly look upon it as an enemy."

"Had you not, in that case, better have one of them removed?"

"Yes. Suppose we send Tiny down-stairs to its mistress? Your aunt, Miss Leslie, is in the cabin, I think—at least, I left her there a short time ago reading a book."

Lord Marchmont advanced to catch Tiny, but the dog, not wishing to be caught, or being afraid of something, refused every blandishment, and ran about the deck to avoid capture.

The lion cub followed his every movement with flashing eyes, and occasionally his lips were raised, so as to show his white, glittering teeth—a not very pleasant sight considering the nature of the beast.

All at once, Tiny dashed forward to where the cub was sitting on its haunches. By this manœuvre it escaped from the clutches of Lord Marchmont, but only to fall into a greater danger.

It was escaping out of the frying-pan into the fire.

The cub looked at the dog for a moment, then, with a slight spring, gracefully and elegantly made, he was by its side.

The dog seemed fascinated and unable to move, as the eye of the cub was fixed upon it.

A sort of mesmeric influence was at work, which it was apparently impossible for the poor creature to withstand.

Haidee, after the secondary pause we have mentioned, raised his paw, which in an instant descended with crushing violence on the dog's skull.

Immediately the blow was given, the head became a shapeless mass.

Tiny rolled over on its side inanimate; and the cub, fixing his teeth in the neck of the carcase, began, with every demonstration of delight, to suck the blood of his victim.

"That is too bad!" cried Lord Marchmont. "I never knew him do such a thing before—better take a stick, my man, and drive him off."

But the seaman addressed stood aloof, and refused tacitly to do anything. He was evidently afraid, and terrified almost, at the angry and ferocious appearance of the cub.

Haidee continued to feast upon the vital current of the unlucky dog.

Lord Marchmont, seeing that his men did not like to touch the cub, thought it better not to press them.

Seizing a sort of marlinespike that lay on the deck, he advanced towards the beast, and hit it a blow on the head, saying, "Down, Haidee—down!" as he had been accustomed to formerly, when he wished it to go down to its kennel.

Haidee, however, would not obey. Quitting its prey, it gave vent to a roar that made its hearers tremble; for, though not so formidable as the roaring of the monarch of the forest, yet there was no mistaking its import.

It evidently intended mischief—that there could be no doubt whatever about.

Having uttered its roar of defiance and anger, Haidee stood in an attitude which had almost more of the offensive than of the defensive in it.

Lord Marchmont retreated a step or two.

Haidee followed him, glaring and roaring at intervals.

Again Lord Marchmont dealt the animal a violent blow, which would inevitably have sent it to visit Pluto and Proserpine in the infernal regions had its owner's intention been fulfilled, and had not its skull been of very considerable thickness.

Agnes stood an alarmed spectator of this singular scene.

A third blow from Lord Marchmont's weapon kept the cub at bay, and a fourth sent him howling towards Agnes, not with the intention of doing her any harm, but with the idea of seeking some refuge from the furious blows that fell upon its devoted head.

Agnes, however, totally mistook its meaning. She thought it was about to make an attack upon her.

Already she felt, in anticipation, its fangs imprinted on her flesh, and she shuddered at the picture.

She stepped upon a seat in order to get out of its way,

but Haidee made for the exact spot, most likely wishing to seek her protection.

But Agnes, with a scream of terror, ran towards the side of the vessel and hastily threw herself overboard.

She preferred a watery death to being torn to pieces by a wild beast.

The treacherous waves opened their arms to receive her, and she sank into their bosom.

She did not remain long under water, for her dress and her crinoline served as a life-buoy.

Fortunate indeed was it that such was the case, for the *Fairy* was progressing at the rate of nine or ten knots an hour, and she was soon left astern.

Now it was too late, the unhappy girl regretted her panic, and wished herself on board again.

But regrets were now of no avail. She had rushed upon her fate, and death was staring her in the face.

It was clear that without assistance of some sort reached her she must sink.

Her clothes were becoming saturated with salt water, and although she threw out her arms frantically to prevent herself from sinking, it was clear to the meanest comprehension that she must soon succumb.

In this moment of extreme peril she thought of Marmaduke, and wished that his strong arm was at hand to support her.

Vain wish! vain hope!

Far away, heavily ironed, in the hold of a convict ship, Marmaduke was totally unable to help her, and not only that, he was unconscious of her peril.

Shutting her eyes, Agnes gave herself up to what she deemed was inevitable, and prepared herself, in no very admirable frame of mind, for the death that awaited her.

She felt herself gradually sinking; she gasped for breath, and in vain endeavoured to prevent the salt water from entering her mouth and choking her.

Just as she gave herself up for lost, and was commending her soul into the hands of Heaven, a strong arm caught her by the waist, and supported her sinking frame as her senses were about to leave her.

This timely rescue was effected by Lord Marchmont, who, with a gallantry peculiar to himself, had only allowed himself time to throw off his heavier garments, before he jumped into the water to save Agnes from drowning.

A few strokes brought him to her exhausted body, and she was saved.

Lord Marchmont supported his now listless burden until the yacht's boat was lowered.

When this was accomplished it was rowed towards him, and they were both taken on board.

By the application of proper restoratives Agnes soon recovered her senses sufficiently to thank her preserver for his generous devotion in risking his own life to save hers.

But he answered her that she was under no obligation to him; he would, he said, have done the same thing for any one. He was, he flattered himself, a capital swimmer, and could keep up for hours in the water, always provided he was not attacked with the swimmer's great enemy, the cramp.

Although Agnes had been snatched from the very jaws of death, she was not so ill as might have been expected, for in the afternoon she appeared at dinner, when she had enough to do to answer all the inquiries of Miss Lavinia as to how the affair happened, and why she did it, with a thousand other senseless and equally unmeaning questions.

Miss Lavinia, if the truth were known, was really rejoiced at the accident.

In her opinion it brought her niece and Lord Marchmont into closer relations.

Now, she said to herself, he has a claim upon her gratitude, and we always take more interest in a person when we have done them a service.

Agnes was, in reality, very grateful to Lord Marchmont for saving her life, and she showed it in her manner, much to his lordship's delight and gratification.

For although Agnes was very much mortified and heartbroken by recent events, and although she had thought two or three times that death would be preferable to life, yet, when the time came, she shrank from it, and was only too glad to spare Charon the trouble of ferrying her prematurely over the murky waters of the river Styx.

CHAPTER XXIII.

DARK CLOUDS—THE HEAVENS ARE OVERCAST—A STORM—
THE ALBATROSS—BY THE MARK SEVEN—BREAKERS
AHEAD—IN THE SHALLOWS—THE "FAIRY" ISSUES
FROM ONE PERIL TO ENCOUNTER ANOTHER—THE
COLLISION—THE "FAIRY" FILLS.

THE day after the occurrences related in our last chapter the weather changed for the worse.

Dark clouds drifted over the surface of the horizon, and the skipper of the *Fairy* augured badly from the signs of the weather.

Neither Agnes nor her aunt knew anything about the laws that regulate cyclones, or the signs of storms.

They were happily ignorant of meteorology.

Had they been otherwise, or weatherwise, they would have had some cause for uneasiness.

Lord Marchmont, who was by no means a bad sailor, shared the somewhat gloomy anticipations of Mr. Long, his skipper.

"You see, my lord," said Long, "this is a dangerous coast, and you often have dirty weather afore you know where you are. The wind drives you on the rocks sometimes before you can cast your reckoning."

Lord Marchmont could not but acquiesce, for he dreaded the coast they were skirting from all that he had heard of it.

Neither himself nor his skipper had ever been the route before, which made them doubly cautious and anxious.

It is true they had the best admiralty charts, and their compass to guide them, and Mr. Long was continually casting his reckoning.

Still neither one or the other were at all easy or secure.

The morning had broken gloomily. The sky was overcast, and towards noon a drizzling rain began to fall.

This, a little later in the day, was succeeded by a dense fog, as white as tissue paper, and quite impenetrable.

A fog at sea is a seaman's worst enemy, nothing is more dreaded by nautical men.

In it occur terrible collisions and frightful loss of life.

In it vessels lose their reckoning, and are cast upon the rocks, where the merciless waves speedily dash them to pieces.

In it hidden, sunken rocks, jagged and piercing, are encountered, which knock a hole in the ship's bottom, when the devoted vessel rapidly fills, and all hands on board perish in the foundering bark.

Lord Marchmont had for some time perceived an immense body of misty light bearing down upon them, before they were actually enveloped in it, and both himself and Mr. Long well knew what it portended.

A tempest was at hand, and one apparently of some magnitude.

For a distant but audible roaring announced the approach of the storm, the indications of whose coming had so long troubled the waters.

The sailors, six in number, who formed the crew of the yacht, were busily occupied, by the skipper's orders, in knotting the reef-points to confine the unruly canvas.

The *Fairy* fell off with her broadside to the sea.

Lord Marchmont remained standing by the side of the skipper, who had for a time released the man at the wheel.

"You have let her fall off a point or two too much," he suggested.

But Mr. Long shook his head gravely, and replied, "The ship is partially unmanageable already."

The canvas which had not been close-reefed, fluttered ominously in the barely perceptible breeze, which was bringing the vapour down upon them.

The sails blew first this way and then that, bellied out one way and another by the uncertain wind.

As they did so a strange cracking noise, like that made by a whip was heard.

Lord Marchmont walked away towards the cabin hatchway in order to talk to the ladies, who might think his absence strange, and Mr. Long, yielding the helm to an experienced sailor, followed him to the centre of the vessel.

As they neared the mainmast something struck it, just above their heads, and fell with a heavy thud upon the deck.

The skipper stooped and picked it up. It was a large bird which had evidently in the density of the mist flown against the mast, and stunned by the concussion and the force of the blow, fallen upon the deck.

As Mr. Long seized it he started.

"What is the matter?" demanded Lord Marchmont, "and what have you got there?"

"Something I wish were a hundred miles away," was the reply.

"Why so?"

"It is a bird of ill-omen. No ship lives long after seeing it, and it is my opinion that we shall soon join Van der Deckin in a cruise in the *Flying Dutchman*."

"What nonsense, man! Don't talk like a woman," replied Lord Marchmont, sternly.

"Ah! you may call it womanish," said Mr. Long, "but I can trust my experience, I should think."

"What is it, then?"

"An albatross," answered Mr. Long, solemnly, "the most unlucky bird to a sailor, that flies."

"Well, well," said Lord Marchmont, "throw it overboard. Do not make fools of the seamen."

With a sigh of relief the skipper flung the bird of ill-omen from him, and watched it for a moment floating on the crest of a wave.

Then, turning to his crew, he exclaimed, "A hand into the chains instantly, to take soundings!"

A man instantly went forward, and Mr. Long awaited his reply with marked impatience.

"Heave away that lead!" he cried.

"Ay, ay, sir!" was the reply.

Unable to bear the suspense, the skipper went up and stood by the man's side to see that he gave the right water.

But the reply was satisfactory. They had water enough and to spare, so they were not as yet driven out of their reckoning nearer the coast than they imagined.

At last the gale came down upon them, and burst with all its fury.

The *Fairy* bowed her head and careened over heavily on one side, but being a thoroughly sea-worthy little craft she soon righted, and was in another moment riding majestically before the breeze.

Lord Marchmont had explained to Miss Lavinia and Agnes that a slight storm was expected, but he begged them not to be uneasy, as no danger was to be feared.

Both ladies were perfectly satisfied with his assurance, although Agnes said, with a laugh, "I hope you will not let me be driven into the water a second time. I assure you my experience yesterday quite makes me dread the sight of salt water."

"Never fear; you are perfectly safe," he replied, "but I would advise you to remain below, as the spray might make you uncomfortably wet, and you might probably be in the way of the men."

"Oh! certainly, we will stay here," they both said, in a breath.

"Very well, then. Another glass of this hock, and I will go on deck again. It will not be long before I rejoin you, however; so do not be alarmed, ladies."

Ascending the companion-ladder, Lord Marchmont stepped up to Long, and said, "Well, how are things looking now?"

Mr. Long shook his head as was his invariable custom when perplexed.

"How does the *Fairy* behave?"

"She will do all that you can expect from teak and iron, *that* you may depend upon."

Endless patches of white foam crested the giant waves that dashed against the sides of the gallant little vessel.

And the wind howled sullenly through the cordage in its onward course.

"I am afraid that we are drifting too far inland, Long," exclaimed Lord Marchmont. "I hardly know why, but I feel strangely uneasy."

The skipper looked dubiously around him without making any reply.

"When did you sound last?"

"Some time ago."

"In that case, have you any objection to do so again? This is so strange a coast, and the mist is so dense, that I confess I am alarmed," said Lord Marchmont.

"Yes, my lord, it shall be done. A man in the chains there!"

The same man hastened to obey the command. The lead was cautiously heaved.

Every one waited the result with evident anxiety; not a word was spoken.

But the tempest roared and surged in undisturbed hilarity.

At last the reply came in clear and piercing tones, which rang out distinctly, and were heard amidst the flapping of the canvas and the crashing of the blast.

"By the mark seven."

"Good Heaven! it is as I thought; we are nearer land than we imagined," cried Lord Marchmont. "What is to be done?"

Mr. Long looked for a moment over the side of the ship, as if calculating the velocity at which she was going, and then replied, "We must tack immediately, or we shall be in the breakers."

"Tack! and in this breeze?"

"The topsail is not enough; and although the breeze is strong, we must fling out more canvas—it is our only chance. I know it is desperate, but it must be done."

"Why not endeavour to anchor?" asked his lordship.

"It will not do, my lord, we must hold on everything; and, in addition to the canvas we have spread, we want both gib and mainsail."

"What!" exclaimed Lord Marchmont, "are you mad? They could not live an instant in this tempest!"

Mr. Long turned calmly to his lordship, and said, "Do you command this ship, my lord, or me?"

"Certainly you do."

"Then cease to interfere with me! Our lives are, I need not inform you, in jeopardy. But, under Providence, I will save them all."

"Well, do so. Have your own way; but for God's sake be careful!"

"The sea casts us to leeward," muttered the skipper to himself; "it must be done quickly."

Seizing his trumpet, in a stentorian voice he gave his commands, and soon the capacious folds of the mainsail were fluttering to the breeze.

Fortunately it was strong enough to resist the force of the blast, and although the mast seemed as elastic as a piece of cane, all went well.

No catastrophe happened; and although every face was anxious and doubtful, still it was a relief to see that so far the measure had been, not only a wise one, but a successful one.

After a while the skipper shouted, "Let her luff."

Notwithstanding the mist, it was easy to see by scrutiny that the ocean, some distance ahead of them, was a sheet of foam.

This was caused by the agitated and boiling water dashing and playing amongst the dreaded breakers.

Not a word was spoken as the ship kept upon her course.

After giving the last command, the skipper went himself to the wheel, and grasped the spokes with his strong and experienced hands.

All this while Agnes was in a state of anxiety; for, notwithstanding Lord Marchmont's assurance to the contrary, she could not help feeling that there was danger in the air.

Miss Lavinia laid herself upon a couch and endeavoured to read a book, while a glass of brandy, which she every now and then replenished, stood by her side.

At length, Agnes could stand the suspense no longer, and without apprising her aunt of her intention, she ascended the stairs, and stood upon the deck.

The wind was so strong, however, that she had to seize hold of a rope to preserve her equilibrium.

She had not stayed to confine her hair in her bonnet, and in a second, she felt her hair streaming in the gale in quite a Grace-Darling sort of style.

But so intent were the crew on the condition and prospects of the yacht, that no one so much as noticed her.

Once or twice the foam rolled away to leeward, and every one indulged a sanguine hope that they were out of danger.

Fresh breakers however rising here and there would soon dispel the illusion.

At length the skipper suddenly, with consummate skill, changed the ship's course, and her head receded from the wind.

"Square yards, and in with the mainsail!" he cried.

The command was instantly obeyed, and the little vessel was quickly riding in comparative safety in the open sea.

Then people had time to breathe once more, and so every one congratulated his neighbour upon the narrow escape they had had.

Lord Marchmont approached the skipper, and shook him by the hand, saying, "Pray forgive me; you have saved the ship; I shall not forget it."

Mr. Long returned his grasp heartily, and turning round Lord Marchmont perceived Agnes. "What! Miss Leslie, you on deck?"

"Yes," said a voice on the cabin-stairs; "and I am coming up too—I want to see the storm."

This was Miss Lavinia, whom the brandy had apparently inspired with what is commonly called Dutch courage.

Mr. Long was about to say something in order to persuade the ladies to go down-stairs again, when a frightful crash was heard.

The Fairy quivered from stem to stern, and appeared about to break up on the instant.

Every one was thrown off their feet, and two sailors standing in the bows were pitched headlong overboard.

What could it be?

That was the difficult question all asked.

But no solution of the problem was arrived at.

"Good God! we have struck," exclaimed Lord Marchmont, as soon as he had recovered his feet and assisted the ladies to theirs.

"Not so; rather say we have been struck," said the skipper.

"How mean you?"

"Look, and you will see!" replied Mr. Long, pointing to starboard.

Gazing in the direction indicated, they perceived a steamer, such as is employed in the passenger-traffic between Aberdeen and London.

The Fairy had evidently come in collision with her, and it was to be feared that from the superior size of the steamer the yacht would suffer.

Such was indeed the case; for one of the crew reported that the Fairy was fast filling with water.

CHAPTER XXIV.

THE CREW OF THE "FAIRY" LOWER THE BOAT—THE LADIES ARE SAVED—WHERE IS THE STEAMER?—THE FOG LIFTS—TAKEN ON BOARD "THE QUEEN OF THE ISLES"—HOSPITALITY OF THE PASSENGERS—THEY CROSS THE BAR AND ENTER THE HARBOUR—ABERDEEN—LORD MARCHMONT AND HIS SKIPPER RETURN TO TOWN.

CRASH, crash! was again heard. Splinters of wood flew in all directions and the timbers of the devoted yacht threatened to separate every instant. With a loud cracking noise the mast fell overboard, and dragged all its tangled mass of sails and rigging with it into the sea. The destruction and havoc of that accident were fearful. The engines of the steamer could be heard puffing and groaning, as with Cyclopean efforts they endeavoured to drag the vessel clear of the rapidly sinking yacht; as yet their efforts had been of no avail, for the bows of the steamer were firmly imbedded in the woodwork of the yacht. Lord Marchmont stood still where he happened to be when his little ship was first struck, and he endeavoured to instil a confidence which he was far from feeling, into the minds of the ladies. Mr. Long was muttering to himself something about albatrosses and the folly of not believing in omens, as if a sailor's life was not made up of superstitions. The crew looked on in blank amazement, waiting for the next event which they knew could not be far off. What their ultimate fate would be, few ventured to predict; all at once Mr. Long awoke from his reverie about albatrosses, and raising his speaking trumpet to his mouth, shouted with all his might, "Stand by there, and lower away the boat!"

"Ay, ay, sir," was the cheery response, as the men went at a trot towards the boat and quickly proceeded to lower it.

No sooner had it touched the water than the steamer managed to draw itself clear of the wreck.

Then the Fairy settled down, making a plunge forward, and in a moment her bowsprit was immersed. Lord Marchmont handed Miss Lavinia to the captain, saying—

"See her safely into the boat, Long; I rely upon you."

"Never fear," replied the skipper.

Laying hold of Miss Lavinia by the waist, he exclaimed, "Come along, ma'am; hold tight to my left arm, and keep your mouth shut; salt water isn't particularly nice at any time if you have to take it internally."

"Oh! in Heaven's name," shrieked Miss Lavinia, "what are you going to do with me?"

"You wait a bit, and you'll see; I am only going to save your life if you will let me."

The old lady was too alarmed to speak, so she contented herself with sobbing hysterically, and wishing she was a mermaid to dwell in coral caves below the angry surface of the troubled sea.

"Now then, ma'am, hold on; here we go!" cried the skipper, who with his arm tightly circled round the old lady's waist, plunged into the sea.

The fall was but slight as the yacht was sinking so fast.

When the pair rose to the surface, Mr. Long made for the boat, whose position, although not clearly defined, he contrived to make out. Having reached it, he placed Miss Lavinia within it, and then got in himself.

Lord Marchmont had followed his example with Agnes, who was clinging to his arm with the tenacity of despair; but his lordship whispered kind words of encouragement in her ear, and she felt that with him she was safe.

In a few moments the skipper assisted them both over the side of the boat, and wet, dripping, and exhausted, Agnes sat down on one of the thwarts by the side of her aunt.

The steamer showed lanterns and lights of all colours, red, blue, green, and white, and lowered her boats, having stopped her engines after she had extricated herself from the *Fairy*.

The seamen of the yacht congregated together on the side of the vessel awaiting Mr. Long's commands, for he had ordered them not to move from the wreck until he told them. Having with Lord Marchmont's assistance got the ladies on board the boat, he stood up and cried, "Now then, lads, overboard with you!"

The men required no further bidding, but instantly threw themselves over the side, and presently came diving and swimming up to the boat, like so many porpoises. There were, however, only four of them, the other two as we have already stated, were unfortunately jerked overboard when the ship was struck; what had become of them was impossible to conjecture. Mr. Long could only hope for the best, although in his heart he had sad misgivings about them.

When all were on board, the skipper pushed off a little from the wreck in order to avoid the vortex.

In a few minutes, with a noise like thunder, the deck of the *Fairy* was burst open by the imprisoned air, which the water compelled to find a vent. Then, with what sounded like a prodigious gurgle and a sigh, the ill-fated vessel gave another lurch and sank for ever.

"She was a good little vessel was the *Fairy*," said the skipper, rubbing his coat-sleeve over his eyes, for he had an affection for the craft he had navigated for so many years.

"Never mind, my man," exclaimed Lord Marchmont, laying his hand upon the skipper's shoulder, "you shall command a better when we get back to Cowes."

"When we do," replied the skipper; "we are not there yet, and I'll be hanged if I can see that long-winded steamer."

"Well, the *Fairy* was not lost by any fault of yours, Long; I don't blame you for an instant. It was the fortune of war, as one may say. It was our luck," said Lord Marchmont.

"Our luck! yes, and cursed bad luck too, I say."

Captain Long turned to one of the men and said, "Get out the oars and row towards the steamer."

"Blow me tight, cap'n, if I can see that there craft," replied the man.

Just as he spoke the mist lifted a little, and then the steamer stood revealed by her lights, and hoarse voices could be heard calling out as if demanding the whereabouts of the survivors of the catastrophe.

"Give way, my lads!" said the skipper, as the sailors placed the oars in the rowlocks. "That's your sort; give way!"

The men pulled with a will, and Mr. Long grasped the tiller.

They were soon alongside, and with assistance the ladies were taken on board. Then the boat was secured, and the rest of its occupants followed.

Mr. Long was delighted to perceive one of his lost men on board the steamer, he had evidently swam in a right direction and had been picked up by the steam-boat. But the other missing one there were no signs of, so that Mr. Long came to the inevitable conclusion that he was lost. He must have swam away out to sea, where he could meet with no earthly succour, or he had gone towards the shore, where he must have been dashed to pieces upon the sharp and jagged rocks with which the coast abounded.

The steamer was the *Queen of the Isles*, bound from the Port of London for Aberdeen, with passengers and cattle on board.

The captain made himself extremely amiable to the crew of the *Fairy*, and some of the ladies took Agnes and her aunt under their immediate protection, which, as they had lost everything they possessed in the world in the shape of clothing, was very pleasant. In a short time they emerged into the state cabin dry and comfortable, having been, in nautical phrase, rigged out from stem to stern by the kindness of their newly-found friends.

Lord Marchmont and Mr. Long were equally well treated by the male portion of the community, and the five surviving sailors found no cause to complain of the hospitality which was extended to them.

Lord Marchmont explained to the captain of the *Queen of the Isles* the dangerous position in which his steamer was, and advised him to turn her head at once and go boldly out to sea, for although the storm had in a great measure subsided, yet the mist was thick enough to prevent their seeing any rocks until the vessel actually shoaled or struck upon them.

This advice the captain without hesitation acquiesced in; and soon they were under steam and making way out of the dangerous locality in which they had hitherto been.

Towards night the weather became more settled, and the mist blew away, revealing the glorious canopy of heaven studded with a galaxy of brilliant stars.

The moon was in her first quarter, and shone faintly upon the brightly glittering waters.

The captain of the *Queen of the Isles* then turned the steamer into another channel, and made her pursue her proper course towards her destination.

About the evening of the next day they crossed the bar and entered the harbour, much to the delight of everyone, and to none more than Agnes and Miss Lavinia, who for some time, that is, ever since the storm and wreck of the *Fairy*, had expected no less a fate than that of Jonah.

Although, if the good lady had had a little discrimination, she might have known that leviathans and monsters of the deep do not disport themselves around the shores of sea-girt Albion.

"What will you do now, aunt?" asked Agnes.

"I don't care, child, what I do, if I can only once more step upon dry land."

"But I mean will you go to some hotel?"

"You know I detest hotels that are not absolutely first-rate, but I suppose we must perforce go to one just for an hour or so, until we can decide what is best to be done," replied Miss Lavinia.

"Will my poor services be of any use?" demanded Lord Marchmont.

"Or mine?" inquired Mr. Long.

"Really you are very good," answered Miss Lavinia, smiling, "and I answer you frankly, yes. You have been so useful hitherto that at this critical juncture we could not positively afford to part with either of you."

Both gentlemen bowed; and Agnes said to Lord Marchmont, with a wicked smile upon her lips, "You know I like to see everyone occupied in doing something, so suppose while aunt and myself drive on to the hotel, you two stop behind and look after the luggage."

"Oh! Agnes," exclaimed Miss Lavinia, "how can you jest about such a shocking thing? I am sure it makes me cry to think of it."

"Why, aunt?"

"Why! because I have lost all my things, and I had such a deal of trouble to buy them. There are all my Macgregor plaids, and my Balbriggan hose, and my Balmoral boots, and goodness only knows what besides. What to do about it I am at a loss to imagine, for I don't suppose this horrible dirty Aberdeen will supply us with what we want."

"Don't be too sure of that," replied Lord Marchmont, "they are very canny down this way, and Scotland can supply people with something besides cakes and haddocks."

A MIDNIGHT CRIME.

Getting into a fly, they drove to the largest hotel, and ordered dinner. Mr. Long returned shortly to the steamer to see after the crew of the *Fairy*, to whom he gave some money. He then told them to enjoy themselves, and find out some lodgings for themselves; but he strictly enjoined them to show themselves every day at one o'clock upon the quay, where he should be ready to inspect them.

This done, he returned to the hotel, and partook of a tolerably respectable dinner with the rest of his party.

After dinner the wine and dessert were put upon the table.

"You are, I think you said, going up the country, Miss Leslie?" said Lord Marchmont.

"Yes, I am," replied Miss Lavinia; "but I shall have to stay here, I daresay, a week, in order to replenish the wardrobes of myself and my niece. We are dependent upon charity for the things we are at present wearing."

"I hope you may find this hotel comfortable," said Mr. Long.

"Well, to expect that would require a stretch of credulity on my part which I really cannot say that I possess," answered Miss Lavinia, with a smile.

"You know," said Agnes, "aunt detests second-rate hotels."

"Yes, that is true," simpered Miss Lavinia. "The only hotels I can tolerate are Claridge's, and some of the private ones about Dover-street. The new railway hotels, and those that belong to Companies, I utterly abominate and detest."

"In that case, why not go into lodgings?" suggested Lord Marchmont.

"Or into a boarding-house?" said Mr. Long.

"Oh! what fun that would be, aunt," exclaimed Agnes. "What do you say to a boarding-house?"

Miss Lavinia shook her head. "No," she said, "I will not rush from the ills I know to those I know nothing of. That would be extreme folly."

Ultimately it was decided that they should remain at the

hotel until they had supplied their numerous wants, and that then they should proceed by railway to Blockhaven, for Miss Lavinia declared that she would never again trust herself upon the treacherous bosom of the deep.

Lord Marchmont arranged that Mr. Long and the crew of the *Fairy* should return to London by the *Queen of the Isles*, and go on by railway to Cowes, and there await his own arrival, for he would return by train in a day or two.

When he found that he would be of no further assistance to either Miss Lavinia or Agnes, Lord Marchmont, after expressing his regret many times at the unfortunate voyage they had made together, put himself into the train, and in pursuance with his engagement with Mr. Long, started on his way to Cowes.

Miss Lavinia and Agnes found the interior of a Scotch hotel much superior to what their somewhat prejudiced imaginations had depicted it.

The food was good and well cooked, the attendance was a little better than they had expected, and altogether they decided that they might have been worse off than they were.

They went out shopping every day, and at the expiration of a week they found themselves in a position to continue their journey.

"You know, of course, my dear Agnes," said Miss Lavinia, "that Blockhaven is a dull, out-of-the-way place, but we make use of it to serve a certain purpose, so that we must not grieve at a little inconvenience."

"No, indeed, aunt, you will not find me grumbling," said Agnes; "I am only too much indebted to your kindness for bringing me here at so much inconvenience to yourself."

CHAPTER XXV.

BLOCKHAVEN—MARMADUKE LESLIE—AN EXCURSION—THE ACCIDENT TO THE PONY-CHAISE—LOST ON THE HILLS—THE THIN, SPIRAL COLUMN OF MYSTERIOUS VAPOUR—DUTCH COURAGE—MISS LAVINIA VANISHES—NATURAL MAGIC—AGNES LOSES HER SENSES.

BLOCKHAVEN was a retired fishing-village on the east coast of Scotland, and on her arrival there Agnes was much charmed with everything. It looked so clean and nice and inviting.

Miss Lavinia had been there before, but her visits dated back a long way. It was when she was younger than she was now.

Agnes asked her how she ever came to find out so lone and retired a place? She replied that her uncle, who was now dead, had a son, who lived a wild life. At the age of nineteen he made a walking tour through Scotland. One night, being in the neighbourhood of Blockhaven, he pushed on rather quickly, as he intended to get a bed, and stay there till morning; but as he neared the village some ruffians rushed upon him and nearly murdered him, robbing him of all he possessed. When he recovered his consciousness he found himself in a cottage, where he had been carefully tended by the inmates. But his leg was broken, and he had sustained many injuries, which the village Æsculapius said would necessitate his remaining in bed for some little time. This boy was Miss Lavinia's favourite, and he knew it. Accordingly he wrote her a letter, telling her the forlorn and lamentable position he was in; saying how he was wounded, friendless, and without money, in a strange country; and with the thoughtlessness and impetuosity of youth begging her to come down to Scotland and nurse him. This she did. "And now, my dear," she concluded, "you know all about it, although, until your little affair cropped up, I had almost forgotten it, for it must be more than ten years ago."

"And what became of the poor boy?" asked Agnes, interested, she knew not why.

"That I cannot tell you. He went to college for a year or so, but while there his father died, and as he was hopelessly in debt and frightfully extravagant, he was obliged to leave, and then, I believe, he became a betting man and blackleg."

"How shocking!" said Agnes.

"Yes, it was very sad, but he had shame enough left to know it, for he has never been near me since he left college in disgrace, although he knew well enough where to find me at any time if he wanted me. Poor Marmaduke!"

"Marmaduke!" cried Agnes, her pulse stopping, and gasping for breath.

"Yes, Marmaduke was his name. But what ails you, child; are you not well?"

"It is only a passing spasm. It will go away directly. I don't think I have quite been myself since the dangers we went through on board the *Fairy*."

"Perhaps not. It was certainly very trying to both of us, but perhaps more so to you than to me, owing to your wild-beast adventure."

"How silly of me to be so agitated," said Agnes to herself directly afterwards. "And yet it is strange. *He* said he was a Leslie. There is something I do not understand. All these mysteries and perplexities quite bewilder my woman's brain. It is, indeed, marvellous how I got mixed up with this extraordinary family of Leslie."

Miss Lavinia travelled by railway from Aberdeen to Blockhaven, and made an arrangement at the latter place with the landlord of the Haddo Arms, to board and lodge herself and her niece, whom she represented as a married woman, whose husband was at present away on business, but who was expected to join them shortly.

The Haddo Arms was a respectable hostelry, and boasted the possession of some hot-water baths and a billiard-room, which in Blockhaven were considered as extraordinary luxuries.

There were bathing-machines on the beach, and the bathing was thought very good, as there was a nice shelving sandy beach and very few shingles.

Agnes and her aunt contrived to pass some weeks at this quiet place pleasantly enough.

Their favourite amusement was walking far into the country amongst the hills; for a spur of the Grampians extended as far as the coast.

Agnes's condition became more critical every day, and Miss Lavinia at last hired a pony-chaise, as Agnes could not bear the fatigue of walking.

In this they still took their long excursions into the country.

They would start in the morning, taking a cold collation with them, and having dined in some quiet, pretty spot, they would arrive at their inn just as the shades of night were descending upon and enveloping the village.

During one of those excursions an adventure befel them.

They started, as usual, after breakfast, and Agnes drove out in a new direction, which was one that they had not explored before, taking what appeared to be an almost disused road, or if used at all, only for agricultural purposes. They pursued it for some distance, until they entered a wild and hilly country. A few pine-trees grew here and there upon the ungrateful soil.

Patches of heather in full bloom here and there illuminated the landscape.

Grouse and black game rose at almost every step, and went whirring away far into the distance, where the foot of the "Sassenach" should not disturb them.

Now they descended a valley, and looked with awe upon the grand old hills frowning down upon them.

And anon they would, by some winding devious path, ascend the steep hills, and gaze from their summits upon the vale below.

The hazy ocean, dotted here and there with the white, glittering canvas of some coasting lugger, or darkened by the fuliginous vapour of a passing steamboat, was perceptible in the distance when standing upon an eminence.

Suddenly they came upon a sort of recess in the side of the hill they were ascending. It offered a protection from the heat of the sun's rays.

Agnes proposed that they should dine there.

Her aunt made no objection, and, alighting, Agnes explored the spot.

She declared it answered their purpose very well indeed; and Miss Lavinia proceeded to unload the provisions, both edible and potable.

Agnes slipped the bit out of the pony's mouth, and permitted him to graze to his heart's content.

A little spring welled up from the ground at a little distance from them, as is so often the case in Scotland, and its tiny stream insinuated itself down the side of the hill to join some river that wound along the valley.

After they had finished their repast, they reclined upon their plaids, and, taking some books from the carriage, began to read.

Suddenly Agnes roused herself from a delicious reverie, for she heard a sound which filled her with dismay.

Their pony had entangled its feet in the reins, and, in endeavouring to extricate itself, it had left the beaten course of the road, and approached the hill-side, which was rather steep.

Here, in his struggles to free himself, he had overturned the chaise, and that instantly began to roll down the declivity, of necessity dragging the pony with it.

The pony resisted this compulsory mode of descending the hill as well as he could, but his efforts were fruitless.

The velocity with which the chaise rolled over and over increased every moment, and at last the pony's head came in contact with a stone, and he ceased his struggles, for he was stunned.

At length the chaise and the harness which bound it to the pony separated, but his release came too late.

Both pony and chaise continued to roll down until the bottom of the hill was reached.

The chaise by this time was a complete wreck.

There was a wheel here and a shaft there, and, in point of fact, it was completely smashed up.

The pony was stone dead—for he had knocked against so many huge boulders which lay as obstacles in his path, that every atom of vitality had completely evaporated from his mangled carcase ere he reached the bottom.

It was the strange winnying noise made by the pony which aroused Agnes, and filled her with alarm and terror.

Running to the edge of the road, she gazed down the declivity, and saw the poor thing rolling from stone to stone, and from heather-bush to heather-bush, startling the birds and the leverets from their lairs.

Her cries brought her aunt to the spot, and she was as much astonished and alarmed as Agnes.

"What shall we do?" she exclaimed. "Here we are miles and miles from home; and you, in your delicate condition, can never walk so far. I think I could find the way, but I could never let you attempt to walk so far."

"Suppose we stay here, aunt, until somebody finds us, or until the people at the inn send out in search of us?"

"No; that will never do," replied her aunt. "You would very soon catch your death of cold out here amongst these bleak, unprotected Scotch hills. What an unlucky accident! I wish we had kept to the old roads."

"Well, aunt, we must do something. Shall we go down the hill, and see if the poor pony is alive?"

"Oh! it is folly to think of such a thing for a moment. The pony must be dead. Look what a distance it is—you can hardly see his body at the bottom—it looks quite a speck."

"Let us, then, pack up these things," said Agnes, "and descend the side. It is no use stopping here."

"Very well," said Miss Lavinia, with the resignation of a martyr, and a sigh which said plainly enough, "See what I put up with for your sake, and be grateful."

They packed up their remaining provisions as well as they could, and threw the plaids round their shoulders; and then they descended the hill by the road which had assisted them to ascend it.

When they had gone a few hundred yards, without either one or the other uttering a word, Agnes suddenly exclaimed, "Oh! look there, aunt!"

"Where, child?—what is it?" queried Miss Lavinia.

"Why, do you not see that smoke curling up the hillside a little below where we are standing?"

Miss Lavinia strained her eyes, and at last perceived what her niece alluded to.

A small stream of white smoke issued, as it were, from the very bosom of the earth.

No hut, no cottage, no shanty, no highland shieling was there from which it could emanate.

It was like an eruption from the side of a volcanic mountain.

Agnes half expected that a stream of lava would presently spring out of the earth and envelope her and her aunt, so mysterious did this circumstance appear to her.

"Oh! it is a cottage of some sort, I suppose," said Miss Lavinia.

"No, aunt—it is not. How can it be a cottage? It comes out of the ground itself."

"Well, I confess I don't understand it, dear," said Miss Lavinia; "but I do hope that it is nothing dangerous or supernatural. They talk in Scotland about wraiths and ghosts and goblins, and goodness knows what."

"Oh! don't talk like that, aunt; I am frightened enough already," replied Agnes.

"So am I. Have you the brandy-flask, or have I? I declare I feel so faint I don't know what to do."

Agnes replied that her aunt had the liquor, and that estimable old lady took a pull at the flask. In fact, candour compels us to relate that she took a very deep pull, so much so that her breath went and came in short gasps, and her face was red with the exertion.

It had, however, a reassuring effect upon her, for she became more courageous than she had been a few minutes before.

"Oh! what shall we do?" asked Agnes, for whom the thin, misty column of smoke appeared to possess a strangely fascinating interest.

"Do, child?" replied her aunt, boldly—"do? Why, go and see what it is."

"Shall we?"

"Yes, who's afraid?—I'm not."

"Very well, you go, dear aunt, and I will stand here and await your return."

Miss Lavinia hesitated as the danger of the expedition flashed across her mind, she rather shrank from fulfilling her half-expressed promise.

In fact, her courage was fast oozing out of her fingers' ends.

"But it might blow up, whatever it is," she said, in a trembling voice.

"I thought you said you were not afraid, aunt," said Agnes, with a sarcastic smile.

"No more I am, and you know it. You ought not to stand there and taunt me. Why don't you go yourself?—there is nothing to be alarmed at."

"I don't know that. I confess I am terribly afraid, and yet I don't like to go away without ascertaining what it is," said Agnes.

Miss Lavinia appeared, a second time, to be attacked with a sudden faintness, for she drew the brandy-flask from her pocket, and turning her back to Agnes slily applied it to her lips.

As formerly, it was some time before it came away again. When it did it appeared to be considerably lightened of its contents.

"Ah!" said Miss Lavinia, smacking her lips, as she replaced the friendly flask in her pocket.

"Did you speak, aunt?" asked Agnes.

"I was merely thinking, my dear, that the air of the Scotch hills is very refreshing—very refreshing indeed, I may say," replied her aunt.

The thin column of smoke still continued to ascend spirally, for hardly a breath of air was stirring.

And so thin and airy was this vapour that it could only be seen when you were within a few yards of it.

"Well, aunt, what will you do?"

"Oh! you are a coward, I can see; you are afraid to go. But I will show you that I am afraid of nothing."

Miss Lavinia spoke confidently; it was easy to see that her second libation had been more copious than the first one, and its effect was decided and immediate.

"Pray Heaven you are running into no danger," said Agnes with some earnestness, for she could not disguise from herself the fact that there was something unearthly about that still, small column of smoke.

Ever ascending, never diminishing, never increasing.

Impalpable apparently as a summer cloud drifting along the surface of the horizon.

What could it be? Was it some exhalation, some jack o' lantern, some will-o'-the-wisp?

It was impossible to answer these questions.

One thing was certain; it was enough to inspire terror in the breast of a young girl alone with her aunt in a wild part of Scotland many miles from any town, or any known habitation.

Gnome-like and mysterious, it continued to rise.

Agnes thought of the fairy tale of the fisherman and the geni, and almost expected to see a huge creature arise and stand before them.

"Well, child, I am going," said Miss Lavinia; "I will soon tell you what it is."

With a reckless laugh Miss Lavinia stepped across the road, and walked towards the extraordinary phenomenon.

Agnes half held out her hand to stop her, but she restrained herself.

Steadily Miss Lavinia walked on without turning round to look at Agnes, whose eyes were riveted upon her every motion.

She neared it rapidly.

Stepping carefully over the patches of intervening heather she was soon within a yard of it.

When what was Agnes's horror and consternation to see her aunt disappear!

Yes, Miss Lavinia vanished in the most wonderful manner from her sight.

Vanished all at once, as if by magic, leaving no trace behind her.

Agnes thought that she heard a faint scream, and then another, and then a series of screams, arising as it were from the solid earth.

Still the thin column of vapour wound unconcernedly upwards.

And Agnes stood rooted to the spot, perfectly mystified.

A few minutes ago her aunt had stood by her side and talked amicably with her.

And now where was she?

In vain she asked herself, over and over again, the sadly perplexing question.

All she could say was, that she had vanished—disappeared —gone from her sight like a flash of lightning.

It was very mysterious.

It was very wonderful.

The sun was high in the heavens, and its scorching beams wandered downwards towards the parched earth.

The birds of the air carolled and sang gaily as they flew lazily along, stopping now and then to rest themselves, or to pick up some delicacy which they espied from afar.

Agnes thought her senses were leaving her.

It was more than she could bear, and with a shrill, piercing shriek, she fell to the earth insensible.

CHAPTER XXVI.

A HIGHLAND STILL—THE PRISONERS—KIND TREATMENT —AGNES IS TAKEN ILL—SHE BECOMES A MOTHER— HER AUNT'S CRIME—MEG RESCUES THE CHILD—AGNES AND MISS LAVINIA LESLIE RETURN TO TOWN.

AGNES had no sooner succumbed to the horror with which her situation inspired her, than the explanation of the apparent mystery was brought to light.

Stepping up as it were from the ground itself—rising from its solid surface—two brawny highlanders stood upon the heather, close by where the smoke continued to ascend.

They were fine sturdy fellows to look at, dressed in the highland costume, the kilt and the tartan. One turned to the other and said as he espied Agnes's body lying on the ground, "Wha is it lies yander?"

"A wee bit lassie, sure eneuch," replied the other.

"Gae ower the ground then, David MacGalliker. We maun hav her wi' the ither."

As they approached her, Agnes sighed and moaned, although she was still insensible.

"Hout! Deil's in the wife," cried David MacGalliker.

"What are you clavering about?" asked his companion. "God sake, mon, lay hold and bring her in. It is na muckle."

The highlanders seized Agnes's inanimate body as if it had been a feather, and carried it to the place from whence they had emerged.

This was an opening in the earth only perceptible when you were close upon it. There were steps cut in the soil, which made a sort of rude staircase.

Descending this for some seconds, they touched the bottom, and going a little distance through a sort of semi-darkness to which they seemed accustomed, they laid Agnes upon a bed of dry heather, and then stood talking together.

A fire was burning at the extreme end of this singular habitation, and some strange-looking machinery was standing by it. A woman was revealed by the light of the fire; she was apparently tending the furnace, or whatever it was.

Presently the men advanced towards her, and she entered with great zest into their conversation. Miss Lavinia was sitting on the ground with her hands bound behind her back, looking very disconsolate and miserable, but still breathing defiance through her flashing eyes.

The fact was, she had advanced without looking before her, so intent was she upon watching the column of smoke.

And before she knew where she was she had fallen into the subterranean apartment, through the aperture we have already described.

The woman, looking first at the ladies, who had been so unceremoniously brought into the apartment, and then at the highlander called David, exclaimed—"We have a bonny family the noo!"

"Ye dinna meet sic friends every night; weel no part wi' them, at ony rate, for a day or twa mair. Eh! Charlie?" replied David.

"The feint a bit of that," said Charlie; "we maun have gold and siller."

The old woman smiled and nodded her head, and, in obedience to the commands of Charlie, went to look after Agnes.

With a little care she contrived to bring her back to consciousness, and Agnes gazed around in astonishment.

"Where is my aunt?" she cried. "Oh! take me to her. Where is she?"

"Wha kens?" said the woman, laconically.

But Miss Lavinia, hearing Agnes's voice, rose, as well as she could, to her feet, and walked, or rather ran, towards her, saying—

"Here I am, child; here I am; but these wretches have tied my hands behind my back."

One of the men here advanced, and seeing what was going on, he himself undid the bands that bound Miss Lavinia, and that lady, going down on her knees, took one of Agnes's hands in hers and began to chafe it.

Miss Lavinia had, during her incarceration, come to her own conclusions about this cave of Adullam—this underground dwelling.

And when Agnes asked her where she was, she replied—

"These people, child, keep an illicit still, and we have been unfortunate enough to fall into their hands; and yet, perhaps, it is lucky after all, for what could we have done, lost on the hills, as we were?"

"That is true," replied Agnes. "I suppose these people will take us back again?"

"Doubtless they will do anything for money, and I will offer to pay them well for it."

Miss Lavinia turned to Charlie, who was standing near her, and said, "We have lost our way, my good man, and although we are much obliged to you for sheltering us here in your house, it is absolutely imperative that we should return home to-night."

The highlander grinned, and appeared to be much amused at this style of address.

"Weel, me leddy, and what then?" he said.

"If you can get us a conveyance, we will pay you well for it."

"Ye ken fu' weel yersel' that we keepit a bit still here."

"Yes," replied Miss Lavinia: "I have, as you imagine, had sufficient penetration to guess the fact."

"And ye will na tell the justice, me leddy?" said Charlie.

"No; I will tell no one—why should I? Your private occupation is nothing to me."

"Aweel, ye wadna like to sleep wi' the tod and the black cock o' the muir?" he asked.

"No; I cannot say I should like to do that particularly."

"Then you must stop here till morning."

Charlie explained in his own peculiar dialect that it was too late for him to think of seeking a conveyance that afternoon, but that he would do so the next day.

He promised that he would do all he could to make them comfortable.

There was, he said, an inner chamber behind the lembeck (or still) where Meg, the old woman, slept, and that was very much at their service.

While Meg would wait upon them, and act in the capacity of lady's-maid, and do everything that lay in her power for them.

What could Miss Lavinia do?

She was in the power of these men, and, in addition to that, there was a great deal of sense and justice in what Charlie said.

Besides, Agnes seemed particularly unwell, so much so that her aunt was quite alarmed about her.

With Meg's assistance, Miss Lavinia took Agnes into the room mentioned by Charlie, who had after his colloquy with "the leddy," gone back to David to assist him in looking after the still.

The two women laid Agnes upon a bed made of heather and plaids, but the poor girl seemed to be suddenly taken so ill that she could scarcely speak.

All she did was to cry and moan.

Miss Lavinia and Meg sat up with her all night in that dreary chamber, cut out of the solid earth, a solitary candle of the coarsest manufacture alone illuminating the darkness.

The next morning what Miss Lavinia had feared took place, and as day dawned Agnes found herself a mother.

For many days she lay ill and weak in her strange abode, carefully tended by her aunt and the Scotch woman, Meg, who constituted herself nurse to the "bairn."

A new difficulty now arose in Miss Lavinia's mind—what should she do with the child?

Agnes could never return to London the acknowledged mother of a baby boy.

Miss Lavinia, therefore, in order to save Agnes from what she considered fatal consequences, resolved upon a deed of horror!

Agnes was in so weak a state as to have been almost unconscious for some time.

Accordingly she would believe anything that was told her.

With this idea, Miss Lavinia made a confidante of Meg, who, on receiving a liberal sum of money which Miss Lavinia had about her, and receiving a promise of more, acquiesced in the plan that was submitted to her, and, without hesitation, delivered the baby into the ruthless hands of its enemy.

One night, when all was still, Miss Lavinia, with the child in her arms, passed up the primitive staircase and emerged upon the moor.

The guilty woman—guilty, that is, of a contemplated crime —paused a moment and shrank back.

But she comforted herself with the reflection that there was no one to watch her in such a remote and desolate region.

Onward she went, at a quick pace, with her unconscious victim asleep in her arms.

When she had gone what she considered a sufficient distance she halted.

Laying the child down upon the heather, she looked at it for a moment—she knew not why.

The stars shed a faint light, but moon there was none.

She could just see the outline of the bundle of plaids that circled the child.

A feeling of pity stole into her heart, and she almost relented of her cruel purpose.

But when she thought of her ambitious designs, and the future she contemplated for Agnes, her heart was steeled.

She smothered all her better feelings, and resolved to let the innocent perish where it lay.

"I will do it no violence," she said to herself; "it shall simply die a natural death.

"So no one can say that I have stained my hands with blood.

"Besides, I do what I do not for myself so much, but for my niece."

And turning round she deliberately walked away.

She had not gone far, however, before she heard a tiny wail issuing from the hapless infant.

Putting her fingers in her ears she ran blindly forward to escape the accusing cry.

But another voice more powerful and louder said something which rang in her ears more shrilly.

This was the voice of conscience, and it said *Murderess*.

Yes, she was, to all intents and purposes, a murderess, and from that day to the day of her death, she had, although she knew it not, aroused an implacable tormentor who would never let her rest.

It was the embodiment of the worm that never dies.

The realization of the fire which is never quenched.

Unhappy woman!

On she ran stumbling now over a bush of heather, and anon setting her foot in the hole of some animal; until out of breath, torn and bleeding, she reached the den of the illicit distillers.

She found the entrance without much difficulty, and going into her apartment with the greatest caution, met Meg, her ally, who, seeing the perturbation she was in, tried to calm her, and gave her a dose of whisky, which was so powerful, and so many degrees over proof, that it had the effect of sending her fast asleep.

Meg then, with many a careful footstep, issued from the room, and thence from the cave itself.

Then, like a bloodhound following up a trail, she wandered about the moor in all directions.

At last the object of her solicitude was apparent.

She was looking for the child that she had betrayed to Miss Lavinia Leslie.

She found it; guided more by its cries than by her own sagacity.

Having found it, she set off at a rapid pace in a totally different direction than the one she came.

The pace she went at seemed quite marvellous for a woman of her age; for in about an hour and a half she had travelled about ten miles.

The country she traversed was of the same wild, desolate, almost uninhabited description that we have previously described.

At last she stopped at a humble-looking shanty, and knocked loudly at the door.

The summons was answered by a woman, who seemed more sleepy than polite.

But when she saw who her visitor was, she evinced every symptom of delight.

Meg whispered a few words in a low tone.

The other replied.

And in a short time Agnes's child was transferred to the arms of the motherly-looking woman, who appeared to be a friend of Meg's.

Meg then set out on the backward trail, and with equal rapidity reached the cave.

This she re-entered with all quiet and secrecy, and not a soul would have imagined that she had accomplished the errand of mercy which she had just brought to so satisfactory a conclusion.

In a few days Agnes was sufficiently recovered to be able to return to Blockhaven.

When she asked for her child, Miss Lavinia and the Scotch woman told her that it had died a few hours after birth.

And she, poor, silly, simple child, knowing no better, believed the inventions that were told her.

Miss Lavinia rewarded the Highland distillers of whisky very handsomely, and did not forget her friend Meg.

After some weeks Agnes pronounced herself strong enough to travel, and, with her aunt, returned to town.

Once more in Hill-street, and numerous modes of spending time were resorted to—such as parties, theatres, and what not—which had the effect, in some measure, of shutting out the horrible adventures that had lately befallen them.

CHAPTER XXVII.

GAIETIES OF LONDON LIFE—THE WORM THAT NEVER DIES—A RIVAL—JEALOUSY—THE HON. MR. CUNNINGHAME — BRIGHTON — THE PAVILION GARDENS — A DECLARATION—AGNES'S CONFUSION—ASK MY AUNT—PERCY CUNNINGHAME INSULTS LORD MARCHMONT—THE CALM BEFORE THE STORM.

AMONGST the gaieties of London life Agnes Leslie found relief from the memories of the past.

When whirling along in the giddy waltz, to enlivening music, she was, in a certain way, happy. The drama afforded her solace, and concerts gave her relief, and in time she came to forget that she had ever been Agnes Wilson.

Not so Miss Lavinia, who could never forget the terrible night in the Highlands when, with heartless cruelty, she had exposed a tender infant to the mercy of the blast and the caprice of the elements. Sometimes she would wake in the night with a terrible shriek, fancying that a legion of infants, armed with sharp, piercing weapons, were about to stab her to the heart, and deprive her of her miserable existence.

She was far from happy. She had sown the seeds, and was now beginning to reap the harvest of crime.

'Tis a crop which never fails the industrious husbandman. It will always bring in three or four fold in return for the smallest sprinkling of seed.

But Miss Lavinia Leslie comforted herself with the assurance that she had been acting in the interests of her niece, and that her reward would be soon forthcoming.

Gold! bright, glittering gold!

Gold with which to purchase every happiness, and, in her old age, to smooth her path down to the grave.

Sinister thoughts would occasionally tell her this was a

delusion, but she spurned such ideas from her mind, and lived, as is often the case, in a fool's paradise.

Lord Marchmont was again in town, and, as before, became a constant visitor in Hill-street. His attentions to Agnes were so marked that no one but a blind man could have mistaken them.

Miss Lavinia smiled secretly at this, and often held secret converse with her niece about it. She told her that she had better in time accept his lordship, as anything more eligible might not offer; and it was an old saying, but a true one, "that a bird in the hand is worth two in the bush;" and there could be no question that one coronet on her brow was worth all the peerage in prospective.

Lord Marchmont was a good-looking man, and one whom any woman might be proud to call her own; and even if Agnes could feel no real, actual love for him, she might respect and look up to him; for he was the pink of politeness and the soul of honour.

Love for her, unhappy woman, was a dream of the past, a phantom that rose into existence only to mock her.

Yet she had her tender moments. What woman has not? Moments when the garden of Hampton Court Palace, glowing in a flood of rich, golden sunset, would pass like a diorama before her dazzled vision. Airy spirits would whisper words of love into her attentive ears. Marmaduke Wilson would be again by her side. Then clouds would gather in the heavens. The wind would rush hither and thither wildly and fiercely as if in furious anger. A terrific storm would burst. But the convulsion of nature would add bliss to the moment.

Then the scene would change, and she would utter a deep cry of endless, passionate yearning for the happiness that had for ever departed from her, for her husband and her child. That husband who was slaving away the best years of his existence in horrible, shameful, and disgraceful drudgery as a convict, without hope. That child whose bones she thought were lying in the soil of a far-off land.

She agreed with her aunt that she could not do better than marry Lord Marchmont, but it was arranged between them that the event should be postponed as long as possible, in order to make his affection for Agnes more ardent and profound, so that he would, when it was at this height, make a very handsome settlement upon her, which he could well afford to do as he was prodigiously wealthy.

About this time, however, a new character appeared upon the scene in the person of the Hon. Percy Cunninghame, who also had more than his share of what is sometimes called the loaves and fishes of this life, and as he was apparently very much smitten by Agnes's charms, Miss Lavinia thought it would not be inadvisable to play one off against the other, although in the end it was decided that Agnes should consent to be Lady Marchmont.

"You see, my dear child," said Miss Lavinia, "there is nothing like a little rivalry to freshen men up a bit, and make them more determined in the chase; and a little, just a wee bit, of jealousy is the finest thing in the world to fan the flame of love. So, by all means, flirt with Mr. Cunninghame, and coquette with Lord Marchmont, although be careful to be always more tender and gracious to the latter. Believe me, I give you good advice, for I have had so many affairs of the sort, that I ought to know something about it."

Agnes followed her aunt's advice to the letter, and it had the desired effect. The Hon. Mr. Cunninghame at one moment thought that he was the favourite; and, at another, he became mad with jealousy, to see Lord Marchmont singled out for attentions equally, if not more, flattering and agreeable. Both gentlemen were constant visitors in Hill-street, and many little parties were arranged between them, and Miss Lavinia and her niece. Sometimes Richmond would be the chosen locality, and sometimes Blackwall or Greenwich.

One day Miss Lavinia determined to go to Brighton. It was such a nice place, she said, you would be sure to meet everybody you know there; and as the London season is defunct, why Brighton is the place of all others to go to; more especially as people are coming back from the Continent. There are certainly a great many men shooting partridges and pheasants, but a true sportsman is never a good lady's man. So the Leslies went to Brighton, and stopped at the Albion Hotel.

"It is much the quietest," observed her aunt to Agnes. "The Bedford is always full of rich city people, and *parvenues*."

Lord Marchmont, after their departure, made the singular discovery that his health was not so good as it ought to be; and his doctor, in consequence, strongly advised him to try the sea air.

The sea air, the doctor said, was so bracing and enlivening, that it would be sure to set him on his legs again in no time. The iodine it contained was such a fine thing; so invigorating, and all that. So Lord Marchmont went to Brighton. As he had a private house there of his own, he did not go to an hotel. What was more extraordinary than this, was the fact that the Hon. Mr. Cunninghame found London insupportable. He declared that there was not a fellow he knew in the place, and he should go to Brighton for a change.

Miss Lavinia was much pleased at this, and she was determined to make the most of it; and the two gentlemen soon paid their respects to Miss Lavinia and her charming niece.

One day, when the band was playing at the Pavilion, Miss Lavinia and Agnes were sitting in the gardens listening to the music, which was chiefly operatic. Now, it would be loud and thrilling; anon, soft and dreamy, like a spirit song.

Agnes was superbly dressed, and Miss Lavinia was no less richly attired. Suddenly Lord Marchmont made his appearance, and bowing to the ladies, took a chair and seated himself by them.

It was a lovely afternoon, and the scene was an inspiriting one. Everybody who had any pretension to be considered fashionable was in the Pavilion Gardens that day; expensively-dressed dowagers and lovely girls, clad as only the best Parisian taste could have devised, such exquisite harmony was there in the blending of the colours.

The officers of the garrison were there in great force, and were much admired by the female portion of the community; as, indeed, soldiers always are, and always will be. For the pursuit of arms always has been, and ever will continue to be, a favourite one with the ladies.

Lord Marchmont felt inspired with love by the gaiety around him, and fascinated with Agnes's peerless beauty, enhanced as it was by the most consummate skill of the jeweller, and the utmost art of the milliner. Her loveliness on the present occasion was positively dazzling. No wonder that Lord Marchmont wished to call so splendid a creature his own. It was hardly a fit and proper occasion to tell her so; but love is blind, and passion sometimes irresistible. His lordship had often been on the point of making a declaration, but somehow or other he had never done so; and now he was determined to delay it no longer. "Who knows," he thought, "who may step in and snatch the prize from me? She is too fair and beautiful to be without suitors; and to lose her I would, I feel, be perdition. Perdition! yes, absolute ruin in body and mind; I could never get over so cruel a blow. She must, and shall be mine!"

Bending his head a little, so that he might converse with her in a low tone, without being overheard by those around, he said—

"I have often, Miss Leslie, been on the point of talking very seriously to you upon a matter of vital importance to me."

"Indeed; your lordship is too good," replied Agnes.

"Not at all. Do not laugh at me, I beg of you. The subject I want to broach is to me a very sacred one; and we ought not to ridicule anything sacred, you know."

"No, I am aware of that; I have, I assure you, a great reverence for sacred things, so much so, that I think, some day, of going to Jerusalem and the Holy Land."

"Oh! you are laughing at me," cried Lord Marchmont, looking very mortified and dejected.

"Indeed, I am not laughing at you," replied Agnes, with a smile; "I would not do such a thing for the world. I don't think I could do so, if I were to try. There is something so solemn and sedate about your lordship, at this particular moment, that your appearance is anything but mirth-provoking."

"If you knew what my feelings are at this moment you would feel for me and pity me," he said.

"I am quite prepared to do so," replied Agnes, with another sweet smile, "if you will condescend to tell me your grief. Come, now, make a sister of me. Let me be your confidant, and pour all your troubles into my ear. Will you?"

Lord Marchmont yielded to the irresistible charm of her manner, and gave himself up to the ecstasy of the moment. To contemplate her beauty was to him like being in the

Elysian Fields—to drink in her smile was to imbibe so much delirium.

"Can it be possible, Miss Leslie," he said, "that you have never perceived that I entertain a feeling for you which is something more than mere friendship?"

Agnes cast her eyes upon the ground, and blushed a little.

"In fact, that I love you!" continued Lord Marchmont. "Yes, my dear Miss Leslie—why disguise the fact—I love you. Love you fondly, dearly, truly, everlastingly, eternally, with a deep, undying, unquenchable love, such as man never before entertained for any woman under the sun. It may seem presumptuous of me to say so, but only put me in a position to prove my love, and then you will be able to judge whether or not I have exaggerated the unspeakable affection I have for your incomparable self. Speak, dear girl, speak, and let me know my fate. Suspense in such a moment is insupportable. So tell me, dearest Miss Leslie, if I may hope?"

Agnes appeared much confused at so lengthy and passionate an address; she had hardly expected so ardent an appeal. Lord Marchmont had spoken quickly and hurriedly, but there was no mistaking the genuineness of his manner, from the heartfelt way in which he spoke.

"Really," said Agnes, playing with her parasol—"really you ought not to speak to me in this manner; it is such a strange place, too, to choose for saying such strange things as you have been saying to me. I declare you have quite taken me by surprise. You know that I have only my aunt to look to to guide me, for my brother is abroad on the Continent, and my father is in the country. So I must ask you to be so indulgent as to permit me to consult her before I give you a decided answer."

"Oh! no, no; now, at once," he said, in a beseeching tone. "Oh! say yes—say you will be mine, and I will bless you for the words for ever."

"I cannot; indeed I cannot; and it is not right or manly of you to press me thus," replied Agnes.

"Oh! pardon me if I have offended you, but I love you so passionately that I am nearly mad. I know not what I do."

"I will consult my aunt, and let you know in a day or two."

"To-morrow. Oh! say to-morrow," pleaded his lordship.

"I cannot be too precipitate," replied Agnes, "but you shall have an answer the day after to-morrow. Will that content you? Will that make you happy?"

"Will you answer me one thing," he said, "and then I will wait patiently?"

"Certainly; what is it?" said Agnes.

"Only this," replied his lordship. "May I, oh! may I hope?"

In his agitation, he took the tips of her fingers in his hand and pressed them.

Agnes, with admirable tact, returned the pressure, and said, in the same low, earnest voice, "You may;" and she smiled kindly, if not lovingly, upon him.

"Oh! thanks, thanks, for that blessed answer," he exclaimed, "Now I am happy. Heaven bless you, dear girl, and favour my suit," he added.

Just as Lord Marchmont gave utterance to these last words, the Hon. Mr. Cunningham walked up to the ladies, and passing behind Lord Marchmont, overheard the latter part of the lovers' conversation. Gnashing his teeth with rage, and clenching his fists with passion, he approached, but good-breeding compelled him to be outwardly calm and serene. Bowing to the ladies, he talked to them in that easy prattling way that is peculiar to well-bred men-about-town, and which at all times makes them such agreeable companions.

Of Lord Marchmont he took not the slightest notice. His lordship's brain was in a whirl, and he thought he would leave the pavilion and go for a ride on the hills. His groom was in waiting with his horse outside, and with that idea he bid Miss Lavinia and her niece good-bye; bestowing a glance of ardent affection upon the latter which did not pass unnoticed by his rival, who was stung to madness by it, more especially as Agnes herself gave him a glance in return, which said, as plainly as if she had spoken it, "You may hope."

The Hon. Mr. Cunningham was standing near one of the windows which lead into the reception-rooms, and Lord Marchmont had to pass through the open window in order to leave the gardens. He might have gone lower down, but he was so agitated that he did not wish to mingle with the crowd, amongst whom he knew he would be sure to meet some loquacious acquaintance or other, who would detain him in conversation for some time. Mr. Cunningham saw his lordship approach him, but did not offer to move to allow him to pass; on the contrary, he remained rooted to the spot, looking straight before him, and talking quietly to Miss Lavinia.

"Will you allow me to pass?" said Lord Marchmont, noticing the obstruction before him.

Mr. Cunningham took no notice of this appeal, but continued his conversation as unconcernedly as if there was no such person as Lord Marchmont in existence.

His lordship repeated his question, but with the same result.

"Ill-mannered brute," muttered Lord Marchmont, pushing his rival on one side by giving him a slight shove on the arm.

This was apparently precisely what the Hon. Mr. Cunningham wanted, for exclaiming, "Oh! this is too much," he added, "your lordship shall hear from me."

"Whenever you like," replied Lord Marchmont, carelessly, walking through the magnificent suite of apartments that the morbid fancy of George the Fourth ornamented with representations of horrible-looking serpents of the largest description.

The Honourable Mr. Cunningham continued his conversation directly, as if nothing had happened; and, if the truth were told, he seemed to be in rather better spirits than before.

This little scene had not passed unnoticed either by Agnes or her aunt, but they attributed it to jealousy, and neither of them anticipated any serious results from an encounter of so apparently trivial a nature. And this contempt for trifles is the great mistake that half the people make in going through life. In reality, there are no such things as trifles, because they always grow into something bigger. You may, if you like, call them great things in their infancy, but never despise them.

Had Miss Lavinia or Agnes known what was about to happen on the morrow, they would not have felt so comfortable and unconcerned as they were at present.

Truly, the morrow was to be prolific in events of startling interest!

CHAPTER XXVIII.

THE HON. PERCY CUNNINGHAME SENDS LORD MARCHMONT A CHALLENGE—HIS LORDSHIP REFUSES TO FIGHT—HIS RIVAL BUYS A DOG-WHIP AND WAITS UPON HIS LORDSHIP—JOHN THE FOOTMAN—A TUG AT HIS COAT-TAILS—LORD MARCHMONT IS HORSEWHIPPED—HE AGREES TO FIGHT.

LORD MARCHMONT'S happiness was so great when he left the Pavilion Gardens at Brighton, that he scarcely for a moment thought of the strange and startling, not to say ungentlemanly, conduct of the Hon. Percy Cunninghame. His thoughts were fixed upon the lovely niece of Miss Lavinia Leslie. Her peerless form was ever before his eyes. His lips could murmur no name but hers. His heart enshrined no image but her own. In fact, he was deeply, irrevocably, in love with her, whom we can only look upon as a fair adventuress. That Percy Cunninghame was jealous, he could not for a moment doubt. Jealous of one who was more favoured than himself by the object of their mutual adoration. Yes, it was even so.

The handsome, rich, and courted Percy Cunninghame, was madly, furiously jealous of Lord Marchmont. So much so, indeed, that he determined to have a terrible revenge—that is, if the fortune of war would grant him the darling wish of his heart. But would it do so? No one could say.

At all events, the Hon. Percy Cunninghame was resolved to risk his own life in order that he might have a chance to take that of his rival. To see Agnes the wife of Lord Marchmont would be worse than death. To think that she was torn away from him, and that, too, only to make the heaven of another, was too much for him to contemplate. He would rather die honourably, like a brave man, sword in hand.

So he thought their rencontre in the gardens could only

result in hostilities. Look at it whichever way he would, he could come to no other conclusion. He would, if he could, take the life of Lord Marchmont. If fate decreed it otherwise, then he would fall a victim to his passion for Agnes Leslie.

He considered that it would be infinitely better that the affair should be conducted privately, without the interference of other persons; of course, he was so well known in Brighton, that he could have got any amount of seconds, if he had chosen to do so, but he thought it would be better not to do so. Duelling in these days is a punishable offence. To kill a man in a duel is looked upon by the law as murder; and any man who does so, no matter what his rank, what his fame, what his wealth, would be hung upon a gibbet, like the commonest and vilest murderer that ever suffered the extreme penalty of his crimes; for the law is no respecter of persons, and this is the great Palladium of English liberty. The Hon. Percy Cunninghame, therefore, considered it advisable that only himself and his antagonist should be aware of their hostile meeting. With this end in view, he wrote a letter to his lordship, couched in the following terms:—

"The Hon. Percy Cunninghame presents his compliments to Lord Marchmont, and begs to submit the following for his consideration.

"Firstly, that as duelling is at present out of fashion and punishable by law, in the event of the death of one's adversary, our own meeting, which is, as your lordship must know, unavoidable, should be conducted by ourselves, without the intervention of seconds.

"Secondly, that we should meet together in order to confer as to a fit and proper place for the encounter to take place in. If your lordship will be so good as to allow the writer of this note to suggest a rendezvous, he would say that the sands at low tide, somewhere in the neighbourhood of Brighton, will be as good a place as is likely to be discovered. Because, if one of us fall mortally wounded, the tide will wash away the stains of blood, and very probably afterwards carry the body out to sea; anyhow, there will be less chance of the surviving party being detected, and hunted down by the myrmidons of the law. The Hon. Percy Cunninghame will feel extremely obliged by the favour of a reply."

This note Percy Cunninghame sent to Lord Marchmont's house, and waited impatiently for an answer. When his lordship received the epistle he was not surprised, but he was undeniably annoyed and vexed at the ominous communication. He was in love with Agnes, and she favoured his suit. Why, then, should he expose himself to the bullet or the blade of a rival in order to gratify that rival's love of revenge? Why, indeed? He asked himself the question a thousand times, but he could not receive a satisfactory answer. It was true that a harsh code of honour commanded him to allow himself to be shot at, if another man chose to fix a quarrel upon him; but why should he defer to that code? Why not inaugurate a healthier and a better state of things? It would be bitter indeed to have the cup dashed from his lips ere he had tasted the sweets it contained. But, as a man of honour, he was bound to give the Hon. Percy Cunninghame the satisfaction he required. Well, for Agnes's sake he would sacrifice his honour—that which hitherto he had held more sacred than life itself. Great, indeed, in this instance was the power of love.

Sitting down at a table, Lord Marchmont hastily scribbled half-a-dozen lines, informing his rival that, for certain reasons, he declined to meet him. He regretted, he said, that he could not afford him the satisfaction he required; but he did not consider that in these days a man was compelled to fight with lethal weapons whenever he was requested to do so by one who had his own private and particular reasons for desiring the death of another. This letter Lord Marchmont signed and sealed, and it was shortly delivered by his servant to Percy Cunninghame. Great was that gentleman's anger and surprise when he read the not very conciliatory contents of his lordship's letter. He even read it twice over before he could believe his eyes.

"Why he must be mad," he said. "That woman has turned his head. Marchmont always used to be considered the soul of honour. What can this mean?"

After a little reflection he could come to no other conclusion than that Lord Marchmont steadily and resolutely refused to meet him.

"Ah!" he muttered, with a bitter smile—"ah! he thinks

to escape me, does he, by this miserable subterfuge; but, by Heavens, I swear that if Agnes Leslie cannot be mine, she shall never be his. No; the thought itself is gall and wormwood to me."

The Hon. Percy Cunninghame considered carefully what would be the best course for him to pursue under the circumstances. An unexpected difficulty had arisen—one which, to tell the truth, he did not expect. For he considered Lord Marchmont a man of strictly honourable principles, and he never dreamt for a moment that he would refuse to meet him in fair and honourable combat. Such, however, had turned out to be the case, and it now behoved him to find some means of *compelling* his lordship to defend his honour. Would it not be best to insult him openly and publicly in so gross a manner that he could not help but resent it? Well, no. Perhaps it would be better were it done privately; and then the scandal would not be propagated by evil speakers and those who delight in canvassing the affairs of their neighbours.

Thinking thus, he left his hotel and walked towards the house occupied by Lord Marchmont. On his way, he purchased at a shop a heavy dog-whip, with which he intended to chastise the man who had refused to fight him.

It was a formidable-looking weapon, and one which, in good hands, would do considerable execution and inflict a great deal of suffering.

Percy Cunninghame, too, was a man "of his inches," as the saying goes, and a formidable antagonist in an encounter like the one he had proposed to himself.

Marchmont was, it is true, a strong man, and well put together; but his strength was inferior to that of Cunninghame and he would be but a child in his grasp.

Knocking at the door, he told the servant who answered the summons that he wished to see Lord Marchmont.

"What name, sir?" demanded the beplushed functionary.

"Tell your master a gentleman wishes to see him," was the reply.

"Beg pardon, sir. But master don't receive anonymous guests," said the servant.

The Hon. Percy Cunninghame bit his lip at this reply, and said, angrily, "If you don't take my message in to his lordship, I shall find a way to make you."

The servant opened his eyes at this threat, and took stock of the imperious visitor who used such peremptory language. Apparently the survey was one which convinced him that discretion was the better part of valour, for he instantly lowered his tone, and said—

"Beg pardon, sir, I'm sure, sir. Didn't mean no offence, sir; not at all, sir; oh, no, sir; by no means, sir."

"Don't stand chattering there like a magpie, my good man. Are you going to keep me waiting in the hall all night?" exclaimed Percy. "Be off with you at once, and tell your master that a gentleman wishes to see him."

The servant lost no time in obeying the commands that were given him.

When Lord Marchmont heard this message, he as it were intuitively guessed who his visitor was, and he said—

"Tell the gentleman that I am too much engaged at present to see anybody."

This, of course, was a transparent fiction, for his lordship was sitting over his wine after dinner, and leisurely picking the rich and ruby seeds out of a deliciously cool and fragrant pomegranate.

The servant went back with his message, which he repeated verbatim to Cunninghame, who, whilst a flush of anger mantled his classic brow, haughtily pushed the servant on one side, saying, "Out of my way, my good fellow," and walked in the direction the servant had just come from.

Stopping an instant and turning round, Cunninghame said, "Where is Lord Marchmont, what's-your-name?"

"My name, sir? yes, sir; John, sir. That's my name, sir. John, sir, at your service."

"Well, John, where is his lordship?"

"In the dining-room, sir. But, sir, don't go to him. He'll be the death of me; I'm sure he will. Don't go, sir; there's a good, real gentleman, sir. You is a real gentleman, sir, I know by the looks of you, and I do hope you will act as sich."

Percy Cunninghame unheedful of John's entreaties walked into the passage leading to the dining-room, much to John's disgust. In fact so much so, that that flabbergasted menial rushed forward and laid hold of Cunninghame's coat-tails, at which he pulled in so frantic a manner that the tails threatened to part company with the parent coat every minute.

A DEED OF VIOLENCE.

So sudden was the attack that the honourable gentleman's progress was arrested for a moment. John took advantage of the retrograde movement; and putting his feet against the wall, gave three or four prodigious jerks which would almost have sufficed to pull a man-of-war from her anchorage.

John had, however, acted rashly, without calculating the consequences of such a proceeding.

The coat happened to be made of the very best cloth, and it had been manufactured by a famous West-end tailor, so that it refused to come asunder in any one part. But the shock administered to the person of Mr. Cunninghame was so great that that gentleman swayed backwards and forwards for a moment like a poplar in a storm, and then fell heavily backwards, almost crushing the unhappy menial in his descent. As the Hon. Percy Cunninghame's somewhat corpulent body fell upon him, the luckless footman uttered a groan which would have moved a heart of stone, so intense and so profound was it; and no wonder, for it typified the departure on a sudden of all the breath his miserable carcase contained.

"Oh! oh!" gasped John, "get up. I didn't mean nothing. I wont do it agin. Get up. Oh! good lord, good lord!"

Cunninghame got up as soon as he was able, purple in the face with rage. Directly he had an opportunity, John did the same thing, and endeavoured to scamper away as fast as he could. But Percy was too quick for him. He resolved that he should not escape with impunity; so, raising his foot, he applied a kick to the man, which not only helped him considerably in his flight, but sent him spinning like a top along the passage.

Then, striding along, he saw through an open door the form of Lord Marchmont in an attitude of listening.

Entering the room, he exclaimed, "I hope I do not intrude. I wrote your lordship a letter which should have told you that I wished so see you."

"But I did not wish to see you, sir," replied his lordship.

"Can't help that," said the Hon. Percy, coolly; "I desired to see you, and here I am."

"Well, sir, now you are here, what do you wish to say?

I am perfectly willing to listen to you, although I must protest against the ungentlemanly way in which you have forced your way into my house."

"I cannot help your protests, my lord. If I have insulted you by so doing, it was your own fault; and most likely I shall insult you more seriously before I leave this room."

Lord Marchmont turned pale at these words, but he replied—

"To your business, sir; to your business."

"Very well; my business is soon explained."

"Good. Proceed, then."

"I am about to do so."

"I am listening."

"Your lordship, I am to understand, refuses to meet me."

"I do."

"This is your determination?"

"My reasons——"

"Never mind your reasons, my lord. Is that your determination?"

"It is."

"Then nothing remains but for me to take the law into my own hands," replied the Hon. Percy Cunninghame, who advanced to his lordship, and, before he could divine his intention, he placed his hand upon the collar of his coat, and grasped it firmly; then he drew the dog-whip from behind his own coat, where he had concealed it hitherto, and applied it vigorously to his lordship's person.

In vain Lord Marchmont struggled, in vain he shouted for assistance; a merciless shower of blows descended upon his devoted and ill-fated shoulders, and his rival did not discontinue the castigation until wearied by the length of its duration.

Then, flinging his lordship from him, like so much carrion, he exclaimed, "Digest that, my lord, in your leisure moments; and now refuse to meet me, if you dare!"

Lord Marchmont shrank cowering, like a whipped hound, into a corner of the room, and there gave vent to low moans of pain and cries of rage.

Suddenly springing up, he said, "Your life shall atone for this."

"Very well," replied the Hon. Percy Cunninghame; "that is right—that is what I wished. Let us then at once arrange the preliminaries of our little affair."

CHAPTER XXIX.

THE DUEL ON THE SANDS—NO SECONDS—THE TOLEDOS—FLOOD BAY—READY FOR ACTION—THE DUEL COMMENCES—THE HON. PERCY IS WOUNDED IN THE ARM—HIS REVENGE—HIS SWORD BREAKS—TREACHERY—A DISCOVERY—THE SUIT OF CHAIN MAIL.

THERE was a horribly fiendish and unnatural expression about the agonized countenance of Lord Marchmont, who had been goaded nearly to madness. The corners of his mouth twitched uneasily, his eyes rolled in their sockets, and he presented all the indications of a man about to have an epileptic fit. But by an effort, the cost of which was known only to himself, he advanced towards the table, and poured out a brimming glass of rich wine from one of the sumptuous decanters which garnished his profuse board.

The Hon. Percy Cunninghame leant with his back towards the mantelpiece, and leisurely took out his cigar-case.

Turning towards his lordship, he exclaimed, "I presume I have your lordship's permission to smoke?"

Lord Marchmont glared at him with the eye of a demon as he replied, "You have not hitherto thought proper to ask my permission as to what you shall do, so why begin the farce now?"

Cunninghame construed this into an affirmative reply, and lighted a cigar, at which he puffed contentedly, waiting for his lordship to commence a conversation which both felt must soon be begun.

They had all the preliminaries of their encounter to arrange. Where they should fight, what weapons they should use, and whether they should be supported by seconds or not.

At last, Lord Marchmont, having drank two tumblers of wine, was sufficiently himself to speak.

"You have this evening," he said, "insulted me so grossly, so unpardonably, that nothing but blood can wash out the stain you have inflicted upon my honour."

The Hon. Percy Cunninghame bowed, as though much pleased at this announcement.

"It follows, then, that we must fight."

"It does."

"Although I refused at first, I did so from no unworthy motive—from no feeling of fear or cowardice."

"I take your lordship's word for it."

"Let us then arrange," said Lord Marchmont.

"Yes; let us make our arrangements. Time presses."

"Shall we fight in the common way, with pistols?"

"There are four ways by which we can get through our little business," said the Hon. Percy.

"And they are——"

"They are, first, daggers; secondly, pistols; thirdly, swords; and fourthly, cudgels."

"Well!"

"Well, which of the four do you choose, my lord? You, as the challenged, have a right to choose your own weapons, as you are doubtless aware."

"In that case, as the choice devolves upon me, I should prefer swords."

"You have selected well. I should have chosen the same weapon. Pistols make a report which might draw attention to our movements."

"Yes, that was one reason. But I am a proficient at sword exercise. Angelo has not guided my arm, and imparted his skill to me all these years for nothing; and I give you fair warning that I am about to kill you. Yes, I feel that I must slay you. Both of us, after this night's work, cannot burden the same planet."

"We are in accord there, my lord," replied Cunninghame; "but as to your threat, why,"—here he smiled scornfully—"the fact is I have sworn to kill you, and I would recommend your lordship to make your will without further delay, as delays are dangerous in these cases."

"Permit me to give you the same advice," replied Lord Marchmont, with a scowl.

"A truce, my lord, a truce to these personalities. We have not yet settled whether we fight with or without seconds."

"With or without seconds?"

"Yes."

"Well, it is a little irregular to do so; but, as you seem to wish it——"

"Yes, I wish it; and for this reason—one of us must fall. Is it not so?"

"It is."

"Very well; it would be inconvenient to be arrested as your murderer——"

"Or myself as yours."

This was said with a short dry laugh, as if his lordship contemplated something serious to his adversary. Could it be that he meditated foul play?

"Certainly as mine. There is the chance, but it is a slender one. Well, do we fight with or without seconds?"

"Without be it."

"Then," continued Cunninghame, "comes the selection of the place to fight. We must have some quiet and secluded spot."

"Yes."

"Away from any dwelling-house or frequented path."

"Certainly."

"Let us, then, as I had the honour to suggest in my note—let us, then, fight upon the sands, before breakfast. It will, as I have ascertained, be low water to-morrow morning at half-past five; at six let us meet."

"I have no objection to make; it shall be as you say," replied Lord Marchmont, who seemed perfectly passive in his rival's hands. "What next?"

"The weapons."

"Ah! yes, the swords."

"I have a couple of Toledos here—as fine a pair of pinking irons as ever got forged; or there are some Damascus blades in that corner, together with the army regulation sword; or else I can supply you with the best Sheffield, our own English manufacture."

"You have quite an arsenal."

"Why, yes; it's a pretty good collection. Which will you have?"

"By all means, the Toledos."

"Yes, the Toledos; I am agreeable."

"We must not be seen leaving the town together," said Cunninghame. "That would arouse suspicion in the event of one of us being missed, as must be the case before ten o'clock to-morrow; for you will give me no quarter, and you have none to expect from me."

Lord Marchmont's lips broke into a ghastly grin at this.

"Well, if your lordship will be guided by me——"

"I will."

"I was going to observe, there is a place beneath the cliffs, after you leave Kemp Town, and pass the first village beyond Brighton."

"That will do. It matters not to me where we meet, so long as we do meet."

"Then, if your lordship will order your horse, and manage to bring these weapons with you, I will join you just through the village, and we can proceed together to the place under the cliffs that I have indicated."

"I will do so," replied his lordship.

Taking his hat, the Hon. Percy Cunninghame made a courteous sort of bow, and left the apartment.

John, as may be imagined, did not make his appearance; indeed, that ill-used menial was solacing himself below stairs with copious draughts of ginger brandy; which, although it burned his throat, warmed his stomach, which was somewhat in want of the generous liquid. Cunninghame let himself out, and went towards his hotel in great glee.

"Lord Marchmont," he said, "in spite of his braggadocio, shall fall by my hand to-morrow; and then, a dangerous rival out of my way, Agnes may, perhaps, consent to be mine. May! She shall, by Heaven! I am not the man to take a fellow creature's blood for nothing."

At an early hour the next morning two horsemen might have been perceived wending their way in the direction of Rottendean, a little way out of Brighton, towards the east.

They were not pursuing the same route, but it was easy to see that they would converge at one given spot.

The shades of night, which had hung like a pall over the landscape, had flitted to that nether sphere to which they belong; and the grey dawn of the morning had usurped their place.

The larks were rising towards heaven's gate, to utter their merry and soul-stirring carols. And it was on such a calm and placid morning as this, when the sun was rising from his bed of azure, that two human beings were about to strive to deprive one another of that existence which a beneficent Providence had given them.

At the appointed spot the rivals met. A brief salutation passed between them, and they dismounted from their steeds. As they did so, the clock of the little village church behind them struck the three-quarters past five.

They left their horses to graze upon the spare herbage which grew upon the cliff, having first of all raised the bridles, so as to take the bit out of their mouths.

Then, Lord Marchmont following his adversary, they descended the cliff by a little winding path, which, after a walk, or rather scramble, of a few minutes' duration, brought them to the beach.

Passing quickly over the shingles, they walked rapidly a short distance along the sands, until they arrived at a part of the cliff which at high water projected far into the sea, a little bay being formed on either side of it. Passing this peninsula, they stood in a quiet and sheltered bay, hidden by the cliffs from the prying eyes of fishermen or villagers; and here it was that the encounter was arranged to take place.

The bay was not of great extent, and there was never more than an hour of low water in it, as it stood so far out that the sea filled its tiny dimensions nearly two hours before it was high water on the beach by which they had arrived. The people called it Flood Bay.

Lord Marchmont drew the rapiers from the leathern sheaths in which he had carried them, and allowed them to rest on their handles on the sands, while their points touched the rock.

Both men eyed them with admiration. They were worthy of it, for they were magnificent swords.

"Now, my lord, to work," cried Cunninghame. "Time and tide will wait for no man."

Lord Marchmont nodded acquiescence, and proceeded to strip. This he did, until he stood in his shirt sleeves. He turned them up to the elbow, and tied his handkerchief round his waist; and, in order to have more elasticity and spring, he took off his boots, and stood upon the moist sand. The Hon. Percy followed his example in every respect, with equal rapidity, and then they stood face to face.

Each advanced and took a weapon. They measured six paces, and "presented."

Then the conflict was about to begin.

The spot they had selected was tolerably free from rocks or boulders, although towards the sea there were several masses of chalk, covered with parasitic sea-weed, which were also incrusted with mussels and all sorts of shell fish. Small crabs played at hide and seek in the little pools with which the immediate neighbourhood abounded.

The sun was hidden by the cliffs, and the combatants were not incommoded by its gleams.

Suddenly the blades flashed fire, as they clashed severely together, and the duel began.

Lord Marchmont contented himself at first with acting on the defensive; but, after a while—seeing, as he thought, some carelessness on the part of his adversary—he made a swift lunge in *carte*, which was beautifully parried in *tierce*.

The Hon. Percy Cunninghame, finding himself hard pressed, retreated a few yards; stubbornly contesting the ground, inch by inch and foot by foot.

While making these retrograde movements, he did not perceive a little piece of granite, firmly embedded in the sand; over this he stumbled, and, with the rapidity of lightning, Lord Marchmont's sword passed through his left arm. The blade was instantly withdrawn, and its holder endeavoured to wound his adversary mortally, by thrusting it through his lungs. But Cunninghame was too quick for him; he parried the thrust, and fought with such determined bravery, that Lord Marchmont was in his turn compelled to give way, and to lose all the ground he had gained.

The wound was not serious, although the blood trickled down in a small stream. It urged the Hon. Percy to greater exertion; because he knew if the duel continued a long time, he should fall a victim to his rival's rage through loss of blood; and then it was not difficult to guess the fate which was in store for him.

During the progress of the duel, the tide had, unnoticed by either of the combatants, made considerable way inland; and if the fight lasted much longer, they would, it seemed, have to fight with their ankles in water.

Cunninghame's wound began to smart, and he pressed his adversary more than ever; and at last, with one brilliant stroke, into which he threw his whole force, he dashed Lord Marchmont's sword from his hand, and sent it flying through the air, until it fell some distance off. Then, with a howl rather than a cry of triumph, he raised his sword, and lunged furiously, with the intention of passing it through his lordship's body. But what was his surprise—his blank amazement, I may say—when his sword broke like glass into a dozen pieces! Lord Marchmont staggered from the force of the blow, but did not fall.

The Hon. Percy Cunninghame stood confounded, and literally astounded at so extraordinary an occurrence. He had struck his lordship full in the breast; his sword should have passed through him—but there it was at his feet, broken in pieces, and his antagonist was unharmed and smiling grimly at him.

Lord Marchmont suddenly made a movement, as if he wished to repossess himself of his weapon; but Cunninghame sprang forward, and, striking him with his fist, dealt him a blow which sent him reeling to the ground like a stricken ox.

"Ha! Traitor! I will explain this mystery," cried Cunninghame, kneeling upon his lordship's breast, and, with both hands, eagerly tearing open his shirt. A sight he was not altogether unprepared for met his gaze. No wonder Lord Marchmont remained unharmed; no wonder the sword was smashed to atoms; no wonder the Hon. Percy was dumbfounded; for Lord Marchmont was encased in a suit of the finest Italian chain-mail!

CHAPTER XXX.

LORD MARCHMONT PREPARES FOR DEATH — HIS LIFE IS SPARED—THE DUEL IS RENEWED—FIGHTING IN THE WATER—THE TIDE RISES STILL HIGHER—LORD MARCHMONT STABS HIS ANTAGONIST TO THE HEART—DEATH OF THE HON. PERCY CUNNINGHAME—PRECAUTIONS—DRIVING THE HORSE OVER THE PRECIPICE—RETURN TO BRIGHTON.

GREAT indeed was the mortification of Lord Marchmont when he found his dishonourable intentions were discovered by his more chivalrous adversary; and his disappointment was more intense and more poignant, because his designs had not only been detected but frustrated, and that in the most complete manner.

He gnashed his teeth with rage, and glared defiance through his eyes. The fear of death was now before him: for, by every rule of the duello in every part of the civilized world, his dastard life was forfeit to his adversary; and could he hope for an instant that the Hon. Percy Cunninghame would grant him his existence—that existence which he had sworn in the most solemn manner to deprive him of? No! all hope of safety and deliverance, by aught but a miracle, was cut off; and Lord Marchmont trembled as he had never trembled in his life before. For Agnes Leslie he had sinned against honour and his fellow men; and now, his plans having failed, he was about to lose Agnes, and go down to his grave, a dishonoured and a disgraced man. And what a grave would be his!—a hole in the sands, where his body would be thrown, unlamented and unmourned—or, perhaps, even six feet of unconsecrated ground would be denied him, and his carcass would be carried out to sea for the element to sport with. These were the uncomfortable reflections which passed through Lord Marchmont's mind, as he lay on the sand of the seashore, encased in that fatal suit of Italian chain-mail, with Percy Cunninghame kneeling upon his breast.

The suit of mail was of the finest workmanship and the most delicate texture; and, rightly enough, his lordship had thought that in it he could defy the skill and the attacks of his adversary, who was now justly incensed against him for his perfidy.

"Lord Marchmont!" exclaimed Cunninghame, "your fate is in my hands, and I see no reason to spare your miserable life."

"I would give much to live," replied the peer; "but I would not beg my life at your hands."

"Your prayers would be useless, were you to do so."

"I know it, and I forbear."

"You do rightly; for you must die—I have sworn it. You stand in my way. Make your shrift, and be quick about it; for the sun is in the heavens, and the villagers will be soon astir."

"If I die," said Lord Marchmont, "you will have the satisfaction of knowing that you were my murderer."

"Murderer! what mean you?" replied Cunninghame, in unfeigned astonishment.

"I mean simply what I say."

"But how can that be, my lord? You are in my power, it is true; but you have, by the rules of duelling, forfeited your life to me; and if I take it, I do only what I have a perfect right to do."

"If you will take your hand from my throat, and your knee from my chest, I will explain my meaning to you," said Lord Marchmont.

Cunninghame complied with this request, and relaxed his hold, exclaiming, "What now, my lord? I give you three minutes to live, and if you choose to employ that brief space in talking to me, why, you can of course please yourself; but were I in your place——"

"Would to God you were!" cried Lord Marchmont, earnestly. "But, were you in my place, what would you do?"

"Oh! nothing. I was but thinking that death is usually associated with priests and prayers—but enough of that. How do you prove me your murderer?"

"If you kill me in single combat, fair and open, well and good; but when you stab me to the heart as I lay, why, after all, it is only a poor sort of cut-throat business—your tavern bully will do the same for five pounds."

"What would you say if I were to give you another chance for your life?" replied the Hon. Percy Cunninghame, who appeared to be somewhat moved by the arguments of the noble lord, who was to all appearances in a few moments doomed to die a cruel death.

"What should I say?" cried Lord Marchmont. "But, no—it is impossible! It is cruel, sir, to mock a dying man. Leave me to myself; I would meditate a moment ere I die."

"My lord, you are free to meditate; I would not interrupt you. A thought merely entered my mind that might have been worth your notice."

"And that was——"

"Only a passing thought, as I have said."

"Name it."

"I will. It occurred to me, that I might give you another chance; always provided you throw off that wretched affair that my sword broke against."

"By Heaven, this is generous!" said Lord Marchmont; "I did not expect this."

"Well, I am not a bravo, you see; I do not care about killing men in cold blood. Rise, my lord."

Lord Marchmont rose to his feet, and replied—

"Your generosity makes me regret that I ever was so infatuated as to wear it."

Cunninghame advanced to where his lordship's sword was lying; and, taking it up, broke it across his knee. Then he picked up the point of his own sword, and again broke Lord Marchmont's, until the two pieces were of the same size. Tossing one to his lordship, he said, "Take this, and follow my example." He then carefully wound his handkerchief round the blade, so as to make a dagger of it.

Lord Marchmont did the same, and they were again prepared for battle. Looking up, Cunninghame perceived that his adversary was still clothed in the obnoxious suit of mail. "How, my lord," he exclaimed, indignantly, "is not that garment thrown into the sea ere this?"

Lord Marchmont had now quite recovered his equanimity, and he smiled disdainfully.

"Off with it instantly," cried Cunninghame, forgetting that they were now on equal terms.

"I part not with it until the spirit departs from my body."

"Fool that I was!" cried Cunninghame. "I might have known that a cowardly wretch like the man before me was capable of any low and disreputable conduct. You refuse, then," he added, "to divest yourself of your mail shirt."

"I do."

"Your fate be on your own head, then," was the reply.

Lord Marchmont stood still, waiting to see the meaning of these words, which was soon apparent—rather sooner, in fact, than he wished.

Putting his hand in his pocket, the Hon. Percy Cunninghame drew out a very small pistol, of curious workmanship. You might almost have taken it for an exaggerated pencil-case. It nevertheless carried death in its diminutive discharge.

"It was fortunate for me that I had this with me," said Cunninghame. "Now, my lord, I am, as you know, a dead shot; and if you do not instantly take off that armour, the bullet contained in this pistol shall crash through your skull."

"Would you shoot me?"

"Would I? Yes, like a dog. Can you for a moment doubt it? What mercy do you deserve at my hands? Did I not extend my clemency to you, worthless wretch that you are? and how did you requite my kindness?"

Lord Marchmont saw that his adversary was in earnest, and he considered that his only chance was to comply with so reasonable a demand. Twice had his dishonourable proceedings been frustrated, and he was covered with shame and confusion. With a cry of rage, he tore off the suit of mail, and threw it into the sea, which was now rolling in rapidly, and washing their feet with its boisterous waves.

"That is right; now we are on equal terms once more. Now, my lord, look to yourself. Guard!"

The duel had assumed a new aspect, and the combatants fought as is the fashion in Italy when daggers are the weapons had recourse to. The left leg of each was advanced, and the foot of one touched that of the other. The body was slightly thrown forward, and each watched his opportunity to strike home.

It was painfully exciting, because the issue did not depend so much upon skill as upon agility and quickness. It was hard and laborious work too,—the sea came in so rapidly that it was already up to their ankles, and when one sprang back to avoid a blow, his movements were necessarily impeded by the water.

Lord Marchmont, as before, was successful in drawing the first blood, for his weapon descended upon his antagonist's shoulder. Fortunately for him, it was the left one, which was already stiff and painful from the former wound.

The Hon. Percy Cunninghame now regretted that he had given Lord Marchmont another chance, for his wounds pained him very much; in fact, so much so, that he became exasperated, and fought wildly, giving his opponent chances which, had he been skilful enough in the use of so crude a weapon to have taken advantage of, would have proved fatal.

Each was becoming a good deal distressed at the length of the combat, and it was clear that it would soon be decided, one way or the other. No one could, however, say who would be the successful combatant, so equally had it hitherto progressed.

Lord Marchmont had received a slight wound in the hand, which caused him some annoyance; but he fought with great resolution and determination—for he knew that, if again conquered, he must die.

Suddenly a huge wave dashed against them, and disturbed their equilibrium.

Cunninghame stumbled a little forward. Lord Marchmont took advantage of so excellent an opportunity, and dashed upon his adversary—bearing him down into the water, before he had time either to divine his intention or frustrate the attempt.

Raising his dagger high in the air, Lord Marchmont drove it to the hilt into his antagonist's back, between the shoulder blades.

Without a cry or an exclamation, the Hon. Percy Cunninghame fell prone upon his face, and instantaneously expired.

Again and again Lord Marchmont drove his weapon remorselessly into the body of the unfortunate man, in order to make sure of his death.

A purple stream flowed from the wounds, and mingled with the already ensanguined stream.

Lord Marchmont then dragged the body to the edge of the rocks, and seizing a huge piece of granite with both hands, he beat the face and head into a shapeless mass.

He then mutilated the body, and left it lying on the strand, as if to indicate that it had fallen there from the cliff above.

It was a horrible, a disgusting, an inhuman thing to do; but when a man once embarks in a career of crime he never knows where to stop, or what he will have to encounter. It was imperative that no suspicion should attach to him as the murderer of the luckless man, and what better could he do than what he had already done?

After this his lordship looked round, to see what else he could do in order to make his position more secure.

His adversary's clothes caught his eye in juxtaposition to his own. These he tore in several places, and then threw the body of the deceased into them as well as he could.

Naturally, after so great a fall, they would be torn and disordered.

Then he thought of his suit of mail; and, after a slight search, he found it, and rehabilitated himself in it.

Putting on his own wearing apparel, and carefully collecting all the tell-tale pieces of the broken weapons—which he made into a parcel, and took with him—he ascended the cliff, trying to look as if nothing had happened.

The morning was now getting on apace. It was near seven o'clock, but there was no one about in the place where they had left the horses.

This was fortunate.

When Lord Marchmont saw the horses, he cogitated for a moment, and then advanced towards the Hon. Percy Cunninghame's, and led it towards the precipice.

The animal neighed, and grew restive.

His lordship, in order to disarm its suspicions, and calm it, tied a bandage over its eyes, and then it walked docilely to the edge of the cliff, whither Lord Marchmont conducted it. Hitting it with the back of his hand, he forced it to advance, till the treacherous soil gave way beneath its feet, and the miserable creature fell heavily down, down, until it struck the flinty shore with a dull crash.

It was now imperatively necessary that his lordship should descend a second time to the shore, in order to take the bandage from the eyes of the horse.

He felt great repugnance to seeing his unhappy antagonist again; but he could not help it, and accordingly he went down the narrow winding path, and stood once more upon the shingles.

Here a shocking sight met his unflinching gaze. The horse was much disfigured and knocked about by so violent a fall, for the altitude was considerable; and, what was strange enough, the animal had fallen exactly on the top of its dead master, and the work of disfiguration which Lord Marchmont had so recklessly begun was effectually continued and finished by the horse.

Had Cunninghame been crushed in the folds of a huge python, or a still more formidable boa constrictor, he could not have been more mangled than he was at present.

Turning with an exclamation of disgust from the sickening spectacle, Lord Marchmont hurried again up the winding path, and breathed more freely when he stood once more upon the cliff. Mounting his horse, he rode rapidly back towards Brighton, and entered his house as if nothing had happened, and as if the terrible events of the morning were but a dream. Fortunately, John had descended into the butler's pantry when he had been so maltreated by the Hon. Percy Cunninghame. Therefore he was not a witness to the severe castigation that his lordship had received at the hands of the former. Neither was John aware of his visitor's name, as Cunninghame had refused to give it him. Had the events we have narrated occurred in a different manner, John would most likely have put this and that together, and have thought it rather extraordinary that his master should be horsewhipped by the Hon. Percy, and that the next morning his lordship should have been up unusually early, and that the body of Cunninghame should have been discovered smashed to pieces under the Rottendean cliffs. But John was only a simple domestic, and, instead of putting two and two together, he bowed to his master, and hoped he had had a good ride.

Lord Marchmont replied in the affirmative, and endeavoured to look as unconcerned as usual. In this he succeeded better than he had expected; and, after disposing of the relics of the combat in a secret cabinet in his study, he ordered breakfast, and thought of Agnes. A serious rival had been removed, and his lordship was master of the field. He had done a great deal for Agnes; and, surely, he deserved to possess her if ever man did. Thus he argued, and endeavoured to shut his eyes to the horrible fate of Cunninghame by saying to himself, "Had I not done so to him, he would, unquestionably, have done so to me. Where, then, is the sin or the harm?"

But dark care, nevertheless, spread her sable wings around him, and enveloped him in meshes he could not escape from.

CHAPTER XXXI.

LORD MARCHMONT OFFERS HIS HAND TO AGNES, AND IS ACCEPTED—HE PROVIDES HANDSOMELY FOR HER—THE AWFUL ACCIDENT—NO ONE SUSPECTS HIS LORDSHIP—BERNARD LESLIE ARRIVES FROM THE CONTINENT—THE MARRIAGE—AGNES BECOMES A BIGAMIST—TROUBLE LOOMS IN THE DISTANCE—LADY MARCHMONT.

DURING the whole of the day which followed the melancholy fate of the Hon. Percy Cunninghame, Lord Marchmont was tormented with doubts and fears.

During the course of the morning the body was discovered, and the news spread like wildfire through the town.

No one suspected the truth.

Every one thought that the horse had run away with the unhappy man, and had rushed blindly over the precipitous cliff.

Thanks to the precaution Lord Marchmont had taken, no one for a moment dreamt of a quarrel, and much less a duel.

His lordship went about as usual, and showed himself everywhere.

In those places where the fashionables of the day most did congregate, there was Lord Marchmont, affable and smiling.

He was playing a part, and we must do him the justice to say that he played it well.

He saw Agnes and Miss Lavinia during the course of his peregrinations, but he merely bowed and spoke a few words, directly afterwards passing on.

"I will not inflict myself upon her to-day," he thought; "it will be better not to. Let her, by all means, have a day to herself to think seriously over my proposition. Besides, the death of Cunninghame may shock her; so, altogether, I shall be doing well to leave her alone for four-and-twenty hours."

Accordingly he did so, and longed for the slow hours to fly quicker, in order that the morrow might come, and then he would know his fate. How his heart palpitated as he thought of the momentous day soon about to approach!—a day which to him was to be so full of interest. His anxiety was naturally great, and that, together with the violent and terrible scenes of the morning, made his cheek a little paler than ordinary, and his eye lacked its usual lustre.

Agnes and her aunt heard of the Hon. Percy Cunninghame's untimely death with the utmost astonishment and horror, and thought how desperately fleeting and precarious life was. They were far from guessing the truth. Agnes had, it is true, noticed that a few words passed between him and Lord Marchmont in the Pavilion Gardens, but she attached no significance to so trifling an incident. She had not even mentioned it to her aunt, and before morning it had faded away almost entirely from her mind. And she, in conjunction with Miss Lavinia, looked upon the young man's death as a melancholy and deplorable accident.

"Well, my child, all flesh is grass," observed Miss Lavinia, by way of commentary upon the circumstance; "and in time it becomes hay, as one may say, for the scythe of Time to mow down."

"Yes, aunt; alas! it is so," replied Agnes, whom the suddenness of the event had affected—not that she felt any tender feeling for the Hon. Percy Cunninghame, but no one can help being a little shocked when an intimate acquaintance comes to a dreadful end so very suddenly.

"Well, well, my dear Agnes, one must be practical, you know, and keep one's tears for one's own troubles," continued her aunt.

"Yes, that is all very well," replied Agnes, with a shake of the head.

"And you don't want a ghost to come from the grave to tell you that he is out of the question now."

"A ghost? oh, aunt! for Heaven's sake don't talk about ghosts! Something tells me that I shall soon encounter one."

"Don't talk such nonsense," said Miss Lavinia, with a sceptical smile, which, however, faded away when she thought of the little baby boy exposed on the wild bleak moor in the north of Scotland.

"I feel even now as if there was one in the room," continued Agnes.

"Be quiet, child! will you? you make one's flesh creep. What is the matter with you, all at once?"

"Oh! nothing. It is only a presentiment, I suppose. Mine is an eventful life, you know."

"Well, let us talk of something else, which will prove more agreeable to both of us."

"Talk of anything you like."

"You give me permission?"

"Perfect permission."

"What of Lord Marchmont, then?" asked her aunt.

"He has proposed to me."

"Proposed?"

"Yes; he made me an offer yesterday in the gardens, and I am to give him an answer to-morrow morning."

"What do you intend doing?"

"What shall I do?"

"You ask for my guidance?"

"I do. I put myself in your hands."

"Very well," replied her aunt; "in that case, accept him; you cannot do wrong. Your brother and myself will take care that he makes you a good settlement."

"It is agreed, then, that I accept him?"

"Certainly. And we shall soon see you a blushing bride," said Miss Lavinia, with a smile of satisfaction.

Had not Agnes's heart become very hard indeed, these words would have brought the tears to her eyes; but she was getting worldly, and she did not feel anything which recalled Marmaduke Wilson and her former happy life, brief though it was. Such are the effects of the lessons of the world—which are hard to learn, but of great use to those who have to fight with the world itself.

After breakfast the next morning Lord Marchmont, with his heart in his mouth as it were, called upon Agnes Leslie. He had sinned for this lovely woman; and now, was he to have her or not? That was the inquiry which he repeatedly addressed to himself. He thought that her compliance with his suit would be too much happiness. He was ushered into the drawing-room occupied by them at their hotel. Agnes was well and effectively dressed, and looked more charming than ever, at least his love-stricken lordship thought so.

Miss Lavinia was reading the paper as he entered. Agnes was engaged in arranging some specimens of sea-weed in an album.

After some unmeaning and conventional conversation about the weather, and a few words about the "late awful accident," which was in everybody's mouth, Miss Lavinia left the room, and the lovers—if lovers they could be called,

when only one of them was animated with the tender passion—were alone together.

An awkward pause ensued, which his lordship interrupted by saying, "Dear Miss Leslie, I have called to receive your answer."

"Really, Lord Marchmont," she replied, with a coquettish smile, "you have given me so little time."

Lord Marchmont looked imploringly at her.

"And it is such an important step to take."

"Did you not mention it to your aunt?"

"Yes, I did."

"And her reply was——Oh! for Heaven's sake let me know the worst at once."

"She left it entirely to me."

"Thank God!" burst from the lips of the enamoured nobleman.

"She said that I must follow the dictates of my own heart."

"And those are——"

"Why ask me?"

"I offer you my hand, Miss Leslie—Agnes; will you accept it?"

Lord Marchmont, like a bold gambler, staked all upon the issue.

"Accept you?" thought Agnes to herself; "why, of course I will." But she made no reply, and only hung down her head in a pretty feminine manner.

Lord Marchmont sprang forward, and seizing her hand in his, exclaimed, "Say yes, darling; say you will be mine."

Agnes faintly murmured the little monosyllable, and then hid her head upon his manly breast.

She little thought, however, that the hand which was pressing hers was even now red with the blood of Percy Cunninghame.

If she had done so, would she have cast him from her? I very much doubt it.

She was now a woman of the world; and the main chance, as it is called, alone engrossed her attention. Lord Marchmont was enraptured at her consent, and he pressed her fondly to his heart, imprinting kiss upon kiss upon her lovely and rosy lips. Agnes suffered his caresses passively, and appeared to be lost in the happiness of the moment.

In a few minutes, which appeared but seconds to his lordship, a very audible noise was made outside the door.

"Oh! leave me," cried Agnes; "here is my aunt."

Lord Marchmont took a chair, and sat by her side.

Miss Lavinia entered the room, and advancing towards them, exclaimed—

"You must pardon an old woman, you know, for intruding upon your secrets; but am I to congratulate you?"

"My dear madam," said Lord Marchmont, "you cannot congratulate me too much—I am the happiest of men."

"I am charmed to hear it, my lord. It is a great weight off my mind, I can assure you, to think that my dear Agnes is settled at last, and in so satisfactory a manner."

And the old hypocrite smiled benignantly, while two crocodile tears stood in her antiquated eyes.

Putting up her hands, she exclaimed, in a theatrical tone of voice, "Bless you, my children! bless you!" and ran from the room, as if overpowered by emotion.

It was arranged afterwards by Miss Lavinia and Bernard Leslie, who returned expressly from the continent on being telegraphed for, that the marriage should be celebrated in six weeks.

Lord Marchmont settled the handsome sum of seven thousand a-year upon his future wife, and, in addition to that, made her almost every day very handsome presents of jewellery, so that all parties were very well satisfied.

By a deed she entered into, Agnes agreed to give her brother, Bernard Leslie, two thousand five hundred a-year out of her settlement; and she also bound herself to allow Miss Lavinia two thousand annually, which left her two thousand five hundred for herself. But what did that matter to her? Her husband would pay everything for her, and that sum would be amply sufficient for her own private and pressing wants.

The day appointed for the marriage drew rapidly near, and Lord Marchmont was unremitting in his attentions; and when the actual time arrived, he seemed transported to the seventh heaven. And he told Agnes that in possessing her he would attain the pinnacle of his happiness.

They were married in great state and with much pomp, and Agnes Leslie, *alias* Wilson, became a *bigamist*.

Little did Lord Marchmont guess this when he fondly called her his own. His own, indeed! She was the wife of another, and that other was even now moving heaven and earth to effect a means of hunting her down, for what he considered her treachery to him.

Truly, Lord Marchmont had plunged deeply into the sea of trouble when he married Agnes Leslie. But she had achieved her object, and was now Lady Marchmont.

CHAPTER XXXII.

LORD MARCHMONT ASKS QUESTIONS—WHO IS MR. LESLIE? —MISS LAVINIA LETS THE CAT OUT OF THE BAG—HIS LORDSHIP SEIZES THE FELINE ANIMAL—INSPECTOR WYMAN AGAIN—THE FINSBURY FOX—THE SCENT LIES.

FOR a time all went merry as a marriage-bell with Lord and Lady Marchmont; but after his lordship's very ardent passion had cooled down a little, he began to descend from his hymeneal heaven, and think a little of sublunary matters.

He knew his wife's aunt, and he knew his wife's brother, but these were the only members of her family with whom he had the happiness to be acquainted. This was, he thought, rather an unsatisfactory state of things.

He had the presumption to suppose that he ought to know the whole family, and, in addition to this, he felt some curiosity to be informed as to his wife's antecedents.

Lord Marchmont, while indulging in these curious reflections, never for an instant loved his wife less than he did when he married her. In fact, his affection for her seemed to grow fonder and more enduring the longer he knew her; but he considered that he had a right to make certain inquiries, and he resolved to do so. Accordingly, one morning when an opportunity presented itself, he did so. Agnes had just returned from bathing.

They had spent their honeymoon abroad, much to their mutual enjoyment, and they had returned to Brighton, where they had resolved to pass the winter.

Agnes, always fond of salt water, went every morning, after breakfast, to the ladies' swimming bath, where she disported herself like an amateur mermaid until she was tired, and then returned to the arms of her expectant husband, who was in readiness to escort her to the pier or the Esplanade.

"My dear Agnes," he exclaimed, as she entered their sumptuously-furnished drawing-room, "I want to ask you a few questions."

"Well!" she replied.

"I am sure you will not be offended at the liberty I am taking; but now that you are my own little wife, you know I have a right to ask you what questions I like."

"I don't know about that," replied Agnes, a little suspiciously.

"Well, we will not argue the point as to whether I have or not. If I have the right, I will waive it, and only ask your permission, in the most submissive manner. Will you grant it?"

"Yes, certainly, if you are not too impertinent," replied Agnes.

"Very well. Shall I begin, then?" he said, looking a little timid.

"Yes," answered Agnes, wondering what made him look so sheepish.

"I think you said you had a father," began Lord Marchmont.

"Well, what if I did?"

"Oh! nothing."

"Nothing! Then why talk about it?"

"Only that I should like to know your paternal progenitor."

"Indeed!"

"Is he still alive?" queried Lord Marchmont.

This was a very difficult question for Agnes to answer; for she positively knew nothing about her father. It will be remembered that she had interrogated Bernard Leslie about him when they first met; but he had refused to tell her anything about him, except that he was alive. Agnes had often thought over the matter since then; and the only conclusion she could come to was, that there was a mystery somewhere. She had questioned Miss Lavinia on different occasions; but that virtuous and antiquated female had steadfastly declared that she was totally unacquainted with the facts she wished to elicit. She told her that she was entirely ignorant of all family matters; and if she wanted to be enlightened on any particular, the best thing she could do would be to address her inquiries to her brother Bernard.

"He will enlighten you, I have no doubt, my dear child," she said; "but, the fact is, I never mixed myself up with the affairs of the family, and, in consequence, I am the very worst person you could possibly come to for information. By all means, my dear, go to your brother Bernard, and I have no doubt whatever that he will give you every possible information that lays in his power."

Of course Agnes knew very well that exactly the reverse would be the case; because Bernard Leslie had on a previous occasion, as we have already stated, refused, in the most resolute manner, to give any information whatever respecting the matter.

Agnes, finding her inquiries had thus been stifled in their very conception, ceased in a great measure to occupy herself about them.

She could not, however, at times prevent herself from feeling a strange interest in this mysterious parent, whom all with whom she was acquainted took so much pains to conceal from her. Who was he?—what was he?—where did he live?—and why was she not allowed to see him? These and a hundred other questions perpetually forced themselve upon her mind, but she could offer no practicable solution to them.

And now, when her husband distinctly and plainly said to her "Where is your father?—why am I not introduced to him?" she felt herself decidedly in a dilemma. What should she do?—Invent some specious lie—some plausible excuse—or at once boldly tell him the truth—or at least let him have the truth with some slight modifications?

She thought the latter course would be the best. After a few moments' consideration, she came to this conclusion.

"You are a long time thinking over my question!" he said, a little petulantly; "one would think you were ashamed of your family!"

"Now, look here!" exclaimed Agnes, boldly; "dont you talk to me like that!"

"Why not?"

"I don't deserve it—and I wont have it!"

"I am very sorry if I have offended you," said Lord Marchmont, thinking he had gone a little too far.

"Perhaps there are things that you are ashamed of?" said Agnes, making a random remark.

"Things that I am ashamed of! What do you mean?" cried his lordship, thinking for the moment that she suspected some foul play with regard to Cunninghame.

"Oh! never mind what I mean; you will know soon enough—perhaps, sooner than you wish," answered Agnes, in that oracular way in which women sometimes talk when they wish to aggravate men, or when "a little bird has told them something."

Lord Marchmont turned pale at these words; but, after an instant's reflection, recovered his serenity. "It is impossible," he argued, "that she should be acquainted with facts that only I and a higher Power are cognisant of." Gathering a little courage from this reflection, he continued, "If you have any particular reason for disguising your family history from me, why, do so, in Heaven's name. I only thought that, as your husband, I had a right to put a few simple questions to you."

"As many as you like," replied Agnes, coolly.

"Oh! you have changed your mind, then?"

"I!—no, indeed. I have not changed my mind; why should I? I am quite ready and willing to tell you all about my family. You have only to question me, I will answer you faithfully, and to the best of my ability."

"Very well, then I will begin."

"Do so."

"You have a father?"

"Yes."

"Where is he?"

"I do not know."

"You do not know?"

"No."

"Are you serious?"

"Perfectly so."

"When did you see your father last?"

"I have never seen him that I recollect," replied Agnes,

innocently—looking her perplexed husband in the face unflinchingly.

"Never seen him!—Oh! this is absurd. I beg you, my dear Agnes, not to joke with me."

"What I am saying is the simple truth. My father may be alive, indeed; and I told you I have every reason to believe he is—but I have never seen him that I can recollect."

"Will you condescend to be a little more explanatory?" said Lord Marchmont, rather coldly.

"Oh! yes; I will tell you all I know, with pleasure."

"Do so."

"My mother died when I was very young," began Agnes. "In short, I do not remember her; I was taken away from home soon afterwards, and placed at a school, amongst strangers; and there I was kept and educated until a short time ago, when I made my entrance into polite society, under the auspices of my respected aunt—Miss Lavinia Leslie. Where my father is at this moment, I know no more than you do; and though I have often questioned my aunt and my brother about him, they would never give me a satisfactory answer. I am as curious as you are to know more about him; so you see I am not deceiving you in any way, as you may have supposed at first from my manner."

"I am convinced of that, darling," replied Lord Marchmont, kissing his lovely and interesting wife; "your manner is too genuine, too sterling, too good for me to suppose for a moment that you could be capable of deception."

Agnes smiled inwardly at this declaration. The fair adventuress knew very well that she could turn his susceptible lordship round her finger like a skein of silk; but it was her intention this time to be candid with him, and she had been so—to a certain extent.

Lord Marchmont religiously believed every word she had told him, and, after thinking for a little time, he exclaimed—

"What you have told me is very strange—very strange, indeed! I wish we could find out something more definite about your father, dear Agnes."

"I wish with all my heart we could," she replied; "but how is it to be done?"

"Well, it is not easy; but if we could only get a clue to his whereabouts at present, the rest would be easier."

"Yes; but this is the difficulty."

"I know it."

"Is it insurmountable?" asked Agnes.

"I think not," he replied. "But leave it to me, and I will endeavour to find a solution of this problem."

"My aunt may probably be more communicative to you than she has been to me," suggested Agnes.

"She may," replied Lord Marchmont, thoughtfully; "at all events I will try her. It will be as well to do so at once, perhaps. What do you think?"

"I quite agree with you. You know that whatever you do is right in my eyes. I can find no fault in you, my own darling!" cried Agnes, fixing her liquid eyes full upon him.

Lord Marchmont clasped his fascinating bride in his arms, and kissed her tenderly; while she, fair creature! made no objection to the osculatory process, but in the words of the old and time-honoured song, "She took it like a lamb."

Lord Marchmont soon afterwards sought Miss Lavinia Leslie, and questioned her as to the position and whereabouts of Agnes's father.

Miss Lavinia was somewhat astonished at first; and hemmed and coughed and looked at the ceiling, and then out of the window, and after that at the carpet—as is the fashion of people when they are perplexed. At last she said—

"The fact is, my lord, we never obtrude Mr. Bernard Leslie, senior, upon our friends, because he is a singular man; he loves retirement and solitude, and we have given it him in the wilds of Carnarvonshire."

"Carnarvon, did you say?" exclaimed Lord Marchmont, interrupting the garrulous old lady—who, for once, seemed to have overshot her mark.

"Did I say Carnarvon?" she stammered.

"You certainly did."

"Oh! it was a mistake then. I meant nothing—I was thinking of something else; you must make allowance for a lady of my age. Old people are sometimes a little inaccurate."

"Yes, they are!" replied his lordship—who was as clever as she was.

He had no doubt but that Mr. Leslie was living somewhere in Carnarvonshire, and he determined to find out where. He knew it would be worse than useless to question Miss Lavinia further on the subject; therefore he pretended to believe her rather lame exculpation—all the while chuckling in his sleeve at having mystified her so completely.

"All of us are a little shaky at times—even the best of us, Lord Marchmont," continued Miss Lavinia.

"Yes, indeed we are," replied his lordship, sympathetically. "Who should know that better than myself?"

"It is rather a sore subject with us," resumed Miss Lavinia—"this of Mr. Leslie; but he is living in the country with some friends, and he keeps himself very much secluded, as I before observed; indeed, he never sees strangers—he has such an antipathy to them. All his family regret his idiosyncrasy; but what can they do? You can bring a horse to the water, but you can't make him drink; and this is the case with poor dear Mr. Leslie—you can bring him into society by force of arms, but you cannot make him fraternize with the people you bring him in contact with."

"How very sad!" said Lord Marchmont.

Soon after this he took his leave, and returned to Agnes to report progress. When Agnes heard his tale, she said—

"You have done something, dear, more than I ever succeeded in doing; and perhaps we may do something with that limited information."

"In what way?"

"Well, it occurs to me that now we know—or, strictly speaking, have reason to believe—that he is living in the Welsh mountains (in Carnarvonshire), we have a clue to his domicile."

"We have, in a certain manner; but the clue is rather vague."

"Never mind that. We have one."

"Well, then. What ought we to do next?"

"Shall I tell you?"

"By all means. I have a great admiration for your clear wit."

"Then let that admiration be increased," she replied, "for I have an idea."

"What is it?"

"Find out a detective, by going to the proper place; and give him money, to induce him to go into Wales to make inquiries."

"Capital!" exclaimed Lord Marchmont; "you are quite a genius. It shall be done this very day. I will go up to town on purpose."

Lord Marchmont did as she proposed. He undertook a journey to Scotland-yard, and had an interview with our old friend Inspector Wyman, who, when he heard the case, said that he had no doubt he could find out some particulars, in a short time, which would be satisfactory to his lordship; but he added—

"I shall not go at first myself. I have a man here who is an adept in such cases. I generally employ him, and I never knew him fail when he had the slightest clue. If it was only as slight and as slender as that which conducted Queen Eleanor into the bower of Fair Rosamond, at Woodstock, he would follow it up with equal sagacity. He hasn't his equal in the force—that he hasn't. I'll back him, all the world over, against any half dozen others."

"What is his name?" inquired Lord Marchmont.

"We call him the Finsbury Fox, because his is the Finsbury district; and he is as cunning as any fox that ever killed a turkey."

"Can I see him?" asked Lord Marchmont.

"Certainly," replied Inspector Wyman. "If he is in the office he shall come up."

On his ringing a small bell a policeman entered, and Inspector Wyman spoke a few words to him. The policeman went away, and presently returned with another of his cloth, who was a somewhat remarkable individual to look at. He was short in stature—rather stout, with a rubicund nose—as if a little addicted to spirituous liquors. But perhaps his nose belied him. If so, his breath was equally culpable, because the aroma of gin was painfully evident throughout the

"SAVE ME! OH, SAVE ME! I SINK, I SINK!"

apartment. His nose was small and podgy, and his eyes resembled those of a ferret.

Inspector Wyman introduced him to his lordship, and said—

"Perhaps his lordship would go outside and talk to him for a few minutes, and then return to him."

This Lord Marchmont consented to do, and, together with the thief-taker, he descended the stairs, and stood in the hall, or ante-room, at Scotland-yard.

The Finsbury Fox walked steadily out of the room and across the road, and opened the door of a public-house which stood on one side of the archway which opens upon Whitehall.

As the Finsbury Fox held the door open, he beckoned his lordship to follow.

At first he felt indignant, but at last he thought that the man evidently did not know who he was, and very probably wanted a glass of ale; so he followed him.

When inside the public-house the Fox said—

"What'll yer 'ave."

"Anything you like," replied Lord Marchmont, considerably amused at the man's odd and quaint manner.

"That wont do," said the Fox; "put a name to it."

"Well, then, a glass of brandy."

"'O de wee,' I calls it; but never mind," replied the Fox, ordering the spirit, and a glass of gin for himself.

Afterwards Lord Marchmont talked to him, and found him a very intelligent man in his way, and told him thoroughly what he wanted done, and the Finsbury Fox undertook to do it.

Lord Marchmont then returned to the office, and gave Inspector Wyman a cheque for expenses which would be incurred, and left Scotland-yard, agreeing to call there again in a week, when he was promised news of the mysterious Mr. Leslie.

CHAPTER XXXIII.

PUFFIN ISLAND—THE RUINS OF THE OLD CASTLE—THE
FLIGHT OF STEPS—AGNES'S TERROR—THE WONDERFUL
RANGE OF SUBTERRANEAN CHAMBERS—A DARK
LANTERN—THE HIDDEN WELL—HOW LORD MARCH-
MONT WAS ROOTED TO THE SPOT WITH AMAZEMENT
WHEN HE OPENED THE IRON-BOUND DOOR.

IN a short time Lord Marchmont was gratified with the
receipt of the intelligence he so much wished for.

The Finsbury Fox, with that sagacity for which the astute
Inspector Wyman so much valued him, had made important
discoveries.

In the recesses of the Welsh Mountains he had searched,
and searched in vain, but he never allowed himself to be
beaten, or his settled purpose to be defeated.

He had travelled from Snowdon to Kader Idris without
discovering any tidings of him he sought. Then he had
crossed over from Bangor to the Isle of Anglesea by means
of the Menai Bridge, and whilst gazing up the Straits, he
had perceived an island.

There was, it is true, nothing extraordinary in the
appearance of an island in that particular spot, at that particular juncture. But its discovery suggested thoughts of a
peculiar nature to the Finsbury Fox. He argued, and very
justly, that the island might be inhabited, and then again,
it might not.

It was his business to determine the point. What else
had he travelled into Wales for?

Accordingly he made inquiries, and found that the country
people knew very little about the matter. He could only
ascertain that there were the ruins of a castle upon it, and
that it was believed that only an old man and his wife lived
there. No one else had ever been seen.

The island was called Puffin Island, from the quantity of
sea-birds, or puffins, that made it their home. It was the
property of a family called Leslie, who once owned a good
deal of land on either side the Straits, and it was thought
that the old man and his wife who lived there were former
servants of the family, and had, in their old age, been pen-
sioned off, and given the ruins of the castle to live in. They
had a boat, and they came occasionally to Beaumaris to
purchase little articles necessary for domestic use. But they
were not sociable, and never made any acquaintances.

Very few people ever went to the island, although sometimes
tourists and visitors, hearing of the ruins, would hire a boat
and sail over. When this happened, John Barr and his wife
Jane would show them over some of the most interesting
parts, and it was said that the old man seemed glad when
they took their departure.

The visitors occasionally declared that while on the island
they heard groans, or something resembling such human
utterances, and subterranean noises which startled them from
their propriety.

In short, the island bore a bad name, and was thought by
the superstitious people of the country side to be haunted.

This was a capital budget of news for the Fox to go back
with.

"I will not visit the place myself," he thought; "there's
no necessity for that. I have collected the information I
wished for, and now I will return to my employers. I am
convinced that on that desolate and sterile rock they will find
him they are seeking."

Returning to London, the Finsbury Fox had an interview
with Inspector Wyman, who instantly telegraphed for Lord
Marchmont.

When his lordship heard the narrative of the Finsbury
Fox, he felt convinced that he was now on the right track,
and rewarding the police liberally for the trouble they had
taken, and the sagacity they had shown, he hastened home
to his wife, and told her everything he had heard.

Agnes was strangely agitated at the news.

"I feel," she said, "that, as you surmise, my father is
dwelling upon that island. Whether of his own free will or
through compulsion I cannot, of course, determine, although
I very much fear the latter."

"I cannot help being of the same opinion," replied his
lordship. "I think that foul play has been exercised in this
case, and I have very little doubt that the unfortunate Mr.
Leslie is detained on Puffin Island against his will."

"Oh! my poor father!" cried Agnes, bursting into
tears.

"Your brother and your aunt must be at the bottom of
this iniquity, my dear Agnes."

"I fear so."

"Perhaps the old man stood in their way, and they
coveted his wealth, and with the hope of getting it, I daresay
that they gave out that he was insane, and, instead of con-
fining him in some private lunatic asylum, they confined
him in the ruins of the castle where no earthly being could
visit him—no one could speak to him or console him in his
misery—no one could comfort him, except the two wretches
called Barr, who are, of course, his gaolers."

"It must be so," answered Agnes. "Oh! what wickedness!"

"It is our duty, as these facts have so strangely come to
our knowledge, to do all we can to rescue him from the
clutches of these miscreants. What say you, will you
journey into Wales, and endeavour to effect the old man's
release from captivity?"

"Oh, yes, yes! A thousand times yes! With all my
heart."

"Very well, then. Let us arrange to go at once," replied
Lord Marchmont, who was pleased at the idea of an
adventure, for the time hung rather heavily upon his hands
since the death of Cunninghame, whose reproachful shade
seemed ever to flit before his astonished vision.

Lord and Lady Marchmont's preparations were soon
made, and a couple of days saw them on their way to
Wales.

They thought it better not to go to any large place where
numbers of people were constantly coming and going, as
their names would get into the newspapers, and people
would wonder what they were doing, and they wished to
keep their proceedings as secret as possible.

To effect this they went to a small village lying under the
brow of a great mountain which frowned upon the sea.
This mountain was nearly opposite Puffin Island, and would
be an excellent place to start from. The village was inhabited chiefly by fishermen, and at the only inn it possessed
Agnes and her husband put up.

The next morning they proceeded to the beach and hired
a boat. Lord Marchmont took a fowling-piece with him,
and said he was going to shoot puffins. He declined the
services of a sailor, and declared he would navigate the boat
himself.

It was a fine day, with a gentle breeze blowing, and the
adventurous couple took their seats in the boat, which was
pushed off by the attendant fishermen.

Lord Marchmont, when they got clear of the shore, found
little difficulty in stepping the mast, and soon their little bit
of canvas was fluttering to the breeze.

After a steady run of half-an-hour, during which, for the
sake of appearances, his lordship killed a few brace of puffins
and a cormorant or two, they drew near the island.

It was an uninviting spot to look at. There seemed to be
very little verdure about it, although what there was was
luxuriant enough.

It must have been a point of some strategic importance
in former times, when it was of consequence to command
the entrance to the Straits, which this effectually did.

The castle was evidently, from its remains, of great
strength when feudal lords and mailed warriors garrisoned
it. But now it was a shapeless mass of ruins. Here and
there a tower remained intact, and in one of these lived Mr.
and Mrs. Barr.

The island itself was not of great extent, and its surface
was uneven.

Looking out for a cove to run his little vessel into, Lord
Marchmont stood with the tiller in his hand directing the
course of the gallant little bark. By good fortune he discovered an inlet which proved to be exactly what he wanted,
and skilfully guiding it, the boat ran gently into the bay he
had detected, and rode calmly upon its placid surface.

Taking in his sail, Lord Marchmont stepped on shore, and
made the boat fast. Then he assisted Agnes to alight, and
together they proceeded to explore the unknown land.

Agnes felt her heart beat hurriedly as she put her foot
upon the rock where her father, like the great Napoleon,
had, in all probability, spent many years of his life, in a
wearisome and hopeless imprisonment.

"Now, my plan is this," exclaimed Lord Marchmont.
"Let us walk all round the island without discovering our
presence, if we can help it, to the Barrs."

"Yes."

"By that means we shall be able to reconnoitre and satisfy ourselves as to the likelihood of any one's being concealed here against his will."

"By all means," replied Agnes. "We have the best part of the day before us, and I do not think we have been observed as yet by the man and his wife."

"I agree with you," said Lord Marchmont. "You see, we approached the island from a direction totally different to one from which boats, I should think, usually come; and we have landed, if you have noticed it, upon a part of the rock in the rear of the ruins, which are, it appears to me, at the other extremity of the island."

Walking on without again speaking to one another, they managed to ascend the rocks that lay in their way, and rapidly neared the summit. Large flocks of puffins flew out of the rocks as they progressed, and countless nests were to be seen in the interstices of the stone. After some toil and trouble they reached the top of the rock which formed the island, and then they obtained a more correct idea of the situation and extent of the old castle.

It was of considerable extent, and must, in its time, as we have already said, have been a formidable stronghold, for its ruins were spread over a considerable space of ground. Ivy and other parasitical plants had not, as is usual with most ruins, been taught to climb over the walls and buttresses. A round tower, which looked something like a cross between a Martello Tower and the Eddystone lighthouse, was a prominent feature in the picture; from the top of this there issued a thin volume of smoke. Upon seeing this neither Lord Marchmont nor Agnes had the least doubt but that it was the one occupied by the Barrs, where Mr. Leslie was confined, if, indeed, he was upon the island at all, of which they had no direct and positive evidence or proof; and they could but of course conjecture.

Going down steps broken and hazardous one moment, ascending similar ones the next, walking upon crazy-looking ramparts, which offered but an insecure footing, they made their way. Moss had covered the stones here and there, and the sea air made it damp and slippery. Agnes would several times have fallen had it not been for the protecting hand of her husband. They were both much pleased with the novelty of everything around them, but their thoughts were engrossed with the importance and magnitude of the affair they had undertaken, and they did not allow themselves to waste much time in admiring the scenery, which on all sides of them was very beautiful.

The morning was clear and fresh, and the air so thin and easily penetrated, that the coast on either side of them was plainly visible. They could see inland for miles. Lord Marchmont repeatedly cautioned Agnes that she would fall if she did not take more care of herself; but notwithstanding his advice, she could not resist the temptation of looking occasionally around her to admire the many beauties which presented themselves. Whilst thus engaged, her foot slipped, and she fell a few yards from the top of a broken wall to the turf beneath. Laughing, she looked up, and Lord Marchmont was just about to jump down to assist her to her feet, when she exclaimed—

"Oh! I have made a discovery. There is a flight of steps here. I should never have seen it had I not fallen, they are so cleverly contrived."

Lord Marchmont joined his wife, and looked at the place she indicated.

In an angle of the wall he perceived an aperture, but no one would have noticed it had they not looked very closely, as the shadows thrown by surrounding blocks of buildings made it look so dark and funereal. Leading down somewhere or other from the aperture was, as Agnes had said, a flight of steps, damp, slimy, dungeon-looking steps, that struck a chill to your very marrow as you gazed on them.

"I wonder where they go to?" said Agnes, hardly able to repress a shudder.

Lord Marchmont gazed carefully at them, and replied—

"Most likely to some dungeon or other, many feet below the level of the sea. Are you courageous enough, do you think, to penetrate the Stygian gloom of the vaults with me?"

"With you I dare do anything," replied Agnes.

"In that case we will venture. Who knows but that we may make some discovery of an important nature?" exclaimed his lordship.

"How dark it will be, though."

"Do you think so?"

"How can it be otherwise?"

"Suppose I have a dark-lantern with me?"

"Have you, indeed?" cried Agnes, joyfully. "That was very thoughtful of you."

"Well, I hardly deserve the credit of it," replied Lord Marchmont. "It was the gift of the Finsbury Fox, the last time I had the pleasure of seeing that gifted individual. He told me that most likely it would be useful, and you see that he was right."

Ascending a few of the steps, Lord Marchmont, with the help of a match, lighted his lantern, and flashed its rays down into the depths below. As far as the gleam of light penetrated the steps continued. No bottom was revealed.

His lordship took his handkerchief from his pocket, and fastening one end round his wrist, he told Agnes to do the same, and then to follow him. This she did, and they commenced their perilous and venturesome descent.

Down, down, down, into the grave-like darkness of those gloomy vaults.

The staircase, or flight of steps, was neither spiral nor vertical, but it went in an oblique direction, so that they walked a long way without going any very great depth.

The steps were in better order than might have been expected, but the atmosphere was close and oppressive, like that of a charnel house.

Suddenly the light revealed a landing, and a few moments brought them to the end of the stone steps.

They stood still to reconnoitre.

The floor they were standing on was beautifully paved with Mosaic, after the most expensive fashion of the Romans. So exquisite was it, that you might have thought yourself among the ruins of Pompeii or Herculaneum.

The light of the lantern showed them a vast expanse supported by pillars of stone. It seemed to be a series of vaults stretching far away on every side.

The limited light they had with them could of course only show them a small part of the immense series of subterranean chambers they were in.

After a little conversation it was arranged that they should explore the strange place they found themselves in, but after going a little way, Agnes felt so horribly alarmed that she expressed her unwillingness to go any further.

Yielding to her solicitations, his lordship retraced his steps, and saw her once more to the light of day.

Agnes thanked him for his kindness, and said that she would run to the boat and prepare the slight repast they had brought with them.

Lord Marchmont made no objection to this arrangement, and promised to join her in the boat at the expiration of from an hour to an hour and a half; and imprinting a kiss upon her lips, he again ventured into the Tartarean blackness of those strange old-fashioned vaults.

Skirting the wall, and flashing his lantern continually before him, Lord Marchmont walked carefully onwards. He calculated that he must be nearing the base of the tower, which he had determined from the smoke he saw, that the Barrs inhabited. He was surprised as he advanced, to see that the stones were all wet and damp, as if they had recently been washed in a shower.

Quitting the sheltering guidance of the wall, his lordship ventured amongst the innumerable pillars that supported the roof, and glided from one to the other, endeavouring to discover some limit to the huge chamber whose depths he was exploring.

At last, a light glimmered far away in the distance. Towards this he made his way. It led him to a mass of brickwork, which had been thrown down either by decay or from other natural causes. Passing over these ruins as well as he could, he approached what appeared to be the solid rock.

The light came through a large hole in this wall of rock, which seemed like a breach made by cannon during some bombardment.

The noise of the sea was distinctly audible as it dashed against the base of the fortress, and a strange unearthly sound it made as it beat against the rocks; for the echo of every wave reverberated through the caverns with a noise like distant thunder. Turning away from this sort of window, Lord Marchmont retraced his steps, and as he was making the circuit of the vault, he came upon another flight of steps. These he ascended without hesitation, although he preserved his footing with difficulty, so wet and treacherous were they.

Upon these steps he perceived, for the first time, some common shell-fish — such as mussels, and those other molluscs that attach themselves to anything submarine—as he got up higher, however, the steps became drier and the footing less precarious. After going up some forty or fifty steps, his lordship came upon an iron door, which apparently barred his further progress. He was about to turn back in despair, so formidable did it look, when he thought of the simple process of giving it a kick. This he did with a will, not because he had any strong conviction that it would open it, but he thought that he would have his revenge upon the inanimate wood, as if it had been a living creature. To his amazement the door creaked—another blow forced it open about an inch—and repeated efforts succeeded in opening it sufficiently to allow a human body to pass through the doorway. It had evidently been unlocked since the lords of the castle had ceased to dwell in their baronial hall.

Lord Marchmont found himself, after passing this door, in a narrow passage, the roof of which gradually narrowed, until it was so low that he had to bend his body, in order to get along with any degree of comfort.

After walking a little distance, the passage widened, and, at length, branched off into two—which to take was now the question. In order to decide this weighty point, his lordship performed an operation which street-boys denominated as "skying a copper." He tossed up a half-crown he had in his pocket, and the result was in favour of the right hand. He was very careful to keep the bull's-eye of his lantern wandering about every part of the passages he traversed; and it was, indeed, fortunate for him that he did so in this instance, as by so doing he escaped a terrible danger. With a cry of horror he suddenly sprang back, for before him lay a yawning gulf, such as tyrants used to make in the more private portions of their castles.

They were generally constructed very skilfully, and placed, like this one, in the centre of a passage, through which the unhappy victim was told to pass. Unsuspecting any plot, he would walk on innocently, until he found himself falling down an endless well, in whose murky waters he was soon stifled. This would have been Lord Marchmont's fate had not his lantern providentially saved him.

Leaving the black and treacherous-looking pit, he retraced his steps; but the sweat started from every pore in his body, and his knees trembled and knocked together. Taking a flask of brandy from his pocket, he drank a deep draught, which restored his shaken nerves. He hesitated when he returned, as to whether he should go back altogether or follow up the other passage.

Agnes would be anxiously expecting him, for he had already exceeded his time of an hour and a half. But as he had gone so far, he thought he would go a little farther. Accordingly he did so; and followed the other passage still more carefully than he had done the former. This was of considerable length, and stopped at a sort of gateway.

In the lock, which was massive and ponderous, Lord Marchmont, to his surprise and delight, perceived a key.

It was old and rusty from time, and a long period of inaction and disuse; so that when he endeavoured to turn it, he experienced no little difficulty. At last, a vigorous wrench made it creak—another moved it—and a third turned it quite round. Then seizing the heavy iron handle, Lord Marchmont pulled with all his might, but the door refused to move. Repeated pulls, however, caused it to oscillate, and, at length, it opened outwards a little.

It was strange, though, that as it moved, a noise of paper or of tapestry being wrenched violently from its hanging-place was heard. But the mystery was fully explained when the door flew open with a jerk, dragging a mass of old time-worn tapestry with it. A flood of light, too, burst upon his lordship, who, gazing through the open doorway, was astounded at the spectacle which met his view.

He had had some remarkable adventures in his life, but this one in the subterranean chambers of the old castle on Puffin Island promised to be the most unheard of. Standing with his eyes wide open, and every lineament of his countenance stamped with the indications of great and irresistible astonishment, Lord Marchmont stood as if rooted to the spot.

CHAPTER XXXIV.

THE OCTAGON ROOM—THE EXTRAORDINARY DISCOVERY OF EIGHT HUMAN SKELETONS STANDING ON AS MANY PEDESTALS—MR. LESLIE IS FOUND AT LAST—HIS SAD STORY—THEY ESCAPE—THE TIDE RISES—MIGHTY RUSHING WATERS—SAVED ONLY TO DIE—MR. LESLIE IS DROWNED—LORD MARCHMONT REACHES THE OPEN AIR, BUT AGNES IS NOWHERE TO BE FOUND.

THE room into which Lord Marchmont had so unceremoniously obtruded himself was of a singular shape. It was what in the language of architecture is denominated an octagon; that is, it had eight sides to it. The roof was vaulted and handsomely embellished with fantastic paintings, chiefly illustrative of monkish superstitions. The wrestling of certain celebrated saints with the devil was a favourite theme for painters and poets in the middle ages, and it was plentifully illustrated here.

The furniture was of old, heavy-looking, elaborately carved oak, the floor was also of polished oak, and the walls were tapestried.

But what caused the intense astonishment, not to say horror, of Lord Marchmont was that in each corner of the oddly-shaped room, standing on a pedestal, was a ghastly-looking grinning skeleton, held together in some cunning manner. These dreadful evidences of decayed and defunct humanity were arranged in the most terror-striking manner.

At each corner of the octagon room was a skeleton. The eyes of the beholder only quitted one of these dreadful objects to encounter another. A lamp suspended by a chain from the centre of the ceiling shed a brilliant light over the room.

After gazing at the eight skeletons until the fascination such a strange sight at first exercised over him had passed away, Lord Marchmont turned his eyes towards the middle of the apartment. Here another surprise, but one he was more prepared for, met his view.

Standing in an attitude of surprise and expectation was an old man. To be more correct, he appeared to have become prematurely old through some severe suffering; his hair was long like that of a hermit, and his beard reached to his waist, its colour, we need hardly say, was silvery. There was a fine expression about this old man's face—an expression which reminded Lord Marchmont of Agnes. Could this man, clad in those loose flowing robes of serge, be his wife's father? He would soon put the matter beyond doubt. Advancing into the apartment, he bowed. The old man cautiously, though rather stiffly, returned his salutation.

Taking off his hat, Lord Marchmont said,

"Have I the pleasure of addressing Mr. Leslie?"

"Leslie—Leslie!" repeated the old man, as if trying to recal some old familiar, but now long forgotten name. "Ay! It was Leslie, if I mistake not."

"In that case, I am happy in the reflection that I have succeeded in the object of my search."

The old man looked at Lord Marchmont, and motioning to him to be seated, he said—

"You mean me no harm?"

"I would free you," replied his lordship.

A smile of incredulity flitted across the old man's countenance, as he said—

"For years I have been shut up here, by the wickedness, I have reason to believe, of a son, and now release comes almost too late."

Shaking his head mournfully, the old man, whom we must in future call Mr. Leslie, relapsed into silence.

By dint of questioning, Lord Marchmont elicited from him that he had about fifteen years ago been seized and shut up in the ruined castle on Puffin Island. He had never from that day seen the light. They had placed him amongst the skeletons in order to drive him mad; and they constantly placed loaded pistols about his rooms, so that he might destroy his life if he felt tired of it, but he had always seen their purpose, and refused to do so. The Barrs brought him his food every day, which was plain but ample. He had books allowed him to beguile his leisure moments, but they seemed to have been selected on account of the horrors they contained. Everything which could deprive him of his senses was studiously resorted to.

Lord Marchmont proposed to the captive that they should retreat through the vaults he had entered a few hours before.

After some persuasion, Mr. Leslie agreed to the proposition; and casting what seemed a look of affection upon his old abode, followed his deliverer.

The interview was necessarily brief, because time was precious, and Lord Marchmont wished to bring her father to Agnes with as little delay as was possible under the circumstances. To tell the truth, his brain was somewhat in a whirl, owing to the marvellous incidents that had befallen him since he left the coast of Carnarvon in the small lugger he had that morning navigated across the Straits.

Following closely on his lordship's heels, Mr. Leslie left his dungeon, passively as a child obeying the orders of his schoolmaster.

He was not exactly in his dotage, but long captivity and brooding over revenge had softened his brain, and the man of once vigorous mind and body was now sadly changed. It was strange to think that this decrepit old man had once been one of the stars of fashion—the agent through whose instrumentality the ill-fated mother of Miriam Moss came to such an untimely end. But so it was.

When they reached the top of the flight of steps descending to the vaults, the old man clutched Lord Marchmont's arm, and exclaimed—

"D'ye hear it?"

"Hear what?" asked his lordship.

"The noise of the wavelets leaping," answered the old man.

Lord Marchmont smiled, as if he thought the old man was not, as the saying is, "quite right in his upper story," and began the descent.

But Mr. Leslie muttered to himself, "He may smile, but I have heard it oft in my chamber, and I know what it means."

The old man's hearing had, as is often the case, become almost preternaturally acute, and he heard what Lord Marchmont's grosser tympanums were not penetrated with.

When they reached the bottom, Lord Marchmont was surprised to find a considerable body of water in the vaults.

It was up to his ankles, and it increased as he proceeded. He thought of turning back, but he considered that they were not far off the steps which led to the upper regions, and as he went boldly onward, the old man clung to him like an infant, and passively allowed himself to be guided anywhere.

Now Lord Marchmont heard, indistinctly at first, but every moment louder and louder, the sound which Mr. Leslie had spoken of as the wavelets leaping. With a harsh, grating noise, water seemed to be entering the caverns somewhere. He was nearly up to his knees now, and moved with difficulty; his lantern showed him nothing but water on every side. Still the noise of mighty, rushing waters increased, and a petrifying conviction broke upon Lord Marchmont.

The tide was rising, and by some means it was entering the vaults; how did not matter; the fact was sufficient. If so, he had conducted himself and the unhappy Mr. Leslie to certain death, without a miracle intervened to save them.

The mystery of the damp cellar was now explained.

It was low water when he first descended the flight of steps, but during the hours he had been engaged in making his explorations, the tide had risen, and flowed into the caverns, as was its wont, through some hidden channel, most likely through the species of window in the solid rock that he had discovered.

The old man trembled in every limb. The danger—the novelty of the scene—the agitation of the last hour, and the coldness of the waves, which rippled around him, to which he was unaccustomed, all combined to frighten the few wits he had left completely out of him.

Lord Marchmont pushed forward manfully, but he could not disguise the truth from his own mind. They were in imminent peril, and he felt much alarmed.

The water was rising with frightful rapidity, and a steady current kept on drifting past them.

At times the force of this current, as some huge wave was precipitated into the vaults, very nearly took them off their legs.

Suddenly the rays of the lantern revealed the wished-for steps, a little distance off.

Lord Marchmont shouted words of encouragement to his companion, and pressed on.

Just as he was about to congratulate himself upon having reached the wished-for goal, the harbour of refuge, a sudden movement of the water dashed them asunder, and with a mutual cry of despair they felt themselves separated.

The shock threw Lord Marchmont towards the steps, upon which he raised himself, and gazed round him in a vain and fruitless search for Mr. Leslie.

His lantern had been extinguished, and nothing now remained to enable him to perceive the position of anything.

It was undoubtedly a matter of congratulation that he had reached the steps in safety.

As he sat on the cold stone, straining his eyes in his efforts to pierce the darkness, a startling cry burst upon his ear.

It was an appeal for help from the old man, whom Lord Marchmont had brought out of his dungeon to perish.

Another and another followed in quick succession, and then for a time all was still.

Then his lordship shouted with all his might, in order that Mr. Leslie might discover the proper direction to walk in; but for some time nothing save his own voice awoke the echoes of the cavern.

But after that sad and solemn pause a loud cry broke through the murky darkness. Far—far off in the distance it sounded, as of some soul in its death agony, and again all was still.

It would have been madness for Lord Marchmont to have attempted to follow Mr. Leslie. In the darkness he would soon have lost his way, and then he would have met the same fate.

It was an accident. It was the old man's fate; and dreadful though it was, Lord Marchmont consoled himself with the reflection that to die at once was better than living in the misery to which he had been condemned for some years past.

But how could he meet Agnes without her father? He was her father's guardian, and he could not give a good account for him. Would she not load him with reproaches, and overwhelm him with her great indignation?—doubtlessly she would do so.

But he shrugged his shoulders, and reflected that he had done his best, and could do no more; and with a sigh he sat down, and waited a little while, to see if there was any chance of his being of any use to the old man.

But that, alas! was now too late to dream of.

Mr. Leslie had been carried away by the water, and speedily suffocated in its death-giving embrace.

At first he had endeavoured to find his way, and had wandered hither and thither, up to his waist in water. But at last a wave knocked him against one of the stone pillars already alluded to, and stunned by the blow, he had sunk to rise no more.

Hastening up the steps, Lord Marchmont thanked his stars for escaping with a whole skin from all the dangers of the day.

When he arrived at the top, he stood still for a moment, and with undisguised satisfaction inhaled the fresh air.

Then he hastened down to the beach, where he had appointed to meet Agnes.

The shades of night were gathering fast, and if they were to return to shore that night they had not much time to lose.

Lord Marchmont wondered whether Agnes would not be terrified out or her wits at his prolonged absence.

Cogitating thus he approached the spot where he had moored his boat.

Yes. There it was, safe enough.

"Agnes, dear Agnes," exclaimed his lordship.

But there was no response to his exclamation, and to his consternation Lord Marchmont found that Agnes was nowhere to be seen.

CHAPTER XXXV.

LORD MARCHMONT CONCLUDES THAT AGNES HAS BEEN CONVEYED INTO THE TOWER—HE ENTERS IT AND MAKES A SEARCH, AT LAST FINDING AGNES BOUND AND GAGGED—THE TERRIBLE SHRIEK—THE MYSTERIES OF THIS "DEVIL'S NEST"—THE FATE OF THE BARRS—AGNES AND HER HUSBAND RETURN TO THE MAINLAND.

LORD MARCHMONT stared around him in utter perplexity. He called his wife, at first gently, and then in a louder tone; but his earnest inquiries met with no response.

At last he was compelled to come to the unwelcome conclusion that Agnes had disappeared. Whether she had been spirited away or not, by some extraordinary means, was more than he could say. He had appointed to meet her at the boat, and on his return to the trysting-place she was not there.

It was a melancholy fact for a fond husband to brood over, but there was no escape from it. It certainly seemed as if she were still on the island, because the boat had remained. In fact, had that not been where he left it, he would have thought that very likely she had sailed over to the mainland to get some assistance for himself, for she was justified in thinking that he had come to some great danger.

It occurred to him also that she might have descended by herself into those gloomy vaults to look for him. If so, he had seen the last of the lovely Agnes.

It would have been madness to have entertained such a thought long, so he dismissed it from his mind. He would not—could not—bring himself to believe that aught had happened to his peerless bride.

"Perhaps," he thought, "she has been taken off the island by some pleasure-seekers, and awaits my coming at our inn. Pray Heaven it may be so."

Suddenly his face darkened, as a new idea entered his mind. It was more than possible that she was still on the island. Suppose that the Barrs had discovered her, might they not for some purpose of their own have made her their prisoner?

The conviction grew upon him until Lord Marchmont could not throw it off. He had been about to hoist the sail and leave the island, but now he resolved, like a knight of old time, to rescue his lady-love or die.

With this resolve firmly embedded in his mind, he walked towards the tower which he considered the one most likely to be inhabited by the Barrs.

He had to walk carefully, for it was growing dark, and he did not reach the doorway leading to the tower without many a tumble, rather more injurious to his person than pleasant. At last he stood before a door leading into what was once the keep of the ancient castle. The door was locked; he tried to open it, but without success. He then seized a stone and beat against its oaken sides with considerable force.

No response followed!

A dull, half-smothered sort of echo alone answered his impetuous summons.

Again and again he struck the door. At last he desisted in his efforts from sheer fatigue. He looked at the impediment to his progress. It was of great strength, and evidently the tower was impregnable to brute force.

He must employ a stratagem!

Walking round the tower he came at last to a window. By looking through this he could perceive a light burning on a table in the centre of the room, which was handsomely furnished in the mediæval style, somewhat resembling Mr. Leslie's skeleton chamber, although those hideous adornments were happily absent. This window, as he might have expected, was fastened. But the stone which had proved useless against the door was available here, for three or four blows sufficed to batter down a large piece of glass. This revealed an aperture sufficiently large for his body to pass through.

Losing no time, he entered the apartment. His surprise was great to perceive it empty.

Not a soul disputed his entrance. Like Robinson Crusoe, he was monarch of all he surveyed; but unlike that unfortunate mariner, he was rather glad to have the coast clear and all to himself.

Whilst looking around him he saw a handkerchief lying on the floor. Stooping down he picked it up. He at once recognised it! It belonged to Agnes!

There was now no doubt that Agnes was in the castle, perhaps a prisoner in the hands of the Barrs!

This reflection spurred Lord Marchmont to greater exertion. These wretches might even now be murdering her for the sake of the few trinkets she possessed!

Seizing the candle in his hand, he rushed from the apartment by a door which led to a winding staircase. This he ascended for some time. It eventually led him into a large chamber. At first the light from his candle did not penetrate far, but, after a while, when his eyes became accustomed to the semi-darkness, and the candlelight penetrated a little

further, he saw something lying in a corner which arrested his attention.

Going towards it he perceived that it was a woman!

Setting the light on the ground, he proceeded to examine. With a cry of rage and alarm he recognised his wife!

He uttered her name but received no reply!

"Good God! can she be dead?" he exclaimed, in the bitterest grief.

The cause of her silence was, however, soon apparent. A gag of considerable dimensions had been stuffed into her pretty mouth, and thus compelled her, much against her will, to remain dumb. Lord Marchmont speedily released Agnes from her uncomfortable position. He had, however, a great deal more to do, for hand and foot she was heavily loaded with chains, as if she had been a malefactor of the deepest dye. These were not locked or fastened, but wound round her limbs in an ingenious manner. One by one he took them off, and threw them, with a curse, to the other end of the apartment, where they fell with an ominous clanking noise.

"Now, my dear Agnes," he cried, clasping her in his arms, "explain this mystery to me; I am dying to learn your adventures."

"I am so glad you have come," she replied, with tears of joy in her eyes. "You have only arrived just in time, for these wretches would have returned to murder me in a short time. They went, as I understood from their conversation, to look after some captive, whom they hold in durance here."

"Indeed."

"Yes. But the way in which I came hither was this. You left me alone, and I returned to the boat; after waiting a little time I fell asleep, as I felt fatigued. Suddenly I felt myself seized, my arms were rapidly bound, and I saw I was in the power of an old man and woman. These were, I conjectured, Mr. and Mrs. Barr. 'You would not murder me,' I said.

"They gave me no answer, but only grinned from ear to ear at my evident distress.

"I was dragged along to the tower in which we now are, and placed in this room, gagged and chained as you saw me. I expect the return of those miscreants every instant, and then you must look to yourself; they are not over scrupulous."

"Never fear," replied Lord Marchmont; "I am a match for an old man and woman, I hope, any day in the year."

As he spoke, a sound of horrible import burst upon their ears. A terrible shriek, speaking volumes of death and doom and frightful accidents, reverberated through the time-honoured walls of the old tower: again and again it was heard, each time fainter and fainter, and then all was still. It froze the blood in their veins to hear it.

"Oh!" cried Agnes, "what dreadful cry is that?"

"Follow me," cried Lord Marchmont, in a frenzy of excitement; "I will soon unravel the mysteries of this devil's nest."

"Oh, be careful. It may be a plot for our destruction," said Agnes.

But his lordship was deaf to her entreaties. Onward he rushed, blind to danger. Down the winding staircase, through the large room on the ground floor of the tower, through a passage which led him into the dungeon formerly occupied by Mr. Leslie.

Agnes followed him as far as this, but when she beheld the ghastly ornaments of the chamber, her overtasked nerves failed her, and she fell insensible at the foot of one of the skeletons.

In her fall she struck the pedestal upon which it stood. The horrible thing oscillated a moment backwards and forwards, and at last fell with a crash upon the inanimate body of the girl.

Fortunate was it for Agnes that she was in a swoon, for she would have surely gone crazy had she known that she was lying on the ground amidst the dust, and bones, and fragments of a skeleton.

Lord Marchmont ran on till he reached the place where the two passages met where he had hesitated that morning in his search for Mr. Leslie. Holding the candle before him, he advanced steadily towards the well.

A horrible suspicion took possession of him!

The Barrs must have discovered the escape of their prisoner, and have rushed in blind fury after him. Of course they knew nothing about the passages and vaults, and they went blindly to their fate.

As he approached the well he heard a subdued groan which seemed to issue from the bowels of the earth. He listened again, but no other sound greeted his expectant senses.

This was then the explanation of the mystery.

The Barrs had fallen down the well, and were now stifling in its fetid waters!

He felt himself powerless to help them, and with a saddened air he returned to see what had become of Agnes. He was horror-struck to perceive her lying amongst the broken pieces of one of the skeletons. Lifting her in his arms he carried her into the ground-floor apartment of the tower, and then administered restoratives which brought her once more to herself. He explained what he had seen to Agnes.

"Horrible!" she exclaimed; "but it is a just punishment for their crimes."

"Shall we venture across the straits to-night, dear Agnes?" asked Lord Marchmont.

"Oh, yes."

"It is dark, and the navigation is somewhat dangerous."

"I would brave anything rather than remain here," she replied.

Lord Marchmont seeing his wife's repugnance to passing a night on the island, agreed to cross over to the shore.

They soon contrived to get their boat clear, and were in a short time paddling across, for wind there was none.

When they were fairly started Agnes exclaimed—

"Well, what of my father?"

Lord Marchmont averted his eyes, and prepared for a trying conversation.

"I discovered your father, Agnes," he began.

"Alive?" she asked.

He was compelled to acknowledge that such was the case.

"And did you tell him that his daughter was waiting to receive him with open arms?"

"I did not, for I had not sufficient time to do so."

"Where is he now?"

"He is dead," replied her husband, solemnly.

Agnes buried her face in her hands, and sobbed as if her heart would break. She wished dearly to see this parent, and she was much prostrated at so sudden and unexpected an announcement.

Lord Marchmont then told her all, and in silence they returned to the little fishing village, where they had temporarily taken up their abode.

CHAPTER XXXVI.

AGNES IS GRIEVED AT THE DEATH OF HER FATHER—A CLOUD WITHOUT A SILVER LINING—THE DEMON OF JEALOUSY—LORD MARCHMONT HAS HIS SUSPICIONS, BUT HE KEEPS THEM TO HIMSELF—COUNT VAL DE GRACE—MESMERISM—THE FIFTH MAN—A TRAVELLING TINKER—JABEZ CLARKE AGAIN.

AGNES felt the death of her father keenly; and she was the more grieved at the untimely event, as he was snatched away just at the time when she was waiting to receive him, and he was hastening to her arms. Of course she acquitted her husband of all blame. He had acted as well as he could in the matter; he had, indeed, behaved with singular gallantry, and even bravery, in penetrating the dark and dismal vaults which led him to Mr. Leslie's prison-house.

Agnes shuddered at her husband's account of the rising tide, which had enveloped them in its stifling embraces as they were hastening through the caverns. The dreadful skeletons she had herself beheld; and she turned pale as she recalled the soul-sickening spectacle.

Lord Marchmont endeavoured to raise his wife's spirits, and to draw her mind away from Puffin Island, and the events that had taken place upon its limited circumference.

"You know, my dear Agnes," he said, "that Mr. Leslie's death could not have been averted by mortal means: his death was doubtlessly decreed as a happy release to his sufferings."

"I would I could think so," replied Agnes.

"But what shall we think of your brother and your aunt?"

"We will forget them—they are unworthy of our thoughts."

It was strange how these two people could affect virtuous indignation.

Lord Marchmont, the murderer of the Hon. Percy Cunninghame, pretended to shudder at the misdeeds of the Leslies. Agnes, the fair bigamist, simulated horror at the crimes of her brother. But so it is; people are always more tender and more compassionate for their own offences than for those of others.

On their return to town it was arranged that they should stay in London for some little time. This Agnes made no objection to, as she was fond of the great city; she liked its dissipation and its gaieties. She could then show off herself and her gorgeous equipages to advantage—and she liked admiration.

She occasionally thought of Marmaduke Wilson, and the reflection disquieted her not a little; but she comforted herself with the idea that he would be unable to recognise in the fashionable Lady Marchmont his former retiring and modest wife. If he did by any chance discover her identity, she resolved to set him at defiance, and put him to the proof, which would be extremely difficult. Where he to lay claim to her as his wife, who would believe him?—people would ridicule the idea—no one would place credence in his strange assertions; for what is the word of a returned convict worth?

Whenever Lord Marchmont thought of the Hon. Percy Cunninghame, he banished the unpleasant idea with wine; or sought the fascinating and enthralling society of his lovely wife, who seldom failed to drive away his care. For, although she did not love him, she raised up a sort of fictitious passion, which did duty for the original. A passion which passed away the time; and afforded her satisfaction, while it threw his lordship into ecstasies.

A cloud, however, was to come between them, hidden in whose dark recesses was a fiend which would soon destroy the little fleeting and transitory happiness their united efforts had sufficed to conjure up. This fiend was jealousy—jealousy, which is at all times the quickest and best destroyer of domestic happiness that Satan and the powers of darkness can find to work with.

Amongst the circle of acquaintances with which Lord and Lady Marchmont had surrounded themselves was a certain French count—good-looking for a Frenchman, and who possessed that indescribable charm of manner that every French gentleman has in so eminent a degree. He was dark, as a matter of course; he wore moustaches of a prodigious length, like the King of Italy: and his coal-black eye had such a penetrating power, that it could pierce through you; and, to tell the truth, the count's great point was his extraordinary eyes. When he looked at you, he seemed to fascinate you in the most remarkable and inexplicable manner.

He had long resided in foreign parts. He had lived for years in Arabia, penetrating its arid plains, and living amongst the strange tribes that inhabit that little known region. There he had picked up curious secrets. In Persia he had made himself acquainted with the lore of the magi.

Paracelsus was not a more profound scholar in all that pertained to the mysterious than himself; in a word, he was a disciple of Mesmer, and a follower of Joseph Balsamo, Count de Caliogstro. He seldom displayed his wonderful powers, but when he did, every one admitted that he was a proficient in the occult art. When questioned as to how he acquired it, he replied that he had studied it long and earnestly. It was to a certain extent like ventriloquism—only one man here and there excelled in practising it; but others would be able to do the same thing, were they to work hard at it for days and weeks and years—never being conquered by difficulties or disappointments.

Picture, then, a tall dark man with black piercing eyes, a consummate gentleman, curt in his manner at times, owing to a sort of abstraction over which he had little or no control, but possessing a strangely insinuating and fascinating manner.

Such was the Count Val de Grace, a constant guest at Lord and Lady Marchmont's.

The count paid Agnes great attention; at times his lordship thought rather more than politeness called for or propriety sanctioned. But he contented himself with watching them, without mentioning his suspicion to any one, or even hinting to his lovely wife that he suspected her of allowing any familiarity which, as his bride, she had no right to permit.

One day it happened that Lord Marchmont, who was a colonel in some militia regiment, had to go away from town for a few days, in order to attend to the training of the men who were called out. He embraced his wife, and told her that he should not be absent long, and that if he was gone more than two days she was to follow him. Agnes promised to do so, and they parted with every demonstration of regret and affection.

Lord Marchmont started early in the morning, and in the course of an hour or so Count Val de Grace paid her ladyship a morning call.

Agnes was attired in a morning wrapper, and was reclining luxuriously in an arm-chair of Parisian manufacture. She seemed pleased at the count's visit, for he was always an agreeable companion, and during her husband's absence she would be able to pass a few hours most pleasantly in his society.

"Good morning, count," she said. "You are an early visitor."

"Not too early, I trust?"

"Oh, no! I did not mean that."

"You are kind to say so."

"My husband," continued Agnes, "has gone into the country for a day or two; and I am all alone, as you perceive."

Count Val de Grace smiled.

Agnes had often heard people talk of the count's extraordinary powers, and she had herself felt fascinated by his gaze on various occasions. But she had wished for some time past to have ocular evidence of his possessing so mysterious and so singular a gift as that of mesmerism. Now, she thought, would be a good time for him to display his talent. Accordingly, she exclaimed—

"By the way, count, your friends say that you are in league with very naughty people."

"What do you mean, Lady Marchmont?" he replied, fixing a searching glance upon her, which thrilled through her.

"I mean that you are able to do extraordinary things."

"Do you think so?"

"I hardly know what to think."

The count smiled.

"The fact is," continued Agnes, "I want to be convinced. I am open to conviction, although I have never had much faith in what is called mesmerism."

The count smiled again, this time sarcastically.

"You want to have an illustration of that little known science; is it not so?"

"It is."

"I shall be glad to oblige you."

"Oh! thank you; how kind of you, exclaimed Agnes, much pleased at the prospect before her.

"But, in the first place," said Val de Grace, "what do you want to see?"

"Ah! that I do not know. I must leave it all to you. It is unknown ground to me."

The count smiled a third time, this time a little bitterly.

"Yes, it is so," he cried. "The people will not take the trouble to investigate a new discovery, but if they cannot at once understand it, they put it down to quackery and empiricism, and the clever inventor is a martyr to his discovery."

Agnes made no comment upon this speech, which was made with much feeling.

"Would you believe in the truth of mesmerism, my lady," said the count, "were I to call a person out of the street—a chance passer-by—and question him as to his former history, dragging everything out of him at the point of the bayonet, as it were?"

Agnes bowed assent.

"Or, suppose I were to throw your ladyship into a trance, and whilst you were in the mesmeric sleep, to extract from you every event of consequence that had ever befallen you, what would you say?"

"Say! Why, that you were a dangerous as well as a mysterious man," replied Agnes, much alarmed.

"Calm your fears, Lady Marchmont. If you possess secrets, they shall remain so for me."

Agnes almost wished that she had never asked this strange man to exhibit his powers before her.

"Well; shall we try the first man who happens to pass by?" asked Val de Grace.

"I have no objection."

"None?"

"None at all. You may proceed as you like, always provided that your experiments are not made at my expense."

"At yours?"

"Yes, at mine."

"How can you suppose, for a moment, that I would be guilty of so ungentlemanly an action? When I spoke just now, it was only for the sake of illustration, putting an extreme case."

"I believe you, Count."

"In order to convince you, Lady Marchmont, that I am about to exhibit no jugglery——"

"Oh, Count, how silly of you to make such excuses! I am prepared to believe in your skill, and I know that you are incapable of such practices."

"I thought," he said, "that you might think I was acting in collusion with somebody."

"Not for a moment."

"Then will your ladyship come to the window with me? and the first man that passes——"

"The first man?"

"Yes. Have you any objection? Take the second or third, if you like."

"Well, say the fifth man that passes by."

"The fifth. Very well, by all means let it be the fifth," returned the Count Val de Grace.

They stationed themselves at the window, and waited for some one to pass by.

It was not a crowded thoroughfare; it was one of those quiet, aristocratic streets in which there is very little traffic until the middle of the day is long past. For a few seconds, possibly for the space of half a minute, they gazed out of the window without perceiving anybody. At last footsteps were heard approaching. The first man was about to pass by the window. With some curiosity they awaited his appearance. He was a baker, with a basket on his arm, and wearing a white hat, which he most likely did, as the riddle says, to keep his head warm. Full a minute passed before the second man came, and then, to use an Irishism, it was a woman. At last the second and third came close together, in the persons of an itinerant organ-grinder and a vendor of "Twelve a-penny walnuts." The fourth was a man of gentlemanly appearance; and as the time approached for the fifth man to draw near, neither Agnes nor Count Val de Grace could repress a feeling of curiosity, which deepened as second after second passed away without any one appearing.

While in this state of expectation "Knives to grind—kettles to mend—scissors to grind," saluted their ears.

"I do believe it is a wandering tinker!" exclaimed Agnes. "I wish it had been that gentlemanly young man who passed last. What a pity I did not say the fourth instead of the fifth."

"Shall it be the tinker?" inquired the count, with a melodious laugh.

"Oh, certainly. If he is the fifth man it must be so."

The tinker's voice was heard coming up the street nearer and nearer, and at last he stood opposite the window. It was clear that he was the fifth man. Seeing somebody at the window, he stopped, and looked up.

As he did so, the count caught his eye, and sent a series of flashes, as it were, of electricity flying through the air from his own person to that of the tinker.

The man stood rooted to the road by the side of his cart, which was standing not more than a few feet from the area railings.

When Agnes saw the upturned face of the tinker she uttered a cry, and, touching the count's arm, she exclaimed—

"Not that one—any one but that—but that one, I implore you!"

But Val de Grace either would not hear her, or he was too much occupied in what he was doing to take any notice of her.

Most probably the latter.

The count's whole figure and expression had undergone a most wonderful change.

He had drawn himself up to his full height.

Every muscle and fibre of his frame seemed to be rigidly distended to its utmost capacity of tension.

His eyes were dilated, and small, tiny sparks appeared to be emitted from them.

His hands were now clenched tightly, and anon thrown open, and held in the direction of the tinker.

The count, by his actions, appeared to be projecting some odic force by a species of animal magnetism through the air

JABEZ CLARKE IS MESMERISED BY COUNT VAL DE GRACE.

towards the travelling tinker, who was perfectly helpless, and unable to resist.

The Count Val de Grace never once took his eyes off his victim, who at last moved towards the door of Lord Marchmont's mansio n—slowly at first, but afterwards with alacrity.

Agnes all this time was gazing at the man with the utmost conste rnation depicted on her pallid countenance.

Who could he be?

How could a man in the garb of a travelling tinker affect the mind or influence the fortunes of the proud and wealthy Lady Mar chmont?

She was much terrified!

She was greatly alarmed!

She evidently wished the count would release the man from the strange thraldom that he exercised over him

This the count would not do.

And she was powerless to compel him.

This was the situation when the man knocked at the door of the mansion.

The count himself went into the passage to admit him.

Agnes threw herself hopelessly into a chair, and waited the sequel of this strange adventure with the utmost impatience, though so quiet was she externally, that you would have deemed her passively patient.

As the count reached the door of the mansion, he found the travelling tinker descending the steps.

By taking his eyes off him, the spell had been broken.

But the count did not intend to let him escape so easily.

"My man!" he exclaimed.

The tinker took no notice of him.

Count Val de Grace again repeated his summons in a more imperious tone, while his features were convulsed with rage.

This time the man apparently could not resist the influence that was at work to compel him to yield his will to that of another. Turning sharply round with a short cry, he retraced his steps, and at last stood in the doorway.

The count kept his eyes fixed upon him, and beckoned him onwards.

He followed without making any resistance, although, at times, short cries, more like the yelping of a dog in pain than anything else, broke from him. He followed Count Val de Grace into the morning room where Agnes was sitting.

The count motioned him to a seat.

The man, in obedience to the tacit command, seated himself.

Then Count Val de Grace approached him, and made several rapid passes over his face with his hands. While doing so, his features became strangely distorted, and he seemed to be animated by the wildest passion.

After the first few passes, the man's aspect changed.

He appeared to suffer acutely.

What little volition he had deserted him, and he was undoubtedly at the count's mercy.

Val de Grace did not desist in his efforts.

The man put up his hands as if to deprecate any further infliction of what was to him evidently a torture.

Val de Grace stopped, still keeping his eyes fixed on the travelling tinker, who could apparently see no one in the room but himself.

Agnes gazed steadily at this individual, and her former suspicions were revived.

In him she recognised an old acquaintance, and the recognition filled her with vague alarms, which was hardly surprising, for the travelling tinker seated before her was no other than Jabez Clarke!

CHAPTER XXXVII.

JABEZ IS MESMERISED BY COUNT VAL DE GRACE—HIS HISTORY IS EXTRACTED FROM HIM WHILE IN A TRANCE—HIS DESIGNS UPON AGNES—THE WONDERFUL POWER OF THE DISCIPLES OF MESMER—JABEZ DEPARTS IN PEACE—COUNT VAL DE GRACE HAS SINISTER DESIGNS WITH REGARD TO AGNES.

YES, the man whom the Count Val de Grace had so strangely introduced into the house was no other than her once reputed father.

No other than Jabez Clarke, coke and potato merchant, in Clare-market.

No other than Jabez Clarke, the murderer of her unfortunate mother.

What a singular chance, what an extraordinary incident in her chequered career!

Agnes was much alarmed at the occurrence.

If Jabez recognised her, he might do her much harm.

He could denounce her as the murderess of her own mother, for as we have already stated that was the report which had got about—propagated, in the first instance, by Jabez Clarke himself. And then Agnes knew, to her cost, that Jabez was a man who had neither the fear of God or man before his eyes.

One who was capable of committing every act of villany for gold, no matter what, as long as he was paid for it; and the higher the pay, the more atrocious the crime. He did bravoism on a graduating or sliding scale, and she now knew that he was a ruffian of the first water.

There was, however, one chance, and that was, that time and various other incidents, would have so altered her, that he would be very sagacious if he were to recognise her.

As for him, she could have singled him out any day from among ten thousand.

His scowling brow, his hardy look, his scrubby, stubbly beard, his bleared eyes, his thick lips, his demoniacal expression of countenance, all put together, gave him a preeminence in ugliness and repulsiveness, that once seen was never forgotten.

Agnes, however, turned from these reflections to watch the progress of the count. He had, it seemed, brought his subject into a proper state of mind, and he was now ready to operate upon him. The count turned a little way round and asked Agnes to come near to the scene of action. Agnes complied with this request, and took a chair by the side of the count. Val de Grace then said—

"I am now about to extract all this man's early history from him. In point of fact, I will, if his face does not mislead me, supply you with materials for a three volume novel."

Agnes had little doubt of this herself, but she made no reply.

"Now, my man," exclaimed the count, "what is your name?"

"Jabez Clarke."

"How did you pass your early years?"

Jabez appeared to writhe violently at this question with the power which held him in its powerful thrall, but the Count Val de Grace perceiving this, made several rapid passes, and with a cry of anguish the man resigned himself to his fate, and replied—

"In thieving what I could lay my hands on."

"Well, what next?"

"I got into a gentleman's service——"

"And got kicked out again, very quickly, I suppose?" put in the count.

"No."

"No! That was a wonder."

"The gentleman, Squire Leslie that was, he had a little business on hand he wanted settled quietly——"

"Oh!" said Val de Grace.

"And he comes to me and gives me the job——"

"Gave you the job, did he?"

"Yes, he did; and as he was pretty liberal with the shiners, I did it for him——"

"No doubt of that," said the count, between his teeth. "Well, what piece of villany was it?"

"No villany. He had got a young woman in the family-way, and he wanted for to get her off his hands, kid and all——"

"Did you murder them?" inquired the count.

"Not I. I married the woman and retired to town, where I started a coke and tater business to get a living, for the squire's money didn't last long; I know how to make the cash fly when I can collar it, and a tarnation bad living I did get out of that ere coke, and them there taters, to be sure."

"Well, what next?"

"I aint going to tell you no more," replied Jabez, sullenly.

"Oh! we will see about that," said Count Val de Grace, who instantly recommenced the rapid passes which had proved so efficacious in a former instance. These had the effect he desired to achieve. Indeed, he seemed to be applying something to his victim which resembled chloroform. When the dose had partially evaporated, he gave the patient another. Jabez Clarke uttered several low moans, and threw his arms about as if he meditated some violence, but the mesmeric influence was too powerful for him, and he soon succumbed to its irresistible power.

"What became of the child you mentioned?" asked the count, relentlessly pursuing his inquiries.

"The child, oh! that lived, and that child's my little game now," replied Jabez, with a cunning leer in his face——

"Well, go on with your story," said Val de Grace.

"Where was I? oh! coke and taters, yes. Well, after a bit I gave my old 'ooman, Squire Leslie's as was, a cut on the side on her head, which sent her to kingdom come; and the child, which her name was Hagnes, hooked it off, slick away from her hum, and so I said as how she had done the bit of murder or manslaughtering, or whatever the lawyer folks call it, and then there was a hue and cry after her, but they none of 'em wornt clever enough to cotch her——"

"Oh! indeed!" said the count.

"Have you not got enough out of him, count?" exclaimed Agnes, who had listened to all this with great interest.

"I think he may as well finish his story, but it shall be as your ladyship pleases," rejoined the count.

"Very well," answered Agnes. "There does not appear to be much more of it, so let us, by all means, hear it, if you wish it, count."

"Not at all," replied Val de Grace; "I bow to your ladyship's wishes."

"In that case, count, pray proceed," said Agnes, who felt bound in politeness to make that reply.

"Go on," cried Val de Grace to Jabez Clarke, as if he were talking to a dog.

"But I'll cotch her," continued Jabez; "if I don't I'll eat my old hat. I have a fancy as how she's better orf now than she was afore, and if there's any money to be had out of her, why I'll have it. If I don't I wish I may die."

"What became of your potato shop," demanded Count Val de Grace.

"I got into a bit of a hobble with some customers of mine," replied Jabez, "about the weights and measures. They swore as how and acted as to insist upon it that I did not serve them as they had a right to be served. I swore as how I did. They made no allowance for a poor chap as 'as to get 'is livin' by the sweat of 'is brow; and so they goes and claps a bobby on to me. The bobby, he says, says he, 'What's the meanin' of this 'ere?' 'What 'ere, says I?' 'Why, this 'ere go about the weights and measures,' says he, a looking hawful spiteful-like at me. 'It's a fine go about nothing,' says I. "We'll see about it,' he says, and went to look at the scales, which had not oughter been as they were, but a cove must live, 'as I said to him; but bobbies aint got no feelin', not a bit o' feelin' for their fellow-creatures; they is the wust sort of blokes there is out. So the peeler he comes up to me, when his examination wor finished, and he says, 'You've been systematically cheating of your customers, so you'll have to come along of me.' 'I says I shouldn't, so I ups with my fist and gives him a bunch of fives right on his left peeper. But there was a lot more bobbies a parsing by, wuss luck, and they comes in with their starves and truncheons, as bloodthirsty as a pirate at the Victoria Theayter with his cutlash all drawn, and they lamas into one amazin'; but I fit for a bit, till at last they drew me into a corner, and took me off to the stashun, where I was locked up, and then the beak he gives me two months. I told him that I would do that lot easily on my head belike. When I comes out it wor no good going back to the coke and tatur line; so I cuts that, and starts a little tinkering, thinking I might possibly light on Miss Hagnes."

Count Val de Grace listened to this as if he took no interest whatever in it. Nor did he. He was simply displaying his skill as a mesmerist to Agnes, who was very much impressed by it. She knew that every word Jabez uttered was true to the letter, and she trembled when she thought that such an abandoned wretch as that was on her track, for she knew that if he could once find her she would know no peace. She would have to spend a fortune in buying him off, and even then she would not be safe from his rapacity, as she would always be in his power.

"Now are you satisfied?" asked the count.

"I am more than satisfied, I am convinced," said Agnes, "that you are infinitely more clever than you are reported to be, and I am very much obliged to you for the trouble you have taken."

"Trouble!" said Val de Grace. "Oh! that is nothing; anything done for you, my dear Lady Marchmont, is a pleasure; it could never be considered a trouble."

"You flatter me, count."

"I! On my word, no."

"Well, let it pass," said Agnes. "But with regard to this man; had you not better get him out of the house in the way in which you brought him in? He might talk about it in the neighbourhood, or he might come here and demand money; or he might be troublesome in some way."

"I will answer for it," replied Count Val de Grace, "that when he recovers his senses he will know nothing about it —nothing whatever. He will be as innocent as a child of all that has occurred in your house this morning, Lady Marchmont."

"Indeed, I am glad to hear it."

"I shall," he continued, "take him out of the house quietly, and he will experience no ill effects from the treatment he has received from me, except a little weakness."

Jabez Clarke's head had sunk upon his shoulder, and he appeared to be in a deep sleep.

The count touched him on the shoulder.

Jabez leaped to his feet, and his eyes rolled about fearfully.

A few passes from the count quieted him, and the chain of mesmerism was again around him more closely than ever.

"Ask him," said Agnes, "if he has any clue to his supposed daughter, Agnes. I am quite interested in the man's story."

The count put the question.

Jabez shook his head.

"Speak, man!" cried Val de Grace, in terrible accents.

This time the unhappy ex-coke and potato merchant replied in the negative.

"You lie," cried the count, passionately.

Jabez hung down his head, and whimpered like a child.

Val de Grace grew furious, and his hands flew about with the rapidity of lightning.

"Now dare to refuse to answer!" he exclaimed, defiantly.

Jabez looked up and said, "Have some pity on me."

"Answer my question," cried the count.

"I will, I will!" shrieked Jabez, who seemed to suffer acutely.

"Well, proceed."

"I don't know nothin' pertickler, but I fancy I see her one day in a carridge. I wont swear to her, but it was a fancy o' mine, and I've stuck to it ever since, and that's all."

"There! are you satisfied?" exclaimed Count Val de Grace.

"Perfectly," said Agnes, "but I hardly think you could make a novel out of what he has told you."

"I don't know that. His story has its romantic side," replied the count.

Rising from his chair Count Val de Grace fixed his eyes upon Jabez, and walking towards the door, motioned him to follow. Jabez did so, and, as the count held the front door open, he passed out and walked down the steps, as if in a trance, following the count, who led the way. When they reached the street, the count made a few swift passes with his hands, and then running quickly up the steps, entered the house, and shut the door behind him.

In a moment Val de Grace rejoined Agnes, and they both watched Jabez from behind a blind.

He gazed about him for a minute or two, as if awakening from a long trance, and every now and then he shivered and trembled like a drunken man, or one who has entered upon that stage of drunkenness called *delirium tremens*. Then he gazed round at the different windows as if trying to recollect something.

Ultimately he beat his brow with his hand, and seizing his cart, walked rapidly up the street.

Agnes followed him with his eyes, and remarked with some little apprehension that he looked at the name of the street, and appeared to be making a mental note of it.

Presently, however, he was out of sight, and she left the window.

"Can you do this with anybody, count?" she inquired.

"With anybody? yes," replied Val de Grace.

"I trust, however, you will never experiment upon me."

"Lady Marchmont," he said, "I promised you once before that you were safe with me. I now repeat that promise."

Agnes smiled and the count left. As he quitted the house he muttered to himself—

"She is a lovely creature. Would I could make her my own."

As he uttered these words a sinister expression stole over his countenance, which boded no good to Agnes.

Agnes, however, was charmed with the count's skill and fascinating manners.

"He is quite a ladies' man," she said to herself. "I have taken quite a fancy to him."

The episode that had just occurred in which the rascally Jabez Clarke had figured so much, only troubled her for a time.

As she was driving in the park that afternoon she heard some bells upon which some men were ringing changes. After a while the changes ceased, and the bells played a pretty little air. It was the "Lass o' Gowrie," and as the chimes gave form and expression to the words, "But now she's Lady Gowrie," Agnes's thoughts were, "Come what may, I can say with those distant chimes whose music floats faintly towards me on the wings of the wind, 'But now I'm Lady Marchmont.'"

And the chimes solaced her as their dulcet tones were wafted along by the breeze, until they fell softly on her appreciating ears. But she little guessed that she had more to fear from Val de Grace than from Jabez Clarke.

CHAPTER XXXVIII

COUNT VAL DE GRACE'S EARLY HISTORY—THE PERSIAN ROSE GARDEN—THE BUL-BUL—DEATH OF FATIMA— THE COUNT'S DIABOLICAL PLOT RESPECTING AGNES— SHE WALKS IN HER SLEEP—A BEAUTIFUL SOMNAMBULIST—LORD MARCHMONT APPEARS ON THE SCENE— THE COUNT DROPS DOWN DEAD.

COUNT VAL DE GRACE had taken more than a passing fancy to Agnes.

His was a strange, mysterious, and not easily fathomed nature.

You might look at him, and endeavour to read him like

a book; but you would be disappointed. There are some men—and women—whose characters, intentions, and designs are easily detected; but Count Val de Grace was not one of these.

He had seen many men and many countries. He had had great and varied experience; and he was more clever and accomplished than even his countenance indicated.

He came of one of the best of the old French families; but he had been exiled on account of his political opinions.

Early in life he had associated himself with a desperate band of conspirators, who had their country's good at heart—but their designs had been discovered and frustrated. And he was, amongst others, condemned to die.

But with his native audacity, he discovered a slender means of escape.

He essayed it, and succeeded.

He knew that whether he attempted to escape or not his fate would be the same.

They could not increase his punishment for making the venture. They could not kill him twice.

He was well off, as the phrase is.

That is, he was much better off than most of his countrymen who sojourn on our shores.

He lived like an English gentleman. He was fond of horses, of driving, of shooting, of the opera, and, in point of fact, he spent his time as a naturalized British subject. He really believed in mesmerism as a science, and he was devoted to it. He had pursued it for many years, and at last he was becoming a proficient in the art. He had had love affairs of course, as most men have; but his grand, his serious passion, had been engendered among the rose-gardens of Persia; and he had whispered his soft words of love while the bul-bul whistled melodiously in the cool and fragrant evening time.

The object of his choice was the daughter of a prince, who, during one of their stolen interviews, had crept upon them with the cunning of a serpent.

But the darkness had enveloped the lovers; and as the infuriated father drew his yataghan to plunge it up to its hilt in the blood of the feringee, he mistook the beautiful Persian girl for the man, and the blood of the peerless Fatima stained the rose leaves, and sank into the thirsty ground.

This shocking incident for a time sickened and disgusted Val de Grace of life, and he wandered from place to place seeking rest and finding it not. Now he was in England. He had found some excitement in mesmerism; and whenever he thought of Fatima expiring at his feet in the garden of Zel-zel, he returned to his scientific pursuits with greater zest and increased eagerness. Perhaps the memory of the unhappy Fatima had faded from his mind, for men are naturally inconstant. I will not undertake to find a reason for his conduct; but he fell very much in love with Agnes. The more he knew her, the more vivid and passionate his love became. With him, to long for a thing was to do all he could to satisfy his inclination. He thought for some time how he could achieve his purpose. Although he brooded over the matter for many days and nights, he had not as yet discovered any infallible means of accomplishing his object. But after his adventure with the knife-grinding tinker an idea struck him. It was this: if he could, by means of his mesmeric powers, compromise Agnes in some peculiar manner, she would most likely consent to leave her husband and go abroad with him.

Count Val de Grace would have made Agnes the partner of his existence.

He had been too long solitary, and after a time men long for women's society. There is a natural craving for it in a man's breast, and he is hardly deserving of the name of man who does not give it full scope.

Count Val de Grace had shunned female society for some time. In fact ever since his dearly-loved Fatima's death. But Agnes had awakened some of his old feelings in his breast.

With the volatile disposition inherent in all the children of Gaul, he argued that he ought to forget Fatima. She had died through no fault of his own, and why should his existence be henceforth a blank?

Certainly Agnes was another man's wife, but he thought nothing of that. That would have been no obstacle in France, where such things occur every day.

He liked her, and he flattered himself he was not wholly indifferent to her. Even if he was he would strive to overcome her repugnance.

He considered, however, that his best way would be to bring his talents into requisition, and, without committing any actual harm, to compromise her to such an extent, that if her husband was a witness to the scene he intended to create, he could not do anything else but drive her from his threshold with ignominy and disgrace. Then, of course, she would accept his advances. So he argued.

In order to put his plan into execution, he called upon Agnes the day after the occurrences related in the last chapter. He found her at home, and asked her to come out for a drive in his mail-phaeton, which was standing at the door. Agnes thought there was no harm in her acceding to his request, and anticipating some amusement from his society, she agreed to go.

Count Val de Grace knew he would be perceived by a great many people who would instantly recognise Agnes, and when Lord Marchmont returned to town he would not fail to hear of it.

It would be a suspicious circumstance which would tell against Agnes, and, of course, in favour of his plans. He thought if Agnes was seen that evening in an extraordinary position by the servants in her household, that would be better than if Lord Marchmont himself was a direct witness. For the count knew that husbands sometimes are dangerous animals to meddle with, and that a bullet, or sometimes a couple of inches of cold steel, now and then fall to the lot of those who endeavour to break up families and to destroy domestic relations.

One thing, however, even his mesmeric experience did not reveal to him, and that was that Lord Marchmont returned to town earlier than he had expected, and instead of going straight home he took a turn in the park, thinking that very likely Agnes would be there.

He saw her there. But when he saw in whose society she was he did not discover himself, but hung in the background watching them; and he determined to watch all day, and all night too, if necessary.

Agnes asked Count Val de Grace to dine with her that evening. As may be supposed he readily accepted the invitation, and was at her house at the appointed hour.

After dinner Agnes complained of feeling unwell. This was owing to the magnetic influence that the count exerted over her. He did it purposely, and was glad to see it work so well.

She felt so sleepy, she said, that the count must excuse her if she retired to rest. She hoped he would stay and finish his wine and smoke a cigar, and she trusted she would be better company next time he did her the honour of visiting her.

The honour, indeed! What a prostitution of the word.

Count Val de Grace bowed, opened the door, let her ladyship out, and then lighted a cigar. He continued smoking till eleven o'clock. The servants all went to bed except the hall porter. The count was well known, and they thought nothing of his staying so late. The butler before going to rest had asked him if he wanted anything. The reply was in the negative. The count was not a great drinker.

As the clock struck eleven, Count Val de Grace commenced his incantations. He had at dinner established an influence over Agnes, so that she was at his beck and call at any moment. He cast his arms about, and he threw his body into all sorts of contortions, in order to increase the power and volume of the magnetic chain he had created between Agnes and himself.

His exertions were successful.

Presently a footfall was heard descending the stairs.

Then a hand was laid upon the handle of the door, and Agnes in her nightdress entered the room.

Count Val de Grace gazed at her with eyes of admiration.

She walked to the centre of the room, and there stood like a somnambulist.

She was evidently unconscious of the action.

She knew not what she did.

The count was so pleased with the success of his plans, that he did not move.

He kept her by his art standing like a vestal virgin before him, as he gloated on her charms.

At this juncture, so critical for the innocent Agnes, the door opened, and Lord Marchmont entered the room.

He held a sword in his hand, and walked deliberately up to the count, with the intention of passing the weapon through his body.

But Val de Grace, strange to say, uttered a cry and fell to the floor insensible.

A small stream of blood issued from his mouth, and Lord Marchmont concluded that he had broken a blood-vessel, and left him to his fate.

He then turned to his wife, and the expression of his face was terrible to behold.

CHAPTER XXXIX.

LORD MARCHMONT SPARES HIS WIFE'S LIFE, BUT DRIVES HER WITH IGNOMINY FROM HIS HOUSE — A DEAD BODY — HOW TO DISPOSE OF A CORPSE IN THE MIDST OF THE BOASTED CIVILIZATION OF THE NINETEENTH CENTURY — THE CEMETERY — A COLONY OF THE DEAD — THRILLING ADVENTURES.

AGNES stood like a beautiful statue, but only for a moment.

Directly the count fell to the ground insensible or dead, the spell which bound her to him was broken.

She opened her eyes.

She looked round in amazement.

Where was she?

How did she come there?

She rubbed her eyes with the back of her hand, to see if she was awake or not.

The whole thing was an inexplicable mystery to her.

She had some time ago, as she thought, gone to sleep in her own bed-room, the door of which she had locked, as was her custom. And now, where did she find herself? In the dining-room of her house. Her husband standing over what seemed to be the corpse of the Count Val de Grace.

Her husband, with a drawn sword in his hand!

Her husband, with flashing eyes and looks of fiery indignation!

She could not make it out.

Her vague ideas, however, were destined soon to be dissipated in rather a rude manner.

Lord Marchmont turned to her, and exclaimed, in the bitterest tones of concentrated irony, with which passion of the most hideous kind was strangely commingled—

"Look, madam! your paramour is dead."

As he pronounced the last word, he spurned the body of the count with his foot, as if to show his contempt for so worthless a piece of defunct humanity.

As her husband made this speech, a new light dawned upon Agnes.

It was evident to her that the count had brought her from her bed to the dining-room by means of his almost magic art. And that Lord Marchmont had returned unexpectedly, which enabled him to be upon the scene at so inopportune a moment.

Truly appearances were against her.

Truly, although in the sight of Heaven she was as innocent as an unconscious child, yet in the sight of man the suspicion against her was very grave.

Agnes had been confounded at the scene.

She had been awakened out of her sleep, and as all these strange incidents crowded upon her senses at once, it was no wonder that the poor girl became confused.

So much confused was she that she did not attempt to exculpate herself with her incensed husband.

And he was boiling with rage and excitement.

One, the adulterer, as he deemed him, had fallen a victim to his just rage; why, then, should he spare the other, the adulteress?

He grasped his sword nervously, and looked at her savagely.

Clad in those white garments, she looked very lovely.

But the sight of her marvellous beauty only sufficed to incense Lord Marchmont to a higher degree.

"She deserves to die," he muttered. "Yes, she shall die!" And rushing forward, he caught her by the hair, and was about to plunge his weapon into her bosom.

He was in a state of frenzy.

He had, at that moment, no doubt whatever that he had discovered a *liaison* between his wife and Count Val de Grace.

This conviction was strengthened by the fact of his having seen them together that morning in the park.

And had an angel from heaven come down to tell him that his wife was innocent of even meditating an offence against his honour, he would scarcely have believed the celestial messenger.

It appeared to him that the proofs were too strong to be refuted, and as he sat, as it were, in brief but terrible judgment upon her, he passed sentence of death upon his charming and innocent wife with as little remorse as he would have done upon the most hardened criminal that ever stood in the dock, on the Crown side, at the Old Bailey.

But he was blinded with passion.

Agnes's life, at that moment, hung in the balance.

The point of the relentless sword was pressing against her alabaster skin.

A little stain of blood tinged the whiteness of her bosom.

With a desperate effort, she summoned up courage enough to say—

"Oh! listen to me. I am not guilty. Believe me, I am innocent."

Lord Marchmont hesitated.

"I am innocent, indeed I am," sobbed Agnes, in an agony of terror.

"Would I could believe it!" said his lordship.

"I swear it. Before Heaven I swear it. I will explain all."

"The thing explains itself," said Lord Marchmont. "No further explanation is wanted."

"Oh! spare my life," gasped Agnes, as the dreadful reality of her position forced itself upon her.

Lord Marchmont was getting a little cooler; and he thought that as the count had expiated his offence with his life, he could with propriety spare the life of his wife. But he resolved never to speak to her or to see her again. She had, he firmly believed, defiled the sanctity of the marriage tie, and that was an offence he could never forgive or forget. So he exclaimed, in answer to her prayer—

"I grant you your life, but perhaps you may live to regret ever having asked it at my hands."

"Oh! what mean you?" asked Agnes, filled with fresh terrors.

"You must leave this house instantly; it is no longer your home."

"Oh! where can I go?—what can I do?" cried Agnes, bursting into an agony of tears.

"I care not. You have sinned, and you must bear the fruit of your offence. Crime is always punished, some way or other. I loved you, and would have done anything in the world for you; but see how you have requited my kindness."

"I have not. It is not true," interrupted Agnes.

"Do not interrupt me; I will not take up much of your time. I was only about to say that no conduct of mine could have provoked this ingratitude on your part. I have ever been a good and kind husband to you."

"Yes, that is true," said Agnes; "and that makes me regret that you should so be led away now by your passion. If you would only listen to reason, I——"

"Peace, woman!" cried Lord Marchmont, sternly.

He was afraid that he might relent in his purpose if he listened to the pleadings of the lovely creature before him.

Agnes determined to make one more effort to move him, and accordingly she threw herself at his feet, and allowing her head to fall upon the ground, while her dishevelled hair lay across her tear-stained countenance, she gave way to a burst of grief which would have moved a heart of stone.

But Lord Marchmont that night possessed a heart hard as stone. It was for the time being composed of granite, of cast iron, of adamant.

He turned his face away from the weeping beauty, and said in a voice colder and sterner than any he had hitherto spoken in—

"Rise, madame. I give you till to-morrow to make your preparations. But I shall expect that by the hour of ten you will have left my house for ever."

"For ever!" echoed Agnes. "And this is the boasted love of men!"

Poor child! hers was indeed a hard fate.

Discarded! disgraced! destroyed! for an imaginary crime.

Oh! how she cursed the hour in which the hapless count had first come to her house!

It was cherishing the viper!

Mournfully she rose to her feet, and with one hand smoothed back her disordered tresses. A shawl lay on a chair; this she took up and placed on her marble shoulders. She looked tearfully at her naked feet; but there was no help for it, she would have to ascend the staircase with them. Lord Marchmont stood with his arms folded, gazing at her with the aspect of an avenger.

Without a word Agnes left the room and sought her own apartment. Then she threw herself upon the bed and wept bitterly. But in the course of an hour or so, she fell off into an uneasy slumber.

Lord Marchmont, after her departure, paced the room uneasily.

The body of the count was still lying where it had fallen.

The pulse had stopped, and to all appearance the count was dead.

Lord Marchmont wished to carry the body somewhere, he knew not where.

He did not wish it to be found in his house; it would tend to an inquiry—a coroner's inquest, perhaps—and that would be extremely unpleasant, and might involve him in serious consequences.

He was on the horns of a trilemma.

He must either leave the body where it was, call up the servants, and state how it all happened; or he must send it to the count's house, saying that he had suddenly fallen down in a fit; or he must take the body somewhere and bury it, or at all events dispose of it so that it would not be discovered. He resolved upon doing the latter.

The question then arose, how was he to effect the end he had in view?

There was a box, he remembered, in his study, which would answer the purpose very well. It had once been used for holding maps and papers that would not bear doubling up. It was of great length, and not unlike a coffin.

If he could force the body of the count into this rude chest, the first great difficulty would be got over.

No one but Agnes was acquainted with the count's death.

When Lord Marchmont had entered the house, about five minutes after eleven, he had sent the hall porter to bed.

He had found that somewhat useless functionary fast asleep in his great hooded chair, and he was not at all sorry to be dismissed to the arms of Morpheus.

Not an inmate of the house had seen Agnes either descend or ascend the staircase.

Not a soul had heard the altercation between Lord Marchmont and his wife.

No one knew that Count Val de Grace had come to an untimely end, which had saved Lord Marchmont from imbruing his hands in blood.

His lordship, however, could not disguise from himself that he was, as it were, the immediate cause of the count's death.

He considered that Val de Grace must have been afflicted with some internal disease, probably heart complaint, and that the unexpected fright which he had undergone must have caused his fearfully sudden death.

Lord Marchmont went noiselessly to his study, and finding the box he was in quest of, opened it. There were a few papers in it; these he put away in different places.

Then he took the box to the dining-room and laid it down by the side of the count. With a shudder and sigh of disgust he raised first the head and shoulders of the dead man, and allowed him to rest on the edge of the extemporised coffin, then he raised the feet in the same way, and after that, placed the entire body in the box.

It fitted, as it were, perfectly. Then his lordship shut down the lid and endeavoured to lock it; but he was surprised to see that the key was lost. He looked for it in every direction, but without success.

At last he gave up the search. It did not matter, after all.

If anybody found the box and wished to examine the contents, they would undoubtedly force open the lock without much ceremony or much difficulty; so where, after all, was the harm of there being no key?

Having shut down the lid, the next thing to be done was to get the coffin out of the house and bestow it in some place where neither the prying eyes of man or woman would be likely to discover it.

Leaving the box on the floor, Lord Marchmont, with the utmost caution, opened the street door and let himself out.

It was a miserable night. The rain came down in perfect sheets of water. The wind whistled and howled round the gables of the houses. The policeman had for once relinquished the task of walking round his everlasting and interminable beat, and was either hiding from the fury of the elements in the capacious recesses of some door-way, or else he had found food and entertainment in the hospitable depths of some area, from whence he had, may-be, penetrated as far as the kitchen, where the society of the cook, and a round of beef, had rewarded his adventurous daring.

Lord Marchmont considered himself very lucky in having such excellent weather in which to carry out his plans.

It was past twelve o'clock.

Everything except the howling of the wind and the splashing of the rain upon the flag-stones was silent, as most things usually are in the dread midnight, "when ghosts do walk and haunt the paths of men."

It was, in truth, a night well adapted for the purpose of Lord Marchmont.

His lordship was on the look-out for a cab.

He stood in the doorway, not exactly exposing himself to the storm, but keeping the door sufficiently open to be able to hear or see any passing cab.

After waiting for half-an-hour, his perseverance was rewarded; a four-wheeled cab dragged its slow length along.

It was one of those seedy and disreputable vehicles known as night cabs.

The driver was enveloped in many a roll of cloth, until he looked like a mummy with all its grave-clothes on.

The horse was steaming like a small muck-heap from the heat of his body and the dampness of the night.

Lord Marchmont ran into the street, and holding up his hand, hailed the cab.

It stopped and pulled up at the door.

The noise of the wind and the rain was so great that the sound made by the wheels of the cab was obliterated by that of the elements.

Lord Marchmont went into the house, and with great exertion managed to bring out the box, which he, with the assistance of the Jehu, placed upon the top of the cab.

Then he returned to the house, and with the utmost gentleness shut the door.

"Where to, sir?" asked the man, in a drowsy tone of voice.

Lord Marchmont slipped a couple of sovereigns into the man's hand, and said—

"Do what I tell you, and you shall have double that amount at the end of our journey."

The cabman looked at the gold, then at his fare, then at the long, coffin-shaped, deal box, and then at the gold again, which he jingled pleasantly together.

"I'm your man, capting," he said.

"Very well, then. Drive towards Fulham," replied his lordship; "and be as quick as you can."

The man jumped on to his seat, and drove with as much rapidity as he could get out of his miserable screw of a horse, in the direction indicated.

Lord Marchmont lighted a cigar, and waited with feverish impatience for the cabman to arrive at the destination he wished for. He could not help feeling that there was a corpse outside the cab, and a dead body is not at any time a very pleasant companion. It is true he had been alone with one before, and one that had died by his own hand; but that was in the broad and open daylight, whilst he was now travelling with a dead body in the middle of the night, which altered the case very materially; for there is something unutterably terrifying about the night time when you have done something wrong and are in constant dread of being detected.

At last the cabman drew near to the outlying suburb of Fulham. Just as they passed the Gunter Arms, his lordship let down a window, and told the man to drive up a dark lane in the direction of Shepherd's-bush.

On one side were nursery gardens, looking black and awful in the darkness, which was only relieved here and there by the faint light shed by some solitary gas lamps placed at intervals along the road. On the other side was a long and gloomy-looking wall of a considerable height. This was the wall of the Brompton Cemetery.

Lord Marchmont stopped the vehicle after it had gone some little distance up the lane, and got out, and beckoned the cabman to come down and speak to him.

"Now, my man, I'll tell you what I want done, and if it is done successfully there is plenty of money to be had."

The man touched his broad-brimmed oilskin hat.

"I want," continued Lord Marchmont, "to get that box on the roof of your cab over that wall into the cemetery."

"Can't be done, sir," replied the man, looking at the height of the wall.

"You think so?"

"I do, sir."

"If we had a ladder I suppose you would not think it so difficult of accomplishment?"

"No, sir, that would alter the case," replied the cabman, wondering what the meaning of the strange proceeding was.

"Those are nursery gardens on the right," continued Lord Marchmont; "and I have reason to believe that the men to whom they belong are gathering apples now. In that case, there would be a ladder or two under some of the trees. They would not take the trouble to remove them, perhaps to some distance, only to have to bring them back again the next morning. There is not much light by which to make a search; but still it must be done. I have a small lantern here, which will help us a little."

"A lantern, sir!"

"Yes; a small dark one."

"Ah! that'll do."

"Well, put your horse up against the wall."

"Yes, sir."

"And come with me. I shall want you to help me to carry the ladder when I have found it."

"Right you are, sir," replied the cabman.

When he had disposed his cab to his liking, he rejoined his lordship, and, with a bow, said "Beg parding, sir."

"What is it?"

"You wont think me a-going too far, your honour?"

"No, no. What is it?" said Lord Marchmont, impatiently.

"I'm to speak up?"

"Yes. Be quick."

"Well, about the blunt as I'm to 'ave?"

"Oh! is that all?" said his lordship, who thought for a moment that the man wanted to back out of the whole affair.

"That's all, sir."

"Very well; here's something to keep you up to the mark." And his lordship took five additional sovereigns out of his pocket, and gave them to the man, whose eyes brightened.

"I'll go through fire and water, sir, for you—as you pays well."

"You shall have some more if the thing is done well. The fact is, there is a still-born child in that box."

"A child!" cried the cabman, who had suspected something of the sort.

"Yes, and I want to put it in the cemetery, out of the way; there is nothing wrong."

"Well, as long as it is all on the square, I'm your man."

"Oh! you need not be afraid."

"You don't look a chap as would do a thing on the cross," said the man, familiarly.

Lord Marchmont turned on his lantern, and led the way over some palings. It was the same dark lantern which he had used on Puffin Island, and which had been presented to him by the Finsbury Fox.

They had not proceeded far before they stumbled on the object of their search. The cabman, who was in advance, suddenly uttered a cry, and fell flat on his face. He had stumbled over a ladder which was resting on its side on the ground, leaning against an apple or pear-tree; it was not easy to tell which in the darkness.

Muttering something about "having taken all the bark off his shins," the man rose to his feet, and with Lord Marchmont's assistance, the ladder was conveyed to the roadside, and placed against the wall. It answered its purpose admirably, as it just reached the top. The cabman then took the chains of his cab, which were used for fastening luggage on the roof, and bound them round the box in which the inanimate body of the luckless Val de Grace was confined; then, with some difficulty, they contrived to hoist the coffin on to the top of the wall. Their united efforts succeeded in doing what one would never have achieved alone. Allowing the coffin to rest upon the summit of the wall, they, standing also on the wall, hoisted the ladder up, and let it fall down gently on the other side. With great care they descended, carrying the coffin between them, making as little noise as possible.

There were not many graves where they had alighted; and the tombs or vaults were further in the cemetery, towards the centre.

After proceeding along a gravel-walk for a little distance,

while the rain beat in their faces and almost blinded them, they, by the aid of the lantern, saw what appeared to be the entrance to a vault.

Lord Marchmont left the cabman in charge of the coffin, and descended the steps.

The door of the vault was shut, but not fastened; a vigorous kick sufficed to send it creaking on its hinges, and a faint odour, as of dead bodies, emanated from the interior. Lord Marchmont recoiled in disgust as the sickening fumes penetrated his nostrils. Then he whistled, and the cabman descended the steps with the coffin.

They both entered the vault.

The light of the lantern revealed coffins piled one on top of the other in dozens. There did not seem to be any room for even one more.

It was evidently a vault which had received its full complement, and the door was left open in the daytime so that the relatives of the deceased might enter this gloomy city of the dead, and gaze on the oaken walls which contained the dust and bones of those who were once dearly beloved by mother, father, sister, brother, wife, or husband.

By slightly disarranging the order in which the coffins stood, his lordship contrived to slip his deal box behind a row of coffins; it fell with a dull sound.

A groan appeared to emanate from its recesses and then all was still.

The cabman trembled a little, but not much; and, in conjunction with his lordship, stood awaiting a repetition of the strange and mysterious noise. But none rewarded their patience.

"It must have been fancy," exclaimed Lord Marchmont, who tried to shake off his superstitious terror. "You have your share of courage, my friend," he added, addressing the cabman.

"You may say that, sir," replied the man; "I have had my turn at body-snatching before now, and this sort of game is not new to me by any manner o' means."

"Oh, indeed," replied Lord Marchmont, who did not know until now that he had been enjoying the society of a resurrectionist.

Leaving the vault, they retraced their steps, and walked towards the wall where they had entered the cemetery.

What was their consternation when they got there to find that *the ladder was nowhere to be seen.*

Locked up in that horrible grave-yard till daylight appeared!

What should they do?

They both paused for an answer.

"Oh, it cannot have been taken away!" cried his lordship. "Who is there here at this time of night, and such a night as this is, too? Who would do such a thing?"

"There are watchmen here," replied the cabman.

Going carefully along the ground with his lantern, Lord Marchmont at last, to his great delight, discovered the ladder, which had been blown down by the violence of the gale.

To lift it up and erect it again was the work of a moment. Then they soon stood upon the summit of the wall and descended rapidly into the road.

They did not trouble themselves to put the ladder back where they found it, but tossed it over the palings into the garden.

Lord Marchmont then got into the cab, and was rapidly driven back to town. He did not consider it exactly prudent to return to his own house, so he drove to an hotel; where he found accommodation for the remainder of the night.

The cabman was liberally rewarded, and Lord Marchmont brought an arduous adventure to a successful termination.

But he was intensely miserable!

His idol had been dashed to pieces; his Agnes—the woman of his choice, and of his love—had played him false; and what was there worth living for after that?

Alas! that he should ever have been credulous enough to have trusted a daughter of Eve.

CHAPTER XL.

AGNES LEAVES LORD MARCHMONT'S HOUSE AND SHAKES OFF THE DUST FROM HER FEET AGAINST HER ENEMIES —A LODGING—A LONG WALK—THE CITY OF THE DEAD ONCE MORE—THE TOMB—THE PILE OF COFFINS —A TERRIBLE APPARITION.

AGNES'S awakening was anything but a pleasant one.

She awoke to grief, to misery, to sorrow!

A discarded wife, in vain could she hope for the forgiveness of her husband, to such a pitch was he incensed against her. Ever the victim of circumstances, when would fate be tired of sporting with her.

As she started up in bed, her cheek flushed and her face reddened as she recalled the scene of the night before, and remembered the fury of Lord Marchmont. "Perhaps," she thought, "he may forgive me in the morning," but after a little consideration she dismissed so fragile a hope from her mind, for although in a very desperate position, she was still too sensible to cling to straws or snatch at shadows.

What should she do?

How often had she before asked herself the same melancholy question, and only by practically looking for it had obtained an answer.

Miss Lavinia's name and house suggested themselves to her imagination, but she recoiled from throwing herself upon the bounty of her aunt. Indeed she had strong reasons for not doing so. She well knew that her aunt was avaricious and mean. To say that she was close-fisted was not to describe her failings adequately. She was penurious to a degree to those who could be of no further use to her; and Agnes could not do otherwise now than class herself amongst this category. If she came to Miss Lavinia in a carriage and pair, dressed in expensive silks, as Lady Marchmont, she would meet with a warm and generous reception; but, as a disgraced woman, a suspected wife, with the circumstantial evidence of her crime so black and damning as it was, Agnes knew that Miss Lavinia's doors would not revolve on their hinges to admit her, and so she, as it were, shook off the dust from her feet against all her relations, and resolved, with a heavy heart, to recommence the pilgrimage of life, solitary and alone.

If everybody's hand was against her, then should hers be against everybody.

She prepared to leave her rich and fashionable home.

"Marchmont," she said to herself, "is doing me an injustice. Some day he will see that such is the case, and then his old passion for me will revive; but as he has chosen to drive me like a dog from his doors, I will not burden him with my presence one moment more than is necessary for me to make my simple preparations."

Agnes had a little money; this she placed in a purse and put in her pocket.

She left all the jewellery that Lord Marchmont had bought her in her jewel-case, retaining only a few simple ornaments which she had possessed before she met his lordship.

She attired herself in an unassuming black silk dress, and packed up a few articles of wearing apparel which were indispensable.

Then she had her portmanteau brought downstairs and placed in a cab, telling the servant she was going out of town for a day or two.

She directed the cab to drive to a railway station; but when she had gone part of the way, she told him she had changed her mind, and, in obedience to her instructions, he drove in the direction of Brompton.

Here she had not much difficulty in finding a lodging; which, by making a payment in advance, she took without the disagreeableness of giving a reference.

She told the landlady she was a governess looking out for a situation, which story the good and unsuspecting old lady fully believed. Agnes added that she did not think she should be an inmate for any length of time, as she hoped to be engaged shortly.

It was yet early in the morning when Agnes had unpacked the few things she had brought with her and disposed them properly in the solitary chest of drawers in her bed-room.

In spite of her desolate condition and the grief she felt at her altered prospects, she felt that she could not afford to neglect the imperative demands of nature. So she sent her landlady to the butcher's, and indulged in the luxury of a chop, upon which she lunched.

After that, feeling restless and unhappy, she made up her mind to go out for a walk and explore the neighbourhood.

Accordingly she dressed herself plainly, in accordance with her altered circumstances, as well as she was able.

But there was that about her which was unmistakeable. She did not look like plain Miss Singleton, as she had called herself.

Her marvellous beauty was enhanced by the simplicity of her attire; and there was a commanding air, combined with an inexplicable something, which was strongly indicative of the admired and fashionable Lady Marchmont.

Agnes walked some distance, plunged in bitter reflections.

Many of the passers-by observed her, and thought what a lovely creature she was; but her depressed air, surmounted as it was with a heavy sadness, commanded for her that respect which she had a right to expect.

After a time, the exercise she was taking had its effect upon her, and she felt a little more lively; her sadness wore off a little, and as she heard the impudent London sparrows chirping all round her, she thought that if they could afford to be happy amidst the smoke and chimney-pots of the great city, surely she could learn a lesson from these little birds, and be happy also.

As she thus grew into a quieter state of mind, her usual serenity returned, and she laughed at the folly of being miserable.

She had often been in desperate positions before, and she had as often extricated herself from them.

Why should she not do so now?

No reasonable answer being forthcoming, she resolved that she would do so. She would triumph over her enemies, and she would laugh at fate till it got tired of persecuting her.

She had been walking for more than an hour, and she thought of turning back; but as she looked up, she found herself exactly opposite some iron gates which led into what appeared to be some beautiful gardens.

The sun was shining—and it was a lovely autumn day. Everything, taken together, invited her entry. She thought she could not spend an hour or so in a better manner. It was, doubtless, some park or other. She did not know much about the suburbs of London. This would be a good opportunity of exploring some spacious spot set apart for the recreation of the people.

She advanced to the open portals; but as she neared them, her eye fell upon an inscription placed upon the lintel. It was to the effect that the public were admitted to walk in the cemetery daily. As she read this, she recoiled a step or two.

"A cemetery!" she exclaimed. "Well, that is not the most agreeable place at the best of times; and I am not one of those sanguine people who can write puns on tombstones."

But after a little reflection, she thought, as the day was so fine, and the cemetery, as far as she could see, was laid out so prettily and invitingly, she might as well turn her footsteps in that direction as in any other.

With a shrinking feeling very natural to a nervous person, she passed over the threshold, and walked along the road which had conducted many a specimen of frail humanity to its last resting-place. And after walking some distance she stood in the centre of this vast city of the dead.

There were graves to the right of her, graves to the left of her, graves in front of her, and graves in her rear. One wide undulating plain, stretching in every direction almost as far as the eye could reach, studded thickly with graves.

With a shudder, she found she was standing on a grave. When her eye moved restlessly from some marmorean satire on a worthless life, it rested upon a mausoleum or travelled to some equally fine triumph of the sculptor's art.

There lay the pauper, and there the peer. Both lay in the same square yard of soil, in the grand equality of death. There was the grave of the miser, and a little further on that of his spendthrift—him who had made his money fly, and in so doing had engendered the disease which killed him. What were they all now? The statesman, the peer, the poet, the man of fashion, the prematurely deceased Magdalene, the miser, the drunkard? Dust, all dust! Turn which way she would, all was vanity.

The vexation of spirit had passed away, but vanity remained and followed them to the tomb. While moralising thus, a few drops of rain fell upon the ground; this shortly increased to a heavy shower.

Agnes was without that useful appendage in our island home—an umbrella—so she looked around for some place of shelter, as she did not care much about getting wet. On her right hand she perceived a vault; some steps conducted into its dark and gloomy recesses. She hesitated at first whether or not to descend them; but the rain came down with such violence that she had no choice. If she stayed where she was at present, she could not avoid getting wet to the skin. So she went down into the tomb—not figuratively, but literally.

AGNES ESCAPES BEING MESMERISED, AND STABS THE COUNT.

The door was open, and as the wind beat the rain down upon her she passed through it, and stood on the floor of the charnel house.

The light which penetrated this subterranean dwelling for the dead was amply sufficient to show her the multitude of coffins on each side of her.

The shower increased its proportions, and developed into a storm.

Agnes congratulated herself upon having secured a shelter, such as it was.

The silence of the grave is proverbial.

Here she experienced it in all its intensity.

A frog or a toad now and then uttered a shrill croak, and hopped about four feet; or a drop of rain water, which had permeated the soil and the brickwork, fell on the damp stones with which the tomb was paved. Save and except these, and the fierce rushing and groaning of the angry blast, nothing disturbed the monotony of her position.

Suddenly she started, as a strange noise fell upon her ear.

Was it human?

Did it proceed from one like herself, existing in the flesh?

Resembling the last groan wrung from the blood-stained lips of some mangled wretch condemned to the torture was this fearful and mysterious sound.

For an instant afterwards all was still.

With trembling eagerness Agnes waited its repetition.

She would have flown from the accursed and mysterious vault, but some strange influence seemed to be at work to prevent her.

The rain still continued to patter restlessly down upon the steps outside.

The occasional drop still fell on the damp floor of the vault.

The frogs croaked and jumped about, as if pleased at the prospect of a little wet and slush to waddle about in.

A second time came that awful and soul-sickening sound.

Agnes's flesh crept, and her hair stiffened.

Yet could she not move.

There, in one corner of the vault, a terrible conflict seemed to be going on.

Heavy blows were rained upon some hard substance.

It was as the agony of a strong man, upon whom the terrors of death had descended.

Then hoarse cries were uttered, and the struggles in the corner of the vault were frightful.

A pile of coffins rocked to and fro.

Agnes would have given the world to have fainted and have become insensible; but this relief was denied her, and rooted to the spot, as she was, she could not fly.

With a horrible shrink, she beheld the pile of coffins fall heavily upon the floor and smash to pieces; while their ghastly contents, only partially wrapped in the cerements of the grave, were exposed to her shrinking gaze. But her eyes soon wandered from these to the corner, where they became rivetted upon something more wonderful than she had ever before witnessed.

There, with one foot advanced from a strangely-shaped coffin; there, with a face upon which was depicted the most acute curiosity; there, with an arm extended as if to feel its way; there, with a lack-lustre eye fixed upon herself; there, in that gloomy cavern, *was the Count Val de Grace !*

Agnes was astounded—she thought herself the dupe of some extraordinary delusion. She was alarmed, terrified, frightened out of her senses.

She stared at the apparition till her eyes ached, and then she reeled against the wall of the vault. She could stand it no longer; and, with a piercing shriek, she fell upon the damp floor insensible.

CHAPTER XLI.

THE SECRET CHAMBER—THE SLIDING PANEL—AGNES COGITATES AS TO WHO HER ENEMY IS—SHE COMES TO THE CONCLUSION THAT SHE IS IN THE POWER OF COUNT VAL DE GRACE—SHE SLEEPS—THE RETREATING FIGURE — STRANGE NOISES—DAY BREAKS — VAL DE GRACE SOLICITS AGNES'S LOVE—SHE REPELS HIM WITH DISDAIN—HIS THREATS.

WHEN Agnes awoke from her lethargy, she found herself in an apartment which was altogether strange to her.

She endeavoured to find out the mystery connected with it, but in vain.

That there was a mystery she could not doubt for an instant.

The furniture was very rich, but of a curious and fantastic pattern. It was not exactly ancient, but an antique pattern modernized. Everything around her denoted that the house she was in belonged to a rich, if not to a great man.

Who could he be? And where was she?

She tried to recal the incidents of the last four-and-twenty hours.

She had been entrapped into a position giving cause for great suspicion, by the acts and machinations of Count Val de Grace, the mesmerist.

She had been discovered by her husband, and he had dismissed her from his home and from his bed with curses.

Then the scene in the cemetery flashed upon her, and she recalled the terrific apparition which had so alarmed her, and ultimately caused her to lose her senses.

What had ensued after that she could not tell: she could only conjecture. What she thought was simply this—

She had seen Count Val de Grace fall down dead, as she thought, at her husband's feet.

Could they have, by any possibility, been deceived?

She knew his marvellous power.

He might have thrown himself into a trance and simulated death.

She had heard of such things being done. And why should not the count have practised this mode of deception to save his life?

He was just the very man to do it.

Agnes was, it must be borne in mind, utterly ignorant of what had happened after she had retired to her room, on the dreadful night when Lord Marchmont discarded her.

If she had known how her husband conveyed the apparently dead body to the cemetery, and placed it in the vault, she would not have had so much trouble to put this and that together.

However, she did, at last, arrive at this result—

She conjectured, and rightly, that when her husband found himself alone with the dead body, he considered it necessary to dispose of it in some way or other.

She was well acquainted with the audacity of his disposition.

What more likely than that he should convey the corpse to some place where it would not be easily discovered.

Then she exclaimed to herself—

"Supposing this to be the case, he must have taken the count's body to the cemetery in the night. The next day, by some strange chance, or by the count's infernal arts, my wandering footsteps were directed thither; and in order to make the whole thing more extraordinary, the shower of rain came on, and I went into the very vault where the corpse had been deposited. Then, while I was standing there, taking refuge from the fury of the elements, the count must have awakened from his trance, and have appeared before me in the appalling manner, the suddenness and the strangeness of which deprived me of sensibility."

This reasoning of Agnes was very clever and ingenious, but what puzzled her most was to discover where she at present was, and how she had come there.

She ran to the two windows which the room possessed, and gazed out.

She saw nothing. A dead wall rose straight up before her. The apartment had evidently been well chosen.

Her eyes wandered upwards. The dingy sky, or more strictly speaking, a patch of sky made dingy by the London smoke, rewarded her efforts in this direction.

Then she looked downwards, only to discover a skylight, covering, perhaps, the kitchen, or some other domestic office.

By the look of the shadows, which were gathering in some parts of the room, it was drawing near the evening.

Agnes felt for her watch.

It was gone!

Somebody had deprived her of it. Their reason she could not imagine; but it was not there. However, she judged that it was about six o'clock.

At last Agnes began to get terribly anxious, she even felt alarmed.

Was she a prisoner in that richly furnished chamber?

She advanced to the door, and tried to turn its ivory handle, but it resisted all her efforts. Certainly they were feminine efforts, but she exerted all her strength, and when a woman is frightened she is stronger than some people think. She imbibes a sort of fury which makes her no contemptible adversary. But in this case her strength was thrown away, for the door would not open.

Agnes stood still, while the beads of perspiration started to her forehead.

What could she think?

Only that she was in the power of some enemy, and as she came to this conclusion, she could conceive no one more likely to treat her in this way than Count Val de Grace. She shuddered as this suspicion entered her mind. To be in the power of that mysterious and unscrupulous nobleman was, indeed, dreadful.

As the terrible and overwhelming conviction forced itself upon her, no wonder that she cowered down in a corner of the room, and covered her face with her hands.

What could she hope?

Absolutely nothing. Count Val de Grace was not a man either to feel or to show pity. He had declared that he loved her, and he had endeavoured, on a former occasion, to force his hateful caresses upon her. The count was perhaps even now watching her from some curiously contrived loophole or crevice in the wall—even now gloating over her misery—watching, with undisguised satisfaction, the uncontrollable tears as they flowed in torrents from her red and swollen eyes.

Would he not now be eager for revenge?

Most likely. He had only escaped the death he merited at the hands of Lord Marchmont by a clever subterfuge—a charlatan's trick, a juggler's device.

But, after a while, Agnes controlled her grief, and dried her tears. She would never, she swore to herself, willingly consent to the desires of the count, and if he attempted violence—if he dared to try to dishonour her—he should fall by her hand, or she herself would never more look upon the light of day.

When she made this resolution she felt happier, and more able to meet the dangers that she felt were environing her.

Her paroxysm of grief had exhausted her fragile frame, and sitting down in an arm-chair fashioned in the most

luxurious manner possible—even to the full extent of a
Sybarite's wishes—she closed her eyes, and tried to snatch a
little rest; but just as she was about to drop off into an
uneasy slumber, she reflected that she would be entirely in
the power of the count if she were to go to sleep. As she
reflected thus, she roused herself, and threw off the somnolent
incubus that weighed upon her.

As she did so, what was her intense astonishment and
surprise, to see that, during the few brief moments of her
semi-consciousness, some one had entered her apartment
and lighted a lamp which stood upon a table covered with
the choicest viands, while a door in the wall, which now
stood open, revealed a small chamber also well-lighted,
furnished with the paraphernalia of a dressing-room.

Agnes stood bewildered, she could scarcely believe her
senses. It looked so like the Ali Baba sort of magic of the
Arabian Nights. However, as she felt faint, she thought
there would be no harm in breaking her fast. Accordingly
she sat down at the table and ate part of some rare and
expensive bird, and washed down her repast with a draught
of wine.

Soon after taking the liquid she felt even more drowsy
than before, and seeking her arm-chair a second time, she
fell soundly asleep.

How long she slept she could not tell, but she was aroused
by an uneasy sensation as of some one near her.

With a cry she started up. The lights had either burned
out or had been removed. A few rays of moonlight penetrated the room and lay pale and motionless upon the carpet.
By the aid of these Agnes perceived a dark figure retreating
through the dressing-room.

She watched it for a moment, and at last it appeared to
have vanished through the wall; for although she strained
her eyes for some time, she saw it no more.

Painfully excited by this strange occurrence, and the
mysteries that surrounded her, Agnes kept awake the rest
of the night; and although at times disturbed and frightened
by strange noises, still she saw no one, and it was with a
feeling of intense gratitude to Providence for its sheltering
care and protection that she saw to her inexpressible relief
the first glimmer of daylight, as dawn broke over the great
metropolis. She welcomed the morning with great satisfaction, because she had reason to believe that the count
would make himself visible, and hold some sort of conversation with her. So firmly had the idea that she was in the
count's power become fixed in her mind, that she never
doubted for an instant that such was the case. Whether
she was right or not in her conjecture will soon be seen.

A few hours after daybreak a knock came on the exterior
of the door she had vainly tried to open the night before.
In as resolute a voice as she could command, Agnes said—
"Come in."

The door then opened, and a gentleman entered. It was
no other than Count Val de Grace.

Agnes's heart beat, and she felt strangely excited, as she
always did when in the presence of this remarkable man.
But she was not in the least surprised at seeing him, as she
had for some time been fully prepared to do so.

The count bowed very low, and hoped that her ladyship
had passed the night well.

Agnes heard him call her "her ladyship" at first with
astonishment, but after a moment's reflection she remembered that the count could not have heard that she had
been separated from her husband; so she resolved to threaten
him with the vengeance of Lord Marchmont, if he offered
to insult her.

"I am surprised you should ask me so absurd a question,
Count Val de Grace," she said, in reply to his query.

"Absurd! why so?"

Agnes pointed to the chair in which she had passed the
night, and said—

"That was my couch."

The count expressed his sorrow that she had not been
better cared for.

Agnes smiled disdainfully.

"Well, count, if you wish to show me any kindness——"

"I do, believe me."

"If so, then order your carriage, and send me home."

"I cannot so readily part with so fair a prize," he answered.

"What!" cried Agnes, "am I to conjecture that I am
to be detained here against my will?"

The count shrugged his shoulders.

"Speak!" cried Agnes, in a still more excited tone of
voice.

"You know how dear you are to me. I have told you
how much I love you," said Count Val de Grace.

"Until lately I regarded you as a man of honour," said
Agnes, pleadingly.

"Honour!" exclaimed the count; "who would not throw
honour to the winds, and character to perdition, to procure
you, lovely Agnes?"

"Leave me, oh! leave me," said Agnes. "Why have I
lived to listen to such insults?"

"You refuse to hear me?" said the count, savagely.

"I do."

"Then will I find a way to tame your proud spirit, and
to make you adore the very name of Val de Grace."

"I laugh at your threats," said Agnes, darting past him
with the quickness of a deer, and endeavouring to gain the
staircase.

But the count was too quick for her. He seized her in his
arms, and bore her shrieking to a chair, in which he placed
her.

He then left her for a time, saying as he went—

"I shall return ere long to receive your answer. Be
mine, and you shall be happy: refuse, and Heaven help
you."

CHAPTER XLII.

THE COUNT PRESSES AGNES—SHE DEFIES HIM—HE
TRIES TO MESMERISE HER, BUT SHE ESCAPES FROM
HIS THRALDOM, AND STABS HIM—AGNES ESCAPES—
THE GALLERY OF STATUES—THE FAIRY ABODE—THE
TREES, THE FOUNTAINS, THE BIRDS—THE GARDEN—
THE SHEET OF WATER—AGNES MEETS AN OLD
FRIEND.

AFTER his concluding remark, Count Val de Grace rudely
and abruptly left the apartment.

At first Agnes's pride bore her up; but when she found
herself in the solitude of that isolated chamber, with no one
to speak to, no one to condole with her, her fortitude gave
way, and she abandoned herself to tears.

She had been brave and determined, as most women are
when the danger is imminent, but when that passes away
their courage oozes out of their fingers'-ends, and they show
themselves to be what they are—women.

Nor were Agnes's fears ill grounded.

Val de Grace was a resolute, and she had every reason to
believe, a bad man. He would not, she thought, hesitate at
any means by which he could accomplish his object, which
she knew well enough was the possession of her person. She
was, however, determined to resist him to the death, if necessary. She had even been virtuous when she had left the
workroom of Madame Cerise; she had resisted every temptation which fell in her way. While Charlotte Saunders,
she had every reason to believe, had succumbed to the force
of the example which Norah Nolan had given her.

In becoming Marmaduke Wilson's wife, Agnes had followed the dictates of her heart. She had given up her
affections unreservedly to a man who was in reality unde-
serving of them. Very likely he was not so black as he was
painted; but he was undoubtedly a thief. And he had been
proved so by a jury consisting of twelve of his own countrymen, who had sat to determine his guilt or innocence: they
had decided against the latter.

Agnes knew that he was a felon, and she had very naturally refused to consider herself a felon's bride.

Marmaduke Wilson had been transported beyond the
seas.

And Agnes had committed her only fault in marrying
Lord Marchmont when her first husband was alive.

But then the temptation was very great.

She had been all her life in a false position.

Miss Lavinia Leslie was urging her perpetually to contract a good marriage, and at last she had fallen in with her
aunt's views, and made one.

Agnes had long ago discarded Marmaduke Wilson from
her mind, although his image would now and then unpleasantly obtrude itself upon her. She hoped and prayed that
she might never in this life meet him again.

She had tried with all her heart to love Lord Marchmont,
and if she had not done so she was not entirely to blame.
She had done her best, and she had behaved honourably to
him at least.

His honour had certainly been safe and untarnished in her hands.

His lordship had in a moment of blind rage and infatuation chosen to believe her false to him; and she had suffered in consequence.

He had driven her from him with every species of ignominy and disgrace. He had not even paid her the poor compliment of wishing her good-bye.

But notwithstanding his insults, his unjust suspicions, and his reproaches, she would not play him false.

"I am Lord Marchmont's lawfully wedded wife," she said to herself; "that is, I am so always provided my first husband never comes back from transportation and claims me, and of that I think there is little or no chance. If he should, he will have to substantiate his claim, and that will not be so easy, even if he should be clever enough to find me out. At all events, I am at present Lady Marchmont, and as the wife of a peer of England will resist every temptation or inclination to evil. Let Count Val de Grace attempt only to put his base purposes into execution, and he shall never live to report the outrage, for he shall fall by my hand."

There was a little bravado in this threat, but Agnes's ready wit would have devised some means of checking the libertinism of the Anglo-French count.

A piece of broken glass would be a dangerous weapon in her desperate hands.

As this idea occurred to her she walked to the window, and drove her fist through a pane of glass.

But the violence with which she struck the vitreous substance sent it flying in all directions into the air, and it fell upon the skylight below with a jingling noise.

Seeing this, she put her hand through the broken pane and smashed another with her elbow from the outside.

This time the fragments fell in the room.

Seizing the most pointed and dagger-like piece from amongst the jagged bits that lay in a heap upon the ground, she concealed it in the folds of her dress, and felt that she was prepared to encounter Count Val de Grace, always provided that he did not put his devilish arts in execution against her.

Hardly had she hidden away the strange weapon she had so cleverly extemporized, than the door again opened, and the count a second time made his appearance.

He had been aroused, and, to tell the truth, a little alarmed, by the noise made by the falling glass, and he had come up to see what had aroused his fair prisoner and driven her to such a pitch of alarm and fury as to break the windows. He was far from guessing the real cause of the disturbance. As he entered the room Agnes exclaimed—

"Once for all, Count Val de Grace, will you let me out of this prison?"

The count replied with a smile on his well-cut lips—

"Candour compels me, my dear Lady Marchmont, to declare that it is utterly out of my power to do anything of the sort."

"This is your determination?"

"Do not be alarmed," said the count; "no harm shall befall you."

Agnes smiled incredulously. She knew the character of the man before her, and she was not to be beguiled with specious speeches.

"You smile," he said. "Why will you not believe and trust me?"

"Trust you!" cried Agnes. "As soon would I stand beneath a tree, and trust to the mercy of the lightning."

"Why did nature make you so charming, my lovely Agnes?" exclaimed the count, who took no notice of her indignant looks or her reproachful tones.

"If I am beautiful," replied Agnes, "nature no doubt had some wise purpose in view in making me so, and as you assure me that I am so, I suppose I am bound to believe you."

"I would not offend you for all the wealth of India," said Val de Grace; "but I cannot restrain myself from declaring the passion I entertain for you. It is like a summer madness; it engrosses all my thoughts. Sleeping and waking I murmur your name, which is ever on my lips. I love you, I have told you so, and not an hour ago you drove me from you with disdain, but love like mine can put up with many slights, and I only adore you more for your cruelty."

"Be silent, count," cried Agnes. "I may not listen to these rhapsodies. You forget that you are addressing a married woman."

The count laughed a wild weird sort of laugh, such as you might have expected to hear from some demon of the Hartz Mountains.

This laugh startled Agnes; with all her courage she could not help being afraid of this man.

"Oh! that you would listen to me," said the count, with an amorous sigh.

"I cannot, will not hear you, count!" cried Agnes, passionately. "Release me, I entreat—I beg of you."

"Never!" he said, firmly.

"If you ever leave this chamber, you do so as my affianced —my——"

"Your mistress, you would say," almost screamed Agnes, her whole frame trembling with rage and indignation.

"We will not cavil about terms," he said, carelessly.

"What do you say, wretch that you are?"

"I was merely observing that one word is as good as another," he said, shrugging his shoulders, as is the habit of Frenchmen when they wish to be sarcastic and freezing in their manner.

"And you think that I will give myself up to your infamous devices, while a drop of blood flows in my veins?"

"I think that you are silly now, and that you may be wiser hereafter," said the count, with a hypocritical smile upon his lips.

"Then learn, once for all, that your time is wasted in talking to me. I would rather die at your feet here in this room, at this very moment, than listen any more to your base proposals and your cowardly insults."

Agnes was much excited, and her rage made her look, if possible, more beautiful than she was in her calmer moments.

The count gazed at her with admiration.

He then moved his hands about uneasily, as he had done in the case of Jabez Clarke.

When Agnes perceived what he was doing, she uttered a cry of terror.

She knew that the count was seeking to envelope her in the enervating toils of the mesmeric trance.

Were she to succumb to the influence that he was trying to establish over her, she would be completely and entirely at his mercy.

A very old illustration is that of the bird and the boa-constrictor. So old, indeed, as to have become almost worn out; but trite and stereotyped as it is, it was applicable in this instance.

As the bird flutters about restlessly, approaching every moment nearer and nearer to the crawling reptile which is about to devour it, so did Agnes endeavour with all her might and main to throw off the thraldom of that power whose secrets Count Val de Grace had learned only too well.

Her cheek blanched, and her lips quivered, but the eyes of the count were riveted upon her, and she could not withdraw her gaze from his hateful countenance.

There he stood, with a remorseless look which partook of the nature of a triumphant one. He was gloating over his victim.

Agnes was alone — alone with this dreadful man in his own house. His servants, even if within hearing, which was somewhat problematical, were no doubt bribed to keep silence as to the misdeeds, and perhaps crimes, of their master; and although she had the will to shriek for help and aid, she had not the ability.

Agnes was in a desperate situation. Indeed, if she lost her consciousness for a moment, what would become of her? She dared not think.

She battled bravely with the magnetic power that the count threw out of his system towards her.

She was strong, and of a vigorous mental organization; but although her strength of mind averted the catastrophe for some time, she felt that she must eventually succumb to the villanous arts and rascally devices of Count Val de Grace.

What could she do? Wave after wave of the odic force went through the air and attacked her system, and she was powerless to do anything which would cancel its effects.

Agnes was perfectly aware that if she did not make a great and prodigious effort, she would, in a few short, fleeting minutes, be in the power of her insidious enemy.

All at once the recollection of the piece of glass which, when she had broken the window, she had concealed in the bosom of her dress, flashed across her mind. With a desperate effort, she seized it firmly in her hand, and wrapped a fold of her dress around one end of it.

As the count saw this, he increased his exertions; and Agnes staggered and appeared as if she were about to fall. The count narrowed the distance between them; but so intent was he on subduing Agnes, that he did not perceive a small hassock lying on the floor. The inevitable consequence of his carelessness was that he stumbled over it, and fell upon the floor.

Up to this time he had followed Agnes with his eyes, but now the magnetic chain was partially broken.

Agnes, in a wild delirium of joy coursing through her veins, felt herself liberated.

She knew that it was only momentary. She knew that Count Val de Grace would recover his footing very speedily, and then he would begin again. With what result she could easily conjecture.

With the rapidity of lightning, like some heroine of romance, she sprang forward and seized the count by the throat.

Then, using the bit of broken glass like a dagger, she dealt him blows with it at random.

With such fury was she animated, that she did not desist from her work of vengeance until the strange weapon she had extemporized broke in her hand, and the pieces fell, covered with blood, upon the carpet, which was absorbing some of the same sanguinary fluid.

The count was motionless as a corpse. Agnes rose and stood beside him.

Was he dead, or was he pretending to be so?

He had simulated death before by throwing himself into a trance. Could he have done so now?

Agnes thought not. The blows she had given him were not exactly serious, although the blood flowed freely from the wounds.

She had stabbed him on the face and neck, and she had dealt him one severe blow on the temple which might have caused his insensibility.

However, now was her chance to escape. She was not so stupid as to neglect it.

The count was bleeding profusely; he might bleed to death, she thought. As the idea struck her, she resolved with great magnanimity not to leave him in such a precarious state. She could not ring or call for the domestics, because that would call their attention to herself, and perhaps they might think it their duty to detain her.

So she knelt down by the side of this man who had tried to do her the gravest injuries, and wrapped a handkerchief round his head; this she tied tightly, so as to prevent any further hæmorrhage.

After this she considered that the most exacting good Samaritan could not have wished her to do more; so she turned away and prepared to leave the apartment.

The door the count had entered by was, of course, unlocked, as he had not thought it necessary to fasten it after him. Passing through this, she found herself in a corridor, along which she hurried. No staircase, however, appeared, and when she reached the end of the corridor she found herself confronted with a door.

There was nothing for it but to go on; to retreat would have been madness. Accordingly she turned the handle of the door, and to her delight a slight push sufficed to open it. When she entered, Agnes perceived a long gallery. There were niches in the wall, in which, upon pedestals, stood some of the finest efforts of the sculptor's art.

There were Venuses in every possible position. There was a sleeping Venus, and a Venus awake, a Venus lying on her side, and one reclining on a couch. Every attitude had been carefully studied, and the result was a singular collection of what were undoubtedly works of art.

Agnes gazed at the statues for a moment, and then pursued her way.

She quickly traversed the marble flagstones of which the floor of the gallery was composed.

Here she met with a novel sort of impediment. A curtain was stretched across the doorway. Without any hesitation, Agnes drew it aside and walked on.

Here an unexpected scene met her view.

She stood in a spacious apartment, furnished and built in a style of the richest Oriental magnificence.

The room was large, and in form square. The ceiling was not very lofty, but supported by pillars formed of what appeared to be the precious metals, gold and silver. Whether it was so, or whether they were only outwardly coated with gold and silver, the effect was the same upon the dazzled beholder.

The ceiling was made in a fantastic manner.

The forms of different animals were cunningly depicted upon it, and their images indented, as it were, in the substance of which it was composed.

Light was admitted through curiously tinted glass, which was placed here and there in the walls, about six feet from the ground.

The floor was paved with what seemed to be amber, or oddly-shaped tiles.

Around the sides of the apartment ran what are called divans, or soft cushions luxuriously arranged. In the centre was a basin which received rose water, which was ejected through the jets of half-a-dozen prettily arranged fountains.

Orange-trees, exotics of the most rare and expensive kinds, and flowers in full bloom, were arranged in profusion in different places. Bullfinches and other melodious birds, which had evidently been carefully taught to sing, fluttered about in the branches of the orange-trees, and made the air resonant with their sweet notes. Gold and silver fish swam about in cool and pleasant basins, which were made for the purpose in the floor of the room, and little fountains played around them.

It was a fairy paradise.

Agnes could not believe the evidence of her senses. She thought that she was bewildered.

She had heard and read of the Alhambra in Spain, and its gorgeous courts and splendid magnificence.

She had read of the Taje Mahal, and the efforts of Shah Jehan at Delhi and at Agra; but here, in the heart of the greatest commercial city in the world, she had stumbled upon all that the wildest fancy, affected with a love of everything Oriental, could desire.

Agnes almost expected to see a turbaned slave make his appearance, and bowing till his head touched his toes, perform what is called a "salaam."

Although she knew that every moment was of consequence to her, Agnes could not resist the temptation of sitting down upon one of the soft and yielding cushions which garnished the apartment.

With a strange feeling of delight she watched the tinkling sound of the fountains and the gentle rippling of the water.

The perfumed atmosphere was grateful to her senses, and the songs of the birds were bewitching.

Count Val de Grace was evidently no common man, and therefore all the more to be feared.

It was strange that he should bring his Oriental ideas into prosaic, commonplace England. But so it was.

At last Agnes summoned up resolution enough to leave this charming abode.

A curtain similar to the one she had removed on entering invited egress on the other side.

Through this she made her exit, and after walking a little distance along a passage, she came to a flight of stairs, and by following them to their base she found herself before a door.

This she opened, and found herself in a garden.

It was the middle of the day, and the sun was high in the heavens.

As it was the beginning of winter, there was not much warmth in its rays, and Agnes felt chilled. But she walked rapidly down the garden without meeting any one.

Her walk led her to a sheet of water.

At first she could not understand such an extraordinary occurrence, but after a little reflection she concluded that she had just made her escape from some villa on the banks of the Grand Junction Canal.

A boat was moored under a willow-tree.

Agnes got into it, and courageously pushed off.

A little paddling brought her to the opposite shore.

She sprang upon the land, and walked a short distance, when she met a solitary pedestrian, of whom she demanded the name of the locality in which she was.

He told her that she was in Maida-hill.

When she heard this she had no doubt whatever that the Count Val de Grace inhabited a villa, the garden of which stretched down to the water.

However, she was free, and she congratulated herself upon her escape.

She resolved to go back to her old lodging, and she walked rapidly, as she thought, in the proper direction.

After proceeding some distance, she found herself in a

fashionable part of the town, and her surprise was great to hear some one exclaim—

"Agnes! can that be you?"

Turning round, she recognised her old friend, Charlotte Saunders, who had taken her side so valiantly at Madame Cerise's.

———

CHAPTER XLIII.

AGNES AND CHARLOTTE RENEW THEIR ACQUAINTANCE —CHARLOTTE'S HOME—A SUBSTANTIAL REPAST—A BRACE OF STORIES—NORAH NOLAN'S HORRIBLE FATE—IMPALED ALIVE—THE DEVIL'S ACRE—GOING SHOPPING —BARMAID AT A CAFÉ—HOLDING A CANDLE TO THE DEVIL.

IT was so long since Agnes had seen Charlotte Saunders, that she was almost oblivious of her existence.

She was a little annoyed, too, at being recognised so easily by her former friend and champion.

It will be remembered that Jabez Clarke had seen Agnes, but he had failed to see in her the lowly drudge, whom he had once so maltreated and abused. Certainly he was in a state of mesmerism; that might have had something to do with it; but Agnes had flattered herself that she was so altered that no one would know her again.

The unexpected meeting with Charlotte Saunders, however, at once dissipated this idea; and Agnes was, as we have said, a good deal chagrined at what she considered an untoward occurrence.

Now that she had met her she could not refuse to speak to her. It would have seemed so strange. It would have appeared so unfriendly; and, indeed, there was, in reality, no help for it.

There was Charlotte Saunders standing before her, extending the hand of welcome, and how could she refuse to take it?

Charlotte had done her all the good that lay in her power when she was a sempstress at Madame Cerise's, and she had extricated her from a most unpleasant position, when Smithers had endeavoured to hold her up to the ridicule and the horror of her volatile companion.

So Agnes shook Charlotte by the hand, and in reply to her friendly greeting, said—

"Is that you? Where have you been, and what are you doing here?"

"I might ask you the same thing," replied Charlotte.

Agnes knew perfectly well that it would be an absurdity to tell Charlotte her history. So she resolved to invent some plausible story, which she had little or no doubt her friend would readily believe.

"My story is soon told," she replied.

"Oh, indeed!"

"Yes. I have not had a very adventurous life since the day you and I left off dressmaking."

"I may say the same thing," rejoined Charlotte.

"What have you been doing, then?" asked Agnes.

"I shall be delighted to tell you."

"Not more so, I am sure, than I shall be to hear your story."

"Story! Lord bless you, I have none to tell you."

"Well, you know what I mean," replied Agnes.

"Well, suppose we adjourn somewhere, and spin a yarn, as my captain says."

"Your captain?" cried Agnes, in surprise.

"Yes. You look astonished."

"Not more astonished than pleased. How long have you been married?"

"Married!" exclaimed Charlotte.

"Yes!" said Agnes, looking up in her friend's face, and awaiting a reply.

"Oh, not very long," replied Charlotte, hesitating a little in her answer.

It was remarkable that as she made this reply her cheek flushed a little.

"Not long. Well, I am very glad to hear it. Is he a nice man? You must come and tell me all about it," replied Agnes, who began to take an interest in her friend's affairs.

"I'll tell you," said Charlotte, "anything you want to know; but we can't talk here."

"Where shall we go?"

"Anywhere you like," replied Charlotte.

"It does not matter to me," said Agnes. "I leave it to you."

"In that case you had better come to my place. It is not anything very grand, but we can talk at our ease, and there will be no one to disturb us. What do you say? Will you come? I think you will like going home with me more than going to any public ——"

"Oh, a thousand times better. Is it far from here?" said Agnes; "if it is we had better have a cab."

"No, it is not far from here. We are close to Regent-street now, and I am still hanging about the old locality."

"The old locality! What do you mean?" asked Agnes, elevating her eyebrows.

"Oh, the Devil's Acre, as they call it."

"What's that?"

"Why, the Market. What a flat you are! you don't know anything."

"What market," said Agnes. "You quite mystify me."

"Oh, you know; come, now, you may be a little green, but you can't be so verdant as all that."

"Do you mean the Haymarket?" said Agnes, upon whom a new light began to dawn.

"Of course I do; but let us be moving. The sooner we start the sooner we shall get there."

Agnes acquiesced in this proposition, and walked by her friend's side.

During their short journey they only indulged in commonplace remarks.

At last Charlotte stopped in a street contiguous to Soho-square, and opening the door of a house with a small latch-key of rather inferior workmanship, ushered Agnes into some plainly-furnished rooms on the ground-floor.

"Now make yourself at home," she exclaimed, giving her an arm-chair to sit in, and bustling about good-naturedly.

She did not say "What will you have to eat or drink," but she went to a cupboard in the corner of the room, and produced the remains of a pigeon-pie, and a couple of bottles of pale ale, and two decanters, one of which contained gin, and the other brandy. She then laid a small cloth upon a tray, and brought out some knives and forks and plates, and the banquet was complete.

"Now," she cried; "you see your food, and if you don't want to displease me, you will set-to and walk into the victuals."

"Oh, Charlotte, how you talk!" said Agnes.

"Oh, that is nothing. I like a little slang now and then; but there is nothing in that. You should hear my captain."

"You are always talking about this wonderful captain; I quite long to be introduced to him."

"Oh, all in good time, my dear," replied Charlotte; "but at present attend to your feeding. Take this wing and this leg; you will find it very good. Some of the breast? A little bit—very well. Here, stop a bit; you have no egg; and you must try the gravy."

"That is very nice, thank you. No more," said Agnes.

Charlotte then uncorked a bottle of ale, and filled her friend's glass.

"Did you make this pie yourself?" asked Agnes.

"I make it?—not I. What do you take me for?"

"Well, in this instance, for something very hospitable—a sort of really sweet thing in friends," replied Agnes, laughing.

"No; I don't make pies," said Charlotte; "and I have two very good reasons for not doing so. In the first place, I don't know how to; and in the second, I have not got the time to spare."

"Oh, I see."

"That's refreshing," replied Charlotte. "I am glad to see you are getting a little cleverer than you were."

"Oh, you think I am. Well, that's something," said Agnes, with a smile.

"Isn't it odd," exclaimed Charlotte Saunders, after a pause, "how old friends turn up?"

"Yes, it is."

"I felt sure I should see you again some day or other."

"Your conviction was well founded."

"Will you have any more?" asked Charlotte.

Agnes replied in the negative.

"Oh, you wont; very well. Have a little cold brandy-and-water, then; or perhaps you prefer it warm. And bring your chair near the fire; I will soon put a match to it. You see I always keep it laid."

Charlotte Saunders struck a match, and stooping down, lighted the fire, which was placed all ready for ignition in the grate.

The "wheel" soon caught, and the resinous matter with which it was encrusted speedily flared up, and in a short time a cheery blaze illumined the apartment; and the young women wheeled their chairs on to the hearth-rug, mixed themselves some brandy-and-water, and prepared for half-an-hour's indulgence in a friendly gossip.

It is remarkable how fond women invariably are of gossiping and canvassing their neighbours, their friends, and their acquaintances, when they get together.

Agnes and Charlotte were no exception to this very general rule. But in this instance they preferred talking about themselves before they discussed the affairs of the nation, or those of their intimates.

"Now, Agnes," cried Charlotte, "'fire away,' as my captain says."

"On the contrary, I want you to begin."

"Me?"

"Yes. I shall never rest until I hear all about this captain."

"Oh, you must wait for that; I am too lazy just now. I am just in the humour to listen to you; so you must be good enough to do as I ask you."

"But," said Agnes.

"Not a word," cried Charlotte; "I am going to be obeyed to-day, so there is no help for you. You had better submit with a good grace."

Agnes pouted a little, and tried to look angry; but after a moment, she said—

"Very well, you shall have your own way."

The truth was, Agnes had wished to gain a little time, in order to concoct a story to tell her friend, but as she was forced to submit, she said—

"When I left you I met a man who married me; he was nothing much. He was a simple artisan, but we got on very well together, until he met another woman, whom, apparently, he seemed to like better, and, in the end, he ran away with her, and left me."

"What was her name?"

Agnes was puzzled for a reply, but thinking there would be no harm in it, she said—

"Miriam Moss."

"Miriam Moss?" repeated Charlotte, quickly.

"Yes. Is she a friend of yours?"

"Not exactly," replied Charlotte, ironically.

"Oh, she is not. How do you know her then, may I ask?" said Agnes, who waited anxiously for a reply.

"Never mind how I know her," said Charlotte; "if you want to see her, and you will come with me, I'll point her but to you this evening, and then you can draw your own conclusions."

"Oh, certainly," answered Agnes.

She was much pleased at the chance of meeting Miriam, because she had vowed to be revenged upon her for her perfidy with regard to Marmaduke Wilson. He was nothing to Agnes now, but she could not help feeling that Miriam had behaved most treacherously to her.

"Go on," said Charlotte; "I am waiting for you to finish your story."

"That is very quickly done," replied Agnes. "After he left me I got some work to do as a maker of the silk fronts of pianofortes."

"Are you still at that?" asked Charlotte.

"Yes; and I make enough to keep myself decently and respectably."

"So I should think," said Charlotte Saunders, with a short, incredulous laugh, as she looked at the handsome silk dress Agnes was wearing, and the expensive bracelet which was clasped round her snowy wrist.

Agnes took no notice of this, but said—

"Now let me hear about yourself. What are you?"

"A barmaid," replied Charlotte.

"A barmaid? Where?"

"In a café."

"A café? What's that?"

"Don't you know? I am a barmaid at a café in the Haymarket."

"Oh!" said Agnes, with an expression of surprise.

"Will you come with me to-night?" asked Charlotte.

Agnes reflected before she made an answer. She did not exactly know what to do with herself, and she thought there

could be no great harm in acceding to her friend's request. She did not doubt for an instant that Lord Marchmont would, sooner or later, acknowledge himself in error, and do her justice, but, of course, she could not tell when the happy period would arrive. It might be to-morrow, and it might be six or twelve months hence—which of the three she could not determine, as she had no power of divination, and she was not possessed of the privilege of looking in Zadkiel Tao Tze's crystal ball.

She knew that it would be folly to go to her husband now and tell him that the Count Val de Grace was alive, and urge him to call upon him and extract the truth from him.

She had left the count in a precarious condition; she had no reason to believe that she had mortally wounded him, but that he would be detained a prisoner in the house for some time through illness was a reasonable supposition.

The count, she felt persuaded, would be animated by a great and overpowering desire for revenge, and if Lord Marchmont should call upon him to ask for the truth, he would, in order to gratify his malice, declare that Agnes was guilty of the suppositionary crime for which his lordship had closed his doors against her.

How unjust this idea was is at once apparent, for she was entirely the victim of the count's diabolical plots.

Although Agnes's first husband, Marmaduke Wilson, was still alive, and slaving away the best years of his life as a convict in Australia, Agnes had always been true to Lord Marchmont in thought and deed.

In the eye of the law, virtually and actually, she was a bigamist; but that was the only offence of which she had been guilty—of which the law could take cognizance, or of which she had to reproach herself.

There were many excuses to be made for the committal of even that one offence. But the future had a heavy expiation in store for her. Of this, however, she was happily ignorant.

She resolved, then, to await the course of events for a week or so, and, in popular phrase, to see what "turned up."

All that Agnes knew about Charlotte Saunders was, that she was the barmaid at a café in the Haymarket. Of the character of such a place, she was without the vestige of an idea. She thought—if she thought at all about the matter—that Charlotte's duties consisted in handing cups of coffee to hirsute Frenchmen, or hairy tobacco-consuming Germans.

She had heard the Haymarket generally spoken of as a place of bad repute; but she was yet to make her acquaintance with that classic locality. So she replied to her friend's question by putting a question, "What time do you go?"

"Oh, I have to be there about seven o'clock."

"Do you stay long?"

"Yes; that's the worst of it. I can't get away till three or four o'clock in the morning. I have to grind at it pretty well, as my captain says."

"What is your captain, as you call him?—I suppose in the army?" said Agnes.

"Oh no, he is not; he is the captain of an Ostend boat. I shall see him to-night; he has just arrived—that is, he arrived the day before yesterday; and he told me that his boat drops down the river to-morrow morning with the tide. So he is sure to come and have a jolly good spree before he goes. He is such a brick! I don't believe there is another fellow like him going. I would do anything for him."

"Of course," said Agnes, who thought her old friend had become rather coarse in her language, and not so elegant in the choice of her expressions as formerly.

She could not help feeling that there was something wrong about Charlotte Saunders—what that something was, though, she could not say with any precision. She particularly wanted to see Miriam Moss, in order that she might overwhelm her with reproaches for her infamous conduct; and Charlotte had said that she was acquainted with some one who bore that name. It was an uncommon name, yet the chance that it was the same was slender.

Agnes resolved to follow the chance up, small as it was.

After a break in their conversation, during which Charlotte Saunders smoked a small cigarette of Turkish manufacture, much to Agnes's surprise, and sipped her brandy-and-water with a persistent frequency which showed that she was accustomed to indulge in the consumption of strong waters and ardent spirits, Agnes said—

"What became of your fast friend Norah—Norah—what was her name?"

"Oh! poor Norah Nolan. Hers was a terrible fate!"

"What do you mean?—is she dead?"

"Alas! yes."

"You surprise me! How did she die?"

"She came to a sad end."

"I wish you would tell me."

"Oh, I will tell you, by all means, if it will gratify you in any way."

"It will! oh! it will!"

"It is briefly told. She went out riding one day. She had left here, and lived in Stanley-street, Pimlico; and she had been to the Park. As she was going through Eaton-square, her horse, which was a restive young animal, took fright at a monkey perched on the organ of an itinerant Italian. The monkey gibbered, and made faces at the horse, and made demonstrations with its paws, uttering shrill cries the while. The horse jumped forward, then stood still and reared, beating the air with its hoofs. After a while, during which time Norah retained her seat with the greatest difficulty, the brute backed towards the railings, and kicked in the most furious manner. Norah, unfortunately, could no longer hold her seat. She was thrown violently from the horse's back, and, as ill-luck would have it, she fell upon the railings of the square. The spikes entered her body, and she was impaled. The spectators of this dreadful scene rushed forward when it was too late. She was lifted down and taken to the nearest hospital; but the efforts of the surgeon, although well meant, were of no avail. From the time she fell upon the sharply-pointed spikes of those iron railings, Norah Nolan was a corpse. I went to her funeral, with many others; and, although I have tried to forget it, her shocking death often haunts me still."

As Charlotte Saunders concluded her narration, Agnes could not repress a shudder.

"How dreadful!" she exclaimed. "Poor thing! how I pity her!"

"Well you may."

The evening now began to draw in, and Charlotte drew the rather dirty-looking damask curtains across the windows, stirred the fire, and lighted a pair of candles. Then she rang the bell and called up her servant, or the domestic of the establishment; for there were other lodgers besides herself in the house.

"Oh! Maria," she said, as the servant answered her tin-tinnabulatory summons, "I want you to go shopping for me."

"Yes, mum," replied the servant. "What will you please to want?"

"Oh, several things."

"Yes, mum."

"Get a couple of penny-farthing bloaters."

"Hard roes, mum?"

"Yes—hard roes. No—one hard and one soft. Get two composites—two for threepence, you know—and half a pound of dips—eights we usually have, I think. Then I shall want a couple of ounces of coffee; and have I got any tea?—just look. Oh, enough for to-night. Well, get an ounce of tea, then."

"Anything else, mum?"

"Well, I think not. You can get, though, one of those sausages seasoned with garlic at that French shop; and I think that will be all."

The servant received some money which Charlotte put into her hand, and promised to get what she had been requested to purchase.

Charlotte afterwards dressed herself, and, accompanied by Agnes, went to her place in the café. Agnes followed her friend with some curiosity; she had often heard of the Haymarket, and she should see it at last.

There could be no impropriety, on her part, taking a peep behind the scenes. It would only be holding a candle to the devil for once in a way.

CHAPTER XLIV.

A CAFÉ IN THE HAYMARKET—BEHIND THE BAR—TWO YOUNG MEN—HOW TO MAKE A "SMALL" PROFIT—A STRANGE TRIO—A YANKEE AMERICAN'S "NOTIONS"—A SLING AND FIXINGS—A ROW IN THE 'MARKET—AGNES IS MUCH ALARMED—THE POLICE ARE WANTED—TWO TO ONE ON THE "BRITISHER."

CHARLOTTE SAUNDERS soon conducted Agnes to the top of the broad thoroughfare known as the Haymarket.

It was just seven o'clock; at that hour there were not many people about, and there was little or no indication of the stream of life which, when the theatres close, rouses everything to animation, and seems to endow the very gas-jets with a sort of tinsel vitality.

The young women passed several cafés having Turkish characters inscribed on the windows, and crescents painted here and there. One was a café Grec, another a café Turc. This one au Milles Colonnes, another to the Palais Royal. Showing that the keepers of the establishments were most probably of foreign extraction—a fact upon which Englishmen may congratulate themselves, and be thankful—thankful that the great national iniquity is fostered and carried on by other than people of English birth and English education.

Charlotte stopped before a Café Turc, which was adorned in a more profuse way than most of the others with the stars, and crescents, and hieroglyphics, and which appeared to burn more gas than its rivals.

Pushing the door open with her foot, Charlotte entered, and beckoned Agnes to follow.

The master of the establishment had already taken his place at what may be called the receipt of custom. He had not far to come, for he slept on the premises upstairs.

He was not a nice man to look at, this Haymarket café keeper. He was dark and swarthy. His hair was black and smoothly oiled or greased; his whiskers were short and stubbly. His nose was flat where the bridge ought to have been most prominent. His teeth were black, that is, what remained of them, for some of the most important appeared to have gone upon some journey likely to be of long duration; that is, they had most probably been knocked down his throat during some disgraceful riot.

He was dressed in black, and the prevalence of the sombre colour gave him a Mephistophelian appearance, strongly suggestive of fiends and flames, and the master he served. A weak imagination would have been partially justified in taking him, or mistaking him, for his satanic majesty himself, and this would not have required a very vivid imagination, or a very elastic fancy.

The room was nearly empty. A couple of Turks wearing a fez each were seated in a corner playing chess, and smoking what is called a narghillé, which is a sort of hookah, or glass bell, filled with rose-water, through which, by some cunning contrivance, the smoke passes before it enters a long tube of india-rubber or gutta-percha, which conducts it all cool and fragrant, to your mouth.

The room was long and narrow. The walls were adorned with looking-glasses, or what are more commonly called mirrors. Glass chandeliers hung from the fretted ceiling, and soft, luxurious sofas disposed comfortably about the room, invited repose. Here and there were little round tables surmounted with a marble slab.

The waiter of the establishment, apparently a Greek or a Turk, by the look of him, was reclining upon a sofa, reading some old Oriental newspaper, and lazily puffing away at a cigarette; a cup of coffee stood by his side, at which he occasionally sipped. Like his master, he had been up till five or six o'clock that morning, and had not been up more than an hour or two; for he had gone to bed directly his duties were over. He was now taking a little refreshment to prepare him for the fatigues of the evening.

When Charlotte entered the room she walked straight up it, and was about to descend three steps which led into a sort of boudoir at the end of the room, which was partially separated from the rest by a curtain. This was a quieter place than the big room, and there the customers and frequenters of the place could play at chess, or talk more at their ease, and be free from the prying scrutiny of others. But her progress was arrested by the proprietor's voice, who exclaimed—

"Why for you not coming soon to your time?"

"What's that to do with you?" replied Charlotte.

"Why for you not coming? eh?" he repeated.

"You shut up Jimmey, you'd better," she said.

"But why for——" he began a third time.

"Oh! shut up, you old fool; it's only ten minutes past seven."

And descending the steps, she pushed open a door in the wall, which admitted her to the higher regions.

Agnes followed her, and they ascended a small spiral staircase, and found themselves in a small room. Here Charlotte took off her bonnet and arranged her hair before a glass, near which a small gas-jet was burning. Then she put

A NIGHT-HOUSE IN THE HAYMARKET.

on a wreath, which gave her the appearance of a ballet-girl.

"What is that for?" asked Agnes.

"Oh! Jimmy will have it. He says it has a good effect. Now I'm ready; are you? I want to get down again. Jimmy is in a bad temper to-day. You see how I'll bully him and tease him. You need not take off your bonnet; you can sit by my side, or near me, and if you feel hot at all you can take it off downstairs. I shall tell Jimmy that you have come to help me, as his custom and business is increasing so largely, and has been getting larger ever since I became one of the ornaments and attractions of the establishment. When I add that you don't want any pay, he wont raise a single objection."

"Wont he?"

"Not he. I know the old sweep: he is as fond of money as a miser is of guineas, or a Jew of old gold. Would you like it, do you think? You need not stop longer than you like. If you feel tired you can have my key and go home."

"Your key?" said Agnes.

"Yes, mine; you are going to stay a day or two with me. Don't say no; because it would be telling an unnecessary story. I must have my way for once. We have not seen one another for a very long time, and I am not going to part with you so very easily. Now, say you agree."

"I agree, then," said Agnes, carried away by her friend's impetuosity, and the torrent of words she rained down upon her.

"That's a good girl. Now, come on. Are you all right? I'll go first. Mind you don't fall down these beastly stairs."

"No fear," replied Agnes, treading carefully.

The door in the wall soon revolved a second time, and the girls were again in the café.

Charlotte walked up to a small bar in one corner of the room, and going behind it, took her place on a high chair, which, but for the canopy, resembled a throne. She had changed her dress upstairs, and now wore a gorgeous brocaded silk, which had an imposing effect, and was likely to impress the silly young and old men who frequented the place.

The counter before Charlotte was covered with little baskets filled with sugar-plums, and with little boxes containing three or more bottles of scent bound with blue or crimson ribbon. These were flanked by some French-made glove-boxes, of no intrinsic value, but pretty and effective outside; a vase filled with flowers stood in the centre, and around it were several plates containing a few bunches of filberts, whose market value was about a penny or twopence. These Jimmy retailed at the price of two shillings a plate! This was certainly one way to out-Rothschild Rothschild.

Charlotte told Agnes to sit down by her side on a sort of sofa-chair. Agnes complied; and by so doing arrested Jimmy's attention.

Walking up to Charlotte, he made an inclination of the head to Agnes, which was supposed to do duty for a bow. "Who your friend is that you here have got?" he said.

"Oh! that's my sister," replied Charlotte; "she has come to have a look at human nature on the loose."

"Ah! pleased she will be moche," said Jimmy, grinning. Going up to Agnes, he exclaimed, "How you pretty be!"

"Oh yes, she'll do, Jimmy," replied Charlotte.

Agnes looked on surprised and amused. The waiter, who had roused himself from the agreeable occupation of reading newspapers and smoking cigarettes, here got up, and brought an urn filled with coffee, which he placed on one side of the bar near Charlotte.

Hardly had he done so, when a couple of young men entered the place, and walked straight up to the bar. They seemed to be slightly acquainted with Charlotte; for they asked her how she was, and continued talking in a commonplace sort of way while they lounged up against the counter.

"Coffee here, Hamet!" cried Charlotte, looking at the waiter, who came up and handed the cups of coffee to the young men. "Have some cigarettes?" said Charlotte, addressing one of her customers.

"No, confound it!" was the reply; "a fellow can't smoke that muck."

"Well, buy them for me; I can smoke them."

"I am always buying you something, confound it!" replied the young gentleman.

"Well, quite right too. Why shouldn't you? Don't you enjoy the pleasure of talking to me? and it is only right that such a high privilege should be paid for."

"Oh, confound it!" was the only answer to Charlotte's address.

Charlotte took the bundle of cigarettes, and lighted one; the rest she put by her side.

"What are you going to buy this evening?" said Charlotte, returning to the attack with indefatigable industry, and addressing the other young man, who had not yet spoken.

"Oh, anything you like," he replied, carelessly playing with his watch-chain, and opening and shutting a little locket attached to it, which shut to with a sharp snap.

"Have one of these glove-boxes," said Charlotte, holding one up to his view.

"One of those?"

"Yes."

"But what's the good? I never wear gloves."

"Oh, what a story! Well, buy it for me, or for your young lady."

"I am sorry to say I haven't got one," he replied, with a slight smile on the corners of his mouth.

"Go along!" said Charlotte. "Which will you have, now?" and she held up two. "Here, you had better have one a piece." And she gave one to each of the young men.

The first one opened his eyes a little, and said, "Oh, confound it!" but made no opposition to the forced sale of which he had been made the victim.

"Now then, who's going to stand my sister some nuts? You want some nuts, don't you, dear?" said Charlotte, with a significant look at Agnes.

"I have no objection," said Agnes, who entered into her friend's plot, thinking it was only a harmless joke.

"Is that your sister?" asked the young man who said that he never wore gloves—an assertion that was broadly and flatly contradicted by a pair of well-fitting lavenders, which showed the dimensions of his small and apparently well-bred hands.

Both of these young men appeared to be gentlemen. They were gentlemanly in their manner; they were well dressed, and had that quiet self-possession and repose which is so eminently characteristic of a well-bred man.

"Yes, that is my sister," replied Charlotte, in answer to the question which had been addressed to her.

Both of the young men had been furtively glancing at Agnes, and admiration of her beauty was plainly depicted on their countenances.

"Don't you think she is pretty?" asked Charlotte, handing some nuts to Agnes.

"Don't, Charlotte; how can you?"

"I cannot presume to offer an opinion," said the young man. "Your sister might think me very rude."

His friend contented himself with uttering his favourite exclamation, "Oh, confound it!"

Agnes contented herself with mechanically cracking a few of the expensive filberts.

"My sister wants some scent; so do I. You had better give us those boxes, old fellow," said Charlotte, making another attack upon the young man with the locket.

"I shall buy all you have got soon if you go on at that rate," he said, smiling.

"Oh, no; plenty more where those came from."

"Now, what would you take for the lot, eh?"

"What would you do with it if you had it?"

"Oh, make a cockshy of it."

"Then I wont sell it. If you like to give it to me you may have it cheap."

"Would you really like some scent?" he said, talking to Agnes.

"Oh, yes; I have no objection," replied Agnes.

Charlotte immediately gave her two boxes.

"Oh, confound it!" said the other young man, who was sipping a second cup of coffee.

"Now we had better square accounts, I think," said his friend, addressing Charlotte, who replied—

"All right. Let's see—three coffee's, two gloves, one nuts, two scents. That'll be one pound three and six together."

"Oh, confound it!" cried the first, pulling out a handful of silver.

"I'll pay," said his friend, putting down a couple of sovereigns.

The young man returned the silver to his pocket, muttering to himself, "Oh, confound it!"

"Will your sister be here all the evening?" whispered the one who seemed to have taken a fancy to Agnes.

"Yes, I think so," replied Charlotte, in the same tone, giving him change.

"I wont say good-night; I shall most likely look in again," he said aloud. And bowing to Agnes, they prepared to leave the place.

His taciturn friend turned round to look at Agnes, and in so doing stumbled over a spittoon. His hat rolled under a table, and his stick fell from his hand.

As he picked himself up amidst the loud laughter of Charlotte, she could just hear him say, in a melancholy tone of voice, "Oh! confound it!"

The young man had hardly left before three men, laughing loudly, and talking in a loud tone of voice to one another, entered the room.

They were evidently some low blackguards out for what they would themselves have called a spree.

Without any ceremony they marched up to the top of the room, and one said to Agnes—

"How do, Mary?"

Another exclaimed—

"How are you, Sally?"

"In our alley," added the third.

At this they all laughed prodigiously, putting their hands on their knees, and bending their heads down.

"What will you take, gentlemen?" asked the waiter, coming up to them.

"Take? Well, we wont take you for one thing," replied one, with a loud guffaw.

"What's Sally a-going to 'ave?" said the one who had bestowed that euphonious name upon Agnes.

"My sister can take care of herself, and you had better leave her alone," replied Charlotte, angrily. "Her husband will be here directly."

"Her 'usban'?" cried the man, with a laugh. "Which of 'em?"

This joke seemed to amuse his companions immensely, for

they laughed so loudly and so long over it, that they all three threatened to go into convulsions.

You might have taken them for laughing maniacs, or for men who had been indulging too freely in that chemical preparation known as laughing-gas.

Agnes's face flushed scarlet, and she felt inclined to serve the wretch as she had some time before treated Mr. Todd, the coffee-house keeper, in Tottenham-court-road.

When the three men had in some measure recovered their serenity, the one who had before spoken to Agnes said—

"Come, Sally, don't take on, one's as good as another."

"Yes, and a good sight better," put in one of his companions, who showed a great deal of Brummagem jewellery wherever he had the smallest excuse for displaying it.

"Do you want to buy a glove-box this evening, gentlemen?" said Charlotte, with an eye to business, thinking she would like to extract a little money from them by way of revenge.

"No; I don't want none of that trash," replied one. "We's old birds, and chaff ain't good for our complaint. Is it, Bill?"

"Not a bit of it," replied that individual, with a cunning leer.

"Give me some brandy-cherries," cried the third.

When he received the glass from Charlotte, he pulled out the cherries with his fingers, and put them in his capacious mouth, exclaiming—

"Them's the jockeys for me."

"Gentlemen generally have a little money to spend," said Charlotte in a bantering tone; "I thought you were gentlemen, or I should not have asked you to buy a glove-box. I am sorry I was mistaken. Perhaps you never wear gloves."

"Don't we!" cried the three, in an indignant chorus, feeling simultaneously in their pockets for their gloves. After some search, each brought out a pair of dirty, common-looking dogskin gloves, a mile too big for them, with a hole here and there, the buttons off, and altogether considerably soiled.

Both Charlotte and Agnes laughed at this display, which seemed to annoy the men more than ever.

Bending down a little, Charlotte whispered to Agnes—

"They are only cads, and cads are always sensitive. You see how wild I will make them. I have chaffed them pretty well already. If they say anything to you take no notice of them. I don't believe they mean anything; it is more their manner, and their education, and their instincts than anything else. Take my advice and don't lose your temper. If they try to insult you, and I see that they mean it, I will protect you."

Agnes promised compliance with her friend's sensible advice, and Charlotte said to the men, who still stood with their gloves in their hands—

"Hadn't you better buy some boxes to put your gloves in? They might get soiled, you know, and that would be a pity."

The men looked at her as if they did not quite know whether Charlotte was chaffing them or not. At last one said—

"What's the damage of that 'ere?"

"Which one—this?"

"Yes, that; the one with the spangle things."

"Oh! it is as cheap as dirt. You can have it for seven and sixpence."

The man whistled slowly.

"Come, have this one; or if it is too much money for you——"

"It ain't that," said the man.

"Well, if it is you can buy it between you—half-a-crown a-piece wont ruin you. It'll hold three pairs easily."

"What do you say, 'Arry?"

His friend after a little reflection responded in the affirmative, and they each pulled a half-crown out of their pockets, looking very grave over the transaction, as if dubious as to whether they had got their money's-worth.

The box, on the receipt of the money, was handed over to one of them by Charlotte, and the trio carefully inspected it; and one of them, by common consent, wrapped a dirty-looking pocket handkerchief round it, and placed it in the pocket of his coat.

"Come over to the Argyll, Sally, and have a dance," said the one who had spoken to Agnes before.

"With you?" asked Charlotte, who had before spoken in behalf of her friend.

"Yes; I suppose I'm good enough for my company."

"What does the man take me for?" said Agnes to herself. "He must have imbibed some erroneous idea respecting me, or he would never talk to me as he does."

"Well then," said Charlotte, "I can tell you, that I for one don't think so. You may be a very great swell, only unfortunately I don't see it. Perhaps you're Lord Palmerston in disguise—only, you see, I don't happen to think so. I wish I had a better opinion of you for your sake, as you seem to set so much store by it; but as you evidently don't think small beer of yourself, perhaps my opinion, in your estimation, may not be worth much."

"No more it ain't—that's the truest word you've said to-night."

"Oh, indeed!"

"Now, what would you take me for?" he said.

"Take you for? Well, if you really would like to know, I should say you were a tailor, in a small way, somewhere down Whitechapel way, Mile-end, or Shadwell; or perhaps, a weaver, or a betting-man in luck."

"You're trying to rile me," said the man.

"Am I? I don't think so; you're not worth it, my dear fellow."

"It wouldn't take me long to smash this 'ere place up," he said angrily, while his face grew red.

"Wouldn't it? Really. Well, it wouldn't take us long to provide you a night's lodging in Vine-street, if that's all."

At this juncture, a tall thin man, with a quid in his mouth, entered the café. He was unmistakeably an American. Coming up to the bar, he said, with the nasal drawl peculiar to his nation—

"You haven't got no Yankee notions, have you, miss?"

"I am afraid we have not," replied Charlotte.

"No slings and fixings."

"No."

"No juleps, or thunder and lightnings?"

"No."

"You've got a cocktail, then?"

"No; I am sorry to say we don't make them. This is not an American bar."

"You've a bad time of it, then, in this tarnation country," said the Yankee, squirting out a volume of tobacco-juice.

"It's as good as old Abe Lincoln's," said the man who had just lost his temper in talking to Charlotte.

"What's that, Britisher?" asked the American.

"Why, talk respectful when you's talking to your betters."

"My betters! Yoop, why I'd squelch you!"

"Would you? It would take a better man nor you by a long chalk," said the Englishman, who was not deficient in bull-dog courage.

"Why, we've whipped you as a nation to eternal smash," said the Yankee. "Why, one Yankee can whip three Britishers, any day in the year. Why, I'd eat *you*, hat and all, let alone boots. Didn't we give you pepper at Bunker's Hill? You think yourself considerable pumpkins, I daresay; but it's all bunkum. You and your bogus aristocracy, you're all bunkum. You think yourself very big taters, I've no doubt; but you're all bogus—you're all bunkum. Why, you ain't fit to walk on Broadway, New York city. They'd eat you in Brooklyn; and Jersey city wouldn't draw you for the draft. Your Irishers can fit a bit, but as for you you're only fit to bully the Brazilians. Why, talk about secesh, you're pigs'-wash to it. We'd wash you out like dirty linen, and hang you up to dry arterwards."

"I'm a better man than you any day," said the Englishman, "and Bill, and I, and 'Arry 'ud mill a dozen on you, one down and t'other come on."

"Here goes for thunder, then," cried the Yankee. "I'll squelch you."

And he turned up his shirt sleeves, rolled his quid over in his mouth, and deliberately squirted a stream of tobacco-juice into the Englishman's eye.

"Come on!" he cried.

And in a minute they were both engaged in a serious combat, which waged with varying fortune.

The Yankee was much taller than his adversary, who was thick-set and strongly built.

But the Englishman was not destitute of that pluck and endurance so characteristic of the race.

The proprietor of the café ran hither and thither frantically, but Bill and Harry kept the ground, as it were, and pushed him back again.

The waiter was as much confused as his master, and did not exactly know what to do.

Agnes and her friend Charlotte Saunders sat still in their places—it was the best thing they could do—and although they were much alarmed, they watched the combat with some curiosity.

Charlotte had often seen some severe fights in the café, and she knew that the police usually came in and restored order, taking the peace-breakers to the station-house.

CHAPTER XLV.

A SOCKDOLLAGER—THE YANKEE IS "FLOORED"—HOW ABOUT BUNKER'S HILL NOW?—THE POLICE ARRIVE—THEY MEET WITH THEIR MATCH—TOM, BILL, AND HARRY—NOVEL WEAPONS—GOING THROUGH A WINDOW—PUTTING UP THE SHUTTERS—MY CAPTAIN—COME WITH US.

AT last Jimmy, the keeper of the café, contrived to elude the watchfulness of Bill and Harry, and darting beneath one of the tables, went out in search of the police.

The Yankee had hit the Englishman two or three stinging blows on the face, which roused his anger, and he felt himself put upon his metal. His friends were looking at him, and would expect him to do his best, so he put out all his strength, and made a desperate blow at the Yankee, which took effect upon his mouth, and made his teeth rattle like castanets.

"That's your sort, Tommy," cried his friends; "that's a sockdollager for him! Warm him! Let him have it! How about Bunker's Hill, eh?"

The Yankee spat out a mouthful of blood, and a bit of a broken tooth, for Tommy's fist was not altogether unlike a sledge hammer, and it had descended with great force upon the American.

But Tommy himself had received a blow, the effects of which were becoming speedily visible. He had been struck upon the right eye, which was rapidly closing up. If this happened he would be a good deal at the mercy of the American. So he gathered himself up, and standing on his toes, "let the Yankee have it," as his friends had advised him. He caught him on the forehead between the temples, and the American went toppling over, like an overgrown oak in a tempest, and fell with a crash upon a quantity of cups and glasses arranged upon a table near him.

The Englishmen applauded violently. But Tommy had not yet done with his adversary. There was a table between himself and the door, which also contained a display of glass and crockery.

Going up to his prostrate antagonist, who was trying to collect his scattered senses, and had just staggered to his feet, he seized him by the waist in a sort of Cornish hug, and swung him backwards and forwards for an instant or two. For although the American was very tall, there was little substance about him, and he was not stout in proportion to his length. Suddenly Tommy let him go, after having given him an impetus towards the table where the glass was.

The Yankee came with his side against the surface of the table, and made a clean sweep of the whole board. With such force was he thrown, that he struck the window of the saloon, and, in the midst of crockery of every description, fell with a crash on the pavement.

"Hurrah!" cried the Englishmen.

But their triumph was short-lived.

A couple of policemen entered the room, and, urged on by Jimmy, attempted to take them into custody.

"Three to two. We'll warm them!" cried one of the three. "Come on—charge through them!"

And all three were quickly engaged in a hand-to-hand conflict with the police.

The battle, while it lasted, was desperate.

Tommy smashed a chair across his knee, and seizing the most formidable part of it, fought like a tiger against the truncheons of the police, who were getting the worst of it.

Blood flowed freely. Wounds were given and received at every blow.

There was no science; all was brute force.

Harry kicked off the top of one of the tables, and wrenched the iron pedestal from the ground, and performed murderous work with it.

Bill put his foot on the marble slab, and smashed it in half, and fought with that.

One policeman lay stretched upon the floor.

Harry staggered, faint and almost insensible, from a blow on the head, into a chair.

But the remaining policeman was, at this critical juncture, reinforced by three more of their fraternity, who, after some fighting, overcame Tom and Bill, and putting the handcuffs on, led them away from the café.

Stretchers were procured, and the policeman and Harry were placed upon them.

The American, after lying stunned for a few minutes, recovered his senses.

His face and hands were frightfully cut about, and he was streaming with blood.

The sympathizing bystanders conducted him across the road to a chemist's shop, where he had his wounds washed, and was attended to.

Everybody said that he must have been prodigiously tough, or he would have thought more of it.

But the only remark he made, as he left the shop with his face covered with plaister, was—"Guess I got gosh that journey."

Then he stretched his arms, much in the same manner that a gamecock flaps his wings, and added—

"Calculate I'll go and see after a cocktail."

When the ruffians who had made all this disturbance had been conducted to the police-station, Charlotte Saunders and Agnes breathed more freely.

Jimmy ran up and down the room in the wildest despair, looking at the destruction of property which had taken place.

The waiter, Hamet, sat in a corner, wringing his hands in the greatest despair.

But neither he nor his master offered to do anything to remedy the mischief.

With the passive fatalism of Orientals, although they felt the misfortune acutely, they thought that what was to be could not be altered. The mischief was done, and could not be undone.

At last Jimmy decided that the best thing that could be done would be to put up the shutters, and wait till the morning. Then he would have an opportunity of punishing the miscreants who had destroyed his shop, and if they had any money, doubtlessly the magistrate would compel them to make restitution as much as lay in their power.

Charlotte Saunders and her friend Agnes were, of course, dismissed for the night, as their services could be of no further use. And going upstairs, Charlotte attired herself, condoled with her employer, and left the shop just as Hamet was putting up the last shutter.

The crowd had dispersed to some extent, although there were still a large number of people standing and canvassing the merits of the "row in the 'Market."

Just as Charlotte crossed the threshold, a voice exclaimed—

"My stars! there's Lotty."

"Oh! that's my captain," cried Charlotte, evidently much delighted.

Agnes looked at the man, who was a tolerably good specimen of a Channel steamboat skipper.

He was of average height, dark, with a moustache and whiskers, white shining teeth, and a good-natured face. He wore a pea-jacket, and a tarpaulin or oilskin hat. He had his hands in his pockets, and was smoking a short pipe.

"You were out of that, Jack," said Charlotte.

"My stars! yes. What was the shindy?" asked the captain.

"Only a fight between a blustering Yankee and some prize-fighting fellows or other."

"I should like to have seen that amazingly," replied the captain. "How did it end?"

"Why, the Yankee got thrown through the window."

"Chucked him through the window, did they? Ah! that's fine. Sorry I was out of that, d— me if I ain't!"

"Then the police came. We were horribly frightened, as you may suppose; but we could only sit still. They fought like tigers, these three prize-fighters, or whatever they were. I think they were drunk when they came in, for they tried to pick a quarrel with me and my lady friend here. Anyhow, they were very cantankerous. And when the Yankee checked them, they were game for a row."

"Game for a row, were they?"

"Oh, yes, no doubt of it. And they had it, too. I hope it will last them for some time to come."

"Not a bit of it. The magistrates will only fine them

forty bob, or something of that sort, and their friends will raise that for them. If, as you say, they are fighting men, they will have a benefit got up for them at Nat Langham's, or Ben Caunt's, or Jimmy Shaw's, or some of those sporting cribs. I know them."

"So it seems," replied Charlotte, laughing.

It was now about eleven o'clock, or perhaps a little past that hour.

The gay butterflies that flaunt in the gaslight were making their appearance in shoals; and Agnes felt that she should like to go home. So she said to Charlotte—

"I think I had better leave you with your husband."

"My stars, no!" cried the captain, who overheard the remark.

"I don't like this sort of thing," said Agnes. "My nerves are a good deal shaken as it is by that dreadful fight; and I can assure you I don't want to witness another such as long as I live. Why, they were more like North American Indians; only I don't think the Redskins would have displayed so much ferocity. I can see that this is not a nice time to be out in the Haymarket, and——"

"What do you mean?" said Charlotte.

"I don't want to offend you, dear Charlotte; you have your husband with you."

As she repeated the word "husband," the captain laughed a small silvery laugh, and showed his white teeth, ejaculating as he did so, "My stars!"

"Why, what's the matter with you?" replied Charlotte. "Who's going to hurt you?"

"Nobody, I hope. But I do not like to be out with a lot of bad women on every side of me; it is not respectable."

"Oh, bother the respectability!" said Charlotte. "Don't be a fool; and come along with us. We are going to have a spree."

"Well, you may please yourself, only if you will give me your key, I will go back to your lodgings."

"That I certainly shall not!" said Charlotte, decisively.

"You will not?"

"No."

"Then you are treating me very badly. You promised me that I should have it, if I stayed with you. I only came at all to please you; and if you don't give me the key, I don't know where to go. I live a long way from here."

Poor Agnes was almost crying, as she then reviewed her position.

"Oh, don't be silly!" cried Charlotte. "Put on your gloves, and come with us. No one will speak to you, if you don't like it."

Seeing there was no help for it, Agnes followed her more experienced friend, who linked her arm in that of her captain.

CHAPTER XLVI.

A NIGHT-HOUSE — HAVING SUPPER — A MOSELLE CUP — AGNES RECOVERS HER SPIRITS — "DO YOU SEE THAT WOMAN?" — MIRIAM MOSS — MIRIAM TURNS PALE — AGNES'S TERRIBLE REVENGE — BEAUTY ONCE LOST IS GONE FOR EVER — CAB! CAB! — ROLLING OVER THE STONES.

AGNES was, to a certain extent, compelled to follow the nocturnal fortunes of her more volatile friend. What could she do? She had not much money in her possession; it was getting on for midnight, and if she had hailed a cab, and returned to her old lodgings near Brompton, her landlady would, in all probability, have refused to admit her; for landladies are "kittle cattle," as the Scotch say, and have their own peculiar ideas about propriety.

To return at twelve or one o'clock at night, after having remained away from your home for a day or a night, is, to say the least of it, a suspicious proceeding. And Agnes felt intuitively, that if she returned to her lodgings, she would have her journey for nothing; and would, by that means, be thrown more upon her own resources than ever. So she put the best face she could upon the matter, and followed the guidance of her friend and the captain.

They walked some distance up the Haymarket, and then crossed over, and entered a small street leading to Leicester-square.

On the right-hand side of this street appeared several open doors, which invited entrance; but there were certain burly fellows standing before each of them, prepared to dispute the entry of anybody who might seem, to their sovereign will, objectionable.

Into one of these houses Charlotte went; Agnes followed her. There were not many people there yet. It was just about twelve o'clock, and it was not their custom to open until that hour.

Going to the end of the room, the captain ordered supper; and Agnes sat down with her new friends to await its production.

It was not long coming; and the captain, who appeared to be afflicted with a good appetite, did justice to the fowls and mushrooms, and various other edibles the length of his purse enabled him to order.

Even Agnes could not help joining her friend Charlotte; and when the waiter brought them a champagne cup, and Agnes had taken a draught of it, her spirits rose, and she could not help feeling a little hilarious. She felt that she had been badly treated by fate and fortune, and that she was undeservedly persecuted; and she became a little reckless of consequences, as the generous wine warmed her blood and circulated freely in her system.

Charlotte laughed and chattered with great volubility; and the captain told story upon story, much to the girls' amusement.

In about half-an-hour the room was full; men and women flowed in streams, and when one departed, another quickly made his or her appearance, and filled the vacant place.

Champagne and Moselle flowed like water — all was hilarity and mad excitement. Suddenly, Charlotte clutched Agnes's arm, and exclaimed, "You wished to see Miriam Moss, did you not?"

"I did."

"Well, look before you. Not that way. There, a little to the right."

"Yes," said Agnes.

"Do you not see? There—just before that waiter."

"Oh!" exclaimed Agnes, drawing her breath shortly. "That is the woman I meant; I have heard her called Miriam Moss the Jewess, and that is all I know about her."

"All?"

"Yes, all."

Agnes looked steadily at the woman her friend pointed out to her.

"Is that the one?" asked Charlotte Saunders.

"It is," replied Agnes.

"Well, now you have found her, what do you want with her?"

"Shall I tell you?"

"Of course."

"Then you remember my saying, this afternoon, that some woman had met my husband?"

"Perfectly."

"That is the one."

"Are you in earnest?"

"Alas! never more so in my life. She separated us. May Heaven reward her for it."

"It was a cruel thing to do," said Charlotte.

"So cruel, that I never can or will forgive her for it."

"But what can you do? You are powerless to harm her."

"Am I?" asked Agnes.

"Well, you are so in my opinion."

"You shall see!" cried Agnes, rising.

"What would you do?" cried Charlotte Saunders, seizing Agnes by the sleeve of her dress.

"Leave go, will you?" said Agnes, who was fearfully excited by the wine, and by the sight of the woman who had worked her so much harm.

"No, I will not leave go."

"You shall, I say," cried Agnes, dashing her friend's hand away from her dress by a blow of her fist.

"My stars!" exclaimed the captain.

"Oh! if that's the way you treat people, you may go to ——"

Well, let us say some hot place, for Charlotte's expression was not very proper or correct.

Agnes walked across the room, and confronted Miriam Moss.

"My stars!" cried the captain, as he watched the proceedings of Agnes, with some curiosity.

"Never mind her; have some more wine?" said Charlotte, addressing the captain.

"All right," said the captain.

"You seem to take a great interest in that woman!" exclaimed Charlotte.

"My stars!" said the captain, taking his eyes away from Agnes, and fixing them full upon Charlotte.

"Well, be a good boy, then, and he shall not be blown up," said that young lady, cooling down a little.

Miriam Moss took no notice whatever of Agnes; she did not appear to recognise her at all.

"Miriam Moss!" said Agnes, slowly, in a hissing tone, for she spoke between her teeth.

Miriam turned round, but although the voice appeared to be familiar to her, she failed to recognise Agnes.

"Do you not know me?" said Agnes.

"Know you? No; and don't want to. What do you speak to me for?"

Agnes looked calmly at her for a brief space, and then said in a penetrating tone—

"I am Agnes Wilson!"

As Miriam heard this she turned pale.

"Agnes Wilson!" she repeated, catching her breath.

"Yes, traitress; and at last I have found you."

Miriam appeared to have lost her former insolent air for the time being, and made no reply.

"I always vowed that if ever I did meet you, Miriam Moss," said Agnes, "I would exact a terrible vengeance."

Miriam trembled a little.

"The day has arrived, and now you stand before me. And I know you to be the wretch to whose infernal machinations I may date all my misfortunes. You poured the insidious poison into my ears—you endeavoured to turn my affection away from my husband—you threw suspicion upon his good and generous heart. Do you hear me, Miriam Moss? you did all this, and you yet live to triumph in your villany, and why? Heaven does for its own wise purposes know. You succeeded in your plots—Heaven curse the hour in which you did so—but so far you have triumphed over me. But one thing you can never obliterate, Miriam Moss, and that is, that man Marmaduke Wilson loved me. Yes; he was my lawfully wedded husband. And if he is away from me now, I can say that I have been blest with the love and affection which you have pined for in vain—yes, and may pine for to your dying day."

Miriam Moss quailed beneath the indignant glance of Agnes during this denunciation of her villany.

Some women had congregated round them, and were listening with much amusement to Agnes's rage, and the outpouring of her reproaches. Some men, too, attracted by her melodramatic manner, also joined the group.

When Miriam saw the eyes of some of her friends fixed on her, she with an effort recovered her presence of mind, and, with a scornful laugh, replied—

"Well, if I did get your thief of a husband away from you, I have not got him now. If you want to join him, you had better go to Australia, or perhaps the Government will provide you with a passage, as it did him, free gratis for nothing—all at the Queen's expense."

"You dare to talk to me like that!" cried Agnes, her whole frame quivering with passion.

"Dare! Well, it looks like it, doesn't it? I'll say it again, if you like it so much."

"You are a bad, wicked woman! Your touch is pollution to me!" cried Agnes, "or I would tear you to pieces!"

"You can try," replied Miriam. "But I think you would find you had your work before you."

The female spectators of this storm in a puddle applauded Miriam, and said, "Slap her face!"

They were no doubt annoyed at Agnes's good looks. A woman will forgive a good deal in another, but she will never forgive another woman for being prettier than herself. This was the case in the present instance. Agnes was, undoubtedly, the prettiest woman in the room.

Agnes was in a terrible passion, flushed and excited with wine, and angry with herself for being in such a place; doubly angered with Miriam for her perfidy in the first instance, and her defiance of her in the second.

She hardly knew what she did.

The counter stood before her, and was studded here and there with bottles; but to get possession of one she would have been compelled to pass by Miriam, who would have unquestionably frustrated her too obvious intention.

A waiter, however, happened to be passing by with a tray, upon which was a bottle of soda-water.

Agnes seized this; and, before any one could divine her purpose, she rushed towards Miriam, and struck her a crushing blow on the face.

The unhappy woman could not scream, for the blow took effect upon her nose and mouth.

With such force had Agnes struck her, that her good looks were gone for ever.

All her front teeth were broken, and her lip was frightfully cut. Her nose had also suffered to a dreadful extent; the cartilage was broken, and the bone smashed.

With a wild hysterical cry, Miriam fell down insensible.

Agnes was standing aghast at the effects of her violence.

Everybody was partially paralysed at the strange scene—one, however, only too common in such places.

Suddenly she heard the voice of the captain saying, "Row, row."

And in a moment the whole room was in darkness.

Directly afterwards Charlotte Saunders's voice sounded in her ears.

"This way! this way!" she said. "Quick! follow me!"

Agnes laid hold of her friend's hand, and followed her at a quick pace into the passage.

The street-door was open.

The doorkeeper, hearing the disturbance, had gone inside to render any assistance that might be required from him.

Darting through this, panting with exertion, Charlotte, Agnes, and the captain stood in the street.

"Cab!" shouted the captain, to one standing close by.

The man jumped down from his box; and the trio got in.

"Drive to the London Docks!" cried the captain. "Quick!—off you go!"

The man required no further bidding; and they were quickly rolling over the stones across Leicester-square, waking the echoes in Green-street and Hemming's-row, and in a few minutes they were driving along the Strand.

CHAPTER XLVII.

HOW THE CAPTAIN DID IT—SMASHING THE CHANDELIER—AGNES REGRETS HER VIOLENCE TO MIRIAM MOSS—WHERE ARE THEY?—THAMES-STREET—THE DOCKS—ON BOARD THE "CITY OF AMSTERDAM"—THE MAIL BOAT—"WE CAN'T TURN IN NOW, SO LET'S MAKE A NIGHT OF IT."

HURRAH! hurrah! my stars! hurrah!" cried the captain, when they were fairly safe from pursuit.

Loud cries had followed them for some little distance; but as the cabman drove at speed, they rapidly distanced any pursuers, and at last the fugitives felt themselves safe.

"Well, how do you feel?" asked Charlotte, addressing Agnes.

"I really don't know," replied Agnes. "I am very excited. What have I done, and how did you get me away?"

"Ask the captain."

"Didn't I do it well?" said that individual.

"Do what? Do explain the mystery to me."

"Well, you remember the room being in darkness all at once," said Charlotte.

"Yes; that is what puzzles me," replied Agnes.

"When I saw what you had done, I saw at once what danger you were in, because I knew that Miriam Moss had many friends in the room."

"Indeed!"

"Yes; and I knew very well that when they had recovered their surprise they would limb you—tear you to pieces—show you no mercy. You were not known in the place, and the waiters, and the porters, and Lizzie herself would not have interfered."

"Who's Lizzie?"

"Why, Lizzie keeps the place."

"Oh! pardon my interruption; go on."

"Well, they might have gouged your eyes out; I don't know what they would have done; nothing would have been too bad for them. You certainly did smash that woman up, you cannot help confessing that. I never saw anything better done in my life, and if she had treated me as she has done you, I think I should have done the same thing. I could never put up with the loss of my captain."

"My stars! no," said that enterprising and affectionate sailor, of what may be called our passenger marine, as he affectionately pressed Charlotte Saunders' little hand.

"Well," continued Charlotte; "I said to the captain, smash the place up while I get her out."

The captain smiled at this.

"He knew very well what I meant; it isn't the first time he has done the same thing. So directly I told him I ran towards you, knowing he would speedily do the rest. Directly I left him the captain took up a chair; didn't you, captain? You tell us the rest."

"My stars! yes," replied the captain. "I collared a chair, and went towards the chandelier at a run, and lifted the chair up in the air; then I brought it down on the glass-pipe in a way I know well how to do. My stars! I believe you. And then the thing was done, for the chandelier fell to the ground with a crash, and I ran to the passage, where I knew I should find Lotty. That's all; and if I have done you any service, why, hang it, you may do something for me some day. You know the story of the mouse and the lion, eh?" And the captain stroked his moustache proudly, as if he were not a bit ashamed of his exploit.

"All I can say is that I am deeply indebted to you, captain," replied Agnes, who shuddered as she saw the magnitude of the danger she had so luckily escaped.

"Not at all. It is nothing. My stars! no. Say no more about it, I beg," said the captain, waving his hand grandly.

But he had forgotten that he was confined within the limits of a metropolitan street cab, and the consequence was that his fist went very, very gracefully through the window nearest to him.

"What an ass you must be, Charlie!" exclaimed Charlotte, after she had laughed at the captain's misadventure.

"My stars! you are complimentary, especially when a fellow's cut his paw."

"Poor paw!" said Charlotte, taking his hand between hers, and tying her pocket-handkerchief round it. "There," she said, "will that do?"

"Thanks, my Lotty," he replied, tenderly. "What should we men do without women? My stars! what?"

"Do you think I have hurt Miriam Moss much?" said Agnes, who had rather vague ideas as to the punishment she had inflicted upon the perfidious Jewess.

"Hurt her, my dear child?" cried Charlotte.

"Yes. You know what I mean."

"If you mean have you disfigured her for life, I answer yes."

"Good God! You don't say so?"

"Say so; yes, I do."

"What did I do, then? What was the damage?"

"Well, I'll tell you as well as I am able," replied Charlotte Saunders.

"Do, please," said Agnes.

"In the first place, you have smashed all her front teeth."

"Nonsense!"

"It is a fact. And her lip is horribly cut; her nose, too, is shockingly fractured. She will have to turn virtuous in self-defence."

"How horrible! I did not know what I was doing," said Agnes, with a shudder.

"I don't know about that," said Charlotte; "you are the best judge of that; but this I can tell you, if you wanted to have your revenge upon her, you have had it."

"My stars, yes!" said the captain.

"You have done a great deal more harm to her than if you had taken a knife in your hand and cut her throat. Then it would have been over with her; but now she will have to live a life of misery and despair, which will be heightened and augmented whenever she thinks how beautiful she was formerly; for she was undoubtedly good-looking."

"For a Jewess," put in the captain.

"For a Jewess, yes. But she was tolerably good-looking. And as for a looking-glass, why, bless you! she will faint at the sight of one. What is a woman with a broken nose and all her teeth out, and what they call a hare lip? Why, she will talk in a sort of lisp all her life. You may certainly congratulate yourself, my dear Agnes, upon having had your revenge in a most signal manner."

Agnes could not help regretting, now that her rage was cooler, that she had suffered herself to be led away by her passion, and that she had, in a moment of frenzy as it were, ruined Miriam Moss's happiness for life. Still she thought Miriam did her great and infinite harm, in a most cruel and refined manner. "I saved her life, too, once, and even after that she plotted against me. Perhaps I am wrong to regret what has happened to her, but still it is horrible—very

horrible. I should not have thought I possessed strength enough to do what I have done."

"Let me give you a bit of advice," exclaimed Charlotte.

"What is it?"

"Only this: you keep out of that woman's way. She might have forgiven you anything but what you have done to her. And if ever she gets a chance to retaliate, she will not let it slip out of her fingers."

"Do you think so?"

"Well, you neglect my advice, that's all, and you will see. You keep out of her path, I tell you. Never cross it."

"My stars, yes! You had better do as Lotty tells you," said the captain. "She is a clever girl, and would not mislead you."

Agnes did not contradict her friends, and the subject dropped, after the captain had said—

"Didn't I do it well, Lotty? By Jove, it is the finest lark I have had for a long time. Sorry for the woman, though. Don't like to see it, you know. My stars, no!"

"Well, old boy, where are you taking us to?" said Charlotte, as the cab drove into rather a dingy part of the City.

"If you particularly want to know, we are at present in Thames-street."

"Thames-street—isn't that near the Tower?"

"Well, it is not far off. I told the fellow to go to the Docks; I thought we would go aboard the vessel."

"Oh! that is charming! As soon as you like," cried Charlotte "I have often wanted to see your steamer. Where is she lying?"

"Not far from here."

"You must, of course, come with us, Agnes; we cannot part from you now."

"Oh! I will follow you. I don't care much where I go," said Agnes.

The captain put his head out of the broken window, and gave the driver more explicit directions; and at last the cab stopped before the Dock-gates.

The captain dismissed the cab; and having told the porter who he was, and where he was going, that functionary, upon seeing his pass, admitted him and his fair companions.

And as it was now daylight, or an apology for it, for the grey dawn had broken, they made their way to a boat; and the captain sculled his female friends on board the *City of Amsterdam*, mail-steamer and passenger-boat.

The watch touched their hats to their skipper, and hid the flask of rum from which they had been imbibing during his absence.

"Well, we can't turn in now," said the captain, "so let's make a night of it. Come into my cabin; I've something very superb in the way of wine."

CHAPTER XLVIII.

MIRIAM MOSS'S HISTORY — A CAROUSE — THE GRACES THAT MAKE LIFE WORTH HAVING — THE CAPTAIN SINGS A SONG — ALL DRUNK — THE FIRST MATE — THE PASSENGERS ARRIVE — THE ANCHOR IS WEIGHED — DROPPING DOWN THE RIVER.

AGNES and her friend Charlotte Saunders were in the captain's cabin on board the steamer.

The rich and generous wine flowed freely.

The captain produced some choice havannas, and smoked and drank, and laughed and talked, and made himself a very agreeable companion.

Charlotte took a bundle of cigarettes out of her pocket, and, I am sorry to say, indulged in the somewhat masculine habit of smoking.

Agnes was not, at first, a very lively companion. She was brooding over her meeting with Miriam Moss, and the terrible revenge she had taken upon her for her perfidiousness.

Unhappy Miriam! Better would it have been for her had she died in the casual ward of the workhouse, in Mount-street, Grosvenor-square. Better, far better, had she been laid beneath the sod, than to recover her senses and her health only to have her beauty annihilated at one fell stroke by the relentless hand of Agnes, her former friend and associate!

Miriam Moss had, in due time, recovered from her dangerous illness, which was superinduced by her immersion in the Serpentine, and the agitation consequent upon her finding her father's lifeless body, with a deep gash in his throat, lying on the floor of the secret room in the old house near the Foundling Hospital.

But when the workhouse opened its doors, and she was cast forth as a convalescent, and told that as she was an able-bodied woman she ought to and must work, she knew not what to do.

Brought up to no trade, she had always lived at home in idleness, and now, at her age, to be told to get her bread was equivalent to being driven on the streets to obtain a livelihood.

She knew that it was the bread of shame, and she shuddered as she contemplated such a disgraceful means of subsistence.

She thought that the first mouthful of food bought by such means would choke her.

Yet what was she to do?

There were only a few courses open to her.

She could either work at some trade, commit suicide, lie down and starve, or accept the fearful alternative we have alluded to.

The first she found impracticable.

As we have said, she knew no trade, and she could find no tradesman sufficiently philanthropic to teach her one and pay her for learning it.

Now she was in her sober senses she shrank from self-murder.

The third course was very hard and very bitter. It was very painful, very soul-deadening. But she thought she would try it in preference to selling herself for gold.

The first day she was brave enough. The second she was sorely tried and tempted; and on the third she was so ravenously hungry from her long starvation and abstinence from food, that she gave way to the cravings of nature, and fell—fell! to rise no more!

Now she was comparatively happy. Men smiled upon her and caressed her.

Now she had what she wanted, almost without the trouble of asking; but her apparent happiness was all a delusion and a sham—she felt that she was degraded. She could not look an honest woman in the face when she met her in the street.

Miriam, although she had money in her pocket, and never really wanted a dinner or a breakfast, shrank from herself with disgust and loathing.

But she had escaped starvation? It is true she had done so, but it is not difficult to say which of the two evils is the lesser and which the greater.

This was Miriam's condition when Agnes met her at a night-house in Panton-street. What followed that meeting I have already related.

Now the wretched Miriam was a thing to shudder at—a veiled monster—a prophet of Khorassan, as it were—something marred and blurred and unseemly. Her once lustrous eyes, and her formerly wondrous beauty were a thing of yesterday—a thing to sigh over and regret, but never more to gladden the eye of the beholder.

Agnes's revenge was indeed complete and faultless. She could not wish for more—she had wounded her enemy in her most sensitive part; for she had destroyed her loveliness and her beauty—that beauty and loveliness by whose means she had hitherto gained a miserable and shameful existence—but still an existence; and now what was to become of her?

It was, indeed, a shocking question. But let us draw a veil for the present over the sufferings of Miriam Moss, victim of a woman's vengeance.

It is time that we quit so painful a theme, and return to Agnes and her gay and thoughtless companions.

"My stars!" exclaimed the captain, "this is a glorious vintage! Another glass of wine, Lotty—some for your friend! Here, pass her glass."

"None for me, thank you," replied Agnes, who was still absorbed in her reverie.

"None for you? nonsense!" cried Charlotte.

"Don't say no, my dear young lady," said the captain. "It will do you good."

"You are very kind, but I would rather not."

"Oh! here, give me a glass," exclaimed Charlotte; "she is a little fool. Fill it up, captain. That's it. Now you drink that, my little teetotaller, and it will warm you like liquid fire."

Agnes could not resist her friend's importunity, and accordingly took the proffered glass, and drained it to the dregs.

"Capital!" said Charlotte. "There is nothing like drowning care, is there, captain?"

"No, that there isn't. There you are quite right, my little fairy," replied the captain, tossing off a bumper of the bubbling, foaming champagne.

Charlotte helped herself to another glass, and watched the sparkling wine as the little beads rose effervescingly from the bottom of the glass to the surface, and then vanished into white froth.

"Sing us a song, captain—there's a good sort," said Charlotte.

"Sing a song a sixpence, a pocket full of rye; will that do?" replied the captain, laughingly.

"Don't be a fool," said Charlotte; "you know you can sing. I wish you would. Come, now; make an effort."

"Oh, do sing!" said Agnes, into whose head the wine was rising.

"Well, I suppose I must, as I am asked to by two such fascinating creatures," he replied.

"Captain!" cried Charlotte, holding up her wine-glass.

"Yes," he said.

"You see this glass?"

"Well!"

"Well, if you don't behave yourself, it will make acquaintance with your head."

"If that's the case, I'm sorry I spoke."

"Now, go on; we are waiting for your song."

"Yes, the captain's song," said Agnes.

The captain disposed of another glass of the generous wine, and then clearing his throat, and putting his hands in his pockets, he sang, in a rich, melodious voice:—

"Oh! here's to the well-built mail packet,
    And here's to the Graces divine—
The Graces which make life worth having—
    They're women, tobacco, and wine.
        Oh! here's to the sea.

"When I land after cruising about, sir,
    And toss off a glass of Schiedam,
I smile, and I say with a shout, sir,
    'By Jove! boys, I know where I am.'

"The women all give me sly glances,
    For they love a true sailor on shore,
And if I just give them a kiss, why,
    They say 'Give me, oh, give me one more!'

"A pipe or a weed is refreshing;
    But when you have taken your whack, oh!
Why, sit down and smoke a small cutty,
    And wont you be fond of tobacco?

"But wine is the grandest invention
    That ever was thought of or made;
Hock or champagne I've only to mention,
    As masters who will be obeyed.

"For they make you both jolly and merry,
    When you feel that you wish you were dead;
And you laugh at all sorrow and care, when
    Champagne, sir, gets into your head.

"So here's to the well-built mail packet,
    And here's to the Graces divine,
The Graces which make life worth having—
    They're women, tobacco, and wine."

he girls laughed at the sentiment contained in the captain's song, and vehemently applauded him.

He really did not sing at all badly, and the wine he had imbibed had given him a fund of good spirits which very much helped his minstrelsy.

The revelry continued for some time, until all the party were more or less intoxicated.

The potency of the wine first showed its effects upon Agnes, who leaned back in her chair, and shut her eyes. Then her head fell a little on one side, and finally she threatened to fall off her chair altogether.

"L-look af-after your fr-friend, L-Lotty," stammered the captain, who was very far gone.

Charlotte got up with difficulty and helped Agnes into an arm-chair which stood in a corner of the cabin.

Agnes was no sooner there than she instantly dropped off in a drunken sort of stupor.

THE DUTCHMAN FORCES AGNES INTO THE DUNGEON.

Charlotte looked vacantly about her, and laughed stupidly, saying—

"Jolly, jolly wine; like joll' wine," and with this exclamation on her lips, she fell down on the floor by the side of Agnes's chair, and slept as soundly as if she had been in her own bed.

The captain tried to get up an idiotic laugh at this strange scene, but he only succeeded in raising a sort of chuckle, which, after many futile attempts to mould it into something better and worthier, died away into a species of imbecile rattle, and the worthy captain followed his feminine friends' example and rolled under the table, where he snored as only drunken men, when lying on their backs, do snore.

The captain might have been in this disgusting condition about an hour and a half, when the first mate of the vessel knocked timidly at the cabin-door.

There was no answer, as may be expected.

He knocked again.

Still no response.

At last, after being a third time unsuccessful in obtaining a reply, he ventured to open the door.

When he entered the cabin, the first mate opened something else.

He opened his eyes.

Then he laughed a shrill, small laugh, as much as to say, "What a fellow our skipper is!"

Then he muttered something to himself.

Perhaps he said, "avast heaving," or maybe "he shivered his timbers," or else he said something about "them there craft," which are, I believe, all stock nautical phrases, not exactly patented like Messrs. Dircks and Pepper's ghost, but free to be used by anybody, either on the stage of the Britannia, Hoxton, or the Victoria in the New Cut—that transpontine temple of melodrama.

After the first mate had taken in the scene, he approached the captain, but he could not help admiring the two sleeping beauties who lay upon the floor of the cabin.

At last he was obliged to concentrate his mind on his duty, and his eyesight on his captain.

So, giving the skipper a shake, rather more rough than gentle, he exclaimed—

"Passengers coming on board, sir; weigh anchor directly."

The captain started up and gazed vacantly about him.

"Bucket, sir?" queried the mate shortly.

The captain, whose hand trembled a good deal, nodded his head, and rolled over on his side again.

As the mate left the room, he saw the bottles of wine on the table—

"Don't see why I shouldn't have a drain as well as those who ain't my betters," he said to himself.

Taking up the bottles one by one and shaking them, he at last found one which was partly full.

Pouring out a large tumbler brimming full, he swallowed it with considerable satisfaction displayed on his countenance. Then he left the cabin.

After the lapse of a minute or so, he returned with a bucket of water; he was evidently acquainted with the skipper's habits.

Placing the bucket on the floor, he again woke the captain, who looked at the water for a moment, and then plunged his head in. Again and again he repeated this, and at last he took the towel which the mate offered him and wiped his dripping head.

"Feel better, sir?" asked the first mate.

"Little," was the reply. "Think I shall do now."

"Try another dip," suggested the mate.

"No, that will do. What is the time now?"

The mate answered the question, and the captain said—

"Are they coming on board?"

"Fast. Five have arrived already."

The captain went to a glass, and although his hands were very unsteady, he put himself as right as he could, and went on deck to look after his official duties.

The passengers all came on board, and the anchor was weighed.

The steamer was soon on her way down the river, and still Agnes and Charlotte slept.

CHAPTER XLIX.

THE CAPTAIN PERFORMS HIS DUTIES WITH AN ACHING HEAD AND FORGETS HIS FAIR PASSENGERS, OF WHOSE PRESENCE HE IS REMINDED BY THE FIRST MATE—SODA-AND-BRANDY — STEWARD — STEWARD! STEWARD!—AGNES AND CHARLOTTE FEEL A LITTLE BETTER—THE MYSTERIOUS STRANGER—"I DON'T LIKE THAT WOMAN."

DOWN the river, past the East and West India Docks, past Greenwich, Woolwich, and Erith, past the Nore, past the forest of shipping at Deal—down, down the river into the Chops of the Channel, and still the girls slept. The captain had forgotten them.

The captain, who had not quite recovered himself in spite of his bath, had evidently overlooked the presence of his fair charges.

They were unconscious—they knew not that they were swiftly steaming to a foreign land. Deep and heavy was their breathing—very heavy and very deep.

The engines creaked and groaned, and the quickly revolving mechanism of the screw and the paddles gleamed and glittered in the sunlight.

Orders were given to the crew in a harsh, commanding voice, and the sails flew out to encounter the freshening breeze.

The thick black smoke came in dense volumes out of the funnel, and hung for many many yards behind like a huge pall.

The sun was rising in the heavens. The passengers began to show what mettle they were made of. Some went below and called in feeble tones for the steward; others, more brave, remained on deck until a stronger wave than usual upset the equilibrium of their stomachs, and they then leant hopelessly over the side of the mail-packet, and began, in mercantile phrase, to cast up their accounts.

There were some, however, who were made of sterner material, who could defy the sea and its terrors; and these walked up and down the deck smoking and talking, and if they called for the steward at all, it was to demand some bitter beer, or Guinness's stout, or brandy.

The captain, after having performed his duties, thought that he might indulge in half-an-hour's siesta. He had received the passage-money, and awarded the proper berths and cabins to every one. He had listened to complaints and adjusted differences; and he considered that he might lie down for a little while without being in any way missed.

As he was about to leave the saloon, where he was making certain entries in his books, the mate approached him and said—

"No offence, I hope, sir, but——"

"But what?"

"Nothing particular, sir, only——"

"Well, speak out," said the captain.

"The ladies, sir," said the first mate.

"The what?"

"The ladies, sir."

As the mate repeated this, the captain suddenly remembered that Agnes and Charlotte were on board.

"The devil!" he exclaimed.

The mate grinned.

"Where are they?" demanded the captain.

"On the floor, sir."

"Where? What do you mean?"

"On the floor of your cabin, sir."

"Oh!" said the captain, "I see. Well, they must go for a cruise, I suppose."

"Yes, sir; wont do 'em any harm. Get the sea-breezes, sir," said the mate.

"Just be so good as to keep your remarks to yourself," exclaimed the captain.

"Certainly, sir."

"And there's another thing you may do."

"What's that, sir?"

"Why, just send some soda-and-brandy into my cabin."

"Yes, sir; directly sir," replied the first mate, who left the saloon.

The captain then made his way to his private cabin. There, on the floor, where Charlotte had fallen the night before, he found her still. Agnes was yet fast asleep in the arm-chair.

"Hang it!" said the captain, "they have slept long enough. I think I'd better wake them."

Going to Charlotte, he shook her by the arm, saying, "Wake up, Lotty. My stars! you've slept long enough to last you a century."

But he had to shake her three or four times before she showed any decided symptoms of vitality.

At last she opened her eyes, and gazed vacantly around her.

"Awake at last, eh, Lotty?" said the captain.

"Oh! it's you, old boy," replied Charlotte. "What's your little game, now?"

"What's yours?"

"Well, I shouldn't object to a little soda-and-brandy, although my little game is the same as usual."

"And what's that?"

"Don't you know?"

"No—what is it?"

"Plunder!" replied Charlotte, showing her teeth.

The steward now entered with some bottles on a tray, and deposited them on a table.

The captain mixed a draught for Charlotte, who eagerly drank every drop of it.

"Now I feel better!" she cried, as she put the glass upon the table empty.

"Oh! do you? Well, that's satisfactory. My stars!" said the captain.

"Your stars! You're always talking about your stars," said Charlotte. "It is about time we went on shore again, isn't it? I must wake up this child. What time is it?"

The captain laughed as she talked about going on shore, but he said nothing.

Agnes was sleeping soundly when Charlotte shook her, and said—

"Get up, dear, or else you will sleep so long that you wont be able to wake when you want to, you will be so used to it."

Agnes opened her eyes, over which hung the heavily weighted lids, charged with blood, and looking red and swollen.

"Lord Marchmont!" exclaimed Agnes, only half aroused.

"Oh!" said Charlotte, under her breath, "that's it, is it? You are a cut above me. I thought there was something."

At last Agnes woke up, and, after drinking the same beverage that Charlotte had just indulged in, she seemed more herself.

The captain poured out a brimming tumbler of moselle with a dash of brandy in it, saying—

"Nothing like a hair of the dog who bit you."

"How do you feel now, Agnes?" asked Charlotte.

"Oh, much better—how are you?"

"Me!—I'm all right. Shall we go on shore now?"

"I think we had better," replied Agnes.

"What a strange noise the ship makes!" exclaimed Charlotte, as the straining of the timbers and the noise and clangour of the engines, with the rush of the steam, and the revolution of the paddles struck upon her ears for the first time.

"Yes; it is blowing rather hard," replied the captain.

"Blowing, is it? Then I suppose that accounts for it."

"Have you made up your mind to go on shore?" asked the captain.

"Yes," they both replied.

"Wont you stay a little while longer?"

"No, I think not. I want to get home and lie down," replied Charlotte.

"But you can lie down here."

"Yes; but not so comfortably and nicely."

"Well," said the captain, "put your hair and your bonnets right and come on deck. I am going upstairs to talk to one of my officers, and I will return in five minutes.'

The girls arranged their attire to their satisfaction, and when the captain came back they accompanied him on deck.

Imagine their surprise—picture their consternation—think of their astonishment—as they saw themselves surrounded on all sides with water.

At first they could hardly believe it.

They could scarcely credit it.

The captain burst into a loud fit of laughter.

He could not help it.

A moment's reflection showed Charlotte what had happened, and she saw the folly of being angry; so she laughed in unison with the captain.

"What is the meaning of this?" demanded Agnes.

"Well, can't you see?" replied Charlotte.

"See! it's all sea!" answered Agnes, attempting a mild pun, such as ladies, when they condescend to be facetious, delight in.

"Of course it is."

"But what does it mean?"

"It means that we are going an excursion—London to Holland, and back. Fare, first class, seven-and-sixpence—steward's fee extra."

"Don't joke, Charlotte," said Agnes. "Do you really mean to say that the vessel has sailed without putting us on shore?"

"Well, it looks like it."

"Is it so, captain?" cried Agnes, addressing the skipper.

"I fear so," he replied.

"Then it is an unjustifiable proceeding on your part, sir!" exclaimed Agnes, very much annoyed; "and one I shall hold you answerable for."

"Indeed."

"Now, Agnes, don't be foolish," said Charlotte. "You can't help yourself. You are on the bosom of the ocean, although not exactly in the Bay of Biscay, where it is occasionally stormy. You had better think yourself lucky that the ocean is not a stormy one at the time when you honour it with your presence."

"Oh!" suddenly exclaimed Agnes.

"What's the matter?" asked the captain.

"The cabin—the steward—the cabin—which way?" said Agnes, her indignation at being carried off merging itself in a stronger feeling.

"Yes—which—which way?" chimed in Charlotte, looking very pale.

The captain, with a smile on his lips, conducted the girls into the ladies' saloon, where the stewardess attended to their wants, which were apparently of a legal character, as they seemed to have brought an action of ejectment against certain substances and fluids with whom the motion of the sea did not exactly agree.

Some hours passed on, and the passengers went to dinner. That is, those who were able to eat any.

The two girls had by this time partially recovered themselves, and contrived to eat a fairy-like piece of fish and a tiny piece of venison.

Although they were still ill and pale, they were much better after they had eaten something, and they looked round them at their fellow-passengers with some degree of interest.

One old woman, in particular, arrested Agnes's attention. She was about forty-five. She was fat, and rather fair than dark, although her hair was of an indeterminate colour. She wore much jewellery, probably of a spurious description. She was accompanied by three young ladies, who might have been taken for her daughters, only they were not a bit like her.

This old lady paid Agnes a great deal of attention, and after dinner she went over to her side of the table, and opened a conversation with her.

By dint of a little shrewd cross-questioning, this amiable old lady extracted the cause of Agnes being on board, and she pretended to sympathise very much with her. She also extended her condolences to Charlotte. Addressing Agnes, she said—

"You will be quite lost, my dear child, in a foreign town, by yourself, and you will have to stay a day or two before the steamer returns."

"Well, I suppose we shall stay on board," replied Agnes.

"Stay on board. Oh! that will be very uncomfortable."

"So it will."

"I will tell you how you can get over that difficulty. I have a house in Rotterdam, and my daughters are not sufficient to fill all the rooms. So if you like, that is, if you will condescend to honour my poor dwelling, you and your friend shall be accommodated to the best of my ability."

"You are very kind, I am sure," said Agnes.

"Kind?—not at all; I am only sorry to see a country-woman of mine in distress."

"Still your offer is very generous."

"You are good, I am sure, to say so," simpered the old lady. "I am going on deck now, with my dear girls; but we will arrange before we leave the vessel. I shall see you again at sea."

"Agnes," said Charlotte, directly she had gone, "I don't like that woman."

CHAPTER L.

A LONG CONVERSATION — AGNES TELLS CHARLOTTE SAUNDERS THAT SHE IS PREJUDICED AGAINST A VERY COURTEOUS LADY—CHARLOTTE OBJECTS TO THE PHRASE "LADY"—OLD FIREWORKS—IN HARBOUR—GOING TO MRS. MORGAN'S HOUSE.

AFTER Charlotte Saunders made the remark which is recorded at the end of the last chapter, Agnes looked steadily in her friend's face, as if awaiting an explanation of so singular a declaration. The amiable stranger was very hospitable, was very kind, was very sociable. However, Charlotte had declared that she did not like her, and although Agnes waited for an explanation, none was forthcoming.

"Why do you not like her?" at length Agnes asked.

"I can hardly tell you," replied Charlotte. "But one thing is very clear, I do not like her, and she is one of those women whom I never should take a fancy to if I were to live a thousand years, and be every day in her society, which, by the way, God and His angels forbid."

"Is there anything extraordinary about her, then?" asked Agnes.

"I cannot say that there is. But I fancy that I have seen her face somewhere before; and in addition to all that she is much too civil to please me. I don't like your very civil people; they may be all very nice and very correct, but they are not so in my opinion, and I always fight shy of them when I do come in contact with them by any accident."

"I think you are very much prejudiced against a good and worthy woman, Charlotte," said Agnes, "and I am surprised at your silliness in objecting to a lady because——"

"A lady!"

"Yes. I said a lady. Why not?"

"Well, all I can say is, that if she is a lady, I am something infinitely superior to that somewhat indefinite title."

Charlotte spoke a little satirically as she said this. She evidently had taken a great dislike to the stranger, and she did not make any secret of it.

"Do you mean to say that you will not go and stop with her when we land?" asked Agnes.

"Certainly not. I would not do so for the world," replied Charlotte.

"Not if I go ?"

"If you go ?"

"Yes."

"But you never will be so silly as to accept the invitation of a perfect stranger ?"

"What motive could she have in asking me ? She cannot do me any harm."

"I don't know about that. As to her motives, they are best known to herself. I could suggest a great many motives, if I liked, but you would, I have no doubt, be offended with me, if I did."

"No, I should not."

"You would not ?"

"No."

"Well, I will tell you another time. But are you determined to go with her to her house ?"

"I am. I do not want to stop on board ship with you and your husband."

"Well, if you are resolute in your determination, I will tell you what I will do."

"What ?" asked Agnes.

"Why, only this—I will go with you."

"Will you, indeed ? Then you have changed your mind."

"No, I have not, indeed. I dislike the old woman, or lady, as you think her, as much as ever."

"Then why do you say you will go ?"

"Because," replied Charlotte, "it was mainly through me that you have come over to Holland in this packet. If I had not taken you out, and my captain had not brought you down to the steamer and made you tipsy, you would have been in London now."

"Yes, that is true."

"Very well. Then it is my duty to look after you."

"You are very kind."

"Besides," said Charlotte, "I never desert a pal of mine; you are an old pal, and I mean to stick to you. You don't know what sort of devilments an old woman like that may have in view in a foreign city, with a lovely English girl like you in her possession."

"But then," said Agnes, "her daughters."

"Her daughters !" replied Charlotte; "there's a family likeness, isn't there ?"

"Oh, Charlotte ! you are incorrigible. You have taken a dislike to this lady because she took a fancy to me first, without noticing you."

"Not I."

"Oh, yes, you did; I can see it, and I wont listen to another word against her."

"Listen or not, you can't change my opinion. I know what's what as well as any woman going, and I have had more experience than you have."

"Will you be quiet, Charlotte ?"

"No; I wont till I've had my say. When I have, I'll shut up; but not before."

"Well, have your say then; but be as brief as you can."

"We shall only stop in the city a couple of days, or three at most, and that wont kill us; and if you are resolved to go and stay with that old—well, I wont say what."

"No, you had better not, if you don't want to offend me," said Agnes, who had really taken a fancy to the amiable stranger.

"All right," replied Charlotte, smiling; "what I was going to say is, that although I am a young girl from the country, they wont get over me, in Holland or any other place—Dutch or not; and as you have made up your mind to make a fool of yourself, why, I will see you well out of it."

"You are unusually obliging, upon my word," said Agnes, sarcastically.

"Oh, you may be sarcastic and chaff," answered Charlotte; "but let those laugh longest who win. It does not matter to me whether I stay on board this ship and have my spree—for I mean to have one since I have tumbled into this adventure—or whether I go into some ‘Hollandsche Lodgement,’ as they call it, and drink vile Schiedam instead of a glass of good Old Tom. Anyhow, I'll stick to you."

"I'm sure you mean me well, dear Charlotte," replied Agnes; "and I am sorry if I have offended you. Well, we will go together, and then no harm can befal us. I think, you know, it is so silly to be prejudiced against strangers just because you don't happen to like their faces."

"Perhaps it is; but we wont talk about the matter any more just now; you may rest satisfied that I am with you. And now you want to go upstairs to join old Fireworks, I suppose ?"

"Old who ?"

"Why, old Fireworks, your new friend. Her nose and her face are so red that they look like a plethoric sort of squib or golden rain, which only wants a spark to set it fizzing."

"Do you mean to say she drinks ?" queried Agnes.

"Drinks ? yes, like a fish. Why, you can see that with half an eye."

"Well, I didn't."

"Perhaps not; but you, as I said before, are not particularly bright."

"Thank you," said Agnes, biting her lip.

"Why, old Fireworks looks," continued Charlotte, "as if she would expire some day of spontaneous combustion."

"Oh ! do be quiet, Charlotte."

"Well, I know one thing. I wouldn't like to put a match too close to her mouth if I were any friend of hers."

Agnes would stand her friend's banter no longer, so she ran upstairs, and soon stood on deck.

It was a fine, fresh afternoon, and the mysterious lady who was so amiable as to excite Charlotte Saunders' suspicions, was sitting down abaft the funnel, where, as the Penny Steamboats inform you, smoking is not usually allowed. And, in defiance of the notification, which was staring her in the face, one of her daughters was talking to the man at the wheel, who did not seem particularly flattered by the notice of the fair girl who was honouring him, if not boring him, by putting some silly questions to him.

As Agnes approached, she heard this young lady say—

"Man at the wheel."

No answer.

"Man at the wheel."

"I'm a list'nin'."

"Oh ! ask your pardon. Are we far from ’Olland ?"

"Good mile and a ’arf," was the reply.

"A mile and a ’alf ?" said the young lady. "Oh, you're making fun of me. You don't take me for a fool, do you ?"

"No, not exactly."

"What for, then ?" said the young lady.

"Next door to it," replied the man.

"Man at the wheel !" began the young lady, indignantly.

"Mum ?" said that individual, in reply to her exclamation.

"Do you know that I am a lady ?"

"Wasn't aware of the fact until I ’erd it from your own lips," said the man, making his wheel revolve rapidly—catching the spokes in a dexterous manner as they went round.

"Rose, dear ! come here," exclaimed the amiable stranger.

Rose obeyed, and took a seat by her side.

"Do you know," said her mother, "that you only demean and degrade yourself by conversing with low fellows like that ?"

"In course," replied the young lady.

"Very well, why not leave such rude, uneducated boors to themselves ?"

"They is unedicated," replied Rose; "and I ’ate any one as ’as ’ad a defective edication."

"Quite right, my dear; but here is our new friend. Cannot you make room on the seat by your side ?"

Rose moved a little on one side, and Agnes, in compliance with the amiable stranger's request, took a seat between the two.

"Well, my dear, have you made up your mind ?" said her new friend.

"I have, thank you. I have been talking to my friend."

"And what does she say ?"

"She will be very happy to come with me."

"Oh ! I am glad to hear it. I will do all in my power to make you comfortable."

"I am sure you will; and it is very kind of you to take so much interest in two girls who are such perfect strangers to you, as we are."

"Oh ! don't mention it. Any one who knows Mrs. Morgan will tell you that it is just her character."

"Is your name Mrs. Morgan, then ?"

"It is so—yours, my dear ?"

"Mine is Agnes Wilson."

"And your friend's ?"

"My friend! Oh! here she is," replied Agnes. "She can answer for herself."

Charlotte, it was evident, had been indulging in some more champagne, for her face was a little flushed, and there was a merry twinkle in her eye.

"Ah, my dear! is that you?" exclaimed Mrs. Morgan.

"Well, I suppose so," replied Charlotte; "I am not aware that I have been changed since I saw you last."

"Oh! how funny you are—quite witty, I declare."

"I wish I could return the compliment," said Charlotte.

"What a dear creature!" said Mrs. Morgan, turning to Agnes. "Isn't she a dear creature? Why she must be quite a treasure to you."

Agnes was about to make some reply to this speech, when Charlotte replied—

"My dear Mrs. Fireworks——"

"Fireworks! Oh! the playful thing—quite like a kitten. What a dear good creature!" cried Mrs. Morgan.

Agnes noticed, however, that the amiable stranger's nose got a little redder, as if she felt annoyed at Charlotte's banter.

"Mrs. Fireworks," persisted Charlotte.

"Well, my dear? If you choose to call me Fireworks, you may, I am sure. What's in a name? By the way, what is your name?"

Mrs. Morgan said this in her blandest and most insinuating manner.

After some conversation, it was finally arranged that Agnes and Charlotte should take up their abode with Mrs. Morgan, when they arrived at their destination.

The steamer went gallantly on its way, and after a quick passage it landed its freight at Rotterdam.

Here Agnes and Charlotte accompanied the amiable stranger to her house.

Charlotte told the captain where she was going, and promised to come down to the steamer early on the following morning; he replied—

"Well, Lotty, you must please yourself; but, my stars! I should stop where I am."

"Oh!" replied Charlotte, laughing, "I am not afraid of old Fireworks, or a hundred like her."

CHAPTER LI.

MRS. MORGAN CATCHES A TARTAR—CHARLOTTE SAUNDERS PROVES TO BE CLEVERER THAN SHE LOOKS—HANS BITES THE DUST AND DOESN'T SEEM TO LIKE IT—FOLLOW ME—CHARLOTTE ESCAPES, BUT AGNES IS DRAGGED FROM THE ROOM IN THE IRON GRASP OF THE DUTCHMAN.

MRS. MORGAN'S house was not a very striking one from the exterior; it was a plain brick-built dwelling, such as is to be seen any day in any street in the towns of Holland and Belgium.

The prosaic money-making people, who are commonly called Dutchmen, are not fond of expending much money in external decorations—they are too practical to do anything so refined.

They have their cathedrals and their town-halls, and a public monument or two here and there; but that is all—beyond that they do not care to go. Therefore superb dwellings, such as are to be met with almost everywhere in London and Paris, are the exception, and not the rule.

Mrs. Morgan's house internally was furnished with great luxuriousness, but there was something very tawdry, artificial, and unsubstantial about the furniture.

There were chairs painted white and gold. There was a satin paper on the wall. Mirrors abounded in the different rooms, and although the effect was striking, the house itself, take it altogether, was not the sort of house that Agnes would have selected to live in had she been free to act for herself.

When the oddly-shaped, old-fashioned carriage had conducted Mrs. Morgan, her three daughters, and her new acquaintances, whom she had in so apparently kind a manner made her guests, to this plain-looking building, the girls were led upstairs into a drawing-room. It was nearly evening, and as they felt tired, and worn out by their long sea-voyage, they laid down upon a sofa, and went to sleep for a little time.

How long they slept they did not know. When they awoke they found Mrs. Morgan standing by their side.

The room was brilliantly lit-up, the window-curtains were drawn, on a sideboard were arranged several bottles of wine and a few boxes of cigars.

The girls started up and rubbed their eyes—the flaring gas rather hurt them.

"Wake up, my dears! Will you not come and have a cup of tea?" exclaimed Mrs. Morgan. "You were so tired after your journey that I did not like to disturb you. I saw how fatigued you were, and I thought that a wink of sleep might do you good. How do you feel now—a little refreshed I hope?"

Charlotte Saunders aroused herself, and recovered the use of her dormant faculties before Agnes had looked around her. When she saw all the preparations we have mentioned in the shape of wine and tobacco, she opened her eyes wider than ever.

"What's all that for, eh?" she said, abruptly.

"What, my dear?" replied Mrs. Morgan.

"Why, all that wine, and smoke and stuff—what's it for?"

"Oh! that is what you mean, is it?"

"Yes, old Fireworks," replied Charlotte.

Mrs. Morgan smiled a little grimly.

"Well, go-a-head, what is it?" said Charlotte.

"The fact is, my dear," answered Mrs. Morgan, "I expect some friends this evening."

"Some friends! Who are they?"

"You are not very polite, my dear. I suppose I can ask who I like to come and see me in my own house?"

"Not if I object to it," replied Charlotte.

"Oh, indeed!" said Mrs. Morgan. "But you must excuse me this time, my dear, as I was not aware of your prejudices. Had I known them sooner I would not have sent out my invitations. As it is they are gone, and my friends will be here shortly. Another time I will pay more attention to your peculiarities."

Mrs. Morgan said this with an almost imperceptible sarcasm in her tone; but if she thought to make a fool of Charlotte Saunders she had made a great mistake, for that young lady was a match for her.

Rising from the sofa on which Agnes was still lying, Charlotte walked towards one of the mirrors, put her hair straight, and then approached Mrs. Morgan.

"Now look here, old Fireworks," she exclaimed, "I'm not such a fool as you take me for. I know your little game perfectly."

"Indeed!"

"Yes; and I have done so from the first moment I set eyes on you."

"Really!"

"You don't get over me, old Fireworks, I can tell you. I'm as fly as you are any day," said Charlotte Saunders, looking her in the face.

Mrs. Morgan shrank from her steadfast gaze, but replied boldly—

"You are treating me very strangely. I have invited you to stay at my house in the most friendly manner, and this is how you requite my kindness. Anyhow it will be a lesson to me in future."

"Now, Mrs. Organ——"

"Morgan, if you please."

"Well, Morgan, if you like. Only I don't suppose you always went by that name, eh?"

"Young woman!" cried Mrs. Morgan.

"Oh, you don't bounce me, you know!"

Mrs. Morgan bit her lip.

"Wasn't it Bet, or Sall, or Poll, down in Whitechapel, before you got on in the world, eh?" said Charlotte Saunders, with provoking pertinacity.

"Get out of my house!" screamed Mrs. Morgan, in an uncontrollable rage.

"I shall go when it suits me, my good woman, but not before," replied Charlotte.

"Wont you? We'll see about that."

"Oh, I'm not afraid of your bullies; I am a match for half-a-dozen Dutchmen or French frog-eaters either, any day," said Charlotte, defiantly.

Mrs. Morgan went towards the fireplace to ring a bell, but Charlotte rushed up to her, and pushed her away, saying—

"Not just yet; I haven't done with you yet, old Fireworks. I'm only just beginning. You've caught a tartar, you know."

"What do you want with me, you brazen thing?" said Mrs. Morgan.

"Brazen thing?" repeated Charlotte. "Come, that's good. Brazen thing, am I? Isn't that something like the story of the pot calling the kettle bad names?"

"You impudent creature!" exclaimed Mrs. Morgan.

"Go it, old Fireworks!" said Charlotte, coolly moving towards the sideboard, and taking up a bottle of Moselle.

"What are you doing there, eh?" said Mrs. Morgan.

"Wait a moment, and I'll show you," replied Charlotte, snapping the wire off with a corkscrew, popping the cork, and helping herself to a tumbler of the sparkling wine.

"You wretch! you dare to drink my wine."

"Well, it looks like it," answered Charlotte. "You see I'm rather thirsty, and as you are so hospitable, I thought you wouldn't mind."

"Why, that's worth half a guilder to me," almost yelled Mrs. Morgan.

"Can't help that. It isn't bad wine, though. Will you have some?" said Charlotte.

Mrs. Morgan got in such a rage that she could not speak; she could only shake her head with inarticulate passion.

"What, you wont! Don't say no, old Fireworks. You didn't get such stuff as this in Whitechapel, did you?"

"It wasn't Whitechapel," at last said Mrs. Morgan, finding the use of her tongue once more.

"Oh, it was down that way somewhere, then? I thought I wasn't far wrong," replied Charlotte.

"Oh, you hussy! you, beast you!"

"Was it Brunswick-street?" queried Charlotte; "that's commonly called Tiger-bay, you know."

Mrs. Morgan foamed at the mouth with rage.

"Oh! too good for you, was it? Well then, perhaps it was Frederick-street, or Flower-and-Dean-street," said Charlotte.

Mrs. Morgan clenched her fists and stamped her foot upon the ground.

"Come, old lady, don't take on so!" said Charlotte, soothingly. "It isn't your fault, you know; it's your misfortune, even if you did live in Gravel-lane."

"Gravel-lane, you—you low, disgusting, vile thing, you!" vociferated Mrs. Morgan.

"I say, draw it mild," said Charlotte.

"I'll give it you, my little beauty!" continued Mrs. Morgan, running to the mantelpiece, and ringing the bell violently.

Charlotte smiled, and retreated near the sideboard.

Shortly after the bell rang a man entered the room. He was a low, sleepy-looking ruffian. He seemed to have been picked up out of the very dregs of the kennel.

"Hans," screamed Mrs. Morgan, "drag this woman downstairs, and lock her up in the cellar!"

"Where I was put the other Fraulein?" asked the man.

"Yes, yes."

"Ya. It is done," said Hans.

"Is it, old boy?" exclaimed Charlotte, placing her hand upon a bottle of wine.

"You come long wid old Hans," said the man, advancing to Agnes.

"Now you keep off!" cried Charlotte. "If you don't, you'll get it, I can tell you."

But Hans, never dreaming of any active resistance, advanced with a lumbering gait to Charlotte, and tried to seize her by the arm.

But Charlotte suddenly lifted up the bottle of wine, and struck him on the head with all her force.

The bottle descended upon his unprotected skull with great violence.

It broke as it struck him, with a loud noise.

The glass fell about in a shower; and the wine mingling with the man's blood flowed to the ground in a ruby stream.

The man tottered.

At last he fell.

The blow had deprived him of consciousness.

"You'll put me in the cellar, will you?" asked Charlotte, between her teeth.

Mrs. Morgan made no answer.

"It looks like it, doesn't it? You put me anywhere! Why, I'll smash your infernal old place up in a moment."

Mrs. Morgan stood like a statue, white and pale and motionless.

Charlotte took up another bottle, and swung it backwards and forwards in her hand, saying—

"I don't like that looking-glass exactly. There is something about it which is not quite the thing. But I will see if I cannot improve it."

Mrs. Morgan sprang forward; but Charlotte exclaimed—"Here goes!"

And before her movement could be arrested or frustrated the bottle left her hand, and went crashing against a beautiful mirror worth forty or fifty guineas.

The glass cracked in every direction, and soon its beautiful surface was nothing but a wreck.

The tears sprang to Mrs. Morgan's eyes as she witnessed this wholesale destruction of her costly and valuable property.

"Now stand still, old Fireworks, or I'll serve you the same!" exclaimed Charlotte, menacingly. "I told you you had caught a Tartar in me, and I think you will be willing to admit that you have by the time I've done with you. I suppose the reason you left England was that there was a warrant out against you, and you were glad to escape with your 'daughters.' But, as I had the honour of remarking once before, you don't get over me, although I may have the misfortune to be a young girl from the country."

Agnes had during this remarkable scene been thoroughly awake.

Very much surprised and astonished, she sat up upon the sofa watching the course of events.

She had heard the altercation between Charlotte and Mrs. Morgan.

She had witnessed the entrance of Hans, and his subsequent fall upon the ground, when Charlotte struck him.

She had seen the breakage of the glass by the champagne-bottle.

But she had not dared to take any active part in the affray.

The fact was, she was too much alarmed; she was not so shrewd as her friend Charlotte Saunders, and she could not exactly comprehend all that was passing around her.

Mrs. Morgan, in a voice of subdued passion, said to Charlotte—

"Go—go!"

"Go! Well, I think I shall avail myself of your gracious permission presently."

"Go—go now!"

"Don't be in such a hurry to get rid of me, old Fireworks," said Charlotte, in a bantering tone.

"Will you go?" repeated Mrs. Morgan, in almost imploring accents.

"Well, I will presently. You don't suppose I mean to stay here all night? Don't flatter yourself. But I should like to give you something to remember me by before I do go."

Charlotte Saunders cast her eyes round the apartment, and at last her gaze rested on some handsome vases of Bohemian glass, which rested upon the mantelpiece. Going towards them, she swept them off the marble slab with one stroke of her arm, and they fell in a shapeless mass upon the floor.

"You had better get a little of Parker's cement," suggested Charlotte—"they'll mend."

Mrs. Morgan made a rush at Charlotte, and cried—

"Fiend! Go from here, or I will have your life."

"Will you? What will you give me for it? It's worth more than you've got to spare, I'm thinking," replied Charlotte.

Mrs. Morgan ran up to Charlotte, with such a furious aspect that it really looked as if she would have murdered her. But Charlotte stepped nimbly on one side, and put out her foot, over which Mrs. Morgan stumbled, and fell heavily upon her rubicund nose.

Charlotte laughed, and going to Agnes, said—

"Well, are you ready to go?"

"What does all this mean?" asked Agnes.

"Can't you see?"

"No."

"Well, you must be blind."

"Pray tell me."

"Never mind about being told now. Put on your shawl and run away. I'll tell you afterwards."

During this scene, Charlotte had not perceived that the man Hans had recovered his senses, and had slunk out of the room like a stealthy snake. She was, however, made unpleasantly aware of the fact, for, when Agnes rose from the sofa, and wrapped her shawl round her, ready to accompany her friend, and the two girls turned towards the door, they were confronted with Hans, and a couple more evil-looking ruffians—doubtlessly retainers of the establishment.

Mrs. Morgan had risen to her feet, and after one look in the broken glass at her injured proboscis, she recoiled from the spectacle with disgust, and appeared to be much pleased at the sight of the reinforcement her small garrison had received.

"Kill them—knock them down—lock them up in the cellar!" she cried. "Give it them!"

The men hesitated a moment, as if they were debating about the plan of the campaign.

"Murder that one—kill that hussy!" she cried, in Flemish, indicating Charlotte.

The three men approached the girls.

"I'll teach her to call me names. I'll give it her hot and strong, I will, presently! She wont tell me I come from Whitechapel again, I'll warrant her."

Charlotte Saunders saw the aspect of affairs, and it did not take her long to discover that they were serious.

"I must take care of myself," she said, between her teeth. "I am afraid that Agnes is so stupid that she will never have sense enough to second me properly, so she must take her chance; if I can only manage to escape from this infernal den, I can look her up afterwards, and rescue her from this old Whitechapel hell-cat."

Charlotte retreated slowly before the three men, and once more neared the sideboard; as she reached it she armed herself, as on the former occasion, with two heavy, massive-looking bottles, called, in the language of the trade, "magnums." With one of these in each hand, she shouted to Agnes—

"Follow me!"

And charged the three men, dealing the first one a tremendous blow, which fractured his skull, and laid him prostrate.

She approached the second; but seeing the fate of his comrade he hung back.

Hans, mindful of former favours, hid himself behind a chair, and with the stolidity of a Dutchman awaited the sequel.

"What!"-cried Mrs. Morgan, in a great state of fury, "and are you afraid of a couple of school girls?"

Charlotte made for the doorway, which she reached in safety, and saying to Agnes—

"If you cannot succeed in following me never mind; I will look after you, and rescue you to-morrow."

She descended the stairs without further obstruction, and after crossing the hall, she opened the street-door, and was at liberty.

Agnes attempted to follow her, but Mrs. Morgan seized her by the arm, exclaiming—

"Not if I know it, young lady; your visit to me is not going to be brought to such an abrupt termination as that of your friend."

"Oh! What mean you?"

"You will soon see."

"Am I not free to come and go as I like, then?" asked Agnes.

"Sit still and hold your noise, will you?" replied Mrs. Morgan, with great asperity.

"Let me go," said Agnes.

"Go! Oh, dear, no! Certainly not. Couldn't part with you at any price."

"But I will go."

"You no part, mine fraulein," said Hans, emerging from behind the sheltering chair.

"You are a bad woman!" said Agnes to Mrs. Morgan. "I see it all now."

"Do you, indeed?"

"Yes; and I wish I had taken my friend's advice, but you will be punished for this."

"Take her to the cellar, Hans," cried Mrs. Morgan. "I had intended that her she-devil of a friend should have passed the night there, but as she has got clear off, perhaps I am well rid of her. However, this young lady shall pay for some of the annoyance I have experienced. Take her away."

"Where, oh, where do you mean to take me?" cried Agnes.

"You'll find out soon enough," replied Mrs. Morgan.

Agnes's protestations were in vain, and shrieking wildly she was borne from the room in the iron grasp of Hans the Dutchman.

CHAPTER LII.

THEN THERE CAME A LOUD KNOCKING AT THE STREET-DOOR—HANS THINKS IT IS THE WATCH—AGNES IS DRAGGED TO THE LOWEST DUNGEON — THE HUMAN REMAINS — RATS, RATS, RATS !— AGNES'S BRAVERY— THE RATS FIGHT OVER THE CARCASE OF THEIR DEAD COMPANION.

AGNES'S reflections, as may be easily imagined, were not of the most pleasant description. She found out—to her cost, when it was too late—that she had been duped and deceived by an artful and designing woman. A woman who belonged to a class, who disgrace, and are unworthy of the very name of woman. A wretch lost alike to all sense of shame and decency. If she had only taken the advice of her friend, Charlotte Saunders, she would not now have been in so unpleasant a predicament. But the thing was done. The folly had been committed, and all she had to do, was to bear the consequences of her stupidity. Hans had seized her with no very gentle touch. His rude grasp hurt her tender flesh, and she had some difficulty to refrain from crying out. But she was well aware that tears or compassion would be thrown away upon the rough Dutchman.

Where was he going to take her to?

What was the meaning of this violence, and why was she subjected to this terrorism?

In pondering over these queries she could only conclude that she had incurred the enmity of Mrs. Morgan, and was now feeling the effects of her spite and hatred. She had spoken of a cellar, which was in all probability equivalent to a dungeon. To be immured in a prison in a foreign country, at the will of an iniquitous old woman, who was as powerful in her small domain as a feudal lord in his castle, was not a pleasant incident in any one's career; and it was perfectly horrible in the case of a young girl accustomed to every luxury that the mind could wish for, or money supply. There were police in Holland, and they would, of course, rescue her, and punish Mrs. Morgan, if they were aware of her cruelty. But they were not aware of it, neither were they likely to be.

How could Agnes communicate with them?

She had no means of doing so.

Her position was very hopeless.

"Oh!" she sighed, "when will fate be tired of persecuting me? When will my troubles be over?"

She had hardly spoken these words to herself, when her captor and herself reached the bottom of the stairs.

The street-door was before her.

The same through which Charlotte Saunders had made her escape a few minutes before.

Suddenly a thundering knock was heard, followed by a violent ring.

Then another, and another.

Hans paused, and listened intently for a repetition of the angry summons.

Agnes was overjoyed at the sound. In her opinion it was like the tocsin of Liberty.

She was sanguine enough to believe that she had been reprieved from her terrible doom.

"Donner and blitzen, it is der watch!" cried Hans, rather alarmed, as another knock, more violent and vigorous than the forerunners, was heard.

Mrs. Morgan put her head over the banisters, and said in Dutch—

"Put her in the lowest dungeon! Quick! Lose no time! It is, doubtless, that cursed friend of hers, with half the police of Rotterdam at her heels. Away with her, Hans! I will reward you. Mind you, she must not be found."

Hans rapidly dragged the shrieking girl down a flight of stone steps, which led to the offices on the basement.

Agnes could plainly hear the repeated knocks on the sturdy oaken door; but with each step that she took they came fainter and fainter, until at last she ceased to hear them at all: and then her last hope of freedom died away like a whisper on a breeze.

Passing the kitchens, Hans entered a small pantry, where he provided himself with a lamp, and then saying, in a rude voice—

"Come along, mine fraulein!" he forced Agnes along a passage, and down a narrow flight of steps, gloomy and terror-striking.

Having arrived at the bottom of these, they reached an

iron door studded with large iron nails. This seemed to defy their further progress, until Hans produced a key, which, once in the wards of the lock, soon caused the ponderous mass to roll back on its hinges.

"Oh! where are you taking me to?" cried Agnes. "For Heaven's sake, have some pity! I am not strong—I am only a weak woman! I shall die in this dreadful place! Let me go, for pity's sake! Let me go, I will reward you!"

Hans grasped her arm tighter, and said, between his clenched teeth—

"You come 'long, Hans will catch the rhumatiz stopping here." And the man shivered, as the cold air struck a chill to his bones.

Agnes, finding entreaty was useless with this savage, gave up the attempt, muttering to herself—

"It will soon kill me, that's one satisfaction. It is a consolation to know that my sufferings will not be of long duration."

The iron door ushered them into another passage, but this was damp and slimy; drops of water rolled through the arched top of the vault, and it seemed as though there was a vast body of water overhead. This was probably the case, for in Holland they have very few streets, as we have in England. They use instead canals and boats and barges. There were a few highways, and that is all.

It was by one of these roads that Agnes and Mrs. Morgan had come from the quay to the latter's house, but the usual mode of transit was, as in Venice, by boats or gondolas, along the placid surface of the everlasting canals.

The passage terminated in a chamber of small dimensions. The only article of furniture it contained was a rude wooden bench. The walls glistened with moisture. The floor had never been paved, and the ground had sunk in several places into little hollows, in which the water had collected, forming so many little pools, fetid and stagnant.

As they approached this dungeon, a scampering was heard, and a whole tribe of rats, frightened at the light and the noise of footsteps, ran away with great precipitation, one large one alone remained sitting upon the wooden bench. At last he followed the example of his companions, and dived down a big hole in the corner, which probably led into some drain.

Agnes shuddered and trembled so violently that she was nearly falling, but Hans struck her violently in the back between the shoulder blades.

This brutality made her sick and ill, but it drove away her faintness.

A rusty chain fixed to a staple in the wall lay like a coiled snake upon the ground, and in its immediate vicinity was something infinitely more horrible than she had hitherto seen.

Several bones lay about the floor!

Bones, which by their shape and formation, she could not doubt were human remains!

What a tale could they have told had they been able to disclose the mysteries of that prison-house!

Horrors were crowding so thickly upon her that Agnes had no time to dwell upon any particular one.

Casting her eyes round, she saw a skull!

The eyeless sockets seemed to glare fearfully at her, and the fleshless jaws did all but jabber warnings.

Hans seemed totally unmoved by these terrifying incidents. He walked up to a particular corner in which was a long stick, this he gave to Agnes, saying—

"Dis will keep de rats away. Better not sleep too much."

"Oh! you are not going to take the light away and leave me here in utter darkness?" screamed Agnes, now really seriously alarmed for her safety.

All the tales she had ever heard or read of rats devouring people alive, came rushing together into her mind, and she became frantic with alarm.

Hans hesitated.

He seemed to be touched with compassion, and then his old brutal, callous feeling came over him, and he was moving towards the door.

But Agnes, with the energy, bravery, and courage of despair, sprang upon him, snatched the lamp from his grasp, and then, with the stick in her hand, stood upon the defensive.

Hans was confounded, so sudden had been the attack, and so complete its success. But with the stolidity of his countrymen, he resigned himself to what seemed inevitable.

He either did not like to risk an encounter for the posses-

sion of the lamp, or else his former feeling of pity cropped up again, for he gave vent to what was a veritable Dutch grunt, and waddled along the passage to the door, leaving the enemy in possession of the field of battle and all the honours of war.

Agnes heard the door fall into its place once more as the old Dutchman closed it securely on the other side, and then as the key grated harshly in the rust-begrimed lock, she was alone with her misery, and, what was more dreadful still, with the rats.

She looked at the lamp, and saw with undisguised pleasure, that it was almost full of oil, and would burn for many hours without replenishing.

This was something in her terrible situation!

She had heard that rats were afraid of light, if so she was safe.

A minute elapsed, and then a rat emerged from a hole. Agnes, with great presence of mind, struck it violently on the head with the stick; it rolled over and over, either stunned or dead. Half-a-dozen or so more rats then followed, but seeing the first, they fell upon and dragged it below, and Agnes heard them fighting over the carcase of their companion.

———

CHAPTER LIII.

A PARLEY—WHO ARE YOU?—ADMITTED AT LAST—OLD FRIENDS—COUNT VAL DE GRACE AND INSPECTOR WYMAN—WILL YOU GIVE THE GIRL UP?—NO—DUTCHMEN *versus* ENGLISH—FOR GOD'S SAKE BE QUICK, THEY ARE MURDERING HER!

MRS. MORGAN went herself to open the street-door. But she stopped a moment before doing so to listen. She heard nothing.

"Who's there?" she said in English.

"Never mind," was the reply.

"But I must know."

"Open the door."

"Who are you?"

"That doesn't matter."

"But I must know."

"You'll wait a long time."

"You'll wait longer."

"Come, open the door."

"I don't let strangers in at this time of night."

"You'll have to let me in."

"Shall I?"

"Yes."

"I don't think so."

This dialogue had been carried on, as it were, through the keyhole.

But at last Mrs. Morgan, seeing Hans reappear at the top of the staircase, knew that Agnes was safely disposed of, and she thought it would only be prudent to open the door and see who her visitors were.

She unlocked the door, but kept the chain up.

She looked out, and saw two men.

One looked like a gentleman, the other like a man in a humbler position in life.

"Come, now, that is something like," said the latter.

"Who spoke to you?" replied Mrs. Morgan, sharply, Then addressing the gentleman, she said, "What is your business, sir?"

"Just let me in, and you shall know, my good woman," was the answer.

There was a something about this man which Mrs. Morgan found irresistible—some mysterious influence—some strange power which she could not interpret—but which she found herself, willy nilly, obliged to obey.

So she opened the door, and the men were admitted.

"You have a drawing-room, I suppose?" said the mysterious stranger.

"Yes."

"Lead the way then."

Mrs. Morgan, although inclined to be indignant, was constrained to do as she was told. And in a short time the two men found themselves in Mrs. Morgan's drawing-room, which bore all the traces of the recent severe conflict which had taken place.

"Ah!" said the shabbier of the two. "Ah! disorderly house—riot—police probably called in—great destruction of property—revoke license at next sessions."

AGNES IS ATTACKED BY RATS, AND RESCUED BY COUNT VAL DE GRACE.

"Will you be quiet?" cried Mrs. Morgan, angrily. "It's no business of yours, I'm sure."

"Independent woman—insolent to police—six months' hard labour," replied this indefatigable tormentor.

Mrs. Morgan felt inclined to cry with rage, but she exclaimed—

"You must be a bad man to insult a lone widow-woman in this way."

"In addition to former sentence, prisoner will pay a fine of forty pounds—to be kept in prison till fine paid," said the man.

"Silence !" cried his superior. "Now, madam."

"Now, sir."

"You have a right to know who we are, and why we have come to your house."

"Yes, I think I have."

"Very well, you shall know."

"Be seated, gentlemen," said Mrs. Morgan, on tip-toe with expectation.

They sat down, and the gentleman said—

"This is Inspector Wyman, of Scotland-yard, of whose fame as a detective you may have heard ; his coadjutor, the Finsbury Fox, is on guard outside, so that no one can leave your house without his perceiving it. I——"

"Who are you?"

"I am Count Val de Grace."

"Your business with me, gentlemen?" demanded Mrs. Morgan, who began to feel slightly terrified as her numerous misdeeds flocked before her vision.

Count Val de Grace bore but few traces of the injuries Agnes had inflicted upon him with the pane of broken glass. A piece of plaster here and there alone indicating that he had been in any way injured.

"By the sagacity of my friend, Mr. Wyman——"

The detective bowed.

"I have been enabled to discover that a young lady of the name of Agnes, amongst others, left England in an English steam-vessel which sailed for this port a short time ago."

"What has that to do with me?"

"Don't be in too great a hurry, and you'll hear," interposed Inspector Wyman.

Mrs. Morgan looked at Wyman as much as to say; "I should like to claw your face down."

"We have traced this girl to your house, and we have come to demand her at your hands."

"I've no girls here," replied Mrs. Morgan.

"We know perfectly well who you are and what you are, Mrs. Morgan, and what your house is," said Count Val de Grace, quietly.

"You do?"

"Yes."

"Then you know that I am a respectable married woman, which I've got a ring on my finger to confirm."

"You said you were a lone widow just now," put in the inspector; "that's a discrepancy in the witness's testimony. Reporter, make a note of it."

"Deception is useless here, Mrs. Morgan," said the count. "I have come over from England expressly to bring this girl back to her friends, and I shall not return without her. She is in your house, and if you do not instantly deliver her up I shall be under the painful necessity of searching your house."

"Search my house!"

"Certainly."

"You'd better attempt it."

"We shall, to a certainty," replied Wyman.

"Will you?"

"Now, you'd better go quietly," continued Wyman. "I mean, give her up quietly; it'll be better for you in the end."

"You shall never search my house with my permission," cried Mrs. Morgan.

"That is your determination?" said Val de Grace.

"It is."

"You have made up your mind—and you refuse to give the girl up?"

"I do; and if you can find her, why, you may have her, and welcome."

"Wyman!" said the count.

"Servant, count," replied the inspector.

"Look to this woman."

Wyman advanced to Mrs. Morgan, and taking a pair of handcuffs from his pocket, said—

"Come, my lady, I must put the darbies on you—just to keep you quiet, you know—you'll look all the better for the bracelets. I thought you and I would be better acquainted. Come now, take it easy."

The inspector, with a dexterous movement, slipped the handcuffs on her, and she was rendered powerless for good or for evil.

She sat down in a chair, gnashing her teeth, and cursing awfully in Dutch and English.

"Now, Wyman, let's have the Fox up," said the count.

Wyman went downstairs, opened the door, and whistled.

Presently, the Finsbury Fox crept up stealthily, and was admitted.

"Right, sir," said the inspector, as he closed the door.

At this, the count descended the stairs, and the three stood together. Hardly had they done so, before Hans, not dreaming any mischief was at hand, walked into the hall.

He looked about him for a moment confusedly, when Wyman exclaimed to the Finsbury Fox—

"Bowl that Dutchman over—he may have keys or something about him."

It was no sooner said than done; for the Fox walked up to his victim, and, without any warning, except "Look out for yourself, old jelly-belly!" he dealt him a blow which sent him rolling like a log into a corner.

"The Fox can do it, count—the Fox can do it!" cried Wyman, in great glee.

Wyman then approached the body of Hans, and searched in his pockets for keys. He extracted all that were there—amongst which was the one of the dungeon where Agnes was confined.

"Offer that fellow something to tell us where the girl is," said Val de Grace.

"It's no good, count—he wont split; they're as obstinate as pigs, these Dutchmen."

Hans, at these words, picked himself up, and after rubbing his Dutch-built nose a little, and spitting out a broken tooth, said—

"What much will you give?"

"Oh, a couple of pounds."

"More?" said Hans.

"More, you avaricious old scoundrel! Why, that's a sight more than you ever came by honestly," replied Inspector Wyman.

"More—one, two, three more," persisted Hans, counting on his fingers.

"Give it him," said the count, impatiently.

Inspector Wyman put his hand in his pocket and gave Hans five sovereigns; and restored him the keys which he had just before deprived him of.

Hans pocketed the money, and after stopping to spit out another broken tooth, led the way downstairs.

The three men followed him closely; and the Fox went first, with his fists doubled, to prevent any attempt at treachery.

The same slimy, wet, chilling steps were retraced, and, in a short time, they stood before the iron-bolted door.

As they reached it, and waited whilst Hans fumbled with the key, piercing shrieks fell upon their ears—horrible cries, and almost superhuman noises, startled them.

"Make haste! make haste! For God's sake, make haste—she is being murdered!" cried Count Val de Grace.

Wyman wrenched the key out of the Dutchman's hand and turned it.

The door swung open, and the detective and the count rushed forward, while the Fox kept guard outside.

CHAPTER LIV.

A BATTLE WITH THE RATS—COUNT VAL DE GRACE SAVES AGNES—INSPECTOR WYMAN SHOWS THE DUTCH RATS THE USE OF ENGLISH BOOTS AND HOB-NAILS—MRS. MORGAN'S TERRIBLE END—THE HOUSE IN FLAMES—FLY! FLY!—ON THE CANAL—THE STEAMER—CHARLOTTE SAUNDERS TURNS UP AT THE RIGHT MOMENT—THE COUNT THREATENS—CHARLOTTE LAUGHS AT HIM.

AGNES on her hands and knees on the cold, damp ground—Agnes battling fiercely with a legion of ferocious and hungry rats—Agnes nearly spent with her exertions, and bleeding from the wounds she had received in this strange, unnatural contest. This was what Count Val de Grace and Inspector Wyman saw when they burst into the subterranean chamber.

The rats reconnoitred the new comers for a minute or so, hesitating as to whether they should depart in peace or stay and fight for the ground they had looked upon as already won.

A good, hearty kick from the inspector's heavy nailed boots determined them upon beating a speedy retreat.

But then ensued great slaughter amongst the predatory horde; for as there were only two holes by which they could escape, and as it stood to reason that they could not all get away at once through those outlets, the boots of Inspector Wyman did very considerable execution amongst them—until quite a hecatomb of killed and wounded lay upon the ensanguined earth.

Count Val de Grace approached Agnes, and lifted her up tenderly—very tenderly—almost lovingly in his arms.

She had not fainted, but she was hysterical, and sobbed like a child who has just undergone some severe correction.

The count pressed her to his heart.

She was powerless to resist. He even went so far as to snatch a kiss from her pallid lips.

This she also appeared to be unconscious of.

The fact was that she had just escaped so great a danger that she could think of nothing else. She was incapable of recognising her rescuers. At that moment she did not know Count Val de Grace from Adam.

Very gently he bore her from the humid atmosphere of that dreadful den up the slimy steps, where the crawling things that always infest underground localities made way for them in a sluggish sort of way, as if only yielding the ground to superior force, and under a very solemn protest. Now and then the scaled back of one would crash with a portentous noise, showing that his efforts to escape had been too tardy, and consequently fruitless. Up the cold stone stairs into the hall. Up the carpeted flight which led to the sumptuous drawing-room, where Mrs. Morgan was constrained to sit on one of her own easy-chairs, manacled and helpless.

But as the party approached, they heard strange stifled cries, such as would proceed from any one nearly suffocated. Very terrible and very awful were those cries, and they froze the blood in the veins of those who heard them.

A moment the count stood listening; then, laying the body of Agnes down upon the landing as carefully as the excitement of the occasion would permit him, and telling Wyman to look to her as he valued his life, for he would surely take it if aught happened to Agnes, he rushed forward and laid his hand upon the door.

A strange smell was emitted from the room.

It was not as though something was burning, yet the count could not divest his mind of the idea that something was on fire.

Something on fire! What in the name of heaven could it be?

He could bear the suspense no longer.

He burst open the door, and stood on the threshold.

Here a sickly vapour, thick and impenetrable, enveloped him. It rolled like a canopy into the passage, and hung over the stairs like a pall.

Thick particles of a fatty matter might have been detected floating about in it.

The stench was overpowering.

"God send it may not be the plague vapour," cried the count, nerving himself to unravel the mystery.

Holding his handkerchief to his nose, as a disinfectant, he groped his way through the cloud.

The gas-lamps burned dimly, and threatened to be extinguished every second.

The vapour appeared to be densest in the neighbourhood of the fireplace.

Towards this goal the count wended his way.

Suddenly those outside heard a strange weird cry escape him, like the voice of a man in deadly terror.

Immediately afterwards his voice rang out, clearly but tremblingly—

"Lights here! lights here!"

The Finsbury Fox hastened to obey the summons, and followed by Hans, who also carried a lamp, he ran to the side of the count.

The flame of the lamps dimmed a little, but they sufficed to show them an appalling spectacle.

Mrs. Morgan was no more.

The Mrs. Morgan as they had left her had vanished—gone—departed, and in her place lay a black charred mass. One large, exaggerated cinder.

Those few faint wails—those few faint, despairing cries—that the count had heard when standing upon the landing, were the last efforts of the miserable woman.

Now she was dead—stone dead—burned to death.

By what means she had taken fire they could not tell.

It was a horrible fate—a terrible fate—a shocking fate—and the men turned from it with gradually increasing horror.

But a new sensation awaited them.

The door had been left open, and the current of air which had penetrated into the apartment in consequence, had fanned into a flame a mass of fire that had hitherto been smouldering.

The house was on fire.

With a frightful rapidity the flames spread, and seized first on one article and then on the other with marvellous speed.

"To the street-door! Fly! fly!" cried the count, dashing out upon the landing, seizing the still semi-animate body of Agnes, and leading the way to life and liberty once more.

Soon they stood in the street.

Count Val de Grace, bearing the body of Agnes, Inspector Wyman, and the Finsbury Fox.

Going down to a canal, they got into a boat, and gave the man some instructions, which he promptly obeyed.

The house of the hapless Mrs. Morgan was now the prey of the devastating element, and its burning rafters threw a ruddy glare upon the water.

After the lapse of a quarter of an hour the boatman neared the harbour, and stopped alongside a steamer.

Paying him liberally, the count ascended the side, still carrying the body of Agnes, and closely followed by his satellites. On the deck he met the steward, and asked if they were correct in supposing that they were on board the London steamer.

The steward replied that they were, and proceeded to allot them their berths.

The count handed Agnes over to the stewardess, saying that she was an invalid, and begging that she might be taken every care of.

As Agnes was carried into the ladies' cabin, a voice exclaimed, "What ever is that?" and Charlotte Saunders went up to the stewardess and peered into the face of her burden.

"Well!" she said, "if that doesn't beat everything!"

Then she ran upstairs and went into the captain's cabin, exclaiming, "I say!" Then she stopped for want of breath.

"What is it? My stars, eh!" said the captain.

"Wait a bit."

"All right, old girl. Take it easy."

"Agnes——" said Charlotte.

"Agnes! What do you mean?"

"What I say."

"Explain."

"I will."

"Go ahead, then."

"She's on board."

"No?"

"She is, though."

The captain looked a good deal astonished, as well he might.

"That saves us the trouble of going after her to rescue her," continued Charlotte Saunders.

"So it does."

"You know we had arranged to go to-night about twelve o'clock and carry her off by force of arms, if they refused to give her up quietly. I must make Agnes tell me all about it when she is better—at present she doesn't seem very well."

"I'm glad she's turned up! My stars, yes!" said the captain. Fact is, I've just received orders to sail for London again at six o'clock to-morrow morning; so a few hours' rest wont do us any harm. Will you go and look after your friend, and when she's well enough bring her in here, and I'll give her a glass of real Old Tom—I dare swear she's tired enough of Schiedam and Hollands."

Charlotte left the cabin and went to look after Agnes, who was soon herself again under the fostering care of her friend. The wounds she had received in her combat with the rats were in no place more than skin deep, and promised soon to heal up.

Charlotte wondered very much at the story Agnes told her, and both the girls thought how singularly fortunate they had been in escaping from so horrible a den. There was one thing that Agnes could not tell her friend, and that was, how she had been rescued and brought to the steamer, or by whom.

While the two girls were speculating over this mystery, the stewardess brought a message to Agnes. It was simply—

"Count Val de Grace sends his compliments to Lady M., and will feel obliged by an interview as soon as she is able to grant him one."

"Count Val de Grace!" gasped Agnes. "Oh! Charlotte, that is my bitterest enemy. If I am indeed in his power, all is lost. I would rather have perished in that dungeon than have fallen a second time into his power. He must have tracked me over here. His power is indeed marvellous."

Charlotte, seeing how the land lay, and her repugnance to see the count, said to the stewardess—

"Tell Count Val de Grace that the lady is too ill to see him at present. He must be good enough to wait till the morning."

The stewardess took the message and brought back a slip of paper. There were some words on it in the Count's handwriting. He said—

"Try to escape me, and you shall curse the hour you were born. I have suffered much for you. I have sworn to possess you; and as there is a God in heaven, I will."

Agnes covered her face with her hands. Charlotte caught the falling piece of paper and read it.

"Oh, indeed!" she muttered, "that's his game, is it? Well, I'm not afraid of any man breathing. I'll back myself to be a match against a dozen French counts any day. Curse the hour she's born, indeed. He'd better look out he doesn't curse the hour he was born." Then she turned to Agnes, and said—"Don't you be alarmed, my dear. If we don't lick that Count What's-his-name, I'll eat my captain's old hat."

CHAPTER LV.

A PLOT—THE VOYAGE HOME—THE CAPTAIN'S STRATAGEM
—HAVE A GLASS OF MY WINE, GENTLEMEN?—LOCKED
IN—AGNES AND CHARLOTTE ESCAPE—NOW FOR A
SPREE!

AFTER a time Agnes recovered herself sufficiently to sit up
and talk to Charlotte, who did all in her power to comfort
her, cheer her, and keep her spirits up.

"One thing is very clear," said Charlotte, "and that is,
we must outwit this count fellow in some way."

"Yes, yes."

"He thinks he has you under his thumb."

"He does."

"He must be very spooney on you, too, to come all the
way over here after you."

"It was lucky he did."

"So it was; but that is not what I meant."

"I hate that man, Charlotte," said Agnes.

"Don't wonder at it, my dear," replied Charlotte. "I
never yet met a good sort of woman that did care for a frog-
eater."

"It isn't that so much, but there is something in the man
himself which I dislike so much."

"Oh, well! it's all the same," replied Charlotte, carelessly.

Agnes sighed and looked unhappy, but Charlotte began to
sing—

"Cheer up, Sall; don't you let your spirits go down,
      There's many a swell,
      That I know well,
Who's looking for you in the town."

"I say, why did he call you Lady M.?" suddenly demanded Charlotte.

"Oh! I don't know," replied Agnes, looking very confused.

"You don't know?"

"No."

"Come, that's a good one!"

"What do you mean?"

"What I say. Perhaps you'll answer my question."

"So I have."

"Yes; after a fashion."

"What more do you want?"

"Shall I ask you again?"

"If you like."

"Well, then, why did that French bloke call you Lady
M.; and in addition to that how did you become acquainted
with him?"

"I met him——" replied Agnes, looking very perplexed and
very stupid.

"Now, look here," cried Charlotte; "what's the good of
humbugging me? A pot's as good as a kettle any day isn't
it?"

Agnes made no answer.

"I suppose you lived with some swell?" said Charlotte.

"Lived with! I? Oh, Charlotte!" exclaimed Agnes,
bursting into tears.

"You? yes you! Who are you more than anybody else,
I should like to know."

"Dear Charlotte——" began Agnes.

"Oh, don't talk to me," replied Charlotte; "I have no
patience with people who give themselves such airs. Not I,
indeed."

"But it's not true."

"Isn't it? You wont make me believe that, my lady."

"Oh! don't, Charlotte!" cried Agnes.

"Don't; but I will. I can see it as well as possible; it's
as plain as a pikestaff. You've picked up with some swell,
and I suppose he cut you when he got tired of you, as men
generally do—they don't live with women for ever, you
know—and then you were on the look-out when you met
me. Perhaps this French fellow isn't good enough for you,
although I don't see why he shouldn't be; but some women
are so difficult to please. There are some people, though,
that say, 'Beggars musn't be choosers.'"

"What do you mean?" asked Agnes, angrily.

"Oh, nothing particular; but when I've got anything on
my mind I like to have it out, that's all."

"I can see what you are now," said Agnes.

"Can you? And what do you think of me after the discovery, eh? Am I good enough for you? Will your ladyship condescend to honour me with your acquaintance."

"I thought you were a respectable married woman."

"About as much married, my dear woman, as you are,"
said Charlotte.

"I am married," cried Agnes, indignantly.

"So am I, then," replied Charlotte.

"But I am," she persisted.

"Over a broomstick, then," replied Charlotte, contemptuously. "But we've had enough of this rot. I don't see
why we should quarrel about such nonsense. You want to
get away from this Frenchman, don't you?"

"Yes. I want, God knows how much," said Agnes;
"but I wont have anything to do with you."

"You wont."

"No."

"Now don't be a fool," replied Charlotte, good temperedly.
"You can never escape him without my assistance. I
suppose I'm fly to pretty well all the rigs out, and if anybody can help you, it's me."

Agnes reflected a little, and saw that the only thing she
could do was to bow to circumstances. She felt that she
could not do much against the magic power of Count Val
de Grace, but she had great faith in the cleverness and
resources of Charlotte Saunders, who had befriended her
and got her out of difficulties that most women would have
shrunk from encountering, on numerous occasions.

So she felt constrained to throw herself upon her friend's
protection.

Besides all this, Charlotte was really the only friend she
could boast of.

She seemed to be environed by enemies.

Her husband, Lord Marchmont, was her enemy.

Marmaduke Wilson, she felt, hated her for what he supposed her perfidy.

Jabez Clarke was in search of her to extract money from
her.

Miriam Moss would have followed her to the end of the
earth to be revenged upon her for the frightful injury she had
done her.

Count Val de Grace had vowed her destruction.

There was a charge of murder—the murder of her mother
—hanging over her!

Was it a time then to be particular?

Agnes thought not, and so she said—

"Forgive me, Charlotte; let us be friends."

Charlotte goodnaturedly took her proffered hand, and
replied—

"Come, now, that's a good deal better than fighting and
slaying one another, and tearing one another's eyes out."

"Yes, it is," said Agnes, between her tears.

"What'll you have?" exclaimed Charlotte, with that
frankness and levity which is so eminently characteristic of
those women who knock about town without possessing the
highest character for morality.

"I don't care," replied Agnes.

"We'll have a drain of some sort. I'm just game for
it."

"What would you like?"

"I'll go and get a bottle of my captain's champagne,"
said Charlotte.

Soon she returned with an invitation from the captain to
come into his cabin and have a glass of wine.

"You had better come," said Charlotte; "you will be safe
there. The frog-eater will never think of following you
down there. Besides, if he did, I should be sorry for him,
poor beggar. My captain hates frog-eaters, and I should
not be surprised if he went head-first out of one of the port-
holes. Anyhow, he'd go upstairs again faster than he came
down, to a certainty."

Agnes fully acquiesced in the force of this reasoning, and
the two girls succeeded in reaching the captain's cabin without being perceived by either of her three captors, or rescuers,
or whatever they ought properly to be called.

The Finsbury Fox, however, was pacing the deck carefully, as if on the watch to prevent Agnes leaving the
vessel.

The count and Wyman had probably turned in. At any
rate it was a reasonable supposition that they had done so,
as they were not to be seen anywhere about.

"Glad to see you again. My stars! yes," said the captain,
as they entered his cabin. "Come and have some liquor.
It'll put a little life into you."

After they had drunk a glass or two of wine, Charlotte said—

"Now, captain, how are we to get this little woman on shore? I told you how that frog-eater wanted to collar her off somewhere or other."

"Yes."

"Well; have you thought of any plan?"

"I have," replied the captain.

"Let us have it, then."

"You shall. All in good time. Fill your glasses."

When this was satisfactorily accomplished, the captain resumed—

"He can't touch you until you land. Well, if I can contrive to shut him up here for half-an-hour or so you and your friend can go on shore and drive where you like; you must look out for yourselves afterwards."

"That'll do stunningly. Shut him up in the steward's cabin, or some hole or other; but you must look after the other two men he has with him."

"I'll take care of that. You haven't any superfluous baggage," he said, with a laugh, "so you wont have much trouble in going on shore."

"No; that's true enough," said Charlotte Saunders.

Soon after they went to rest, and did not make their appearance again until they were far on their way up the Thames.

The captain took the passage-money from all of the passengers except the three Charlotte had told him of. These he passed over till the steam-boat was off Greenwich. Then he went into a sort of state cabin, and sent one of his mates to them to ask if they would be good enough to step down and settle their fares. The captain had somehow or other forgotten them, and as he was now busy making up his accounts, he would be much obliged if they would come down and pay their passage-money, and the mate added—

"Cappen told me to say, sir, as he could give you gents a good glass of wine and a prime cigar, if you would like a chat for five minutes."

The count, suspecting nothing, went down to the cabin, preceded by the mate; Wyman and the Fox, attracted by the prospect of something to drink, followed.

Count Val de Grace had waited impatiently for Agnes to make her appearance during the voyage, but finding that she avoided him, he had arranged with Wyman and the Fox that she should be seized as she landed, by the detective, handcuffed, put into a cab and taken to the count's residence; if she resisted or appealed to the people, Wyman was to say that she was a thief and a pickpocket, and that he had arrested her for felony.

When the trio entered the little state cabin they found the captain entering some figures in a book. He took their money, and then said—

"Excuse me, gentlemen, for a moment. I have some very good Moselle on board—I import it, and I should esteem it a favour if you would try a glass. Gentlemen often buy a dozen or two of me. It's such wine as you don't get in England."

They expressed their willingness to wait while he fetched his wine. And he left the cabin for that purpose.

Directly he was outside he double locked the door; and the three men were prisoners.

"I don't half like that skipper fellow's mug," said the Finsbury Fox.

"Nor I," replied Wyman.

The count fidgeted uneasily, he hardly knew why.

They waited and waited.

The minutes flew away, and no one came.

Then they tried the door, and found it fastened.

The fact that they were imprisoned flashed across their minds.

Their curses were loud and deep; but all their efforts to extricate themselves were fruitless.

In the meantime, the ship steamed into St. Katherine's wharf.

The passengers landed: Agnes and Charlotte amongst the first.

When the captain saw them depart safely, he sent one of his men to unlock the door of the cabin where the count was confined.

As soon as they were let out, they rushed on deck like madmen.

But Agnes was nowhere to be found.

The count walked up to the captain, his face white with passion, and attempted to strike him; but the captain was well on his guard, and dealt the count a blow which sent him rolling over a heap of boxes.

The policeman picked him up; and finding that all attempts at obtaining redress were hopeless, they disconsolately left the steamship, determining to find Agnes again, if she were a thousand miles away from them.

"I shouldn't object to a drop of gin, Mr. Count," said the Finsbury Fox, as they left the gangway.

The captain was close behind them, and he exclaimed—

"Wouldn't you like a glass of my wine better?"

They scowled at him, but walked on in silence.

Charlotte drove Agnes straight to her lodgings, saying, as she went along—

"Now we'll have a spree. I'm so jolly glad to get back to old England; there's no place like it. I'll take you to lots of places. We'll go to the Holborn and the Argyle, and to Caldwell's, and to Mots', and heaps of places I know. What do you say?"

But Agnes made no answer.

CHAPTER LVI.

MARIA AGAIN—CHARLOTTE'S LANDLADY—A DROP OF GIN—AGNES DISPLAYS HER IGNORANCE OF MIDNIGHT LONDON—AN HOUR'S SLEEP—ONLY TEN O'CLOCK—WHAT SHALL WE DO?—CHARLOTTE'S IDEA.

AGNES was at a loss to understand what her friend Charlotte meant by having a spree.

But there were many things of which she was ignorant, and of which she could not have had a fitter exponent than Charlotte Saunders.

If she wanted a guide to certain places in the neighbourhood of the Haymarket which have acquired a notoriety of an unenviable description, she could not have had a better one, for Charlotte was thoroughly acquainted with them all—for she was what Agnes had truly imagined her to be—one of those women who indulge in the flirting gaieties of a butterfly life, without being trammelled in any way by the holy rites of Mother Church.

Agnes was shocked at the discovery, but what could she do?

Charlotte treated her with every kindness, and whilst every man's hand was against her it was not the time for her to stick at trifles—at least she thought so.

She had little or no money.

Lord Marchmont would not receive her back again; and she did not feel at all inclined to trust to the tender mercies of Count Val de Grace.

This was an alternative to her mind much worse than any which had yet presented themselves to her.

So she resolved to become Charlotte's guest until something turned up.

People of an indolent disposition always wait for something to turn up. Sometimes it is kind enough to do so, but more generally it is not.

The girls returned to the lodging-house in the neighbourhood of Soho-square. The door was opened by the servant, Maria, who expressed the greatest astonishment and delight at seeing Charlotte once more.

"Do come in!" she exclaimed.

"All right. Light a glim."

The servant lighted a candle, and led the way into the apartment which Charlotte formerly occupied.

"The bills has been up," she said; "but we aint had no applications."

"Oh!"

"Missus she would have the bills up," continued the servant.

"She must be an old faggot," said Charlotte. "Why, I only owe her a week's rent, and I'll soon knock that off."

"Of course."

"What did you think had become of me?"

"We thought you was locked up for a week."

"No?"

"We did, though, and I went to Bow-street to find out, but couldn't hear nothing of you."

"What a lark!" cried Charlotte. "We've been to Holland, Maria. What do you think of that?"

"To 'Olland? nonsense!"

"We have, though," said Agnes, who ventured to speak.

"Don't stand gaping there," cried Charlotte. "Go and get a quartern and a half of gin."

" Where shall I go ?"

" Oh! go to the Nell Gwynne. Pearson's gin is too sweet for me."

" Better have half-a-pint," said Maria.

" You want a drop, don't you ?" replied Charlotte, sarcastically.

" Shouldn't object to a drain."

" Then you wont have it—not a smell."

Maria picked up the shilling Charlotte tossed towards her, and made her exit.

While she was gone, the girls took off their bonnets and shawls, and made themselves a little comfortable.

" Fancy putting up the bills !" cried Charlotte; " there's an old wretch for you !"

" Well, it was rather hasty," replied Agnes.

" I'll tell her what I think of her, though, when I meet her."

" I wouid, if I were you; only don't treat her as you did that poor woman in Holland."

" I'll tell you what I will do," replied Charlotte; " I'll have those two bills down."

And as she spoke she went to the window and pulled down the obnoxious notices.

As she turned round, the door opened, and her landlady entered the room.

She was a short, fat woman; very unctuous and very oily.

She wore a shabby black silk dress, which she had probably seized some time ago from one of her lodgers who was unable or unwilling to pay her rent.

" Oh !" she exclaimed; " you have returned. I am glad to see——"

" Sorry I can't return the compliment," replied Charlotte, gruffly.

" Maria told me you were back," she continued.

" Did she? Maria had better mind her own business."

" Well, you don't seem to have come back in the best temper."

" No, I haven't."

" Oh ! indeed."

" And when I want you," said Charlotte, " why, I'll send for you."

" But I'm here now," said the landlady.

" Yes, I know; and it'll be bad luck for you if you stay here much longer."

" I suppose you can pay your rent, as you're so cockey ?" said the landlady, boldly.

" No, I can't pay my rent, either," replied Charlotte, with a defiant gesture.

" Oh, Charlotte," cried Agnes, " do be quiet !"

" Hold your tongue."

" But——"

" You'll get it, if you don't look out."

" I? What have I done ?" said Agnes.

" Never mind what you've done; hold your tongue."

" I can't afford to let my rooms for nothing," continued the landlady.

" Who said you could ?"

" I must live."

" So must other people."

" And when you bring lodgers home with you, why I ought to raise the rent."

" You may raise it as high as St. Paul's, for what I care," said Charlotte; " only perhaps the higher you raise it, the more difficult it will be for you to get it."

The landlady softened a little. Perhaps she saw that bullying was no use. Anyhow, she looked blandly at Charlotte.

" It's no good bullyragging me," said Charlotte.

" Certainly not, my dear."

" You may lead me, but you can't drive me."

" Well, you will pay some day, wont you ?"

" Oh, I'll pay you all right enough."

" Of course, my dear. I always said you were the best lodger I had."

" I ought to be, considering how you rob me."

" I rob you !" cried the landlady, holding up her hands.

" Rob me, yes, you old cat."

" Old cat ! well, I'm sure."

Charlotte went on pinning up her hair before the glass, without taking any further notice of the unfortunate landlady, who, after a time, subsided into comparative good temper, and said—

" Well, my dear, now you've come back, what are you going to stand ?"

" Stand ! oh, stand on my head if you like."

" I don't mean that."

" Well, what do you mean ?"

" Wont you stand a drop of white satin ?"

As Charlotte was about to reply, Maria returned with the gin, saying—

" I got unsweetened gin. I thought you would like it best."

Charlotte took the bottle out of her hand, and, seizing a wine-glass, poured out some of the fiery liquid, and handed it to Agnes.

" Drink this, Cocky," she said; " it'll warm you."

Agnes took the gin and drank it, although she stopped once or twice before she drained the glass, and when she had done so her eyes were full of water.

The landlady looked on wistfully.

Charlotte noticed this, and said—

" Don't be in a hurry, old lady; your turn has not come yet. All in good time."

If it is possible to look marlingspikes, the landlady did look them.

Charlotte again filled the glass brimming full.

It was a night for a stimulant. The evening was just drawing in. The candle gave a faint light, and the cold was penetrating.

" You like gin, missis, don't you ?" said Charlotte, addressing her landlady.

" I don't mind a drop now and then," replied she, blandly.

" Well, then, see me drink it."

And with a laugh, Charlotte tossed off the gin, much to the old lady's disgust.

With a grunt, she got up, and was going to leave the room; but Charlotte overtook her, and gave her some of the cheap poison which the poor and reckless drink for their own destruction.

The landlady drank it with avidity, and said—

" Don't mind what I said, dear, about the rent. But it looked odd your going away like that, without any warning, don't you see."

" But I left my togs."

" Yes, you left them. But the duds weren't worth much."

" Never mind what they were worth to you, they were worth a good deal to me."

" Certainly."

" Well, then, what are you grumbling about ?"

" Nothing, my dear, but——"

" Oh, I've no patience with such avaricious old cats," cried Charlotte. " You're as close over a penny as a mouse is over a bit of cheese-rind."

Muttering something that was unintelligible, the landlady went her ways, and Charlotte returned to her parlour.

" Now then, Maria, light that fire," cried Charlotte. " What are you standing there like a fool for ? One would think you were a perfect child."

" Yes, mum," replied Maria, setting to work.

When the fire was alight, Charlotte said—

" I must have something to eat, but what to have, I'm sure I don't know."

" Have an Ostend rabbit ?" suggested Maria.

" An Ostend rabbit !" repeated Charlotte. " Can you cook an Ostend rabbit in five minutes ?"

" No."

" Well, then, don't be such an idiot. Why, Maria, one would think you had only just left school, instead of being five or six and thirty."

Maria made no reply.

" Fish cooks quickly," said Agnes.

" Yes," replied Charlotte; " but don't you know to-day's Monday, and there's nothing but Saturday's leavings to be had. I'm not going to eat stale fish, if you are."

" What will you have, then ?"

" Will you have a golden herring, mum ?" said Maria.

" Ah ! that'll do. Go and get some of them and a couple of eggs, and if you're long over them, why, I am sorry for you."

Maria shuffled off to execute her errands, and the two girls sat over the fire and finished the gin between them.

Charlotte drank because she liked it, and it was habitual to her; Agnes because she wanted to keep her spirits up.

After tea, Charlotte said to Maria—

" Have you washed that white-flounced dress of mine ?"

" Yes, mum."

" Has it gone to the mangle ?"

" No."

" Then why hasn't it ? You are enough to provoke a saint; you are the most aggravating woman I ever came across. What am I to do ?"

" I'll soon get it done, mum. There's that woman in Brewer-street."

" Well, you'd better go to her."

" What will you do, Agnes ?" asked Charlotte.

" Do! What for ?"

" Why, for to-night."

" To-night !"

" Yes; you are coming with me, aint you ?"

" Where are you going to ?"

" Oh! lots of places. You come and you'll see."

" But I've got nothing to wear !"

" Oh, yes, you have."

" What ?"

" Why, that brown moire you've got on will do. Wear that."

" This old moire ?" cried Agnes, in surprise.

" Yes; it's lots good enough."

" But you are going to wear a muslin."

" No, I am not. It's too cold for that. I only spoke about it to wake Maria up; she always goes to sleep when I'm not here. I shall wear my black silk."

" Oh! I see," replied Agnes. " Where do you intend to go, though ?"

" Well, I shall go to Kate's."

" What's that ?"

" That's a night-house. Same sort of place as you met Miriam Moss at."

At the mention of Miriam's name, Agnes shuddered.

" Ah, you may well shudder," said Charlotte. " Poor devil! my flesh creeps for her."

" Is it just the same sort of place ?" said Agnes.

" Not quite; rather more swell, if anything."

" Do you pay anything to get in ?"

" Pay anything !" echoed Charlotte, contemptuously.

" Well, how should I know ?"

" They are very glad to have decent women there."

" What do you mean by decent women ?"

" Oh! don't ask so many questions," replied Charlotte; " you'll find out everything fast enough."

Agnes was obliged to be contented with this answer, and as she had imbibed some of the reckless feelings of her companion, she was satisfied to take things as she found them. She soothed her conscience and smoothed over her scruples with the sophistical reasoning—

" That there would be no harm in her seeing a little life— digging, as it were, below the surface. If she saw people who did things that were wrong in her eyes, that was no reason why she should do wrong also."

As she was reasoning in this fallacious manner, Charlotte said—

" I shall lie down for an hour or two: shall you ?"

" Lie down! What for ?"

" Well, I don't know. What do people generally lie down for ?"

" Because they're tired, I suppose."

" Well, then, I'm tired."

" But I thought we were going out."

" So we are," replied Charlotte.

" It must be seven o'clock now."

" Well, what if it is ?"

" Why, it's getting late," said Agnes.

" Oh, no! not for the places we are going to. Any time will do for them."

" Really !"

" And you had better follow my example, and see if you can't get forty winks !"

The girls both disposed themselves to sleep in Charlotte's bed-room.

The bed was a large four-poster, with long, capacious curtains, and there was plenty of room for both of them.

They slept some time.

Agnes was the first to wake; she rose half up and rubbed her eyes.

" Charlotte! Charlotte!" she exclaimed.

Charlotte woke up and said—

" Well, what is it ?"

" Why, it's ten o'clock," replied Agnes, looking at her little Geneva watch.

" Only ten ! Why, you must be a fool to wake one up so soon !"

" Soon ! I call it late."

" Never mind what you call it. What are we to do ?"

" I'm sure I don't know," replied Agnes.

" Oh! I'll tell you," said Charlotte; " we'll go to the drum at the corner for an hour."

CHAPTER LVII.

AUNTY AT HOME — A NAUGHTY PARROT — VENDING SPIRITUOUS LIQUORS WITHOUT A LICENCE—CAPTAIN SMASH—A SLIGHT DISTURBANCE—A NEW USE TO PUT DEVILLED KIDNEYS TO—AUNTY MEETS WITH HER MATCH—A JEWESS IN A WASHING-TUB.

WHEN the girls were ready they left the house, Charlotte taking the precaution to carry a latch-key with her, for the hour at which the "women of London" return to their homes, varies according to their several propensities. Some will return at tea-time, and never leave the house till the next morning. Some will come back from their work at seven or eight o'clock, and retire tired-out an hour later; but there are others who, like bats, prefer the darkness and revel in the small hours. Of this number was Charlotte.

They threaded several small streets and courts and alleys, until they reached Coventry-street. They then crossed Leicester-square, and passing Panton-street, stopped before a house in James-street.

This was fitted up, externally, as a coffee-house; but if a labouring man ventured to task its hospitality at five or six o'clock in the morning, he would be told that coffee was a shilling a cup, and a slice of bread and butter sixpence. This, of course, would not suit his book, and he accordingly went elsewhere.

This house was kept by a man and woman, who passed as man and wife. Their customers called them Uncle and Aunty.

Aunty was a tall Jewess, with a forbidding countenance. The man, who was completely under her thumb, looked the low, contemptible wretch he was. He merely got his board and lodging. Of the profits of the establishment he saw nothing. When he went out he had a shilling or so given him by Aunty to spend.

Aunty sold champagne at twelve shillings a bottle to her customers, and retailed brandy and other spirituous liquors in small glasses at a large profit.

It is needless to say that she had no licence, but as she kept her liquors in small bottles in a cupboard, and dispensed them in a friendly sort of way, it was difficult to prove anything against her.

This was what Charlotte had called the drum at the corner.

Charlotte opened the door, and as she did so, a small bell tinkled.

They entered a room with tables set out around the sides; here and there were little boxes; thick blinds prevented any scrutiny from those without, as the windows were all draped in the same way.

Aroused by the tinkling of the bell, Aunty emerged from an inner chamber, and advanced to meet them.

Agnes saw before her a swarthy Jewess, and felt almost inclined to draw back, but she remembered that she had come out with her friend in quest of adventures, and she determined to go through with everything she might encounter.

A parrot sat on a perch in a cage which stood on a table, and occasionally uttered exclamations not quite proper for ears polite.

" How do you do, my dear ?" exclaimed the Jewess to Charlotte, whom she instantly recognised as a friend and customer.

" Oh! I'm all right; how's yourself, Aunty ?" replied Charlotte.

" I've been very bad, my dear—dreadful. I've had the rheumaticks so awfully bad."

" So have I," replied Charlotte, wickedly.

" Lor' now, have you ? Well, come in and sit down. There's no one here yet, and I was just having a bit of a nap."

"Where's uncle?"

"'Arry? Oh! he's gone over to Surridge's to get a drain, if he can cadge one. I wouldn't give him anything."

"Quite right, too," said Charlotte. "Men will drink one out of house and home, wont they, Aunty?"

"That they will; but I say, come here."

"What's up now?"

"Nothing. I only want to speak to you."

Charlotte got up and followed the Jewess into a little room, leaving Agnes standing in the coffee-room.

There was a cheerful fire burning on the hearth, a sofa stood along one side of the wall, and there were several arm and other chairs disposed in various places.

"Well, Aunty," began Charlotte; "got any kid on hand, eh?"

"No, nothing of the sort. There's no kidment going now; but I want to know who that party with you is. It's a new face."

"Yes; she has never been about."

"Oh!"

"She has only come out to see a little life. So none of your games, Aunty."

"Certainly not, my dear, if you wish it."

"Didn't you see me give you the office just now."

"Yes; but I didn't know what you meant exactly."

"Well, you know now?"

"Yes."

"Let her alone, then, and perhaps we'll stop an hour in your den."

"What'll you have?" asked the Jewess.

"Some soda and brandy," replied Charlotte, "and a couple of kidneys."

"Wont you ask your friend in?"

"Agnes!" cried Charlotte.

"Where are you?"

"This way—in here," was the reply.

Presently Agnes made her appearance, and on being asked what she would have, said "A glass of lemonade."

This was given her, and the trio were sitting very amicably together, when a man entered.

He was a debauched-looking man, with the traces of good looks on his florid countenance. There was a cunning light in his eyes, and he might have been Charles Dickens's Artful Dodger, arrived at man's estate.

He shook hands with Aunty, nodded to Charlotte, and stared rudely at Agnes.

She cast down her eyes beneath his impertinent scrutiny.

Agnes was sitting on a sofa, Charlotte was reclining in an arm-chair near the fire. Charlotte beckoned to Agnes to come near her. This she did, going to the end of the sofa nearest the fire. Charlotte leant forward and said—

"That's Captain Smash; don't offend him, he's got lots of money."

"How does he get it?" said Agnes.

"How should I know? I suppose he's a smasher, or cardsharper, or something. It don't matter how he gets it, as long as he's got it."

"Oh! I don't know that."

"Don't you?" said Charlotte, "then you'd better make yourself civil to him. Be a brick; have some chaff with him, and get him to stand a bottle of champagne."

"Will he?"

"Yes, like a bird."

During this colloquy Captain Smash had seated himself on the sofa by the side of Agnes.

When Agnes turned round he exclaimed carelessly—

"This your first visit to these parts?"

"Not exactly the first."

"Oh, you have been here before, then?"

"Once."

"And you liked it well enough to come again, eh?"

"My friend brought me," said Agnes.

"Oh, she did," replied the captain; "very sensible of her. It would be too bad to shut up so much beauty."

Agnes blushed.

"I think," he continued, "we ought to call you 'Queen of the Night.' No one ever deserved the compliment better."

Captain Smash spoke as if he had once been something better than a midnight prowler about the Haymarket.

"Now, old fellow, what are you going to stand?" exclaimed Charlotte.

He looked up.

"You can't enjoy our society for nothing, you know."

"What will you have?" he said.

"Oh, the usual thing, something for the good of the establishment."

The captain took a sovereign out of his pocket and said—

"Bring a couple of bottles of Moselle, Aunty."

"Oh, you're a swell, I should think," cried Charlotte.

"I?"

"Yes; you've been in luck, I suppose?"

The captain looked a little annoyed, but said—

"The only luck I've had is meeting you."

"Indeed; well, after that, I don't mind if I drink your wine," said Charlotte, with a laugh.

The captain, as he called himself, bestowed his attention almost exclusively upon Agnes, who seemed uneasy and restless, as if she did not like his assiduity.

Charlotte perceived this, and said—

"Come on, Agnes; let us go somewhere else."

"What do you want to go for?" asked the Jewess. "You are always running away the moment you come here."

"I suppose I can go and come when I like?"

"Oh, certainly; but——" here the Jewess telegraphed with her eyes towards Captain Smash, as much as to say, "He's got plenty of money; make him stand some more wine before he goes." But Charlotte was like the deaf adder; although Aunty charmed very wisely she could not make her hear.

Captain Smash said to Agnes—

"Where are you going to? Can I come with you?"

Agnes stammered a little, for she did not know what reply to make; but Charlotte overheard his question although it was put in a low tone, and not intended to reach her ears, and she came most opportunely to the rescue.

"No, you can't," she exclaimed, decisively.

"I was addressing my remarks to this lady, not to you," replied Captain Smash, quietly.

"Really. Well, you see, I'm talking to you, and there's the difference."

"I suppose this lady can do what she chooses," he said.

"She wont choose to go five yards with you."

"Wont she?"

"No."

"How do you know?"

"Because I wont let her."

Captain Smash was evidently losing his temper. His eyes moved restlessly, and the corners of his mouth twitched nervously.

Charlotte looked contemptuously at him, as if he had been so much dirt under her feet.

"Do you think," she said, slowly, "that I would allow any friend of mine to go about with a fellow like you?"

"A fellow like me, eh?"

"Yes, like you."

"Well, I suppose I'm as good as my company," he replied, with a sneer.

"Oh!" said Charlotte, in a provoking manner, "if I am nothing particular, I'm not a low, swindling thief."

"Now be quiet," he said, turning pale.

"Who have you been robbing to-night, eh?"

He made no reply.

"Perhaps you've been chousing some unfortunate man at cards, in one of those Jew holes."

Still no answer.

"Or you've been picking up a drunken man in the street. I know you—I know your game. You low, dirty scoundrel."

The captain turned very red and very angry at her repeated insults.

Aunty had been superintending the cooking of the kidneys which Charlotte Saunders had ordered, and she now made her appearance with them, all hot and smoking, in her hand.

She had stopped a moment at the door, as she heard the angry voices, and catching the last two or three phrases Charlotte had employed to abuse the captain, she said—

"Come, I can't have that, you know."

Charlotte, who was excited by the wine she had taken, squared up to the Jewess immediately, and said—

"What?"

"Can't allow that sort of thing in my place."

"You can't allow it. Who are you?" cried Charlotte.

"Never mind who I am."

"Shall I tell you who you are?"

"There, take your kidneys," said Aunty, soothingly,

THE "COLONEL" IS PLACED IN AN UNPLEASANT PREDICAMENT.

looking a little frightened, for she knew what Charlotte was when she was in a rage.

Charlotte took no notice of her.

"Shall I tell you what you are?" she repeated. "Perhaps you wouldn't like to hear it? You dare to talk to me, an infamous old wretch like you, who ought to have been transported for life long ago. Why, you old hag, I'll murder you."

As she said these words, she snatched the dish of kidneys from her hand and dashed it in her face.

It struck her on the forehead, but did not do much damage.

Charlotte knew very well that in a disturbance of this sort the Jewess would not dare to call in the police, because, in the first place, they would put it down as a disorderly house, and a note to that effect would be made in the books at the station-house; and, in addition to that, they would see the glasses and bottles, and know at once that she sold liquors without a licence.

"Oh, Charlotte!" cried Agnes, "do be quiet; do, for Heaven's sake."

Charlotte did not seem to hear.

"Oh! let me implore you to be quiet," she continued.

But Captain Smash took her by the arm and forced her into a seat, saying—

"Don't say anything. Leave her to herself; she's a bad woman. They must fight it out."

Under this constraint, Agnes remained passive and quiescent.

Not so the two combatants.

The Jewess returned Charlotte's assault by giving her a blow in the face.

But Charlotte, with the ferocity of a tigress, twined her fingers in her long black hair, and dragged her, shrieking and screaming, into the other room.

The gas was alight here, and shed a sickly glare upon the scene.

Every now and then Charlotte knocked Aunty's head

against the wall, or a table or chair, or whatever happened to be nearest.

The Jewess's face was now covered with blood.

Captain Smash and Agnes followed, to see the end of the quarrel.

They stood in the doorway, anxiously watching.

Agnes, in her trepidation, nervously clutched Captain Smash's hand.

He passionately returned the pressure, and cast a look upon her full of admiration.

She, however, did not notice this bye-play; she was too intent on what was going on before her to take any notice of any one else.

"She will murder the poor woman!" she exclaimed.

"Not she!" replied her companion. "Too good a judge, my dear."

"Do you think so?"

"I know women better than you do; and I know they have the greatest possible objection to appear outside Newgate at eight o'clock on Monday morning."

"I hope you are right."

"I know I am; don't you alarm yourself, and it'll be all right presently. I know them so well. They can't deceive me."

There was a tub of water standing on one of the tables. It was half full of dish-water. It was muddy and dirty, and the savour which arose from it was not exactly like the atmosphere outside a Bond-street perfumer's shop.

Charlotte's eye alighted upon this.

She dragged the Jewess towards it, and in spite of her tears, her oaths, her resistance, she plunged her head in again and again, until she had nearly smothered her.

The Jewess struggled frantically; but Charlotte would not relax her grasp.

CHAPTER LVIII.

AUNTY DECLARES THAT SHE WILL BE "ONE" WITH CHARLOTTE SAUNDERS—NEW ARRIVALS—MAID MARIAN AND SALLY-COME-UP—A PARTING BENEDICTION—POOR-POLLY!—CAPTAIN SMASH TURNS UP IN THE HAY-MARKET—HELP!—KANGAROO—THE CAPTAIN IS ROUGHLY HANDLED.

At last Charlotte had compassion upon her victim. She loosened her hold, and allowed her to get up. This she did all dripping wet. The moisture fell from her in a shower, like a fall of rain. She shook her head in a savage manner, and glared fiercely around.

Charlotte, without being in the least daunted by the ferocious expression of her countenance, bravely stood her ground.

Suddenly the Jewess uttered a cry.

The soap-suds had got into her eyes, and she stamped on the floor with the pain,

"My eyes! my eyes!" she cried, in agony.

"Oh!" said Charlotte, with a laugh. "D——n your eyes."

This was not very pretty or elegant language for a woman to make use of; but in the Haymarket they are not very particular about the adjectives and expletives they employ.

Charlotte stood with one foot advanced, holding a handful of hair in her tenacious grip.

Long, lank, greasy-looking hair it was. But it was a trophy; and she regarded it very much as a North American Indian looks upon a scalp which he has snatched from his adversary in honourable warfare.

When the pain of the soap-suds had a little subsided, Aunty sprang forward, crying—

"A knife!—a knife! I'll stick a knife into the wretch!"

Captain Smash advanced a step or two to see that no positive mischief was done.

"I'll knife her!" vociferated the Jewess. "By the living God I will, if I have to serve seven years for it!"

Captain Smash stood prepared to dart forward at the slightest warning.

It was fortunate that he did so; because Aunty espied a knife lying upon the table near the parrot's cage, and, seizing it, she advanced to where Agnes was standing with the aspect of a Fury or a Fate.

The Jewess brandished the weapon.

Captain Smash then ran forward, and, at a very critical juncture, interposed his masculine strength.

It was truly fortunate for Charlotte that he did so. Her career might have been ended there and then.

The captain caught hold of the arms of the Jewess and pinned her. Then he forced her into a seat.

"Let me go—let me go!" she screamed, foaming at the mouth.

"Be still," said Agnes, persuasively. "You will thank him for it afterwards."

This brought Aunty's attention particularly to her. She eyed her furiously for a minute, and then said—

"It's all through your low banter. If you had not been here this wouldn't have happened."

"What have I to do with it?"

"Say nothing," said Captain Smash. "Leave her to me."

Agnes made no answer.

"I'll be one with you," said the Jewess, again turning her attention to Charlotte Saunders.

"Very kind, I'm sure!" replied Charlotte.

"You may sneer, but I will."

"Will you?"

"All you say," cried Aunty, "goes for nothing with me."

"Doesn't it?"

"No."

"Well, I'm not a Christ killer," said Charlotte, coolly. The Jewess said nothing.

"Or a crucifier either," continued Charlotte.

"Ah! I'll be square with you."

"Will you? Then perhaps you will give me that umbrella you stole."

"Ah! you may say what you like. But do you know what it comes to?"

"No. Nor don't want to."

"Well, I'll tell you—nix."

"What's that?"

"Of no account—something like yourself."

"Oh!" said Charlotte. "What will you take for your chance of vengeance?"

"Nothing!"

"Nothing?"

"No. Not a pension."

"Oh! I would, if I were you."

"No. I wouldn't sell it for a diamond as big as a brick."

As she said this the door opened, and two women entered.

They were gaudily dressed, and seemed partially intoxicated, as is the custom of frail femininity in the Haymarket. They were full of a vicious hiliarity—one was dark, the other fair.

The fair one was a little stout woman, and as she entered, she was singing—

"Good St Anthony kept his eyes
　Firmly fixed upon his book;
Devils black, and devils blue,
Devils of every colour and hue."

Here she broke off abruptly, and exclaimed—

"Hullo! Here's a shindy."

Then she made use of a word which is better expressed by another—namely, sanguinary. With her everything was sanguinary.

Her eyes and other people's eyes, if not condemned by her to everlasting torment, were sanguinary; and in the present instance she evinced a great desire to know what the sanguinary disturbance was.

Charlotte threw down the handful of hair, and, shaking herself very much as a bird does when its plumage is ruffled, gave an explanation of it in her own particular way.

"This old Jew cow," she began, "cheeked me, and I slipped into her, and gave her an uncommon good hiding, which I have no doubt will do her all the good in the world; and if she wants another hiding, why, I'm ready for her. And she may come on as soon as she likes. The sooner the better. I'm not afraid of her, or anybody else. I don't care a hang for anybody—not for the whole lot of you put together. I brought my friend here, and I wont have her insulted by any pocket-picking ruffian who chooses to go sloping about the 'Market."

Charlotte cast a look of defiance at everybody, and then went up to Agnes.

"Who are those women?" asked Agnes.

"Oh! I know them well enough. I'd serve them the same as I served that old Jewess for two pins. They'd better not say anything to me. I'm just game for a row, I can tell them."

"But what are they called?"

"You seem to have taken a great fancy to them all at once."

"Not I."

"Well, it looks like it."

"Can't you answer my question?"

"I can," said Charlotte. "But suppose I don't choose to?"

"Oh! it doesn't matter. I didn't know there was any secret about it," replied Agnes. "If I had known it, I, would not have asked."

"There is no secret."

"I only asked because I thought they seemed to know you, and they might go about with us, and stick up for us in case we get into any more rows."

"Go about with them? Not if I know it."

"Why not?"

"Well, they're too good for me."

"Good? You mean the reverse, I should think, by the way you look."

"Well, what if I do? I have not come down to their level yet."

"Who are they, then?"

"Do you want to know particularly?"

"I suppose I do, or I should not have asked."

"One's Maid Marian," replied Charlotte, condescending at last to be communicative; "and the other's Sally-come-up."

"Sally-come-up?"

"Yes."

"Well, that's an odd name, anyhow," replied Agnes.

During this brief colloquy, Aunty had been getting very restive in the paternal grasp of Captain Smash.

He had some difficulty to hold her; but he took the precaution of disarming her, and throwing the knife she held in her hand to the other end of the room, where it lay glittering in the gas-light like a thing of evil.

"Now, get out of my place, both of you!" cried the Jewess, suddenly, to Agnes and Charlotte.

"I shall go when it suits me, and not before," replied Charlotte, coolly.

"Hook it out!"

"I shan't."

"Step it, will you?"

"When I choose—not before."

"Well, you've got to go. Your name's Walker out of this."

"You'd better go," said Captain Smash, in a low voice. "Wait at the corner of the street, and I will join you directly."

Charlotte either saw the wisdom of this advice, or she felt tired of the amusement, and wanted to go elsewhere; so she moved towards the door.

But as she passed the tub of dirty water, she could not resist the temptation of seizing it, and throwing it with all her force against the parrot's cage.

The tub struck it in the centre, and doubled it up.

The bird had a miraculous escape, flying unhurt over the débris, and perching unconcernedly upon the gas chandelier, where he sat making most sepulchral noises.

The water flew all over the Jewess, wetting her from top to toe.

"How's your poor feet?" cried the parrot.

Captain Smash saw the missile coming, and cleverly avoided it, so that he escaped unhurt.

Charlotte and Agnes then made for the door as fast as they could.

The parrot called out—

"There's another guy! Run along! Police—police!"

The girls soon found themselves upon the pavement once more; and the clock of St. Martin's church struck eleven.

"Oh! it's quite early," said Charlotte. "What shall we do?"

"I'm rather hungry," replied Agnes.

"Hungry, are you! Well, so am I. That reminds me that I never had my devilled kidneys, worse luck. Well, we will go somewhere and get some oysters."

"Where will you go?"

"Oh! let's go to Scott's; that's the jolliest place I know."

"All right," said Agnes. "How you frightened me in that coffee-house place. I thought you were going to kill the old party, or that she was going to kill you."

"The first is the most likely," replied Charlotte, with a laugh. "I am an old stager, you know, and they don't come the old soldier over me; not they. I'm a match for a dozen of them, any day, one down and t'other come on."

"So it seems," replied Agnes. "I didn't know you were such a fury."

"Oh! I'm a perfect demon when they set my back up."

"In that case I shall take care how I offend you."

"Oh! you need not be afraid; I don't treat my friends like that."

"I'm glad to hear it."

"I'm sure I'm the milk of human kindness to most people; but one must draw the line somewhere."

"Of course."

"Well, I draw it at Jewesses."

"Do you?"

"I can't stand a Jewess. I hate them like poison."

"I'm not much fonder of them than you are. But I say, isn't that our friend, Captain Smash again?"

Agnes, as she spoke, pointed to a man who was advancing towards them.

They were now in the Haymarket, having traversed James-street.

It was the dark, badly-lighted side of the thoroughfare, and so it was not very easy to distinguish a person's features at a distance. But Agnes was right in her conjecture, that Captain Smash was approaching them.

Lifting his hat, he said—

"I've been looking everywhere for you. When I left Aunty's I went up Panton-street, thinking you had gone that way, but I am glad I have found you at last. I never like to be beaten at anything, and a moment ago I had almost given you up."

"Had you?" said Charlotte. "A good job too."

"Why so?"

"Because we are not going with you."

"No one asked you."

"Well, never mind; where I go, my friend here, goes with me."

"I suppose she can take care of herself. She doesn't want leading-strings."

"That is just what she cannot do, and I am going to take care of her."

"Quite an interesting infant," said the captain, with a sardonic grin, taking advantage of the opportunity in the darkness to squeeze Agnes's hand in a very tender manner.

She indignantly withdrew her hand from his, but said nothing.

"Now, don't you stand there and cheek me, old fellow, or you'll get it," said Charlotte, flushing up.

"Really! shall I?"

"Yes, that you will."

"Why can't I go with you?" he asked.

"Because we don't want you."

"Is that all?"

"No, it isn't. If you are so very anxious to know, you shall. I don't choose to be seen myself with any flash fellows of your description, and I'm sure my friend does not either!"

"What do you mean?"

"I mean that you are nothing better than a low thief and a gaol-bird. Why, your hair looks now as if it was only just recovering from a county crop."

Captain Smash lost his temper completely at last, and with an oath, he gave Charlotte a rude push which sent her reeling up against the wall, and taking Agnes by the arm, he said—

"Come with me, will you? I'll take care of you. You can do without that mad friend of yours for five minutes, can't you? An aunt of mine lives round the corner, we can go in there and have a glass of wine."

Agnes pulled her arm away from him and shouted "Police!" with all her might.

She had not vociferated the magic word more than once, before a tall, dark man, who was standing near one of the flaming cafés over the way, rushed with great speed across the road, and stood beside them.

No wonder he appeared dark, for he was a Mulatto!

Thick-lipped rather, and with the general half-caste sort of face which the intercourse between white and black produces; he stood six feet two and a half about, he was lithe and supple, and with his long arms, looked a very formidable antagonist.

"What's up?" he exclaimed, in very good English.

Agnes was about to speak when Charlotte Saunders, who had just recovered herself, replied—

"Punch that fellow's head."

"Which one?"

"Why that. Give it him, and you shall have a skiv for your trouble. The low, cowardly ruffian! Give it him, Kangaroo!"

The Mulatto, whom Charlotte called Kangaroo, turned up his sleeves in a regular pugilistic manner, and faced the redoubtable captain.

The latter looked rather crest-fallen at the prospect of an encounter with the man before him, but seeing there was no help for it, he, too, made his preparations.

But he had hardly time to complete them before Kangaroo dealt him a tremendous blow in the face, which sent the blood spurting up in streams.

"That's your sort!" cried Charlotte, rubbing her hands.

She seemed like a Spanish lady at a bull-fight, or a Roman matron at a gladiatorial exhibition.

It was rather dark where they were, and very few people passed that way.

The other side monopolized the midnight traffic.

But a few persons, attracted by the noise, crossed over, and looked on at the combat.

A sleepy-looking cabman or two left the rank, and looked on in a deliberative sort of manner, as if the affair had not very much interest in their eyes.

Perhaps it was of too common an occurrence to excite more than a passing remark or so, and a momentary attention.

The captain staggered, but soon gathered himself together, and before Kangaroo could repeat his blow, he contrived to deal him a forcible blow on what is sometimes called the bread-basket.

This had very little effect upon the Mulatto, who fought remarkably well, and never again gave his adversary a chance to get within a mile of him.

Captain Smash fought bravely. But the fight degenerated into a mere slaughter, for the Mulatto had it all his own way.

CHAPTER LIX.

KANGAROO IS VICTORIOUS—THE POLICE AWAKE AND EMERGE FROM A BOOZING-KEN—CAPTAIN SMASH COMES TO GRIEF—THE BLACK PRINCE—THE JEWESS AGAIN—BONNET HIM—THE COLONEL'S LUDICROUS POSITION.

AGNES contemplated this pugilistic encounter with open mouth and eyes.

She was not so much surprised, though, as she would have been before she met with Charlotte Saunders.

Before that event happened she was, to a certain extent, unsophisticated; but lately events had been crowding themselves upon her, and no exhibition of brutality, however glaring, appeared so absolutely repugnant as it did at first.

The eels are said to get used to being skinned, and after a time to take a certain amount of pleasure in the operation.

In the same way Agnes had been accustomed to scenes of violence, and she watched the encounter between Captain Smash and the Mulatto with some interest, wishing that the latter might be victorious, of which there was little doubt.

The captain's attentions to Agnes were far from being agreeable to her, and she thought, from the pertinacity with which he followed her up, and pressed his suit, that he was not only a bad but a dangerous man.

If Kangaroo, then, gave him what Charlotte kept on telling him to do—to wit, "a thundering hiding," he would, in all probability, be only too glad to slink home and hide his diminished head.

This reflection gave her undeniable pleasure, and when Kangaroo hit his antagonist harder than usual, she could not help joining in the applause which Charlotte Saunders showered upon him in a lavish manner.

At last Kangaroo gathered himself up. Standing as erect as a young sapling, he drew back his arm, and prepared to strike out well from the elbow.

Captain Smash was beating the air feebly with his hands. He could hardly see. Both his eyes were bunged up. His nose was like a stumpy and irregular potato, whilst his lips

were very much like those of the Mulatto, who had, for the last five minutes, been inflicting incessant punishment upon him.

The captain's arms moved about like the sails of an inebriated windmill, if ever a windmill can be said to be in that sad and lamentable condition.

The cabmen and others who formed the ring around the combatants considered the affair a foregone conclusion.

"Lam in, lam in!" cried one.

"Slog him!" said another.

"Go it!"

"Hurrah! hurrah! Now's your time."

And other exclamations of a similar nature resounded on all sides.

The guardians of the public peace had not thought fit to put in an appearance as yet.

The fact was that the regular constable, whose beat was the Haymarket, together with the two extras who patrolled the same pavement, were, at the urgent solicitation of a friend of theirs, indulging in a drain at Carter's, a public house in the immediate vicinity.

Consequently, if murder was being committed, it might have been done with impunity, as far as these intrepid custodians of public morality, law, and order were interested.

Kangaroo at last delivered the blow he had been preparing.

He caught the unhappy captain between the eyes, just above the bridge of the nose, and Captain Smash went spinning along like a teetotum, until he finally kissed his mother earth, close to the wheels of one of the cabs on the rank.

"That's the knock-down blow," cried one spectator.

"He's give him Tommy this time," said another.

While a third invoked a terrible end for his optics if it weren't stunning well put in."

"May I drop down dead," said a fourth, "if the nigger don't know how to do the trick."

"Let's see who I've been a-peppering," exclaimed the Mulatto, who went up to Captain Smash, and dragged him to a lamp-post.

When he saw who it was, he said, in astonishment—

"Why, it's the captain. Here's a pretty bit of fakement."

The captain opened his eyes, and said, in a voice in which sadness and melancholy, together with a pathetic humour, were commingled—

"You needn't have laid it on so nation thick. You might have let a brother pal down easy."

"Wish I may die," began Kangaroo, "but I never knew it was you, cappen."

He had not time to say more before a cry was raised that the police were coming.

"Come with us. This way," cried Charlotte to Kangaroo.

He followed her, leaving his victim to his fate, because he wanted the sovereign she had promised him And, in addition to that, he had a lively dread of being locked up all night, with, perhaps, the pleasant prospect before him of being sent to prison for a week, as it would have been by no means his first appearance in Marlborough-street, and the "beak" preserved a very vivid recollection of his West Indian physiognomy.

The police had just emerged from the "boozing-ken," in which they had been fortifying themselves against the effects of the night air, and nerving themselves for the due and proper execution of their nocturnal duties.

They walked along with the air of a peacock when he hopes to pick up a caterpillar, and they held their heads so very upright that there was every prospect of their breaking their somewhat swan-like necks.

Policemen, as a rule, seem to have a very slender knowledge of the English language.

They appear to be possessed of two or three stock phrases which they bring out on every occasion.

They may be possessed of a good deal of wit, but, like Hudibras, they don't always carry it about with them, for fear of wearing it out or losing it.

"Now, move on!" is a very favourite phrase with them, and "What's this 'ere?" is also of frequent assistance to them.

On the present occasion they said, "What's all this 'ere about?"

Captain Smash staggered to his legs, and he was instantly collared, while the other two policemen ranged themselves on either side of him, placed their hands upon their truncheons, as if they were prepared to resist any attempt at a rescue, and glared round them at the crowd, which increased every minute, with a sort of vinous courage in their glance, which spoke volumes of goes of gin-and-water.

Some one in the crowd volunteered an explanation of the occurrence, and at last it became clear to the official mind, that the public peace had been broken; one of the combatants had disappeared, but one had remained behind.

It should be their especial business to see that he did not escape like his more fortunate companion.

Accordingly, after uttering another oracular phrase, "You move on!" they put themselves in motion, and marched in solemn phalanx towards the Vine-street police-station.

Captain Smash walked passively between them, knowing that it would be of no use to say anything to them. He would be able to tell his tale to the inspector on duty, and he would possibly refuse to take the charge.

The crowd increased every moment, and as they reached the Circus, the traffic was impeded by the mob.

Thus Captain Smash was dragged along, wounded and bleeding, with a howling mob yelling at his heels.

But he bore it all with philosophical calmness.

When he reached the station it turned out as he had expected. The superintendent refused to take the charge. The policemen had not seen the disturbance, but Captain Smash averred that he had been set upon, and brutally maltreated.

The police said that they came up directly they heard of the disturbance, and hoped they had done their duty.

The superintendent congratulated them on their zeal, and Captain Smash was liberated according to custom.

He adjourned to the nearest public-house, which was the Man in the Moon, in the alley round the corner, and there stood brandy-and-water cold to his three captors, who were full of apologies, and as jolly as possible with their late prisoner.

Then Captain Smash went to a chemist's, got his hurts and bruises looked to, and then getting into a cab, went home to lay up for a couple of days till he was fit to be seen about once more in broad daylight, which he certainly was not at present.

Kangaroo followed Charlotte and Agnes closely, and at last all three entered a public-house in Arundel Court where Charlotte called for half-a-pint of gin. She then gave Kangaroo the sovereign she promised him, and said—

"You're a brick, Kangaroo, and now you've got some money you are flush enough to pay for this white satin I should think."

Kangaroo changed his money, paid for the gin, and shortly after took his departure, saying with a bow, that he was always very happy to oblige a lady.

Charlotte had some money which her captain, as she called him, had given her, and consequently she could afford to be generous.

"I am glad," she said to Agnes, "that Kangaroo came up so opportunely. I don't know what we should have done without him."

"Nor I either," responded Agnes.

"It was very lucky."

"That it was. But who is this Kangaroo? What a funny name to give a man."

"Well, he is like a kangaroo in everything, isn't he, barring the tail?"

"He is tall and dark."

"He is sometimes called the Black Prince," said Charlotte.

"Why?"

"Because he came from Jamaica, so the story goes, with a lot of money, which he ran through over here. He is an interpreter when he can get anything to do; but he is generally to be seen loafing about here of a night, and picking up what he can from men and women."

"Really!"

"Yes, and he is a very good sort, too. I like Kangaroo; he is a woman's friend all over."

"So it seems."

"He will stick up for a woman at any time as he did for you and me to-night, and he can fight splendidly."

"Yes. There is no doubt about that," replied Agnes. "I feel quite interested in your description of the Black Prince."

Charlotte smiled.

But just at this moment a great noise was heard outside, and suddenly a woman's voice exclaimed—

"I tell you it is them, 'Arry, I saw them. Let me go. I will get at them."

Charlotte and Agnes with some consternation recognised the voice of the Jewess, whom they could not help supposing had left her café, and come in search of them.

"That's her husband with her, I suppose?" said Charlotte.

"Her husband?"

"Well, the man who lives with her; he is generally supposed to be her husband. They call him the 'colonel' generally. He is quite a character; he was an officer's servant, or something of that sort, once upon a time, and he has a certain military air about him, with a dragooning look when his wife's not thrashing him. But when she does, which is pretty often, he twists his long moustache and takes it very quietly."

The scuffle outside still continued. The "colonel's" voice was heard saying—

"Now, Fanny."

"I won't. You let me go."

At last he got angry apparently, for he exclaimed—

"Bust my gall——"

But she stopped him by giving him a push, saying at the same time—

"By my father's life, I'll give it them. By my life, I will."

"Bust my gall!" again said the colonel, and the infuriated daughter of Israel rushed into the place.

Charlotte Saunders made for a second door which opened to the left and led into the court towards Coventry-street, pushing Agnes before her as she did so.

Then she took up her glass which was full of hot, steaming gin-and-water, and laying the spoon down, threw it point blank into the Jewess' face.

Aunty uttered a piercing scream, for the burning liquid nearly blinded her.

Charlotte hastily followed Agnes out into the court.

The "colonel" was standing close to, not venturing to follow aunty, who was roaring like a mad bull.

He was just recovering from the effects of the push she had given him, and did not see Charlotte, as his back was turned towards her.

She knew who it was, by the size and look of him, and going softly behind him, she bonneted him with all her might.

With a dull crash, his hat slid over his face, and the brim at last touched his shoulders.

It was a hat rather too small for him. Probably one of his customers had left it in the café.

Anyhow, it was much too small for him, and all his efforts to get it off were of no avail.

He pulled at it frantically, while low, smothered cries proceeded from the inside of the hat.

It was like the moaning of a wild beast *in extremis*.

Fortunately for the colonel there was a ventilator in the top of the hat, or it would have gone hardly with him.

He would inevitably have been smothered.

At last his terrific efforts sufficed to tear the brim of the hat off all round.

This he dashed upon the ground and danced upon it.

His struggles were of course worse than useless after this, because he could not possibly move the hat now he had nothing to lay hold of.

Charlotte and Agnes laughed at this ludicrous scene till the tears trickled down their cheeks.

Getting into the shadow of the wall they watched the colonel's evident distress, without the chance of being seen by any one.

At last a voice from inside the public exclaimed—

"'Arry!"

Of course there was no answer.

"Colonel!"

The wretched man was still silent perforce.

"'Arry," she cried, a third time.

This time the colonel heard her shrill voice, and tried to go in what he thought was the direction of the door, but after groping about without success, he ran his head against the wall with some violence.

Then he kicked the wall spitefully till he hurt his toes and limped on one leg.

Low whines came from the interior of the hat.

This was his lamentable condition when the Jewess emerged from the public-house to look for him.

Her face was as red as fire.

Fortunately the gin-and-water which Charlotte had thrown at her was not boiling; if it had been, the consequences would have been very serious.

As it was, the liquid was only warm, and it did her no particular injury. It rendered her very uncomfortable, for it trickled all down her bosom, and, as she herself afterwards declared, "made her as wet as muck, it did."

When she saw her husband, in spite of her misfortunes, she could not help laughing.

There he was with the brimless hat over his head, holding his foot in his hand, and shaking his head as if he was going into a fit.

She took him by the hand and led him into the public-house, where the landlord nearly went into convulsions, and the two or three men who were drinking there, held their sides with laughter.

CHAPTER LX.

AN OYSTER-SHOP—A NEW ACQUAINTANCE—THE MYSTERIOUS SIGNALS—GOING TO KATE'S—RASCALLY JACK AND SPLAWGER—THE MAMMON OF UNRIGHTEOUSNESS — THE LONG CORRIDOR — THE ROOM — KATE HAMILTON.

THE colonel struggled, the colonel kicked; the colonel did all that lay in his power to extricate himself from the unpleasant predicament that Charlotte Saunders' malicious and mischievous propensities had placed him in.

But Fate was against him, and in this instance she was inexorable.

"What's to be done?" said the Jewess.

Aunty was as much puzzled how to get him out of the scrape, as he himself was.

She tried to raise the hat up with her hands, but she might as well have tried to raise the dome of St. Pauls.

It stuck to him like a leech, or a Jew when he holds your acceptance after doing a bit of stiff for you.

At last an idea came into the landlord's head.

"Cut it off!" he exclaimed.

"What!" said Aunty, aghast, "cut it off?"

"Yes."

"You don't mean it."

"I do."

"What! can you stand there and have the abandoned brutality to tell me to cut his head off," she said.

"No, not the head, I meant the hat."

"Oh, that's another thing."

"To be sure it is."

"Give us a knife, then."

"All right. Wait a moment."

The word "knife" fell upon the colonel's ears.

This was the only part of the conversation he had heard except "cut his head off," and it may readily be supposed that he was terribly alarmed.

He threw himself down on the ground like a child, and in an agony of apprehension, howled like a demon.

"That's pretty, certainly!" she said.

"He's in a fit," suggested some one.

"Ah! it is likely," returned Aunty. "Perhaps he'll go off like that. Make haste with that knife, will you?"

Two men volunteered to hold him during the operation, and it took them all their time and all they knew to do it.

Aunty with great care made a slit in the hat near the ventilator. This she gradually widened until she was able to tear the hat down the back of his head with her hands.

In another second the colonel was as free as air.

For a moment or so he could not speak. He gasped for breath.

His eyes rolled fearfully, and he had the appearance of a man who was hesitating as to whether he should go into an apoplectic fit or not.

After a time, he decided that he would not.

His features gradually recovered their wonted expression and tone. His eyes remained a little distended, and that was all. He took in several copious draughts of air, as if he was glad to inhale that element again as freely as he was accustomed to.

"'Arry, 'Arry," said his tender spouse.

His lips moved spasmodically, and then he said, in tremulous accents—

"Bust my gall!"

When Aunty heard him utter his favourite oath, she was satisfied that he was in a fair way to become himself again.

Soon after, "the colonel" said—

"Give us a drop of gin, old woman."

And after drinking the beverage that was speedily handed to him, he got up and threw his arms about, letting them fall by his side like an old hen flapping her wings.

Charlotte Saunders and Agnes had watched all this with great amusement, and now they considered it prudent to move away to some other, if not distant, quarter of the Haymarket world.

"What about those oysters?" said Agnes.

"Oh, I had forgotten them."

"So I thought."

"Will you come and have them now?" asked Charlotte.

"Oh, yes; nothing I should like better."

"Wasn't that fun?" said Charlotte.

"Fun, I should think so. I don't think I ever laughed more at anything in my life. I'm sure I shall never forget it. Poor fellow! I can see him now, with his brimless hat, and his——"

As she recalled all the funny incidents of the preceding quarter of an hour, she laughed again involuntarily, while her companion joined in her irresistible merriment.

"I think," said Charlotte, "that they will remember me for some time to come. So it will be only prudent in me to avoid the Café de Cagmag for some few weeks, or they'll make it too hot to hold me."

"The Café de what, did you say?" asked Agnes, much puzzled.

"Café de Cagmag. Don't you know what cagmag is?"

"No, that I don't."

"Well, I'm surprised. It means any muck—garbage, or something nasty and uneatable."

"Well, I'm sure. What a name to give it. Who invented it, I wonder?"

"I think the nun did."

"The nun! Who's she?"

"Oh, a woman who goes about. I don't like her; I think she's very cocky and disagreeable. But you may see her to-night at a place I'll take you to."

"Well, you are teaching me something," said Agnes, with a smile.

"Aunty's place has another name I myself gave it," said Charlotte.

"What's that?"

"Why, the Café de Fried and Boiled. Because they have always got a lot of soles and flounders ready, fried or boiled, for you. But here we are at Scott's. How many dozen can you manage?"

"How many? well, I should think one would be enough."

"Not for me," replied Charlotte. "I always eat two or three dozen when I begin. Suppose I order four?"

"Very well; do as you like," said Agnes.

They entered a shop, the window of which was filled with shell-fish of every description; a long marble counter ran along the shop, at which several men were standing eating oysters as fast as the assistants behind the bar could open them.

Passing through this, Charlotte led the way into a long room divided into little boxes with tables in them—five on each side. These were mostly occupied, but as they proceeded they found one near the fireplace at which only one man was seated.

As Charlotte passed the looking-glass over the mantelpiece, she could not resist the temptation of stopping and putting her bonnet straight.

The man at the table looked up and said, with a good-natured smile—

"You'll do."

"I'm glad you think so," replied Charlotte, sitting down at the table, where Agnes had already taken up a position.

The man who had spoken to her was a gentlemanly-looking man, tolerably well dressed, and about thirty years of age.

"You see how I'll work him," said Charlotte, to Agnes.

"Work him? what do you mean?" she replied, in the same low whisper Charlotte had made use of in speaking to her.

"Look on, and you will see," was the reply.

"I suppose you have been to the Argyle, old fellow?" said Charlotte, addressing him.

"No, I have not."

"Oh! Well, where have you been? I'm sure you would be a loss to any society."

He smiled, and replied—

"I'm sure I can return the compliment. But won't you and your friend have some supper?"

"I have ordered some oysters, but I don't mind having something to drink," said Charlotte.

"Have what you like," he said.

Charlotte tinkled a little bell, and when the waiter came, she said—

"Bring a bottle of champagne."

This duly made its appearance, and Agnes looked very pretty and interesting as she raised the thick Maltese veil she wore, to sip the wine that Charlotte gave her.

"Is that your sister?" asked the gentleman.

"Yes. Do you think we are alike?"

"That's hardly a fair question."

After supper, Charlotte said—

"We are going to Kate's; will you come?"

"With pleasure," replied the gentleman.

"Well, if you are going with us, I should like to know who you are, old fellow?" said Charlotte, coolly.

He smiled again.

"I can't go about and be seen with a man I know nothing of."

He showed his pearly teeth this time.

"Well, who are you?" she continued.

"Oh! I'm not a bad sort."

"That's not the question. If I didn't think you were a good sort I shouldn't take you about with me. What are you?"

"I'm a painter and glazier by trade," he said.

"Nonsense!" cried Charlotte. "You can't sell me. Are you in the service?"

"No."

"Well, what are you?"

"I've told you."

"Yes, you've told me a lie."

"You call things by their names."

"Yes, I do, and people too, as you'll find out if you are not a little more communicative."

"Well, I'm under Government," he said; "will that suit you?"

"Not quite."

"It won't?"

"No."

"Then you are very hard to please."

"Well, I admit it. I am rather particular."

"I'll make you a promise!"

"What is it?"

"That you shall know who I am before we leave Kate's!"

"All right. On those conditions we will make friends again. Waiter!"

When the waiter came, she said—

"How much?"

He mentioned the amount, and the gentleman paid the sum with the greatest readiness.

"I told you I would work him," said Charlotte to Agnes. "A woman never need pay anything, without she is the biggest fool that ever lived. If a woman's ladylike to men, and has got plenty of cheek, she can always get a man to pay the shot for her and stand Sam."

They then left the oyster-shop and emerged in the street. A couple of men, who seemed to be standing about as if they had nothing particular to do, looked at the gentleman, and with their fingers made a rapid sign, which they accompanied by slight nods of the head.

The gentleman held up two fingers!

They nodded again.

All this was lost upon the two girls, so quickly and cleverly was it done.

The two strange men then rapidly left the spot, and were soon lost to sight in the darkness.

"I say, I must call you something," suddenly said Charlotte, as they were turning round the corner of Princes-street.

"Call me what you like."

"Well, let me see, what shall I call you?"

"Call me anything but Moses."

"You have a pretty good coat on!" said Charlotte. "I think I shall call you Coat?"

"All right."

"Will that do?"

"Yes, capitally."

"Oh! Charlotte, how can you!" exclaimed Agnes.

"Well, it's a good coat, and I don't see why he shouldn't be called Coat."

The man, whom she called all the rest of the evening by this singular nickname, took her badinage very good-naturedly, and in a few moments they approached a door.

It was like the door of any private house, with this exception, there was a little loop-hole in one of the top panels. A piece of wood was pushed across this, but it was easy to see that it could be removed at will, so that any one inside could reconnoitre those without before the door revolved on its hinges and gave them admittance.

A man with a woollen comforter tied round his neck stood outside this door and just in front of it.

He was a tall, thick-set man, with a battered nose and forbidding features.

Close to him was another man, short and stout, whose chief characteristic was his ugly, ill-shaped, splay feet. These were the porters.

"Who are those men?" asked Agnes.

"Those! Oh! the porters. One's Rascally Jack and the other they call Splawger."

Rascally Jack touched his cap to Charlotte, and said to her in a whisper—

"Who's the bloke?"

"It's all right."

"Is he all square?"

"If he wasn't he would not be with me."

"No, of course not, but—"

"But what?"

"Well, look here."

"Go ahead!"

"You see," said Rascally Jack, "we've got strict orders to-night, to look out for the slops."

"Is there anything up?"

"Well, I know nothing. But them's my orders."

"Oh! he's all right."

"You're sure of that," said Splawger, joining in the conversation.

"Does he look like a fellow on the cross?" said Charlotte.

The men eyed him attentively. He bore the scrutiny very well, but there was the least sign of anxiety upon his countenance, as if he rather wished to be admitted, and dreaded a refusal on the part of the two porters.

"Well, what do you think of him?" asked Charlotte.

Splawger and Rascally Jack conferred together for a little time.

"Do you know his face?" said Rascally Jack.

"Can't say I do," replied Splawger. "I think I've seen him before, though; but I couldn't swear to him."

"Now, how much longer are you going to keep us standing here; I'm getting cold," said Charlotte, giving Rascally Jack a poke in the ribs with her umbrella.

Seeing the men still hesitated, the man went up to Rascally Jack and gave him a sovereign, saying—

"I suppose the fact is I ought to pay an entrance fee, as I have never been here before. Is that what you are waiting for, eh?"

Rascally Jack turned the money over in his hand, and said to Splawger—

"It's all right, I think. He's square."

Splawger shook his head a little dubiously, but the sight of the gold pleased him, and he acquiesced.

Rascally Jack then rang a bell, and a man inside opened the door and admitted the party.

"Come on, Coat," said Charlotte. "Sorry those two fools kept us waiting so long."

And she gaily darted along a lengthy passage, and, after passing through another door, which opened at their approach, led them into a brilliantly lighted room.

It was long rather than broad. It extended from Princes-street to Leicester-square, and was a very handsome room.

There were a great number of people in it, although not so many as there were on some occasions.

There might have been eighty women, and as many as five-and-fifty gentlemen, of all ranks and of all professions.

Here was a barrister—there a soldier—on the other side a physician—to the left an architect—to the right a City man—at that end a tradesman, at the other a merchant —and in that corner a stockbroker. A little higher up a betting man—lower down a "welcher," or low, swindling betting man. Sitting at that table a thief—opposite him a receiver of stolen goods. By his side a horse chaunter, and within a few paces of him a peer of the realm. Near that window an honourable—by the other a baronet. And, in fact, you might distinguish every character that Proteus, in his wildest and most sportive moments, could wish to personate.

At a bar at the end of the room was seated the queen of the festivities.

Raised on a sort of dais, or throne, sat Kate Hamilton, the mistress of the revels.

CHAPTER LXI.

THE UNKNOWN IS TACITURN—TWO STRANGE PEOPLE—ROMANY—WHAT IS IT?—THE LANGUAGE OF THIEVES—THE BELL RINGS THREE TIMES—THE CLOCK STRIKES TWO, AND THE POLICE ENTER—WYMAN AGAIN—THE DIAMOND ROBBERY—FLY-BY-NIGHT IS ARRESTED—CHARLOTTE AND AGNES ARE IN AN UNPLEASANT POSITION.

SOME were smoking, some were talking, some were silent, and may be, some were sad, but everybody was drinking—drinking wine, drinking brandy, drinking gin, more frequently drinking Moselle.

Charlotte did not go into the centre of the room, she sat down at the side. Agnes disposed herself close to her, and the strange man they had met at the oyster-shop sat by the side of Charlotte.

A small marble-topped table stood close to them.

The unknown, as he may very truly be called, took out his cigar-case and lighted a very decent cigar.

"That's a good weed, I know," said Charlotte.

"Well, it's not bad! But how do you know?"

"Oh, by the smell of it! Do you suppose I can't tell a good weed from a bad one?"

"I might have supposed so at first, but now I don't, because you have given me a proof of your sagacity."

"What's that?" asked Charlotte, elevating her eyebrows.

"That?"

"Yes. I don't understand your long words."

"But everybody, surely——"

"Well, don't use long words to me, or else I shall think you're a cad—only cads use long words, and they don't impress women at all, I can tell you; they only disgust them! Hullo! what's that?"

This exclamation was caused by a sudden commotion in a distant part of the room.

There was apparently a great breakage of glass, for a noisy clatter was heard, and the sound of falling tumblers and plates jingling together was plainly audible.

The stranger seemed perplexed, and looked round him anxiously.

"Here, I say, Coat!" exclaimed Charlotte; "you're taller than me, just get upon this table, and tell us what is going on."

"Certainly," he replied, mounting, by the help of a chair, upon the nearest table.

"Well, what is it?" demanded Charlotte, impatiently.

"Only a couple of women fighting!" he replied.

"Oh, that's all! There's nothing very wonderful about that! Woman are always fighting in these places!"

"Are they?"

"Yes. I wonder who it is, though? Oh, here they come!"

As she spoke a couple of waiters appeared, dragging a woman along the centre of the room. She struggled a good deal, but they held her by the arms, and compelled her to go forward.

"I'll go!" she kept on saying; "but I wont be turned out. Leave go, will you? Let me alone! I'll go, but I wont be turned out!"

"Now, come on! Come quietly!" said one of the waiters. "You've got to go, and it's no good making a fuss over it."

"What's the row, Spurgeon?" demanded Charlotte of a waiter standing near her.

"Only a fight, miss. She is always making a disturbance."

Spurgeon was a playful appellation for the head-waiter, because he was supposed to resemble the popular minister of that name.

Soon afterwards, in spite of her resistance, the woman

was turned out, and speedily made her way to some other nocturnal resort.

"Ah! you would not get much by it, if you tried that sort of game on with me, old cock!" said Charlotte to the waiter.

"Oh, I don't know! We are not particular," replied Spurgeon.

"Why, you old swine!" said Charlotte; "I'd mark you if you were as big as Goliah."

"Would you?"

"Would I? Yes!"

"Ah! you'd have your work before you if you tried."

Charlotte made a face at him, saying—

"Who cares for you?"

"Now, Coat!" she said.

"Well!"

"What are you going to stand?"

"Anything you like."

"All right; order some wine then!"

"Waiter!" said the unknown.

"Coming, sir!" said Spurgeon.

"Bring some wine."

"Wine, sir—yes, sir. What wine, sir?"

"A couple of bottles of Moselle."

"No—not bottles," said Charlotte.

"Well, what then?"

"Why, bring a Moselle cup."

"Right, miss," replied Spurgeon, who hastened to obey the command.

It was worthy of notice that the unknown did not talk much; his eyes kept roving about the room. Now, he was scrutinizing the face of a woman; anon, that of a man. No countenance escaped him. He answered Charlotte, when she spoke to him, in monosyllables. At last he fixed his gaze upon a man and a woman, who were sitting together nearly close to where he himself was seated.

Perhaps this proximity to him had prevented his noticing them before. They occupied rather a quiet out-of-the-way table, and it was evident that they did not think that they were observed. They were conversing eagerly in a low voice, but their conversation was conducted, in what to most people would have been an unknown tongue.

It was also worthy of note that the mysterious unknown appeared to understand their lingo.

Once or twice he started, as if something they said surprised him.

It was not wonderful that their conversation was unintelligible to most people; for they were holding a dialogue in Romany—*the language of thieves.*

The preoccupation of the unknown did not escape the penetration of Charlotte, who exclaimed—

"What's the matter, Coat?"

"Eh!" he replied, looking up.

"What's the matter? You look as if you'd found sixpence and lost a shilling."

"Do I?"

"Yes. Can't you be lively? If you are not I shall go and talk to somebody else."

Agnes was very silent during this scene. She drank some wine; but she had no one to talk to. There was plenty of occupation for her, however, in watching the various people with whom the room was filled.

"Oh, I'm lively enough," replied the unknown, who could not drive away the expression of care which sat upon his countenance, although he tried hard to do so.

"Well, Coat, give me some wine."

While the unknown held the cup in his hand, and as the sparkling wine bubbled inside its silver receptacle, a sharp ring was heard in the passage; this was repeated at intervals of five seconds.

Instantly the greatest confusion took place—the waiters ran about with the utmost alacrity—all the spirits in the room were immediately concealed, sometimes under the crinolines of the women, sometimes in out-of-the-way cupboards, and under the counter—anywhere, everywhere in fact, where they could possibly be stowed.

What could be the cause of this sudden commotion?

What could make all these men and women exhibit so much consternation?

The waiters, after hiding away all the intoxicating drinks they could find, placed a few bottles of lemonade and soda-water on the different tables, and with their napkins on their arms awaited the sequel.

THE ARREST OF "FLY-BY-NIGHT" AT KATE HAMILTON'S.

Then Spurgeon, with a half smile upon his lips, spoke a word to Mrs. Katherine Hamilton, who nodded her head in return.

Then he touched a bell-rope which made a corresponding signal. The unknown's face now brightened up—he seemed totally changed; his hands felt something in the pockets of his coat, which he clasped nervously.

Agnes happened to look round, and she thought she saw the glitter of brass or steel, but she said nothing.

The few people who had been talking Romany seemed rather apprehensive, and slunk into the background as much as they could. The unknown kept his eye fixed upon them.

"What's going on?" asked Agnes.

"Don't you know?" replied Charlotte.

"No."

"You don't?"

"How should I?"

"Oh! I forgot."

"Well, what is it?"

"Why, the bobbies are coming."

"What for?"

"Why, to see what they can find."

"Oh! that is it, is it?"

"Yes. You know they can't get a licence at these places, so they have to look out."

"Of course."

"But the police are well paid for keeping their eyes shut, so their hearts are soft. If they were not smoothed over, they would be as hard as nails."

"Look there!" said Agnes, all of a sudden.

"What?"

Charlotte turned her attention to where Agnes's finger was pointed, and saw something which rather surprised her.

We have said that the two people who were talking Romany were seated near the unknown.

The woman, who was well-dressed, had noticed the peculiar

glitter of something in his pocket which had attracted Agnes's attention.

Gliding up to him like a snake, she had put her hand in his pocket in the most skilful, subtle, and accomplished manner.

She had raised something half out of the pocket, when she uttered a startling cry, and let it fall again as quickly as she had touched it.

Going back to her companion, she exclaimed, in a terrified whisper—

"'Ware hawks."

He clutched her arm nervously, but said nothing.

Both their faces were ashy pale, and they seemed stricken by a sudden panic.

"Well, that's a funny start!" said Charlotte.

The unknown took no notice of this little episode. He appeared perfectly indifferent to anything.

After the lapse of a couple of minutes the police were heard approaching.

Every one listened.

Conversation was at an end, and all waited to see what would happen next.

First a sergeant entered the room. He was followed by a common policeman. Then came another, and another, and another.

Presently six policemen, besides the sergeant, stood in the room.

They drew up in a line before the door.

At this juncture the clock struck two.

The vibration had scarcely departed from the atmosphere where it lingered, when the unknown started to his feet.

The policemen saluted him in military fashion.

With a sudden movement the unknown took off his hat, dashed a wig and a pair of whiskers upon the floor, and unbuttoning his coat, stood revealed in his true character.

Spurgeon uttered an exclamation of surprise, and then said—

"Inspector Wyman, by——!"

With an easy, confident step, he advanced towards the two people who had been talking Romany, and taking a pair of handcuffs from his pocket, he exclaimed—

"John Coon, alias Whitney, alias Fly-by-night, you are my prisoner."

"Never!" he replied, boldly. "I would rather die."

"Rescue! rescue! What's the row?" exclaimed some drunken young gentlemen, rushing up and crowding round.

At this demonstration the six policemen drew their truncheons, and stood on the defensive.

Wyman waved them back.

"Gentlemen," he exclaimed, "I arrest this man for felony."

At this they all started back in horror and amazement.

"Give it him!" cried one.

"Lock him up!" said another.

"This is the celebrated Fly-by-night," continued Inspector Wyman, "and I arrest him for a diamond robbery in Regent-street. I have reason to believe that he came here to dispose of the plunder—for stolen goods have been received in this room before now."

Here the inspector looked sternly around him. As he did so, a sudden report was heard, and a bullet whistled past Wyman's ear.

The shot would have been fatal had not the woman pushed his arm up, and prevented the leaden bullet taking the effect he intended it to.

"No!" she exclaimed; "you shall not add murder to your other crimes."

Fly-by-night, with a curse, flung the pistol from him, and with his clenched fist struck the woman in the face.

"D—— the women!" he cried; "they are at the bottom of all mischief that happens!"

"Shame! shame!" arose on all sides.

The unhappy creature fell prone upon the ground, her face smothered in blood.

"Poor thing! Bring her here!" said some one. "Give her a drop of brandy."

"Sorry, sir, I can't let her out of my sight," said Wyman. "You may give her the brandy, and welcome; but as she is an accessory after the fact, it is my duty to see that she does not escape."

"Quite so."

"As for this ruffian, I'll put the darbies on him for that little piece of work."

Fly-by-night made no further resistance—he sullenly and passively allowed himself to be handcuffed.

Then the inspector searched him, and, in an inside-pocket, cunningly contrived, he found a packet.

Eagerly he opened it. It contained a magnificent tiara of diamonds, and several loose stones of great price.

Exultation might have been read upon every lineament of the inspector's features.

He replaced the diamonds in his pocket, and handed his captive to the sergeant. The woman had by this time partially recovered, and had risen to her feet.

The inspector, without handcuffing her, gave her also into safe keeping. Then he advanced towards Kate, and said—

"Mrs. Hamilton, I beg to state that the ladies who brought me here knew nothing about me—I was a casual acquaintance of theirs. They were totally ignorant that I was in any way connected with the police-force."

"That does not matter to me," she replied. "I neither want to see you nor any of your friends."

"But they are not my friends."

"Oh, never mind; anybody who comes here with you must be a pal of yours."

Wyman said no more; but approaching Agnes and Charlotte, said—

"You can come out with me, if you like."

"Not I," said Charlotte. "You have infernally well sold me, and you had better take some of your wine with you."

With an angry gesture, she threw the champagne-cup he had ordered at him.

He was deluged with the wine, and the cup hit him on the lip, cutting it rather severely. He took out his handkerchief, but said nothing.

Putting himself at the head of his men, he left the room. The dull tramp of the police sounded in the corridor, and soon all was still.

When they had fairly departed conversation again began; people recovered themselves, and a great many went away to disseminate the news, and because they rather wished a change of air after what had occurred.

The waiters, and some others connected with the establishment, regarded Charlotte and Agnes with a sinister expression.

But Charlotte looked as unconcerned and as jovial as ever; not so Agnes—she was deadly pale.

CHAPTER LXII.

A GREAT CONFUSION—AN ATTEMPT AT RESCUE—"THIS WAY! THIS WAY! TO THE WINDOW!"—FLY-BY-NIGHT ESCAPES—THE TERRIBLE FATE OF HIS MISTRESS—CHARLOTTE IS IN A BAD TEMPER—KATE HAMILTON'S IS CLOSED—"LET'S GO TO BARNS'S, FOR I MEAN TO GET AS TIGHT AS AN OWL!"

THE people in the room began to comment upon the strange scene which had just taken place in the fashionable night-house.

"Unpleasant affair!" said one.

"Dem'd awkward for the wobber!" lisped a young ensign with a silky moustache.

Charlotte Saunders looked intensely annoyed. She had been completely taken in by the insidious stranger, who so strangely turned out to be a detective.

It was a very humiliating fact for her to dwell upon.

It must seem to every one that she had acted in bad faith in bringing him to the night-house.

Of course no one would believe Inspector Wyman's account of the affair.

The proprietors of the place, the waiters, the people therein assembled—every one, in short—must look upon her as an accomplice, who had been bribed by the police to betray the confidence which had hitherto been reposed in her.

Charlotte even thought that she noticed looks of aversion. Certainly, threatening glances were bent upon her.

Agnes was as much annoyed as Charlotte, and she said—

"Oh! Charlotte, fancy our having brought a detective to this place!"

"Oh, don't talk to me!"

"Why not?"

"Because I'm in a rage."

"Are you?"

"Can't you see?"

"Isn't it dreadful, though?" persisted Agnes.

"I wish you would hold your tongue! I am in such a state of mind, I can't trust myself to speak to anybody."

"Well, you need not be so cross with me! I am sure I couldn't help it. It was not my fault, now was it?"

"Oh, it was nobody's fault but my own, I suppose!"

As she spoke a commotion was heard in the passage, slight and muffled, as it were, at first, but gradually increasing. It might have been remarked that during the brief space which elapsed before the noise we have spoken of was heard, that all the waiters, with one exception, had left the room. Where they had gone to was a mystery, but that they had gone somewhere or other was plainly evident to the meanest comprehension.

The faces of one or two people who were connected with the establishment were gravely anxious. Somehow or other a sort of gloom seemed to hang over the assembled company. Suddenly, a rush, a stamping of feet, and all the evidences of a scuffle fell upon the ear.

Those people who had left the room with a view to leaving the place altogether, came hurrying back in great trepidation. There might have been a score of them; they flocked into the room like so many panic-stricken sheep.

They reached the centre of the apartment.

People crowded round them, and asked questions.

Then there was a great confusion of tongues. A perfect Babel, or a second Pentecost, or gift of tongues, for English, French, German, and Spanish were spoken in different parts of the room by the representatives of those countries.

The noise in the passage increased.

Hoarse cries were heard.

Blows resounded, and a dull noise now and then told of a severe stroke evidently given by the oaken truncheon of a policeman.

It was as the sound of many men in mortal combat struggling together in a confined space, and fighting as only desperate men do fight.

The voice of a woman, raised in lamentation, was heard. Then followed a shrill, piercing cry, such as one associates with some deed of bloodshed—with *death*. As the echoing cadences of this shriek floated with melancholy sadness upon the impure air of the casino, every voice was hushed, heads were inclined forward to listen, and fingers held up to enjoin silence—for a moment all was still.

A sigh emanated from many a breast, and joined the fetid atmosphere. It was a requiem to a departed spirit.

After this momentary pause, the riot again commenced with fresh vigour, with renewed ardour.

Suddenly, with a noise and a rush like that of a whirlwind, a man ran into the crowded and brilliantly lighted room.

He was covered with blood.

His clothes were torn, and he presented a sorry spectacle.

The people made way for him. For one moment he hesitated, and glanced around him with the look of a tiger or a cougar.

There was then heard, from the other end of the room—

"This way! this way! To the window, quick!"

The crowd opened to allow him to pass, which he did with incredible swiftness.

Like a flash of lightning he came and went.

It was Fly-by-night—the man whom Inspector Wyman had so cleverly arrested for the great diamond robbery in Regent-street—the man who had been the friend and associate of Marmaduke Wilson, the Surrey Wolf, and the dwarf Stubbles—the man who had struck the unfortunate woman who was with him at the time Wyman made the arrest, so foul a blow in the face, that one and all cried shame upon him.

But now that seemed to be forgotten; every one moved on one side, and seemed anxious that he should escape.

The public generally take the side of the culprit against the police; and if a man breaks from prison, people usually say—"Oh, I hope the poor fellow will not be caught!"

This is not right, but it is the prevailing sentiment of a maudlin age, where capital punishments are looked upon as something dreadful, and to be abolished, and where tickets-of-leave are granted unsparingly to the greatest criminals.

When Fly-by-night reached the extremity of the room, he found a window opened for him by the man who had called to him to come in that direction.

There was no area. All he had to do was to leap upon the pavement, and he was free.

With a leap and a bound he dashed through the casement, and stood in the street.

His hands were manacled, but he was free.

Scarcely had he made his successful spring, when the window was shut to, the curtains drawn, and everything was in its normal condition once more.

With such celerity was this done that only a small fraction of a minute had passed away since Fly-by-night first made his appearance.

Soon it was evident that a rescue had been attempted, and actually made.

The police came into the room, driving the waiters and door-porters before them.

No sooner had they entered, however, than the gas was turned out, and a scene of the most indescribable confusion ensued.

It was pitch dark.

Most of the visitors, both male and female, stayed where they were.

Some who tried to grope their way out in the darkness were rudely repulsed by the police, who had taken possession of the doorway.

After a time Inspector Wyman succeeded in lighting the gas.

But his prisoner had gone.

The bird had flown; and although he searched every corner of the room, searched the cupboards and the cellars, searched the house from top to bottom, he was nowhere to be seen.

His rage and disappointment at so unexpected a reverse were very poignant; but he concealed his private feelings as best he could, making a virtue of necessity.

Splawger and Rascally Jack he took in charge, owing to their having taken a conspicuous part in the rescue.

The waiters he could not identify, so they escaped scot free.

At last the inspector retired, with traces of great and infinite disgust upon his countenance.

All he could do was to place a couple of policemen as sentries before the door, and retire, with the rest of his force, to Scotland-yard, discomfited.

But while this was going on a melancholy cortège was wending its way along Whitehall towards Westminster Hospital.

It was the body of the wretched woman, whose only fault—whose one misfortune—was that she loved a brute in the semblance of humanity.

It was the mistress of Fly-by-night, the thief, the robber, the pickpocket, the burglar, the *murderer*.

There may be some sort of romance about Jack Shepherd, Dick Turpin, and the Knights of the Road, but there is very, very little about your murderer-thief—no romance, no chivalry.

The poor thing was frightfully disfigured.

In his blind fury Fly-by-night had, in the passage, dashed his handcuffed hands in the woman's face, mutilating her horribly, and dashing her head with such violence against the wall that her skull was fractured.

When she reached the hospital, the house-surgeon looked at her, and said—

"She may live two hours, but then, God rest her soul!"

Inspector Wyman was a spectator of this brutal outrage of a mad and selfish poltroon; and he exclaimed, with vehemence—

"He shall swing for this, or my name's not Wyman."

They took her into one of the wards. They laid her upon a small bedstead, where a paralytic had died of inanition the night before.

They stripped her of her gaudy, meretricious finery, and laid it by—she would want it no more.

There was a bracelet on her wrist—it had been stolen. Very pretty was this golden toy.

The rubies with which it was profusely set and studded had, strange to say, lost all their brilliancy—dull and colourless were they.

There is a superstition—a tradition—call it what you will—that rubies pale before misfortune. Here was a strange confirmation of a monkish fable. This bracelet they did not touch.

There were rings upon her fingers—some of them containing stones of price—and she wore a wedding-ring, the symbol of matrimony.

Clinging to a respectability she had for ever forfeited—the mistress of a thief—she yet tried to deceive her aching heart into the belief that she was an honest woman in the eyes of a critical world.

The surgeons did what they could for her.

They brought out plaster and strapped it round her in various places—they gave her stimulating mixtures. But she never spoke more; and ere day broke she was a corpse, and, in a few hours, would lie upon the table in the dissecting room, ripe and ready for the knife.

Such was the end of one of the women of London.

Soon after the police had taken their departure the night-house was closed.

The people turned out to go elsewhere, and the business brought to a close for that night.

Agnes and Charlotte walked up Panton-street arm-in-arm.

"Well, Charlotte, if this is the sort of thing that goes on in night-houses, I must say, people who frequent them get plenty of excitement."

"I never saw such a thing before," replied Charlotte.

"Oh!"

"No. It is quite an adventure. But I wish I had not been mixed up in it."

"So do I; but it wasn't your fault."

"What a brute that Fly-by-night fellow was to smash the woman up as he did."

"Yes; I'd hang him for it," replied Agnes.

"It would serve him right. I'm sorry they collared old Splawger and Rascally Jack off, though."

"What will they get?"

"Oh! fine them forty bob, perhaps, or give them a week. They'll do that on their heads."

"Well, I think all we have seen to-night is very disgraceful."

"Do you. What did you expect to see in the Haymarket?"

"Nothing very good, of course."

"Well, then, don't be a fool."

"A fool!"

"Yes; don't be an idiot. You came to see a little life, and you've seen it. And who are you more than anybody else that you should set up your back?"

"Well—" began Agnes.

"Oh! I forgot!" said Charlotte. "I forgot about Lady Marchmont. Perhaps your ladyship would like to return to the arms of his lordship!"

Agnes sobbed and replied through her tears—

"Yes—yes—yes. I should—I should, indeed."

"Well, I'm in a bad temper. You needn't cry like that. I didn't mean anything, only I hate a woman who's nothing particular herself, to go saying places are not good enough for her, and all such as that."

Agnes still sobbed.

"Oh! come on. I'm going to Barns's to get a drain. I mean to get as tight as an owl before I go home. You've never seen me blind drunk, have you?"

"No."

"Oh! it'll be a caution to you when you do."

And the two girls went across the Haymarket, in the direction of the "Wyndham Arms."

<h3>CHAPTER LXIII.</h3>

BARNS'S—PATSY—MR. WYNDHAM BEHIND THE BAR—AN ALTERCATION—AN EXTRAORDINARY BONNET—ALL THE COLOURS OF THE RAINBOW—SNUFFLES—HOW TO GET A BOTTLE OF MOSELLE WITHOUT PAYING FOR IT.

AGNES was rather alarmed at the reckless state of mind into which Charlotte Saunders had fallen; but as she had come out with her, and could not go home without her, she resolved to stay with her and see that she did not get into any trouble, if she could help it.

Agnes had seen a great deal that night in a few hours; and she was a little curious to know what the place Charlotte had spoken of as Barns's was like.

She conjectured that it was a night-house, somewhat similar to those she had already been in; but without asking any questions, she followed her companion, who, having crossed over to the west side of the Haymarket, led the way up a small court.

A door in the wall was opened for them by a shock-headed ruffian, whom Charlotte addressed as Patsy.

"How are you, mum?" said Patsy, in return to her salutation.

Charlotte made no answer, and was just about to descend two steps which admitted those without into the sacred precincts of the bar, when Patsy exclaimed, "Wyndham's here to-night!"

"Eh!" said Charlotte.

"Yes, and he is a-going it."

"Come on, Agnes," said Charlotte. "Wyndham's here; we shall have some fun."

Passing through the door, the young women found themselves in a brilliantly lighted room, which was filled almost to overflowing with men and women—talking and gesticulating in the loudest and wildest manner.

Two waiters ran about, pushing their way through the throng as well as they could, attending to the wants of the customers.

The scene was like Pandemonium in its cups; and Agnes hesitated after she had crossed the threshold. What she had seen before was nothing to what she now witnessed.

A partition and a curtain divided this room and its bar from the other part of the public-house, which faced the Haymarket.

None but the initiated would have imagined the scene that was taking place such a short distance from a public thoroughfare.

Charlotte whispered something to Agnes, which the noise and din prevailing at the time prevented her from hearing, but from her manner she gathered that she was about to push her way to the bar, and was beckoning her to follow.

Their progress was rather difficult—no one would make way for anybody else, and the women resented a push, however slight, with rather strong language, and occasionally a blow.

Charlotte was not in the humour, however, that night, to be thwarted by any one; and it was easily apparent, from her appearance and her manner, that she would stick at nothing.

One woman in particular seemed resolved to impede Charlotte's progress as much as she could.

She was a little woman, who possessed no good looks to speak of; but who based her pretensions to notice on the fact of her wearing all the colours of the rainbow.

Her bonnet was black, and it was trimmed with blue and yellow, with a dash of white here and there, by way of variety, while quite a nosegay of flowers flourished in the front.

And these flowers included amongst them almost every celebrated botanical favourite—from a rose down to a sprig of sweetwilliam.

Her dress was a pea-green silk, and she wore a light grey cloak.

Her gloves were mauve; but it was to be observed that they fitted her badly, and had been worn on more than one previous occasion.

Charlotte gave this woman, who had her back turned towards her, a push, and exclaimed at the same time, "Get out of my way."

"Out of your way!" said the woman, turning round; "who are you?"

"I'll soon let you know who I am," replied Charlotte.

"Will you?"

"Yes, I will."

At this moment, Charlotte happened to look up. She perceived the extraordinary floral combination, and cried out, laughingly, "God help us!"

"What's the matter?" said the woman; "you seem as if you had found something."

"Oh! oh!" said Charlotte, laughing more than ever.

"Well, you must be a silly fool to go laughing like that at nothing at all."

"Nothing! do you call that nothing?"

"That! what?"

"Why, the bonnet! Oh! oh!" replied Charlotte.

Agnes had followed her friend, and was close behind her; she had overheard this altercation, and could not help being amused at the singular spectacle the bonnet presented.

She wished, however, Charlotte would move on; for they were in the vicinity of a large fire, and the heat, at such close quarters, was anything but pleasant.

"Where did you get it?" at length asked Charlotte, when she had recovered her gravity sufficiently to be able to speak.

"What's that to you?" replied the woman, colouring up, as if she was afraid that there was something wrong somewhere.

"What's that to me? Oh! a great deal."

"What?"

"Well, I think I should like to have one like it."

"Would you?" replied the little woman, angrily, hitting Charlotte in the face. "Would you like to have another one like that?"

Without saying a word, Charlotte sprang at her adversary, and dexterously, as if she had performed the feat on more than one occasion before, tore the remarkable bonnet from the woman's head, and flourished it for a moment in the air. Then she walked to the fire-place, and threw it on the fire.

The flames leaped around, and soon wrapped it in a fiery embrace, as if they considered it a good joke.

The little woman was too much astonished to do anything until her treasure was reduced to a piece of cinder.

She then played nervously with a glass she held in her hand, and looked as if she were about to hurl it at Charlotte, but a woman, who seemed to be a friend of hers, tried to calm her.

She was a common-looking woman, and had the misfortune to speak through her nose.

"My dear, don't put yourself out," she said.

"But my bonnet?"

"Ah! it was a beauty—but never mind."

"It was a beauty," cried Charlotte, coming up to them. They made no reply.

"Something like you," I suppose.

The little woman was going to say something, but her friend laid her hand upon her arm, and said—

"I wouldn't talk to such low women if I were you, dear."

"Low women!" repeated Charlotte. "Why, you dirty old rag-shop!"

"Rag-shop!"

"Yes. Why don't you speak through your nose?" said Charlotte.

The woman muttered something about low wretches.

"Speak out, Snuffles," said Charlotte.

Agnes could not help laughing at this. Charlotte evidently had the best of the altercation.

"I'll give it you!" cried Snuffles.

"Eh, what?" said Charlotte, pretending not to hear.

"I'll make you remember me."

"No necessity for that, I am sure. Couldn't forget you if I tried, Snuffles."

"I'll make you——"

"No—don't!"

"I'll give you something you'll carry to your grave."

"It had better be a coffin, then, Snuffles. I hear they are likely to rise in price soon. It might be useful to me."

Snuffles had put herself in such a passion that she could hardly speak, and she had talked so much and so loudly through her nose, that that ill-used organ could stand it no longer without entering a protest. Snuffles sneezed.

"Sign of rain when a cat sneezes," said Charlotte.

"You hook it," cried Snuffles, "or it will be the worse for you."

"Will it? Sorry to hear that."

"I'll make the place too hot to hold you."

"No necessity for that, I'm as warm as a woolpack already," replied Charlotte. "You wouldn't be any the worse for being a little cooler."

"You low str——," began Snuffles.

"Now, don't," interrupted Charlotte; "I've just come from Billingsgate."

"You may go to blazes," said Snuffles.

"Oh! Snuffles, I'm ashamed of you!" replied Charlotte, playfully.

"My name ain't Snuffles.

"Isn't it?"

"No."

"Well, it will do, I suppose."

"Perhaps that will do for you," cried the little woman who had been robbed of her bonnet, and who now saw her friend being made fun of.

As she spoke she threw the tumbler she had held nervously in her hand all the time at Charlotte.

Her intention was very plainly to hit Charlotte, and do her as much injury as she could.

But her hand was very unsteady. So much so, that instead of hitting her, as she intended to, she struck one of the waiters on the head.

His skull was made of good material, as it did not break, but it evidently caused him considerable pain.

In addition to the blow he had received, he was further annoyed by some of the gin-and-water the glass contained going into his ear, and afterwards gliding gracefully down his neck.

Rushing up to the little woman, he laid hold of her by the arm, and exclaimed—

"You shied that tumbler at me, did you? Think I'm going to have my 'ed pretty well cracked and gin-and-water put in my ear 'ole for nothing?"

"I didn't shy it at you."

"It 'it me."

"I'm very sorry."

"Werry sorry; I should say so. But it's no good; I'll have to put you out."

"No, you wont," said Snuffles.

"And you along with her," cried the waiter. "I'll be shut on the pair of you."

"That's right, Harry," said Charlotte Saunders. "Put them both out. They are low, quarrelsome women. They have been making a disturbance for some time past. I saw them shy the glass at you; and one of them, Snuffles, said—'It was a d—— fine joke.' How you can let such women into the place I can't imagine."

Snuffles ground her teeth with rage, and shook her fist at Charlotte, who took no notice of her.

Another waiter came to the first one's assistance, and in spite of their struggles, the two women were ignominiously expelled from the establishment, and Patsy was strictly enjoined not to allow them to come in again.

The waiter wiped himself down with a cloth, saying, in an injured tone—

"Think I'm going to have my 'ed pretty well cracked, and gin-and-water put in my ear 'ole for nothing?"

So common were these rows and expulsions, that the people assembled took little or no notice of it.

Agnes and Charlotte laughed till they were fit to cry almost, and then they went on to the bar, where Charlotte met some women she knew.

Over the bar, written in large letters, was the following inscription—"The Wyndham Arms."

An elderly woman was behind the bar, drawing beer and gin, and various other liquors.

Charlotte spoke to her, and was about to answer her question of "What will you have to-night?" when a noise, as of some one descending a staircase to the right, was heard; and in a short time a young man, with dark hair parted in the middle, rather stout than otherwise, with a little hair on his upper lip, not at all bad-looking, but with a restless—almost vacant—expression of countenance at times, and a very unpleasant habit of twitching his lip nervously, made his appearance; and pushing those who were near him rudely on one side, entered the bar, and proceeded to officiate as barman.

"That's Wyndham," cried Charlotte to Agnes.

He went about his novel occupation with great earnestness, as if the situation really belonged to him, and he was trying to do his duty as well as he was able.

"What for you?" he asked, speaking to Charlotte.

"Well, some Moselle, I think, if you intend to stand it."

"I'm not here to stand anything; I'm here to give you what you want."

"Well, I want some Moselle."

"You'll have to pay for it, then."

"Oh no, I shan't! I never pay for anything when a gentleman is talking to me," said Charlotte.

Wyndham moved away to attend to some one else, and drew some things for the waiters, who paid him over the bar.

"Have you been driving any engines lately?" asked Charlotte.

"No," he replied. "Have you?"

"I don't know. You had better ask my friends the Llewellyns, in Duke-street, St. James's."

Wyndham scowled.

"I say, don't slobber," cried Charlotte, laughing.

"There—there, that'll do," said the old woman who had been in the bar all the time, and who did not like so good a customer as Mr. Wyndham to be annoyed.

His eccentricities were nothing to her or to the establishment, as long as he paid for them.

"What did you say you wanted?" said Wyndham to Charlotte, as if he wished to escape her persecution.

"Now you are listening to reason. You had better give me some Moselle, I think."

Wyndham took down a bottle of Moselle from a shelf, uncorked it, and placed it before Charlotte and her friend Agnes.

CHAPTER LXIV.

GLOOMY FANCIES ARE SUCCEEDED BY MERRY MOMENTS—
DON'T GO MAD—SANE OR INSANE—BROAD ACRES AND
ACCOMPLISHED COURTESANS—THE AMATEUR BARMAN
RETIRES IN DISGUST—ON THE TRACK—WYMAN AND
THE FOX AGAIN—"WHERE, WHERE SHALL WE GO?"

THE girls drank the sparkling wine, and each glass she took made Charlotte Saunders more reckless and more madly hilarious.

The effect upon Agnes, after imbibing the generous beverage, was different. She felt depressed and sick at heart. She wished herself miles away from the giddy throng surrounding her. She was at war with herself. She blamed herself for many things when she was but the child of chance—a blind mole, as it were, groping in the dark—searching for a clue to guide her to the open daylight once more.

But that clue was in the hands of Fortune; and until the fickle mistress of her tangled, complicated destiny chose to give it to her, she might grow grey in the search.

Agnes was sorry that she had ever penetrated to the haunts of low and fallen women, in one of which she now found herself.

Everything around her seemed so hollow and unsubstantial—it was like a masque of death, and all the people round about her were but the poor and sorry mummies.

The gay but unreal laugh—the wan and sickly smile—the loud and blasphemous oath—the feeble ribaldry, so dreadful, so sickening, when proceeding from feminine lips—the flaunting air—the occasional sigh and half-repressed tear—the entire absence of that self-respect that ought to characterize every word and every movement of a woman, were all—all so distasteful, unpleasant to Agnes, that she longed to be at peace anywhere, she cared not where.

At one time she thought that even the gloomy precincts and sepulchral catacombs of a churchyard would be preferable to an existence passed as only too many were passing theirs, and in whose society she had been brought by Charlotte, who in her friend's estimation was but a moth fluttering round the fatal flame, too soon to scorch her wings and lay her charred and withered trunk in the transparent globe beneath it.

But as she drank more wine her tenebrious fancies were eliminated, and her spirits rose once more.

She caught the infection of the merry moment, and joined Charlotte in a loud laugh which bespoke the vacant mind which gave it birth.

Charlotte continued her badinage with the gentleman barman who attended to the wants of every one with so much cordiality and promptness.

At last he got tired of his occupation, which was no sinecure; and, jerking a pot of ale down upon the counter, he exclaimed—

"I've had enough of this fun!"

"Have you?" said Charlotte.

"Yes. I think I shall shut up now."

"Barns ought to give you a medal, I should think."

"I shouldn't mind. I'll back myself to work as hard as you can talk."

"Will you?"

"Yes."

"But talking is a woman's privilege, you know."

"You make it your privilege, anyhow."

"Now, don't get angry, because—"

"Oh, chain up," he answered angrily.

"Don't go mad, because I shall be afraid of you if you do."

He looked angrily at her.

"I shall telegraph to Colney Hatch," said Charlotte.

"Don't be a fool."

"Perhaps they keep strait-waistcoats on the premises."

In order to escape from his indefatigable tormentor, the young man in whose sanity all England, Ireland, and Scotland took so deep an interest some time back, made a

rush up the stairs and took refuge in a room above, where he could indulge in a game of blind hooky or lansquenet, with a moral certainty of rising a loser by many pounds—that is, always provided the luck was not with him but against him.

Agnes was laughing at the undignified disappearance of the quondam owner of those broad acres in Norfolk which the ability of a well-known courtesan assisted him so soon to dissipate.

Whether he had occasion to congratulate himself on his acquaintance with so accomplished a "Woman of London" is a question for himself to decide. There is no accounting for taste, and it is said that some people of the Gladstone school prefer a glass of sour French wine to a foaming tankard of English ale.

Agnes was still standing, with a smile on her lips and a mixture of spirits-and-water in her hand, when a middle-aged man, who may be very well described as of the shabby genteel sort, insinuated himself through the throng, and going to the bar called for a glass of whisky—hot, sweet, and strong. He was followed by another not quite so respectable in appearance, but with a great amount of sagacity discernible in his face. Nor was his companion, who had preceded him, wanting in facial evidences of acuteness.

When these two men were supplied with what they wanted, they commenced a conversation in a low voice, but they were so close to Agnes that she couldn't help overhearing part of their conversation.

The one who seemed to be the subordinate of the first one, said—

"Long odds on the covey having written Walker agin his name."

"I don't know; cannot tell yet. I've seen 'em come back lots of times, but there's hardly a move on the board that fellow's not up to."

"You're right there."

"But we'll spot him."

"Spot him! I rather reckon we will," returned the superior. "My professional reputation's bound up in that man's capture."

Agnes listened intently to this dialogue. She could not help thinking she had heard the speaker's voice before somewhere, and his features did not seem altogether unfamiliar to her.

Suddenly he spoke again.

She bent all her faculties upon the task of listening.

"Marmaduke Wilson!"

"What?" she was on the point of saying, but she repressed the inclination with an effort.

"Marmaduke Wilson was the first of the gang I nabbed; and that go was all through his spoony woman, a young Jewess who split upon him."

"Ah! I remember. And the Surrey Wolf's gone across the Herring Pond a fourteen year journey."

"The Dwarf's the only one at large, except Fly-by-night, and I mean to let him bide."

"He's gone into the undertaking line, I've heard tell."

"Yes. He's getting an honester livelihood now than he ever did before. But lor', there are tricks in that trade, as well as every other."

Agnes now knew that the two men who were talking close by her were detectives.

One she recognised as the inspector who had endeavoured to arrest Fly-by-night in the night-house called Kate Hamilton's.

The fact was, Inspector Wyman had gone back to Scotland-yard, in order to deceive any one who might be following him. He then changed his dress, picked up the Finsbury Fox, and left the office by the private entrance in Whitehall place.

He never allowed himself to sleep when he thought there was the least chance of following up his victim, and he imagined that very likely Fly-by-night would brazen out the affair by hanging about the vicinity of the Haymarket, as less likely to be closely watched than Whitechapel or Spitalfields.

Wyman was a terrible foe when he was fairly aroused, and anybody who was acquainted with the inspector's character for indomitable perseverance, would have bet a hundred to one on Fly-by-night's capture eventually.

Agnes shuddered when she found that she was so close to her first—her real husband's—enemy.

She did not as yet know that Wyman was the Count Val

de Grace's ally, and that he had accompanied that noble-man to Holland, or she would have been more alarmed than she was.

She had learned one thing conclusively from Wyman's conversation, and that was, that Marmaduke Wilson had been betrayed into the hands of the police by Miriam Moss, and she did not now regret the shocking injury she had done her. She even felt a wild, fierce feeling of satisfied vengeance thrill through her.

"There is another little job I have on hand," said Wyman to the Fox.

"What's that?"

"Why, you know we have only just come back from Holland after that girl the French count was so sweet on."

"Yes."

"Well, the count has offered me a handsome reward if I find her, and I never mind killing two, or three, or half-a-dozen birds with one stone."

"That's my motto."

"Not a bad one either, I can tell you. Well, after we put the count into a cab, you know we went back to see the stewardess."

"We did so."

"And I did all I could to pump something out of her."

"Well!"

"She told me about that other girl—the captain's friend."

"I know."

"The one who whipped the count's young tit away so cleverly from under our noses."

"Well, 'twasn't badly done."

"Now there's no question about her being a little fishy."

"Of course not."

"In fact nothing better than the women who form our earthly paradise at the present moment in this charming garden."

"Bear garden, I should think," growled the Finsbury Fox.

"Something like it."

"But what of it?"

"Don't you see?"

"No, I don't; else I shouldn't ask."

"Well, you needn't be grumpy."

"All serene; go ahead."

"What more likely," said Wyman, "than that she should be in one of these dens with her fast friend?"

"Stunnin'," cried the Fox, rubbing his hands, "stunnin'."

"You think it a good idea, then?"

"Stunnin', I tell you."

"Well, while we are looking after Fly-by-night, let's have an eye to this beauty."

"How'll you work it, supposin' we light upon her?"

"In this way," replied Wyman: "I have a warrant in my pocket to arrest her for an attack on Count Val de Grace, with intent to do grievous bodily harm."

"It's a precious bit of bisness," said the Fox.

"Well, it ain't as square as it might be, as far as we are concerned. But then look at the swag there is to be made."

"That's true."

"We should never lay by a penny for our old age, if we didn't take a chance when it came in our way," said Wyman.

"No. We must study ourselves," replied the Fox, trying to look virtuous.

"Should you know her again?" asked the Inspector.

"I think I should."

"Should you?"

"Well, I wouldn't swear, but I think I've got her phiz pretty well drawn out in my mind."

As Agnes heard this, she thanked her stars that she had been standing with her back to the speakers all the time they had been conversing.

Plucking Charlotte's sleeve, she said, trembling all over—

"Come outside. For God's sake, come. If you have the very least atom of regard for me, come, I beseech you. Don't stop for anything."

"What is it?" asked Charlotte, in amaze.

"Oh, come—come. I will tell you outside."

"Oh, what a funny girl you are!" said Charlotte, following her out of the room and into the little passage.

Then keeping close up against the wall, Agnes told Charlotte all that she had heard. And Charlotte agreed with her in thinking that they would be safer elsewhere than in the Wyndham Arms.

Inspector Wyman was undoubtedly clever, and so was the Finsbury Fox, but they had forgotten two wholesome maxims—that silence is golden, while speech is but silver; and that walls have ears.

Charlotte and Agnes walked hurriedly up the Haymarket without any fixed idea and without any settled purpose. Charlotte was drunk, and Agnes was shaking with terror, apprehension, doubt, and fear.

CHAPTER LXV.

45, STRAND—THE COCK AND BOTTLE—RUM AND MILK —MARIA ONCE MORE—RUNNING THE RULE—HOW TO GET EGGS AND BACON—MARIA EXCHANGES BAD EGGS FOR GOOD ONES—CHRISTMAS ARRIVES BEFORE ITS TIME, AND THE SNOW COVERS THE HOUSETOPS.

DURING the evening there had been a decided change in the weather, and as the two girls walked along the street, they wrapped their shawls closer around them, as the cold was intense.

Owing to their just having left a warm room, they felt the change more severely than they otherwise would have done.

The air was clear and crisp, and a few snow-flakes fell upon the ground, heralding what was speedily to follow.

Agnes shivered, and she could not help thinking of the lovely summer weather that had passed away, and of one day in particular, when Marmaduke Wilson had whispered words of love in her ears, in the gardens of Hampton-court palace.

But now the winter had come upon them.

How many changes had taken place since Agnes first began the battle of life in company with Charlotte Saunders, the woman in whose society she had once more been thrown, by a combination of the strangest incidents.

All at once the snow began to descend heavily.

The air was bitter cold, and a white sheet seemed to have been laid on everything. There was no wind, so the flakes floated steadily downwards.

"This is pleasant," exclaimed Charlotte, who did not feel so intoxicated in the sharp, fresh air, as she did in the close room she had just left.

"Pleasant!" replied Agnes, with a shiver. "I am of a different opinion. The old woman is picking her geese rather early this year."

Charlotte made no answer, but called a cab from the rank.

"What are you going to do?" asked Agnes, a little surprised.

She thought they were going home, and they had such a short distance to go before they reached Charlotte's lodgings, that she wondered what her friend wanted a cab for.

"Well, if you want to know particularly, I am going to do three or four things."

"What?"

"Get into the cab first, and I will tell you."

The cab now drove up. The man opened the door.

The two girls got in, and the cabman asked where he was to drive them.

"45, Strand," said Charlotte.

"45, mum, yes, mum," replied the cabman, and getting on his box again, he drove off.

"What in the world are you going down to the Strand for?" inquired Agnes. "You are doing such strange things, Charlotte, that I really don't think you ought to be out any longer. You are hardly responsible for your actions. Let us go home, there's a dear. Let me tell the man to drive to your lodgings. Shall I?"

"My dear woman," answered Charlotte, patronizingly, "I know I'm drunk, but I'm not such a fool as you take me to be. I know perfectly well what I'm about."

"Do you? Well, I'm glad to hear it."

"Don't alarm yourself," said Charlotte.

"But I should feel more satisfied if you would explain."

"Explain! All right, I can easily do that."

"Go on, then."

"In the first place, you want to know why I got into a cab?"

"Yes."

"Very well, then, I will tell you. One of my reasons was that Wyman might have followed us out of the place we have just left, and pitched upon us at an inconvenient moment. He evidently either does not know your features very well, or he did not have a good look at you. Probably the latter. You were standing with your back towards him, were you not?"

"Yes, I was."

"Ah! that accounts for it, then. But if he had met us he would very likely have found you out, and have carried you off to that precious scoundrel, Count Val What's-his-name. You know who I mean—the frog-eater."

"Yes," replied Agnes, "there is a great deal of sense in what you say."

"My second reason was, I object to getting wet, and I have a very strong aversion to getting frozen."

"Frozen!"

"Yes. I should have been a perambulating iceberg in about five minutes."

"Well, what else?"

"Oh! a good deal."

"But why go to 45, Strand?"

"Because it's the only place to get good gin at. Do you mean to say that you have lived in London so long, and never heard of that place?"

"Well, I must confess that I have not," said Agnes, with a smile.

Charlotte looked at her with an expression of pity, as if she was deserving of it for her lamentable ignorance.

As they passed through Charing-cross they heard a clock strike.

"One, two, three, four, five," repeated Charlotte, "and a bore. It is too early; they will not be open yet. Confound it! I'm done out of my gin."

"No great loss, either. You have had enough, I think."

"Ah! what you think doesn't matter to anybody."

"Doesn't it?"

"Not a bit."

"Well, don't get angry over it. What will you do?"

"Oh! I know."

"What?"

"Well, I wont be done. We'll go to the Cock and Bottle, and have some rum-and-milk."

"Where's that?"

"Oh! not far; a little higher up in the Strand."

"Is it a nice place? asked Agnes;" "and are you sure of getting in there?"

"Yes, it's always open."

Charlotte let down the window, and told the cabman where to go; and in a short time they stopped at a public-house.

The two girls got out, went into the place, and called for two glasses of rum-and-milk, which were duly given to them.

Then they re-entered the cab, and were driven back to their lodgings.

The snow came down faster and faster, and the autumn seemed not only to have expired, but to have been laid out and covered with a winding-sheet.

After the rum-and-milk, Charlotte entirely succumbed to the force of her potations, which had, during the evening, been more numerous than select.

Agnes took the latch-key out of her pocket, and opened the door, afterwards helping her into the house.

She then dismissed the cabman, paying him liberally for his services.

But although she gave him three times his fare, he grumbled and growled over it like a discontented dog over a bone.

But such is the nature of cabmen, whose ingratitude is proverbial.

Soon afterwards the young women were fast asleep, and it was late—very late in the day, before they woke.

Maria did not venture to call them, because she knew that Charlotte never allowed herself to be disturbed.

When she got tipsy she always liked to sleep as long as she could, because she had an idea that it helped to restore her wasted energies, and her somewhat shattered constitution, which was none the worse for being a little invigorated now and then.

Maria once, in an evil and imprudent moment, had the hardihood to rouse the Sleeping Beauty, but a ponderous bolster, thrown with great precision, had the effect of causing her to beat a retreat with all the quickness imaginable.

When Charlotte woke up she did not leave Maria long in ignorance of her recovered vitality.

That ill-used, under-paid, and over-worked domestic was sitting in her kitchen anointing her somewhat elephantine hands with a composition known as goose-grease, the hands in question being afflicted with chaps in cold weather and suffering much in consequence.

Consequently Maria did not make her appearance so quickly as she might have done; indeed that worthy female was generally what is denominated a slow coach.

She had once had an attack of rheumatism, and the malady had taken such an affection for her that it refused to leave her, and obstinately settled in her left hip.

This caused her to do what school-boys call "dot and carry one," and her progress up and down stairs was not of the quickest.

The imperious beauty upstairs rang the bell a second time, and with such violence that the rope came down with a run, and she lay in bed with it in her hand, regarding the long coil of rope mournfully, not to say tearfully.

Maria opened the door with the assurance peculiar to a London servant, and exclaimed with a very good assumption of innocence—

"Did you ring, mum?"

"Ring? well, I like that!"

Maria looked the incarnation of every virtue.

"Yes, I did ring," continued Charlotte, "and I not only rang, but I pulled the bell-rope down."

"Sorry for that, mum."

"Are you? Well, you'll be a deal sorrier before I've done with you. What are you standing there like a fool for? Why don't you speak?"

"Yes, mum."

"Yes, mum? That's all you can say, you silly beggar. Now why don't you go and get some white satin? Don't you see I'm dying for a drop of gin."

"Money, mum," said Maria.

"Money? what a harpy you are! I haven't got any money. You must borrow a bob from somebody, or stick it up. They'll tick you; I should think they ought to. You're a pretty good customer."

"Yes, mum."

"Now off you go, old hop and go one."

"Yes, mum."

"And don't let the grass grow under your feet, or it'll be bad luck for you."

"Yes, mum."

"What time is it?"

"Four o'clock."

"Well, bring some lights up. I've had a jolly sleep."

Maria went away to execute her errand, and Charlotte shook Agnes, and woke her up.

"How have you slept," asked Charlotte.

"Oh, I feel so bad," replied Agnes, in a faint voice.

"Yes, I suppose you do."

"Oh, don't talk to me."

"Oh, nonsense! Who are you that you should not be talked to?"

The only answer Agnes gave was a groan.

"Besides, it will do you good. You must rouse yourself."

Agnes moaned.

"I've sent for a drop of gin, that'll make you as right as ninepence; but I suppose that thundering old fool, Maria, will be an hour getting it."

"Has Maria gone for it?"

"Yes. There are only two things Maria is fit for."

"What are they?"

"Why to fetch a drop of gin, and go to the pawn-shop for one."

As she said this, Maria again made her appearance, and produced a bottle containing half-a-pint of gin.

"How did you get it?" demanded Charlotte.

"Cheeked an old bloke for it," replied Maria.

"No?" said Charlotte, much pleased.

"I did, though. He was standing in the bar, and he asked me what I would have; I said 'a drop of gin, if you please,' and he stood it like a bird; and then I said, 'I think as you're so generous I'll have a little drop in a bottle.'

"Oh yes," he replied; "have what you like." So I asked the bar-maid—the squint-eyed one, you know—for half-a-pint of Old Tom; and when I got it, I lammased."

"You'll do, Maria," said Charlotte, in admiration. "The best of you is that you're a stunner when anybody is hard up. What do you think she did one day, Agnes?"

AGNES SURVEYS THE MYSTERIOUS CHAMBER.

"I don't know—what?" replied Agnes, languidly.

"Why, she saw a man who was tight in the street, and she helped him into a cab, and ran the rule while she was about it."

"Ran the rule! what's that?"

"Why, she found a little loose silver in his waistcoat-pocket, and she thought she might just as well be paid for her trouble."

"Do you mean to say she took the poor man's money?"

"Took it!—yes. She'd have been a fool if she hadn't taken it."

"But that's thieving!" said Agnes, much shocked.

"Oh, no!—running the rule's fair enough. Men shouldn't get drunk; they are fair game for a woman when they do. Why, look at the police; there is hardly a man in the force who hasn't got a watch, and how do you suppose they get them?"

"I don't know."

"You don't suppose they buy them out of their eighteen bob a week—do you?"

"No; not exactly."

"Very well, then. They pick up some drunken man, and relieve him of all his superfluous valuables. But I say, Maria, what are you standing there like a fool for? You're worse than a child—I am always obliged to tell you everything."

"What is it, mum?" asked Maria.

"Why, pour out the gin—what did you bring it for? Do you suppose I wanted it to look at? You must be a fool! Now then, don't go to sleep—pour some out, and give it to Lady M——."

Charlotte said this with a sarcastic smile, which was not lost upon Agnes.

The gin was duly poured out and consumed; after which, the girls got up, dressed themselves, and went into the parlour.

"Oh, I've got such wolves!" exclaimed Charlotte.

"Wolves! what do you mean?" said Agnes.

"Why, a sinking feeling about the abdominal region; which being translated, means a pain in my stomach. It's like a lot of wolves waiting to be fed. Where's that dreadful Maria? she must go out and get something. Have you got any money?"

"A shilling, I think. I gave the cabman all I had."

"Well, I haven't a rap. Let's ring for Maria—can't do anything without her."

When Maria came up, Charlotte said—"Are you flush, Maria?"

"Haven't got a mag."

"More have I; what's to be done?"

"Would you like some eggs and bacon?"

"Yes—that'll do."

"All right, then."

"But how will you manage it?"

"Why, look here. The first floor back's got a very nice bit of bacon; I can cut half-a-dozen fine rashers off it."

"Well!"

"Well, I'll swear the cat had it."

"But the eggs?"

"I'm coming to that. There's a bad egg downstairs."

"A bad one! Well, what's the good of that? I'm not going to eat rotten eggs."

"No; but look here——"

"Look here! Who are you talking to? I suppose I've got a handle to my name, of some sort," cried Charlotte.

"Yes, mum."

"Ah! you stick to that—or it will be the worse for you."

"Yes, mum. But I shall take this bad egg to all the shops about here, and tell them I bought it yesterday, and cheek them into giving me a fresh one. I'll bet I get twelve or thirteen."

"Thirteen! that's a baker's dozen. Well, if you can manage that, you are the cleverest devil out of Newgate. Cut along, then, and see what you can do—I'm dying for something to eat."

Maria vanished, but in about half-an-hour returned with a smoking dish of eggs and bacon.

She had succeeded, as she had predicted she would, in changing the egg.

She went to nine shops, and got as many fresh eggs; but at the ninth shop, the man threw the egg into the street, and smashed it, saying, "It could not be of much use to anyone." And so Maria was unable to display her skill any more that day.

The snow-storm was over. But as Charlotte looked out of the window after tea, she saw that the snow was still lying on the ground, and cresting the housetops.

The cold had increased, and it was freezing hard.

Charlotte made up a large fire, and turning to Agnes, said—

"This is Christmas before its time, and no mistake."

"Yes," replied Agnes, drawing closer to the chimney-blaze; "it is, indeed."

It promised to be the sort of night that would fill the Field-lane refuges.

CHAPTER LXVI.

CHARLOTTE AND AGNES RUN UP AGAINST INSPECTOR WYMAN—THE WHITE BEAR—CHARLOTTE'S STRATAGEM—AGNES ESCAPES, AND WYMAN IS TAKEN FOR A THIEF AND CHASED DOWN THE HAYMARKET—THE BLUE POSTS.

IT might have been about eight o'clock when the two girls had finished their tea.

Charlotte Saunders appeared to be merry and hilarious, for she talked incessantly, and occasionally sang snatches of songs, and diversified the evening's amusement she was affording Agnes by telling her interesting anecdotes and stories of adventures she had had.

Agnes was quiet and thoughtful, although occasionally she could not help laughing at Charlotte's quaint humour and fun.

"Are you going out again to-night?" asked Agnes.

"Yes, I should think so. What is the use of stopping at home? You will never pick up a purse in that way. I am just in the humour for it."

"I suppose you will not go back to your café any more?"

"No; I'm sick and tired of that. It was all very well at first, but now the novelty of the thing has worn off, I don't care about it any longer."

"That is just like you. You never stick to anything long."

"Don't you begin to sermonize. Put on your bonnet, and we will just run down to Jimmy's and have some chaff with him."

"Don't you think we might meet that dreadful man Wyman, though?" suggested Agnes.

"We might, and we mightn't."

"That's not an answer."

"What I mean is, that it is best to leave it to chance. If we do meet him, we must try to escape him as well as we can."

"Perhaps he will not recognise you?"

"It's no good being afraid of anything; I don't care for anybody."

"Ah! you are a wonder."

"Well, I believe I am sometimes. A short life and a merry one, eh?—that's my motto. I suppose, when my time comes, I shall go under the turf; but until then, why, I will have my fling. If I had been born a man I might have done something that would have made my name famous; but as I am only a poor devil of a woman, instead of famous, I suppose you must read infamous, for any feat that I may be celebrated for. Well, what's the odds as long as you're happy. I don't care. Give us another drain of that gin. Put it in my cup. I like a drop of gin in my tea."

Charlotte's eyes were a little moist in spite of her bravado. Perhaps some tender passage in her life cropped up and turned on the fountains of her heart. We all have a soft spot somewhere.

The girls attired themselves and went out.

It was bitter cold, and Charlotte took a muff with her. It was a pretty little Chinchilla muff, and she offered it to Agnes, but she would not deprive her friend of it.

They walked on briskly until they came to the Haymarket.

Suddenly Agnes started, and grasping Charlotte's arm nervously, she exclaimed in a terrified whisper—

"Look!"

"Where?"

"Why there!"

"What is it?"

"Don't you see?"

"No."

Agnes whispered one word in her ear, and that was—

"Wyman!"

Facing them, hardly two yards distant from them, was Inspector Wyman!

He stopped and scrutinised the girls closely.

A satisfied sort of smile stole over his face.

He was near a lamp-post.

The gas-jet gave but an indifferent light, but it was sufficient to enable him to glance at a dirty bit of paper he took out of his waistcoat-pocket, and he slowly deciphered what was written before it.

"'Light hair,'" he said, in a low tone. Then he looked at Agnes.

"Yes. That's it."

"'Rather wavy at the top.'"

"Answers the description exactly."

"'Blue eyes.'"

"Has she got blue eyes? Hang me, if I can see at this distance."

"'Small hands and feet.'"

"Yes. No doubt about that."

"'Gloves sixes.'"

"I should think so. Small mouth. Answers to a T. That's her, that's her!"

Agnes was terribly alarmed.

She was terrified beyond conception, because she knew from what she had overheard the night before, that the crafty and avaricious inspector had been bribed by Count Val de Grace to capture her and take her to his house, from whence she had escaped in so remarkable a manner on a previous occasion.

Charlotte Saunders now proved herself a friend indeed, because she was a friend in need.

"Don't you be in a funk," she exclaimed.

"Oh! what shall I do?"

"Leave him to me."

"What can you do? I do not doubt your good intentions, but I don't see what you can do for me," said the unhappy girl.

"Never mind what *you* can see. I'll tackle him."

"Heaven help you."

The inspector was a cautious man. He was not one of those blunder-headed fellows who would go up to any one on the merest suspicion and say, with an air of authority, "You are my prisoner." He had very much refined on the old method of thief-taking. He was a sort of spider. He would spin a web, and envelope you in its silvery meshes, which were so cleverly woven that you did not know that you were entangled in them until you were actually caught, and then your most strenuous endeavours would not suffice to extricate you. He had a smattering of law, too, and counsel were always so well and ably instructed by him, that a prisoner never escaped through a flaw in the indictment.

Wyman went cautiously up to the two girls, and addressed them in a polite tone. He wanted to make sure of his quarry before he let fly his shaft.

In reply to his trivial remark, Charlotte said—

"As you seem to have taken a fancy to us, you had better stand something to drink."

"Certainly," he replied. "Come in here," and he led the way into the White Bear.

They passed through the bar, and by means of a small door entered a private compartment, where they were all alone.

Wyman called for three soda-and-brandies, as the girls said they would prefer that to anything else.

Suddenly an idea seemed to strike him. He said—

"I think I had the pleasure of seeing you last night."

"No, that I'm sure you didn't. You might have thought you saw us, but you didn't."

"I don't think I am mistaken."

"I don't think at all about the matter," replied Charlotte. "I know it; for I was with my mother at Camden-town. She was taken very ill with the spasms, and I had to go to her all at once, and my sister went with me."

"That's your sister, is it?" said Wyman, looking intently at Agnes, and evidently comparing the description he had just read with the original before him.

"Yes. Have you any particular objection to the relationship?"

"Oh dear no. Then it wasn't you I saw last night."

The inspector was not deceived, although he pretended to believe what Charlotte told him.

He was morally certain that the two women before him were the two who had so cleverly given him the slip on board the steamer, and whom he met at the oyster-shop when he was waiting to find some means of capturing Fly-by-night. Perhaps he did not recognise them on that occasion, owing to his anxiety to secure the burglar. But he had since fortified himself with a carefully-written description of Agnes, given him by the count himself, and he was positive that he was not mistaken this time.

While Charlotte was talking to the inspector, she gave Agnes what she herself would have called the "office," to go away as cleverly and as quickly as she could.

Agnes understood, and waited for an opportunity.

"I say, old fellow, I want to tell you something," said Charlotte to Wyman.

"What is it?"

"Come here."

He approached.

"Bend your head down, I want to whisper to you."

He did so, and Agnes slipped out of the bar.

"What is it?" he said again.

"Only this," replied Charlotte, with a laugh—"sold a second time!"

Inspector Wyman looked around him, hardly knowing what to make of Charlotte's strange speech.

Then he discovered Agnes's flight, and he saw at once that he had been foiled by the ready wit of the clever woman before him.

Charlotte placed her back against the little door, through which they had entered, and through which Agnes had just taken her departure, so that the inspector could not follow her.

He grew furious, and gnashed his teeth with rage.

Charlotte did all she could to worry and annoy him.

"If you are Inspector Wyman," she said, "you are not everybody, you know."

"Let me out," he said.

"Oh no, not yet. I can't part with you so very easily as all that."

"Let me go."

"Not just yet. You are tired of me rather suddenly."

Wyman was almost beside himself with rage. He danced about the floor of the little compartment, but Charlotte would not let him out.

At last he could bear it no longer, so he jumped over the bar, and rushed into the street.

When Charlotte saw this, she thought she would amuse herself still more at the inspector's expense.

So she screamed out, at the top of her voice—

"Stop thief! stop thief! stop him!"

Some people who were standing at the bar thought that he really had robbed Charlotte, and his going away in such an odd manner made it seem more than probable.

Three or four men plunged into the street after him, and cried out, loudly and hoarsely—"Stop thief."

The pedestrians took up the cry, and Inspector Wyman ran down the decline of the Haymarket at full speed, with a crowd of men, women, and boys baying at his heels.

He was half-mad.

He did not like to stop and face his pursuers, he was afraid he might be roughly handled, so he tore along, hoping to run across Trafalgar-square and get to Scotland-yard where he would take sanctuary.

Cries, yells, shouts—a fierce, panting, striving crowd; the inspector running as hard as he could, and going over the ground like a hunted hare with the greyhounds at his heels; Charlotte laughing immoderately.

That was the state of things when a man who was standing on the steps of the Blue Posts put out his foot, over which the inspector fell with a dull, heavy crash.

The foremost of his pursuers was running with such velocity that he could not stop himself, so he fell over the inspector, and these two bodies made a barrier over which about a score of persons fell.

Then there were blows, and oaths, and fierce cries.

It was a heavy, seething mass, from which the steam arose in a cloud in the cold night air.

At last they got up, and Wyman was dragged into the Blue Posts.

He was not much hurt, but a good deal shaken.

They gave him some brandy, and he felt better.

The mob and cries of his captors brought a policeman, who entered the place exclaiming—

"Where's this 'ere thief? he'll have to come along of me."

But he started back in surprise, for he immediately recognised the inspector.

He was one of the A, or Whitehall division, and he was perfectly acquainted with the inspector's features.

An explanation ensued, and the crowd went about its business.

When Wyman felt well enough he started once more upon the trail of Agnes.

He never gave up a chase.

Nothing could subdue him.

But this time he was destined to have a more adventurous pursuit than he imagined.

He walked some distance and searched a great many places, but he did not discover the least trace of her he was in search of.

CHAPTER LXVII.

LITTLE WONDER—BONES, UNDERTAKER—THE DWARF, STUBBLES—AGNES IS SURPRISED TO MEET HIM—MAKING COFFINS—THE DWARF OFFERS SHELTER TO AGNES, AND SHE ACCEPTS IT—THE BLACK DOOR—A PROFOUND MYSTERY—SATAN—AGNES CANNOT SLEEP FOR THINKING OF THE BLACK DOOR.

As Agnes nervously and tremblingly walked along she perceived that a change had come over the weather—it was no longer cold and frosty.

The snow was rapidly melting beneath the influence of a sudden thaw.

A gentle south-westerly wind had taken the place of the fierce, cutting, wintry blast, which blew so relentlessly from the east a short time before.

The change was grateful to her, but she had not much time or inclination to notice meteorological changes.

She was in dread of Wyman.

Events had crowded upon her so much within a few short weeks that she seemed in them to have lived a lifetime.

She had sense enough, however, in spite of even her nervousness and all her trouble, to know that to escape Wyman was a matter of life and death with her.

She knew that Count Val de Grace was an unprincipled villain.

Notwithstanding his courteous manner, his winning smile, his gentlemanly address, his amiability — notwithstanding all these advantages and accomplishments, she knew him to be unscrupulous and bad at heart.

She was, however, resolved—firmly resolved—to suffer a thousand deaths, a thousand dangers, a thousand persecutions, rather than be dishonoured by this French voluptuary.

She had plenty of cause for fear.

She did not exaggerate the danger of her position in the slightest degree.

The count was clever, cunning, and rich; and he had employed the chief of the detective police force to capture her and bring her to his house, in order that she might be delivered into his hands.

What her fate would then be she could not doubt; she shuddered as she contemplated.

It was too dreadful to dwell long upon, so she concentrated all her energies, mental as well as physical, upon her present position.

She was alone in the world once more.

She could not return to Charlotte Saunders, because she felt assured that Inspector Wyman would be on the look-out for her there, so that she would, perforce, be separated from her gay and careless companion for some time to come.

Agnes cudgelled her brain for an idea, but none came to her succour.

While wandering about she sought the shelter of the darkest and quietest streets—and some of the thoroughfares about the "Dials" are dark and dismal enough.

The parish authorities do not burn much gas in them; but some good Samaritan might, peradventure, discover the haunts of crime, disease, and misery that there abound.

Fever, ague, and leprosy, have there taken up their abode; and Azrael, the Angel of Death, with his glittering scimitar, hovers perpetually over the houses, ever ready to cross some threshold whereon the vital spark is dying out.

After half-an-hour's melancholy wandering about—ever anxious, ever apprehensive, dreading the rough grasp of a policeman—she, a peeress, if a bigamist, for she was the wife of Lord Marchmont, a peer of Great Britain, with a seat in the House of Lords, found herself in a narrow, evil-smelling, badly-lighted thoroughfare.

There might have been grass in the roadway, but it refused to grow in such a pestilential atmosphere. Even larks and linnets, those ever-welcome companions of the poor, were absent—suffocation in smoke, filth, and fog, soon disposed of them.

The name written in white paint, now brown, upon the corner was "Little Wonder."

It was a wonder, certainly, that it did not fall down and bury the inhabitants amidst its ruins. It was a wonder anybody lived there for more than a week, but the poor are long-suffering, and take a great deal of killing. It was a wonder that the inspector of nuisances did not make a clean sweep of all the inhabitants; but perhaps he valued his health too much to do anything half so foolhardy as to put his nose inside any place so plague-stricken and grave-beckoning.

Agnes walked a little distance down Little Wonder.

Then she got frightened at the appearance of the place, and was about to retrace her steps and try to get into fresher air, which her lungs could breathe without danger of congestion, when she thought she perceived the dim outline of a figure which was familiar to her.

She looked again more intently.

Yes, there could be no doubt of the fact.

She was close to an undertaker's shop. A coffin with shining brass-headed nails was exhibited in the window, and a paper informed the inhabitants of Little Wonder that funerals were conducted at stated charges. At the end of the paper was—

"N.B.—Horses with false tails charged for extra."

The undertaker, whose name, as written over the door, was Bones, must have been a man wise in his generation, for certainly no other trade could have flourished so well in so hideous a locality.

There was work going on within, as Agnes could see through the open door, and the figure which had arrested her attention was busily engaged in wielding a ponderous hammer, with which he was knocking up a common deal coffin. Presently, while Agnes was still engaged in scrutinizing him closely, he threw down the hammer, and walked towards the door of the shop, as if he wished to have a look at the night.

Agnes immediately uttered a cry, as much as to say, "Yes, I am right. That is the man."

He was a strange, uncouth monster; strangely misshapen and malformed. As horrible and as repulsive a dwarf to look at during ghostly hours as could be found anywhere. But his heart was in the right place if his body was distorted and hideous.

Agnes seemed pleased, and no wonder, for the dwarf standing before her at the shop-door of Bones the undertaker of Little Wonder was her husband's, Marmaduke Wilson's, faithful friend Stubbles—Stubbles the dwarf, who had once been the guardian of the subterranean haunt in Bluegate-fields, where the Surrey Wolf, Marmaduke, and Fly-by-night, were wont to hide from the police when the hue and cry was particularly fierce.

Stubbles did not appear to notice Agnes.

She, however, was resolved to make herself known to him. He might help her, she thought, in this her hour of need.

She approached him.

Then she accosted him.

"Stubbles!" she said.

"Who calls me Stubbles?" he exclaimed, as if he were alarmed.

"I do."

"Then it is a lie. My name is not Stubbles."

"I know you by no other."

"Who are you?"

"A friend."

"Speak, then."

"Know you the name of Marmaduke Wilson?" she said.

At the mention of his old friend and patron's name, Stubbles started, changed colour visibly, and going up to Agnes, took her by the hand, saying, in a voice tremulous with expectation and anxiety—

"What of him? Have you come to summon me to his side? I am ready."

There was something very fine in the chivalrous devotion of the dwarf to Marmaduke Wilson, and the tears started to Agnes's eyes.

"But no," he added, before she had time to speak; "it cannot be. He is far, far away in hopeless drudgery and shameful servitude. But it will not be long before he returns to his native shores. I dreamed a dream, and my visions always come true—sometimes too true. But who are you? Methinks I have seen your face somewhere?"

"I am his wife," replied Agnes, in a low voice.

"His wife?"

"Yes; alas, yes!"

"Then your place is at his side."

"You say truly. But I have had strange adventures. I am now in need of sanctuary. I cannot now talk to you, Stubbles, but you were ever faithful to my husband. Do for me now what you would have done for him."

"You can command me," replied Stubbles; "anything in reason, anything that can or may be done by man shall be done by me for the wife of Marmaduke Wilson."

"Thank you," replied Agnes, feelingly. "I ask but little at your hands—a little food and shelter for a day or so until I can mature my plans."

The dwarf hurriedly explained that his master would not suffer him to entertain any one in the house did he know it. Bones was a hard man, but the dwarf had entered his service because he wished to be out of the way, and get an honest living if he could.

People took a dislike to him generally on account of his appearance, and the trade of an undertaker was the only one he could find employment in. He added that his master was out at present, but he expected him back soon.

There was no one in the house but another dwarf, if anything more ugly and terror-striking in his appearance than Stubbles himself.

He was a foundling, he had never been baptized, and he commonly went by the name of Satan.

Satan, he said, would do anything for him, as they were great friends. They both slept downstairs in the cellar, but the rooms, if they could be called rooms, they occupied were dry, if not comfortable and elegant.

Stubbles would ask Satan to allow him to sleep in his

room, and Agnes could have his for a night or two, or as long as she liked to stay.

Bones never came into their apartments, so she would be perfectly safe from detection.

Agnes did not like the idea much, but she could not help herself, so she gladly acquiesced in the dwarf's plan, thanked him again and again, and thought that she had been really very fortunate in meeting him in so odd a manner.

"If your master is coming home soon, had I not better descend at once to lower regions?"

"Certainly; it would be wise."

"Lead the way, then, and I will follow you."

The dwarf lighted a candle, and led the way down a flight of stone steps.

They soon reached the bottom, and Agnes perceived several long passages.

One of them the dwarf threaded, and stopped before one of three doors.

The centre door was painted black, the two other white.

"This is my room," said the dwarf, pointing to one of the white doors; "the other white one is Satan's."

"And what is the black door?" asked Agnes.

The dwarf made no reply, but looked seriously at her.

"The one in the centre, I mean," said Agnes, thinking he had not quite understood her question.

The dwarf laid his hand gently, but respectfully, upon her arm, and replied gravely—

"Never seek to know the mystery connected with that room."

"Mystery?"

"Yes."

"But why?"

"Ask me no questions."

"Oh, speak!"

"I may not."

"But——"

"As you value your peace of mind for ever," said Stubbles, "be contented to know that it is an enigma. Leave it so, and all will be well; disobey me, and the terrible punishment you will bring upon yourself, dear lady, will be no fault of mine."

"I would give worlds to know."

"And I, lady, would give worlds not to know."

Stubbles shuddered as he spoke.

Agnes looked at the black, funereal, pall-like door, and followed the dwarf into what he called his room.

There was a common-looking bed upon the stone floor, which was covered with a ragged bit of Dutch carpet. No window, no fireplace, a few chairs, a table, and that was all.

"It's a cheerless place for a lady," said Stubbles.

"It is security from pursuit," said Agnes, "and that is all I want."

"Needs must when the devil drives," said Stubbles.

"Yes, indeed."

"I will seek food for you, and make you as comfortable as I possibly can," said the dwarf.

There was genuine feeling in his tone; and Agnes caught his rough, hairy hand, more like the paw of a bear than aught else, and shook it heartily with her slender fingers, saying—

"You were my husband's friend—you are now mine. You have a good heart, I am sure, in spite of your rugged exterior."

"Let my actions speak for me," he replied; and putting down the candle, he went in search of provisions.

After a time he returned with something substantial. Not rich, expensive fare, but good and solid, some bottled ale, and a little spirit.

"I had a few shillings wages," he explained. "You will not mind my spending it in your service," he said, kindly.

"Mind, my friend? No. But here——"

The dwarf watched her movements inquiringly. She unclasped her bracelet from her wrist, and said—

"Take this to-morrow and sell it. It will supply us with more money than we shall want."

"It shall be as you wish, lady," replied Stubbles, concealing the glittering bauble securely about his person.

Then he added—

"Satan has come in, and is upstairs. I have explained everything to him."

"And what does he say?"

"He is quite agreeable."

"To your arrangement?"

"Yes."

"That is capital."

"He will allow me to sleep with him to-night," said Stubbles.

"And he will not tell your employer anything?"

"Not a syllable will pass his lips."

"That's good also. I should never forgive myself were I to get you into any sort of trouble."

"Fear nothing. I must go to work again now, lady, but in the morning I will be up early, and you shall have some tea or coffee, when you feel inclined to breakfast."

Wishing her good night, Stubbles took his leave, and Agnes was alone in her strange apartment.

She congratulated herself upon her escape from Wyman, and thought she would avail herself of the dwarf's hospitality for a day or two, and then employ him to find her a lodging.

She found herself rather tired, and soon retired to rest, throwing herself on the bed, dressed as she was.

But it was some time before she could sleep.

The black door, which Stubbles had spoken so strangely and mysteriously about, haunted her imagination, and she could not rest.

Why would the dwarf not speak when she questioned him? There must be something dreadful connected with that chamber.

The more she thought of it the more restless she became, and as the hours passed she was still awake and wondering.

CHAPTER LXVIII.

AGNES RISES AND GOES TO THE BLACK DOOR—THE DWARFS AT WORK—THE DROP OF BLOOD—IN THE CHAMBER—LIGHTING THE LAMPS—THE ENDLESS SUCCESSION OF HIDEOUS COFFINS WITH THEIR GHASTLY CONTENTS—THE STRANGERS—A PASSAGE—ESCAPE—THE NOISE OF DOGS, CATS, HORSES AND COWS.

IT is strange, but nevertheless true, that curiosity is always excited by restrictions. The more fetters you place around it the more power you seem to give it wherewith to break the bonds with which you have just bound it.

So it was with Agnes.

The black door so strangely and mysteriously placed between the two white ones—which led to the rooms occupied by Stubbles and Satan, and in one of which she then was—so excited her imagination that she could not sleep.

She turned uneasily upon her bed, and wondered what strange secret lurked behind that door. The dwarf had hinted vaguely at something very dreadful, and shuddered as he spoke. No light thing could cause Stubbles, the former companion of Marmaduke Wilson, to shudder.

All the wonderful events that had lately happened to her paled before the all-engrossing passion which possessed her to know something of the mystic crypt, or chamber, that she had been forbidden to enter. It was the story of Blue Beard and the rusty, blood-stained key over again.

Wyman was forgotten, and Count Val de Grace ignored.

After more than an hour's restless tossing about upon the anything-but-luxurious couch, it became a mania with Agnes to solve the riddle, and to know what fell secret lurked behind that ominous and funereal, black-painted door.

Whatever the terrible reality might be, she felt that she could better bear it than her present state of maddening suspense.

Once across the dreaded threshold—once through the awful portals—might she not regret her hardihood, and lament not having heeded the friendly advice of the well-meaning and good-intentioned dwarf, Stubbles?

She might.

But an all-engrossing passion, desire, longing to know more, and to achieve the adventure, had taken such an irresistible hold of her mind, senses, and inclination, that she was no longer mistress of her own actions.

There was a strange light in her eyes as she rose from her bed and uneasily paced the floor of what may truly be called her cell, for there was very little difference in size, shape, and appearance between a prison-dwelling and the room in which, through the kindness and hospitality of the dwarf, she was enabled to pass the night, and take shelter and sanctuary from the never-ending pursuit of her indefatigable enemies.

She had lain down in her clothes, as we have already said,

so that she was fully equipped for her nocturnal, perilous, and, we may safely say, foolhardy adventure.

The candle stuck in the neck of a ginger-beer bottle with which Stubbles had embellished his apartment, was still alight.

Agnes clutched it nervously. Her hand shook and trembled so much that drops of evil-smelling tallow fell upon her fingers, her dress, and also bespattered the stone floor.

She had taken off her bonnet, and she allowed that to remain on the chair at the foot of the bed where she had placed it. She could not stay now to replace it.

Her long fair hair had escaped from its fastenings and fell in rippling, golden waves over her shoulders and down her back.

It was such lovely hair that had a satyr met her in some sylvan bower he would have fallen down and worshipped so great a wealth of auburn tresses, and have remained rooted to the spot with rapture at having been permitted to contemplate such loveliness.

Her locks were unadorned, but still no pearls, no flowers, no diamonds could have imparted more grace, more beauty, more charm than at present lurked within the simple silken coils, all dishevelled as they were.

Like little mice her feet escaped from beneath the hem of her dress—so small and tiny that a Chinese lady might have envied their proportions.

Nerving herself for the effort, Agnes prepared to leave the room, and dare the terrors of the forbidden chamber.

Opening the door firmly, yet with a natural shrinking and hesitation, she stood in the doorway.

Another step and she was in the passage.

The wind blew down in stormy gusts from the upper stories of the house, where the dwarfs were still hard at work, making receptacles for the diseased, emaciated, poverty-stricken bodies of the unhappy inhabitants of Little Wonder.

The flame of the candle flickered.

Agnes shaded it with her hand, and then it burnt steadily again.

The heavy thud of the hammers, wielded by the powerful hands of the two dwarfs, struck like a knell upon the timid heart of Agnes.

With a hollow, sepulchral sound, the noise of those hammers at the hour of midnight reverberated through the subterranean caverns amongst which Agnes had been rash enough to venture.

And as each fresh stroke rang out clearly in the nighttime, an echo was heard in the heavy pulsations of the young girl's heart, which beat in unison with the blows of the elfin workmen upstairs.

She turned her eyes in the direction of the black door. They had not far to wander—a few yards, that was all; half-a-dozen steps brought her close to it; and then she stood gazing at it, half fascinated with its uniform colour presenting so strange and striking a contrast to the doors on either side of it.

The handle was made of wood and painted black. There was not one speck of white upon that door which could for a moment relieve the awful monotony of its universal blackness.

Stay! there is something upon the handle which catches the eye of Agnes, and arrests her attention.

She approaches closer and more closely still, in order that she may examine it; she stoops down, that she may see it better.

Her eyes distend and the pupils dilate.

It is as she thought.

With a cry she springs back, for there is *blood* on the handle of that door!

A vivid stain of rich red blood!

Not one—not two—not three—but a multiplicity of stains; and ineffaceable spots are at length revealed, as if some gory, blood-stained, blood-embrued hand, all wet and dripping with the ensanguined stream, had seized the handle, to close or open the door of that ill-omened chamber.

It is not a pleasant thing to touch or come in contact with blood, wet or dry, and Agnes shared the general repugnance to what we know is necessary to our existence when it flows beneath the surface of our skins, but which we shrink from when it flows from a hideous gash in a human body, and bespatters surrounding objects with its crimson globules.

When she had sufficiently recovered her equanimity, she again seized the handle of the door, and with a sudden motion turned it.

She pushed the door.

It yielded.

But then again she was checked in her onward career.

She felt afraid to enter.

She knew not what she was about to encounter, and for the moment she almost wished she had not undertaken the adventure, but had remained quiet and passive in the little chamber the well-disposed dwarf had placed at her disposal.

However, her hesitation was but momentary.

Eve, in the Garden of Eden, plucked the fruit of the Tree of Knowledge of Good and Evil, simply because she was strictly enjoined not to do so. Pity she had not eaten of the Tree of Life, which stood close by, at the same time.

Perhaps, if the dwarf had not said a word about the dark chamber, Agnes would now have been sleeping quietly in her bed, instead of proceeding on an expedition that even Don Quixote would have delegated to Sancho Panza.

Breathing heavily, Agnes advanced.

The door, which was made of heavy, ponderous oak, swung slowly backwards, and, holding the candle high above her head, Agnes advanced to the centre of the apartment.

A sickly glare was diffused throughout the room.

The faint rays of the tallow candle dimly illumined the immediate space around it.

Suddenly, her foot stumbled against something.

Stooping down, to her horror, Agnes perceived that it was a human bone, with some particles of half-putrid flesh adhering to it.

A few more steps and she was in the centre of the room.

And now she became conscious of what had only been partially perceptible before—a strange, unnatural smell, as of decaying or decayed humanity, not in its last stage, but rather in its primary one—still overpowering, brain-deadening, soul-sickening.

By her side Agnes perceived a table; upon it were two oil-lamps, shaded, as if to throw down and concentrate the light upon the table.

She removed the shades; then, without a moment's hesitation, she lighted the two lamps, which were already cut and trimmed and filled.

At first they burnt slowly, but after a while they burst out into a fierce, glowing, scintillating flame, which illuminated the whole apartment, even to the uttermost and most secret corner.

Then Agnes raised her head, and gazed around her.

Poor child! she saw a sight which might have appalled a stouter heart than hers.

She gazed upon a spectacle which might have wrung a shriek from the lips of many a man who considers his nerves well strung.

She did not cry out; she merely gazed on, unable to remove her eyes.

Gazed as if paralysed with the extraordinary spectacle that she had sought out amongst the funereal vaults of villanous St. Giles's.

Upon some rude supports, roughly but firmly put together, running along two sides of the chamber, were an endless succession of hideous coffins, all filled with human corpses, their ghastly and cadaverous faces upturned and rigid.

Agnes tried to count them,

One, two, three, four—she could get no further—she gave up the attempt.

It seemed too horrible that the grave should give up its dead in this way.

Men and women—women and men. Young, old, middle-aged; handsome, ugly, plain, repulsive—all ranks, all classes, apparently.

Agnes felt her brain reeling.

She could attach no meaning to anything so singular.

She was utterly at sea, completely lost.

She did not faint; her nerves were too highly strung for that.

If she had done anything, she would have lost her reason—she would have *gone mad!*

The table against which she was standing was chopped about and hacked like a kitchen dresser.

Here lay a scalpel, and there a double-edged knife.

Traces of blood upon the bricks, with which the room was paved, were numerous.

Of a sudden Agnes heard the sound of voices, at first distant, but gradually coming nearer.

Then footsteps were audible descending the stairs; not one, but many, as of a concourse of people.

What could she do?

She did not wish to be detected; she would not be seen there for worlds.

She might, in those lonely dungeons, be horribly ill-treated, dishonoured, and perhaps murdered.

She dared not go back to her chamber; she might meet them in the passage.

It was a frightful moment—a period of terrible suspense!

She looked around her.

She saw a door, it was her only hope.

She rushed towards it.

It yielded to her touch.

With her candle in her hand she entered a narrow passage, and ran along it.

She cared not what the coming crowd would think of the door of the chamber being open, or the lamps being alight.

Her only object was to escape and hide herself anywhere till morning.

As she continued her journey along the damp, mouldy, and seemingly interminable passage, she heard the yelping and barking of dogs, the mewing of cats, and occasional neigh of a horse, mingled with the lowing of a cow, and the bleating of a lamb.

Mystery succeeded mystery in this strange part of underground London.

What could it mean?

As she approached nearer the noises increased.

Agnes was mystified; and well she might be.

She asked herself a thousand hurried questions, without receiving one practical or intelligible answer.

Still she went on.

CHAPTER LXIX.

AGNES SURVEYS THE MYSTERIOUS CHAMBER, BUT WHILST SHE IS SO ENGAGED SHE HEARS A CROWD OF PEOPLE APPROACHING—SHE HIDES HERSELF—THE VIVISECTORS —HORROR UPON HORROR—AN ATMOSPHERE OF BLOOD AND CRUELTY.

AGNES boldly penetrated through the passage and entered a large room.

As she advanced the strange noises increased in intensity, until the din was perfectly deafening.

If the sight she had encountered in the first apartment she had visited had astonished her, it is but fair to say that what she now saw astounded her.

Let in to the walls were stalls and pens of various descriptions; in some were confined horses, in some cows, and in the other and smaller ones, dogs and cats, and even poultry.

One misguided and credulous game-cock, seeing the unwonted light, began to crow with all his might, thinking it was daylight, and fondly supposing that the sun was shining.

This was a stretch of belief and an evidence of faith that would have done him great credit had he been other than he was.

Agnes walked all round this large room, which was of great extent.

The light she carried did not shed much of a glare around.

It was but a faint and sickly illumination at the best, but by stepping every now and then and holding it aloft, to allow its rays to descend, she managed to see everything, and could in turn have taken a very good and correct inventory of the living contents of this singular place.

She patted the horses on the necks and stroked their noses, as is the manner of females whenever they come in contact with an animal of the equine species. She petted the cats, and made friends with the dogs, which she remarked were rather noticeable for their noise than their breed, but there was little or no reciprocity about them. They did not appear glad to see her; they shrank from her caresses, and some of them slunk into the corners of their cages, as if to escape some terrible fate which they had instinct enough to know was impending over them.

Agnes was surprised at this, but she was so bewildered at everything that she did not attempt to explain any of the strange things she saw.

Perhaps, she thought, the undertaker upstairs is a rich man, and has a fancy or a fondness for animals. He may have collected all these creatures down here to have a sort of subterranean Zoological Gardens. Who knows? By the time she had three pars made the circuit of the room, she heard groans and short yelps as of dogs in pain.

Raising her candle, she went in the direction from which they emanated, and was shocked beyond measure to see several dogs lying upon their sides, with large, gaping wounds upon their carcases, as if they had been fighting.

Going close to them she saw that the skin had been cut open and the flesh and bones laid bare.

A quantity of clotted blood had collected here and there, and there were extensive stains of coagulated blood on various parts of the stone floor.

"Oh, this is too horrible!" she exclaimed.

One poor dog lay panting and wining, too weak from ill-treatment and loss of blood to yelp or cry outright. Its tongue, parched and fevered for want of water, lolled out of its mouth.

Agnes saw some water in a basin in the next apartment and humanely took it away, giving it to the dog, who seemed so much in want of it. The poor creature was too weak to drink it; Agnes poured a little down its throat, and the dumb animal turned its eyes full of thankfulness upon her. She had preserved its life by this timely assistance, but whether she had done it a good action or the reverse, was a moot point. Perhaps it would have been better for it to have died outright; yet she had but obeyed the dictates of her conscience, for it was totally repugnant to her nature to see anything suffer. She passed on, and saw a sheep which was stone dead. It appeared to have been cut in half almost. Its ribs were bare, and its carcase presented the most sickening spectacle that it had been Agnes's lot to encounter.

After she had gone completely round the room she advanced to the centre, where she found a series of tables, very much resembling in form and size those in the first room. They were blood stained, but there were no remains of anything upon them; some smaller tables stood close by, and upon them were some sponges and bowls of water.

While she was examining these, she once more heard the sound of footsteps. The noise made by the animals had prevented her hearing it before. Voices were also raised in hilarious conversation, and the party who were approaching seemed to be animated with all the elements of merriment and good companionship.

Agnes rushed towards the door.

But then she heard the coming phalanx more distinctly than ever.

What was she to do?

It was a moment of great peril. But her nerves did not fail her.

She cast about in her mind for some place of security. She found it sooner than she expected. On her right hand, almost under the shadow of the door, was a sort of cell, evidently intended for the prison of some wretched animal. In that she would hide.

She had no sooner conceived the idea than she proceeded to put it into execution.

She blew out the light and crept in.

It was large enough to hold her, but she was obliged to stoop. The position was painful and uncomfortable, but it was better than falling into the hands of a parcel of people of whom she knew nothing, and of whose intentions she could divine still less, if it were possible to extract anything lower than nothing.

The footsteps and the noises advanced, and drew nearer every second.

Agnes could hear her heart beat.

It was a moment of frightful suspense.

At last Agnes saw the door open and a crowd of men flocked into the room—some were young, but there were many who had grey hair—old, hoary-headed men having the most respectable and interesting appearance.

What could be their mission there at that strange time of the night?

This it was that puzzled Agnes, and well nigh drove her distracted.

She had one consolation, however, and that was, that by keeping quiet she stood some slight chance of making a discovery.

There were, perhaps, fifteen men in all—young and old.

The dwarfs accompanied them, both Satan and Stubbles.

Satan was, if possible, more ugly and repulsive in personal appearance than Stubbles, who, God knows, was hideous enough, in all conscience.

But Satan was a hunchback as well as a dwarf, and strongly recalled the familiar demon of Notre-Dame to one's imagination.

The new comers went to the tables and took sundry small boxes or cases out of their pockets.

The dwarf lighted some lamps they had brought with them, and set them on the tables; afterwards putting paper shades over them in order to concentrate the light and prevent it from wandering abroad.

Then Agnes, from her hiding-place, could see many an oddly-shaped and curiously-wrought instrument glittering upon the deal boards.

Some of the men took off their coats and turned up their sleeves; others went to the different places where the cattle were confined, and looked at them with a careful, not to say a critical, eye. Others, again, regarded the poultry wistfully, while some evidently had an eye to cats, and the rest took a decided interest in dogs.

The truth all at once flashed across Agnes's mind!

She had heard of the dreadful practice of *Vivisection*.

She had read of the horrors that were daily perpetrated in France, and the apathy of the Parisians on the subject had always surprised her.

Vivisection is one of those things which medical men declare that the exigencies of modern science imperatively require.

They assert that they cannot ascertain the true and proper action of the nervous system unless they operate upon the body while it is alive and in a state of animation.

That these men were vivisectors she could not for a moment doubt; everything pointed towards such a conclusion.

She shuddered at the discovery she had made—it was too shocking to dwell upon.

She would have run away there and then, but she could not; she was for the time being a captive, and an involuntary spectator of the brutal experiments of a band of unprincipled doctors.

She asked herself repeatedly, "Is this possible? Have they no compassion for the dreadful and horrible sufferings of dumb and defenceless creatures, who cannot help themselves?"

These were all idle questions.

Their pity, their compassion, their feeling—all these collectively were where last winter's snow is. In other words, they existed nowhere.

They had once, flourished in all their native purity, but now, it was little more than a dream. They had vanished—and other sentiments had usurped their place. It was a reflection sad and humiliating for human nature, but it was a fact.

The reason of their coming to such an out-of-the-way and secluded spot was apparent to the meanest comprehension.

The law in England would have stepped in to prevent the perpetration of the cruelties they had in view; Public Opinion—that grandest of all palladiums—would have raised its powerful and irresistible voice, and the practice would have been condemned and abolished almost before it had begun to exist; for the voice of the people, when united to that of the Press, is all-powerful. May it ever remain so, and prove itself superior to the wishes and intentions of any oligarchical body.

The surgeon had soon selected the victims, and the dwarf proceeded to take them out of the pens for them. One body of four had made up their minds to experimentalize upon a horse.

The unhappy quadruped was fettered in such a manner that he could by no possibility resist, and then the diabolical proceedings commenced.

Tendons were severed, fibres laid open, veins cut, masses of flesh hacked and hewn until they hung only by a bit of skin to the parent carcase. Groans and sobs and sighs and strange inhuman cries proceeded from the poor tortured creature, but the surgeons heeded them not. They persisted in their diabolical work without the least compunction or remorse. The other tables were quickly occupied, and the fiendish work became general. Blood flowed everywhere, and soon the floor was a thousand times worse than that of a slaughter-house.

No *abattoir* could have equalled it in its revolting details.

The smell of the warm blood was peculiarly disgusting to Agnes, and she would have given worlds to have escaped from her disagreeable position.

She now wished that she had not given way to that irresistible curiosity which had prompted her in the first instance to penetrate through the black door into the midst of those mysteries the dwarf had in the most friendly manner advised her to avoid. Repentance, though, as is generally the case, came a little too late.

The shrieks of the animals became quite appalling.

The operators were used to such a medley, such a Babel of horrible sounds, but Agnes was not.

It was, after a while, a perfect Golgotha, a place of skulls; but the most striking part of the whole *programme* was that, after some of the surgeons had cut a living subject all to pieces, they would put it back into its cell, or its kennel, in order that in another day or two they might see how the pulse acted, when loss of blood had reduced it to something little better than a bloodless hide, or a bag of bones.

Agnes could stand it no longer. She determined to make an effort to escape. She did not exactly know how it was to be done, but she looked around her to see if such a thing were feasible.

The door which admitted people into this chamber of horrors—this den of groans and sighs and suffering—was open.

The cell that Agnes occupied was facing the open door.

The focus of light was the centre of the room, consequently there was not much of the illumination wasted upon the outskirts.

Every one was intent on his brutal work.

The dwarf was busy attending to the wants of the surgeons, getting them new subjects or replacing those they had done with.

It was a chance, perhaps a slender one, but Agnes resolved to try it.

She would make an attempt to escape, for she felt she should die if she remained any longer in that atmosphere of blood and cruelty.

CHAPTER LXX.

THE ATTEMPT TO ESCAPE—SATAN SEES AGNES—HER ALARM—HE TAKES HER FOR A GHOST—LOST AMONGST THE DEAD—IN THE ARMS OF A CORPSE—THE SURGEONS COME BACK, TAKE AGNES FOR A SUBJECT, AND PREPARE TO CUT HER OPEN.

AGNES did not hesitate long before making the attempt to escape from the presence and the society of the vivisectors—those detestable men who found a pastime in cutting and maiming the living.

Agnes could understand anatomy.

She could sympathize with surgeons who, in order to become intimately acquainted with the structure of the human body, had recourse to surreptitious means to do so.

She could make allowances for fair and legitimate science, but she fairly believed that these men were going much beyond that.

Her impression was that there was no real necessity for men to lame and cripple and torture dumb animals in order to see how many pulsations a minute the heart made when the rest of the body was writhing in indescribable torment. Or whether the tendons of a dog contracted when cut, or remained the same length.

With a shudder and an inward loathing, which made her flesh to creep, she looked out of her rather insecure hiding-place.

All were intently occupied with their disgusting work.

No eyes were turned towards the door. This was very fortunate.

Creeping, gliding, crawling like a snake — steathily, warily, cautiously, she emerged.

She stood in the doorway.

One of the dwarfs turned his head. He looked in her direction.

Agnes thought she should have fainted.

Her face, already frightfully pale, if possible, turned paler.

It was Satan.

Stubbles was engaged in another part of the room, in staunching the blood that came from a wounded horse.

He held a sponge in his hand, and wiped away the ruby fluid as it flowed, in order that the operators might more readily perceive the action of the muscles.

"I FEEL I MUST DIE," CRIED THE DWARF TO AGNES AND STUBBLES.

Satan stood transfixed to the ground, as if he had seen an apparition.

Agnes was at a loss what to do, or how to escape.

The danger was very imminent, but when she saw that the dwarf did not cry out, or give any alarm, but stood still as if he was alarmed and frightened, an idea came into her head.

Perhaps, she thought, he takes me for a ghost. If so, nothing could be better. I will work upon his superstitious fears, and he may consider me the spirit of some of the dead bodies in the other chamber.

The idea was no sooner conceived than acted upon.

She abandoned her former attitude of timidity, and assumed one quite the reverse.

She drew herself up to her full height; she extended her arms in a terror-striking manner, and looked at the dwarf in the manner she thought most likely to intimidate him.

The effect was as magical as it was instantaneous.

He threw up his hands. He staggered to and fro for a moment, as if he were drunk, or as if he were a poplar in a hurricane; and then with a short, half-articulate cry, fell down upon the cold, hard floor in a fit.

Agnes immediately ran forward, and was soon lost to sight in the dark and mazy intricacies of the passage.

What became of the dwarf she knew not, nor did she care whether he came to life again or not. Whether he told his extraordinary tale or not—or whether they believed him, or thought him the victim of some hallucination, was a matter of most perfect and utter indifference to her.

All she thought of, all she cared about, was to remove herself to a distance from the horrible and sickening atmosphere of the shambles she had just left, and companionship of the scientific butchers in the slaughterhouse.

It was so dark, that she was obliged to grope her way. She now wished she had her candle with her; but that—as it was useless to her without a light—she had left behind.

The agonized cries of the poor animals, who were dying by inches under the relentless knives of the granite-hearted vivisectors, grew fainter and fainter.

Agnes thanked God for it.

Her brain would have given way had she been compelled much longer to witness the dreadful inhumanities she had fortunately escaped from.

But although she had escaped one danger and one unpleasantness, she had another to encounter.

She found her way through the passage into the first chamber where all the corpses arrayed in coffins were, but for the life of her she could not find her way out again.

She was in a trap.

She did not know which way to turn, or what to do.

The whereabouts of the black door was a mystery to her, and she was afraid to move lest she should stumble up against some coffin or other, and touch the cold, clammy bone and flesh of the dead with her own warm, living hands.

She shrank from the touch of a corpse as she would have done from that of a viper.

And no wonder.

He is a bold man who can walk about amongst dead bodies, and handle them in the dark.

She was in a quandary.

She had gone a certain distance into the room before she hesitated. If she tried to go back again the chances were that she would not find the door she came in at.

Not a ray of light of any description penetrated into that gloomy vault. The gay and gladsome sunshine had never since its creation illumined its tartarean depths.

Agnes trembled.

But anything was better than inactivity.

She pushed on, feeling her way very carefully. Her hands were extended before her.

She only moved one step at a time. At last she touched something.

She shivered, started back, and clasped her hands.

Then after a moment's pause, and a hastily muttered prayer, she moved in another direction.

Step after step she took—all measured, all calculated.

She thought she heard strange noises, but she put them down to the effect of the surrounding influences, and her overwrought fancy.

Suddenly her foot struck against something, she fell instantly forward, and in vain threw out her arms to save herself.

There was a momentary silence, but that was broken by a terrific shriek from Agnes.

She had fallen upon a corpse.

She felt its cold, dead cheek pressing against hers, and the contact sent a sensation through her as of an iceberg being suddenly launched into her system, or as if she had suffered her blood to become congealed and turned into ice.

She dare not move; new horrors might await her; and there she lay, a living soul chained, as it were, to an empty shell.

After the lapse of a few seconds she gave way entirely. She could no longer hold up against the accumulated horrors of that terrible evening, and she became for a time unconscious.

Whilst she was in that state, some of the surgeons, who had finished their labours in the vivisecting-room, came into the other, which may be correctly designated the dissecting-room, for the bodies there accumulated were stolen from coffins by the undertaker, and he perpetrated his thefts in carrion in the most clever and dexterous manner.

He did it in this way.

Mr. Bones, as we have said, employed the two dwarfs as his assistants, but Satan was his agent for the most diabolical part of his work. He had his hearses built in a peculiar manner, and near the upper end, close to the driver's seat, he had a box constructed where Satan could hide himself. He was even provided with tools necessary for the work he had in hand; and before the hearse went to the door of the dead person he would conceal himself in his box. The unsuspecting relatives of the deceased would allow the coffin to be placed within the hearse, but as soon as the machine was in motion, Satan began his operations. Carefully lifting the coffin-lid and doing everything with as little noise as possible, the dwarf would take out the dead body and put it in his box, then he would fill up the empty coffin with bricks and stones to make it sufficiently heavy, and as the hearse stopped outside the cemetery-chapel, he would retreat into his box, sit upon the corpse, and patiently wait for the time when he would be liberated.

The parson would read the burial-service over a box of bricks, and, in reality, although he was totally unconscious of it, make a farce of Christianity.

Mr. Bones the undertaker of Little Wonder was a clever man, and Satan the dwarf was the most accomplished of resurrectionists.

The hearse would return home, and the dead body, over which fond friends supposed that they were weeping, would very shortly repose in peace and quietness, if not in consecrated ground, in the vaults below the undertaker's dwelling.

The surgeons who were returning, were doing so with the intention of cutting up a corpse or two before they went to their lodgings, and completed their labours for the night. The dwarfs did not accompany them. They carried their own lights, and walked slowly round the room.

They stopped before Agnes, and by mutual consent they laid hold of her.

They were not murderers.

They were not wrong or evil-doers; but they took her for a corpse.

There was every excuse for the supposition.

She was on the top of a dead body, and half in a coffin.

She was pale and cold and motionless, and if she did not wear the ghastly lineaments of the grave there was very little difference between her and an inhabitant of a grave.

Dragging her to the table, they laid her upon it, and began rudely and roughly to deprive her of her dress.

They laid bare her bosom, and one who seemed the most experienced of the number, displayed several sharp instruments, wrapped up in a leather-case.

He took up one.

His friends crowded round to see the result of his experiment.

He held the glittering knife in a scientific manner, and, baring his arms, prepared to plunge it into her fair and spotless breast.

CHAPTER LXXI.

A TERRIBLE MOMENT—THE MEDICAL STUDENTS HESITATE —THEY FEEL HER PULSE—A REPRIEVE AT THE LAST INSTANT—THE RETURN OF THE VIVISECTORS—THE DOCTORS SUSPECT AGNES AND STUBBLES—THEIR DANGER—PRUSSIC ACID—THE ALARMING ATTITUDE OF CAMPBELL, BALDWYN, AND THEIR PARTY.

IT was a terrible moment for Agnes—a moment fraught with danger great and imminent.

There she lay upon that plain but blood-stained deal table, where many a mute and insensible body had been hacked and hewn in pieces.

She was in the hands of the vivisectors, but they little thought that they were about to cut in pieces the loveliest specimen of humanity that they had ever met with dead or alive. They dreamt not that she was *alive*. So solemn, so deadly did her faint appear, that they took her for one of the corpses with which the room was stocked.

As two of them stood with their terrible knives, sharp as razors, and glittering like daggers whenever the light caught their polished blades, they were not aware that they were endeavouring to add the stain of murder to their other offences, if other offences they were guilty of. They simply thought that they were executing and carrying out their legitimate functions as surgeons. It was in no way different from a post-mortem at the hospital.

The eldest of the two surgeons, to whom the lead appeared to have been delegated, was, as we have said, ready to plunge his knife into Agnes's fair and lovely bosom, looking like driven snow in the sickly glare of the tallow candles, but as he gazed upon her peerless form some irresistible feeling seemed to take possession of him. Was it Agnes's guardian angel battling with his good angel? invisible spirits holding converse together in impalpable air? Possibly. It is hard to say. At all events, he stayed his hand, like Jacob when he was about to offer Esau as a burnt sacrifice. It was a miracle, for in another moment the cruel, relentless knife would have drank deeply of her heart's life blood—it would have gone through that tender skin that Marmaduke Wilson once loved to press, and that Lord Marchmont doted on—that white and delicate skin that Count Val de Grace raved about—and, severing cartilage, fibre, muscle and flesh, it would have gone direct to the seat of all pulsation, of all vitality—the heart.

But it was not doomed so. So horrible a fate was not destined for Agnes Leslie.

Throwing his knife down, the doctor said—

"It's odd, but I think I saw her bosom heave."

"Nonsense, Campbell!" replied the second surgeon; "it's impossible."

"It may appear so to you," said Campbell; "but I saw it with my own eyes, Baldwyn."

Baldwyn laughed incredulously, and picked up the knife, which had stuck in the floor, handle upwards.

"Get out of the way," he said. "Let me see what I can do; I'm not a woman, if you are. The girl's good-looking enough, but what's the use of her good looks as she's dead? If she were alive, now, it would be another thing."

"I don't believe she's dead," replied Campbell, positively.

"Not dead? That's ridiculous; she wouldn't be here if she were not. Old Bones knows what he's about. You don't suppose he'd give us a treat in vivisection?"

"What do you mean?"

"Why, he wouldn't give us a fellow-creature, all alive and kicking, to operate upon without charging something more for it."

"Oh, I don't know; he might—he's capable of doing it."

"I don't doubt his capability; all I say is, he'd charge more for it."

Baldwyn flourished the knife in his hand, and was about to rip up the skin and lay it in a flap over the side, as is the custom in anatomy, when Campbell exclaimed, in a tone of entreaty—

"For God's sake feel her pulse! she may be in a trance."

"Oh, trance be hanged! No more trance than you are, Campbell. You've drank too much whisky to-night, that's about the size of it."

"Is it? I don't think so, and I am not going to see murder committed before my eyes."

"Murder! Who talked about murder?"

"I did."

As he said this, Campbell drew himself up to his full height, and looked like a man who was bringing a reprieve to a criminal condemned to die by the hands of the hangman, and who had already mounted the scaffold, renouncing life.

The lights in the sepulchral chamber burned dimly; they had not been attended to lately, and the snuffs of the lamps were thick and heavy.

The group of student doctors bore the appearance of a lot of fiends who had gathered together to witness some inhuman rite, some ghastly sacrifice, like ghouls clustered together, to devour the body of some newly-buried woman, standing out in bold relief in a deserted churchyard, with the freshly dug up mould piled up all around them in heaps, and the corpse stretched out in the moonlight all white, and fair, and moribund, not yet discoloured by corruption—like vampires were they grouped around the catacombs of some suburban cemetery—repulsive, horrible, detestable.

Campbell's persuasive arguments had not had much effect upon his companions, but when he uttered the magic word, "Murder," they all turned round and listened attentively to him.

"Yes, murder," he continued, in a loud, sonorous voice. "I believe, as firmly as I ever believed anything in my life, that that woman is not dead, but sleeping—in other words, in a trance; and if you kill her after this solemn protest, blood will be upon your heads: I wash my hands of it."

"You're something like Pontius Pilate," said Baldwyn. "But if you are in earnest in saying what you do, the question is soon set at rest."

And going up to Agnes, he took her hand in his, and felt her pulse. He took out his watch—it was an old professional habit and he couldn't help it; he looked at the watch, and held the vein between his fingers—the blood pulsed through it—slowly and faintly, but still it pulsed.

"By God!" he cried, in the most intense astonishment, "her pulse beats."

"Beats?" cried all around the table, in a chorus of surprise.

"Yes, beats. If you don't believe me, come and feel for yourselves."

"Oh, we believe you," cried some; but others, more unbelieving, went up to Agnes and tested her pulse themselves.

"Well, there is something odd about this," cried Baldwyn. "I did not think anything about the woman being dressed,

because many of old Bones's subjects come to us in that state, and it isn't the first time we have cut up a woman who has worn a crinoline; you know Bones gets lots of suicides, and that accounts for it. But this woman is alive—decidedly alive—and I am very glad to think so, for she is far too pretty to be lost to the world at so early an age."

"So she is," replied Campbell; "and I am very much pleased to think I found out the symptoms of vitality which you had ignored."

"Better bring her to," said some one.

"Yes, and let her give an account of herself," said another. "She may be some prisoner, or some victim of old Bones; and if she is, and I find he has treated her badly, I'll break every bone in the old villain's skin, and crucify those two devilish dwarfs into the bargain."

Baldwyn concurred in the opinion that it would be better to bring her to, and he intimated as much to Campbell, who felt in his pocket and produced a case of lancets. Selecting one, he made preparations for operating with it. He turned up Agnes's sleeve, and laid bare her dazzlingly white arm almost up to the shoulder. When he had done so, he pinched the arm to find the vein he wanted, and having done so, exclaimed—

"Hold a basin, some one."

"Oh, hang the basin! Fire away," returned Campbell. "If her blood does fall on the ground it wont be the first time that the same fluid has done so."

"I know that; but I want to measure how much I take from her."

"Guess it."

"Yes, that's all very well."

"Go ahead, then."

"But I don't want to take above a couple of ounces."

"Will you do it, or shall I?" said Baldwyn.

At this Campbell set to work, and skilfully inserted his lancet. The blood flowed slowly at first, but presently the sluggish dimensions of the stream changed, and the blood flowed briskly. The purple current ran on to the table and sank through the chinks till it dropped on to the floor, and formed into little puddles, where it clotted.

"That'll do," cried Baldwyn, as he saw Agnes open her eyes.

Campbell took a handkerchief out of his pocket, and bound it tightly round the wound, tying it over her arm.

"That will do the business, I think," he said.

Agnes first moved one arm and then the other, the latter was the one which had been lanced, and it seemed stiff and painful. Uttering a low wailing cry, she let it sink by her side again.

"Where am I?" she moaned feebly.

"You are all right; don't be alarmed," replied Campbell.

He lifted her up gently, and made a sort of arm-chair for her by supporting her with his arm, for there was not a single chair in the place, and that was the best he could do.

"Give her some brandy," suggested Baldwyn, extracting a flask from his pocket, and handing it to Campbell.

The stimulant revived Agnes, and she petitioned to be placed upon her feet. She staggered a little at first, but her giddiness soon went off, and she saw at once the strange situation in which she was placed.

"Excuse the question, but it is a natural one under the circumstances," said Baldwyn; "but how did you come here? We were very nearly cutting you up by mistake."

Agnes was very much confused, and hardly knew how to answer; but while she was hesitating, to her inexpressible relief she heard the sound of footsteps coming from the inner chamber, where all the dogs, and animals of various descriptions, were kept by the vivisectors. The surgeons also turned their attention in that direction.

After a moment's suspense, Agnes perceived Stubbles approaching; she did not doubt that the vivisectors were following him, and that he was leading the way, for he held a candle in his hand, as if he were lighting those that came after him.

When Stubbles saw Agnes, he stood and rubbed his eyes. He could hardly believe his senses, but after a few seconds' consideration, the truth flashed across his mind; he thought that she had been so worried and excited with anxiety to know what lay behind the black door, that she could not resist the temptation which beset her, and that she had penetrated into the tartarean depths of the mortuary chamber.

He saw that the danger would be great if the doctors thought that she was not in some way connected with the establishment, for to have their secret betrayed and published in newspapers, would be utter ruin to most of them.

He devised on a plan.

Advancing with a smile on his lips, he went up to Agnes, and said—

"My dear sister, you might have waited upstairs for me; I should not have been long."

Agnes stared.

"You have come into something worse than Madame Tussaud's Chamber of Horrors," he continued.

"Is it possible that such a monster should have so pretty a sister? I'll not believe it," exclaimed Baldwyn.

"Nor I!" echoed several others.

"And that she could love him is equally absurd and out of the question," said Campbell.

An ominous frown gathered on the brows of the doctors.

At this juncture the vivisectors entered and demanded what the altercation was about?

Campbell assumed the part of spokesman, and said—

"We think we have discovered a plant on the part of this dwarf to sell us. This woman we found fainting, insensible, in fact, on the top of one of the coffins; we took her up, thinking she was dead, in order to operate upon her, but from certain indications, I considered that she was in a swoon, or in a trance, but not dead. I took some blood from her, and she revived. Now, my impression is, and I think it is pretty generally shared by my friends here, that the dwarf wishes to get up a case against us, and has bribed this woman to watch our operations, and afterwards give evidence in a police-court, as perhaps his own character is so bad that his testimony would not be worth much. Probably overcome by the unaccustomed sight of dead bodies, the loneliness of our place, and its other accessories, she lost her senses, and it was only by a lucky accident—that of our selecting her for a subject to begin with—that we have been enabled to discover the plot."

A murmur of anger, of surprise, of indignation, ran all round the circle of listeners.

"More than that," cried Baldwyn; "who knows but that this is an organized system of espionage? How can we tell? Perhaps there are police spies even now concealed on the premises."

Fists were clenched, and lips were pressed tightly together at this, as if the vivisectors were not men to be trifled with; and more than one heavily loaded life-preserver was brought out from its resting-place.

"The question is," resumed Campbell, "what is to be done with the traitor and traitress? For they are so, I do not doubt for an instant."

"Prussic acid," cried a voice in the crowd.

"Yes; a drop of 'Shield's,'" said another.

Shield's is the strongest preparation of prussic acid that there is, and a drop of it would not only instantaneously kill a man, but an ox, a buffalo, or rhinoceros.

"I've got some cyanide," said another, "in my pocket. It'll soon settle a dozen dwarfs."

"She is too pretty to die," exclaimed one of the students; "turn her up in the street and let her go. I don't think she's a spy, and if she is, what of it? Who's afraid? No one knows our names, or who we are, not even Old Bones the undertaker."

"Yes, that's true enough," replied Campbell; "but we should have our scientific experiments stopped; and what should we do then?"

"Ah! Campbell's thinking about that book he is writing," said a voice.

A stormy discussion ensued. The medical men were divided on the question; some thought that the dwarf and the girl ought to die, and others were in favour of sparing their lives.

Campbell and Baldwyn and their followers pressed towards the dwarf, who had placed the girl behind him so as to be out of harm's way.

Stubbles retreated, pushing Agnes along.

"Oh!" said Agnes, clasping her hands together; "what shall we do? They will kill us!"

"Leave it to me," replied the dwarf, who gradually retreated towards the door which led into the passage from which the vivisectors had first emerged.

CHAPTER LXXII.

THE DOCTORS AND STUDENTS BECOME ENRAGED—
—STUBBLES TRIES TO FIND A SECRET DOOR, BUT
CANNOT DO SO IN THE DARKNESS—THE BATTERING-
RAM—SATAN APPEARS WITH A LIGHT—THE KNOB IN
THE WALL—DISAPPOINTMENT—SATAN SHOWS FIGHT.

CRIES and exclamations arose on all sides, and the confusion became deafening.

Stubbles, however, seemed to have some definite purpose in view.

What that was it was difficult, if not impossible, at present to say. But it could not be doubted that his whole heart was set upon securing Agnes from the horrible fate that some of the students had suggested, both for her and for himself.

And what was there to prevent it?

The subterranean haunt of the vivisectors was utterly and completely unknown to the police; it might have been in Madagascar as far as they were concerned, and the infamous and revolting practices carried on there would have put even King Radama the Second, or the King of Dahomey to the blush.

Prussic acid is wonderfully quick in its execution.

Put a drop on your tongue and you will not live long enough to tell anyone of it.

This was what alarmed Stubbles.

These lawless young men might with the greatest facility poison any one they liked, and after the deed was accomplished, what was easier than to throw the bodies into a corner?

No coroners inquest awaited them.

No jury would set upon them.

The public press could not take cognisance of the iniquity, because it would never come beneath its notice.

From the determined aspect of Campbell and his party, Stubbles feared the worst.

He could see that some of the students would like to see him get away with Agnes, but others, and by far the more numerous part, were of one mind, and their inclination was to kill them both—the dwarf and the girl—like rats, and throw their carcases amongst the coffins which lined the dismal vault.

There might be a fight for it.

There probably would; but Stubbles, who was by no means a fool, could see at a glance which would be the victorious party, and then, when his few adherents were vanquished, he knew very well what would become of Agnes and himself.

It also occurred to him—it was a grotesque idea—that the young men would have no objection to dissect a dwarf —a hunchback, for such a subject seldom, if ever, came beneath their notice. Of course they would do it under cover of the highly-sounding phrase, "the interests of science," but that would be poor compensation to him, and he resolved, if he could, to frustrate their kind intentions; for although he had a great respect for science, he did not care to further its interests by his own martyrdom.

He kept on backing to the door we have before called attention to, and at last succeeded in reaching it. As he did so, Baldwyn and Campbell and their party rushed forward in a body.

The other phalanx, which was in a manner favourable to the refugees, interposed, and a conflict began.

Blows were delivered and received.

Fists were clenched and a great deal of execution done in the King and Heenan style.

Stubbles took advantage of this, and pushed Agnes through the doorway. Then he closed the door with a bang, and after groping about in the dark for a moment or so, shot the bolts into their sockets.

For a few minutes they were safe, but after the expiration of a short time there was but little doubt that the infuriated mob in the dissecting-room hungering and thirsting for the blood of the fugitives, would batter down the door and wreak their vengeance upon them in a sanguinary manner.

"We are safe," whispered Stubbles.

"Safe! Oh, no!"

"Trust me."

"I do—I will."

"You may with the most perfect confidence."

"You were my husband's friend," said Agnes, thinking of Marmaduke Wilson.

"That's a painful topic," said Stubbles; "and the less said about it the better."

His voice trembled and his tone was sad as he spoke.

"But to the business in hand," he continued.

"Yes; what shall we do?"

"Do not be alarmed."

"How can I help it? Those dreadful men will kill us."

"Not they. You wouldn't take my advice, you would go and achieve the adventure of the black door, and you see what trouble it has involved."

"I could not help it," replied Agnes, moodily.

"I have a plan," exclaimed Stubbles. "It's no use talking over what has happened, let us turn our attention to our own position, which, it must be acknowledged, is none of the pleasantest."

"That it isn't."

"Follow me," said the dwarf, holding Agnes's hand, and drawing her along the passage.

The sound of the strife in the room they had just left, grew louder and louder, and cries of triumph rent the air.

It was plain that Agnes's friends were getting the worst of it. She was very sorry, but she was powerless to assist them.

Stubbles continued to draw her along the passage, and she remarked that he appeared to be feeling his way, as he touched the walls with his hands repeatedly.

Perhaps he was trying to discover something — a door or knob in the wall—a secret spring; but his efforts were fruitless, for he found nothing. He stamped his foot and uttered a curse in his vexation.

Tremendous echoes now reverberated through the passage. Baldwyn and his friends were evidently trying to batter the door down.

Would they succeed?

Agnes trembled as she thought of it.

"What are you doing?" asked Agnes, addressing the dwarf.

"Trying to find something," he replied.

"What?"

"A door; but it is so dark, I cannot distinguish anything."

Agnes breathed a fervent prayer that his researches might be crowned with success, although she was not very sanguine about it.

The noise at the door redoubled, and a sound like that of a sledge-hammer, wielded by strong and willing hands was heard.

"I am afraid we must submit to our fate, and give ourselves up," exclaimed Agnes, in a tone of deep despair.

"What!" cried Stubbles, in astonishment.

"It is an unequal contest."

"Do you talk so despondingly, and are you serious?"

"Alas! yes."

"Can it be possible that any friend of Marmaduke Wilson's, or any one connected with him, can show so cowardly a spirit?" replied the dwarf, indignantly.

Agnes's face flushed in the darkness, and she felt ashamed of her pusillanimity.

"Forgive me, my friend," she said; "I am but a woman."

"Try and be brave then."

"I will. You shall not hear another complaint pass my lips."

"If I could only find this cursed door," exclaimed the dwarf, "we should be all right. Ah! what was that?"

A terrific blow was aimed at the door, which took effect upon the lock, and sent it flying along the passage. A faint, dim stream of light flowed in through the aperture.

The doctors hurled themselves in a body against the door, thinking that every obstacle to their passage had been removed; but they were disappointed to find that the bolts at the top and bottom barred their further movements.

"Listen!" suddenly cried the dwarf, catching Agnes by the arm, and griping her tightly.

Agnes listened intently, and almost held her breath as she did so.

The sound of footsteps was heard approaching from the vivisecting-room.

Who could it be?

Gradually they drew nearer and nearer.

Then a feeble light illumined the damp and slimy walls of the passage.

"Thank God!" exclaimed Stubbles, "it is Satan."

The dwarf had been left in the vivisecting-room to put the wounded animals away and to feed those that had been spared for a future occasion.

He had finished his work, and was walking slowly along, thinking of retiring to rest, as he was tired and worn-out with the numerous fatigues of the day and night.

Stubbles ran forward to meet his friend.

Satan stared a little when he saw him advancing.

"Your candle! Make haste! Give it me!" cried Stubbles, hurriedly.

"What is it?"

"We are in danger."

"Who from?"

"The doctors."

"How so?"

"You shall see presently; I have not time to talk now," replied Stubbles.

The roar of voices in the vivisecting-room, and the clanging of hammers, had partially ceased.

Stubbles was more alarmed at this calm than he would have been at the loudest noises.

"What can they be doing?" he thought. "Some devilish device no doubt has occurred to them."

While thinking in this way he kept on looking for the whereabouts of the secret door; but owing to his agitation, or the dimness of the light, or some inexplicable cause, he could not find it.

"Confound it!" he cried. "If I cannot find the door we are lost."

Agnes shuddered.

Satan did not know what door Stubbles alluded to, as he was not so well posted in the mysteries of the place as his companion, so he merely looked on wonderingly.

"Is it more towards the place where the animals are?" said Agnes.

"No; it is in the other direction."

"You are sure of that?"

"Positive."

They gradually approached the room in which the doctors were.

An ominous calm pervaded the apartment.

"There is something going on," said Stubbles. "Those doctors are not the fellows to let us escape so easily. There are several men and students from the Veterinary College, and they are always ready for any devilment. The worse it is the better it pleases them."

They were not long kept in suspense.

In another moment the sound of feet rushing over the pavement was heard; and something soon afterwards came with a dull, heavy crash against one of the panels of the door.

The panel creaked and bulged inwards a little.

Then the footsteps retreated into the middle of the room, soon after again advancing.

It was clear that they were using something like a catapult, or a battering-ram.

The stoutest door, had it been made of oak, could not have withstood them for any length of time.

Stubbles saw that after one or two more efforts the panel would fall through, and leave an aperture sufficiently large for a man's body to pass through.

If all the students were desirous of following them up, assisting in their capture, they could easily do it.

First one would go through, then another, and after him a third.

Stubbles saw the danger, and was nearly frantic with apprehension.

Turning to Satan, he said—

"Are you with me?"

"To the death."

"This is the wife of an old pal—I must save her."

"Yes."

"Will you help me?"

"With my life."

"Good," said Stubbles. "You know how to use your fists."

The dwarf bared his brawny arms at this, and smiled grimly, as if he would say—"No fear, I could crush a man's skull between my two palms."

"That panel must go," continued Stubbles, "and then we shall be at their mercy."

"Yes, yes."

"But if you stand by it, and when any one ventures

through the hole, catch him by the throat, and put the hug on, he will never speak more."

"Never," replied Satan, solemnly.

"Do so, then; and when you have silenced the first one who is hardy enough to venture, throw his lifeless body back again amongst his companions, who will be deterred by the spectacle from following him. All I want to do is to gain time. I know the secret door I am looking for is hereabout somewhere, because I have seen the guv'nor bring the bodies in through it. A few minutes more will enable me to do it."

As he finished speaking, the weapon of offence the doctors were using rattled up against the already loosened panel, and smashed through it with a tremendous noise.

The shattered wood went flying about in all directions, and a splinter struck Satan in the hand.

With such force was the ram urged against the door, that it slipped through the hands of those who were using it, and flew through the panel, sliding several yards along the passage, and stopping at Stubbles' feet.

He started when he saw what it was.

They had been using one of the strong elm coffins with which the room was filled, and so careless were they, and so brutalized were their minds, that they allowed the corpse to remain inside. Possibly they thought the additional weight would assist them.

However, there it was, lying with its upturned face and its closed eyelids, with its tightly stretched skin a little discoloured, for it had begun to swell.

Satan advanced at a run to the hole in the door made by the battering-ram.

He was not a moment too soon, for a head and shoulders was speedily thrust through, and the dwarf caught the head of the rash intruder under his left arm, and held it as if in a vice, while he administered punishment with the other hand.

In a very short space he had battered the poor fellow's face into a pulp; and so disfigured was he that his own mother would not have known him if he had been suddenly confronted with her.

Giving him a parting squeeze, the dwarf, with a fiendish laugh, threw the body back into the room, and awaited the coming of another.

There was a cry of surprise, alarm, and fierce anger when it was discovered how he had been treated.

The doctors held a council of war.

It was hardly safe to dare the chance of encountering that terrible hug, the effects of which were plainly visible.

What should they do?

It was a weighty question, and one which required mature deliberation.

While they were discussing the matter and attending to their wounded companion, Stubbles was not idle.

Suddenly he uttered a cry of joy; he had discovered what he had so long been in search of.

"It is here," he cried. "I have found it at last."

"Found what?" asked Agnes.

"The knob in the wall."

"Thank God!"

"Come on; I have only to press it and the door will fly open."

He pressed it, but no movement took place.

Again he tried, but with no better success.

"The devil!" he muttered between his teeth, while a cold sweat burst out all over him.

"What is it?" said Agnes.

"The door wont open."

"Wont open?"

"No."

"Try again."

"I have, but it's no good."

"Oh! what shall we do?"

"Keep at it, I suppose. Satan!"

"Yes," replied the dwarf.

"Keep them employed," said Stubbles.

"All right. I've slogged one of them. He'll have dead bodies on the brain, I think, for the rest of *his* life."

The surgeons, no way discouraged, resolved to batter down the rest of the panels, so that more than one of their number could enter at a time, and then, armed with knives, they would be a match for the dwarfs.

The warfare was becoming interesting, and the position of the fugitives was more critical than ever.

CHAPTER LXXIII.

THE SECRET DOOR DISCOVERED—SATAN FIGHTS GALLANTLY, BUT IS STABBED FROM BEHIND—HE RECEIVES HIS DEATH WOUND—STUBBLES BEARS HIM INTO SAFETY—HIS DEATH—THE PURSUERS BAFFLED—THE WAY TO FREEDOM—THE DARK PIT—AGNES MISSES HER FOOTING, AND HANGS SUSPENDED OVER THE GLOOMY SIDE OF THE CHASM.

THERE was not much noise now: both parties were in earnest. Blood had been shed, and the doctors were anxious to revenge it.

They were angry also at being held at bay by two dwarfs and a woman; but contemptible as the dwarfs appeared in their eyes, they had hitherto been a match for all of them.

The blows dealt against the devoted door followed one another in quick succession; and it was not difficult to divine what the end of it would be.

Stubbles continued fumbling and bothering about the knob in the wall. He was certain that he had found the right one, but he did not know the secret. He had pressed it and pushed it, and tried to move it, first on one side and then on another, but all to no good.

Satan stood with his fists clenched and his eyes wide open, ready to pounce upon the first who was foolhardy enough to venture through the hole.

This was the state of affairs, when a woman's ready wits came to the rescue.

"Have you tried everything, my friend?" exclaimed Agnes to Stubbles.

"Everything," he replied, in a desponding voice, "and the brutal thing wont move an inch."

"Not one?"

"Not the eighth of an inch, in spite of all my efforts."

"Then it is clear you are going the wrong way to work."

"You think so?"

"I do."

"What shall I do, then?"

"You have pressed it?"

"Yes."

"Pushed it on all sides?"

"Yes, yes."

"Have you tried to pull it towards you?"

"No," he replied, "I have not."

"Then try, my friend; for I have an idea that that will be the solution of the difficulty."

"I should be only too happy to think so."

"Try it; it can do no harm."

"Certainly not."

At that juncture another panel went with a crash into the passage. A cry of triumph resounded in the vivisecting-room. They could distinctly hear the students encouraging one another. There was no time to be lost.

"Pull at it, Stubbles; pull at it!" cried Agnes in an agony of apprehension.

He did so.

He took the knob between his fingers and thumb.

Then he pulled it as well as he was able.

It moved.

It gave a little.

Another effort, and another and another, and the door opened slowly outwards.

Agnes could almost have fallen down on her knees there and then in that cold stone passage, with the irate mob in the next apartment thirsting for her blood, and that of her companions; but the dwarf caught her by the shoulders and thrust her through the open doorway.

Stubbles caught up the light, which had hitherto rested upon the ground, and waved it in the air as a signal to Satan.

Satan saw it, and prepared to follow; but as he moved away two of his assailants made their appearance, one at each breach of the door. It was important that they should not know in what way they had effected their escape.

He stood by a moment, and then dashed his fist into the face of the foremost one.

The blow fell with crushing effect upon the luckless man's countenance, and battered it into a shapeless mass. He fell back with a groan into the arms of his friends.

Satan was about to turn round to serve the other in the same way, but before he had time to do so the doctors had contrived to pull his body through.

Springing to his feet, he observed a long knife in the air.

It was not long in descending upon the devoted shoulder of the ill-fated dwarf.

Deep, deep did it penetrate into his thick hump, which, like that of a dromedary, stood out like a conspicuous mark for an enemy.

The dwarf uttered a loud cry of pain, and fell prone upon the ground, where he moaned and wailed like one of the animals in the adjoining room when under the knife of the vivisectors.

Stubbles hearing the noise hastily gave the light to Agnes, and rushed forward to rescue his friend.

The man who had stabbed him in so assassin-like a manner kept on probing the wound with the knife, trying to thrust it further in, and screwing it round remorselessly with a crisp crunch as the particles of bone yielded before the sharp edge of the razor-like knife. So intent was he on his bloody work that he did not hear the approach of Stubbles, who glided along as noiselessly as a serpent, who, when about to spring upon his prey, does not even allow one of his scales to rattle.

Stubbles saw the condition of his friend. With a sudden feeling of anger his face flushed, his heart beat quicker, the blood rushed to his head, and he felt as if he were losing his senses.

The dwarf was usually a quiet man; but when calm people do lose their tempers, God help those who incur their resentment.

With a spring and a leap that would not have disgraced a tiger in the wild jungles of India, Stubbles was down upon his victim before he could offer the least resistance.

He first of all brought his fist down with a frightful amount of force upon his face. The blood spurted up in streams from the numerous wounds that that one blow inflicted. But he had not done with him yet. He seized him by the hair, and dragged him to the wall. He might have used his own knife and have killed him with that, but he was too much excited to use any but Nature's weapons. Drawing himself up till all the veins and muscles on the surface of his body were swollen and distended almost to bursting, he threw all his force into his right arm, and dashed the unhappy man's head against the wall. It cracked as if it had been a filbert, and his brains flew about in every direction—it was like the collapse of a cocoa-nut beneath the stroke of a heavy hammer.

Then stooping down affectionately, Stubbles lifted up the body of his friend, and carried it to the secret door, while the blood dropped down in a stream from the terrible wound that the student had inflicted upon him.

Once inside the said passage, Stubbles drew the door to after him; then he laid Satan down for a moment, and seizing the candle looked around for any bolt or other contrivance for fastening the door inside; but he found none. He had been so rapid in his movements, that none of the besiegers had been able to notice in which direction he had gone; he put his ear to the door and listened to see if they were still pursued. He was soon set at rest upon that point; he heard a noise as if all his assailants were scrambling through the breaches they had made. Then a loud wail arose. They had discovered the dead body of the man who had stabbed the dwarf. After that, when they seemed to fully comprehend what had taken place, and that their companion was really dead, there came from the lips of one and all a yell such as savages might make use of.

Stubbles, excited as he was, could not help feeling his flesh creep as he heard it.

His impulse to see what they would do next was intense and indescribable.

They did not stop long lamenting over the dead man—they were too anxious for vengeance.

Fortunately they never dreamt of the existence o a secret door; they imagined that the girl, accompanied by Stubbles, had taken refuge in the vivisecting room, and in a body they rushed pell-mell along the passage.

Stubbles congratulated himself upon their escape.

When the footsteps died away in the distance, he stooped down, and once more turned his attention to Satan.

His wound was bleeding frightfully, and it caused him the most excruciating pain.

Stubbles almost wept as he contemplated the wreck a few minutes' sanguinary work had reduced him to.

"Try and stanch the blood," said Agnes.

It was a wise suggestion, for the effusion was very great, and much danger was to be apprehended from that.

"It is of no use," said Satan, with a feeble utterance; "no earthly power can save me."

"Oh, say not so!" replied Agnes, stooping down like a ministering angel, and putting her white cambric handkerchief over the gaping place.

It was, as he said, of little or no use, for the ruby current welled up in a stream, and soon the kerchief was wet through and through, and Agnes's fingers were covered with the warm and crimson fluid; but in her endeavours to aid him she heeded it not.

"The spine is injured," murmured Satan; "I feel I must die. Stay with me till my spirit departs."

"I will, I will," replied Stubbles, in a quivering voice, for he was deeply attached to the ungainly but kind-hearted monster.

"We must all die some day," he continued, "and I don't know that I am sorry. I rejoice that your friend has escaped the murderous crew."

"Oh, you will not die," said Agnes; "you will live a long time yet, to enable me to thank you and show my gratitude for your heroism in saving me."

"No, no."

"Oh yes, you will; you deceive yourself. Your wound is not mortal."

The dwarf shook his head sadly, uttered a sharp cry, as if the spirit was passing reluctantly away from the body where it had so long abided, and the dwarf closed his eyes.

"I killed him," whispered Stubbles in his ear, "so it is blood for blood."

Satan opened his eyes once more for an instant, as if the spirit had been recalled, beamed a look of thankfulness from the orbs already beginning to lack lustre, and then, with a few convulsive, spasmodic contractions of the limbs, the dwarf straightened himself out, and was dead.

Stubbles threw himself down by the side of the body, and his tears flowed apace.

Agnes respected his sorrow, and did not disturb him by sign or word.

At last the fit passed away; it was very poignant while it lasted, and left its traces upon the countenance of the mourner.

"He was a good friend," he said, as he rose to his feet; "I shall never meet his like again until Marmaduke Wilson once more lands on the shores of England. Men will not be friendly with me on account of my malformation; but Satan was more hideous than myself, and we were drawn together owing to our being companions in misfortune. But there is some sort of curse upon me—the sins of my father are being visited upon me. From my birth I have been ill-treated and persecuted, and if I love anything it will most surely die."

"Do not give way so," said Agnes, gently.

"Ha! are you there? Pardon me; I had forgotten you. We must away from here. The body can remain until I have time to give it decent sepulture. On, on; follow me."

Snatching up the candle once more, he led the way up the passage, which was more musty, damp, and mildewed than the other. It was very close and narrow, but as they ran up it the air appeared to be a little fresher, as if they were approaching some open space.

After going some distance, they slackened their pace.

The dwarf walked very cautiously, as if looking out for some obstruction in the path.

"It should be about here," he said.

"What?" asked Agnes.

"The pit."

"What pit?"

"The pit wherein the bones and carcases of the animals are thrown when the doctors have done with them. We have an opening here into a sewer, and we precipitate all the remains down the pit; they fall into the sewer, and are swept into the Thames."

"How dreadful!"

"Yes; everything connected with this place is so."

"What is your master?"

"A body-snatcher, a rogue, a rascal, a nigger-driver—everything that's bad."

"Why do you stay with him, then?"

"Because I cannot help myself; the police persecute me to such an extent that I can do nothing else. No respectable person will speak to me because I am a dwarf, and no woman ever looked kindly on me, because I am so hideous, so ugly, so repulsive. And yet I did not make myself: the same Creator who made others also made me."

"For some wise purpose, believe me," said Agnes.

"I am willing to think so."

"Ah!" suddenly exclaimed Agnes, as a loathsome effluvium was wafted towards her. It emanated from the pit Stubbles had spoken of. Agnes grasped the arm of the dwarf, for it made her feel faint and sick, and there was something so horrible and disgusting in the emanations connected with it that she felt a strong inclination to draw back, but he led her forward.

They advanced to the brink!

They could hear the sound of water rushing swiftly along, as if many thousand gallons a minute passed the hole.

It was one of the main sewers of London, and the volume of water was immense.

"How do we pass it?" asked Agnes.

"There is a ledge to the right of you," replied the dwarf.

"Must I pass along that?"

"I know no other way."

He held up the light as he spoke, and Agnes saw a small space which connected one end of the passage with the other; on the left was the chasm yawning deeply and ominously before her.

"Oh, I shall slip; I shall fall!" she said, in alarm.

"There are nooks in the wall for you to lay hold of," replied Stubbles; "there is no danger."

"I dare not venture," she said, in a terrified whisper.

"There is no help for it."

"I would rather die, then. Leave me, my friend; preserve yourself."

"No, I shall not leave you. Summon up your resolution."

"I cannot."

"I will go first; you can follow me, and I will extend my hand for you to help you across."

Agnes looked irresolute.

"Oh! I wish I were dead!" she cried.

"Have a little of this," said the dwarf, kindly taking a bottle from his pocket.

"What is it?"

"It is only gin, but the spirit may revive you; in this damp place, it cannot do you any harm, that's certain. I always carry some with me, because the filthy offices I am obliged to perform in the vivisecting-room, make my blood curdle and my flesh creep, and were I without a stimulant I think I should not be able to bear it."

Agnes took the cordial he proffered her, and drank deeply; then she handed it back to him.

"A little more?" he said.

"Not a drop, thank you. I am better already; my faintness has gone off."

"Come then, let us try to cross." He conducted her to the right-hand side, and placed her hand upon one of the nooks in the wall, and told her to grasp it tightly.

She did so.

He then passed her, and said—

"Let me get safe over before you attempt to follow me; I will take the candle with me, and then place my foot firmly upon the other side and hold out my hand for you to grasp."

Agnes nodded her head, and the dwarf commenced his perilous task.

It was not so dangerous for him, however, as for Agnes.

He had crossed the narrow causeway before, but she had never dreamed of doing such a thing until a moment or two before.

Agnes watched him, and saw him effect the crossing in safety.

Then she breathed more freely. He at least was safe, and that was one comfort.

It was now her turn.

He encouraged her with his voice. She advanced one foot and then the other, laying hold of the nooks as she did so. One false step and she would be precipitated to the bottom, and smothered in the fetid water of the sewer.

Three parts of the way was safely accomplished!

He held out his hand till she grasped it!

But as she did so, her foot slipped, and she swung over the side of the gloomy chasm!

CHAPTER LXXIV.

AGNES IS SAVED BY THE DWARF FROM FALLING INTO THE SEWER—THEY PURSUE THEIR WAY AND AT LAST SEE DAYLIGHT ONCE MORE—THE LEGEND OF THE CAPUCHIN MONKS AND THE SISTERS OF ST. GILES'S—IN THE PARK—A STRANGE, STARTLING, AND MYSTERIOUS SOUND, WHICH CHILLS THE HEARTS OF THE LISTENERS.

THE water bubbled and rushed and gurgled, and the fetid fumes arose, poisoning the air, which at the best of times was not too pure in those filthy passages under St. Giles's.

Agnes was at first paralysed with fear and astonishment. She could not shriek, she could not utter a sound. She felt herself falling, falling, but suddenly her downward progress was arrested.

The dwarf had caught her by the hand, and was pulling her up again with all his might.

She swung backwards and forwards.

The foul slime of the walls contaminated her dress.

Foul insects sprang and leaped upon her, running all over her face and hands as if she was a corpse and her flesh of right belonged to them.

The dwarf stood with his feet firmly planted upon the ground; he had dropped the candle in his alarm, and heard it fall with a splash into the sewer below.

In the darkness, in that terrible opaqueness, which in such a situation seems almost like a foretaste of hell, he exerted all his strength, which was at no time despicable, and gradually hauled Agnes up to the brink; then he caught her by the waist, and laid her gently down upon the soft and slippery floor.

She had not fainted, but she was in a semi-inanimate condition. She was physically exhausted.

The blood which had flowed from Satan's wound, when like a good Samaritan she had endeavoured to stanch it, had clotted and coagulated upon her fingers, upon which here and there large clots of blood might have been detected. Her hair was loose and hung down behind her back, lank and limp; the moisture of the vaults had taken every bit of wave out of it. It was so dark that Stubbles could not see all these things, nor could he see whether she breathed or not. He was only too thankful to think that he had saved her life. Holding her hand in his, he said—

"It is so dark here that I cannot see whether you are insensible or not? If you have your senses about you, speak!"

Agnes could not speak; she tried to move her lips, but they refused to obey her commands.

"Can you not speak?" he continued.

She made a desperate effort, but her tongue clove to the roof of her mouth.

Stubbles took the gin-bottle out of his pocket, and feeling for her mouth in the funereal gloom, he, when he found her lips, put the neck of the bottle between her teeth and poured some of the spirit down her throat.

She swallowed it, and although it was not an atom more potent than publichouse gin usually is, it had the effect of reviving her.

She sat up, and as the gin flowed into her system and warmed her blood, she felt better. She rose to her feet and leaned on the arm of the dwarf.

"That is better," he said; "are you well enough to walk?"

"Yes; I think so," she murmured.

"Try what you can do, at all events."

"I will."

"It is worse than anything to remain here. You had a narrow escape, but I am glad to say I caught hold of your hand just in time."

"That you did."

"Come along, then," he continued.

"Have we far to go?" she demanded.

"Not very far, now."

"That's a mercy."

"Trust to me."

"I do."

Taking her along by the hand, he led the way at a slow pace. She followed as well as she could, although she was obliged now and then to rest, in order to obtain a fresh supply of strength, of which she stood very much in need.

After traversing the passage for about a quarter of a mile,

THE ALARM OF AGNES AND STUBBLES ON DISCOVERING A PYTHON IN THE PARK.

they came to an iron grating. It was secured to its frame by chains and padlocks of vast size; anyone unacquainted with the secrets of the place would have considered it hopeless to attempt to open it, but the dwarf, without the least hesitation, caught hold of a defective link in the chain, which was so composed that by a little pressure it allowed itself to open, and the enigma was solved.

After loosening all the chain in this way, the dwarf caused the grating to swing back upon its hinges, which were so well oiled that they did not creak at all, showing how frequently it was made use of as a means of ingress or egress.

Agnes passed through the aperture, and with a little assistance from the dwarf, stood in the open air.

The morning was breaking, and by its dim, grey light, she could see that she stood in a churchyard. Graves surrounded her on every side.

Stubbles soon joined her, and exclaimed—

"Now we are free, and I am not sorry to get out of the pestilential air of those vaults, and that horrible darkness which was so thick and impenetrable that you migh have cut it with a knife."

"Where are we?" asked Agnes.

"In a churchyard in Holborn. The sexton is a friend of the guv'nors, and we often use this as a method of bringing corpses into the dissecting-room for the doctors. Some of the animals are also brought in this way, for the vivisectors or cutters-up-alive, as I call them. There is a singular history connected with that long passage you have just traversed."

"What is it?"

"They say that, in the olden times, a monastery stood here where we are now. A church has since usurped its place, but it was a refuge for heart-broken and pious men in the good old time, and occupied by Franciscans or Capuchins, I forget which."

"How singular!"

"Yes it is, but strange changes take place in the world.

These monks were celebrated for the austerity of their order, but very often the more outward show there is, the worse people are in reality."

"So it is," said Agnes.

"Well," continued the dwarf, "the report goes on to say, that where Little Wonder now stands, when St. Giles's was a village some way distant from *chère Reine* or Charing-cross, there was a nunnery, and in order to establish a communication between the two religious houses, the monks wielded the trowel, became their own workmen, excavated, and finally made this long passage, through which they used to visit one another, when the superstitious and believing laymen thought them at prayers. It was many years before the scandal was discovered, but when it was, the disclosures were so horrible and revolting, that the primate ordered the nunnery to be rased to the ground, which was done, and the monastery was turned into a church. There is the story; I give it you for what it is worth."

"It is likely enough," said Agnes.

While talking, they had both sat down upon a tombstone. Having related his anecdote, the dwarf turned to Agnes, and exclaimed—

"Excuse me, dear lady, but what will you do now? Have you some home to go to?"

"Alas, no!" replied Agnes, sadly.

"Can I, then, be of further assistance to you?"

"You can, indeed."

"I do not seek to win myself into your confidence," continued Stubbles; "but if you will impart a little of your grief and of your private history to me, perhaps I shall be better able to advise you."

"I will."

"I am listening."

"Do you remember Marmaduke Wilson's bringing me to the old house in Bluegate-fields?"

"Yes, perfectly."

"I have not seen you since then, but strange adventures have befallen me. I need not recapitulate them, as they would not interest you. They are painful to me, and time is valuable."

"It is."

"However, I am persecuted by a foreign nobleman, named Count Val de Grace, who is possessed of marvellous power, and I fear him as I do the arch fiend. If I were a Catholic I should cross myself whenever I mention his name. He has followed me from place to place with the most indefatigable and unremitting energy. He has also employed my husband's foe——"

"What, Wyman?" cried the dwarf.

As he mentioned the name, an expression of intense hatred passed over his features.

"Yes, the same."

"Ah! a day will come when I shall square up accounts with the inspector. He is clever; but a man must be very clever indeed, and have a long spoon, who sups with the devil, and I would league myself with the Prince of Darkness to be revenged upon him for more than one foul deed."

"Wyman," resumed Agnes, when the dwarf calmed down a little, "has followed me up with all that astuteness for which he is so justly celebrated. He's doubtless bribed—heavily bribed by the count to capture me, and I am almost afraid to show myself in public lest he should do so."

"Ah!"

"When I came into Little Wonder, and so providentially met you, I was flying from Wyman, who had hunted me down and had tried to capture me in order to deliver me into the hands of the most unscrupulous nobleman that ever disgraced his patent of nobility."

"Scandalous!" ejaculated the dwarf under his breath.

"So you see, my friend, that I am still in a most perilous position," continued Agnes. "I would rather die, I need not tell you, than fall into Count Val de Grace's hands; and I would do anything to avoid so revolting a contingency."

The dwarf nodded.

"Wyman will no doubt circulate my description amongst his myrmidons at the different police-stations in London."

"Most likely."

"Yes, it is most likely; and if so, my capture will be inevitable. I never wanted a friend more than I do at present, and I throw myself upon your generous protection."

"You do?"

"Entirely."

"Without the least reserve?"

"Without the slightest reserve."

"Very well, then," replied the dwarf; "we must see what can be done. I too am homeless and adrift once more. I had often made up my mind to leave the undertaker, but as long as my friend Satan lived I would not. I was happy in my way while he was with me, for his was a kindred nature, and we understood one another. Now that dream is passed, and I must begin my life anew, and vegetate somehow and somewhere until the return of my friend Marmaduke Wilson."

"He recurs to that theme with a strange pertinacity," thought Agnes. "Can he have any ground for his assertions? I should think not. God grant he may not. What should I do? It would be worse than all my other troubles put together."

The dwarf's eyes were moist as he spoke of his dead friend Satan, and he brushed the tear-drops from them with the rough sleeves of his freize coat; but when he spoke of Marmaduke his eyes glistened again, and he evidently was thinking of old times, and indulging in the hope of a happy future. He was very much like a horse which has been stolen or sold away from a master to whom he has attached himself, and his fidelity to his former chief could not for a moment be questioned.

It was a good point—a redeeming one in his character, which contained more good than bad in it; and it showed the folly of judging people by their external appearance, for although his outside was ungainly and repulsive there was good stuff within.

"I will share your fortunes, lady," said Stubbles; "and perhaps together we shall be a match for our mutual enemy."

"Heaven prosper our friendship," she replied.

The dwarf echoed the sentiment.

"It is early morning," he said, "and I know not what to do at present."

"Nor I."

"I have only one plan to suggest, and that is, to go to a coffee-house and get some food, for I am faint and famishing; and you, dear lady, must be in the same prostrate condition."

Agnes's pale face gave a very plain answer to the question.

"There are many coffee-houses that open about here at half-past five to enable the workmen to get a cup of coffee before they proceed to their daily toil. Let us go to one of them."

"And what then?"

"Then we will walk up to the Regent's-park, select some quiet spot, and discuss our future plans."

"Yes; that will do admirably."

The dwarf smiled.

"No wonder Marmaduke Wilson trusted you, for you have a genius of your own," she added.

The dwarf smiled again, this time fondly and with pleasure.

They contrived to open the gate of the churchyard, but it was fastened in a peculiar manner, which was understood by Stubbles; and they passed out of the funereal precincts and into the street between the lights, so that they were unobserved by any policeman.

A coffee-house standing close by invitingly opened its door just as they neared it, and, along with one or two other men and women, they entered.

Having satisfied their hunger and their thirst for a small sum, they left, and wended their way to the Park, which they reached in a short time.

They went in at the gate near Portland-place, and wandered up the road until they came to a gate which led them into the long avenue going up to Primrose-hill.

They followed this for some little way.

The Park was only just thrown open to the public, so that there were very few legitimate travellers or pedestrians in it. But here and there dark forms dotted the grass, and Agnes could distinguish the bodies of many unfortunate people—both men and women—who had been compelled by poverty to find a night's lodging in the Park.

This is the nightly dwelling of many of our surplus population.

After going some distance, they turned on one side and went to the left, taking a direction leading to the Zoological Gardens.

Near the palings which surround these spacious grounds, they rested, and sitting down upon the grass, gave themselves up to contemplation.

It was cold and chilly. The distant sun had not yet made its appearance; the grass was wet and damp, so they arose and found a seat, which they appropriated.

Their backs were turned to the Gardens, and by that they were debarred from a view of the spacious domain; but the undulating plain stretched in a long vista before them down to the ornamental water, which was so prettily laid out in the time of the Regent, afterwards George the Fourth, after whom the park was named.

Taking in the beauties of the landscape, they sat for some time in silence.

Their reveries were interrupted in a most singular manner; a low, rustling noise was heard by them. It was as of some elongated body drawing itself—or being drawn—over the grass, and it struck a chill to the hearts of the listeners.

CHAPTER LXXV.

THE HORRORS OF SUSPENSE—THE HUGE PYTHON—ITS UNDULATING LENGTH AND GLITTERING SCALES—AGNES FALLS DOWN, BUT THE MONSTER PURSUES STUBBLES AND THROWS ITS COILS AROUND HIM—THE RESCUE—THE SAD STATE OF THE DWARF.

AGNES felt her flesh creep as the monotonous rustling sound drew nearer and nearer.

She grasped the hand of the dwarf nervously, and pressed it convulsively.

He in his turn became much alarmed.

It was a steady, gliding, rustling noise, as if two or three bundles of sticks, or faggots, as they are usually called, were being dragged over the surface of the grass.

Both of them had an undefined presentiment of coming evil; they hardly knew why, but some occult influence seemed at work to warn them.

Agnes was so terror-stricken that she dared not move.

But the dwarf, who was made of sterner stuff, and possessed more courage, turned his head, in order to ascertain what sort of an enemy was approaching them.

He was not long kept in ignorance.

A sight met his eyes which blanched his cheeks and made his blood stand still in his veins.

"What—what is it?" gasped Agnes, in an agony of terror and apprehension.

The dwarf made no reply. He could not. In his great dread he was as powerless as a child.

"Oh, speak, speak! for God in heaven's sake, speak!" said Agnes.

But he made no response.

He was incapable of doing so.

No wonder he was mute; no wonder he was horribly alarmed; no wonder his energies were paralyzed; for within a few yards of him was *a snake of the most formidable description*—a python, covered with glittering scales which refracted the light, and sent a thousand glittering, scintillating particles into the morning air. It did not seem at home; it was uneasy and restless. The atmosphere was uncongenial; but still it moved on perseveringly. First its head and neck resolved itself into coils, then the centre of the body, and lastly the tail. It went with prodigious swiftness.

Its length must have exceeded fifty feet, and its bulk was enormous.

Its girth in the middle was the size of a stout man's body round the abdomen.

The dwarf had never seen so terrible a monster in his life before, and as its flat head reared itself up ever and anon, and th dark flashing eyes moved angrily in their sockets, he cowed down in terror at the foot of the seat.

"Oh, speak! I conjure you, speak," cried Agnes.

He could only hold up his shaking hands and point in the direction of the serpent.

Agnes broke the spell which had hitherto bound her, and turned her eyes in the direction indicated.

Shriek after shriek pealed from her lips at what she saw.

There was no room for doubt.

There it was—a huge, unwieldy python, coming towards her with incredible celerity.

In the heart of London; in the Park in which people are accustomed to take exercise and recreation!

She could hardly believe her senses; but there it was—there was the one great damning fact before her.

The forked tongue of the snake went in and out of its mouth, and suggested horrors unutterable.

"Oh, would to God I had died in the vaults from which I have just escaped!" murmured Agnes.

There was little or no doubt in the minds of both Agnes and Stubbles that the snake had escaped from the vigilance of the keepers in the Zoological Gardens, and had made its way into the Park.

Often had she shuddered on winter nights, when crouching around the fire, she had read stories of snakes in foreign lands, of travellers crushed to death in the irresistible folds of a boa-constrictor, or bitten to death by the sharp and venomous fangs of the dreaded rattlesnake.

But a snake in London—a huge rolling beast in one of the most frequented parks!

It was unprecedented, undreamed of, and she would as soon have thought of meeting the devil and all his angels drawn up in battle array, with the pomps and vanities of this wicked world making up an allegorical host in the rear.

With every demonstration of the most utter and complete alarm, terror, and fear, with her senses numbed, and her heart sinking, Agnes uttered one long, despairing cry, and fell upon the dew-burdened grass. She did not faint, but there she lay, still and motionless—incapable of action; she could not have moved a muscle had a king's ransom been her reward for doing so.

The snake approached and reared its dreadful head as if reconnoitring the prey before it.

Stubbles rose to his feet and staggered along—he was trying to escape.

The snake fixed its terrible gaze upon him, and, although his back was turned towards it, he was compelled to stand still and reverse his position. Then the serpent established as complete an influence over him as Count Val de Grace had on former occasions over Agnes and Jabez Clarke. He was rooted to the spot as thoroughly as if he had been a tree whose roots had taken fast hold of the ground in various directions.

In a foreign country, in the tropics, in the parched and arid plains of the sunny East, he would have anticipated such a meeting, but within a mile and a half of Charing-cross, why, the thing seemed preposterous.

However, there it was, advancing rapidly with its horrible crest and glittering scales that rattled strangely as the serpent moved.

Agnes, although unable to move hand or foot, was a witness to all that had hitherto happened.

She awaited the sequel with feverish impatience.

The snake brought itself up to where the dwarf was standing trembling like an aspen, and shivering every now and then with violent terror.

Raising his flat and loathsome head to a level with the dwarf's, it gazed in his face, as it were, for an instant, completely fascinating him. Then, with a sudden movement—so quick, so rapid, so lightning-like, that you could not follow it—the reptile threw its coils around the luckless body of the unhappy dwarf.

Fold after fold enveloped him until he had the appearance of a gigantic Armstrong gun spirally coiled before the iron is welded.

Agnes closed her shrinking eyes.

She could bear it no longer.

She expected to hear the crunching of bones, the snapping of tendons, the last cry of the dwarf in his death agony; when she again looked up she feared to see the faithful fellow an unrecognisable heap of mangled flesh and blood and bones, smothered in the foul saliva which snakes expectorate and cover their victim with in order to assist deglutition.

The dwarf gave himself up for lost.

He was afraid no earthly power could help him.

He felt the hot and fetid breath of the snake upon his cheek, and he dreaded lest every moment the huge mouth might open and engulf his head.

His horror was so great that he fainted, his head fell back upon his shoulder, slipped a little on one side, and rested on the rough scales of the serpent, which had not as yet exerted its strength.

It had contented itself with encircling the dwarf.

It was waiting for some reason or other before it contracted its muscles.

All seemed dark, hopeless, and gloomy; but there was a break in the clouds—a speck on the horizon which no one suspected.

Suddenly a loud noise arose in the rear.

Men appeared round the corner blowing flutes and beating drums and clashing cymbals.

They were the keepers of the Zoological Gardens.

The escape of the reptile had been discovered, and they had sallied out in a body to effect its recapture.

The method usually employed by them when a snake got away was to charm it.

This they had learned from the Orientals.

There is nothing a snake likes so much as music; you can do anything with him when you employ it.

The python had contrived to get out of his cage, owing to a square of glass having been cracked by the intense frost and cold that had prevailed for some time past.

When the serpent heard the musical sounds, he raised his head and listened.

When the keepers saw that they had attracted his attention, one of them with a flageolet, and another with a violin, advanced to within a hundred yards of him.

The rough music instantly ceased, and the two keepers began to play plaintively upon their instruments.

The python turned its head first on one side, then on the other, and kept time to the music.

After a bit its coils relaxed, its muscles became pliant, and it gradually drew away from the dwarf. It was like unrolling a huge rope from the capstan of a ship.

The dwarf fell to the ground.

He was saved; but at what a cost!

Perhaps in those brief but shocking moments, during which he had endured the embrace of the python, his senses might have deserted him for ever.

When the keepers saw how successful their efforts were, they commenced retreating, and changed their tune into one more lively.

It was "Limerick Races."

The snake seemed immensely pleased with the air.

If St. Patrick had not driven all the snakes out of Ireland, we should have said that the serpent in question was of Irish parentage, so delighted did it seem with the inspiriting strains.

The keepers retreated slowly, but surely, and led the snake after them.

The ungainly monster was delighted beyond measure, and showed his appreciation of the efforts which were made to amuse him by moving his head up and down, as he had done when he first heard the musical sounds.

They led him into the Gardens by a private entrance, near the reservoir, and, after a time, the python was safely shut up in another and a securer cage, which was shared by the redoubtable boa-constrictor.

Agnes watched all this with the utmost satisfaction, and when the monster which had caused her so much alarm and suffering had disappeared, she ran up to Stubbles and raised him gently in her arms.

He breathed heavily.

It was a consolation to notice that, for it showed her that he still lived.

At last, the cold air brought him to himself. The first few words he uttered were incoherent.

Agnes spoke to him soothingly, almost lovingly—in gentle tones recalled him to himself.

He raised his hands and covered his face with them, as if to shut out some horrible vision—some terrible nightmare.

"Oh God!" he cried, in a tremulous tone.

"Be composed," said Agnes; "it is all over now. Providence interposed in your behalf."

"Never shall I forget the horror of those few moments if I live to be a thousand years old!" he cried, with a shudder.

"Oh, come—come! Let us away from this spot," exclaimed Agnes; "the air seems to stifle me."

"It was a dreadful adventure," he replied.

"Most wonderful. But it has ended well."

"Oh! what is that?" he cried, in a shaky voice.

The branch of a tree, dried and withered, moved by the wind, fell down upon the ground. This it was that had startled him.

When he saw what it was, he sighed and said—

"Alas! I shall never again be like my former self. Those moments of suspense and torture have made me worse than a woman. God help me!"

And Agnes echoed the prayer.

CHAPTER LXXVI.

THE "BLACK SHEEP"—THE DWARF RECRUITS HIMSELF—AGNES RECOGNIZES AN OLD ENEMY—JABEZ CLARKE CLAIMS HER AS HIS DAUGHTER—THE FIGHT—STUBBLES IS THROWN A "CROSS-BUTTOCK"—JABEZ CARRIES AGNES OFF TRIUMPHANTLY, BUT THE DWARF DOGS HIM.

How the dwarf left the Park, after his horrible adventure with the python, he knew not; but with the friendly assistance of Agnes he did so, and it was a great relief to him when he found himself in the friendly shelter of a public-house.

Agnes had conducted him along many a narrow, devious, and winding thoroughfare, avoiding the principal thoroughfares as she would have done a pestilential, plague-stricken neighbourhood, for fear of Inspector Wyman and his satellites.

The public-house they entered was near the University Hospital, in the vicinity of Fitzroy-market, which is not the quietest or most genteel part of London to wander into or to reside in.

The sign of the tavern was the Black Sheep, and, if one might judge from the countenances of those who frequented it, there must have been quite a flock of black sheep, with a few adolescent ones—the lambs if possible—giving greater promise in their guilt-garden of infamous deeds to be achieved than did their sires.

The dwarf and Agnes attracted a little attention as they entered, but the topers—they could not be called revellers—soon returned to their pots and, their quarterns and left the new-comers to themselves.

Agnes ordered a pint of gin and paid for it.

The dwarf drank greedily, and felt his sinking courage reviving as the kindly mixture sank into his stomach.

Agnes followed his example, and their tongues being loosened, they conversed together in a low tone.

All mention of the python and that terrible hug, which had so nearly proved fatal to Stubbles, was avoided.

There was a seat in a corner just large enough to hold two; it was unoccupied. They took possession of it and rested their weary limbs. They were both much in want of sleep, but knew not where to go and get it.

The dwarf was still fearfully pale, and well he might be. Many a time in his after life did he wake up in the night time, the victim of a terrible nightmare, and scream out with all his might, that a huge constrictor was coiled up upon his chest, hissing at him and protruding his forked tongue till it seared and burned his cheek while its poisonous breath stifled him.

Agnes was little better in spirits and condition than he was, but with the fortitude of a woman while any necessity exists for her to show it, she held up bravely and only succumbed when she could no longer be of use to anybody; this time had not yet arrived.

The dwarf required her care and her attention. Her kindly ministrations prevented his mind from dwelling on the danger he had just escaped; her voice, all gentle as it was, soothed him, and she proved herself, to him at least, a ministering angel.

The men in the public-house were drinking, talking, and swearing, as is but too often the case. They were mostly costers and people in that condition of life; they had come in to have their "morning drain" before they commenced their peripatetic career.

Although they were all noisy, there was one who excelled all the rest, not only in the loudness of his voice but also in the blasphemous nature of his language.

He was a dark and grizzly ruffian to look at, and had Agnes seen his face instead of his back, which was turned towards her, she would not have sat so still and so unconcerned as she was at present doing. As it was, something in the man's voice seemed to strike her. Her attention was arrested, she laid her hand nervously upon the dwarf's arm, and stretched her body forward in an attitude of listening.

"What is it?" demanded Stubbles, anxiously.

"I have heard that voice before," she said.

"Where?"

"I cannot at this moment tell, but it is strangely familiar to me."

"Try and recollect."

"I will."

"Which man is it?"

"The thick-set one."

"That burly man with his back towards us?"

"Yes, yes."

At this moment the man turned round.

Agnes caught sight of the bloated features she knew only too well.

Those ferret eyes, those red and swollen cheeks, that thick-lipped and widely-cut mouth, extending nearly from ear to ear, that podgy, prize-fighting nose, all these she knew as well as she did the handsome and calm features of Lord Marchmont.

"Oh! save me," she whispered to Stubbles, in a terrified voice.

"From what?" said the dwarf.

"From that man."

"Let him dare to lay a finger upon you——"

"Oh! he will—he will. You know him not."

"Let him try, that's all."

"What can you do?"

"Something he wont like, I know."

All of a sudden the man saw Agnes, his eyes scintillated with pleasure, his flat nostrils distended, his mouth opened; he recognized her in a flash of lightning as it were.

"Why, strike me blind!" he cried.

"What is it?" asked one of his friends.

"What is it? Summut I wouldn't lose for huniverses."

"Eh!"

"It's Hagnes."

"Who?"

"It's my darter."

The man advanced to Agnes, who shrank back with her hands before her eyes, as if to shut out some dreadful vision.

"My dear, how are you? how are they all at home? Sorry to part with you, eh?" he exclaimed.

"Oh! go away, go away."

"Not at all. You're my darter, and I'm Jabez Clarke," he said, with a malicious accent in his voice.

"Oh! why am I to be persecuted in this way?" said Agnes.

"Persekewted! Come, that's a good 'un. Who's a persekewting of yer? Ain't a bloke got a nat'ral and a legal right to his own darter—his own offspring, his own flesh and blood?"

Agnes made no answer.

"What do you say, mates?" he said, appealing to his companions; "ain't a cove got a right to his own darter?"

"Sartinly, that's right, that is," was the unanimous reply.

"Wery well, then; what's the use of crying out afore you're hurt? Come on."

This command was addressed to Agnes, who did not think fit to obey. She shrank still further behind the dwarf—to him she looked for protection in this, her hour of sore need and trouble.

"Stop where you are," said Stubbles, sternly.

"Eh! You a speaking to me?"

"Yes, I am."

"Stand a one side, then, if you don't want a prop in the eye."

"She's under my protection, and I shan't let you or any other man meddle with her," boldly returned Stubbles.

"You ugly little knock-softly," cried Jabez Clarke, in a rage; "who are you? Think I'm going to knock under to you? Are you a going to come atween father and darter? A pretty story, aint it? Why, you're little better nor a cripple; crutches are cheap now, I should recommend you to go and get a pair."

"You'll want some if I begin with you," said the dwarf.

"What! an abortion like you?"

"Yes."

"Come on; I'm game for a dozen dwarfs. Come on; I'll warm you. Look out, mates, and you'll see sport."

Jabez Clarke spoke in a confident tone.

His friends gathered round him to watch the end of this strange contest.

Agnes sank into a seat, powerless to do anything, her whole soul and system crushed with a horrible dread.

The dwarf, knowing the value of "first blood," hit out straight at the unwieldy figure of the costermonger.

The blow, which was a heavy one, dealt by the strong hand and arm of the dwarf, took effect upon Jabez Clarke's forehead, between his eyes.

It would have made an ox wince a little; but upon Jabez it had no perceptible effect. He shook his head, laughed, spat on his hands, rubbed them together, jumped about on his toes, and seemed as lively as a grig.

"D—— the fellow!" said Stubbles between his teeth; "his head's made of cast-iron."

Seeing a good opportunity, Jabez struck out at the dwarf, hit him a blow which, strictly speaking, was a foul one, for it was as nearly as possible under the right ear.

Then, as Stubbles reeled under the effects of the stroke, Jabez Clarke caught his head under his arm, and with the full exercise of his prodigious strength, amidst the applause of his associates, flung the dwarf a cross-buttock, sending him spinning through the air, and causing him to fall, shattered and bleeding, at the other end of the bar.

The applause at this was tremendous. The rafters of the old house rang again. Some patted Clarke on the back, some shook him by the hand as if he had vindicated the character and fame of their class, and others pressed drinks of all descriptions upon him.

Jabez shook off all his admiring friends as soon as he could, and advanced to Agnes, who was still sitting in her old position, stupified with grief at the accident to her faithful friend and protector, and utterly prostrated at the sad and dangerous condition in which she found herself. She felt that she was once more in the hands of the ruffianly fellow who slew her mother.

What should she do?

Could she escape?

Alas! no.

Jabez Clarke did not give her much time for reflection. She had only time to think of her first experience of Count Val de Grace's marvellous powers, and how he drew all Jabez's secrets from him, in spite of his resistance.

Agnes knew that the fellow had been upon her track for some time past with the sole end, aim, and view, of extorting money.

By a very remarkable coincidence she had stumbled upon him in the bar of the Black Sheep, whither fate had that morning directed her footsteps.

Her cogitation was cut short by Jabez Clarke's coming up to her and saying—

"You've got to come along of me."

"Oh, no, no."

"But I say yes."

"I would rather die," cried Agnes.

"Oh, I daresay. That cock wont fight. Perhaps you'll tell them ere mates o' mine as you ain't my darter."

"No more I am," said Agnes, indignantly.

"Never passed as such, I suppose?" he said, jeeringly.

"Yes, I have; but still——"

"You'll say next your mother wasn't my wife."

"She was your wife, I admit; but that doesn't make you my father," replied Agnes.

"Doesn't it? The old woman knew better than to look anywhere else for one," he replied, coarsely.

Agnes made no further remark; she was too heart-sick to do so.

Jabez Clarke went up close to her and said, in a sibilant whisper—

"If you don't come along of me, I'll gi'e you in charge for *murdering* of your mother."

"Oh, God!" cried Agnes, wringing her hands; "what shall I do?"

"Come with me, and don't be a fool," said Jabez.

He took hold of her arm, and dragged her out of the public-house.

His associates cordially concurred in what he was doing; one of them said—

"I'd larrup her if she wor mine."

"Gi'e her the strap, Jabez," cried another.

Jabez Clarke grinned sardonically at these suggestions, and led Agnes into the street.

They had not been gone more than half a minute, when the dwarf, whom nobody had noticed since his defeat, staggered to his feet, looked wildly around him for a moment, and then left the Black Sheep. He caught sight of Agnes and her brutal captor, and with all the sagacity he possessed, he followed them a short distance, watched them go up a court, and noted the house into which Jabez Clarke took her.

Then Stubbles looked all around him, as if he were making landmarks to guide him on some future occasion. He even crept along the walls of the court and stopped before the house which Jabez had entered. As he stood there, a long, smothered shriek seemed to ascend from the very ground; a door slammed heavily, and all was still.

The dwarf stole away upon tiptoe, emerged into the street, and walking along, was soon lost in the distance.

CHAPTER LXXVII.

IN THE DUNGEON—JABEZ CLARKE QUESTIONS AGNES—SHE REFUSES TO ANSWER—HE CHAINS HER TO THE WALL—STRIPPING HER OF HER DRESS—THE BEDSTEAD—THE STRANGE AND EXTRAORDINARY TORTURE OF THE DROP OF WATER—AGNES WILL CONFESS NOTHING.

WHEN Jabez Clarke led Agnes into the house in the court which Stubbles had so carefully reconnoitred, he conducted her down a flight of steps into what seemed the domestic offices. But avoiding anything in the shape of a kitchen, a scullery, or a servant's-room, he dragged her along a passage which seemed to extend some little distance under the street. The poor girl was too much knocked up, too fatigued, too tired, too much alarmed and terrified to cry out. To make any resistance would, she knew, be fatal.

At last Jabez stopped before an iron-bound door, opened it with a key, and thrust her in.

He quickly followed, closing the door after him.

They were in darkness.

Jabez, however, stretched out his hand, and found a lucifer match upon a shelf.

This he struck, and the faint flash of the match partially lit up the dungeon.

A piece of candle, stuck in an old black bottle, was revealed.

This he lighted, moving the match about in the grease to make it burn quicker.

When the candle was thoroughly alight, Agnes could see the dimensions of the subterranean apartment into which she had been brought.

It was a vault about ten feet by twelve in size—it might have been six feet high, not an inch more.

In one corner lay a quantity of potatoes; in another some bunches of parsnips and carrots.

It was Jabez Clarke's storehouse.

It was evident that he had given up tinkering and turned costermonger.

The walls were bare and damp; the floor was the plain earth, without brick or tile.

The trace of many a snail was left in all its silvery slime upon the walls. In the wall facing the door was a large iron staple. Affixed to this was a chain of great weight and size. At the end of it was an iron girdle, which, from the look of it, appeared to open and shut like a dog-collar, and was fastened by a key.

"Do you see that, my lady?" cried Jabez Clarke.

"What?" said Agnes.

"That 'ere chain and fittings."

"Yes, I see it," she replied, as her heart beat quick.

"Well, that's for you."

"Oh, no!"

"Oh, yes!"

"You can't be in earnest."

"Can't I? We'll see. Come on!"

He seized Agnes rudely, brutally by the wrist.

She fell to the ground, but he still continued to drag her along until she was at the foot of the iron staple.

"Now then!" he exclaimed.

Taking a key from his waistcoat-pocket, he unlocked the girdle, and clasped it round Agnes's waist.

Then he relocked it.

There was a considerable collection of moisture in one part of the roof or ceiling, and this dripped down in drops, which followed one another in quick succession—probably two seconds elapsed between each one.

Jabez Clarke looked at this fixedly for some time as if it had not arrested his attention before.

At last he said, in a satisfied tone—

"That will do. Yes, that'll do stunnin'."

Agnes did not at the time understand the meaning of the remark; but the unhappy girl was not to be kept long in ignorance.

Sitting down on the heap of potatoes, Jabez Clarke took out his pipe, filled it, and lighted it.

After puffing away for a few minutes, he exclaimed—

"I say, you gal there, what ha' you been a taking me for all this long time?"

No answer from Agnes, who did not know what to say.

"For a tarnation fool, I suppose?"

Still no answer.

"But I'm not, as you've found out. I've got you hard and fast; and what I want to know is, what you've been a doing with yourself?"

"I shall tell you nothing," replied Agnes boldly, feeling it would be better to speak than to remain silent.

"Oh, you wont?"

"No, not a word."

"Very well; we'll see."

Agnes glared defiance at him.

"What ha' you got on—any bracelets, jewels, or sich like?"

"No," she said, resolutely.

"Nothing of the kind?"

"No."

"That dress is a good 'un, though; it'll lumber. You'd better take it off."

Agnes, chained to the wall as she was, felt like a tigress at bay.

"It is mine, and I shall not let you have it."

"Wont you? Don't say that."

Advancing towards her, he attempted to unfasten her dress; but she flew at him, scratching his face, making deep long furrows, and using her nails with great dexterity.

"Drat the varmint!" he cried, in agony, stanching the blood as well as he could with a dirty snuff-coloured pocket-handkerchief.

Directly he found the hæmorrhage had partially subsided, he raised his hand, and with his open palm gave her a box on the ear, which nearly stunned her.

She reeled against the wall.

"I meant to knock you silly," he exclaimed. "I'll make you smart for this. I'll make you pay for it. I'll be one with you, curse you!"

Then he again endeavoured to unfasten her dress with his coarse hands, and this time successfully.

She was too faint and ill to resist his brutal attack.

When he had undone all the fastenings he drew the dress over her head, and folded it up into a neat, small parcel, saying—

"You'll be warm enough as you are. You wouldn't mind a father taking your gown to pawn? I'll bring you the ticket. What's this? some money in the pocket. Let's have a look at the posh, One, two, three, four, and a kick—four bob and a kick. That's luck. I'll have a little blue ruin on the strength of it."

Putting the money in his pocket and the dress under his arm, he once more sat down on the potatoes, mopped his bleeding face with his handkerchief, took a whiff at his pipe, and then said—

"Where ha' you been all this time?"

Agnes was fairly roused, her giddiness arising from the blow had passed off, and she replied, defiantly—

"What's that to you?"

"A great deal."

"You will never know from me, then."

"Wont I?"

"No."

"I'll try then."

"You may. It will take you all you know to do it."

"I know a great deal," replied Jabez; "more than you think for, perhaps."

"I'm not afraid of you."

"You will be before I've done with you."

"If you think so, I don't."

"Wait a bit."

"You may kill me," said Agnes.

"I don't want to do that."

"I don't care for you a bit. You killed my mother, and you may kill me! It is only what I may expect."

"I'll put you to a better use than killing of you," replied Jabez Clarke.

"You'll never get a farthing through my instrumentality," said Agnes, resolutely.

"Don't be too sure."

Agnes, in her great rage, spit at him.

He scowled at her, and getting up went out of the dungeon.

"Thank Heaven, he is gone?" said Agnes, sinking to the ground, and leaning against the wall.

Jabez Clarke was not long absent; when he returned, he bore a small iron bedstead in his arms, such as you buy in Tottenham-court-road for eight and sixpence; upon it was a paillasse.

"My arguments have had some weight with him; he is growing merciful," said Agnes, to herself.

But she little divined the intentions of the bad-hearted and relentless ruffian before her.

He placed the bedstead in the middle of the room, then he moved it towards Agnes. At last he got it into the position he wished to.

Sitting down on the paillasse, which he placed on the bedstead, he exclaimed, looking at Agnes furiously—

"There's more ways nor one of getting secrets out of people, and if fair means don't succeed, there's nothing like trying foul ones."

"What are your intentions?"

"You'll see time enough."

"Oh, tell me!

"Not I. You'll find out time enough, I say.

Agnes grew alarmed.

"Would you murder me?"

"No, it wouldn't suit my book. A woman alive's worth more than one dead."

"Oh, kill me at once, and put me out of my misery! I am tired of living," said Agnes, despondingly.

"Certainly not. If you wish to die it is all the more reason why I should make you live. Come here!"

Agnes refused to move.

Seeing this he undid the chain.

Then, taking her in his brawny arms, he lifted her on to the iron bedstead.

He laid her flat on her back. Then he drew a coil of rope out of his pocket, and proceeded to bind her to the bedstead.

He succeeded in doing this in spite of her struggles, her cries, and her resistance. He fastened her so that she could not move.

He particularly bound her head in such a way that she could not stir it, either to the right or to the left.

Then he looked up at the ceiling and watched the course of the drops of water we have before alluded to. By moving the bedstead a little more towards the wall, he brought Agnes's face directly under the drip, drip of the water.

A drop fell with a splash upon her cheek.

Jabez Clarke moved the bedstead again, and the drop splashed upon her forehead; another movement, and it fell in the very centre.

He watched the falling drops narrowly, critically for a time, and seemed to be perfectly satisfied.

Going to his corner, he filled his pipe again, sat down on the heap of potatoes and smoked contentedly.

He watched Agnes with the eye of a lynx.

Agnes did not know it, but the crafty brute, with his low fiendish cunning had invented a torture worthy of the Inquisition.

At first the patting of the drops of water upon her forehead tickled her; then it ran into her eyes, and down her neck; but that was nothing.

After a time, the water seemed to grow heavier, and to fall with greater volume and force.

It made her head ache.

She writhed uneasily upon her rude couch, but she was unable to extricate herself from the horrible position in which she was.

The water continued to fall with a monotonous splash upon the *same spot* on her forehead.

At last it was like a drop of lead falling on her.

Her head ached and throbbed.

Her eyes flashed and grew bloodshot.

Every drop which fell upon her made a vibration all through her body.

The torture was becoming unbearable.

Jabez Clarke looked on with gratified malice, and not one ray of pity penetrated his heart for the unhappy condition of his victim.

The torture grew unbearable, Agnes uttered low moans of pain.

It was music to Jabez to hear them.

"I'll make her speak," he muttered; "or I'll know the reason why."

The low moans increased to loud exclamations.

Then she gave utterance to piercing, sickening, soul-penetrating shrieks, but they fell like blunted arrows against Jabez Clarke's breast.

And still the steady pat, pat of the dropping water was audible amidst the lamentations of the girl, and the heavy-breathing of the man.

Drip, drip.

Patter, patter.

It was driving her stark, staring, raving mad.

Human nature, flesh and blood could not bear that maddening, everlasting throb, throb, thirty times in every minute.

The skin was already becoming sore and excoriated.

A wound was forming, and were not madness to release her from her sufferings the brain would unquestionably in time be laid bare.

Agnes shrieked.

Jabez watched her sufferings, and the water fell as monotonously as ever.

CHAPTER LXXVIII.

JABEZ CLARKE PROVES HIMSELF TO BE A SCIENTIFIC TORMENTOR—AGNES'S FORTITUDE—HE QUESTIONS HER—AGNES WILL NOT CONFESS—JABEZ CLARKE IS ENRAGED THEREAT—HE THREATENS AND LEAVES HER TILL THE NEXT DAY—SHE HEARS A MYSTERIOUS NOISE—SUSPENSE.

THE moments that passed while Agnes was in the power of Jabez Clarke were terrible ones indeed.

That cruel relentless man did not appear to have the slightest pity. He did not seem to feel for her sufferings an atom of that sympathy that anyone, not hardened in an extraordinary manner, would naturally entertain for anyone tormented as she was being.

Strapped securely to that plain iron-bedstead, what could she do? She was unable to move—unable to stir hand or foot.

If she could have moved her head a little—very little bit on one side, she would have given worlds to purchase the privilege. The torture consisted in the drop of water falling continuously upon the same spot.

If the drops had been distributed equally over her face, it would merely have caused her a little inconvenience, and that is all.

She would have felt wet and uncomfortable; but the maddening pain would have been spared her.

At last the torture became so dreadful, that every drop of water which fell upon her poor defenceless forehead, felt like molten lead sinking deep into her brain.

Jabez Clarke sat upon the mass of vegetables in the corner, smoking carelessly.

Agnes's shrieks disturbed him very little indeed; for he took no notice of them. Perhaps, he was satisfied with the thickness of the door and walls; after awhile, he rose and took his pipe out of his mouth, shook the ashes out, using his finger as a tobacco-stopper. Then he advanced to Agnes, and gazed curiously at her, as if she presented a singular spectacle, in which he took a great and unmistakeable interest.

She turned her swollen blood-shot eye-balls towards him with such a piteous gaze, that the archfiend himself would have entertained some commiseration for her, had he been in Jabez Clarke's place.

After he had satisfied his curiosity, the man gave the bedstead a careless kick, which made it slide a little to the left of him. This sufficed to remove Agnes from the place where the drop of water continually fell.

Words of thankfulness rose to Agnes's lips. All her resentment faded away; she could at that moment entertain nothing but gratitude towards the man who, although the author and originator of all her sufferings, had, at the last moment, taken compassion upon her, and liberated her.

Jabez looked at her savagely, and exclaimed in a gruff voice—

"None o' your thanks, young woman; you ain't got nothing to thank me for."

"Oh, yes, I have."

"Well, some dogs—curs I oughter say—will lick the hand as whacks 'em."

"I do thank you for releasing me from that torture," said Agnes.

Jabez smiled.

"I could not have borne it much longer."

"Warn't it nice?" he exclaimed, with a sardonic grin.

Agnes shuddered.

"Would you like some more on it?"

"Oh, no, no!"

"It don't cost nothin', it be the cheapest amusement as I knows on."

"Oh, don't; please don't," said Agnes.

"It be fine fun," he continued.

Agnes said nothing.

"It be about as good to me as going to the Great Mogul, down in Drury-lane—and I do love that place; what a many sprees I 'ave 'ad in that there crib to be sure!"

He appeared plunged in reflection as he said this, as if the reminiscences he called up pleased him.

Now and then he laughed.

Presently he looked up again, and said to Agnes—

"I'll lay summat now as you would like to know what my little game is wi' you."

"I know."

"You do?"

"Yes, I think so."

"What is it, then?"

She hesitated.

"Let's have it."

"You want to get money out of me," said Agnes, timidly.

"Right you are," he replied, rubbing his hands together.

"But I haven't got any," she pleaded.

"Aint got none?" he repeated, with an air of incredulity.

"No, I have not."

"That's all my eye."

"Indeed it's true."

"I aint a marine; I'm an able-bodied seaman, and that sort of thing wont do for me. If you want to tell me lies, you must make better 'uns than that."

"I give you my word of honour," said Agnes, "that what I tell you is the truth."

"Your word of honour? What's it worth?"

"You can rely upon it."

"Not I."

"My honour is all I have left now, and that is more tarnished than I could wish it," said Agnes, mournfully.

"Look 'ere," suddenly exclaimed Jabez.

"What is it?"

"You see that water a dripping?"

"Yes, yes."

"You'll be under it again uncommon quick, if so be as you don't answer my questions."

"What questions?"

"Don't you 'urry yourself; you'll hear fast enough, I'll warrant."

The ruffian smiled grimly.

"Speak," said Agnes; "I will answer your questions truly."

"That's right—that is; that's the way a daughter should answer a father."

"You are not my father," cried Agnes, indignantly.

"Aint I? Well, it don't matter—you're nothing to be proud on, so we wont quarrel over it."

Agnes with difficulty repressed the angry response which was rising to her lips.

"What ha' you been a doing on since I last had the pleasure of meeting wi' you?" asked Jabez quietly, accompanying his query with a searching glance at the helpless girl before him.

"I can't answer you," she replied, timidly, but resolutely.

"You can't?"

"No."

"Then I'll make you."

"Oh, what would you do?"

"You'll have another taste of that water dodge of mine. It's as good as the ghost invention. I think," he added playfully, "I shall go and get it patented. It licks Pepper's ghost, 'cos it's my own idea, and the ghost wasn't his'n, they say, but another bloke's."

"Oh, do not torture me any more," almost gasped Agnes, in an agony of apprehension; "have some pity upon me. Remember that if you are not my father, my mother was your wife. Think of that, and think of how she died."

"Curse you!" cried Jabez Clarke, rising to his feet, "you'll throw that in my teeth, will you?"

"I meant nothing."

"Then keep your tongue between your teeth in future, or it'll be the worse for you."

"Oh, spare me!" cried Agnes.

"I'd kill you with pleasure, curse you! I allers hated you," he replied. "I'd kill you now in this ere place if I didn't think you'd be useful to me. I think I can make something out of you; and that's the only reason I let you live. Come now, answer my questions, will you?"

"I cannot; I do not feel justified in doing so."

"You won't speak?"

"No."

"Think again."

"I am resolved. You may kill me; a little more of that terrible torture will soon do so, but you cannot make me speak."

"Kill you will it?"

"I hope so—I care not about my life."

"It will not kill you," said Jabez Clarke, with cruel emphasis, but I can tell you what it will do."

"Oh! what is that?"

"It will make you a drivelling idiot for the rest of your existence."

"Do your worst!" said Agnes, in desperation; "Heaven may have mercy upon me, if you have none; and I will pray it to release me from my sufferings."

"You may pray," he cried with a loud blasphemous laugh, "but you won't get much by praying."

"You cannot tell that."

"I've got you 'ere," he hissed between his teeth. "No one knows of it; no one can help you. There's no getting out of lions' dens now-a-days; so you needn't think it. Once more, Miss Hagnes, tell me who your friends are? and give me their addresses, and I'll let you go after a time."

The temptation to send the man to Lord Marchmont was very great, but Agnes did not like to do it.

Jabez might, and probably would, make certain revelations which would make his lordship dislike her more than anything else; and she valued his esteem as much as she did his regard.

She could not bear the idea of being despised by the proud aristocrat. She did not mind being shunned and hated so much, but the idea of being scorned and looked down upon, was excessively distasteful to her.

Her pride, even at that critical moment, stepped in, and prevented her from adopting those measures to save herself which the man presented to her.

"You're a long time making up your mind," said Jabez Clarke, impatiently.

"It is made up."

"What will you do?"

"Nothing."

"What do you mean?"

"I will trust in Providence."

He laughed loudly, perhaps a little bitterly.

"I know a way to tame you, my lady," he cried, brutally, pushing the bedstead underneath the dripping water once more.

The spot where the drops of water had descended before was easily noticeable, because the flesh was not only discoloured, but much swollen.

Clarke, with devilish ingenuity, adjusted the bed to his satisfaction.

Agnes closed her eyes, and seemed to be resigned to her fate; her lips moved occasionally; sharp, spasmodic twitches passed over her face now and then as if she were in great agony, but that was all. Nor sound nor cry escaped her.

Jabez Clarke watched the monotonous drip of the water, and noted its effect upon his victim with ill-disguised dissatisfaction. He walked up and down the floor of the cell and stamped upon the bricks with his heavy nailed boots, as if he could hardly control his rage. Once he advanced to Agnes with his fist clenched, and shook it in her face; her eyes being closed, she was spared the degradation of seeing herself threatened in this brutal and cowardly manner. An angelic sweetness stole over her pallid countenance, which had hitherto been so anguished.

Jabez Clarke saw it, and despaired of making her speak on that occasion.

With a kick, he sent the bedstead against the wall, and exclaimed—

"Curse you! again you think to thwart me, do you? We shall see. You think you've beaten me this time, but you haven't—not a bit of it. I'll be one with you. Lie

JABEZ CLARKE MEETS WITH AN UNEXPECTED ATTACK FROM THE DWARF.

there till this time to-morrow; perhaps by that time you'll want something to eat—and you may want."

"I am faint and ill now," said Agnes, opening her eyes.

"Answer my questions, and I'll feast you like a princess," he replied, eagerly.

"Never."

There was a look of resolution, and strength to bear a great deal, stamped upon her face.

"Then you may die and rot in this 'ole," he said; "for, so help me, you never shall leave it alive, unless you confess."

Agnes sighed, and Jabez Clarke took up the light, unlocked the door, and passing out, locked it on the outside.

Soon his heavy footsteps were heard growing fainter and fainter in the distance.

When he was gone, Agnes was inexpressibly glad that she was alone once more. It was something to be relieved of the monster's presence.

She was confined to the bedstead; he had not taken the trouble to untie her. Her position was most uncomfortable —most desperate. But still, in all her misery, she could not help feeling rejoiced that Jabez Clarke had departed. She entertained no hope of ever leaving that gloomy vault alive; she thought that Jabez Clarke would surely kill her, either by inches or in his rage; but she was resolved, nevertheless, to suffer and undergo anything, rather than let him know a line of her history. You may call it obstinacy, but very often women are obstinate, and allow their interests to suffer through it.

The rest of the day passed wearily for the captive.

Sleep refused to visit her heavy eyelids; the watches of the night had commenced and she was still awake.

Suddenly a strange noise aroused her attention.

It came from above.

What could it be?

She listened.

CHAPTER LXXIX.

AGNES FINDS HELP AND SUCCOUR WHEN SHE LEAST
EXPECTS IT—THE TRAP-DOOR IN THE TOP OF THE
CELLAR—STUBBLES APPEARS LIKE AN APPARITION—
WHAT HAPPENED TO JABEZ CLARKE—THE ESCAPE.

THE noise continued.

It could not properly be said to increase, because it was a cautious, never-varying noise.

The author of it, whoever or whatever he was, evidently did not wish the sound of his operations to be heard at any great distance.

Agnes strained every nerve to listen.

The sound seemed to her to be some gracious evangel, sent her in the hour of her direst need.

She was very ill.

Stiff and sore all over, owing to the brutal way in which Jabez Clarke had confined her limbs.

The cords with which he had bound her could not be described as eating into her flesh, but as they had been round her delicate and tender flesh for many hours, the pain they caused may be imagined.

The blood was unable to circulate properly, and the result was quickly apparent in every part of the girl's body where the bands touched her.

At first, the noise resembled some one probing the earth overhead; but after some time had elapsed, it was more like grating and scraping against stone or masonry, with some hard substance—possibly a trowel or a knife.

Agnes gave herself up to every sort of speculation.

Who could it be? what could it mean?

She prayed devoutly in her inmost heart, that if any extraordinary means of deliverance was at hand it might be brought about quickly.

She did not know whether she would be able to survive the night. If she did so—if her constitution proved strong enough, and enabled her to bear up against the innumerable horrors that surrounded her—she felt sure of one thing, and that was she would not be strong enough to stand much more torture and ill-treatment at the hands of Jabez Clarke.

A thousand times Agnes wished she were a man, and able to cope with the cowardly ruffian. She would have shown him little or no quarter.

He had treated her in the most barbarous and inhuman manner, and at the moment she believed she could have heard him condemned to die upon the gallows without much inward shrinking or compunction.

More than that, she could have seen him expire without extending a hand to save him.

In her calmer moments she would have banished such ideas from her mind at once; but now she had gone through so much she had not that self-control which she formerly possessed.

Suffering and misfortune had caused bad and evil passions to enter her mind, and partially take possession of it.

But this was extremely natural.

Without any warning that such a thing was about to happen, the noise, whatever it was, ceased—ceased suddenly.

Every germ of hope that had sprung up in Agnes's heart was instantly smothered.

It was as if an early summer had taken place and given birth to premature rosebuds, which an unsuspected frost had withered and cut off in all their hopefulness and youth.

It was hard. It was another drop in the bitter cup which Agnes held to her mouth, and was compelled repeatedly to drink of.

Everybody, however, who has made any part of our earthly pilgrimage knows that disappointment is the lot of mortals.

Happy those who get through the world with the least number of annoyances.

Still, as we have said, it was very hard that Agnes should have her hopes darkened at the very commencement. She had been foolish enough to think that some one was trying to deliver her.

When the noise ceased she blamed herself for her excessive credulity.

Who could have found her out in that damp dungeon?

Would Lord Marchmont have believed it possible that such a thing should happen to her or any woman in a civilized country? Or if he were really certified of the fact would he care to go after her?

It was extremely doubtful.

Thinking of Lord Marchmont turned Agnes's thoughts into another channel.

She dwelt with a sort of painful pleasure—half pleasure, half pain composed the feeling which animated her—upon the time she had lived with her aunt, Miss Lavinia Leslie, and subsequently with Lord Marchmont. With pleasure because she had been happy with the man who believed himself to be her husband, but who was, in reality, the usurper of another man's right. With pain, because she was afraid that she had forfeited his love and regard for ever, and for no fault of her own. Here was the sting of it all.

While carried away by her reflections she had almost forgotten the mysterious noise, but she was reminded of it by the sound of footsteps overhead. They stopped, as it appeared to Agnes, just over the very centre of her dungeon.

A moment of suspense followed.

A harsh sound struck upon her ears. Immediately afterwards a draught of cool air fanned her flushed and fevered face.

Looking upward she perceived that a hole appeared to have been made in the ceiling or dome of the vault.

A little starlight penetrated through the shaft, if we may call it so, which led the way from the roof of the dungeon to the pavement outside.

This starlight, faint as it was, did not illumine the black depths of the vault very long.

A shadow fell upon the opening, and a voice exclaimed—

"Mrs. Wilson!"

Agnes started.

Her convulsive movement had the effect of making the cruel cords chafe her flesh, but she was so astonished that she could not resist the movement.

She recognised the voice—it belonged to the dwarf.

"Yes," she replied, in a voice soft and low from exhaustion.

"All right," said Stubbles, cheerily.

Then his head was withdrawn from the aperture.

The starlight penetrated the dismal place once more, and Agnes had time to congratulate herself upon having found a friend at last.

A rope fell into the vault. It touched the floor.

Not very much time elapsed before the dwarf made use of it, and descended.

It was dark, with the exception of the light which came through the hole, which was little better than none at all.

Feeling in his pocket, Stubbles produced a taper and a box of matches. The chamber was soon illuminated. When his eyes got accustomed to the light, he gazed around him and saw Agnes extended upon the iron bedstead as if she had been a corpse.

When the dwarf comprehended how ill she had been treated he ground his teeth and clenched his fists.

Opening a knife, he lost no time in cutting the cord and liberating Agnes, or Mrs. Wilson, as he had called her.

Agnes was too weak to rise at first, but the dwarf, ever ready with an expedient, administered a stimulant to her, and she sat up.

"How did you find me out?" she asked.

"I followed you when he took you off."

"How did you know I was here?"

"I guessed it," replied the dwarf. "I saw him take you into this house, and I thought he would put you into some cellar, so I came back about an hour or two after he first took you, and pretended to fall down in a fit on the pavement; I did this, because I thought if you were in any dungeon underneath I should hear voices, or hear you scream if you were being ill-treated."

"Yes, yes."

"And I did hear you; I knew your voice well enough, and I was sure you were confined underneath where I lay. The next thing to be done was to find out how to get at you."

"How did you do that?" eagerly asked Agnes.

"By perseverance," replied the dwarf.

"Tell me how!"

"I found that the vault directly beneath me was a coal-cellar, because I saw the plate close by. Having made that discovery, I got up and went away. The sympathizing bystanders never for a moment supposed that I was not seriously ill. I acted my part well."

"I can believe that," said Agnes.

The dwarf smiled, and continued—

"I came back half-an-hour ago, and began operations on the cellar trap."

"I heard you."

"No doubt."

"But why did you go away for a time and then come back?"

"For a very simple reason."

"What?"

"I saw a policeman in the distance, and I prefer avoiding a blue whenever I can; they are enemies of mine. When the policeman had gone away to some other part of his beat, I began again, soon got the plate up, and the rest you know."

"Thanks to you," replied Agnes, "I am free."

"Not yet," said the dwarf quietly, almost sadly; "there is much to be done yet."

"In what way?"

"How are we to get you out of this place?"

"Through that aperture," replied Agnes, rather surprised at his question.

"I am afraid not."

"Oh, do not say so!"

"I don't say it to alarm you," replied Stubbles; "but you cannot climb up a rope like a sailor."

"No."

"I do not think I could haul you up safely, and yet it might be tried."

"Before you make any attempt to liberate me," said Agnes, "would it not be better to fasten this door in some way?"

"A good thought," said the dwarf; "but how?"

The dwarf looked in vain for any bolts or fastenings inside with which he could secure the door; nothing of the sort could he find. The door was utterly destitute of any bars inside. Probably Jabez Clarke had removed them if any had previously existed. It was not his plan to allow his prisoners to bar themselves inside a dungeon whenever they heard him approach.

"No," exclaimed the dwarf, "no; I cannot find a hasp or a staple, let alone anything else."

"What is to be done, then?"

"I know not."

"Jabez, the man who took me away——"

"Ah, I owe him one for that!" cried the dwarf, bitterly; "I have not forgotten that cross-buttock throw he gave me."

"Jabez may come in at any moment," said Agnes, "and mar our plans."

"Do you think so?"

"I do."

"Well, in that case, endeavour to go to sleep again for an hour or two; I will watch carefully. The ruffian will not suspect that I am here; he will come in carelessly—probably he will be smoking or drinking. I shall then knock him on the head, bind his hands and feet, take the key of the dungeon from him, and we will make our exit together in the way in which he usually leaves you."

Agnes hastily expressed her acquiescence in this plan, and after some urging consented to follow the dwarf's advice, and endeavour to snatch a few hours' or a few minutes' repose, as the case might be. She felt literally worn out—she had had so much mental excitement and physical fatigue that an hour's sleep would be worth a bag of gold to her.

She laid down upon her uncomfortable bed, and closed her eyes.

She had hardly done so, however, before the quick ears of the dwarf detected the sound of approaching footsteps.

He listened intently.

Yes, he was not mistaken.

They drew nearer and nearer.

Stubbles gently touched Agnes on the shoulder.

The poor girl was asleep; as soon as she closed her eyelids she had fallen into a heavy slumber.

She awoke at his touch, and looked at him inquiringly.

The noise made by a key being inserted in the lock made everything apparent to her, and she prayed inwardly for the dwarf's success. She dared not look on, but, burying her face in her hands, she awaited the result with much anxiety and impatience.

The key turned in the door.

The dwarf got into a corner; his lips were compressed tightly together, and his fists were as hard as balls of iron.

Jabez Clarke came into the cellar whistling. He did not in the remotest degree suspect the sort of reception he was about to meet with.

The dwarf allowed Jabez to enter the room and to reach the centre of it, before he molested him in any way; then he crept along on tiptoe until he stood just behind him. His eyes literally blazed with fury.

Agnes was in a fever of apprehension. She was sitting upon the bed holding the dwarf's candle in her hand.

Jabez had been drinking, his mental faculties were obscured, and he had not remarked the fact of Agnes's being possessed of a light until he was close to her. Suddenly it struck him as being very singular.

How could she have got it? Where did she obtain it from?

It was a riddle.

The dwarf's breath came thick and fast; he could not help it.

Jabez Clarke turned half way round as he heard the deep breathing of Stubbles.

This was what the latter desired. He raised his fist and delivered a blow under the ear which would have floored any ordinary ox ever exhibited for sale in Smithfield; but it did not seem to have much effect upon the burly costermonger—he shook his shock head as if to enter an energetic protest against the attack, but that was all.

He did not stagger.

He did not fall.

Stubbles, however, had this advantage over him.

He was a good deal confused at the suddenness and the unexpected nature of the attack.

The dwarf repeated his onslaught—if possible more furiously.

Again and again his fist hit Jabez Clarke in the same tender place, and at last the Hercules of the costermongers fell to the ground, completely knocked out of time.

The dwarf stood over him with his fists doubled, to see if he was shamming.

When he had satisfied himself that he was really stunned and defeated, he turned to Agnes and said—

"You need not be afraid now; he is quite harmless."

"Quite?" said Agnes. "Oh, make yourself perfectly sure."

Stubbles spurned the body with his foot, and rolled it up against the wall.

"Will that satisfy you?" he said.

Agnes replied in the affirmative.

"For Heaven's sake, then, let us get away from this place."

"With all my heart," responded Agnes.

"Shall we confine this fellow here?" exclaimed the dwarf.

It was an idea that occurred to him.

It would be only a just retribution.

Jabez Clarke was not the sort of man to lead captivity captive, and it would serve him right were he to be confined for any length of time, in the same dungeon in which he had doomed Agnes to dwell.

"He may starve!" said Agnes.

"And if he does it will be no more than he deserves."

The dwarf was thinking of the scene in the public-house, where he had been tossed from one end of the room to the other.

"No!" exclaimed Agnes. "I cannot consent to that; he has been my bitter and determined enemy, but I should not like him to starve."

"Well!" said the dwarf, "he shall not starve; I promise you that, but let us leave him here for the present, for our own safety? He will not hurt, there is bread and water; fare quite good enough for him. Besides, if he looks out, he may catch a frog somewhere about the floor, and they eat frogs in France, I believe."

Agnes saw the force of the dwarf's remarks, and it was arranged that Jabez Clarke should be locked in his own potato-cellar.

The dwarf could not repress a chuckle of exultation as he turned the key and knew that he had left the brute safely confined within.

The dwarf led the way along a passage which brought them to a flight of steps. This conducted them to the open air, and Agnes breathed freely for she was out of the power of Jabez Clarke, and she was happy, although she had, as the saying is, all the world before her once more. This had occurred to her so often that she did not feel so much alarmed as she would have done some years ago.

Her present feeling was one of unadulterated joy.

She was not to be tortured to death as Jabez had threatened her.

A reprieve had reached her, in the shape of her husband's friend, Stubbles—the ever faithful companion of Marmaduke Wilson.

CHAPTER LXXX.

AGNES PROPOSES CHARLOTTE'S LODGINGS AS A PLACE OF REFUGE—SHE GOES THERE—MARIA IS FRIGHTENED AT THE DWARF—CHARLOTTE WELCOMES AGNES—HOW THE "CAPTAIN" GOT LOCKED UP—A TRIPE SUPPER—THE DWARF TAKES A GREAT LIBERTY.

ONLY those who have escaped some great danger or obtained their liberty after many weary years of hopeless captivity, know what a blessed thing it is to be free. They alone have realized the ecstatic feeling of the blood dancing up and down in one's veins in the mad hilarity of the moment.

The longing after freedom is at length gratified, and the consciousness of freedom is the one touch of nature which makes the whole world kin.

Poerio must have felt this when he left the Neapolitan dungeons.

Trenck must have felt it when he defied the fortress of Milan.

The captives of the Bastile, the victims of St. Angelo, must have felt it and rejoiced in their new-born liberty.

Agnes felt it in all its glorious entirety, when she turned her back in virtuous indignation upon Jabez Clarke, his evil machinations, and the cruel prison-house, in which he had made her undergo so much unmerited suffering.

She seemed to tread upon air.

Had the streets been paved with gold she would not have stopped to gaze at them, her soul felt so sublimated at the thought that she was free.

A voice recalled her to herself.

It was that of the dwarf.

She hastily turned round and encountered his gaze fixed rather sorrowfully upon her.

She was at a loss to account for this, but when he spoke she saw at once that her faithful though deformed companion was sorrowing over her forlorn position.

In her joy she had totally forgotten that she was without a home, that she was environed on all sides by enemies, who were no doubt eagerly running along her track like bloodhounds, who are thirsting for the blood of the fugitive they are hunting down.

"What will you do, now?" he said.

It was a simple question, but how was she to answer it?

"I know not," she replied, sadly.

"And I cannot think of anything at this moment," said Stubbles, thoughtfully.

"I was so entranced at the idea of escaping from the perfidious and brutal wretch who held me captive," said Agnes, "that I thought of nothing else. I cannot tell where to go; can you advise me, my friend?"

"Alas! no."

"What are we to do, then?"

"You say, we!"

"Yes. You will not leave?"

"Never of my own free will," replied Stubbles, warmly, and with some feeling. "I thought you might have driven me away from you."

"Oh! no."

They walked on in silence for some time. They had crossed Oxford-street, and having come down Charlotte-street and Rathbone-place they found themselves in Sohosquare.

Morning was breaking, dull, cold, and gloomy.

There were few people about.

The police patrolling their solitary beats looked suspiciously upon the dwarf and his companion, but did not offer to molest them; they did not know them.

Suddenly Agnes thought of Charlotte.

She knew very well that her old friend would be delighted to see her, and would do what she could for her, but would it be safe to seek shelter and sanctuary there? Would not Wyman, the indefatigable inspector of police, be soon upon the spot, informed by some spy he had very probably set to watch the neighbourhood of Charlotte's house?

This was a question that only the future could reveal.

According to human calculation, nothing was more likely.

Yet there are two sides to every question, and there was another side to this.

Wyman might have to a certain extent relinquished the chase in the neighbourhood of the Haymarket.

He might be looking out in other quarters; or he might have given up the chase altogether!

Perhaps he had other things to occupy his attention!

Then another consideration which forced itself upon Agnes's mind was, that the luck which had attended her hitherto might still favour her, and enable her to defy Wyman and the Finsbury Fox put together.

She was also becoming a little reckless. A conglomeration of misfortunes very often has that effect upon people; they become desperate, and chance things which they would not do had the ordinary routine of their lives not been disturbed.

Turning to Stubbles, Agnes said—

"A friend of mine lives near here."

"Indeed!"

"She will give me shelter I have reason to believe—we are old friends."

"That is fortunate," said Stubbles.

"Yes, it is; because we have really no other place to go to."

"You can call me your servant; I will wait upon you," exclaimed Stubbles.

"As you like, my friend; you shall not leave me."

Agnes conducted the dwarf to the house in which Charlotte lodged. There was a light in the parlour, and another in the kitchen, which could be distinguished through the chinks in the shutters.

Agnes rapped gently at the door; she waited for some one to come and admit her.

Presently Maria's pit-a-pat was heard on the stairs and along the passage.

The chain was taken down in a leisurely manner; for Maria always made a point of never hurrying herself over anything.

Then the bolts were shot back, the key turned, and the door opened a little bit.

"Who's there?" cried Maria; adding to herself, "I hope it aint thieves or police."

"Me," replied Agnes, timidly.

"Oh! you don't lodge here—wrong house, my good woman," replied Maria, hearing a woman's voice, and not recognising its owner.

"No, I don't lodge here."

"What do you want, then?"

"It's me."

"Who's me?"

"Agnes."

"The party as went to 'olland?"

"Yes—yes."

"All right," replied Maria, and she opened the door.

Agnes stepped in, the dwarf was about to follow, when Maria gave him a push, and exclaimed—

"Not if I know it."

The push sent him on to the step outside, where the light of a lamp fell upon his hideous features. When Maria caught sight of him, she screamed out "Oh!" in a way which reached Charlotte Saunders' ears.

"There, now, if you'll believe me, which you aint got no call not to do," Maria afterwards exclaimed to her intimate friend and acquaintance, Mrs. Webster, who was wellbeknown in Whitcomb-street, having often done a good day's charing there, "when I see that there devilskin I was that took aback I thought I should have dropped —if I didn't, may I die this minute—it regularly shook my nerves to rags, it did. I was a bit flustered before that all along of missus coming home tight as a drum, and blowing of me up about the mashed taturs which weren't full of lumps, as she swore they was. Why you know Mrs. Webster, as I'll mash taturs, and make onion sauce either for boiled tripe, stewed rabbits, or shoulders of mutton — leastways shoulders of mutton, I should say—you know as I'll do it again anyone 'bout the Dials. But to see that there dwarf there now, it took away my breath, and made me that bad, that an hour afterwards, when they'd sent me to bed, I got out at the airy-door, and went down to 'Arry Obery's to get a quartern of their best. But they wasn't open, so I went to Surridge's, and then I saw Bill—you know him as works up at Waghorn's—and I cheeked him into standing half a pint of Old Tom; and I never went back home again till five o'clock in the afternoon, and all along of that dwarf. There, if I don't 'ate 'em, Mrs. Webster, if you believe me—which you aint got no call not to do—I can't abear dwarfs; and I didn't like the style of that one, as I'm telling you about, no more than I like that of a nigger—and they're hawful."

Charlotte came out into the passage and exclaimed—

"What's all this row about? You'll jolly soon get the sack, Maria, if you go on in this way. The idea of your having friends at this time of the night!"

"It's me, Charlotte," said Agnes.

Charlotte was quite astonished to see Agnes, but she was nevertheless much pleased. She shook her by the hand and asked her in.

"You must let my friend in, too," said Agnes. "Maria seems to have taken a great objection to him."

"Never mind Maria; Maria's a fool," cried Charlotte. "Tell him to come in. Don't stand there with the chain in your hand, Maria. Let the man in, can't you?"

Thus adjured, Maria shrank on one side, and allowed the ungainly monster to pass by her—a privilege of which he at once availed himself.

When he entered the sitting-room, and the gaslight lit up, his distorted figure, Charlotte herself was a little shocked.

"Why, Agnes," she cried, "what is it?"

Agnes laughed.

"Don't laugh; is it a monkey?"

"No; a man—a dwarf."

"So it is."

"A very good friend of mine he is, too."

"Will he bite, or anything?"

"Bite! don't be so silly," replied Agnes.

"Well, I didn't know. Give him a chair."

"Sit down, Stubbles," said Agnes.

The dwarf did so, ensconcing himself in a corner.

"Well, my dear, where have you been? I was almost afraid that inspector fellow had collared you off, as I didn't hear anything of you," said Charlotte.

"Oh! no, here I am."

"What will you have? I'm just having some tripe boiled in milk, with onion sauce. It's a favourite dish of mine. Will you have some?"

"Yes, with pleasure. I am very hungry," replied Agnes.

"My captain likes it too," continued Charlotte. "It was his ordering. But we went out on the spree. I have only just come back. Well, we went to the Café Regence, and there was a row. Of course the captain must be in it, and he got a fellow who cheeked him and stuffed him regularly up the chimney. Never saw such a thing in my life. It took two policemen to pull him down again, and then he was as black as a crow. Laugh! I laughed till I was fit to faint. It was a lark, if you like. One of the blues said something after that to my captain, and he fetched him a lick in the eye. The bobbies all came down on the captain then, and hauled him off to Vine-street, where he's got a night's lodging for nothing."

"Locked him up," said Agnes.

"Yes. I tried to bail him, but I couldn't knock anybody up, it was so late, and there he is. Maria! Where's that infernal woman? Just touch the bell dear, will you, Maria?"

Maria's voice was heard in the depths of the kitchen, saying—"One moment, mum."

"One moment," said Charlotte. "Yes, it's always one moment with you. If a man asked you to marry him, you'd say, 'One moment, sir,' before you gave him an answer. Come on, make haste, else you'll have me after you. Maria!"

"Coming, mum!" replied Maria, half up the stairs.

"Can I get anything?" asked Stubbles, civilly.

"Yes, I don't see why you shouldn't do something for your living," replied Charlotte, coolly. "Run down to the kitchen and get some plates and some knives and forks."

The dwarf instantly left the room to do as he had been directed; but, as it happened, Maria was coming up with the very articles that Charlotte was waiting for.

The dwarf met her in the passage.

Maria screamed, and let the plates and knives and forks

fall. This made a great clatter, which brought Charlotte Saunders to the door in a minute.

"Why, you silly fool. Did you think he was going to eat you," she cried, angrily.

"No, mum," gasped Maria.

"Well, what then?"

"Oh! he startled me so."

"I suppose the truth of it is you're drunk now."

"May I——" began Maria.

"Don't tell me," cried Charlotte. "I can see you're eyes swimming."

"May I drop——"

"Why, you nasty, drunken beast, get down stairs, do."

"May I drop down——"

"Oh! don't talk to me."

"May I drop down dead——"

"Get out of my sight," said Charlotte, giving her a push which upset her equilibrium and sent her rolling along the passage.

She would have inevitably fallen down the stairs, had not the dwarf caught her in his arms and carried her down to the kitchen.

I must do her the justice, as a veracious chronicler, to say that she kicked and struggled a good deal; but Stubbles held her in a grip of iron, and did so on purpose.

He was having his revenge for the aversion she had displayed towards his personal appearance.

When he got her into the kitchen he had the unparalleled audacity to touch her chaste lips—with which such a liberty had never before been taken—with his own.

With a cry of rage, not to say despair, Maria liberated her arms, and with her nails made two deep furrows on each side of the dwarf's countenance.

"You'll do it again, will you?" she exclaimed, passionately. "You ugly brute, you dare to touch me again. Keep in your proper place, will you? I'll get your head punched for you to-morrow. I wouldn't let the Prince of Wales touch me, let alone an abortion like you. Your mother must have had bad dreams before you were born. I wonder they didn't put you in a caravan and show you, that's all you're good for. But I'll be one with you, you nasty, low, disgusting brute!"

The dwarf took no notice of Maria's angry diatribe. He wiped his face with a dishcloth. He was not much hurt.

Then he took up some more plates, and other things which were wanted, and re-ascended the kitchen stairs.

After Agnes and Charlotte had finished their supper, they gave the remains of the tripe on the dish to the dwarf, and told him to eat it—a command he was very quick in obeying.

Afterwards they sent him downstairs, and told him to make himself a shakedown somewhere.

He went, and the two women disposed themselves by the fire, and became cosy and chatty over their spirits and water.

CHAPTER LXXXI.

AFTER SUPPER—CHARLOTTE SAUNDERS RELATES THE MISERABLE END OF MIRIAM MOSS—AGNES IS INDUCED TO TELL HER HISTORY—WYMAN AND THE FINSBURY FOX ENTER THE HOUSE—THE DWARF IS CAPTURED—AGNES'S IMMINENT PERIL.

ALTHOUGH Agnes sat very quietly by her friend's fireside, she was far from easy in her mind. She knew that at any moment the myrmidons of the law might pounce down upon her and carry her off. One of her enemies was for the present safely disposed of. Jabez Clarke was utterly powerless to do her any harm. There was every chance of his starving to death in that terrible dungeon, unless she chose to reveal his whereabouts to some one, which she did not feel inclined to do until he, like herself, had experienced some of the bitterness of enforced captivity.

Agnes's repugnance to Count Val de Grace had acquired new strength, she felt that he was the cause of all she had been obliged to go through, and also of her present forlorn and unprotected condition. She felt this, and she hated him for it. The idea of again falling into his hands was like gall and wormwood to her. So bitter was it that she dismissed it whenever it came into her mind. It was too bitter and too revolting to dwell upon.

"What do you intend doing now?" said Charlotte, inquiringly.

"I am at a loss to tell," replied Agnes. "I shall be obliged to trespass upon your hospitality, I am afraid, until I can either find or make myself a home."

"You may safely do that."

"You are always kind."

"I only do what you would do for me."

"Oh, yes."

"So you see it is nothing," replied Charlotte, laughingly.

"It is still an obligation."

"I don't see it in that light."

"Nevertheless it is."

"Well, it shall be, if you like so to consider it."

"Am I not keeping you up?" said Agnes.

She looked very sleepy herself, and Charlotte remarked it.

"I suppose," she replied, "the fact is, you are beastly tired yourself, and you want to go to roost; isn't that it?"

"No," replied Agnes, telling a very palpable falsehood.

"No? Well, I am glad to hear it."

"But you have not answered my question," Agnes persisted.

"What's that?"

"Whether," said Agnes, with a yawn, "whether I am not keeping you out of your bed?"

"Not at all. I never let anybody interfere with me, my dear child. If they are in my way, I freely tell them so, and very plainly, as I dare say you know. If you were keeping me up, you'd soon hear of it—you wouldn't be long finding it out. I was very tight when I came in; but since I have had some supper I feel better, and I am just in the humour for a little quiet conversation; only for half an hour, you know."

"I have no objection," replied Agnes. "What shall we talk about?"

"About yourself."

"You wont find that very interesting," replied Agnes, with a sickly smile.

"Oh, I don't know that! You appear to have seen something since we parted, some time ago, at Norah Nolan's."

"Ah! I remember."

"And that reminds me of something else."

"What?"

"Why, Miriam—Miriam—what's that woman's name—the one you smashed up so awfully in at Sams's one night?"

"Oh, Moss—Miriam Moss."

"Yes. Well, Miriam Moss is dead."

"Dead!" cried Agnes, in unfeigned amazement.

"No mistake about it!" replied Charlotte.

"How did she die?"

"As loose women very often do die."

"How's that?"

"She took rather more cold water than was good for her."

"Do you mean to say she drowned herself?" asked Agnes.

"It looks uncommonly like it."

"Tell me the particulars."

"They are soon told."

"What are they?"

"They picked up her body, stone dead, somewhere down the river; Millwall, I think. They had an inquest upon it, and they brought her in 'Found drowned;' but how she came into the water, there was no evidence to show."

"She committed suicide, no doubt," said Agnes.

"Most likely. You see, her face was so bad and so disfigured that I suppose she couldn't bear to look at it, so she must have thrown herself over some bridge in the nighttime—possibly over Waterloo-bridge. She lived in Stamford-street."

"What a sad thing!" exclaimed Agnes, feeling penetrated with remorse for the injuries she had inflicted upon the unhappy woman.

"Ah, never mind," said Charlotte; "she's out of it now, and that's the best thing for her. Besides, I'd have served her the same, if she had done to me what she did to you."

Agnes sighed.

"By-the-bye, you never told me the rights of that."

"Did I not?" asked Agnes.

"Never. I have often asked you; and really, Agnes, if you were to repose some confidence in me, I might be better able to advise you. I have shown my friendship for you in more ways than one, so why should you hesitate to trust me?"

"I know not, except that I don't like to allude to some passages of my life."

"But to me," said Charlotte; "I am your friend. Come now, tell me your history. No lies, you know. Tell me everything on the square. What did you do first when you left old Cerise's, and cut the dressmaking business?"

"Oh, it's a long story. I cannot go into all the details," replied Agnes; "but I will tell you enough to prove to you that I am very unhappy."

"Go ahead, then, and drink this."

As she spoke, Charlotte mixed Agnes a stiff glass of brandy-and-water. Agnes sipped a little of it, and said—

"I have been married twice, Charlotte. My first husband, Marmaduke Wilson, was transported through Miriam Moss."

"The wretch!" cried Charlotte.

"After that I married Lord Marchmont."

"Really?" ejaculated Charlotte, as if she did not more than half believe her.

"Upon my honour, I am speaking the truth. I know I am a bigamist for so doing; but I did it in ignorance. When I engaged myself to Lord Marchmont I thought that Marmaduke Wilson had ceased to exist."

"That's odd," said Charlotte; "but go on."

"I lived happily with his lordship and tried to forget Marmaduke and everything connected with my early life; but a serpent crossed my threshold and instilled his venom into my home."

"Who?"

"Count Val de Grace."

"The Frenchman who followed us to Holland?"

"The same."

"He wont forget me in a hurry," laughed Charlotte, in a satisfied manner.

"He is a mesmerist, Charlotte; and he once placed me in a singular position. My reputation was compromised, and Lord Marchmont turned me out of his house."

"He wouldn't have turned me out, I think," muttered Charlotte.

"My conscience was as pure as driven snow. I had nothing to reproach myself with."

"More fool you if you liked the man."

"Which one, Val de Grace?"

"Yes."

"I hated him."

"Well," said Charlotte.

"The count is even now seeking for me, as you know. Lord Marchmont I have heard nothing about. Marmaduke Wilson will most likely shortly return from transportation."

"Why don't you say abroad? it sounds better," suggested Charlotte.

"What is the use of quarrelling about words? He is a convict," said Agnes.

"Well, my dear, there is one consolation for you."

"What is that?"

"His hair will have time to grow during the voyage home."

"Oh, Charlotte, how can you?" said Agnes, almost crying.

"It's no use worrying yourself, my dear child," exclaimed Charlotte. "Wait for what turns up. How do you know what may happen? Perhaps somebody will be obliging enough to die just at the proper moment. One thing I can tell you, you will never do any good by grizzling and growling. Look at me!"

"You are a miracle, Charlotte," replied Agnes. "Never saw anything like you."

"Have you told me all?"

"All the main facts. Of course, I have had lots of adventures; but those you don't care about."

"Not much, just now. They will keep for another time. At present, I think I shall go to seepsiby, as my captain calls it."

"I am quite ready to do that," said Agnes, yawning again. "I am as tired as a dog."

"So am I," replied Charlotte. "Come on; let us lie down."

Charlotte led the way through the folding doors into her bedroom.

Both the girls were too tired to undress themselves, so they laid down on the bed in their things, just pulling some of the bed-clothes over them to keep them warm. Soon they were sleeping soundly.

Stubbles contrived to make himself tolerably comfortable on the hearthrug before the kitchen fire.

Maria relented after awhile, and gave him a counterpane off her own virtuous couch. He wrapped himself up in this, and was soon snoring loudly. Exhausted nature was repairing its shattered forces.

Maria was putting her kitchen straight before going out the back way to get something to drink; for she was very honest, and never touched a drop of anything belonging to her mistress. When she heard the dwarf snore, she exclaimed—

"Lor', how he do snore! ain't it orful!"

She went up to him, and gave him a kick in the ribs.

Not even with a grunt did Stubbles resent this indignity. He was too fast asleep to take any notice of feminine insults.

Without putting on her bonnet, Maria went out at the area door, which she left, as she called it, on the latch, and walked along the street. Her leaving the door open was the cause of a catastrophe, which she would have been amongst the first to avert had she had the slightest suspicion that she should be instrumental in bringing it about.

Scarcely had she disappeared round the corner, than two men, who had been watching the house, emerged from a doorway on the opposite side of the street, and crossing over, they descended the area steps, lifted the latch, pushed the door open, and stood in the kitchen.

Maria had left a tallow-candle burning. This faintly illumined the room. Although the light was bad enough, it was sufficient to show the form of Stubbles stretched out on the hearthrug.

The two men advanced towards his unconscious body. They regarded it inquisitively for an instant; then one said to the other, "That's him."

"Right you are," was the reply.

"Clap the darbies on him," said the first.

This was soon accomplished, and Stubbles was a prisoner.

A rough shake aroused him. He sprang to his feet, and glared fiercely around him. He caught sight of the two men who had so cleverly captured him. His countenance fell; and no wonder, for he was confronted with Inspector Wyman and the Finsbury Fox. They knew him well, and he also knew them. He was their prisoner, and he saw that to resist them in any way would be useless. Wyman smiled complacently: the Finsbury Fox rubbed his hands gleefully together.

The dwarf sat down in a chair, and looked gloomily in the fire. He had been so persecuted by fate that he did not care much what became of himself; but he was anxious and apprehensive for Agnes, over whom he could not help thinking some great danger was impending.

CHAPTER LXXXII.

INSPECTOR WYMAN MAKES AGNES HIS PRISONER—CHARLOTTE ATTEMPTS A RESCUE, BUT IS ONLY PARTIALLY SUCCESSFUL—MARIA GETS THE MILLER—AGNES LEAVES A MESSAGE FOR THE DWARF, WHO LOSES NO TIME IN ACTING AS SHE DIRECTS.

THE two policemen satisfied themselves by a careful scrutiny of the place that Stubbles was alone.

Once assured of the important fact that he had no confederates near at hand who might endeavour to effect a rescue their course was clear.

They had seen Agnes, accompanied by the dwarf, enter the house.

They could then and there have gone across the road and have effected a capture, but that was not what they wished to do.

They were desirous of as little publicity as possible attending their operations.

It is true, that if a crowd had collected in the street, which was not very probable at so early an hour in the morning, they could have brazened it out, and have made everyone believe that they had lawful authority for the capture.

A policeman is very often in himself a tower of strength.

People are afraid to trifle with the majesty of the law, and to a certain extent a policeman in his own proper person, when attired in uniform, represents the majesty of the law, which, when vindicated by him at the point of the truncheon, is irresistible.

Inspector Wyman had waited until he saw what he considered a good opportunity.

The maid-servant had gone out, and had in all likelihood left the door open, or if not open at least unlocked.

This suspicion proved to be correct.

Now all that Wyman and his subordinate officer had to do was to arrest Agnes. She was, he surmised, asleep upstairs.

Addressing Stubbles, the inspector said—

"If you dare to move or speak but one word—" then he stopped and looked at him significantly. A glance from the inspector very often spoke more than words.

Stubbles nodded his head sulkily, as if in token of acquiescence.

Leaving him on a chair, Wyman, followed by the Finsbury Fox, taking a candle in his hands, carefully ascended the stairs.

Agnes was far from having the remotest idea of what awaited her. The poor child was fast asleep and roving in the land of dreams.

Wyman determined to search the parlours first. He could not of course tell in which room Agnes was, although from the light which he had noticed in the parlour window, he had a strong presumption that he should find her on the ground floor.

He first opened the door of Charlotte Saunders's sitting-room.

Holding the light up, he saw that the fire was just glimmering.

The glasses and other things stood upon the table, flanked by two long-necked bottles, one containing brandy and the other gin.

To the first of these the inspector applied himself with great assiduity. The Finsbury Fox imbibed a sudden affection for the other, and subsequently imbibed the gin, which might have been heard undiluted gurgling down his throat in large quantities.

Considerably refreshed as to the inner man, the two men looked at one another and smiled. Wyman was generally an abstemious man when he had any work in hand—but to-night he allowed himself something to drink as he had been standing some time in the cold, and he felt that he stood in need of it.

The Finsbury Fox always drank, but what was very remarkable, he seldom, if ever, drank to excess. He could take a great deal; some men can, while others can scarcely bear the smell of intoxicating liquors. Before he went into the metropolitan police he had been a porter in the London Docks and went about with people who had tasting orders. It is always strictly enjoined and written on the orders that the men are not to be allowed anything to drink, but they care very little about that and generally help themselves to as much as they want.

The Finsbury Fox in his merry moments, when he laid the majesty of the law on one side for half an hour, and strolled over to a celebrated house-of-call for policemen, used to calculate that he had cost the company three pipes, one hogshead, and a quarter-cask of wine during the time he was in their employ.

On the present occasion the Fox wanted to replenish his glass, but his superior restrained him, saying—

"Not now. Afterwards."

Wyman next reconnoitred the bed-room through the folding doors; there he perceived the two women fast asleep.

Charlotte was talking in her sleep—

"Where—where's that devil Maria?" she muttered, then turning uneasily over on the other side, she went off again with sundry snorts and grunts, rather more porcine than elegant.

Going up to the bed-side, the inspector said in a whisper to the Fox—

"This is our bird, I think?"

"That's her," replied the Finsbury.

The two men stood for a few seconds admiring the surpassing loveliness of the sleeping beauties.

"Do you admire the count what d'ye call's taste," exclaimed the Fox, slyly touching the inspector on the arm.

Wyman made no reply, but gently shook Agnes.

She was sleeping so lightly that his touch aroused her instantly.

Starting up, she looked around her.

The first object she encountered was the stolid, indifferent face of Wyman.

Too well she knew it.

In it she read no trace of pity—no symptom of commiseration. She could see in a moment what she had to expect.

But what was she to do? How was she to extricate herself from the trying dilemma in which she was placed? How, indeed?

She fell back again upon the pillow, stupified with grief at this new disaster.

"Fool that I was," she thought, "ever to come here at all. I might have known that I should be hunted down."

Wyman laid his fingers on his lips to enjoin silence.

But Agnes heeded not the gesture.

She turned hastily to Charlotte, and shook her violently.

Charlotte muttered something, and would have gone off to sleep again, but Agnes repeated her attack.

Then Charlotte sat up.

Agnes had come to a sudden resolution.

Putting her mouth down to Charlotte's ear, she whispered, in a slow but distinct tone—

"Send the dwarf to Lord Marchmont, and tell him that I am in the power of Count Val de Grace."

Although Charlotte was very much surprised and confused at everything she saw, she heard this, and was sufficiently awake to understand it.

"Send the dwarf to Lord Marchmont, and tell him that I am in the power of Count Val de Grace."

This was what Agnes had said, and she remembered it.

In order to impress it more firmly on her memory, she repeated it to herself more than once.

Agnes had not time to say more before Wyman seized her rudely by the arm, and compelled her to stand by his side on the floor.

"Why use this violence?" demanded Agnes.

"You are my prisoner," replied Wyman.

"Yes, you've got to come along of us," put in the Fox.

"I can see that I am your prisoner," replied Agnes, "but is that any reason why you should treat me in a barbarous and inhuman manner; and what is more than that, I should like to know for what you have made me a prisoner, and upon whose authority you are acting?"

Inspector Wyman made no answer.

"Why do you not speak?" she continued.

"I did not come here to talk with you."

"Of what am I guilty?"

"You will learn soon enough."

"Tell me now."

"You'll hear soon enough."

"I have a right to know."

"Then it is a right I do not recognise," said the inspector. "I can remember nothing about it in my instructions."

"I firmly believe that you are acting illegally," persisted Agnes.

The only fear was that Jabez Clarke had, some time or other, denounced her as the murderer of her mother, and that Wyman had a warrant for her arrest on that ground. She was anxious to find out why he had captured her. Her real idea was that Wyman was but the passive instrument of Count Val de Grace. If that was the case, she had a right to resist to the utmost, because the inspector was being guilty of a gross breach of his professional duty. He was perverting the great power with which the Chief Commissioner of Police had entrusted him into a wrong channel.

"Will you come quietly, or must I use force?" said the inspector.

"Let her alone," suddenly exclaimed Charlotte, recovering her wits.

"She is my prisoner," was the reply.

"Your humbug. What has she done?"

"Quite enough."

"What?"

"I am not here to answer your questions," said Wyman, surlily.

"Oh! it's you, isit," she cried, recognising him. "You have forgotten me, have you? I have not forgotten you though, and you'd better get out of my house, without you want to be kicked out."

"Sorry to intrude," said Wyman, quietly, when he saw he could get nothing by bullying Charlotte.

"What do you do it for, then?"

"Always sorry to disturb or inconvenience a lady."

"Let my friend go."

"Couldn't think of it," was the quiet and decided response.

A rapid glance travelled from Agnes to Charlotte.

The former did all she could to impress upon the latter the uselessness of resistance at the present juncture.

But Charlotte was not to be restrained. She was quickly on her feet. Then she looked round her. The washandstand stood close by her side. She took up the water-jug, discharged its contents full in the face of the Finsbury Fox, and drenched him from top to toe. The jug itself she hurled at the inspector. It struck the wall just above his head, and the broken pieces fell around him in a shower.

Hastily pushing Agnes along before him, he made his way out of the room, telling the Finsbury Fox to guard the rear.

The next weapon which Charlotte made use of was the water-bottle. This was thrown with unerring aim, and hit the unfortunate policeman just above the right eye. Fortunately it was empty. Had it been full, the consequence would have been very serious. As it was, it laid open a considerable gash on the side where it had struck him.

Before Charlotte could seize anything else, the Fox left the room, and went after his companion.

Charlotte rushed after him, seizing a box full of powder, which stood upon the dressing-table. This she threw after the retreating figure of the Finsbury Fox.

Maria had the moment before come in. Hearing the noise, she came upstairs, and entered the room as her mistress sent the powder-box flying after the policeman. Missing its intended mark, it took effect upon Maria's forehead; the top came off the box, and the powder fell as thick as hail all over her.

She was white all over. It was a floury baptism.

Her hair, her dress, her face, her arms, were all covered with the whitening.

Charlotte burst out laughing when she saw the effect of her random shot. Maria wiped her eyes, and exclaimed—

"You *have* given me the miller this time!"

When Charlotte recovered herself, she went into the passage, but the birds had flown. There was no one there. She looked up the street, but it was nearly deserted. It was clear that if she wished to help Agnes in any way she could only do so by following her instruction to the letter.

This she resolved to do. Taking the candle from Maria's hand, she went to the kitchen.

The dwarf was still sitting there, with his hands handcuffed. He had heard the sound of a scuffle going on upstairs, but manacled as he was, he knew he could have done no good; so he remained, still determining to work by stratagem. It had stood him in good stead before, and he was resolved that it should do so again.

"They have got her," said Charlotte.

"I know it," he replied, laconically.

"But she said I was to tell you to go to Lord Marchmont, and let him know that she was in the power of Count Val de Grace."

"It shall be done. But first——"

"What?"

"Give me a file to remove these things."

He held up his hands, and showed the handcuffs.

Maria brought him one.

Charlotte went to bed; and Maria worked for an hour to liberate the dwarf.

Her hatred for him had partially gone off, and she was also sorry for the plight in which he was; but although her will was good, her strength was weak, and it was found necessary to call in the butcher-boy from over the way, who had more strength in his wrists than she had. For a shilling he consented to work at it.

Maria explained that the dwarf was "own brother to the gent as had the best attic; but he'd been a larking and had put the handcuffs on without knowing how it was done, and his brother had gone away with the key." So she added, "it was a case."

The butcher-boy succeeded in doing what Maria could not; and after some hard labour his efforts were crowned with success.

The dwarf no sooner felt himself liberated than he thanked Maria, and left the house.

His first visit was to some reading-rooms in Leicester-square, where he could see a Peerage.

He looked over it till he saw the name of Marchmont.

Having found it he copied down his lordship's address in London, and left the place, muttering to himself—

"Now I am upon the track!"

"COME TO MY WIFE'S CHAMBER!" CRIED LORD MARCHMONT, SEIZING THE COUNT BY THE COLLAR.

CHAPTER LXXXIII.

THE DWARF DELIVERS AGNES'S MESSAGE TO LORD MARCH-
MONT AND DEPARTS—HIS LORDSHIP SEEKS COUNT VAL
DE GRACE—THE COUNT DENIES THAT HE KNOWS ANY-
THING ABOUT THE LADY, AND REFUSES TO MAKE ANY
REVELATION WHATEVER.

IT was raining when the dwarf halted before the residence
of Lord Marchmont—a dreary, drizzling rain, such as we
are accustomed to meet with in England, the home of fogs,
mists, and pluviose clouds.

The streets presented a dreary, muddy appearance.

But few people were about at the West-end; and those
that Stubbles saw in the streets, were out because they were
compelled to be, and could not help themselves.

Perhaps they were agents for coal merchants or brewers,
seeking for orders.

Perhaps they were town travellers, going about in the
commercial interest, to increase the trade of their employers,
and make their names famous, whilst they obtained a paltry
pittance for their own services.

There are many people in London who obtain a living in
this way.

Stubbles did not stop to speculate as to the occupation
and means of obtaining a livelihood of the solitary pedestrians he met with.

His mind was exclusively occupied with the condition of
Agnes.

He did not require Charlotte Saunders to tell him more
than she had done.

He had heard quite sufficient to make everything intelligible to him.

That message which Agnes had in the midst of her great
peril and her terrible apprehension thought of and conjured
Charlotte Saunders to deliver to the dwarf was full of
meaning—

"Tell Lord Marchmont that I am in the power of Count Val de Grace."

It was more than enough.

Stubbles could guess the rest.

He looked up at the palatial residence of John, ninth Lord Marchmont, and regarded it with some interest.

It was an old-fashioned house, built of red brick, in the most substantial manner of the period, which was probably that of Queen Anne.

The strange-looking horns, for extinguishing the torches borne by the linkmen, were to be seen on either side the flight of steps leading up to the hall door.

Raising the knocker, Stubbles beat a loud rat-tat-tat.

The door was opened by a powdered footman, in all the glory of plush breeches, silk stockings, and buckle shoes. He did not condescend to ask Stubbles what his business was.

He waited for him to speak.

"Is Lord Marchmont within?" said the dwarf.

When he spoke, the footman descended from the pedestal of his mightiness, and looked superciliously at the ill-shapen figure of the dwarf. Apparently not very much pleased or satisfied with his careless scrutiny, he exclaimed—

"Go to the airy door."

Stubbles, however, did not move.

"Go on," continued the footman; "first gate on the left."

"But I want to see his lordship."

"He wont see the likes of you."

"Is he within?"

"Yes; but he wont see you, I tell you."

Stubbles put his hand in his pocket and took out half-a-crown, which he gave to the footman.

The man pocketed the coin, with a smile of satisfaction.

"Will you take a message to him for me?" asked Stubbles.

"Well, I will, to oblige you," replied the footman; "although, to tell you the truth, his lordship hasn't liked being disturbed the last week or two."

"How's that?"

"Why, he lost his wife, and——"

"Did she die?"

"Oh, no! ran away like, or something, and he's took on awful."

"Indeed."

"What's your message?"

"Only this," replied the dwarf, and he wrote on a piece of paper—

"Agnes is in the power of Count Val de Grace! She is in need of succour."

Giving this to the footman, the latter took it in to Lord Marchmont, desiring the dwarf to wait.

It must be remembered that the dwarf imagined Agnes to be the wife of Marmaduke Wilson.

He was not aware of her intimate relations with Lord Marchmont.

He thought that his lordship might be able in some way that he could not understand to help her; and it was sufficient for him to be told to do a thing by the wife of his old friend without asking any questions; for although he was both brave and faithful, the dwarf was not very clever at putting this and that together.

On the present occasion he had delivered his message, and he thought that he was at liberty to go.

His simple plan was to allow Lord Marchmont to work in his way for the liberation of Agnes, while he would do what he could to find out the residence of Count Val de Grace, and assist her as much as he could single-handed.

He forgot the famous maxim—"Union is strength."

When the footman came back to desire him to come into Lord Marchmont's private apartment, he found him gone.

The dwarf had opened the door and let himself out, and was trudging along once more in the blinding rain.

"Fool!" cried Lord Marchmont, when the servant returned without the dwarf, "what did you let him go for?"

"No fault of mine, my lord; man went without telling me."

"Go; leave me."

The footman went away, and his lordship read and re-read the scrap of paper.

The fact was, that since Agnes's flight he had experienced a strong feeling in favour of her innocence.

Absence makes the heart grow fonder, and every extenuating circumstance he could think of he brought up in Agnes's favour until at last he brought himself to believe that she was not guilty.

His astonishment was great when he heard in this unexpected manner that she was in the power of Count Val de Grace.

He deemed the count dead.

Had he not fallen down lifeless at his very feet, just as he was about to plunge his naked sword into his breast?

Had he not packed his dead body up in a box and buried it at night in the Brompton Cemetery?

These were incontrovertible facts.

How then could the count be alive?

Yet here he was solemnly assured that Agnes was in the power of the subtle and mysterious count, and earnestly imploring his succour!

It was passing strange; it was almost marvellous.

Who could have any interest in deceiving him?

Who could have the slightest motive for telling him an untruth on the subject?

He was strongly inclined to believe that his services were required, and that promptly!

Required to deliver the woman he had a few short weeks ago been proud to call his own from the devilish arts and devices of an unprincipled and unscrupulous scoundrel.

As the count had been an intimate acquaintance of his lordship's, the latter, of course, knew that he lived at Maida-hill, and he determined to call upon him.

Ordering his carriage, he drove at once to the count's residence, so hardly five hours had elapsed between the capture of Agnes and the arrival of Lord Marchmont at the count's pleasant little villa on the banks of the Grand Junction Canal.

"Was the count in?" asked his lordship.

"Oh, yes!" replied the servant. "He was always in to his friends, and would be very glad to see Lord Marchmont."

He was conducted into a handsomely furnished and, in all respects, elegant room, which if it had a fault, it was only through being a little too Frenchified—a recommendation to some people.

Lord Marchmont had hardly seated himself before Count Val de Grace entered, smiling.

His visitor returned his salutation stiffly.

"Ah!" muttered the count, "I see how the cat jumps; he has heard. She has communicated with him in some way."

"I thought," exclaimed the count in a suave and gentle voice, "that you had been cruel enough, my friend, to give me what you English call the cold shoulder—ha! ha! excuse my mirth, but finding that cold steel was of no use—no good at all—you present me with cold shoulder."

"I never expected to see you alive again, count."

"No! ha! I am like one of your cats, I have nine lives; you cannot kill me."

"So it seems," replied his lordship.

"I have a good fairy watching over me."

"Pardon my abruptness, count," said Lord Marchmont, "but I came here to have some serious conversation with you."

"Yes. I am ready."

"You will remember when you simulated death so well, or when you swooned, or when you did something which resembled death?"

"Something which resembled death!" repeated the count, with a sardonic grin. "Very good; go on."

"You will remember that I found my wife and yourself in a very equivocal position?"

"Ha!" said the count, showing his white teeth.

"Was it not so?"

"My friend, you must not trust too much to appearances."

"But I may believe what I see with my own eyes."

"Believe one half you see, and nothing that you hear," replied Val de Grace, sententiously.

"Sir!" cried Marchmont, angrily, "I did not come here to be schooled by you."

"My lord," replied the count, with an affectation of submission, "I am dumb."

"I have reason to believe," continued his lordship, "that by some means or other, my wife is in your power."

"Oh!" said the count, laughing, as if much amused.

"You may laugh, Count Val de Grace, but I am not joking, as you will learn to your cost."

"Pray go on. It is excellent—quite farcical," said the count, still laughing.

"And I am afraid she stands much in need of my assistance. I have carefully considered the circumstances under which I saw you together, and the result of my deliberations is an acquittal of her, but I strongly condemn you, and think you meditated not only her ruin but the destruction of my peace of mind."

"Have you done?"

"Not quite."

"I listen."

"I have come to you to demand my wife, for I am firmly of opinion that you have her in your custody."

"Permit me to assure you," said the count, "that you are entirely mistaken."

"I do not think so."

"I will explain."

"Do so."

"I was sitting in your dining-room—being your friend it is not surprising that I should do so—your wife, not feeling well, had retired to her chamber. Considering myself, in a certain manner, at home in my friend's house, and being invited by her ladyship to do so, I stayed for a little while smoking and drinking your wine—which, by the way, my dear lord, allow me to assure you, is excellent—'pon my word, excellent."

"Never mind my wine, sir, proceed with your story."

"You lose your temper," said the count; "I am calm. Well, you are English, I am French; there is a difference certainly, so I make allowances."

"Will you proceed?"

"In my own good time."

The count took out a cigar and lighted it leisurely.

Lord Marchmont fretted and fumed inwardly with impatience, but the stolidity and self-possession of the Frenchman increased rather than diminished.

"Well, I was sitting in your dining-room, my lord, smoking very much as I am now; my legs were crossed thus!"

He crossed his legs as he spoke.

"I was occasionally sipping your excellent wine, when to my surprise, I heard a footfall on the stairs."

"Well?"

"Like the footfall of a fairy, it was the patter, patter of little slipperless feet."

"Yes, yes."

"Presently the door was pushed open, and what was my astonishment to see——"

"What did you see?" demanded his lordship.

"Her ladyship!" calmly responded the count.

"Then you mean me to infer from that," cried Lord Marchmont, "that my wife sought you?"

"You may infer what you like," said the count, shrugging his shoulders.

Lord Marchmont rose from his chair, took three or four paces, and stood close to the count.

"If you mean to say that she sought you, you disguise and pervert the truth!" he hissed between his teeth.

"Oh! these English!" said the count, quietly knocking the ash off the top of his cigar.

"Count, I demand my wife!"

"She is not here."

"Will you give her up?"

"I do not provide wives for people, my friend."

"I am in no mood for joking," said his lordship.

"Nor I."

"Then deliver up my wife."

"She is not here," again replied the count.

CHAPTER LXXXIV.

THE COUNT PERSISTS IN HIS DETERMINATION NOT TO GIVE ANY TIDINGS OF AGNES — A HAND-TO-HAND COMBAT—THE COUNT PROPOSES A DUEL AFTER THE FASHION OF THE MEXICANS — THE CHALLENGE IS ACCEPTED, AND THE TWO NOBLEMEN GO TO THE ARMOURY.

THE position of affairs was becoming serious.

The count knew very well that Inspector Wyman had, some three hours before, brought Agnes to his house, and he was fully aware that she was then confined in a room which she had occupied on a former occasion.

But it was not his intention to allow Lord Marchmont to divine this. Far from it. He intended to do all he could to throw him off the scent.

It was pretty clear that he *was* on the scent, and it was a mystery to the count how on earth he could have discovered that Agnes was in his power.

The count was of opinion that, in spite of his confident manner, his lordship was only partially informed.

"Once more," exclaimed Lord Marchmont, "will you or will you not give up my wife?"

"Can you get blood out of a stone?" replied the count, quietly.

"That is no answer to my question."

"It is the only one I am able to give."

"You either have my wife in your possession, or you are able to give me tidings of her."

"Neither one nor the other."

"You refuse to speak?"

"I do not refuse anything, but I am unable to do what is impossible," replied the count, confronting Lord Marchmont with an apparently open and truthful countenance.

"I insist!" cried his lordship, imperiously.

"You insist," repeated the count, interrupting his noble visitor. "You forget, my lord, that you are addressing your equal in rank and position. Probably my patent of nobility is of as ancient a date as your own, and my 'scutcheon may be as free from blots as yours."

Lord Marchmont started at this. His thoughts reverted to the Hon. Percy Cunninghame, lying mangled and mutilated beneath the brow of the rock near the little village of Rottendean.

"Count," exclaimed Lord Marchmont, "these personalities are idle, and but waste time which might be much more profitably employed. You tell me frankly and plainly that my wife is not under your roof."

"I do," replied the count.

"I assert the contrary, without meaning to insult you; so we are at issue."

"Well?"

"The only way that occurs to me of settling the matter is for you to permit me to go over your house."

"A modest proposition, certainly."

"I can then satisfy myself."

"Anything else?" said Val de Grace, in a sarcastic tone.

"If I find nothing," continued Lord Marchmont, "I shall only have to apologize to you for my suspicions."

"Yes."

"And admit that I have been misinformed."

"What if I refuse?"

"It is a fair and reasonable proposition."

"Oh! certainly, very much so," said the count, still more sarcastically than before.

"If you refuse, I shall know what to say to you, and how to treat you."

"Lord Marchmont," began the count, "I have assured you, on the faith of a gentleman, that your wife, the Lady Agnes, is not here. What more do you want?"

"I am sorry to say that I do not believe you, and I want to satisfy myself."

"That you cannot do."

"Cannot?"

"No. You have insulted me in refusing to take my word, but I pass it over. I am magnanimous. I make every allowance for the irascible state of your temper, and I sympathize with your feelings. You have lost your wife; I am sorry for you. But for you to propose to search my house, as if you were a police-officer and myself a criminal! The idea is too absurd; no one but an Englishman in a bad temper would have thought of such a thing."

"I can accept no other satisfaction, count."

"Then, my friend, you must please yourself. I am sorry to be rude, but you must do your worst—do what you can, in fact! Put the machinery of the law in motion against me; bring an action against me for unlawfully abducting your lawfully wedded wife. Marchmont *versus* Val de Grace. How amusing it would be! What fun for the clubs! they would gossip over it for days. It would be as good as the Yelverton case, or the Crawley Court Martial."

"A truce to this," cried Lord Marchmont, angrily. "I am not to be mocked at like a schoolboy."

"As you please. You are in my house. I may talk in it without your permission. If my remarks are unpleasant or distasteful to your lordship, it is in your power to go away at any moment. Probably your carriage waits; if not, my servant will get you a cab."

"I shall not leave this house until I have satisfied myself, beyond the shadow of a doubt, that my wife is not within its precincts," exclaimed Lord Marchmont, firmly and with great decision.

The count looked equally determined, and replied, while a malignant scowl stole over his face—

"You shall not pass this threshold, my lord, unless you do so with the intention of removing yourself from a house where your presence is very obnoxious."

"Then I will pass over your body!" cried his lordship, his face glowing with passion, and his body trembling with rage.

With a bound, Lord Marchmont sprang upon the count, caught him by the throat, and a fearful struggle began.

They writhed in one another's grasp one moment; the next, you would have taken them for a pair of Cornish wrestlers.

They were so closely locked in each other's arms that they were unable to deliver straightforward blows.

Lord Marchmont was strong, thick-set, and well put together. His adversary was a much smaller man, but lithe and nimble.

At last he succumbed to the fierce strength of his antagonist, and was hurled into a corner of the room breathless, and feeling as if he had just escaped from the tender and close attentions of a grizzly bear, whose hug, like the embrace of that old instrument of torture, the "Scavenger's Daughter—which may even now be seen in the Armoury of the Tower of London—is far from pleasant or agreeable.

Lord Marchmont stood in the centre of the room and wiped the perspiration from his forehead.

The count raised himself upon his elbow, and said—

"At least, my lord, we might fight like gentlemen. One would think that we were a couple of costermongers who had just received their wages, and were out for an hour's holiday. I do not admire your English way of fighting with the arm and the fists."

"I am willing to accommodate you," replied his lordship.

Both the noblemen saw very plainly that a battle of some sort must take place between them. Their blood was hot, and they were eager for the fray.

Count Val de Grace was certain in his own mind that he would never be able to enjoy Agnes in peace as long as Lord Marchmont lived; and that nobleman saw that he had little or no chance of rescuing Agnes unless the count was in some manner or other put out of the way.

"How will you fight?" demanded Val de Grace; "I have had enough of your English fighting."

"I shall be perfectly agreeable to any way of settling our little difficulty that you like to propose," said his lordship.

The count rose to his feet, walked to a mirror which stood over the mantelpiece, adjusted his ruffled shirt, smoothed his hair with the back of his hand, and, with the utmost composure, lighted another cigar.

The one he had been previously smoking had been dashed from his hand, and was now lying extinguished upon the floor.

"Have you ever heard of a way the Mexicans have of fighting?" asked the count, looking his late antagonist steadily in the face.

There was a ferocious twinkle about the count's eyes as he spoke, as if he were contemplating, or rather gloating, over something extraordinary.

"I cannot say that I have studied the habits and customs of the Mexican people," replied Lord Marchmont.

"Shall I tell you?"

"Certainly."

"First they quarrel."

"We have done that."

"Yes; that is an unnecessary remark to make."

"What next?"

"Next they arm themselves."

"In what way?"

"With pistols—that is to say, revolvers, each containing six chambers."

"Yes," said Lord Marchmont.

"With swords."

"Yes."

"And with knives—sharp two-edged knives, with edges like a razor, and points as sharp and penetrating as those of a Venetian dagger."

"Is that all?"

"All! Enough to make sure of the death of one or both of the combatants."

"Where and how do they fight?" demanded his lordship.

"How do you like my programme?" said the count, with a grim smile.

"Oh, well enough. I do not care how I kill you, as long as I accomplish it by some means."

This was said carelessly.

"You ask me how they fight?"

"Yes."

"I will tell you. A room is selected which is perfectly destitute of furniture of any description—there is nothing to be seen but the bare floor and the bare walls."

"Well!"

"The shutters are drawn close to the windows so that not one ray of light can penetrate into the chamber. Some drapery is hung over the shutters to make it more impossible for the light to enter."

Lord Marchmont could not repress a shudder.

"The combatants——" continued the count.

"Well, the combatants."

"Strip themselves to their drawers."

"Yes."

"A belt circles their waists—in this the knife is stuck."

"Are they then equipped?"

"Almost. They hold the six-chambered revolver in the right hand, the sword in the left. They then enter the room arm-in-arm, cross the threshold, shut the door, and once in the darkness the fight begins."

"In the dark?" cried his lordship.

"Yes, all is as dark as Erebus," replied the count.

"That is, indeed, a terrible method of fighting a duel."

"Are you afraid?" asked the count, with a sneer.

"Afraid!"

"Yes. It sometimes happens that peculiarly constituted individuals succumb to the feeling."

"I am so far from being afraid, count," replied Lord Marchmont, "that I assent to your proposition."

"You assent?"

"Yes."

"Unhesitatingly?"

"Quite so."

The count turned a shade paler. He had hardly expected this. He had proposed the most terrible way of fighting a duel of which he had ever heard, in order to see if he would decline. If he did so, he virtually gave up Agnes. But the count was wofully disappointed.

However, there was no help for it.

The count was far from being a coward. In a duel like the one he had proposed, there was, of course, a great deal of luck; every shot, every thrust, was made in the dark. The count trusted to his luck.

"Very well, then, my lord," he exclaimed, "we had better get this affair over as soon as possible."

"Certainly."

"I have a room upstairs which will answer our purpose admirably."

"Nothing could be better. But the arms?"

"I can supply those also."

"Indeed!"

"Yes; I have an armoury on a small scale. This is not the first affair of honour that I have been engaged in."

"Really!" said Lord Marchmont.

"Come," said the count—"come to my armoury; we will select our weapons."

CHAPTER LXXXV.

LORD MARCHMONT AND THE COUNT SELECT THEIR WEAPONS — TRACES OF AGNES — LORD MARCHMONT GROWS FURIOUS—PREPARATIONS FOR THE COMBAT— THE DARKENED ROOM—THE APPEAL TO CHANCE—HIS LORDSHIP WINS THE TOSS.

WHAT the count called his armoury was in reality a small room containing a few swords, pistols, cutlasses, sabres, rifles, fowling-pieces, guns, and other arms, reposing in cases, or hanging against the wall, suspended by hooks and leather straps.

Val de Grace, as we have had occasion to observe once before, had led a very adventurous life, and he had found some use on some occasion or other for most of the weapons he treasured up. One, perhaps, was famous with him for saving his life amongst the Moors; another for similarly befriending him in the arid deserts of Arabia; that pistol, maybe, had shot a poisonous snake in some swamp of the

West Indies; the rifle over there might have checked the impetuous career of a buffalo; while the shining glass dagger by its side may have—well, when a crime is not proved against a man? Is it not the commonest sort of slander to mention it?

"Choose for yourself, my lord," exclaimed the count.

Lord Marchmont ran his eye critically round the apartment, and mentally cursed his thoughtlessness for not bringing with him his coat of mail. Had he thought of it, it would have been an important auxiliary to him.

"Shall I tell you an anecdote?" said the count.

"I have no objection."

The count took up a handsomely-embossed pistol, and snapped a cap, in order to see that the bore was not foul; and while he was talking he proceeded to load the costly weapon which he held in his hand.

"You shall hear my story," he began. "What I am going to describe happened in Mexico, in the environs of Puebla."

"You have travelled, then?"

"A little, my friend. I had made an acquaintance in the city, and he was one day insulted by an American. The duello was proposed and accepted. They fought as we are going to fight. Well, we gave them a room; they were armed. We heard shots, twelve in all, fierce cries, and groans, and shouts. An hour elapsed—two hours—then we entered the room."

"Well!" exclaimed Lord Marchmont.

"Well, my lord, they were both dead."

"Both?"

"Yes, riddled with balls."

Lord Marchmont drew his breath shortly.

"Perforated with swordthrusts."

"Ah!"

"Bathed in blood."

"Horrible!"

"Nothing extraordinary, and yet it was not a pleasant spectacle to look upon."

As the count finished speaking he raised the pistol he held in his hand and took aim at a spot of mildew on the wall. He held his arm bent a little, and altogether showed himself a master of the weapon. He fired. The spot of mildew disappeared, and the bullet embedded itself in the brickwork.

Lord Marchmont watched the shot, and thinking that the count had fired it out of bravado to show how good a shot he was, loaded a revolver. When the six chambers were filled, he looked around him for something to aim at.

The count watched his movements with a smile upon his lips.

Lord Marchmont was determined to prove to Count Val de Grace that he knew how to handle a pistol. A fly stationary upon the ceiling caught his eye. He never reflected that there might be some one in the room above. Raising his arm, and pointing the muzzle of the pistol upwards, he fired.

Count Val de Grace rushed forward to stay his arm, but he was too late.

"Stop! stop!" he cried.

But his warning voice was not heeded. The fly had disappeared, but the bullet had gone through the ceiling; a moment afterwards, and before the cadences of the report had died away, a terrific shriek sounded above their heads, and penetrated to where they were standing; it was not repeated. It was followed by the fall of something or other upon the boards above. Then all was still. Nothing was audible except the deep and heavy breathing of the two men.

"Her voice!" cried Lord Marchmont, when he had recovered from his surprise; "her voice; I would swear to it among a million."

"Whose?" asked the count, coldly.

"My wife's, scoundrel—my wife's," replied his lordship.

"You are mad."

"Come to her chamber, come!" cried Lord Marchmont, seizing him by the collar.

He dragged the count out of the room, up stairs, and stopped on the landing, at the door of a room which, by its situation, appeared to be just over the armoury.

The count was unable to resist his passionate strength; he did what he could, but for any practical purpose he was as powerless as an infant. The infuriated nobleman dragged him along as a giant would a pigmy.

"Now," he exclaimed, "open that door."

"Impossible!" he replied; "I have not the key."

The count pretended to feel in his pockets, as he spoke, in order to lend the more truth to his words.

Lord Marchmont furiously assaulted the door, but without succeeding in opening it.

"My lord," exclaimed the count, as an idea struck him, "if you think to put off our duel in this way, let me tell you——"

"Put it off!" interrupted Lord Marchmont, "believe me, I have no intention of doing so; make yourself easy on that score. But I heard my wife's voice, man; it was she who cried out. I may have shot her when I fired that cursed shot!"

"If she be dead?" said Count Val de Grace, incautiously.

"If! Then you admit that she is there?" cried Lord Marchmont, triumphantly.

"I—I did not say so."

"Prevarication is useless now you have as good as admitted that my wife is in your house—in this room, perhaps?"

"Well," returned the count, assuming an insolent and defiant air, "suppose we go upon that presumption, and I at once admit that she is; what then?"

"What then!" repeated Lord Marchmont, "why let me have access to her."

"Certainly not," replied the count, slowly, and with emphasis.

"But she may be dead?"

"If so, you cannot be of any service to her whatever."

"She may be wounded?"

"If so," replied the count, "she is in good hands; she is not left without attendants."

"By heaven! I will kill you where you stand," cried his lordship, "if you dare to talk to me in that cold-blooded way."

"My lord, do not talk to me like an assassin," said the count, with dignity.

Whatever his ideas may have been with regard to honour, when connected with that of a woman, he was strictly honourable in what are usually called affairs of honour.

"If," he continued, "you wish to kill me, come upstairs; you will have plenty of opportunities. You may succeed in your wish—always provided I do not kill you, which I have a strong presentiment I shall," he added, in a muttered tone, which did not reach Lord Marchmont's ears.

"Lead on," said his lordship, folding his arms; "the sooner one of us ceases to exist the better."

"Precisely my view of the case," replied Val de Grace, cheerfully. "Come, my lord, follow me."

They descended to the armoury once more. Lord Marchmont was biting his lips with impatience; the count was as cool as a cucumber. They selected their weapons; a revolver containing six chambers, which each loaded; a sword of the finest temper, the best steel, and the most perfect workmanship; and a knife whose sharpness and edge no one could call in question for an instant.

Each, armed like this, ascended the stairs side by side, carefully watching each other, lest either one should steal a cowardly advantage.

The count assumed a careless, jaunty air, which sat well upon his finely-cut features. It was not the first time he had been engaged in an affair of honour. So great a traveller had he been, that he had not only seen many men and many things, but he had studied the manners and customs of nearly every nation on the face of the globe. He had chosen the strange way of settling his difference with Lord Marchmont, which we have detailed, probably because he wished the affair to be final, or, perhaps, he had been engaged in a similar duel before, and had profited by the experience he had then acquired.

Lord Marchmont, although inwardly determined, did not exhibit outwardly the assurance of the count. He felt—as, indeed, who could help feeling—that he was engaged in an affair of life and death, the issue of which it was impossible to foretel, and he was a little grave at the prospect. His visible paleness did not arise from fear, but only from that natural apprehension, that the near approach of death in any shape is calculated to cast over any man—I care not who he is—prince or peasant, high or low.

At length the top of the staircase was reached, and the count led the way into a large unfurnished room. He left the door open and advanced to the window; drawing the blind down, he next proceeded to put to the shutters.

Having accomplished this, he looked around him; some light streamed in through the doorway from the passage, but to all intents and purposes the room was effectually darkened, and had the door been closed even a mole would have had some difficulty in finding his way through the very thick darkness.

Not a ray of light penetrated through the smallest chink in the shutters.

Seeing this, the count said—

"I think that will do."

"Perfectly," replied Lord Marchmont.

"If you are satisfied," continued the count, "I am also."

"I am quite satisfied."

"I asked the question," said the Count Val de Grace, "because if you had any lingering doubt as to the thorough exclusion of the light, I could very soon have hung some thick damask curtains over the window."

"It is unnecessary," replied Lord Marchmont.

"Very well; in that case nothing remains but for us to prepare ourselves."

Lord Marchmont made an inclination of the head, and the two noblemen began to strip themselves of their clothing; at last they stood in nothing but their shirts and their drawers.

They adjusted their weapons in the manner each fancied would be most serviceable to them, and then the only remaining ceremony to be gone through before the bloody work commenced in real and startling earnest, was that of shutting the door.

It was a difficult thing to arrange, because if one shut the door, directly he had done so the other would, of course, fire at him; but it had to be done.

If they had had any one to second them it would have been altogether different, but they were, as we know, left entirely to their own resources.

The count, however, was equal to the occasion. He said—

"We are in a slight dilemma here."

"Yes," said Lord Marchmont.

"But I think I can surmount it if you consent to my plan."

"Yes."

"If we were seconded by some friend he would place us equi-distant from one another in different parts of the room and close the door. The sensation of being in the dark would be the signal for us to commence hostilities."

"Of course."

"But we are left entirely to ourselves; had we not better toss up some coin and decide it by chance?"

"As you please," returned Lord Marchmont, carelessly.

"So be it, then. Will you toss something in the air, and I will endeavour to guess which side it comes down? If I win, of course the task of shutting the door devolves upon you."

"Certainly."

Going to his clothes, which were lying in a heap in the passage, Lord Marchmont took a sovereign out of one of his pockets.

The count followed him into the passage so that they might have more light.

Lord Marchmont put the coin on the top of his thumbnail and sent it spinning into the air. It fell with a clank upon the boards.

Lord Marchmont instantly placed his foot upon it and eagerly demanded the count's selection—

"Man or woman?" he cried.

The count contemplated for half a minute, and then replied—

"This quarrel is about a woman, so I will stake my chance upon her. Woman, I say—woman."

Lord Marchmont removed his foot, and both the men, holding their breath with anxiety, stooped down to inspect the unconscious piece of gold which was to exercise so much influence over their destinies.

"Man!" they exclaimed, simultaneously.

"By God!" cried Count Val de Grace, "you have won the toss."

As he spoke he turned a shade paler.

Lord Marchmont's face beamed with exultation.

CHAPTER LXXXVI.

THE DUEL IN THE DARK BEGINS—IT PROCEEDS WITH VARYING FORTUNE—THE COUNT SUCCEEDS IN DRAWING FIRST BLOOD — THE LAST SHOT — THE SWORDS ARE BROUGHT INTO REQUISITION—THE FIGHT WITH KNIVES —THE SHADOW OF DEATH.

LOSING that toss was as good as signing the count's death-warrant. Without question his adversary would mark his position, level his revolver, and fire the moment darkness enveloped them. He would, while the light lasted, be enabled to take *aim*, which was everything in the sort of warfare in which they were about to engage. They would, after the door was closed, be obliged to allow themselves to be guided by sound; and that is at all times calculated to mislead people.

Lord Marchmont could not restrain a smile of exultation and of triumph. He felt his heart leap to his mouth, and he involuntarily uttered the word "Agnes."

A deep bass voice, close to him, exclaimed—

"Shall yet be mine."

He started, and looked up. It was the count who had spoken.

A grim smile was playing round the corners of the French nobleman's mouth. An expressive smile it was, too, which, he could not tell why, struck a chill to the heart of Lord Marchmont.

It was just possible, it occurred to him, that his exultation and his joy were premature.

It is a good old saying, that it is imprudent to reckon without your host; and it is also true, that it is impolitic to count your chickens before the process of incubation has been brought to a satisfactory termination—in other words, before they are hatched.

Lord Marchmont thought of those homely adages, and in his turn turned pale.

"Come, sir," exclaimed the count, "let us to business!"

"I am at your service," was the reply. "Lead on."

The count needed no further adjuration. He led the way into the room, and stood with the handle of the door in his hand.

Lord Marchmont took up his position near the darkened window, distant from the count about ten paces.

At such close quarters his shot was sure to be a murderous one.

It was a terrible moment for both of these men; but more terrible to the count than to the English peer.

The lips of both were compressed together, as if they were frightfully in earnest.

They were battling for a fair prize—a lovely woman—and their lives.

Who, on such an occasion, when two such dearly-prized things were at stake, would allow his thoughts to wander, or allow any opportunity to pass?

"Are you ready?" asked the count, in a voice which, in spite of his determined look, trembled a little.

Lord Marchmont noted the tremulous accents of the count; but his own voice was not one whit firmer when he replied, "I am."

The count closed the door a little, then a little more, keeping his eye all the time fixed intently upon his antagonist, who had raised his pistol, and levelled it dead at the forehead of his adversary.

As Lord Marchmont ran his eye along the highly-polished and gleaming barrel of his weapon, he endeavoured, as far as was in his power, to concentrate the focus upon his adversary's forehead. He wished his ball to enter his brain, and so end the duel at once.

The count kept his eye upon Lord Marchmont, and he did not shrink when he saw the deadly preparations which were made for him.

The door closed a little more; then again a little more, until only a small space remained for the light from the passage to enter by.

Suddenly the count slammed to the door with the greatest quickness.

They were in the dark.

Lord Marchmont was taken by surprise.

The count had cunningly counted upon this being the case. He had cleverly consumed at least five minutes in partially closing the door; and his adversary supposed that he would take his time about the remainder.

Keeping the pistol levelled, too, tired Lord Marchmont's arm a great deal; but, nevertheless, directly the door was slammed to, he fired. The shot went crashing through the door, flattening itself against the wall of the passage, whose hard exterior was opposed to its further progress.

A little round hole, through which a faint ray of light entered, was revealed; but so small was the hole, and so faint the ray of light, that it was not of any advantage to either of the duellers.

It sufficed, however, for one purpose, and that was to show Lord Marchmont that he had, somehow or other, missed the count.

That nobleman had, with instinctive cunning, dropped flat upon his face on the ground directly he had shut the door.

He calculated with great reason that Lord Marchmont would not think of lowering his pistol, and he was right in his conjecture.

Winning the toss had not benefited his lordship in the slightest degree.

He had wasted a shot, and he had tired his arm; and, in addition to these two evils, he had put himself in a passion at his ill success.

Suddenly it struck him as only prudent to move a little on one side.

It was lucky he did so, for the next moment a ball whizzed past his ear and struck against the wall.

The flash of the pistol revealed the count's whereabouts to a certain extent, and Lord Marchmont immediately let fly another shot.

No cry of pain, no sound, resulted to indicate that he had been successful.

The fact was, the count had cleverly contrived to lie on the ground, but when he fired he had raised his arm as high as he could, and the flash coming from a certain distance from the floor, Lord Marchmont had been deluded into the belief that he should inevitably hit the count if he fired in the direction from which the flash had emanated.

A moment before they had fired shot and shot; now the advantage was in favour of the count.

He had one more deadly missile in his possession than had his adversary.

Both, of course, had denuded themselves of their boots, so that if they walked with great caution their movements would be inaudible. The only thing which would in the slightest degree betray the position of one to the other would be the breathing.

Lord Marchmont endeavoured to walk round to where he thought the count was.

His plan was to stand still after he had gone a little distance, and then see if the count moved.

He did so.

Walking with the utmost carefulness, he skirted the wall, reached the corner, which he distinguished by its angular formation, advanced two paces more, and stood still.

Not a sound broke the horrible stillness that reigned in that room, soon to become the chamber of death; the scene of a murder, or perhaps of a double tragedy.

Lord Marchmont could not help his breath coming thick and fast, the agitation of the moment would otherwise have choked him.

The imprudence of not checking his sensations, at any cost, was, however, too soon apparent.

There was a flash of light close to him almost, a report, then a sharp, stinging sensation in his left arm.

Some hot fluid trickling down his shirt sleeve next aroused his attention, and he knew that he was wounded.

Before he had time to think, another shot thundered in his ear, but this time the bullet missed him.

Dropping on his hands and knees, Lord Marchmont crawled noiselessly away.

When he thought himself out of danger, he rose to his feet, and listened.

The drip, drip of his blood upon the floor only too well betrayed his position to the count.

A fourth shot left his opponent's revolver, but by some chance flew harmlessly past his lordship, who saw that unless he could stay the effusion of blood which betrayed his locality only too well to the count, he would be slaughtered in a very short time.

He moved again, and continued to walk round slowly, so as to mislead the count in case he fired again.

While moving he tore a piece of his shirt off, and wrapped it round his arm tightly, tying it as well as he was able in the darkness.

This had the effect of stopping the hæmorrhage.

When the count heard the ripping noise made by the linen, he fired his fifth shot, but owing to Lord Marchmont's moving about, the shot did not hit him.

The count had drawn first blood, and he hoped that, as his lordship had not returned his last three shots, he had wounded him in some vital part.

This made him bolder than he otherwise would have been.

Lord Marchmont had decidedly the advantage in one respect, and that was, that he had only fired two shots, whereas Val de Grace had fired five.

His lordship determined to hazard a shot on the first opportunity.

But, in order to succeed better than he had hitherto done, he resolved to let his opponent take the initiative, so he remained ensconced in a corner, in a crouching position. Minutes passed, and all was as still as death.

The men had obtained more command over their breath, and no deep respiration broke the sepulchral stillness of that room.

Lord Marchmont could not help his thoughts reverting to Agnes, who was pining in her enforced captivity downstairs.

"Perhaps," he reflected, "she is lying dangerously wounded by my own hand."

The idea of his wife writhing in pain caused by himself—the idea of his hand being red with his wife's blood—was very shocking to him!

He was aroused from the partial reverie into which he had fallen, by hearing a noise like the rustling of a piece of silk close to him. It came apparently from the right of him. It struck him immediately that it must be the count coming in search of him. He listened. He heard it again. He levelled his revolver, and held himself in readiness.

A third time he heard it. Then he fired. A loud cry of pain rewarded this effort.

In that exclamation the count acknowledged himself hit.

Lord Marchmont had sense enough to leave the wall directly he had fired, and to go into the middle of the room. He saved his life by his forethought and decision, for the next moment a bullet struck the wall with great force. His lordship congratulated himself upon his narrow escape, and wondered where he had wounded the count.

The drip, drip of blood now proceeded from the unfortunate Frenchman, who had fired his last shot, and was now in a manner at his antagonist's mercy—at least, Lord Marchmont thought so. He little knew, as the sequel proved, the almost unlimited resources of Count Val de Grace.

It is true that he had fired his last shot, and that three chambers of his opponent's revolver were charged; but he still possessed his sword, and were that to fail him, his two-edged knife would no doubt stand him in good stead.

Guided by the noise of the blood which the count continued to lose, Lord Marchmont opened fire with his fourth barrel. No sound resulted, so that he was unable to tell whether he had succeeded in hitting his adversary. Perhaps the count had schooled himself, and, by an heroic effort, prevented his agony finding utterance; but, on the other hand, it was more than possible that his shot had not hit the mark it was intended to reach.

This last discharge placed the two men more on an equality than they were before; the odds against the count were only two to one—not three to one, as they had stood formerly.

Lord Marchmont's wounded arm pained him a good deal, but as it was his left arm he did not care about it. He looked upon it as an insignificant scratch.

Certainly the limb might be of use to him in the event of his coming to close quarters with the count; but he could only think of his luck in escaping any serious damage to his sword arm, which would have been a misfortune indeed; and one it would have been out of his power to remedy in any way whatever.

The count must have been losing blood very rapidly, for the monotonous drip continued.

Lord Marchmont thought that as this was the case he would get more by delaying than by taking instant and immediate action.

He remained passive and immobile.

The minutes went by once more; but very slowly—so slowly that their tardiness was painful.

In moments of great danger one's wits are sometimes preternaturally sharpened.

It was so with his lordship.

He was in great—in the greatest danger, and he racked his brains continually for some means of out-manœuvring and out-generalling his opponent.

He knew the count to be a man fertile in resources, to be possessed of indomitable courage, and what alarmed him most was that he knew him to be treacherous and crafty to a degree.

Lord Marchmont was constantly in dread of being shot through the head or heart without a moment's warning, or of being pounced upon from behind, before he knew what was going to happen to him.

If the count once got to close quarters with him, he very well knew that he would not hesitate to use that murderous knife he had in his belt; and in all likelihood he was more expert in its use than most men.

These reflections gave birth to an idea which did Lord Marchmont credit. It was worthy of the Count Val de Grace himself.

The idea was this. The count would, it was probable, endeavour to force his lordship to come to close quarters. In order to do this, he must discover in what part of the room he was standing.

The only way to accomplish this was to feel his way cautiously along the sides of the room until, by some indication, he discovered in what position he was.

Lord Marchmont, in order to gain an advantage, laid down upon his back, with his head to the window, his feet towards the door, so that if Val de Grace pursued him he would inevitably trip himself up over the prostrate body, and fall down upon the floor.

Having taken up this position, Lord Marchmont waited impatiently for the result.

The count's wound did not bleed so quickly as it had done; he had, perhaps, stanched it in some way. Whatever the reason was, the fact remained the same. The blood only dropped occasionally on the floor, once or twice in a minute, perhaps, certainly not more than twice.

Time flew away; ten minutes had elapsed, when Lord Marchmont thought that he heard something. He held his pistol ready for the first chance. From the tremulous creaking of the boards, there was no doubt that the count was approaching. This was Lord Marchmont's opportunity; he watched eagerly for it. It was not likely to slip through his fingers when it did come. It came sooner than he had expected.

The count was either not proceeding with his usual care, or he was taken by surprise at the novel impediment. He stumbled over the body of Lord Marchmont, and fell upon the floor.

The peer was on his feet in an instant, and his two barrels were discharged in quick succession at what he supposed to be the count's carcase. He would have leant over him and have made sure of his foe's death, but he remembered that the count still had one barrel which had not been discharged, and instead of killing anyone, he might have been killed himself.

It was this dread which held him back, and made him fire more at random.

The count, directly after the discharge of Lord Marchmont's remaining two barrels, let fly the only one he had left, and the duellists were equal again in the matter of pistol shots; although it was impossible to tell without light and inspection who was the most severely wounded.

The count's last shot went wide of its mark, and Lord Marchmont was unscathed. With a cry of triumph he threw away his still smoking, but now useless, pistol, and transferred his sword from his left to his right hand. Then he rushed forward to where the count ought to have been lying, in order to continue this duel in the dark with the deadly toledo.

The count had risen to his feet. He, too, had dropped his revolver, he looked upon it as practically useless; he might have dealt a few blows with the butt end of it, but what was a revolver when compared to a sharp knife?—as a wooden ship to an iron-clad—as an old-fashioned blunderbuss to a Minié rifle—so he threw it on one side.

Lord Marchmont had not hurt Val de Grace with either of his last two shots, but he had done what was of great use to him—he had succeeded in accomplishing the next best thing—that was, he had struck the count's sword with a pistol-ball, and shattered the blade so that it had broken in two, and was of no more use than the kitchen poker.

The count would have been utterly defenceless but for his knife, and this he determined to make good use of.

Lord Marchmont held himself on guard in the most approved fashion. He moved about more fearlessly now, because he was not afraid of a bullet.

He walked round the room without finding the count. Then he got, as near as he could guess, into the centre of the apartment.

He lunged in every direction.

His sword's point touched something.

He had found him at last.

It was the count.

Lord Marchmont pressed forward, and was surprised at not feeling the count's sword clashing against his own. He did not know that it had been disabled and broken, so it was a mystery to him.

As he was wondering as to the meaning of this strange circumstance, something struck his sword; the blow was repeated higher up, and by a skilful twist his weapon was wrested from his grasp, and sent flying up in the air towards the ceiling. It fell upon the floor with a dull thud, which showed that it had descended upon the point, which was, probably, sticking in the flooring.

Enraged, perplexed, and annoyed at so distressing a calamity, his lordship sought for his knife; it was in his belt; in another moment it was in his hand. Hardly had he grasped it firmly before he encountered the blade of the count's knife against his wounded arm.

A struggle of the fiercest and most desperate character now commenced.

They were both equally armed.

Lord Marchmont had somehow or other lost all the advantages which he had formerly gained, and he was upon exactly the same footing as Val de Grace.

They stabbed one another here, there, and everywhere.

The terrible knives did frightful execution.

The contest was appalling in the extreme.

Sparks of fire flew into the air whenever the finely-tempered blades crossed one another.

The combatants grew faint with the loss of blood. The floor was slimy and gory with the sanguinary fluid. They were continually losing their footing.

Thrust after thrust was blindly dealt in the darkness.

But the efforts of the two maddened men grew feeble and yet more feeble.

Lord Marchmont gathered himself up for a final and decisive blow, when his foot slipped, and he fell into a puddle of hot and steaming blood. He expected the death-stroke, and yet it came not.

He commended himself to Heaven.

He thought his last hour had come.

But it was not so.

CHAPTER LXXXVII.

LORD MARCHMONT ESCAPES DEATH—HE OPENS THE DOOR OF THE DARKENED ROOM, BUT IS ASTOUNDED AT PERCEIVING NO TRACE OF COUNT VAL DE GRACE—THE SECRET DOOR—THE PASSAGE—THE ORIENTAL APARTMENT—THE COUNT'S DEATH.

LORD MARCHMONT may be truly said to have given up all hope. There he lay upon the floor of that sombre and funereal apartment at the mercy of Count Val de Grace, whom he expected to spring upon him with the ferocity of a wild beast every moment. And yet the death-stroke did not come; what could be the meaning of it?

Lord Marchmont puzzled and racked his brains for an answer, but in vain; an answer was not forthcoming. Then it struck him that the count might be too exhausted to continue the combat, or to take advantage of the extraordinary chance which the vicissitudes of the combat and accident had thrown in his way. As this idea gained ground in his mind, Lord Marchmont determined to rise to his feet and see how things really were; if the count was dead or mortally wounded, then he had conquered.

His lordship was sick and faint; for he had lost a great deal of blood. He was strong enough as yet to walk, and he could have fought some minutes longer, had it been necessary to do so. But was it necessary? that was what he was now going to endeavour to discover. He was afraid

JABEZ CLARKE TORTURED BY THE DWARF IN THE DUNGEON.

to walk straight up to Count Val de Grace because he was perfectly well acquainted with the count's treacherous and perfidious character; and he was quite prepared for some subterfuge, such as the count springing up on his approach, taking him off his guard, and plunging his knife up to the hilt in his heart; but there was in reality little or no fear of that.

Lord Marchmont, thinking that he was justified in so doing, opened the door of the room. At first the light nearly blinded him; but in a few seconds he became accustomed to it. A terrible spectacle the room presented. There were the empty pistols, and the swords smothered in blood, which also covered the room in innumerable places. But what literally astounded Lord Marchmont was, that *the count was nowhere to be seen.* He looked to the right and to the left; he looked up and he looked down; he rubbed his eyes, but he was not deceived; Count Val de Grace had vanished. He walked to the window, and, after some trouble, undid the shutters.

A flood of light poured in; but it revealed no Count Val de Grace either dead or alive. It was passing strange. Lord Marchmont, for once in his life, could not—wouldnot believe the evidence of his senses. The holes in the wall, caused by the bullets, were visible; so were the weapons, and so were the blood-stains; but where was the man with whom he had just been engaged in mortal combat? he asked himself, aloud, Where?—and echo answered, "Where?"

Could he be asleep or awake?

He had expected to see the count stretched out a corpse before him, rigid in death, pierced in twenty places by the double-edged knife he had wielded so well against him.

It was more than strange—more than wonderful—more than marvellous.

It was miraculous.

At least Lord Marchmont thought so.

A vague suspicion that he was in league with the devil flitted across his startled mind, and had he been a Catholic he would have devoutly crossed himself at the diabolical supposition.

But it was necessary just at present to allow this mystery to stand over for elucidation later in the day, for the state of his lordship's wounds was becoming serious.

Sitting down upon the ground he examined himself.

He was wounded in many places, but most of the places where the knife had struck him were but skin deep. In the dark it is difficult to deal a deadly blow. Nevertheless, he was much hurt.

The remainder of his shirt was applied to the work of stanching the effusion of blood, and his lordship soon had bandages over the more serious of the cuts with which the count had favoured him. Then he staggered to his feet once more.

He had good blood in him had Lord Marchmont, and he would not give up anything as long as he had a leg to stand upon.

His common sense told him that the count could not have been spirited away. He could not have gone out at the door, nor at the window; and yet he had disappeared in some way.

The ceiling was too far off for him to reach it!

There remained then but the walls.

The walls!

Lord Marchmont no sooner thought of them than he began to think of trap-doors and sliding panels and all the machinery which in every-day life we associate with the stage. But the stage has borrowed most of its appliances and contrivances from real life.

Lord Marchmont extracted his sword from the floor and holding it steadily in his hands, began to probe the walls.

Nothing but brickwork rewarded his efforts for some little time, but unexpectedly his weapon, instead of coming in contact with some hard substance and being turned on one side, penetrated the paper up to the hilt.

This explained the apparent mystery.

There was a door in the wall!

Throwing down his sword, Lord Marchmont felt about in every direction for some secret spring.

He felt convinced that there was one somewhere, and he made it his immediate business to discover where.

He was very irate with the count for treating him in the way he had done. It was clear and evident that Val de Grace, finding himself worsted and beaten, and most likely knowing that his already wasted strength could not hold out many minutes longer, had availed himself of the secret door, with whose existence he must have been previously acquainted.

Having opened it while his lordship was lying upon the floor, he had gone through the aperture, closing it again upon the inside.

What had become of him subsequently it was for his lordship to discover. Lord Marchmont was something dreadful to look at. Half naked, covered with blood, bandages, and wounds, with his hair matted with blood, he would have frightened any one who had met him into fits.

After a minute examination of the door, he discovered a spring.

He pressed it.

The door flew back inwards an inch or two.

A kick forced it to open wider.

Without staying to put on his coat, Lord Marchmont plunged into the secret passage; first, however, taking the precaution to see if the door could be opened on the inside.

He found that it could.

He shut it after him, and groped his way along a dark and gloomy corridor.

He pursued it for some time. Once or twice he thought he trod upon something soft and wet; it might have been the count's blood, he could not say it was not.

After travelling about five-and-twenty yards, he came to another door, which was open. He took advantage of this, and stepped into the Oriental apartment that Agnes had once traversed with such astonishment and admiration.

The birds were still flying about amongst the fragrant orange-trees; and their gaudy plumage glittered in the subdued sun-rays which the windows gave entrance to.

The fountains tinkled melodiously in their marble basins as of old, and the water fell with a pleasing cadence.

The rare exotics, some worth their weight in gold, shone out in all the wealth of their beauty and their sweet blossoms.

The gold and silver fish darted to and fro in the clear streams in which they lived and found sustenance.

The gilded ceiling was as lovely as ever, and none of the fairy aspect of the apartment had departed from it.

Passing a group of orange trees, all white with their flowers, Lord Marchmont saw what he had expected all along.

Count Val de Grace had penetrated to this delightful place; once arrived, his strength failed him, and he had fallen upon one of the cushions with which the floor in some places was covered.

While his lordship was looking on, he thought he heard a groan.

Val de Grace, then, was not dead.

Rushing forward, he chivalrously determined to render him whatever assistance lay in his power.

On arriving at the place where he was lying, Lord Marchmont bent over his body, and exclaimed—

"Count!"

The count opened his eyes—they were becoming glassy. He had some difficulty in discovering who was speaking to him. When he recognised Lord Marchmont he smiled sadly and shook his head.

"You are not dying?" said Lord Marchmont.

In faint, almost indistinct tones, the count replied—

"I have not many minutes to live."

"You will be better presently."

"Never. The seconds are numbered."

"Would to God it were not so."

"I feel it," said Val de Grace, solemnly.

"Can I be of any service to you?"

"Alas! none."

His eyes closed as he spoke. The death-rattle rumbled in his throat, and he was dead.

Thus expired Count Val de Grace, the most determined enemy that Agnes had yet had to encounter.

———

CHAPTER LXXXVIII.

LORD MARCHMONT SEEKS AGNES AND FINDS HER— MUTUAL EXPLANATIONS ARE FOLLOWED BY FORGIVE- NESS—HOME AGAIN—THE HUE AND CRY—THE POLICE AT FAULT—AGNES HAS VAGUE TERRORS, AND SEES VISIONS IN HER SLEEP—SHE GOES SHOPPING, AND MEETS AN OLD FRIEND—MARMADUKE WILSON STANDS BEFORE HER.

THE count was certainly dead, his jaw drooped, his head fell back, and he showed all the symptoms of inanimation and death. His spirit had departed from him, and had gone to that land where the souls of the departed are at rest. His had been a stormy existence, which had been crowned by a stormy end. There was one point in his character which did him infinite credit, and prevented him from being utterly base—in all affairs of honour between man and man he had ever been the pink of propriety. He had fought Lord Marchmont fairly; he might have assassinated him in some manner, or have put him out of the way, but he had not attempted to do anything of the sort, nor had he attempted at any time to mesmerize him and put him under that terrible and enervating influence which had proved so efficacious in many instances.

The mortal remains of Count Val de Grace were not pleasant to look upon, and Lord Marchmont shrank from any prolonged contemplation of them. The dead man bore the traces and evidences of the severity of the conflict in several places. His face was scarred, and a long and hideous gash all down his right cheek, spoke of a slashing cut when the swords were thrown away, and those terrible long knives resorted to. He had been shot through the lungs, and if his lordship had been able to spare time for a more pro- longed and critical examination, he would have discovered many a gaping and discoloured wound. But this he had neither time nor inclination to do. The count was dead, that there was not the least doubt about, and it behoved him now to attend to his own affairs.

His thoughts flew at once to Agnes. He dared not con- jecture in what state she was. He was possessed with a wild longing desire to see her. How was he to get at her? He imagined that she was in the house, but he had no positive proof that such was the case. The myrmidons of the count might have removed her to some other prison. The very idea of such an occurrence distracted him. He could not bear to think of it.

In order to set his doubts at rest, he endeavoured to make his way out of Count Val de Grace's luxurious, costly, and splendid Oriental chamber.

As he passed by the orange trees, the birds, the fountains, the fish, and the marble basins, he could not help moralizing on the vanity of human wishes. A few short hours before, the count had been master of everything except a woman's affections, and in order to gain them he had plunged into a hundred arduous enterprizes, and at last he had lost his life. Lord Marchmont felt saddened and chastened as these ideas swept through his brain, but he saw the paramount necessity of extricating himself from the mazy intricacies of the Paphian groves in which he found himself; so he looked diligently around for an exit. He was not long in finding one. Some crimson curtains drew aside, and disclosed a corridor; without any hesitation he followed it; and, at length, after traversing a suite of rooms handsomely furnished in the style of Louis XIV., he emerged upon a landing.

Then he stopped.

There were flights of stairs leading up to the highest regions, and there were flights leading lower down.

Knowing that he had ascended to reach the chamber in which the fatal duel had been fought, and remembering that the room in which he had heard Agnes's voice was on the first floor, he thought it would be better to go down and see where the staircase would take him to.

Accordingly he descended one flight and paused again.

As yet he had seen or met no one.

A door stood open.

He looked in; it was apparently a dressing-room of Count Val de Grace's, for brushes, combs, razors, pomades, and clothes of various descriptions were lying about in pleasing confusion.

It occurred to Lord Marchmont that if he were to enter this apartment and make himself more like a Christian, it would assist him materially should he meet any of the domestics of the establishment.

Indeed, he was not in a fit or proper condition to return to his own house even in a cab.

Pushing the door wide open he walked in, closing it again after him to prevent any interruption.

The first thing he did was to go to the basin and wash himself, as well as the gradually increasing stiffness of his wounds and hurts would allow him.

He arranged his hair, put on one of the count's shirts which he found in a drawer, and attired himself in such things as he thought most becoming.

They fitted him indifferently, but he thought nothing of that.

He opened a sort of wardrobe to discover a hat if possible. On the ponderous oaken doors swinging back he saw several, put there to keep the dust away from them.

Another thing caught his attention, and that was a black bottle with a silver stopper to it.

Taking it down he hastily uncorked it.

A glass of wine at that moment would be to him like manna to the Israelites in the wilderness with a brace of quails for supper.

To his delight he found it was port wine. Applying the neck of the bottle to his mouth he drank deeply of its generous contents.

It seemed to put fresh life and energy into him.

Again and again did he drink, each time receiving fresh invigoration from his hearty application.

The fourth time finished the bottle, and Lord Marchmont, like King Richard, was himself again.

Having fully equipped himself he took his departure and recommenced, in more civilized attire, his search for Agnes.

The next landing he reached was, he thought, the very one upon which he had so furiously requested the count to give him admittance to the chamber in which Agnes was confined.

Lord Marchmont's perceptions had been quickened by the wine, and he thought he recognised more than one insignificant object here and there.

He tried to open the door but, as before, it was locked. He rapped with his knuckles upon one of the painted panels. Then he listened to see if his summons was responded to by any one.

He heard footsteps approaching.

They drew gradually nearer.

A key turned in the lock.

The door revolved on its hinges and a woman's voice said in a whisper—

"She sleeps."

The next moment Lord Marchmont was face to face with a middle aged woman of respectable exterior, who was one of the creatures and dependents of the late count.

When she saw Lord Marchmont she uttered a short scream and would have shut-to the door again had he given her the opportunity. But this he did not do.

He grasped her by the arm gently but firmly, with his right hand; his left he could not use.

He had with the greatest difficulty, donned the count's habiliments, but now for all practical purposes he was about as efficient as a London commissionaire—that is, he had only one arm to use.

The woman looked up in his face in a frightened way, hardly knowing what to do. From the expression of her countenance, which was one of terror, Lord Marchmont concluded that she was about to cry out.

It was necessary at all events, at the present juncture, to prevent this.

He did not want any disturbance.

There was the ugly fact of Count Val de Grace, lying stark and stiff upstairs upon the luxurious cushions of his Oriental divan.

According to the code of honour existing amongst duellists the count had been fairly killed, but in the eye of the law Lord Marchmont was a murderer, and would be treated as such should the commission of his crime be brought home to him.

"Silence!" cried Lord Marchmont, "for your life, silence."

The woman held her peace, although strongly against her inclination, but the determined aspect of the man before her awed her into complete submission.

"What do you want of me?" asked the poor woman.

"I want you," replied his lordship, "to conduct me to the lady you have under your charge."

"I cannot do so," she replied, in a tremulous voice.

"Why not?"

"The count, my master, would be the death of me."

Lord Marchmont thought that he had been the death of him, but he did not say so.

"You must do as I tell you," he said.

"Oh! do not ask me."

"I will not harm you if you comply with my wishes."

"I cannot—I cannot."

"No harm shall befal you."

"How can I be sure of that?"

"Take my word for it I do not speak without reason."

The woman reflected for a time, and then said—

"I consent, on condition that you do not say I assisted you to gain an entrance into the secret chamber, as it is called."

"Not a word shall pass my lips."

"Follow me, then."

She led the way through the room in which they were conversing, which was plainly, if not meagrely, furnished, and after ascending some steps at the end of the room, and pushing aside a curtain, his lordship found himself in the most elegant and sumptuous boudoir it had ever been his lot to enter.

His eyes did not rest upon the triumphs and the excellencies of the upholsterer's art. He caught sight of Agnes lying upon a couch, wrapped, apparently, in a deep slumber.

So quiet, so still, so wax-like did she look, that a horrible suspicion crept into his lordship's mind.

He recollected all at once, with terrible distinctness, the shot he had fired when in the count's armoury.

Could it have taken effect? Could it be possible that she was dead. Turning hastily to the attendant, he said—

"She lives?"

He put this interrogatively.

The woman replied in the affirmative.

"Oh! yes, she's alive enough, or rather she was before I left her," said the woman. "Something like a lobster before it is boiled I should have called her. Thought she'd have gone into a fit once or twice."

Lord Marchmont walked upon tiptoe to the couch upon which Agnes was reclining.

She was a good bit altered since she had left his house—or more properly speaking, since he had driven her away from his abode because he deemed her unfaithful to his bed.

She was paler and thinner. Her face wore a more harassed expression, and there were traces of tears scarcely dry upon her pallid cheeks.

Lord Marchmont bent tenderly over her.

Stooping down yet lower, he brought his lips in contact with hers.

He kissed the unconscious girl rapturously.

She must have slept very lightly, for the act awoke her.

Springing up, she sat on the sofa, resting on her elbow. She looked in a scared and startled manner around her.

"My darling, my long lost darling!" exclaimed Lord Marchmont.

"You here," she said, assuming an air of injured innocence and insulted virtue.

"Yes, Agnes, I am here. I received your message. I only want your assurance to perfect and complete my belief in your innocence. Say that my suspicions were groundless. Tell me that you are guiltless of any thought or intention to wrong me, and I will at once forgive you."

"Oh! how could you ever doubt me?" she said, bursting into tears. "I have ever been true to you."

He was by her side in an instant.

"It was cruel to have such suspicions," she continued. "Circumstances and appearances were against me, but I swear before Heaven that I never wronged you either in thought or deed."

"I believe you. As God is my witness, I believe you," cried Lord Marchmont.

The sound of his voice recalled her to herself.

"Thank you for that," she said, raising his hand to her lips.

"This is not the place, my sweet pet," resumed Lord Marchmont, "for conversation. Let us leave it at once."

"Oh! yes, yes."

When the woman who had conducted Lord Marchmont to Agnes heard this she pricked up her ears and found her tongue.

"You can't go out of this!" she exclaimed.

But his lordship took no notice of her remark; he pushed her away, saying—

"Stand on one side, my good woman," and taking Agnes by the hand, led her from the apartment.

Descending the stairs, they reached the hall, but without being molested by anybody. The street-door speedily gave them egress, and they walked rapidly away.

Hailing the first cab, Lord Marchmont ordered the man to drive to his residence, and, in a short time, Agnes was once more under the friendly shelter of his lordship's roof-tree.

For some days Lord Marchmont remained at home; he did not wish to expose himself to popular observation. He saw, through the medium of the newspapers, that the lifeless body of the count had been discovered.

It was a moot point with the journalists and reporters whether the count had been assassinated, whether he had committed suicide, or whether he had been killed in a duel. Each theory found its partizans.

The police, of course, were said to be acting upon information which they had received; and it was firmly believed that this startling mystery would speedily be elucidated.

That indefatigable officer, Inspector Wyman, and his energetic colleague, the Finsbury Fox, were actively engaged in following up a clue which had been supplied them.

That the police held some links of the long chain of evidence no one would venture to deny, and before long the missing links would, without doubt, be supplied, &c., &c.

But in spite of all this flourish of trumpets, nothing was elucidated; and the mystery was consigned to the limbo where the Road murder, the Waterloo-bridge mystery, the Soho tragedy, and a hundred others are sleeping—and will continue to sleep, until the last trump shall reveal many things that are now hidden from the eyes of man.

Had the dwarf read the paper, he might have had his suspicions; but this he was not in the habit of doing. So Lord Marchmont had twice embrued his hands in a fellow-creature's blood and escaped detection.

Some weeks elapsed, and Agnes was again installed as the mistress of his lordship's mansion. Again servants bowed down before her; and an unlimited supply of money placed everything within her reach.

A carriage was, as before, at her disposal, and she began to think that her troubles were over, and that, at last, she had found rest.

But a calm always precedes a storm. Occasionally dark thoughts and fears would flit across her mind, and startle her with their ominous forebodings.

She was troubled in her sleep, and the image of her husband over the sea was constantly before her eyes.

Sometimes her mind would revert to Scotland, and she would grow gloomy over the sudden death of Marmaduke Wilson's child; at other times, she would think of Jabez Clarke, and wonder whether the dwarf had kept his promise to liberate the wretched man, or whether he allowed him to starve to death. Her mind became sorely troubled, and she dreaded some evil. It came sooner than she expected it.

One day she went out shopping, and her carriage stopped before one of the most famous shops in Regent-street.

She went in, made her purchases, and, followed by the obsequious shopman, with the packages in his arms, she returned to the brougham.

She had hardly touched the pavement before, exactly in front of her, she saw the dwarf, Stubbles. He was not alone; another man accompanied him.

This man was still young, but he looked as if he led a hard life. His brow was somewhat corrugated, and his face was covered with hair. His eyes bore a subdued, not to say sad, expression; but, with all this, his bearing was upright and manly.

Agnes turned pale.

She trembled all over.

She felt her legs giving way beneath her, a film came over her eyes, and had not the shopman rendered her some assistance she must have fallen to the ground.

How she got to her brougham she knew not.

It was strange that the sight of this man should have agitated her in so striking and visible a manner.

Stubbles would not alone have caused such a tumult in her mind, for she had met him often before, and he had always shown himself friendly disposed towards her.

What, then, could it be?

The dwarf hastily whispered some words in his companion's ear.

The man was almost as much agitated as Agnes had been a few moments previously.

He pressed his hand to his brow, but the voice of the dwarf, as he said—"Courage, my friend—courage," recalled him to himself.

The dwarf ran to the horse's head and held the bridle in order to prevent the coachman driving suddenly away.

Then the other man, nerving himself by a great effort for the task he had before him, advanced to the door of the brougham.

Agnes saw him coming, and waved her hand, as if to repel him.

But he heeded it not.

The shopman had deposited the things on the front seat of the carriage, and had gone away.

There was nothing singular in a gentleman recognising a lady and speaking to her through the window of her brougham.

When the coachman saw Stubbles at his horse's head he was very indignant, and cried out—

"Now you haporth o' ugly, let go, will you?"

But the dwarf pointed to the carriage-door, as if he would say—

"My master is talking to your mistress."

The man nodded, and remained quiet.

The stranger put his head in at the window, and Agnes leaned back upon the luxurious cushions.

She knew what was about to happen.

Her cheek did not blanch without cause.

Her breath did not come quickly without reason, nor did all the blood in her heart leave it for nothing at all.

In that sunburnt, hirsute man, who had so coolly and deliberately intruded his head into her carriage, she had recognised an old friend, with a sickening feeling of utter horror and a presage of some dreadful occurrence.

She knew that her HUSBAND was before her.

Her husband, lawfully so by the rites of the Church of England, as by the canons enjoined in such cases.

Marmaduke Wilson!

The convict!

But none the less her lord and master.

CHAPTER LXXXIX.

AGNES HAS A TRYING INTERVIEW WITH MARMADUKE WILSON—SHE REPUDIATES HIM—HE LOVES HER STILL—THE DWARF ELICITS A FEW FACTS—THE HUSBAND AND WIFE PART, BUT TO MEET AGAIN.

AGNES had expected this.

She had always entertained a vague feeling of terror whenever she thought of Marmaduke.

She had striven, but ineffectually, to drive his image from her heart; but although it was not shrined there, yet it would intrude occasionally.

During the time he had been away she had taken up new fancies and new ideas, and she could not tolerate for a moment the idea of being a convict's bride, and condemned to a life of misery and poverty.

For what money could the man have, and what honest pursuit did he follow?

So Agnes determined to repudiate him.

He was her husband, but she would brazen him out.

If she could make it so, it should be a case of mistaken identity.

Marmaduke Wilson spoke first.

It was with a great effort that he did so.

"At last I have found you," he said.

She was silent.

"Have you no welcome for me?"

"Who are you?" she plucked up courage enough to say.

"Who am I?" he gasped.

"Yes. This intrusion on my privacy is unwarrantable."

"You do not know me?"

"Certainly not," she replied; "nor do I want to."

"Oh, Heaven!" he cried, "can this be possible? or may I be after all mistaken? But no; those features are too well impressed upon my memory. It is my wife."

"Who do you take me for, sir?" demanded Agnes, becoming a little more courageous, and determining, now she had begun, to play her part as well as she could.

"Can you ask me such questions?"

"Speak, sir."

"For my wife."

"Your wife!" echoed Agnes, laughing a silvery laugh of scorn.

"Yes, yes. Have I not said so?"

"Oh, this is too much!" she exclaimed. "You must be some lunatic who has escaped from his keepers; I pray you remove your head from the window, and allow my coachman to drive home."

"Woman," cried Marmaduke Wilson, "this subterfuge shall not avail you. I am positive that I am not mistaken; you are my wife, and as such I claim—I demand the possession of your person."

"Your pertinacity, sir, is very annoying. I tell you plainly that I never saw you before in my life, and, after that assurance, if you had one spark of gentlemanly feeling in your breast you would go away and cease molesting me."

"Listen to me," he began.

"Oh, yes; I will listen to you," she said. "Perhaps it is best to humour your strange insanity. Perhaps if you talk the matter over you will find out your mistake."

"You will listen to me?"

"I told you so. Proceed."

"I married you," said Marmaduke Wilson, "and for some time we lived happily together, until that she-devil, Miriam Moss, came between us. You remember Miriam Moss?"

Agnes shook her head, as if to indicate that the name was utterly strange to her.

"You do not?"

"No," she replied; "I have no Jewish acquaintances."

"I went abroad——"

"Then you left your wife?"

"No—that is——"

"Pray go on."

Marmaduke reddened to the roots of his hair, but did not speak.

"Certainly your story is very lucid," she said. "Does your memory fail you?"

"Oh, no; but——"

"Well, I am awaiting your explanation."

There was a pause.

"You say you were married," she continued, relentlessly; "that you lived happily until some Jewess—I forget what name you mentioned—separated you. Then you went abroad. But yet you did not leave your wife! Did she leave you? What am I to understand from all this?"

"She did not leave me," he replied, gloomily.

"I really must trouble you to do one thing or the other," said Agnes: "either go on with your rambling story, or allow me to go home. My time is valuable, and I cannot afford to waste the whole of the morning in listening to your conversation, which is no doubt excessively agreeable to your own friends and acquaintances—that is, people in your own walk of life—but you can hardly be so exacting as to expect me to take much interest in your somewhat romantic history."

"Are you a fiend?" he asked, grating his teeth and rolling his eyes wildly about.

"Oh, no, I hope not. I am a woman—at least, I have always been considered one."

His rage made him silent.

"Come, are you going to speak?" she said, with an impatient gesture. "I think I am excessively good-natured; anyone but me would have called in the assistance of the police long ago, but I always think that we ought to have some consideration for people with aberrated intellects. Come, now, tell me—why did you leave your wife?"

This was a home-thrust with a vengeance, but he had no alternative but to reply.

"I will tell you."

"That's right."

"Because——"

He hesitated.

"Well, go on."

"I—I went to Australia, and couldn't take her with me."

"At whose expense did you go?"

"What do you mean?"

"At the Government's?"

"What need for concealment?" he said, frantically. "Yes, woman, I was transported, and you know it."

"I know it now you have told me."

"You knew it before."

He glared fiercely and savagely at her.

"Don't look at me like that; perhaps you are a dangerous man—you may do me some harm."

"Fear not," he replied, with a loud laugh; "I shall not hurt you. But rest assured of one thing."

"What is that?"

"You haven't seen the last of Marmaduke Wilson."

"That is unfortunate," she replied; "for, from his behaviour to me to-day, I never could wish to see him again."

"I shall leave my card upon you some day when you least expect."

"Your what?"

"My card."

"Oh, indeed! Mind it isn't your ticket-of-leave."

"You dare to talk to me like that?" he cried.

"It seems so."

"And yet I love her!" he exclaimed. "During my long and weary captivity, which was never enlivened by one line from her. Even when I knew her to be fickle and false, I loved her; I love her now, and I must teach her once more to love me. She is mine. The law will assist me."

"Yes," cried Agnes, "and the law will protect me. Will you go?"

"Yes, I will go."

"Then you save me an unpleasant task. It is intolerable that ladies should be annoyed and insulted in open daylight in a public thoroughfare by such fellows as you."

"Fellows as me?"

"Yes. By your own admission you are a felon."

"And I am seeking a felon's bride," he returned coldly. "That cuts both ways."

Agnes felt her heart sinking as she heard those words; they were spoken with great deliberation and emphasis, and she knew well enough what they portended.

"You have repudiated me, you have repulsed me, and you have made sport of my misfortunes and my necessities," he continued.

"Your list of grievances is rather long," she replied, with a sarcastic smile.

"And yet I love you," he added, musingly.

"Indeed!"

"Yes, do what I can, I am unable to drive you from my affections."

"That is flattering."

"And remember, Agnes," he said, "that although you have refused to obey me to-day, the time will come when you shall do so."

"That is more than you can tell," she said, in the same bantering style.

"I wish you good-bye now," he concluded. "Think of me; I shall be by your side again shortly."

She smiled incredulously, almost disdainfully, but she would not have thought herself so secure if she had overheard a little conversation between her coachman and Stubbles. It was fraught with peril to her.

"Who do you work for?" asked the dwarf.

"What's that to you, ugly?" replied the Jehu.

"Nothing much, only——"

"What?"

"Why, I like to know who the governor's female acquaintances are."

"Oh! I see."

"Do you?"

"Yes."

"You've been a long time about it."

"Not more than usual."

"Well, are you going to tell me?"

"Yes, if you'll tell me who your governor is."

"My governor?"

"Yes. Who is he?"

"Oh! he's a great swell, but not much known in these parts."

"Oh! indeed."

"He's ex-chaplain to the forces," said Stubbles.

"Is he now?" replied the coachman. "Shouldn't ha' thought it; he don't look like a parson."

"You shouldn't go by looks in this world."

"Well, so they say."

"But look here, you haven't answered my question yet."

"What, who am I a working for?"

"Yes, that's it."

"Well, it's Lord Marchmont's livery."

"Oh!" and the dwarf gave vent to a prolonged whistle.

"I've pumped him," he added to himself; "but he ain't pumped quite dry yet. I'll work the handle up and down a bit more before I've done with him."

"Lady inside his daughter?" asked Stubbles, carelessly.

"Daughter! Lor bless you!"

"What then? Nothing that way?"

Stubbles pointed over his left shoulder.

"Oh, no. She's his wife."

"Eh!"

"His wife, I say. Is there anything wonderful in that?"

The dwarf thought there was, but he did not say so.

At this moment Marmaduke Wilson returned from the carriage-door and rejoined his faithful companion.

Agnes put her head out of the window and said to the coachman, in a voice not quite so melodious as was usual with her—

"Home!"

He applied the whip to his horse, and was soon rattling over the stones towards her ladyship's fashionable residence.

The dwarf and the convict were together.

"Well," said Stubbles, "you have seen her."

"I have," replied Marmaduke, moodily.

They walked on in silence.

CHAPTER XC.

MARMADUKE WILSON AND THE DWARF HOLD A COUNCIL OF WAR—THE DWARF GIVES GOOD ADVICE—THEY RESOLVE TO CALL ON LORD MARCHMONT—STUBBLES HAS A LITTLE BUSINESS ON HAND.

AFTER proceeding some distance, Marmaduke Wilson and Stubbles, by mutual consent, adjourned to the tap-room of a publichouse, where they could discourse over the strange event which had just happened.

Marmaduke had not been many days in England. His term of transportation was considerably abridged by his good conduct, and in addition to that he had had the good fortune to save the life of the governor of the island, who was so grateful for the service he had rendered him that he instantly granted him, upon his own authority, a ticket-of-leave. He had returned to his native country with two objects, one was to claim his wife wherever she might be, the other to renew his acquaintance with Stubbles, for whom he entertained a sincere regard.

During the first few months of his enforced captivity he cherished feelings of revenge—almost of hatred—towards Agnes; but after that his heart had softened and absence made it grow fonder. He came in time to forgive her, to make all sorts of excuses for her, and to cherish the most sincere regard for her.

"She might have come to see me in prison," he said; "she might have made inquiries; and she might have written to me to cheer me in my exile."

But he spent his time in finding palliating circumstances to extenuate her conduct; and the consequence was, that he came back more in love with her than ever.

Her repudiation of him, during their accidental meeting in Regent-street, was a great blow to him—a very great blow, and one he would not easily get over.

But he made up his mind to bring her away from wherever she might be living, and then he would, if it were possible—and what is not possible to a strong man's love?—he would, by all sorts of kindness, endear himself to her, and break through that icy barrier which she had, in their late interview, set up between herself and him.

This was a praiseworthy resolution; but would he be able to effect so much?—that remained to be seen.

Marmaduke had returned to England determined, if he could, to lead an honest life. He felt he could not, with any conscience, ask Agnes to return to the arms of a man who habitually spent his life in defying the laws of his country and the regulations of society. He would endeavour, as far as in him lay—and he was a man of great energy and resolution—to turn over a new leaf, and lead an honest existence. He had brought home a little money with him, for the unhappy prisoners in our convict stations are allowed to earn a few small sums by their own industry at stated times. He had gone to a haunt in Westminster where he knew he should hear news of Stubbles, and that accounted for their being now together.

"You have seen your wife?" said Stubbles, by way of beginning a conversation.

"I have, and that is all I can say!" he returned, bitterly.

"How so?"

"She repudiates me."

"You!" cried Stubbles.

"Yes; I know it too well."

"It is strange."

"It seems so to me."

The dwarf mused a moment, and then exclaimed—

"I think I can explain this apparent mystery."

"Do you, indeed!" said Marmaduke Wilson, looking up attentively.

"I think so. Listen to me.

"I will."

Marmaduke disposed himself to listen to the dwarf, who began—

"While you were conversing with the lady inside the carriage, I was not idle."

Marmaduke's attention increased.

"I talked to the coachman and put some questions to him, cunningly framed, so as to throw him off his guard——"

"Yes, yes."

"He replied incautiously, and I learnt something that will be of use to us."

"What is that?"

"I will tell you. It struck me as being singular that your wife, whom I had been seeking for before I saw you, as I have already told you, should be riding in a carriage. The count who is dead, now, carried her off; but it is clear she would have derived no assistance from him."

"Certainly not."

"Who then could be her protector? I asked the coachman. He told me Lord Marchmont; but he added that she was his lordship's wife."

"His wife!" exclaimed Marmaduke Wilson, horror-stricken.

"Calm yourself, my friend."

"Oh, yes; I will! I am calm; go on."

"He said so; and if she really is married to this lord, she has committed bigamy. Perhaps she thought you dead—who knows?"

Marmaduke, crushed by the weight of this new sorrow, was silent.

Stubbles continued—

"What will you do, supposing this information to be true? Supposing that she has been living with another man as his wife—not as his mistress, mind you—I say, what will you do?"

Marmaduke cogitated.

"Would you take her back, or leave her with her new love?"

"You ask me if I would forgive her?"

"Yes."

"Then I answer that I would! She has much to forgive in me, and I cannot blame her for anything that she may have been driven to during my absence from her. Oh yes, I would forgive her with all my heart things worse a thousand times than that!"

"That is right. That's what I expected you would say," replied Stubbles. "Women are weak without a man's guiding arm. But now what course of action will you pursue?"

"I am not yet resolved."

"You say she denied everything to-day?"

"Yes, in the most decided and emphatic manner," replied Marmaduke Wilson.

"That I can understand," said the dwarf.

"In what way."

"In this. She is comfortable, if not happy in her present home. She has wealth and a title, she has carriages and horses and houses, and servants to wait upon her, with every appanage of a nobleman's establishment."

"Yes," said Marmaduke.

"Very well, then! Is .it likely that she would be prepared, at a moment's notice, to come back to—excuse me—a broken man, without a penny, without a character, who could only offer her poverty and a garret. It is too much to expect from any woman."

"Stubbles," replied Marmaduke, "I feel that you are right. I have no right to expect her to do all this."

"I do not say that I think you have a right, but the thing must be done gradually, rather by diplomacy than by open warfare."

"What do you propose, then?"

"I propose this. Let us call on Lord Marchmont and see what he has to say to the justice of your claim."

"Well."

"And let our future course be guided by what takes place at that interview."

"Yes."

"I fully agree with you," replied Marmaduke Wilson; "we will do as you say. Possess her again I must; I feel that I cannot live longer without her. Let us go at once."

"Stop!" cried the dwarf; "I have a little business on hand in which I shall require your services; afterwards you shall have mine."

CHAPTER XCI.

THE DWARF CONDUCTS MARMADUKE WILSON TO THE DUNGEON IN WHICH JABEZ CLARKE IS CONFINED—THE DWARF'S TERRIBLE REVENGE—HE PUTS OUT JABEZ'S EYES WITH NITRIC ACID, AND SENDS HIM FORTH INTO THE WORLD BLIND.

MARMADUKE WILSON was at a loss to conjecture what the nature of the business the dwarf had in hand could be; his thoughts were so much occupied with Agnes, and his late adventures in Regent-street, that he did not dwell very long upon the matter.

Stubbles had asked his assistance, and he had declared himself to be at his service. Passing along Oxford-street, they hastily threaded some small and devious thoroughfares, which eventually brought them to the neighbourhood of Fitzroy-market. Turning up a court, the dwarf led the way into a house, afterwards descending some steps, closely followed by Marmaduke Wilson, and stopping suddenly before an iron-bound door.

Marmaduke was at a loss to understand the meaning of his friend's eccentric movements, but he had seen so many things in his life, and gone through so much, that he rarely wondered at anything. Taking a key from his pocket, the dwarf opened the door, and invited Marmaduke to enter. The dwarf ignited a match by striking it against the wall, and immediately afterwards lighted a couple of candles, which he disposed in different places so as to illumine the dismal apartment.

It was the gloomy vault in which Jabez Clarke had confined Agnes, and where he had treated her with such horrible and revolting cruelty. He had, in his turn, been a prisoner there for many weary weeks, and he now knew the bitterness of captivity.

The dwarf had not suffered him to starve to death; he had punctually supplied him with food of the commonest and coarsest description. It was not his intention to *kill* the man; he reserved him for a more terrible fate.

When Marmaduke Wilson was inside the dungeon, the dwarf carefully closed the door, and locked it on the inside. In a short time the eyes of the visitors became accustomed to the light, and they could plainly distinguish the once burly form of Jabez Clarke. How altered now! His eyes were sunk deeply in his head, his cheeks were thin and emaciated, hollow and sunken, his hair was long, dark and matted, his beard was stubby and unkempt, his flesh had fallen away, and he was no longer the stout and powerful man he had been a month ago. The dwarf looked complacently upon what was his work, and smiled in a satisfied manner.

The wretched man was securely confined, he could not spring upon those who had come to gloat over his misery; he was as helpless as a baby. Jabez Clarke was fastened to the wall by the iron girdle and chain which had once cinctured the slender waist of Agnes. He looked up meekly as he saw the dwarf, but said nothing.

The iron-bedstead which had served as an instrument of torture, when the water descended upon Jabez Clarke's prisoner, was still there; upon this the dwarf sat down, motioning Marmaduke to follow his example, which he was not slow in doing.

"You do not know that man?" began the dwarf; "but I can tell you much about him that will interest you."

"Indeed!" said Marmaduke.

"I extracted his history from him one day in this vault, and I will repeat it to you."

"Do so, my friend."

"He married your wife's mother."

Marmaduke started, but made no remark.

"She was betrayed by a Squire Leslie."

"Leslie!" cried Marmaduke, "my own name. That is very strange."

"This man," continued the dwarf, unheeding the interruption, "was Squire Leslie's groom. When the squire got tired of his mistress he deserted her, and, for a consideration, this fellow married her. His cruelty drove Agnes from his home."

"It must have been then that I met her."

"Probably; Jabez Clarke—that is his name—killed his poor unoffending wife by continued brutality and repeated blows of his fist."

Marmaduke's fingers trembled convulsively.

"He then fixed the murder of his wife upon Agnes, and she was sought after by the police; had they found her, they would have hanged her like a dog."

During this recapitulation of his enormities, Jabez preserved a stolid demeanour.

Marmaduke Wilson breathed heavily, as if under the influence of great excitement.

"But, as we know," said the dwarf, resuming his narrative, "she had the good fortune to defeat the machinations of her enemies, and to escape."

"What perils she has had to encounter!" exclaimed Marmaduke.

"More than you are aware of," replied Stubbles. "But the worst part of my story as regards this man is yet to come."

Jabez looked at him almost piteously, as if beseeching him to have some mercy; but there was a look in the dwarf's eyes which bade him dismiss the idea from his mind ere it had hardly been born.

"Chance threw your wife in his way; he confined her in this dungeon, and tortured her in the most brutal manner, with a view of extorting money."

Marmaduke looked up incredulously.

The dwarf, in a few words, told him in what the ill-treatment consisted, and ended by saying—

"If you cannot credit me, ask the man himself. He confessed it to me, and he will not dare to deny it if you question him."

"Is what I have just heard true?" demanded Marmaduke, addressing Jabez Clarke.

The man hung his head, and made no answer.

"Speak!" cried the dwarf, furiously; "or shall I find a means of making you?"

"Do not threaten him," interposed Marmaduke; "let him speak of his own free will."

Jabez looked up, and in a quavering voice replied—

"It be all true enough."

"Such a wretch ought not to live," said Marmaduke.

"Death is too good for him; but as he is the murderer of his wife, by the law of the land his life is forfeit."

"Yes," replied Marmaduke; "a life for a life—blood for blood."

While this conversation was progressing, Jabez Clarke, with unwonted excitement, gazed from one to the other of the speakers, and hung upon their words, as if his existence depended upon them.

And so it did.

"He shall not die!" exclaimed the dwarf, after a pause.

When Jabez heard this, he began to sob and cry like a little child; the revulsion of feeling was so very sudden. He had thought his death deliberately planned and previously determined on.

"But he shall not escape my vengeance," continued Stubbles. "The villain gave me a throw which I remembered, and felt the effects of, for many a long day; but I will do something to him the effects of which he will feel as long as his miserable life lasts. How long that may be, I will not pretend to say; but what I am about to do will not, I am of opinion, have the effect of prolonging it."

There was a demoniacal expression about the dwarf's face which augured no good to Jabez Clarke.

The unhappy man caught sight of it, and shuddered—it chilled his very blood, which seemed to freeze in his veins.

Marmaduke Wilson was also surprised at his friend's vehemence. He had never seen him like that before.

The two candles flickered and flared, and no sound was heard save the deep breathing of the three men.

Taking up a piece of rope, Stubbles advanced to Jabez Clarke, and tied his hands firmly behind his back. He accomplished this without any trouble. The man was passive as a lamb on its way to the slaughter. He treated his legs in a similar way. Then he undid the padlock which fastened the chain, and the iron fell with a clanking noise upon the damp bricks.

The dwarf then caused Jabez to lie down on his back upon the bed. When he had done so, many a coil of thick rope bound him down so that he could not move.

He fixed his head in the same way in which Jabez had fixed Agnes's when he allowed the water to drip down upon her marble forehead.

Then his preparations were nearly complete. Taking a thick handkerchief, he stuffed it into his victim's mouth to deaden his cries.

A cold sweat broke out all over Jabez Clarke's body. The pain and terror of death fell upon him, and he gave himself up for lost.

Even Marmaduke Wilson's flesh crept, in anticipation of some unspeakable tragedy.

The dwarf next felt in his waistcoat pocket, and produced a small phial. It was filled with a liquid of a dull colour.

Jabez strained his eyes to watch every movement of the dwarf.

"What are you about to do?" exclaimed Marmaduke.

"You will see presently," replied Stubbles, imperturbably. He drew the cork from the bottle, and held the latter up to the light.

There was a label upon the glass. A piece of common white paper, such as surgeons use for writing prescriptions. Upon it were scribbled two words.

Jabez Clarke with some difficulty read them. They were—

"Nitric Acid."

"The Lord help me!" murmured Jabez, inwardly. "I am in the power of man, and I can expect no help unless it come to me from on high."

Marmaduke Wilson stood up with his back leaning against the wall, a silent spectator of what was about to ensue. He felt sure that the dwarf had invented some especially awful mode of vengeance which he had neither the inclination nor the power to thwart.

"He has said he will not kill him," argued Marmaduke, "and whatever he does is no business of mine. That shrinking, cowering wretch has provoked his fate. He

must suffer and endure the penalty his misdeeds have brought upon him, for I neither can nor will render him the slightest assistance."

The memory of Agnes, and all she had endured at that man's hands, steeled Marmaduke Wilson's heart against him.

The dwarf seated himself upon Jabez Clarke's chest, and peered inquiringly into his face.

The ferrety eyes shrank from meeting his glance.

The dwarf, satisfied, apparently, with his scrutiny, commenced his operations.

He placed one finger of his left hand upon that eye of Jabez Clarke's which was nearest to him. Then with his finger and thumb he seized the lid and held it up.

Jabez was unable to move any part of his body the eighth of an inch, so securely had he been bound to the bed.

Raising the bottle of nitric acid, the dwarf poised it for an instant over Jabez's eye, and dexterously allowed a drop of the burning fluid to fall upon the pupil.

An agonized expression stole over and convulsed the features of the unhappy man, as the acid touched the tenderest part of the human frame.

The dwarf gazed on his exploit with a fiendish satisfaction. He watched the skin of the eye contract and frizzle up before the action of the powerful drug which was consuming it.

Jabez's countenance became horribly distorted. The intensity of his suffering made him endeavour to shriek and scream, but the gag in his mouth prevented him from uttering anything but a short squeal such as a whipped dog gives out.

Marmaduke Wilson closed his eyes, and turned his head. He had beheld many dreadful things in his lifetime, but nothing to equal the scene that he was now witnessing.

At last the eye became all eaten away and honeycombed. A frothy sort of film grew over it, and the sight was gone for ever.

Stubbles next turned his attention to the other eye, which he treated in the same way. Lifting the lid, he let fall a drop of the pungent acid, and the same horrible drama was enacted over again.

But this time Jabez Clarke was insensible to pain—he had fainted. It was a mercy that he had done so.

When the dwarf had effected his purpose, he threw the bottle of nitric acid against the wall. The glass cracked and broke, and its contents ran hissing and steaming down the damp wall. He had no further use for it now.

"Is it over?" asked Marmaduke Wilson, in a sad and trembling voice, as he heard the crash.

"Yes," replied the dwarf, with a careless laugh. "I have had my revenge, and in a way he is not likely soon to forget."

When Jabez Clarke came to himself, the pain that still lingered nearly forced him back again into insensibility, but with an effort he mastered it. At first he seemed to have some difficulty in collecting his thoughts. Taking a knife from his pocket, the dwarf cut his bonds, and removed the gag from his mouth.

Jabez sprang to his feet as he felt himself free, took two steps forward, put out his hands in a groping way, and exclaimed—

"What, no light! Have they gone away again and left me in the dark?"

Seizing a candle, the dwarf advanced with it to Jabez, and held it under his hand for an instant. The flame scorched his flesh.

"Fire!" he cried, "and I cannot see it. Oh, how my eyes burn! It is as if molten lead were eating up my eyeballs."

"Jabez Clarke!" exclaimed the dwarf.

He started at the sound of his voice.

"Who calls me?" he said.

"I, the dwarf—I who have been your executioner. From this day forth until the breath leaves your body, you are blind; do you hear me?—blind."

"Blind! blind!" repeated Jabez. "Oh! no, no, no. Say not so. Blind! anything but that."

He shook his head, as if he did not believe the fell and evil tidings.

"I would not kill you," continued the dwarf, "because that would have put you out of your misery at once; but I have blinded you."

The once strong man moaned feebly, like some poor

THE FATE OF JABEZ CLARKE.

stricken wretch whom the disease has brought to the verge of the grave.

The feelings, the thoughts, the anticipations, which animated Jabez Clarke were horrible beyond conception. Could it be possible that he was really blind, that for him the sun no longer beamed, no longer shone?—That to him in future nature was a sealed book—No sun, no flowers, no shrubs, no smiling landscapes should ever gladden his eyes again. —That his sense of sight was utterly and irrevocably eradicated—That he would have to grope his way in an ever-lasting, never-ending darkness, black as night—That to the end of his days it would be *all* night—That he would not gaze upon the lovely face of woman, nor see her rosy lips as they formed themselves into smiles, nor gaze upon her rippling, glossy hair? He would not believe it. He could not for a time, and yet it was so.

"Come," cried Stubbles, unlocking the door of the vault; "you must wander forth into the world, and know what it is to live upon the charity of your fellow-men. Summer will give place to winter, and winter to spring; and yet it shall be all one to you, except when you swelter in the heat or shiver in the cold. Come, come, you must begin your penance."

Jabez Clarke trembled all over like an aspen; but he allowed the dwarf to grasp his arm, and lead him forth to the light of day.

The sun was shining brightly, and penetrated with its glowing beams the dirty, smoke-begrimed precincts of the court. But it shone not for Jabez Clarke; all to him was as a funeral pall.

The dwarf conducted him to the street; and, hissing in his ear the words, "Blind, blind, for ever blind!" left him holding on by the railings, trembling like a leaf with rage and apprehension.

After going some distance he turned round, and looked back. The unfortunate man was still there. His future was, indeed, a blank; but the dwarf gloated over what he had done.

Some good Samaritan subsequently took Jabez to the Ophthalmic Hospital. The surgeons there allayed the inflammation produced by the nitric acid, but that was all they could do for him. His sight was gone for ever.

He may now be seen in a leading thoroughfare in the great metropolis, guided by a dog, with a basket round his neck, and helping his weary steps along with the assistance of a thick stick. It is thus by soliciting the alms of the charitable that he gains a miserable and meagre subsistence; and sometimes he finds a piece of gold in his dog's basket, and although he knows it not, it is placed there by the commiserating hand of Marmaduke Wilson.

CHAPTER XCII.

THE OLD BAILEY—TEN SHILLINGS A HEAD—AN EXECUTION—CALCRAFT—FLY-BY-NIGHT IS HANGED—MARMADUKE HAS AN INTERVIEW WITH LORD MARCHMONT—AGNES FAINTS AT THE SIGHT OF HER HUSBAND—IN THREE DAYS.

MARMADUKE and the dwarf walked on for some time in a purposeless way. They were both occupied with their own thoughts. The day was wearing now. It was too late to pay Lord Marchmont a visit, so they postponed that until the coming day. By mutual consent they returned to their lodgings, which were in a part of the town near old Smithfield.

The dwarf, whose culinary art was anything but limited, cooked a steak with onions in an excellent manner. They dined; and afterwards, over a bottle of gin, discussed their future plans.

They retired early to bed, as they wished to be up betimes in the morning. Marmaduke's dreams were all of Agnes; and it was with a firmer determination than ever to possess her again that he awoke. The morning sun was streaming in through the half-closed shutters, and seemed to reproach him for his inertness.

Breakfast over, the dwarf and himself were soon on foot. It was about half-past seven. The dwarf was acquainted with Lord Marchmont's residence, as he had been there when he delivered Agnes's message about Count Val de Grace.

They intended to walk down the Old Bailey and along Fleet-street and the Strand, but when they got to Snow-hill they found all the approaches to the Old Bailey thronged with an excited mass of people. The blackened walls of Newgate looked down and frowned upon them. Policemen were conspicuous here and there. A large wooden structure, just above the governor's door, with something more ominous still on the top of it, spoke plainly enough of an execution.

Having penetrated so far, the two men resolved to await the sequel; and, with a morbid feeling, allowed themselves to see a fellow-creature launched into eternity.

It was close upon the hour, and they had not long to wait before the melancholy cortége made its appearance.

The dwarf could see nothing; but Marmaduke, being a tall man, was better able to reconnoitre the proceedings.

They were close to a coffee-shop, and a voice behind them said—

"Come up-stairs, gentlemen; come up-stairs; fine places, and a splendid view. Ten shillings a head! only ten shillings a head!"

Marmaduke had the money in his pocket; and although he could ill spare it, with a recklessness peculiar to his nature, he paid the man what he demanded, and both Stubbles and himself ascended some rickety stairs, and found themselves at length in a small room looking out of an open window along with several others.

The condemned man, accompanied by Calcraft, now made his appearance on the scaffold. He eyed the gibbet narrowly, but apparently without fear. Stepping forward and looking over the railings of the scaffold, he made a low bow, to what may not be inaptly called the audience. They returned his salutation with cheers and ironical laughter. Many of them had been there all night, having come early to get a good place, and were partly if not wholly intoxicated. Suddenly, the dwarf caught Marmaduke Wilson convulsively by the arm.

"What is it?" asked Marmaduke.

"Look!" cried the dwarf.

"Well, I see nothing."

"Nothing?"

"No."

"Look again. It is——"

"Who?" abruptly asked Marmaduke, catching some of his friend's excitement.

"Fly-by-Night!" replied the dwarf, in a terrified whisper.

Yes; it was Fly-by-Night. Inspector Wyman had at last hunted down his prey. The man had been tried and convicted, and was now about to pay the extreme penalty of his crimes.

Fly-by-Night did not appear to recognise his two former companions amongst such a vast crowd of people. How could he?

Calcraft adjusted the rope round the culprit's neck, pulled the cap over his eyes, shook hands with him, and placed him upon the drop.

The drop fell.

There was a sharp cracking sound, audible to those in the immediate vicinity.

It was the man's neck breaking.

The legs twitched up and down convulsively.

A tremor pervaded the whole body, and Fly-by-Night was a corpse.

Cut off in the prime of his manhood.

Bulwer says, "The worst use you can put a man to is to hang him." But the State does not think so.

And Fly-by-Night added another page to the already swollen volumes of the Newgate Calendar.

"Come away!" said Marmaduke, almost stifled. "The air this day or two has teemed with horrors. Let us get out of this!"

"Poor Fly-by-Night!" murmured the dwarf; "he was not a bad pal. A little hasty, perhaps—but not a bad pal."

They hurried down the stairs and forced their way through the mob—the members of which were trying with all their might and main to get into the publichouses in the neighbourhood, which were on this morning driving a roaring trade.

A long and brisk walk brought the dwarf and his companion to the door of Lord Marchmont's house.

The dwarf it was arranged should wait outside until Marmaduke's interview was over.

The servant, in answer to Marmaduke's application, said that his lordship had just finished breakfast. He would take his name in, and perhaps he would see him.

The servant shortly returned and conducted Marmaduke into a small study, where he desired him to wait.

Five minutes elapsed, and then Lord Marchmont condescended to remember that some one was waiting to see him.

"To what am I indebted for the honour of this visit, Mr. Wilson?" said the earl, as he entered the room. "Pray don't move, be seated."

The nobleman and the convict sat facing one another.

"My business is of a delicate nature," began Marmaduke.

"Oh! perhaps you are collecting for some charity. If a guinea is of any use, I shall be very happy."

Marmaduke smiled, and said, "No."

"You are, perhaps, a gentleman of literary pursuits, temporarily out of employ?"

"No, my lord."

"Or a purblind artist?"

"No."

"Ah! let me see; are you a beefeater on half-pay?"

"No, my lord, I——"

"Pardon me," said Lord Marchmont; "I see now. You are a curate in Wales on thirty pounds a-year. You want some old clothes, eh? My servant shall have orders instantly to——"

"I am none of these," replied Marmaduke, interrupting his lordship.

"What are you, then?"

"That you will know presently. I wish to have some conversation with you about a matter of great and vital importance to both of us."

"In-deed," said Lord Marchmont, with a vacant stare.

"I hardly know how to begin. You will, I have no doubt, consider me an impostor."

"Not without cause, sir. I never prejudge any man."

"Some years ago," began Marmaduke Wilson, "I married."

"Remarkably interesting, I'm sure. Fact that ought to be recorded," replied his lordship, insolently.

"And *is* recorded, my lord," replied Marmaduke, a little sharply; "as you will find to your confusion."

"'Pon my soul, I don't understand the fellow, can't make head or tail of him!" said Lord Marchmont, looking very perplexed.

"I was obliged, through circumstances over which I had no control, to leave England for a time, and as I could not take my wife with me she remained here."

"What! here, in this house?" demanded Lord Marchmont.

"No, my lord, I don't mean that," replied Marmaduke Wilson. "But she is here *now*."

"What!"

"I repeat, my lord, she is here now."

"Do you mean it?" gasped his lordship.

"I have reason to believe so. I do not speak without good grounds for what I say, my lord."

"Come, you must either be mad, or you want to extort money from me," said the peer, recovering his equanimity by a violent effort.

"I am neither the one nor the other," replied Marmaduke, calmly. "I am not mad, nor do I want money."

"In Heaven's name, then, what do you want?"

"Simple justice."

"In what way?"

"Shall I explain?"

"By all means. You mean to assert that—but, perhaps, it is one of my chambermaids that you are after? How foolish of me not to have surmised that at first!"

"Wrong again, my lord."

"Do you mean, then, seriously to say——"

"I will tell you what I mean," said Marmaduke.

Lord Marchmont had risen from his chair in his excitement, but he now sat down again.

Marmaduke Wilson looked steadily at the man he was about to humiliate, humble, and crush, and said—

"My lord, you consider yourself married, when in reality you are not."

"How so?" he cried, convulsed with rage.

"It is as I say."

"Who are you, who dare talk to me in this way?"

"I am Marmaduke Wilson," was the calm and collected reply.

"Well, I have yet to learn what Marmaduke Wilson is to me," said the peer, proudly.

Marmaduke rose from his chair, and drew himself up to his full height, then he said—

"I am the husband of her whom you call your wife."

Lord Marchmont, on hearing this, lost all control over himself. Dashing at his visitor, he endeavoured to seize him by the throat and strangle him; but Marmaduke was too quick for him. Catching him in his arms, he held him in his powerful embrace until the paroxysm was over, afterwards leading him back to his seat.

"Be calm, my lord," he said, in soothing accents.

"Your proofs," sullenly demanded his lordship.

"I can propose a test which may satisfy you."

"And that is——"

"Call my wife."

"Your wife! ten thousand devils, sir!" screamed Lord Marchmont, foaming at the mouth.

"Well, call her Lady Marchmont, if you will. Summon her ladyship to your presence, and see whether or no she will be unmoved when she sees me."

"It shall be done."

A bell was hastily rung, a servant appeared, a message was given him; and the two men waited impatiently for the arrival of the woman whom both claimed as the legal partner of their bed.

The minutes flew by.

At last she came.

The door opened.

Marmaduke Wilson was still standing erect and dignified in the middle of the room; his eyes were fixed upon the door.

She entered. She cast her eyes around her. Her gaze alighted upon Marmaduke, upon her *husband*. She glared at him for an instant, then with a half-uttered cry upon her lips, she fell forward, and lay upon the ground insensible.

He had kept his promise, and Agnes now knew that she had to fear the worst. He had told her in Regent-street that it would not be long before they met again; but she had disbelieved him—she had thought that he would be unable to find her out. He had tracked her, however, unerringly, and now she saw that all her deception, all her trickery, and all her heartlessness, was of no avail.

Lord Marchmont sprang forward when he saw Agnes fall, and bore her from the room in his arms. When he returned, he exclaimed to Marmaduke—

"There is more in this, sir, than I at first thought. What do you propose should be done?—of course, you have proofs, witnesses, &c."

"Yes," replied Marmaduke.

"You can, then, produce them?"

"Certainly."

"I will summon the—the lady's relations. Will you meet them here in three days?"

"Yes."

"The subject can then be fully gone into."

"I have no objection."

"Her relations!" thought Marmaduke.

It was a new mystery for him, for he knew nothing about the Leslies, or their recognition of Agnes.

"And now good-morning," said Lord Marchmont. "This occurrence has so taken me by surprise, that I am quite ill, quite unnerved, quite unhinged. I must be by myself; I am nearly distracted. If I have treated you with unnecessary rudeness——"

"Oh, no," replied Marmaduke, generously.

"If I have, forget it, and now go. In three days."

"Yes, in three days."

In two minutes, Marmaduke was again with Stubbles.

"Well?" said the dwarf, interrogatively.

Marmaduke looked at him.

"What news?"

"Excellent."

"Have you seen her?"

"Yes."

"And the result?"

"My dear friend, at present all goes merry as a marriage-bell."

Turning the corner of the street, the dwarf and his companion were lost to view.

CHAPTER XCIII.

THE MEETING AT LORD MARCHMONT'S HOUSE—AGNES CONFESSES THAT SHE IS MARMADUKE WILSON'S WIFE —MISS LAVINIA MAKES AN IMPORTANT DISCOVERY— LORD MARCHMONT RUSHES FROM THE ROOM—THE LESLIES DEPART, AND THE MAN AND WIFE ARE ALONE.

THE three days passed rapidly away, but how differently to all the persons with whom this history has to deal.

Lord Marchmont was distracted between doubts and fears; at one moment he believed Agnes to be his lawfully wedded wife, at another he was ready to spurn her from him as a traitress and a deceiver.

He absented himself from his home until the mystery was cleared up; until that time when the matter should be decided one way or the other, either for or against him, he would hold no sort of intercourse with Agnes.

Leaving a note to this effect for her whom it most concerned, Lord Marchmont went to Richmond and stayed at an hotel there.

Miss Lavinia Leslie was summoned to meet at his lordship's house, and his letter found her at her old residence in Hill-street, Berkeley-square.

The summons, coming as it did so unexpectedly from Lord Marchmont, alarmed her terribly, for Lord Marchmont and Agnes had kept the Leslies at a distance since they had discovered old Mr. Leslie upon Puffin Island, that lonely rock upon the Welch coast.

But the sum Agnes had promised to pay to her aunt and her brother on her marriage had been faithfully and scrupulously paid, and Miss Lavinia was afraid that something was going to happen which would have the effect of putting a stop to Agnes's munificence and liberality.

The same thought occurred to Bernard Leslie, who happened to be in town when the letter arrived at his chambers in the Albany. He immediately got into a cab and drove to Hill-street. In five minutes he was there.

He found his aunt with Lord Marchmont's letter in her hand, looking very much alarmed.

Her face was pale and her cap a little on one side, a sure sign that she was unusually disconcerted.

A thoughtful expression pervaded her features.

She was most likely, as was her favourite custom, "considering the position."

Bernard Leslie flung himself into a chair, threw his hat into a corner of the room, and without giving his aunt the usual greeting when people meet, tossed over Lord Marchmont's letter in a cavalier way.

It fell short of its mark, but he never troubled himself to pick it up.

The old lady stooped down and possessed herself of it, read it slowly, and then gave her nephew the one she herself had but a short time before received.

"So they want us at a family council, eh?" exclaimed Bernard. "Hang me if I know what it all means, do you?"

"I know no more than yourself," replied Miss Lavinia.

"They can't mean to stop the supplies, eh?"

"I don't think they can do that," said his aunt, shrewdly. "It was all arranged by deed."

"Oh, yes, they could if they chose," was the gracious reply; "don't talk nonsense. If they chose to go to law they could upset those deeds to-morrow."

"Why?" she demanded.

"Because there was what the lawyers call no consideration."

"Well; you know more than I do about it, Bernard; but I know one thing, I don't like it at all. It has put me out very much, I'm sure I feel quite ill."

"You'll go, I suppose?" said Bernard Leslie.

"Go! Oh, yes; it will be but prudent. What's your opinion?"

"I think so too. There is nothing like sticking up for our rights."

"Nothing, my boy, nothing," replied Miss Lavinia, with a chuckle which only sufficed to show her toothless gums.

"What time shall you go then?"

"It is impossible for me to get there before three at the outside. I don't get up till one as you know, and I must breakfast before I start."

"I never liked that Marchmont fellow," exclaimed Bernard Leslie, savagely. "You know how he cut us when he found out the old man down in Wales?"

"I remember. It was a lucky thing too that he died, or we might have found ourselves in a mess."

"Yes; it was a bit of luck. We have been fortunate so far, and we must take care of ourselves in the present instance."

"Leave us alone for that," replied Miss Lavinia.

They both laughed at this sally.

"Good-bye, aunt," said Bernard Leslie; "I shall meet you there at three."

"At three, very well; good morning, Bernard."

When he was gone the old lady leaned back in her chair and began once more to consider the position.

On the eventful day, Marmaduke Wilson was the first to arrive at Lord Marchmont's house. The dwarf accompanied him as far as the door, and then left him to go and wait at a neighbouring pothouse.

He was shown into a small room, where he amused himself with a newspaper for a short time.

He heard several knocks at the door, and at last he was requested to step into the drawing-room.

On entering it he saw two people.

They were the Leslies.

Almost immediately Lord Marchmont entered the room, leading Agnes by the hand.

She kept her eyes firmly fixed upon the thickly piled carpet.

She had been anxiously communing with herself during the past three days, and the result of her self-communion was a slight revulsion of feeling towards Marmaduke Wilson.

Yet she dared not look him in the face.

The expression that the faces of the Leslies wore was a mixture of defiance and of perplexity, with just a dash of apprehension in it.

Lord Marchmont's face was gravely expectant.

Marmaduke Wilson was the only person in the room who was at all self-possessed or confident.

Lord Marchmont was the first to speak; he said—

"You will excuse me for entering without ceremony upon the business we have in hand. I will not preface what I am about to say with a long speech, I need only confine myself purely and simply to facts. You are aware," he added, addressing Bernard Leslie, "that when I married your sister——"

"His sister," exclaimed Marmaduke Wilson, under his breath; "can I be mistaken after all?"

"I did so under the impression that she had never in her life before contracted a matrimonial engagement. I can only say that as far as I am concerned I never had the remotest intention of assisting her, or any other woman, to commit bigamy."

"Who alleges she has done so?" cried Bernard Leslie, fiercely.

"I do," replied Marmaduke Wilson, calmly.

"You!" exclaimed the infuriated young man. "Who are you, sir, that dare to thus disturb a family, and hurl a foul slander at the fair fame of an innocent lady?"

"I think that's not so bad," he said to himself, when he had finished.

"I am her first husband," answered Marmaduke, with the same gentlemanly quietness.

"This is too bad," said Bernard Leslie, really becoming furiously indignant.

He believed it to be false, although he had his secret misgivings.

Miss Lavinia had not taken the least share in this conversation. From the first moment that Marmaduke Wilson entered the room she remained mute as a stone. Her eyes were fixed on Marmaduke, and she seemed unable to take them off again.

Lord Marchmont turned to Marmaduke, and said—

"You will, of course, give us some proof of the truth of this allegation?"

"Yes, yes, the proof," cried Bernard Leslie.

"Certainly," responded Marmaduke, drawing a paper from his pocket. "Here is the certificate of my marriage; it is signed and attested by the proper officers, as you will perceive."

Lord Marchmont seized the document, hastily unrolled it, and began to read it. Bernard Leslie looked over his shoulder.

"Ha!" he suddenly exclaimed, "what's this? The spinster's name here is Clarke—Agnes Clarke."

He looked around him triumphantly, after the manner of an Old Bailey barrister who has discovered a flaw in the indictment.

"I never knew her by any other name," said Marmaduke. "When I married her her name was Clarke; I know not how many times she may have changed it since."

All eyes at this speech were turned towards Agnes. Her eyes were still fixed upon the ground. She looked the picture of irresolution and despair. She hardly knew what to do. She was afraid that she was hunted down, but she was not sure of it.

Marmaduke Wilson walked up to her and took her hand in his. It was cold as ice or marble.

Lord Marchmont noticed the action, and walking up to them, gently removed Agnes's arm, saying—

"Pardon me, but I cannot permit that familiarity until you have substantiated your claim. At present this lady is Countess of Marchmont. Whether or not the title belongs to her we are met here this day to decide."

Marmaduke Wilson fell back a step at this rebuke.

Raising his voice, he said—

"Agnes, do you not know me?"

She looked up for the first time since she had entered the room. Her eyes were red and swollen, and her cheeks were wet with weeping. She encountered his burning glance levelled full upon her. It acted like an electric shock. She uttered the word "Yes."

The next moment she regretted it.

"You see, my lord, she knows me," cried Marmaduke, triumphantly.

"You say you know this man?" exclaimed Lord Marchmont, sternly.

"Oh! yes, yes."

"How? In a casual manner?"

"Oh! do not ask me any more questions," she said, in a piteous tone.

"I must. It is a painful duty, but it is imperative that you should answer my question; the happiness or unhappiness of all of us depends upon your replies. Now, in the first place, did you ever go by the name of Clarke?"

"Yes," she answered.

"When?"

"Before I found out Bernard Leslie, and he acknowledged me as his sister."

"So, sir," cried Lord Marchmont, angrily, addressing Bernard, "so, sir, it appears you had a hand in this business."

"Go on with your queries," he replied; "I will explain what share I had in it, when you have finished."

"So be it," replied his lordship.

Then again to Agnes—

"Now I ask you, solemnly and seriously, whether you married Marmaduke Wilson under the name of Clarke?"

"I did," was the faint response—so faint as to be almost inaudible.

Lord Marchmont struck his forehead with his clenched fist, and said—

"Perdition! It is even as I thought. Oh, how basely has my name and title been prostituted! how have my affections been trifled with! and how have I been made the sport and the tool of designing people!"

"It is time now, I think, that I should explain a little," exclaimed Bernard Leslie. "My father had an illegitimate daughter——"

"Is—is she——" asked Lord Marchmont in a choking voice, pointing to Agnes.

"That lady is the natural child I allude to. My father married her mother, his mistress, to one of his grooms, by name Jabez Clarke. Agnes came to me, proved her identity, and I agreed to acknowledge her as my sister, never dreaming she had a husband alive. I introduced her to my aunt, Miss Lavinia, and she brought her out; your lordship took a fancy to her, and married her, and that is all I know about the matter. Now you have heard all, I will, with your permission, take my departure."

He picked up his hat, and was about to go away, when Miss Lavinia jumped up from her seat as if she had suddenly come in contact with the electric eel at a moment when that interesting fish was highly charged. Rushing to her nephew, she clutched him by the arm, and pointing eagerly towards Marmaduke, cried, in startling accents—

"'Tis him, 'tis him!"

"Him! Who?" replied Bernard, thinking his respected relative had taken a temporary leave of her senses.

"Marmaduke Leslie," she said; "the boy I was so fond of years ago."

Bernard stared, and muttered—

"Relations creep up like mushrooms after a shower of rain."

"Yes, I will swear it," she continued. "It is my uncle's son. Ask him, Bernard, ask him."

Marmaduke listened to all this with some curiosity, and said—

"My name is Leslie—Marmaduke Leslie. Wilson is an assumed name: since I left Oxford, and since the days Miss Lavinia is talking of, I have done many things of which I am ashamed, and I disguised myself under the fictitious name of Wilson."

"It's all very odd, that's all I can say," muttered Bernard Leslie.

Miss Lavinia continued to feast her eyes upon Marmaduke.

Agnes was in a stupor of grief and irresolution.

Lord Marchmont's features were convulsed with sorrow and rage.

"Are you all of one mind?" he said, in a husky voice. "Have you any doubt that these two people are man and wife?"

The Leslies replied that they thought everything was conclusive.

"Then I wish you good morning."

With these words, Lord Marchmont rushed from the room unceremoniously.

Miss Lavinia extracted a promise from Marmaduke that he would come and see her.

"Come along, aunt, if you are coming. I think our pig's pretty well killed," said Bernard, coarsely.

She followed him out of the room, and Marmaduke and Agnes were alone together.

Alone! after so long a separation, fraught with much peril, much misery, to both of them.

The feelings which agitated the man and the woman are to a certain extent sacred, so let them rest.

CHAPTER XCIV.

MARMADUKE WILSON RECEIVES A NOTE FROM LORD MARCHMONT—HE HANDS IT TO HIS WIFE—LORD MARCHMONT ANNOUNCES HIS INTENTION OF LEAVING ENGLAND, BUT PROVIDES FOR AGNES—AGNES GOES TO CHARLOTTE SAUNDERS—LIKE THE CLOWN IN THE PANTOMIME, MARIA APPEARS AGAIN.

MARMADUKE WILSON had regained his wife; but it appeared that her affections were either alienated from him, or that she was so enamoured with the gilded trappings with which Lord Marchmont had encircled her, that she did not care to come back to him and poverty. Marmaduke was a good deal surprised that his lordship should have left the room in so quiet and undemonstrative a manner. He fully expected some personal attack, some violent effort to eject him from the house; but none happened. He was unmolested. Another source of wonder, not to say bewilderment, was Miss Lavinia Leslie's recognition of him. He remembered perfectly well how kind she had been to him when a boy, and his heart smote him when he thought of the disgrace he had brought upon his family. He found some little consolation in the fact that his family had not treated him well, and that he had in a certain measure been driven to do what he had done; at all events, he had done it more through poverty and distress than through inclination. After all, he had been a famous thief: he had made some little noise in the world; and there is a sort of pride amongst thieves to be a successful thief. A Turpin or a Jack Sheppard is a distinction amongst the fraternity, between whom honour is said to prevail, on the principle, I suppose, of dog refusing to eat dog.

Agnes was still seated in that richly-furnished apartment. Although Marmaduke Wilson had been born and educated as a gentleman, his family had not been very well off, and he had never been in so sumptuously garnished a room in his life before. He had not seen such luxury at home, nor had he met with it amongst his friends and acquaintances.

"It is hardly reasonable," he said to himself, "to expect my wife to fly into my arms, to be eager and willing to come back to me. I cannot disguise from myself that I am a felon—a returned convict—a ticket-of-leave man. That in addition to all this I have deceived her from the first—I have misrepresented myself, and that now I have nothing to offer her but my love. It appears that she has found some one else to do that, and to back up his love with a pile of substantial sovereigns and every creature comfort Yet she is mine—the law has made her mine! And however hard it may be for her to come back to me, I can compel her to do so. And why should I hesitate to exercise the authority with which I find myself gifted? who is to prevent me? why should I pay any attention to the silly scruples of a woman who perhaps does not know her own mind? I love her. I feel that I love her more now than I ever did. She is mine legally. She has been mine positively and actually, and she shall be so again."

Marmaduke Wilson uttered these words in a decided tone, which would have shown anybody acquainted with him that he meant what he said, and would in all probability give some practical interpretation to his words. He turned his attention to his wife.

She still preserved her attitude of grief. Her energies seemed completely paralysed by the mighty blow which had come upon her. A few days ago she was the happy companion of a man who loved her, and who had the power and the inclination to minister to her wants and make her happy, and now, what was she? The wife of a felon hunted down and brought to bay—confronted with her husband, whom she hardly knew whether to hate or tolerate—apparently deserted by Lord Marchmont, and looked coldly upon by the Leslies—those people who had hitherto made a tool of her, and found her most lucrative.

Marmaduke walked up and down the room with his arms folded and his head bent. He was in deep thought; much had occurred to make him indulge in cogitation. He was thinking how he could approach his wife so as not to meet with a rebuff; such as would be most unpleasant to him, and most prejudicial to his plans. After pacing the room for some time, he stopped, and bent his gaze upon Agnes. Her face was buried in her hands, and she did not, from her manner, appear aware that he was in the room. He determined to speak to her.

"Agnes!" he exclaimed.

She did not evince the slightest symptom of having heard him. He was about to touch her hand, and accost her a second time, when the door of the room opened.

A servant entered, and approached Marmaduke Wilson. The latter looked at him inquiringly.

The domestic carried a silver salver in his hand, and upon it was a letter. When he came to where Marmaduke was standing, the servant held up the salver, and presented the letter to Marmaduke.

The envelope was blank. There was not the vestige of a superscription upon it. Under those circumstances, although he thought the epistle was meant for him, Marmaduke hesitated to take it. His hesitation, however, was cut short by the servant's saying—

"Note for you, sir."

"Who from?" hastily demanded Marmaduke.

"Lord Marchmont," replied the servant.

Marmaduke, upon hearing this, took the letter, and the servant, after making a low bow, departed. He saw, no doubt, that something peculiar was going on in the house, but he was too well trained, and had too much sense to evince any symptom of curiosity, or to show the slightest atom of disrespect to anyone who happened to be under his master's roof. He was fully aware that gentlemen have an unpleasant way of rewarding impertinence, on the part of inferiors, by an occasional kick in a region where such violent salutations are far from pleasant, and still farther from being conducive to one's personal and corporeal equilibrium.

Marmaduke found that the blank envelope contained two short notes. One was evidently intended for himself. It was to the effect that the writer having discovered that some one had a prior claim to the affections of the lady who had for some time gone under the name of Lady Marchmont, he begged to resign his pretensions in favour of his rival, and would thank him to peruse the accompanying note, and then give it to the lady whom he had a right to call his wife.

Lord Marchmont's letter to Agnes ran as follows—

"To Agnes,

"The discovery I have this day made has proved a very great blow to me. Perhaps you will never know how severely I feel it. I have done a great deal to win you, and I dreamed at one time of ending my days in your society, which at all times was very pleasing and agreeable to me, but which latterly I grew to look upon as peculiarly fascinating. My heart will not break. I believe that broken hearts are poetical fictions, but I may, after a time, pine away and die. Should such be the case, you may breathe a sigh to the memory of one who loved you ardently and devotedly—how much so, you will never know; perhaps it is better that you should not. Perhaps a knowledge of what I have done for you, and what I was fully prepared to do for you, would not be conducive either to your future serenity or peace of mind. I cannot stay longer in England—every street, every house, and every public place, would bring vividly before me memories of you; and as I want to forget you as quickly, as thoroughly, and as effectually as I can, to stop in London will be the worst plan I can adopt. No, Agnes—I almost wish I could prefix some of the old epithets—darling pet, or—but no, I know and feel that you are no more to me now than yonder cloud floating across the surface of the horizon, which looks so bright and gauzy as I view it from my window. It is a melancholy reflection for me, but I must not shut my eyes to what is—to what actually exists. I wish I could; but that solace is denied me. I pray that you may be happy, and as I utter the prayer, a contradictory spirit rises up within me. I am half distracted. At times I wish you happy, at others I wish you miserable, wretched. I could, without remorse or shrinking, see you dying on a dunghill, and that detestable fellow, who has torn you from me, broken upon the wheel. I could see you, in my moments of frenzy, perishing of starvation in one of the streets of the metropolis; and if a penny would save you from the most horrible death, I would not give it you. These ideas are bad and wicked, and I intend going away in order to avoid them—they might lead me into crime. It would not be the first time that a man had imperilled his neck for the sake of, and for love of a pretty and engaging woman. Agnes, I am going to leave you. You will never see me again. By the time this letter is in your hands, I shall be far away from the house which contains you. Another sun shall not rise and see me in England. I will fly to the land of the luxurious and volup-

tuous Orientals—to the land of the dreamy East, where you can more nearly realize Paradise than upon any other portion of the habitable globe. If I survive the rude shock which I have this day received, I shall turn Mohammedan, and die a true believer. But be not alarmed, I shall provide for you amply and beneficently before I leave my native land. I intend on my way through the city to call upon my lawyer, and instruct him to draw up a deed in your favour, in which you will be allowed five hundred pounds a-year; and through whose provisions you will receive a thousand pounds down to embark in any undertaking you should fancy. I will not ask you to think of me or to pity me, although God knows I deserve everyone's pity. If I were to ask you to commiserate me, my parting words might so affect you, that you would not behave with becoming courtesy to him to whom you legally belong; and this is an eventuality I should be very sorry to bring about."

Here the letter ended abruptly; there was no signature, no adieu, no good-bye.

Marmaduke had read it carefully, and he went a step nearer Agnes to deliver it to her. He spoke to her as before, but she would not reply to him. He was naturally enraged at her prolonged silence or obstinacy, it was difficult to say which. Seizing hold of her arm, he shook it.

She roused herself up a little at this, her eyes opened, and her hands fell down from her face and rested upon her knees.

Without a word Marmaduke gave her the paper to read.

Wiping away her tears, she endeavoured to do so; she perused the document with some surprise, and her astonishment was final and complete when she saw that Lord Marchmont really intended to give her up without a struggle. She had hoped, faintly, that he might have discovered, through his superior intelligence and ingenuity, some means of thwarting Marmaduke Wilson. Lord Marchmont's declaration that he would settle five hundred a-year upon her smoothed the way for her a little, for there was nothing she dreaded so much as poverty; she had experienced it, she had tasted of its bitterness; she knew full well what it was, in all its terrible and fearful reality, and as long as Lord Marchmont did not leave her penniless, she did not care so particularly about losing the title she had once been so proud of.

When Marmaduke Wilson saw that she had read the letter, he addressed her.

"My dear Agnes," he said, "is this the way in which you treat your husband?"

She looked at him with her red and swollen eyes, but made no answer.

"Is this the only greeting you have for me?"

"Oh, don't talk to me now," she said; "I am not able to bear it."

"But I must talk to you; with me it is now or never."

"What do you wish to say?"

"Many things."

"What are they?"

"I will tell you."

Agnes looked at him as if she was prepared to hear the most bitter reproaches pass his lips.

"Lord Marchmont," began Marmaduke Wilson, "has recognised the justice of my claim; he believes you to be my wife, and you can no longer hope for any assistance from him. He is even now, perhaps, on his way to a foreign land, or at least making preparations for his departure. We took one another for better or for worse; the worse came, and do you now shrink from fulfilling your marriage vow? If you do, tell me so, and I shall know how to act."

"I might have been happy if you had left me alone," replied Agnes, tearfully.

"And can you not be happy now?" he exclaimed, raising her gently from the chair, and placing her upon his knee.

Her head rested upon his breast, and her tears rolling down her cheeks, fell upon his hand.

"Do you hate me because of my misfortunes?" he asked.

"I have had many things to try me," replied Agnes.

"Do you regret you are my wife, and that I have returned once more to clasp you in my arms?"

She was mute.

"Oh, Agnes!" he continued, "if you knew how I have loved you during my dreadful captivity, you would pity me. If you knew how I longed and panted for your loved society during my inglorious exile, you would not try to drive me from you in this way."

Agnes seemed to be recovering some of her former love for Marmaduke Wilson—some of that love which had evaporated for a time before the influence of the sun of Marchmont—for she placed her tiny hand in his, and looked up like a timid dove in his face.

"Speak, my darling, speak!" exclaimed Marmaduke, enraptured at this symptom of returning affection.

"Marmaduke," began Agnes, slowly; "leave me for a day or two; my mind is such a chaos of ideas, that I cannot think, I cannot form any definite plan of action. Leave me to myself for a short time, and I have no doubt that I shall look upon you as I did formerly, but just now so many recent events are fresh in my memory, that I don't feel capable of any action whatever. Let my mind have a rest—give it time to recover its accustomed energies, and I shall be in a better condition to talk to you."

"What will you do?" he asked.

"I have a friend who will be glad to see me; I will go to her for a short period. You can come and visit me at her house—you can even accompany me there now, if you would like to."

"It shall be as you wish," he replied. "I defer to your request. I will take you to your friend's at once. I will visit you every day, and we shall, I hope, soon be as good friends again as ever."

They left the house together. Agnes took none of her things with her; she left word that she would not be gone more than a day or two.

Calling a cab, Marmaduke Wilson put her into it, and followed himself. Agnes desired the man to drive to Charlotte Saunders's lodgings in Soho. Marmaduke accompanied her as far as the door, promised to call upon her the next day, saw her enter, and then went back in the cab to the place where the dwarf was waiting for him.

Maria opened the door as usual, and exclaimed when she saw Agnes—

"Oh, my! wont the missus be glad to see you!"

Agnes smiled, and followed Maria into the parlour.

CHAPTER XCV.

MARIA, AS USUAL, IS FAVOURED WITH A BIT OF HER MISTRESSES MIND—A CONVERSATION AND A LITTLE FRIENDLY ADVICE—CHARLOTTE SAUNDERS IS MARRIED TO THE CAPTAIN—AGNES AND MARMADUKE ARE RECONCILED—THEIR REGRET FOR THEIR LOST CHILD—SOMETHING OF AN UNEXPECTED NATURE IS HAPPENING IN ANOTHER QUARTER.

CHARLOTTE SAUNDERS was apparently in her bedroom, for a thick, bass voice issuing therefrom, exclaimed—

"Maria!"

"Yes, mum," responded that long-suffering individual.

"What do you want to go trapesing about the house for in that way?"

"It's a lady friend of yours, mum."

"Oh!" cried Charlotte, coming out.

"Glad you aint got no dwarf with you this time," said Maria quietly to Agnes.

Agnes smiled and Charlotte entered.

"Well," said Charlotte, "you're like a bad penny, always turning up, and no good to misers."

"Are you glad to see me?" asked Agnes.

"Glad! of course I am. Come in, don't stand out there in the cold."

Agnes followed her friend into the sitting-room, and they were soon hobnobbing together by the fireside.

"Maria!" cried Charlotte, in a shrill treble.

"Coming, mum," replied that highly reputable and much injured domestic.

"Well, why don't you come?" said Charlotte. "I'll be hanged if you are not always coming; something like Christmas, only you are an infernal long time about it."

"Yes, mum," answered Maria, with all the humility she possessed forced into her ingenuous countenance.

"Yes, mum, you fool," cried Charlotte, sarcastically. "Why can't you say something else? It's always, Yes, mum, with you. I'm jolly well sick of your one note. You're just like a parrot who's only learned to say one thing."

"Yes, mum," said Maria, getting a little confused.

"Now, if you say that again I'll break your head," exclaimed Charlotte, getting greatly incensed.

Maria looked around her for sympathy, but finding none, she looked as if she was perfectly willing to go into some wilderness, and live upon locusts and wild honey—anything, in fact, as long as she escaped from the haunts of men.

Charlotte Saunders could not help laughing at Maria's evident perplexity, and Agnes positively roared, the whole scene was so amusing.

"Now, Maria," said Charlotte. "Once for all——"

"Yes, mum," replied Maria, this time with a look of mock humility, for she was losing her temper at being badgered, only she was afraid to show it.

"Confound you! If you say 'Yes, mum' again I'll be the death of you."

This threat terrified Maria, who replied—

"I wont, mum. It's all right, mum."

"Is it?" said Charlotte, a little mollified. "I don't know about that. Now pay attention to me."

"Yes, mum. That is——"

Maria had been betrayed into her familiar exclamation, and for the life of her she could not get out of it without a little stuttering and stammering.

"Just hold your tongue, will you?"

"Yes, mum."

"I never saw such a woman," said Charlotte to Agnes. "She does it to aggravate me, I'm sure."

"Listen to what's said to you, Maria, and don't answer," exclaimed Agnes, in a friendly way.

"Yes, mum," replied Maria, for about the tenth time.

"Oh! my God!" gasped Charlotte, "that woman will be the death of me, I know she will. It's no use talking to her."

Maria cast down her eyes, and looked as penitent as she was able to.

"You wont do it again, Maria, will you," said Agnes, in a kind tone.

"No, mum."

"Come, Charlotte, that's better," continued Agnes.

"Well, it is a little; but I've no patience with such silly beggars. I suppose she's gone out and got tight along with a lot of fellows. You've been on the mouch, haven't you? I know you had no money, and you couldn't have got it in any other way. Now, look here, just give me your attention for a minute, if you can."

"Yes, mum."

At this Charlotte turned to Agnes, and said—

"Isn't she enough to provoke a saint, let alone a devil like me?"

"Yes, it is provoking."

"Maria! now, don't answer me, all you have to do is to listen. Is there any liquor in the house? If there isn't go and get some."

"Yes, mum, plenty," replied Maria. "The captain sent some in. Brandy, rum, gin—all sorts."

"Oh! when did it come?"

"Early this morning."

"Was it paid for?"

"Yes, mum, bottles and all."

"That's jolly. Go and bring some up."

"Yes, mum."

Maria departed in peace. Charlotte Saunders was too much pleased at seeing Agnes, and at an event which was to come off on the morrow, to blow her up any more.

"Well, Agnes," said Charlotte, "what's the best news with you?"

"I hardly know."

"What do you mean?"

"Why, I've lost a man and found a husband."

"You're lucky, then."

"Do you think so?"

"Of course I do. A husband's better than a man any day."

"How do you know?" said Agnes.

"Because I'm going to be married."

"You?" cried Agnes, astonished.

"Yes," replied Charlotte, quietly.

"Who to? You must tell me."

"Who do you think?"

"How should I know?"

"You have seen him."

"Do you mean the captain?" said Agnes.

"Who else should I mean?" replied Charlotte, with a gratified smile.

"Well, I am glad," said Agnes, "upon my word I am glad. And so you are going to get settled at last?"

"Yes, I hope so."

"I always thought your captain was a jolly fellow."

"Jolly! he's the biggest brick out."

Agnes smiled, and Maria entered with a bottle of gin.

She placed it on the table, and proceeded to take some glasses off the sideboard, when Charlotte exclaimed—

"Who told you to bring gin up?"

"I don't know," said Maria.

"Don't know, eh? What is it you ever do know?"

"I'll take it back again."

"Of course you will. I'm perfectly aware of that fact."

"Yes, mum."

"I suppose the fact is you want a glass of gin. You have had a little, and you want a drop or two more just to make you square. Is that it?"

"I haven't had any at all, mum, yet."

"Don't tell me, I know better. I can see it. Do you take me for a fool?"

Maria took hold of the bottle of gin, and was about to carry it off and substitute something else for it in its place, when Charlotte Saunders again interrupted her, and frustrated her attempt, saying—

"Who told you to touch that?"

"You did, mum."

"I?" cried Charlotte.

"Yes, mum," said Maria.

"You must be drunk. Get out of my sight."

"Yes, mum," answered Maria, leaving the room.

But she had hardly crossed the threshold, when Charlotte cried after her—

"Bring a bottle of brandy, and the corkscrew."

When this little episode was over Agnes asked her friend when she was going to be married.

"I was going to tell you, dear, only that woman always puts me out so infernally."

"Perhaps you only confuse her by bullying her."

"I can't help that. If people are fools they must be told of it."

"Yes, of course."

"Well, then, you can't wonder at my losing my temper with Maria."

"She is tiresome."

"Tiresome! I should think she was. But never mind, she's not a bad sort, so we'll not say anything against her behind her back."

"That's right, Charlotte. Tell me about yourself."

"I will, dear. I am going to be married to the captain to-morrow at St. Martin's church. Isn't it jolly? You know I always liked him, and he is going out to China with Captain Sherard Osborne, in the Anglo-Chinese expedition, and it is rather a good thing for him."

"Shall you go with him?"

"Yes. I am to be stewardess on board his ship."

"How happy you will be."

"I hope so," replied Charlotte. "Now tell me something about yourself?"

"What do you want to know?"

"Oh! everything."

"About Count Val de Grace?"

"Yes. How is the frog-eater? Did you get away from him?"

"I am glad to say I did. Lord Marchmont rescued me and killed him."

"Is he dead?"

"Yes, and buried by this time. Don't you read the papers?"

"Not I? I sometimes look at the Police in the Sunday paper—that's Lloyd's—but I never saw anything about it."

"Well, Lord Marchmont's left me, and my husband, Marmaduke Wilson, has come back from transportation."

"That's something like," cried Charlotte. "It's quite a romance."

"I want to ask your advice."

"What about?"

"One or two things," replied Agnes. "First of all, shall I go back to live with Marmaduke Wilson?"

"Do you like him?"

"I think I do; I used to," said Agnes, hesitatingly.

"Has he got any money?"

"No. Not a rap."

"Any trade?"

"No. But that doesn't matter so much. Lord Marchmont has left me some money, and we could set up in business very well with that."

"Oh, in that case you wont hurt."

"What do you advise me to do?"

"Why, stick to Marmaduke."

"You really mean that?" said Agnes, raising her eyes to Charlotte.

"Certainly I do. Perhaps the man is none the worse for having been unfortunate. He will be able to appreciate you better than he did before he went away."

"I also begin to think it is the best thing I can do," replied Agnes. "Marmaduke dotes on me, I am sure, and I cannot forget that I was once passionately attached to him."

"I suppose the truth is, that you were pleased at the idea of being a lady?" said Charlotte, with a smile; "that idea ruins more women than you have any idea of. If any friend of mine were to come to me to be put up to a few wrinkles to help her through life, I should say 'Don't go setting your cap at high game.' Where one woman succeeds, nine hundred and ninety-nine out of a thousand fail, and when they do fail, they come to horrible grief. If you can find a man who likes you, never mind how humble he may be, as long as he is a good sort; stick to him, and you'll be happy all the rest of your life."

Agnes tacitly assented to this proposition.

A loud knock, as Charlotte finished speaking, was heard at the street door.

Charlotte ran to the window to reconnoitre her visitor. Drawing aside the blind, she peeped out.

"Hurrah!" she cried, "it's the captain."

Tripping lightly into the passage, she opened the door, and admitted the man who was to lead her to the altar to-morrow.

He was smiling, and had a jovial expression on his good-looking face. He caught her in his arms, and imprinted a hot kiss upon her pretty pouting lips. But this was in the passage where nobody saw it, and perhaps I am not doing right in divulging an occurrence of so delicate a nature.

The captain greeted Agnes very kindly, and said—

"My stars, how well you're looking!"

This was not exactly true, but the captain always told women they looked well, he thought it pleased them.

Agnes was looking in reality ill and anxious, and the traces of the recent agitation she had gone through were only too apparent on her face.

"So you are going to China, captain," said Agnes.

"Yes. Will you come with us? Make you comfortable on board my ship! My stars, yes!"

"That's a good idea," said Charlotte. "Come to China, Agnes; your Marmaduke might get on very well out there."

Agnes smiled, and said—

"You are very kind, both of you, but I cannot leave England; I have gone through so many adventures and trials lately, that I want rest and peace. I think I shall recommend Marmaduke to take a public-house somewhere in the suburbs, somewhere out Fulham or Walham-green way."

"I wouldn't go there, if I were you," said Charlotte.

"Why not?"

"Because I've heard that publics are so numerous in that neighbourhood, that there is one public to every male inhabitant."

"Oh, what nonsense!" said Agnes, laughing.

"At all events, my dear, the thing's overdone. If you want to go into the public line, go to some other locality."

"I should like to be a publican myself," said the captain.

"Would you?" remarked Agnes.

"Of course he would," laughed Charlotte. "Because he'd always have the liquor handy."

"It isn't that," he said. "The reason I think a publican's business the best thing going, is there is no surplus stock—no waste; everything is consumed, and very quickly too."

The day passed very quietly with Agnes. Her friends went to the theatre in the evening, but she retired to rest early. The next day they were married. There was no fuss about a wedding breakfast, although that necessary adjunct to a wedding was not altogether forgotten. Charlotte came back to her lodgings, changed her dress, and, with her husband and Agnes, went to Epitaux's, in Pall-mall, where something had previously been ordered. After this, the newly-married couple went down to the Isle of Wight to spend the honeymoon, which could only last a fortnight, as at the expiration of that time they were to sail for China in the *Thunderer*. The captain liked the name, and said—

THE JOY OF AGNES AND MARMADUKE AT THE RECOVERY OF THEIR CHILD.

"My stars! that's something like a name for a ship which carries Armstrong guns.".

They parted regretfully with Agnes, who, after Charlotte's departure, felt the sense of desolation and oppression which troubles everyone at the loss of an old friend, and Charlotte Saunders was one of Agnes's very oldest friends.

And this was the end, as far as I am able to relate it, of one of the "Women of London."

When Marmaduke Wilson again saw Agnes, she met him in a more conciliatory spirit. He told her how he loved her, and how he would endeavour to compensate for his faults by devoting the rest of his life to her happiness.

Agnes said she believed him, and, for the first time for ever so long, she allowed him to kiss that velvet cheek which was now more than ever his own.

"We are friends now," he said, as their long and earnest conversation was brought to an end.

"Yes," she replied, smilingly, "yes, Marmaduke, we are friends again, and I hope we shall ever remain so."

"There is one thing I cannot help regretting," said Marmaduke.

"What is that?"

"That our child did not live to assist at our new-born happiness."

The tears sprang to Agnes's eyes. She sighed.

In the meantime something was happening which was destined to astonish them not a little.

CHAPTER XCVI.

A STRANGE AND MOST UNEXPECTED VISITOR — GOOD TIDINGS—MISS LAVINIA IS OVERJOYED AT HEARING OF THE EXISTENCE OF AGNES'S CHILD — MAKING FRIENDS WITH BRUCE—A GREAT LOAD IS TAKEN OFF MISS LAVINIA'S MIND—OLD MEG IS HAPPY.

MISS LAVINIA LESLIE had hardly returned to her home in Hill-street, Berkeley-square, after the exciting interview she had recently had with Lord Marchmont, than another adventure befell her which did not fail to excite her astonishment quite as much as that which she had recently encountered.

She was reclining in an arm-chair, having recourse to that stimulant which she found of so much use to her on the bleak Scottish hill-side, when she had fallen down the entrance to the Highland still, much to her own disgust and the dismay of Agnes.

A ring came at the area-bell.

Miss Lavinia heard it, but she took no notice of it.

What did it matter to her? Anyone who came to see her knocked at the door and rang the visitors' bell. Pouring out another liqueur-glass of brandy she took up the paper, and was about to read it, when she heard an altercation in the hall.

Some one had been admitted, and was talking loudly; the accent was Scotch, the dialect broad Scotch. Miss Lavinia listened intently. Surely she had heard those tones somewhere before. They were certainly familiar to her ear. Where could she have heard them? She racked her brain, but she could not remember.

The noise increased.

"I tell you," she distinctly heard the footman say, "she can't be disturbed. She wont see you; so it's no good your waiting."

"Hech, mon, but I must see her."

"She is engaged."

"I dinna care."

"Will you go?"

"Will I gang? Nae, mon! I've come all the way frae Scotland, just beyant Aberdeen."

"I can't help that."

"Tell your leddy as a puir Scotch lassie wants to see her."

The man was still hesitating when Miss Lavinia touched a small hand-bell. The footman hearing the summons said—

"Wait here till I return."

"Eh, mon! I'll bide," she replied.

"Who is that?" asked Miss Lavinia, when the man entered.

"Some Scotch person, ma'am, who wants to see you. I thought you were tired, and wished to be alone, so I told her she could not see you."

"What did she say?"

"Said she wouldn't go till she did, ma'am."

Miss Lavinia cogitated a moment, and then said—

"Show her in."

Leaving the room, the servant said—

"You're to come in."

"Eh! and that's gude," replied the raw-boned Scotchwoman, following him into the apartment where Miss Lavinia was."

"You're looking bonnie!" she exclaimed on entering, and coolly taking a chair without waiting to be asked to do so:

"Who are you?" asked Miss Lavinia, abruptly; "and why do you seek me?"

"You dinna ken who I am?" said the woman, with a grin.

"I am utterly and entirely ignorant of who or what you are," replied Miss Lavinia, with dignity.

"I must remind ye."

"Pray be as quick as you can."

"Dinna fash yersel, my leddy."

"Will you come to the point?"

"All right; all in gude time."

"Who are you?" demanded Miss Lavinia, fiercely.

"I'm Meg."

"Meg who?"

"Scotch Meg, frae Blockhaven."

Miss Lavinia gasped for breath at this announcement. She felt that something was about to happen to her which would be far from pleasant. Misfortunes seldom if ever come single, and she had met with one already that day. This was to be the second.

"What do you want?" she said.

"I want you," replied our old friend Meg, with another and a wider grin upon her hard, rough face.

"You want money, I suppose?"

"A little siller wont hurt me."

"You shall have it."

"You have nae forgotten that nicht, my leddy?"

"What do you mean?" asked Miss Lavinia, blanching, in spite of the brandy she had been taking.

"Ye dinna forget the bairn?"

Her auditor shuddered visibly.

Forgotten it!

Had she ever forgotten that dreadful night, when she had committed a shocking and detestable murder.

The worst of all murders—infanticide.

The worst, because the cruelest.

The poor babe cannot help itself, and the heart must, indeed, be stony which refuses to be moved by its plaintive wails.

Miss Lavinia felt so faint that she was obliged to pour out a glass of brandy, which action Meg noticing exclaimed—

"I will nae say no to a wee drap o' liquor."

Miss Lavinia pushed the bottle over to her, and the Scotchwoman took a draught which would have brought tears into the eyes of an ostrich, with a cast-iron throat and stomach, but she did not so much as wink.

Taking her purse from her pocket, Miss Lavinia exclaimed, as she held it out—

"You want money; I know that must be your object. Take this. You would not have come all the way from Scotland for nothing. You were actuated by the motive that influences all human actions more or less. You wanted money. You have cleverly found me out, and there is some to go on with; you shall have more when you want it."

Taking the purse with the utmost composure Meg put it in her pocket without looking at it. Its weight satisfied her, and said with a satisfied smile—

"Puir bairn!"

"Why do you harp on that string, woman?" cried Miss Lavinia, angrily. "You have obtained what you want, now go."

"Not yet, my leddy."

"Go, I tell you."

Meg shook her head.

"Go at once!"

"Would you like to see the bairn?" she said, with a cunning leer.

At this question, Miss Lavinia Leslie started from her chair, and clutched her visitor by the arm—

"What do you mean?" she exclaimed.

"Leave go, and I'll tell ye."

"Dare to trifle with me, and——"

"And what, my leddy?"

"Say on."

"The bairn lives!" said Meg, with the air of a person who is making an important announcement.

"Lives! you lie!" cried Miss Lavinia.

"Nae, my leddy, I never lie!"

"You do, I say!"

"Nae, nae; you thought you killed the bairn, but I saved it."

"You! How did you do that?"

"I did it."

"But how? tell me how?"

Meg thus abjured, gave Miss Lavinia the history of the whole transaction, and told her how she had saved the child, and taken it to a friend's house.

Miss Lavinia's astonishment was intense. She could scarcely credit the good news that she was not after all a murderess.

"This account is strictly true?" she said.

"As God is my witness!" replied Meg, solemnly, turning up the whites of her eyes in the true conventicle manner.

"Where is the child now?" was Miss Lavinia's next question.

"In London," replied Meg.

"Indeed!—whereabouts?"

"Would you like to see the bairn?" Meg said, with glances of pleasure at seeing Miss Lavinia's joy at the news she brought her.

"Oh, yes, I should."

"You can."

"When?"

"Now, my leddy."

"Oh! bring it at once. Where is it?"

"In a cab, as you ca' your coaches, at the bottom of the street."

"Run and fetch it!" cried Miss Lavinia, eagerly.

Meg needed no further bidding. She left the house; shortly returning with a handsome boy in her arms. He could just walk, and contrived to lisp a few words of Scotch. His hair was light and curly, his cheeks red and rosy, and, altogether, he was a picture of health and good bringing up.

Miss Lavinia took him from Meg's arms ond kissed him; but whether he was used to Meg, or whether his instincts warned him against the lady, he cried so violently that Meg had to take him back again and soothe him the best way she could.

It was a great load off Miss Lavinia Leslie's mind to find that she was not guilty of the midnight murder, which had lain heavily upon her conscience for a long, long time. She could almost have embraced Meg in her transport of joy and gladness. She insisted upon the old Scotch woman's taking up her abode in her house, and she could not make fuss enough either with her or the little fellow, whom she petted in every conceivable way. She was apparently trying to make up for the great wrong she had endeavoured to do him.

It was arranged between Meg and Miss Lavinia, that when the child was restored to Agnes, the former should say that the child was supposed to be dead, but that it recovered in an extraordinary manner after it had been given over.

This was to prevent Agnes utterly casting off her aunt, who did not wish to be made contemptible in the eyes of those most nearly related to her.

After some time, the child took a fancy to the old lady, whn was so kind to him, and eat her lollypops with becoming co descension.

Meg had christened the boy "Bruce," and Miss Lavinia and Bruce became great friends. If Agnes had only known how near she was to her boy, how she would have flown to him!

CHAPTER XCVII.

MARMADUKE WILSON REFUSES LORD MARCHMONT'S BOUNTY — THE "HAPPY COUPLE" — AN UNEXPECTED VISITOR — BERNARD LESLIE'S DEATH — THE RESTORATION OF THE CHILD — CONCLUSION.

WE are approaching the end of our story: but little remains to be told now.

Marmaduke Wilson not only regained his wife, but her affections flowed again in the old channel. She took her husband back to her heart, and forgave him his bonds and his disgrace.

The money that Lord Marchmont intended to give to Agnes never reached its destination. And for this reason. Marmaduke no sooner heard of the gift than he called upon the agents of his lordship and flatly declined it.

"I will not, gentlemen," he said, "be indebted to Lord Marchmont for anything; he is the last man in London that I should think of applying to in any difficulty. No doubt it is extremely generous of him to make the offer to my wife, but I beg respectfully to decline it."

"What!" exclaimed one of the agents; "you refuse the money?"

"I do!" replied Marmaduke.

"You surprise me."

"I can work," said Marmaduke, drawing himself up proudly. "It is time that I endeavoured to retrieve the errors of my youth. I can see a hard future before me, but I do not shrink from facing it."

"Your determination does you great credit," said the agent, regarding Marmaduke with a kindly glance.

Marmaduke looked resolute.

"May I ask what you purpose doing?" the agent observed.

"Certainly; my plan is to obtain some money from some friend, or some money-lender, with which I can take a publichouse."

"I like your independence, and I shall be glad to assist you in any way, if you are not too proud to receive assistance from me I am not a friend of Lord Marchmont's, I am only his professional adviser in matters of business, which I conduct for him to the best of my ability. How much money do you want?"

"About twelve hundred pounds; I could buy the goodwill of a very respectable house for that," replied Marmaduke. "I thank you very much for your offer."

"Will you accept it?"

"I will. I speak plainly to you. I will accept it; you have offered it me in a generous spirit, and I will promise you your money again in twelve months, or at least half of it."

"Then," said the agent, with a laugh, "excuse me, but you'll have to water the gin."

Marmaduke smiled.

"Publichouse profits are very great, I know," continued the agent, "but keeping a tavern is not like having the wishing cap of Fortunatus. I should not mind lending you this money at five per cent., just by way of an investment; you can pay me half-yearly, and keep the principal until I see something better, and call it in."

The result of this interview was that Marmaduke Wilson borrowed the twelve hundred pounds from the agent, and took a publichouse in an eligible situation. By dint of perseverance and politeness he soon increased the business.

Agnes was a great attraction, and by her good looks and her pleasing manners she assisted her husband materially. Everything they sold was good and of the best quality.

The sign of the house was the "Happy Couple," and it acquired such notoriety that people went out of their way to call there. If one man remarked to another—

"Which is the best house about here to get a glass of gin or of beer."

The reply was sure to be—

"Oh, the 'Happy Couple!' Best house in London!"

One morning, about a month after they had been installed in their new home, Agnes and her husband were sitting in the bar-parlour, Agnes was hemming pocket-handkerchiefs, Marmaduke was quietly smoking his first pipe, and reading the *Morning Advertiser*. The barman put his head in at the door, and exclaimed—

"A lady wishes to see you, please, sir."

"Who is she?"

"Says her name's Miss Lavinia Leslie, sir."

"Oh!" cried Marmaduke. "Show her in."

Agnes threw down her work, and Miss Lavinia entered.

"Well, my dears!" she exclaimed; "how are you? I have had such trouble to find you out. You have never been to see me as you promised, and I thought I should never have discovered your whereabouts, but you see I persevered, and I have succeeded at last."

"Sit down," said Marmaduke, handing her a chair.

It was worthy of note that Miss Lavinia was not dressed so finely as usual. She wore very little jewellery, and her boots were dirty, as if she had no carriage now, and had walked some part of the way. The fact was that Lord Marchmont, finding he was not legally married to Agnes, considered the marriage settlement null and void, and had discontinued the payments Agnes had always made, according to the arrangement with her aunt and her brother, in days gone by. The consequence was that Miss Lavinia had to give up many luxuries, and put down many expenses— much to her disgust. But it seemed like a judgment upon her. After all her scheming, and all her deep-laid plots— what was she?

Bernard Leslie had been obliged to go abroad.

Miss Lavinia was in deep mourning.

"Why, aunt," cried Agnes, "what's the matter?"

"I have had a great loss."

"Who, may I ask?—not Bernard?"

"Yes; Bernard is dead."

"Really! How did he die?"

"He was so worried by his creditors that he went to live abroad. He went to a gambling-house at some German place, and there lost the small sum he had left. In his desperation he blew his brains out."

"How terrible!" said Agnes. "What a dreadful end!"

"But," said Miss Lavinia, with a smile; "if I bring bad news I also bring good."

"Well, that is consolatory!" said Agnes, smiling. "What is your good news, aunt?"

"Yes," observed Marmaduke; "let us hear it."

"You shall; but I must tell it you gradually. Suppose now, that any one you thought dead was to come to life again."

Agnes started, changed colour visibly.

Marmaduke began to grow interested, he knew not why.

"You see, I am a little obscure, but you must remember our tour in Scotland, Agnes?"

When Agnes heard this she grew uncontrollably excited. Rising to her feet she ran to her aunt, and grasped her hand nervously, saying, in tremulous accents—

"My child! my child! What of it?"

"There! there!" said Miss Lavinia, soothingly.

"Tell me, I insist. I must know. I shall die. This suspense——"

Marmaduke was visibly affected at this strange scene.

"My dear child!" said Miss Lavinia, whose eyes were moist; "sit down and you shall see him."

"See him!" cried Agnes. "Oh, Heaven!"

As she uttered these words she fell down upon the carpet, and lay so pale and motionless that you might have supposed the spark of life to be extinct.

Marmaduke was by her side directly, and by the judicious application of proper remedies she was brought to herself.

Just before she unclosed her eyes Miss Lavinia slipped out of the room, presently returning with a fair-haired boy.

When Agnes's gaze fell upon him she looked affectionately at his pretty face.

"Is it, indeed, he?" she murmured.

Guided by some instinct, the little fellow took her hand in his, and said—

"Mamma."

"Yes, my darling," she replied, springing to her feet, clasping him in her arms, and straining him to her breast.

Miss Lavinia's eyes ran over like a gutter in a rainstorm.

Marmaduke himself was visibly moved.

Kisses were showered upon the boy in the most profligate manner. After a time—when all had had a good look at him and some had declared him to be like his mother, some like his father, and others that he bore a wonderful resemblance to a distant relation, innumerable questions were asked and answered—old Meg was called in.

She had been waiting outside, and the story which had been concocted between Miss Lavinia and herself was duly told.

Agnes and her husband were too much pleased at recovering their boy, whom they both often mourned over secretly as dead, to criticize very closely the history they had just been favoured with.

The lost had been found. The dead had come to life again.

Marmaduke produced a bottle of his best champagne, and all filled their glasses to the brim, with the exception of Meg, who said—

"She would rather hae a glass of gude whisky than all the French rotgut in the cellar."

And she toddled off into the bar, and in defiance of the barman, helped herself, and so frequently that she at last set all the taps running, and began to shout out—

"A man's a man for a' that."

And then she drank the baby-boy's health, and called him "Burns."

Her mind was confused, and she was at length forcibly removed to an old sofa in the kitchen, where she lay for hours hissing through her teeth like a snake, because she fancied herself a tea-kettle on the boil.

The curtain must now descend, and shut out the domestic bliss of Marmaduke Wilson and his wife, Agnes, than whom a happier pair, or one more amiably disposed towards one another never claimed the Dunmow flitch of bacon.

The bell rings. The curtain falls. The drama is at an end, and the public are at liberty to applaud, or—well, we wont give them permission to do the other thing. It is a habit that geese have, and to do what a goose does is to possess the attributes of a foolish creature.

THE END.

Lightning Source UK Ltd.
Milton Keynes UK
UKHW050747030323
417983UK00012B/499